THE MEMORY OF SKY

D0873715

OTHER BOOKS BY ROBERT REED

MARROW SERIES

Marrow
The Well of Stars

VEIL OF STARS SERIES

Beyond the Veil of Stars
Beneath the Gated Sky

OTHER NOVELS

The Leeshore
The Hormone Jungle
Black Milk
Down the Bright Way
The Remarkables
An Exaltation of Larks
Sister Alice

COLLECTIONS

The Dragons of Springplace
Chrysalide
The Cuckoo's Boys
Eater-of-Bone and Other Novellas
The Greatship

CHAPBOOKS

Mere
Flavors of My Genius
Eight Episodes
The Next Invasion
Our Candidate
Swingers

THE MEMORY OF SKY

A GREAT SHIP TRILOGY

ROBERT REED

PRIME BOOKS

THE MEMORY OF SKY

Copyright © 2014 by Robert Reed.
Cover art by Benoit Penaud.
Cover design by Sherin Nicole.

Prime Books
www.prime-books.com

Publisher's Note: No portion of this book may be reproduced by any means, mechanical, electronic, or otherwise, without first obtaining the permission of the copyright holder.

For more information, contact Prime Books:
prime@prime-books.com

ISBN: 978-1-60701-426-3

To the memory of Bette Boellstorff.

CONTENTS

BOOK ONE

DIAMOND

PROLOGUE

"Standing on two feet and calling yourself human does not make you so," says the man. "True humans are a noble, glorious species—an eternal family that has always been mortal and flawed, but keenly beautiful in that multitude of hearts."

Then he pauses for a moment, forcing the numbers and nothingness to listen to silence.

"Ages ago, humanity stood against miserable odds," he says. "Yet we managed to defeat a host of enemies as well as our own worst natures. As a prize, we were given a rich corner of the Creation and one long deceptive peace. But war is an endless business. War always returns, and not every battle will be won. A new enemy arose, rising straight from the souls of humans: immortal monsters, perfect and astonishingly lovely. Those monsters only pretended to be human. Instead of violence, they used smart words and charm and musical, intoxicating voices that unleashed every kind of wild promise. Bullets and nuclear plumes were nothing compared to those endless corruptions, and worst of all, the false humans could make every promise come true.

"Immortality was the most bewitching lure. Traditions and scruples were helpless against one soothing voice offering endless life and perfect health. A young man might listen to the siren call and then drift away before breakfast, never to return. Old women would pack their bags at midday, shamelessly limping off to claim vibrant new bodies. Fathers and mothers picked up their little ones, entire families slinking off in the night, repudiating honorable life to claim ten thousand years of monstrous existence.

"Ageless bodies demand superior minds. There are kinds of knowledge and knowing that only dense, eternal machines can master, and the lost people shamelessly mated with those machines—another abomination in the endless, one-sided struggle.

"The colossal war was unleashed, and true humans were losing.

"But the shreds of humanity gathered, and with old-fashioned minds, they decided on a bold strategy. Creation was full of places. One or two little corners had to exist where an honorable species could find its well-earned peace. This was why people joined together, marching into long forgotten realms. Humanity passed through and around and over and beneath every obstacle. Accidents killed many. New attritions came with every temptation. But the solemn, clear-eyed survivors arrived in a place that seemed nothing but perfect, and the last best souls settled down to make their final home.

"Except the Creation was relentless, and after a long age of safety, the great sanctuary grew porous, imperfect.

"Good souls stood on honorable legs, discussing and debating their miserable options. For three generations, wise scholars offered every moral solution. None were accepted. Then the fourth generation fell into an ugly slow war, the species collapsing into tribes, the tribes murdering one another with the age-old relish.

"And that was when one small boy drowned.

"His name and circumstances would soon be forgotten. True humans have brief perishable memories, which is as it should be. But the bare facts are that he slipped beneath a volume of chilled water, his last breath lost in a panic of bubbles. Blood grew purple and cold inside that shell of flesh. His mind fell away into darkness. Then a parent or perhaps an uncle grabbed a handful of hair and dragged him to the surface and pushed fresh air into his lungs, and somehow that cold dead mind remembered to live and came back from the Afterlife.

"Smothering water came up with the phlegm.

"His first words were, 'I heard a voice.'

" 'You heard my voice,' his savior agreed. 'I was shouting at you, you careless shit.'

" 'No, I heard a new voice . . . while I was dead and gone,' the boy said. 'The voice told me what has to be done to save my people.'

"True humans can be intense believers, shamelessly superstitious to the brink of foolish. Yet it had been ages since any of them were instinctive followers of gods or wise demons. Suspicious citizens had gathered in a circle, watching and listening. 'So whose voice was it?' one bystander asked. 'Do you know who was talking?'

"The boy nodded weakly, but he said nothing.

" 'And what did this voice tell you?' another person asked.

"The boy wasn't known as being especially bright or well-spoken, but the voice must have said quite a lot because he spoke without interruption, laying out a new journey and a fresh destination that none in the audience, not even the oldest wisest scholar could have imagined.

"Nobody believed him.

"Obviously the drowning had made him crazy. But the body quickly recovered its health, and as boys did in that day, he trained as a warrior, preparing to defend his tribe and his personal honor. But he never forgot the voice or its very clear message. On the eve of his first adult battle, he stole away fifty children and left the enclave. No great journey is easy. That little band endured forgotten adventures, defeating and confounding a host of monsters, but in the end, as their reward, they were allowed inside a place too remote to be named.

"This would be their home, just as the voice promised.

" 'But who was talking to you?' asked one little girl. 'When you were dead in the cold, who told you about this hiding place?'

"For the first and only time, the boy named their benefactor.

" 'The Great Ship spoke to me,' he said with a soft voice.

"It was an unexpected joke, and it seemed funny. Everyone else laughed while the boy smiled patiently, and then everyone joined together in a communal embrace, and ten generations later, nobody could remember that day or any day that came before."

ONE

The boy was real and his room was real but nothing else was. Other rooms and spaces larger than any room stood somewhere beyond the walls, but he couldn't believe in what refused to be seen. He was the one authentic person and the one true life. Even Mother and Father existed only when they stood beside him, their giant faces covered with silken white masks, gloved hands cradling his tiny misshapen body. They told him that he was a beautiful baby despite his appearance. They wanted him to relish a long pleasant life, despite frailties and the endless fever. Their words began as slow senseless noise, but there was no mistaking the devotion and fear woven through their voices. Learning to love those giants, the boy grieved when they left him and he wished they could be real even if he was alone, and one day his door was closed and locked and he let himself imagine his parents standing inside a second room just like his own—an inspiration, an epiphany, born from his growing love.

Then he wasn't a baby anymore. The boy was walking and discovering his own urgent voice and how words were attached to ideas. The first lesson taught to him was that the world was dangerous and often horrible but he was blessed with a fine sweet life. Good sons needed to remain behind the door that almost never opened, and regardless how unfair this existence might seem, he was told that those same good sons needed to obey every rule.

Disease was the first enemy. Germs rode on fingers and breath, ready to kill what was weak. Other than his parents, the most frequent visitor was the doctor—a man smaller than his parents, dressed in a white gown and white mask and thin gloves that stank of disinfectant. The doctor always smiled, even when he was worried. The smile showed in the watchful eyes and musical voice. Every examination began with the question, "How do you feel today, Diamond?" Diamond felt the same every day, but adults never believed that answer. So he claimed he was better here and worse there. The doctor nodded, carefully writing down each lie, and he took his patient's temperature and listened to the malformed heart and slow lungs, and he might measure a hand and short arm, or he would put a long leg into the air, studying the arched foot and stubby, nearly useless toes. Nothing important would change between visits, but at least the doctor felt certain of that before he gathered up his tools and wished his patient well, locking the great door behind him.

Diamond's parents always waited in the hallway, and the boy always jumped off the bed, putting an ear to the heavy wood, listening to three adults using quiet, serious voices. This was how he learned that children born tiny usually died. His modest fever was an old problem, but at least his breathing and pulse didn't seem any worse. And he was managing to grow, though slowly. Sluggish growth was another sure sign of weakness, like his odd skin and the narrow bones. But at least the quarantine was working, and the doctor congratulated his parents for their vigilance. Even the best people sometimes had odd babies, he reminded them. The Creators' hands were at work, and who could say why? Their son was surviving and seemed content enough despite his infirmities. There were fine reasons to celebrate. And if Diamond found the strength, he could someday visit other rooms inside the house, and should he become an adult—unlikely as that seemed—he might risk little journeys into the open air, feeding his soul with the beauty and perfection of the world.

The boy grew a little older and a little taller, and people came to visit the house—friends and neighbors wanting to wish the old couple well, and if possible, catch a glimpse of their remarkable, doomed child. Some spoke about the Creators and what was wanted for this boy. Sometimes they stood outside his door, reciting ancient words that might or might not bring blessings to the suffering. The best friends let his parents speak about the burdens and joys that came with sharing their lives with this small quiet gift of a child. Those good people were most likely to meet Diamond. If they were free of sniffles and fevers, and if they washed their hands and faces and dressed properly and touched nothing, they were allowed inside his room, if only for a very brief visit.

One lady was especially nice.

"Diamond," she said. She always said his name lovingly. "It is so good to see you," she said, her eyes smiling above the mask. "What have you been doing today?"

Unlike every other visitor, she acted patient, remaining quiet while the boy named his toys and told their life stories while explaining the furious little games that he had invented for himself.

The woman was younger than his parents, but she had two boys of her own. Diamond never asked about anyone's children. There was still too much baby inside him, and even though he was curious, he couldn't find the best words. But he listened intently when she mentioned her youngest son, how smart and special he was, and once, in an offhand fashion, she suggested that the two of them should meet and play games together.

That it would never happen. But being so young, Diamond accepted his solitude just as he knew that tomorrow or the next day some horrible sickness would find him, and his scrawny weak body would perish. That was the way of the world, and that was the Creators' will, and in the meantime he loved his toys and adored his parents, and each day had its little pleasures and trusted routines—a happy creature by nature, and why should Diamond question any portion of his great little life?

One day the young mother came to the house and spoke to the boy for a pleasant while and then left again. She shut the door but neglected to lock it, and Diamond sat on the floor and played with soldiers. A hand knocked lightly before trying the heavy brass latch. Then the door swung inward and a stranger entered. The stranger didn't wear any mask or gloves, or for that matter, any kind of smile. He was the lady's older son—a very big boy pulled into the room by curiosity. Saying nothing, he watched the toddler set down a block and a wooden soldier and then stand up, remaining where he was. The large boy studied Diamond's ugly long legs and that wrong-shaped face with the tiny nose and those odd pale eyes and the teeth that were too white to be real.

Diamond said, "Hello."

With a dismissive sneer, the stranger said, "You don't sound right either."

The little boy decided to say nothing.

"You aren't sick," the stranger said. "That's just a story, isn't it? I know what you really are. You're some kind of monster."

Diamond shifted his weight from one leg to the other, wishing this person would leave.

Then the stranger came close, and when Diamond backed away, the big boy said, "Don't. Stay where you are. I mean it."

The boy's voice was angry, and it was happy. He sounded both ways at once, unlikely as that seemed. And he was smiling now, except it wasn't a normal smile.

"Guess what I'm going to do," the stranger said. "Guess."

Diamond said nothing and did nothing.

"All right, I'll show you." Then he reached into a pocket riding his trouser leg, pulling out a long bright knife, and he drove the blade into Diamond's belly, watching the tiny boy squirm and bleed, using a quiet happy voice when he told him, "This is what you do with monsters. You kill them."

• • •

After that day, people were forbidden to see Diamond, and very few friends visited the house anymore. The only other guest was the doctor, but there were fewer examinations after the stabbing. The boy didn't seem to require the same exhaustive care. And the doctor used a new voice with the parents, hard and skeptical and sometimes loud. There was no good explanation for these phenomena, he warned. He was doing quite a lot of research, and certain old writings mentioned strange births and ancient children displaying the occasional odd power. But he doubted that his patient was like anyone ever born before.

One day, the doctor demanded to be left alone with his patient. That final examination lasted a long while. Little knives and steel hooks were involved, as well as gruff warnings to be quiet, and the tests might have continued all day if Father hadn't come through the door.

Stepping away from the bed, the doctor pulled off one his gloves.

"What are you doing?" Father asked.

"What I should have done hundreds of days ago," said the doctor. Then he put the surgical tools back into their case, and in front of Diamond, he warned that disease might kill eventually the boy, but that wasn't the worst problem. What his parents needed to fear, honestly and with all of their heart, were the mysteries wrapped around the creature living in their midst.

Mother stood beside Father now, her hands wrestling with one another.

"Are you all right?" she asked Diamond.

"I'm fine," he said, sitting up, showing them marks that weren't even wounds anymore.

Then the doctor said, "I've asked before. But maybe this time, you'll convince me. Was the pregnancy normal?"

Mother muttered a few soft words.

Turning toward Father, the doctor said, "I want to examine your wife. A careful, thorough assessment would only help."

Father stepped forward, towering over the doctor. And with a voice louder than Diamond had never heard, he told the little man, "We've seen enough and heard enough from you, sir. Before I throw you on your ass, leave. Climb away, and don't come back, and if you talk about this to anybody, I'll gut you. I will gut you while you live, which is what you deserve. Believe me."

• • •

Nobody visited anymore, and that wasn't the only change. Diamond's parents stopped wearing masks and gloves, though they were still careful about dirt and sniffles. His mother boiled his drinking water and cleaned his clothes in scalding, soapy water and fed him nothing but thoroughly cooked food. Nervous enough to tremble, his parents sat on his bed, explaining that he wasn't sick in normal ways but it would be best for him to remain inside the room. New dangers were on the prowl, but Diamond was safe when the door was closed and locked. They told him that people would soon forget what they couldn't see, and with time, the story about the knife and wound would seem too wild to believe. Their shared dream was that Diamond would grow out of this phase, and though they never said it to him, those two old people could imagine no greater blessing than an ordinary boy, happy like he was today, but unremarkable by every other measure.

They never stopped apologizing for his circumstances, and they never stopped asking what they could do to make his home better. And Diamond was almost honest, telling them that he couldn't think of anything that would improve his room. His room was supposedly the largest in the house. Storage chambers had been linked, creating a complex landscape full of hollows and corners, little tunnels and dead-end holes. The walls were living wood, dark and fragrant. The furniture was built from dead wood that had been cut and shaped carefully, joined together with glue and heavy pins. There were chairs too large for his body and chests full of heavy drawers, and strong shelves were fixed to the smoothest walls, the highest shelves holding dusty books left behind by people who lived long ago. Tubes of polished metal brought light from outside, each tube ending with a round plate of glass that changed color and brightness as day passed to night. Diamond's bed—a wide platform woven from soft silken fibers—stood within sight of the door. On the bed were his best friends, including a big lump of pale brown cloth and stuffing with jeweled eyes and a smiling mouth made from black thread and white insect shells. For some reason the doll was called Mister Mister, and the boy loved him and held tight to him when he felt most alone, and Mister Mister spoke to him with those quiet staring eyes and the grin that was like his grin, including the many white teeth.

Toys and other distractions littered the central chamber. Every leaping ball had its unique color and size, and there were rubber figures cut into geometric shapes and thousands of simple wooden blocks. He had an army of wooden figures shaped by hand and painted by hand and played with by his father and his father's father, time and busy fingers blurring the paint while smoothing every old wooden nose. Several mirrors supplied much fun. The boy liked to hold the largest mirror before his face, staring at the nose and eyes and mouth that were not that different from his parents' features. A circle of heavy glass was fixed to a wooden handle. The glass was thick in the middle and thin on its edges, and it meant nothing to him until he held it to his eye and looked at the wall. What had been small became wondrously large. The wood was full of giant ridges and cavernous pits. But even more fascinating was the landscape on the back of his bare hand. Thin hairs towered above smooth young flesh that was pink and stretched across a network of purplish veins and bumpy bones. He spent a full day comparing one hand with its mate and the tops of both legs with each other and the amazing unique whorls riding the tips of every finger and thumb. In his dreams that night he was a giant, so vast that tiny people walked across him—hundreds and maybe thousands of people—and he woke in the morning smiling even more than usual.

A narrow passageway led to the most remote chamber inside his room. This was once a back entrance to the house, but the chamber's original door was gone, the living wood pricked and prodded until the hole closed. The only furniture was an old chest built to fill a round space. The chest was full of drawers. Every drawer had its lock, but one lock had been broken and no one but Diamond knew it. That intriguing space was filled with fancy tools, some with sharp edges and pointed tips and handles designed for careful adult hands. He took what he needed and went back to the main chamber, setting the hand lens on the edge of a table and weighing down the handle with one of the old books. Then he held his left wrist under the lens while the right hand manipulated the knife. This was what the doctor had done to him many days ago. Feeling more pressure than pain, he cut into the biggest vein. Eager blood fled his body, turning a bright beautiful red in the open air. Then the edges of the cut reached across the gap, clasping one another, knitting the separated tissues back together, and the blood dried to something that was harder than any scab, and the dead blood soundlessly dissolved back inside the healed, unmarred flesh.

His parents' skin was beautiful, decorated with wrinkles and spots and old cuts never quite healed, and he asked them why this was. They would try to laugh at the question. Time had its ways of eroding and sculpting the body, they explained. A long pale scar defined his father's face, running from just beside the right eye down under the serious little mouth. It was a handsome mark—an intriguing remnant of some important, violent event. What could have done such lasting damage? The boy asked that question several times, and sometimes he would touch the scar or stared fondly at it for too long. But the man explained nothing. Some deep pain still had its hold, and Father would find some gentle means to deflect their conversation toward more pleasant topics.

Food and games were safe, happy subjects. Father was clever that way. He couldn't be tricked and never spoke without thinking first. And that was one reason why the boy adored the man and wanted to be like him.

One morning Diamond sat before the biggest mirror, using the sharpest knife to cut his face. He was trying to replicate that wonderful scar. But the cut refused to remain open. On his fifth attempt, Diamond discovered that he could ignore the pain, stabbing himself to the cheekbone and jerking down. Shoving his free hand into the gore, he managed to yank at the loose tissue. If the wound were too wide, it wouldn't heal. That was what he was hoping. But his mother happened to come along. Before he could hide the knife, the door was unbolted and open, and she saw the horrific gouge in his face and the whiteness of his naked cheekbone, the bright knife tight in his hand. In a miserable low voice she said his name, coming close and taking the knife while kissing the five fingertips of her other hand, using those blessed fingers to carefully close the hole, helping his face heal itself.

"Diamond," she whispered. "You must not. Don't do that. Never again, please."

He cried. The pain was small, but the disapproving sound of her voice made him sick and ashamed.

"Where did you find this?" she asked, holding the knife carefully.

Diamond showed her the drawer and watched as she stole away the sharpest, best tools.

"Are you going to try to hurt yourself again?"

He promised he wouldn't.

She accepted those words, vanishing with the tools and returning with a bowl of sweet nuts and warm fresh milk. By then, his face was normal again. She smiled at his face. She liked to watch her son eat. After a while she told him, "You're perfect as you are."

"But I'm not like you," he said.

She didn't respond.

"Or like Father," he whispered.

She nodded sadly. Then she told him what she always said at moments like this: "You are my son, and you are beautiful as you are, Diamond. So beautiful you make both of us ache."

• • •

He loved those two old people, but Diamond was leaving the days when little boys surrendered to their parents' every wish. He didn't feel trapped inside the room, and he still believed the old explanations and half-defined fears. But more of each day was spent with eyes closed, trying to imagine what he had never seen.

He knew the world was enormous. Enormous to him was a great room with tall walls and a distant ceiling—a volume too large to walk across in one long day. His visitors had mentioned the world, and his parents said quite a lot in passing. That was why he knew there were trees and wild animals and tame animals and many, many people, and every person wore a different name and special clothes, and everybody enjoyed busy, important lives. There was bright light to the day and deep shadow at night, and by stitching together tiny clues, Diamond understood that the great room had corners and holes where not even the bravest man would willingly go.

Father was brave. During one of her long-ago visits, the woman with two sons held the sterile mask across her mouth, telling the strange little boy, "You should be proud of your daddy. His work is special and rare, and he's one of the best. He might be the very best alive today."

Work was something that carried fathers away from home. Diamond was proud of the man, honestly fiercely proud, but he knew almost nothing about what his father did. The man usually rose early, leaving the house before the day began. If he was gone for four meals, he returned happy and relaxed. But he often wasn't home until late, six or seven meals into the day, and sometimes Diamond didn't see him for days and nights. On those occasions he always came home exhausted, his face dark brown except for the pale circles around his reddened eyes. The house door would open and close and Diamond would listen. He heard quite a lot. His parents used private voices, and then the hot water would run, his father washing his entire body with scented soaps. Only when he was clean would he finally enter his son's room. His face was still dark and tired, but despite his miserable mood, Father made himself smile and say happy words, and Diamond would notice the stink clinging under the perfumes—animal smells, musky and rich and very peculiar, often carrying the salty aroma of something that wasn't blood.

Asking Father about his work was useless. The man's only answer was a shrug and distant stare, and sometimes a little joke about sitting in a quiet place, doing as little as possible.

Mother said much more. People weren't visiting the house anymore, and she wouldn't leave her boy alone. That meant she was lonely. She had nobody except Diamond to speak with, and that's when little doses of truth leaked out. She admitted that she worried about Father. Much of the world was wild, and every wild place had its monsters, and she mentioned fire spiders and chokers, man-traps and jazzings, each of those monsters happy to prey on the small and careless. Then one day she used the word "papio." Diamond didn't know the word, but sometimes saying nothing was a good way to tease more words out of a person. He stared at his floor and odd toes, remaining quiet, and then she said that word a second time, explaining that the papio were smarter than men and they ruled the edges of the world.

He asked if the papio were monsters.

The question made her uncomfortable. Straightening her back, she said, "They aren't, no. In fact they're just another kind of human. But they must be handled with exceptional care."

"Does Father handle them?" asked Diamond, his right hand grabbing a piece of empty air.

Mother seemed ready to laugh at his joke. But then she stopped herself, saying, "That was the wrong word. Sorry. But yes, he gets along with the papio quite well."

On a later day, Diamond asked, "What is the worst monster of all?"

Mother thought for a long moment. Then she said, "He would never agree, but I think it's the coronas."

Diamond asked what the coronas were, and when she didn't answer, he hastily asked again.

She regretted her words. "No, no. Forget what I said."

Diamond forgot almost nothing. "Who wouldn't agree? Is it Father?"

She didn't seem to hear the questions. Her wide eyes stared into the wall, picturing the monstrous coronas. Diamond imagined something enormous and powerful but with no definite shape. Mother's fists made him nervous despite her confident noise. "There are no monsters," she said at last. "That's a word we strap to what we don't understand."

Yet that night Diamond dreamed of an enormous mouth that ate his house and his parents before gobbling him down.

One day Mother was angry. The boy noticed and asked why, and she said, "No, it's not because of you. It's never you, honey."

Diamond was playing. She was sitting on one of his big chairs, watching the floor. Without prompting, she said, "Sacrifice."

He looked up at her. "What does that mean?"

"It means giving up your life and well-being, doing what's right for others." Then with a sneer, she told him, "Sacrifice used to be honored. It used to be celebrated. But those were different times."

Father had missed three last-dinners and three nights. Diamond asked when he was coming home.

The old woman dipped her face and smiled sadly at her bunched up hands, not quite crying. "Soon," she said. "It won't be long."

"I miss him."

"And I wish he were here," she said.

"Why does he have to work?"

Why indeed? She asked herself that same question and thought hard before falling back to a trusted answer. "People need work to live," she said with a resigned, hopeless voice.

To the boy, that answered nothing.

Then she added another conundrum. Sighing, she told him, "Some people do impossible, important jobs. They are very good at those jobs. But that doesn't mean they don't hate the work with all their heart."

• • •

Father stayed home late enough one morning to bring Diamond the second breakfast. Sitting on a big chair, he watched his son gobble down the salted meal and milk while they talked about the usual matters: dreams and toys and the boy's plans for his gigantic day. Then with his most matter-of-fact voice, Diamond asked about the weather outside. Father considered, as he always did at such moments. "It's a wonderful day indoors," he said, and then he stood and asked if the chamber pot needed to be emptied. It did. "Well, I guess I'll dump it."

Father was the tallest person Diamond had ever seen, and despite his age, he was still quite strong. Lifting the pot by one handle, he held it as far from his face as possible. Then he set it on the floor and opened the door and went through with the pot and closed the door behind him. But he didn't use the lock, and he didn't wish his son a good day. Father was coming back. Diamond waited on the bed with Mister Mister. After a minute, a bell sounded. It was the bell that meant somebody was going to talk without being inside the house or at the door. Bad news often came with that bell, and the bell stopped and he listened, hearing nothing. But Father didn't return. He had left too quickly to say good-bye, and that bothered the boy in many ways.

The door was still unlocked. This had happened before, on rare occasions, and nothing else had happened. Diamond was safe inside his room; safety was the finest possession to have in your life. How many times had he been told that? But he was still bothered because his father hadn't wished him well on his day, and that changed his mood, his nature. He listened for his mother and heard nothing. She could be in some distant room or chamber, and she had no reason to think about him. Anything could be waiting beyond these walls, and without locks and bolts that heavy old door was no barrier at all, and that's why Diamond pulled it open and slowly, slowly stepped into the hallway.

What startled him first was how normal everything was. The walls and ceiling were the same living wood, the floor smoothed by generations of feet, and the air itself was no fresher or sweeter or brighter than the air he knew. A familiar green glow fell from round lights fixed to the walls and ceiling. He felt as if he belonged inside this short straight hallway. Another ten steps put him beside a second door that used to be sealed but now was held opened with a slice of thick golden rope. Beyond was a second hallway, wider and running perpendicular to his hallway. That's where Diamond stopped. He touched the open door and breathed before turning, looking back at his bed and happy Mister Mister, marveling at the distance he had covered.

And Mother found him.

The empty chamber pot dropped and rolled, and she hollered in surprise and then let out a nervous, brittle laugh.

Diamond jumped back and wished he hadn't.

"What are you doing?" she asked.

"Nothing," he said, which happened to be a little bit true.

She stared at him. Surprise became reflexive anger, and the anger was quickly swallowed up by deep old pities. "We know this is difficult," she said at last. Then she reached for his face, leaving her long hand in the air as he backed away. "For you and for us, this is such a burden. But it won't be forever, Diamond."

His life felt like forever.

"When you grow up," she said. "I promise. When you're big enough and know how to act . . . when you aren't a little boy who cuts his face for no good reason . . . you'll walk out of here. And if you wish, you'll never have to return to that room again."

She wanted him to feel thankful.

The rule, the tradition, was to dip his head as people did toward their superiors, and he would say, "Yes, Mother. Thank you, Mother."

But Father had left without warning, and Diamond's anger wasn't going away. Squaring up the little shoulders, putting his odd feet apart, he shook his head and said, "I won't. No, I won't ever do that."

Her blackish-brown eyes grew huge. "You won't do what?"

"Leave my room," he said. Then to prove his words, he retreated up the little hallway. "The world sounds awful. I won't go. I want to stay here forever."

His parents were very different from one another. Mother wasn't able to secure every thought, parsing out her sentences with clear authority. She was the parent who suffered doubts and second-guesses. Nothing her son could have said would have struck harder. Did he really not want to leave this room, this prison cell? Had their warnings been given too many times and too well, and now the child didn't have any curiosity left? That was an awful, unbearable prospect. And that's why she didn't hesitate, grabbing up one of his thin arms, dragging her barefoot son back to the second door and then into the long hallway.

Looking over her shoulder, she told him, "A quick glance then. Have a glimpse."

Diamond was stunned and very scared. This would be momentous, and he wasn't prepared. Never leaving his tiny familiar place was only words, only noise, and when the hallway curved before both of them, he muttered, "No."

She pulled harder. "One look out the window," she told him. "You deserve that much."

He meant to shout, "No."

But the hallway had come to an end. A tall pane of clear glass stood before them, and beyond the window was a great reach of air filled with green light and flickering shadows and objects moving too quickly to be seen clearly.

Diamond jerked his hand away.

Mother looked down at him. Didn't he understand? Couldn't he appreciate what she was doing? She was breaking the most important rule, and he was spoiling the moment with a toddler's stubborn idiocy.

She grabbed his little shoulders.

And Diamond swung—a reflexive hard sweeping motion with his right fist.

Mother shouted and stumbled and fell.

Now their faces were at the same level. Both faces were crying. With her right hand, the injured woman touched her ribs gingerly, and she winced, and she tried twice to stand before giving up. The pain was too awful. But with her other arm, she managed to pull her son close and hold him until her misery subsided part way, and he gradually fell back into quiet, exhausted sobs.

"We've always told you that you're weak," she said. "But that's a lie mostly meant for others. You're just small and not built for trees."

People were climbers. But Diamond wasn't a climber.

"For your size, you're really very strong. Amazingly strong. And now you know."

But what did he know?

She rose slowly and breathed as if nothing could hurt worse. But she managed to guide him back to his hallway and into his room. "Please, shut the door for me. Would you?" she asked. Then as it closed, she added, "And don't tell your father. For today, for always, this has to be our secret."

• • •

One secret led to others, building a conspiracy that brought mother and son closer. Children weren't supposed to begin reading and writing until they were a thousand days old. That was the rule and had been the rule forever, which made it only sweeter when she brought in the big-worded books intended for school children and simple people. While his father worked, Mother taught Diamond about letters and the very important marks that went between the letters, creating meaningful words that could be strung together in endless sentences. And she gave him black markers and bare pages, pleased with his successes and quiet when he failed. But he made few mistakes, particularly on matters of memory. Everything inside his head seemed eager to be found, and every day he amazed the old woman with what he had learned and how he found the patterns inside each of these secret lessons.

That a book could hold pictures was a revelation. The fat old volumes on his shelves were filled with long, impenetrable words, but one of his learning books was built from brightly colored drawings. Diamond studied strange faces and bizarre objects. The faces belonged to the Creators. Painted scenes showed the bright blackness that existed in that timeless time before the world. Mother sat beside her strange boy, describing how the Creators tried to weave perfection out of shadow, out of nothingness. Each of their works failed and had to die, but the gods learned and learned, and in a show of genius, they managed to piece together this Creation, this splendid, beautiful world without end.

The Creators loved the world and knew they could never do better, and celebrating what they had accomplished, those titanic beings kissed one another before dissolving into the same nothingness from which people and trees had come.

One Creator was named Marduk.

Patting the floor, Diamond said, "Our tree is named Marduk."

Important trees had important names and long histories.

His mother nodded. "But how do you know that?"

"I heard so."

"Someone told you about our tree?"

"No. You and Father were talking, and I was listening."

She looked at him and then at the closed door. "What else have you heard?"

The world was full of noises that never found his ears. "I haven't heard much," he claimed, not really lying.

"There are reasons we tell you so little," she said.

He nodded.

"Why we don't dare explain more."

Diamond waited.

"But if you live in the dark too long, your mind will be crippled."

Mother's plan, imprecise as it was, involved teaching the boy just enough—a string of tiny lessons to feed his mind, and perhaps, with luck, ease his transition into the world. Some days were full of reading and counting, and he never got tired. But she was tired or she was scared, and there were days when he taught himself, reading common words and writing them with his right hand. She also taught him manners and some mathematics and little songs for children. Diamond was rarely bored, but if he let his gaze wander, she would relent, giving him larger skills and bigger views. And every day, no matter the circumstance, lessons began and ended with a solemn promise not to share what was happening. Father was busy and had many problems, and no, Mother wouldn't explain the poor man's burdens, but Diamond needed to believe her and please stop asking those questions.

So he stopped asking, for days and days. And then one day, without urging, Mother began to talk about their home tree. Marduk was a blackwood, and more than a thousand families lived inside its carved tunnels and rooms. Some neighbors were her cousins, and others were friends or at least had been friendly in the past. She saw few people anymore. But hearing sadness in her own voice, Mother promised that if something was important and necessary, then there was goodness to find, and that's why this isolation was endurable.

Sitting in a chair, she named dozens of people and her ties to each of them, and she mentioned some of the larger trees by names or species, ending with the famous old bloodwoods growing in the District of Districts. But no tree was better than Marduk.

"Why, mama?"

Because her ancestors claimed the tree when it was little more than a sapling and she was born inside its wonderful wood, and she felt nothing but pride for the home that had fed and sheltered her without complaint. No other blackwood grew such sweet nuts, and that's what Father believed too, and he wasn't even born here. He came from the District of Mists, and he was a hornbeam man. Diamond asked what that meant, but she didn't hear him. Her face tilted backwards, eyes watching what only she could see. Then she smiled, and it was a different smile than any he could remember. Suddenly she was telling how she was a girl and Father was a beautiful soldier stationed in the nearby wilds, and that was how people from different places could meet and fall in love.

"The courtship and our marriage," she said wistfully. "It seems so long ago, my parents alive, standing beside me at the ceremony . . . "

Her voice trailed away.

"How long ago was it?" he asked.

That question she heard. Thorough calculations ended with the number, "Our wedding was five thousand and fifty-five days ago."

The number made little sense. Trying to measure it against something familiar, Diamond asked, "How old am I?"

She started to answer, but winced and put one of her hands into the other and held it snugly, as if comforting herself.

"I'm past nine hundred days," he said confidently. "But I haven't reached one thousand yet."

She found a smile. "Nine hundred and thirty days ago. That's when you blessed us by joining our lives."

How many of those days could he remember? Diamond looked into a bare wall, thinking back as far as possible.

"That was a very long day," his mother mentioned.

Diamond looked at her.

"Sometimes that happens," she continued, talking as much to her clenched hand as to him. "There are days that feel as if there might never be another night in the world. But night is inevitable."

Night was a presence. It was something that lay beyond the reach of men, plunging the world into shadow whenever it wished. And the darkness was a mystery to the boy.

"And the dawn always follows night, bringing us rain," she said.

Rain sounded beautiful, and it sounded terrible.

"You don't understand what I'm saying," she said hopefully.

Diamond didn't know what he understood. But after a few moments of silence, he asked, "How old are you?"

New calculations were made. "I'm ten thousand, six hundred and twenty-three days old."

That was an enormous number. He nodded and dipped his head.

She misunderstood. With a laugh, she said, "Don't worry. My parents lived past sixteen thousand days. They enjoyed good long lives, strong to the end."

"The end," he repeated.

She said nothing.

"When you die, what happens?"

She looked at her hands again. The fingers began to wiggle. "Those left behind will cry," she said. "Beyond that, I do not know."

• • •

Father was a careful speaker, but even silent men are full of lessons.

He often wore special clothes, heavy clothes covered with deep pockets and sturdy loops. He had a favorite pair of boots with armored flaps over his exposed toes, and padded undergarments helped protect his heart and belly and groin. The gray work shirt and trousers often came home needing to be mended, particularly when he had been gone overnight, and after Mother washed them, Father would sit in his son's room, expertly sewing up the long, unexplained tears.

Every person carried himself in a certain way, and Diamond studied how his father sat and walked; and later, in front of the big mirror, the boy would try to move like the scar-faced man.

When he was tired and smelled of death, Father's words were less guarded. He might mention a distant tree or some other landmark, and Diamond knew that if he put on a curious expression, some detail might be offered about a distant, unknowable piece of the world.

One evening Father sighed and said nothing, exhausted eyes staring at the floor. Then he sighed again, and with an important tone he warned the boy that coming home always took longer than leaving.

"Why would that be?"

The man thought for a moment. "For every reason you can think of," he said mysteriously.

Knots were their shared passion. Father showed the boy how tie the bright needle to the thread and pull it through the ripped fabric. He taught him how to marry two threads together and how to make one rope into a trustworthy slipknot. Every knot had its name, though he didn't know where any name came from. And he was impressed when Diamond practiced on his own, mastering even the most intricate knots.

Father left late one morning and came home while the day was beginning to fade. The room lights were softening, signaling night's arrival. Diamond was sitting on his floor, playing with the wooden soldiers. Father came through the door and smiled. He was wearing green clothes, soft and cut differently than his serious work clothes. This was what he wore when he didn't have to go away for a long time. Unlike every other day, he knelt on the floor in front of his boy, waiting for something. The room's door was ajar. He was listening. After a while, Mom called to him. She said that she was going to Cousin Ollo's, and Father instantly shouted, "Fine! Your men will defend the fort in your absence."

Something here was funny.

The two "men" laughed while Father reached into a front pocket, winking at

Diamond. "I shouldn't. Don't tell her. But I saw this outside, and I thought . . . well, I don't know what I thought . . . "

There were colors in the pocket. A patch of blue appeared, brighter than any blue Diamond had ever seen, and around the blue was a thin gold ring, and on the other side of his father's finger was a startling green—radiant and metallic, possessing depth, as if the greenness only increased as the eyes peered deeper into the beauty. The painted wooden soldiers were drab in comparison to this astonishment. Diamond giggled until his father held the colors close to him, and then he saw the dull black eye in the middle of the blue. The eye remained open, even as the man's thumb pulled across it. A pair of matching triangles, orange and tiny, stood near the eye, and the boy realized that the triangles formed some kind of mouth and the blue color was the head of a tiny animal and that rich metallic green was a body unlike anything that he had ever envisioned.

"What is this?" Diamond whispered.

"An usher bird." His father held the body and head in his long palm. "I found it on our landing. Poor thing flew into the window, probably just before I came home." Using his other hand, he eased one of the little wings away from the body. Its underside was white as cold milk, and each feather was a little different from its neighbors. "He's still warm," Father mentioned. Then after some thought, he asked, "Do you want to hold him?"

Diamond nodded, and the bird rolled off into the cup made by his tiny hands. The body weighed next to nothing, and the open eye was matched by another open eye on the opposite side of that narrow head. Diamond turned the bird and looked down the mouth, admiring a tiny tongue, and he turned it over and looked at the golden feet with their long toes and curled claws. Returning to the face, he studied the eyes while holding all of it tightly. Then quietly, more puzzled than worried, he said, "I don't think he's breathing."

"He isn't," Father agreed.

The boy looked up.

"He's dead, sweetie."

Diamond looked at the bird again, but differently.

"His neck is broken. Like I said, just before I got home, the poor boy flew into our window."

Yet the creature looked alive. That was Diamond's sense of things, and Father was mistaken.

"I'll have to take him with me. By tomorrow, he's going to stink. And nobody wants that."

The world was full of life. Little insects and millipedes occasionally found their way into this room, and Diamond had studied them with the hand lens and his tiniest tools. Tearing apart bugs taught him what death was, but it was never sad. This was sad. He stared at the usher bird, and finally his father said something about Mother coming home soon, carefully easing the corpse out of the boy's hands.

Diamond was close to crying.

Father looked at the wet eyes and then at the floor. "Maybe we shouldn't have."

"Shouldn't have what?"

"Never mind." Then a little later, he told him to do what was impossible. "Forget it," he said.

The bird vanished back inside the pocket.

"I'm glad you showed it to me," Diamond said. But he wasn't glad. Suddenly and for no reason he could name, he was angry.

Father didn't notice, or he ignored what he saw. Either way, he stood stiffly, knees sore from sitting on the floor, and after glancing at the half-open door, he turned back to his son. "We had good reasons," he said. "Everything we have done has been for you."

Then he left.

Diamond got to his feet and stood before the door as it was carefully re-locked, and despite trying to think about anything else, his mind was filled with that gaudy gorgeous almost-alive bird. He felt sick with fury. If something as beautiful as an usher bird could be found and thrown away in the same day, then the world outside had to be astonishing, and he didn't know anything about anything, and he feared that he was going to live forever, trapped inside a tree that he would never see for himself.

• • •

In one of his dreams, Diamond found himself out in the world, walking under the wide strong arms of what he assumed to be trees, and strangers spoke to him, and they had faces like his face, and there was light in the world and green shadow with distant walls and a ceiling made of a dark scented wood, and he liked all of it, even when he was awake again, lying in his familiar bed.

But there was another dream, an old piece of nonsense that always left him curious and terrified. It began inside his room. He was playing with his favorite toys when a sound interrupted his fun. Sometimes it was a voice, and sometimes it was music—a few bright little notes beginning some melody that felt familiar. And the voice was familiar too. Sometimes it belonged to a man, but usually a woman was talking. He heard his name called, except he wasn't Diamond, and he tried to remember the name but his usually perfect memory failed him, losing it before he woke.

That night, after Father brought the bird and took it away again, the dream returned. The woman called to him, using the other name. He always recognized her voice. Diamond got up from his toys and listened until she called again, her voice more urgent than usual. Of course he followed, and like every other time he ended up inside the side chamber where the big chest stood with its many locked drawers. The chamber was the same as in life, except for a tall door that didn't belong. The door was bright and gray, slick like a mirror but strong to the touch. His touch triggered a hidden mechanism, or maybe the door opened for no reason. Either way, it would pull aside, revealing another room, unsuspected until now. The room was Diamond's secret, and that night, when he touched the door, he expected what always happened. A great wash of light would pour over him, and he would see wonders, and the shock and his amazement would yank him out of his sleep, leaving him unable to remember any details.

This would be the same dream, he assumed. With that thought, he touched the door and watched it fall away. But there was no flash of light this time, no visions too wondrous to recall. There was just a long gray hallway, and standing before him was a powerfully built man who stared hard at him, as if angry to find a boy where he expected someone else.

Diamond tried to talk but couldn't.

Then the strong man knelt and greeted him with the other name.

The boy recognized the voice.

"This is just for the little while," said the man. "Just to keep you safe."

"I am safe," Diamond said.

"Until you can leave and come find us."

"Come find who?" Diamond muttered.

The man had different features than Father. His face had no scars or wrinkles, but it was an uneven, ugly face just the same. He had short arms thick with muscle and long legs and the wrong-shaped feet that Diamond knew well, and the boy stared at those feet until boots formed around them. Then the strong man touched him on the face, fingers warm as a fever.

"When you come find us, bring them," said the man.

"Who do I bring?" Diamond asked.

But the man didn't answer. A smile broke out on his unhandsome face, and a voice that sounded rough and sturdy and never quite friendly said, "One bit of advice. Everything is even stranger than it seems."

And with that, Diamond fell awake.

• • •

Night was its darkest, deepest. Mister Mister agreeably went with the boy, riding under one arm as he climbed through a passageway that smelled of sap and living blackwood, two friends slipping into the chamber with the old chest and the many locked drawers and round walls that held no secret door, and that's where the boy was when dawn broke. Metal tubes carried the day inside that little space—a blood-colored light that meant rain—and he sat on the bare floor, long legs crossed, feeling the slow, majestic sway of Marduk as the world began one more day.

TWO

Tomorrow Diamond would be nine hundred and eighty-three days old.

He mentioned this while making ready for bed and his mother nodded as if listening. She was kneeling, picking up blocks and putting them into their special big box with the hinged lid and rope handles. That was unusual. Mother was diligent about cleaning his dishes and the chamber pot, but this was his room and his world, and she demanded nothing but enough space for a person to walk wherever she wanted. Yet there she was, on her knees with her long back bent, working her way toward a stout little building guarded by wooden soldiers.

"This was a quick day," Diamond mentioned.

She nodded again, finding a place for a long cylinder. Then she hesitated, focusing on her fingertips before looking at her son sitting on the edge of his bed. "What did you say?"

"It was a short day."

"It was," she agreed.

He asked, "Why?"

"Because." She took a breath and held it deep, golden teeth shining in the dim green light. She was trying to devise a worthy answer, or she was thinking about something else entirely. There was no telling. Then the air leaked out of her, and she attacked the big fort. His soldiers fought as hard as they could, accomplishing nothing. She swept them aside and quickly dismantled what Diamond had built today, dropping blocks into the open box until sharp corners and whole pieces were sitting above the rim.

"He won't be home tonight," said Diamond.

Again, she didn't seem to hear him.

But when he started to repeat himself, Mother interrupted. "Your father is working all night. Yes."

There was a long pause. Diamond wasn't certain why, but the evening silence felt wrong. The person on his floor wasn't her usual self, and that bothered him and fascinated him and he watched her as carefully as he could.

Mother noticed. Her mouth tightened again and the black-brown eyes looked through him. Then with a careful slow and almost angry voice, she said, "I want these little men picked up."

"The soldiers?"

"Get them off the floor."

He didn't complain, but working slowly, he snatched up the figures one by one, studying each face before finding the perfect place for his friends to stand on the various shelves. Every soldier had a name and rank, and they were lumped into smaller units composed of good close friends. Hundreds of battles had been fought and won by this army. These good brave men always stood united against the common foe. No soldier had ever died forever, and they had defeated a host of monsters, including an agreeable Mister Mister. They were his army and the worn faces meant quite a lot to him, and more than once his father had mentioned that nobody had ever played as hard with them as Diamond had.

"When will he come home?" he asked.

Mother was struggling to fit the blocks into their box. "Tomorrow, and maybe in the morning."

"Oh, good," he said.

The best soldiers deserved the highest shelf, but Diamond couldn't reach all the way up. He pulled the stool out from under the bed and got up on his toes, setting twelve warriors in a row, near the edge, each holding a sword or a gun, ready for the next war. Swords were long knives, and he knew about knives. But his parents never talked about guns, which made them mysterious and intriguing.

Old books were propped on that shelf. Diamond pulled one book down and dragged a thumb across the dusty binding, enjoying the rough cool leather and its considerable age. Then he opened the cover, glue cracking with the abuse. Unlike the books for children, the binding was on the side, not on top, and the words ran in straight flat lines across the gray pages. Not one letter was familiar. He knew the full alphabet for people, but he couldn't even guess how to piece together what was being said here.

"Why can't I read this?"

Mother was staring at the box overflowing with blocks. What could have been pain started to show in her face, and then pain turned into a sigh. She picked up a triangle and put it down where it had been, reminding him, "I told you. Those books aren't ours."

"Then we should give them back."

"No, they belong to us. But others wrote them."

"What others?"

She tilted her head and looked at him. Then her face turned away and she said, "No."

Diamond put the book back and climbed down.

Talking to the blocks, she said, "These won't fit."

"They do," he said.

"I don't believe you." A smile came from somewhere. "Show me."

Diamond pulled off the top few rows, sorting the blocks as he worked. Then he put them back inside their box. This was a puzzle with many answers, but there were many more ways to go wrong. He liked the task. He liked how his mother frowned when he worked his fastest. When he was done, there were little gaps in the top row. "I'm missing a triangle and two cubes," he said.

"Lost by my father," she admitted.

These used to be his grandfather's toys. Mother didn't play with them when she was little, and that's why the dead man was blamed.

Diamond shut the lid and went back to rescuing soldiers.

But then she said, "Stop. I don't care about that, honey."

He finished with the soldier in his hand before sitting on his bed. What was very peculiar was how quickly it had grown dark, in the world and inside his room. He could see Mother's face and what she was doing, but the gray-green light was blackening by the moment. Maybe she read his thoughts, or maybe it was chance. Either way, she warned him, "It's going to be a long, long night."

Days and nights were the never same twice. He nodded and said, "All right," and waited to be put under the sheets.

But she didn't want to leave. She stood and brushed the hair on his head and then ran those same fingers through her stiff gray hair, smiling in an odd way before saying, "Does your pot need to be emptied?"

"No."

"I should do that anyway." She looked at the mostly closed door. "You have water and something to eat?"

"Cold crescents and oil," he said. "And you filled the pitcher."

She said, "Good."

He waited.

"What was I going to do?"

"My pot."

"Yes. How did I forget?"

He wondered that too. But he said nothing, watching her carry the chamber pot out the door. He was nervous but unsure why. A very bad feeling made his breath quicken, and then she returned with the clean pot and everything was better again. His mother drifted through the gloom. Suddenly it was full night, only the faintest glow coming through the five tubes that led into this chamber. Diamond recognized his mother from her shape and the walk and how she still favored the ribs that were lazy about mending.

"Good night, Diamond."

"Good night."

She kissed him. Then she touched the top of his head, saying, "Such a marvelous brain."

He waited.

"Is it inside your head?"

"Is what inside my head?"

"Your brain. That mind of yours." She bent low, and a tear fell from her face onto his cheek. "Can you tell where your thinking comes from?"

He touched his temple.

"Maybe so," she said, sounding skeptical.

Now he was crying, and he had no idea why.

"Nine hundred and eighty-three," she said, laughing too loudly. "That's a fine wonderful perfect age."

"Mother?"

"Yes."

"I want to sleep," he lied. "I'm tired now."

"Of course." She kissed his wet cheeks and his silly little nose and then ran her hand through the curly brown hair that wasn't like anyone else's. "Sleep as long as you can, honey. Your father comes home in the morning."

• • •

The night was exceptionally long.

Diamond woke twice to relieve himself in the chamber pot, memory guiding him through the seamless dark. But he got careless once, stumbling and then catching a bare foot on the pot itself. Nothing spilled, but the near-disaster felt like a warning. After finishing, he cleaned himself and went slowly through the blackness with both hands leading. The pitcher was a heavy cool piece of varnished wood, the water warm and delicious. He drank until full and remembered his way back to his bed, crawling under the sheets with Mister Mister, touching the cloth eyes and teeth and those simple two-fingered hands.

There never was a longer night, not in his life. Diamond was scared but not in a bad way. Not so that he wanted to call out for Mother. He was worried but excited and there wasn't any sleepiness left in him, and for a long while he lay there thinking. His mind jumped from subject to subject. In his head, he played with his toys, but that wasn't much fun. He replayed everything his mother said before bed, word after word, and he imagined Father arriving in the morning, the sound of his voice and running water in the shower and hearing him walk down the hallway to his son's room. Then Diamond didn't feel scared. But sadness ran in his blood, and he tried to decipher where that feeling came from, and that's what he was doing when he heard the noise.

He heard the noise, and he felt it.

The sound was distant but drawing closer. He started to sit up as the floor shook and the bed swayed, as a great rumbling engulfed him. Dark strong wood was being pushed. Enormous forces were testing Marduk's trunk. This was something new, something Diamond hadn't imagined. He remained upright, grinning with nervous amazement, and then the tree gradually quit moving while each of the room's five lights began to glow.

A deep brownish red light was the first sign of the day. Like every morning, it came slowly. No moment seemed brighter than the moment before, but the transformation was steady and smooth. Vague lines became simple shapes that turned into walls and furniture and the shelves. It was as if a hand and paintbrush were adding details everywhere at once. When he could see his floor, Diamond jumped down and set his stool under the lowest light, and standing on his little toes, he put his eyes up next to the pane of thick round glass. He had done this before, this careful watching of the dawn. Red was always the first color. The dawn rain would last for a little while or a long while. Long nights usually brought long rains. Pushing an ear to the glass, he heard a smooth steady sound louder than the usual rain sounds, and he closed his eyes, working to imagine what was happening outside.

What always came to mind was the image of water spilling from a giant wooden pitcher.

He had mentioned that guess to his parents, more than once.

Father usually responded with a sober nod, saying, "It's something like that. And it's something else entirely."

Mother preferred to look away, telling the walls, "I don't like rain. Let's change the subject."

Diamond stood tall until his calves ached. By then the light was bright, the blood color thinning toward pink once the heaviest rain was done. Jumping down from the stool, he returned to bed and pulled the sheets over his body and lay down, ready to pretend sleep. That was one of his best tricks, eyes closed, body limp and dreamy. He lay there a long while, sharp ears listening to the pumping of his heart and his blood. The wood overhead offered a slow majestic creaking. Marduk was adjusting to the weight of water and the vanished winds, and one shift triggered others, a much louder groan coming from behind his head. Then he heard his mother's footsteps. He was certain. Familiar bare feet were slipping along in the hallway, and he smiled into his pillow, waiting for the locks to be turned. Father always flipped the knob's lock before releasing the two long bolts. Mother used the keys first, probably because the knob was hardest for her. He listened for the rattle of big keys, but there wasn't any. He couldn't hear the feet on the floor anymore, and nobody called through the massive door. Nobody was saying, "Good morning, my darling. How did you sleep, my love?"

Eventually Diamond sat up, staring at the door.

Abandoning his bed broke an important ritual. He slowly approached the door, setting his right hand on the cool knob. Nobody was standing on the other side. He was as certain of that as he had been about his mother's arrival. The red and pink of dawn had vanished, replaced with the searing green-white glare of full morning. Maybe he had fallen back asleep. The footsteps could have been a dream. But just to be sure, he said, "Good morning," to the door. "I'm awake, Mother. Are you there?"

There was no answer.

To the silence, he said, "You're late, Mama."

She was very late. He couldn't remember the day being this far along and not have at least two visits from her or Father.

"Where are you?" he asked.

The great tree gave a sorry long groan—one of those early-in-the-day tremors signaling the flow of sap in response to the sun. Marduk was with him but that meant so little, and Diamond settled to the floor with his legs crossed and put his hands on his face and cried.

• • •

The crying didn't last.

No bravery or special courage dried his eyes. Tears didn't help, and he gave up on them. Father would be home soon. He stood and wiped his eyes and went to the table with the water pitcher and the little plate with two cold crescents and the blackwood bowl full of golden oil. That Mother left such a large treat was unusual and suddenly ominous. But she always had reasons for doing what she did, and he assumed there were good wise perfect reasons behind the gifts. Father was coming home. He might arrive in the next breath. Mother had to step out early this morning, and she would be back in another moment, full of apologies. Those were the stories that allowed Diamond to feel hungry.

He wouldn't let himself worry, eating both of the crescents, using their charred ends and his fingers to soak up the last drops and smears of the sweet oil. Once again, he used the chamber pot, and he brushed his teeth with his special brush and the bitter gray paste, and he considered dressing but decided to wait. A game seemed necessary, and so he brought down his soldiers and lined them up on the floor and opened the box of blocks and stared at the top layer for a long time. Then he invited Mister Mister to sit beside him, and together they studied the loyal warriors with their swords and fierce guns and uniforms unlike what his father wore for work, and to no one in particular, he said, "I don't know what to do now. I don't."

He returned to the door, pressing an ear to the cool wood.

Nothing.

Early in his life the door's edges had been covered with foam, sealing out germs and unnamed poisons. But the foam below had worn away, leaving a long gap. Through his left eye, the hallway was a plain of smooth wood, vast and empty. Nobody was standing quietly on the other side. He looked at every angle, making sure. Sitting back, his mind wandered where it wanted, and it was as if he was watching his thoughts from some safe high place, uncertain where they would lead next.

The image of his mother returned to him—bent over, ribs bruised, her face filled with tears. Old people were subject to injuries. His parents proved that, what with scars and creaking joints and the way they stood up slowly and carefully after too much sitting. Mother wasn't gone; she was hurt. A sloppy misstep caused her to fall, and she was somewhere else in the house, too sore to move or help herself. That was the perfect and very awful explanation, and the boy leaned against the door and cried for both of them.

Again, tears didn't last.

He got to his feet, and quicker than ever in his life he dressed. He put on yesterday's trousers and a favorite long shirt that he tied with a one-knot on his left side, and he slipped on the sandals that Father had refitted for his feet. Then he hurried up into the round chamber with its chest full of locked drawers and the one drawer that still had a few tools that weren't forbidden to him.

He pulled out the entire drawer and carried it to the door.

Once more he looked through the gap and with a loud worried voice called out, "Mother. Are you there? Can you hear me?"

Nobody answered.

That made everything worse. He couldn't know how badly hurt and helpless she was, so he had no choice but work fast. Little steel prods and screwdrivers and a hammer meant to shape soft metals offered their services. Diamond didn't know what to do with any of them. But he remembered another day—almost two hundred days ago—when the knob became too difficult for Mother to turn. Father kneeled beside the door, using various tools to remove the old brass plate and fix the workings, adding lubricant and a few hard curses before closing it up again. Then he winked at the little boy who was watching every motion, asking, "And how can this be interesting?"

Everything was fascinating, if you paid attention.

Diamond set out his tools and studied the door before picking up a screwdriver, attacking the two broad screws that held the plate in place. He turned the left screw until it tumbled to the floor. But the other screw was worn and partly stripped, and it refused to come free. And even if this worked, he wondered what he would do with the dismantled knob. Two enormous bolts were set deep into the adjacent wall, each ready to fight him to the end. Diamond touched the dead wood and the lowest cross bracings and each wooden pin that held the stubborn door together. Three hinges were on the left side, each filled with a long iron pin. The pin on the bottom hinge had worked partway free. That seemed important. With his little hammer, he struck the pin from below, trying to lift it free. Soon the pin's head was shiny, and he made so much noise that he heard it in his head after he quit. But nothing had changed. Nothing was different. So he stepped back and looked at everything but the door, searching for the hardest toughest strongest object in the room.

Then he saw himself in the mirror.

Tools always broke, but the boy was an enduring constant. He attacked the door's wood with screwdrivers and steel prods and other small, nearly useless implements. Then he set the hand lens on the floor and broke it with the leg of a chair, and wrapping the biggest shard inside his heaviest shirt, he sliced long narrow gouges into the softest board. Pressing as hard as possible, the sharp edge peeled out slivers, and he cut up the shirt and himself and finally stopped to heal. Then he went back to work and cut himself again and forgot to stop. Time didn't matter. But it was still early morning and still very bright and nothing useful had been accomplished. So he dropped to the floor and stared at the bloody mess of his right hand, watching the blood pull back inside him before the skin closed and turned pink again. He was deciding if he should sit here and cry or cry in bed. Both plans had their merits, and he hadn't decided. And that's when a voice said something about the knob.

He didn't know the voice. And to say that he heard words would overstate what happened. But there was a presence, both distant and exceptionally close. It came from the world or surfaced from his brain. Whatever the source, he felt it for a moment and then there was nothing to feel, and as if for the first time, he stared at the knob.

Rising to his feet, Diamond took two deep breaths. Then he grabbed the round brass ball with his unbloodied hand, and the repaired, well-lubricated mechanism turned easily, and not only wasn't the knob locked, but while he was sleeping, sometime during that very long night, someone had taken the trouble to unlock the long bolts as well.

The door swung toward him.

And for the second time in his life, Diamond stood inside the larger world.

• • •

Barely more than whispering, he called for his mother.

Silence.

He walked to the end of the first hallway. A little louder this time, he said, "Mother?"

The silence held for a few moments. Then came a sharp click from somewhere close, and after a pause, two more clicks.

Diamond entered the second hallway and stopped. He stopped and looked back into his room, seeing Mister Mister sitting on the floor, waiting for him. He wanted to go back again and grab him up, and he might have done that. But a small quick shape burst out of another room or chamber, running out into the hallway, and seeing the boy standing a few steps away, the shape let out a bright musical yelp.

Diamond jumped backward.

The animal leaped straight up, dropping whatever was in its hand.

"What are you?" asked Diamond.

No bigger than his biggest stuffed toy, the animal was covered with dense short fur that was orange on the face and scalp and almost black on the body. The feet were like hands, and it stood on all four hands, showing the human a set of fearless yellow teeth.

On the floor between them lay a big ripe luscious. The purple skin had been pierced, revealing sweet cool white flesh. Diamond glanced at the fruit. The animal snarled and ran forward, grabbing up the treasure with its front hands, sticking the luscious into its mouth before backing down the hallway, finding that perfect distance where it could sit on its haunches, enjoying its meal while keeping close watch over its competitor.

"What are you?"

The creature was a surprise. Diamond couldn't guess its name or where it fit among the animals of the world, much less how it got inside the house. He supposed that it could have always lived here, but wouldn't there have been clues? His parents would have mentioned the creature, and he definitely would have heard anything so noisy. Yet in little ways, the face and body were familiar. Some of his stuffed animals were similar. That long face and the little hands had human flavors. Diamond watched the animal consume the luscious. Then he took one small step forward, and the animal noticed, lowering its front hands while the orange fur lifted, making its face appear bigger than before.

"Where's my mother?"

Diamond expected a response. He deserved an answer, and the animal seemed to understand him. Every time he spoke, it reacted, sneering at him, yellow teeth and bluster proving that it was in a very foul mood.

"Have you seen my mother?"

It snarled.

"Are you a monster?"

Maybe it was. But Diamond's imaginary monsters were enormous. Bulk and strength made them terrors, and this little beast was nothing compared to the dreams that made him afraid.

Green daylight was behind him. Diamond had come into the hallway ready to look outside. But he stepped away from the window, one stride and another, and reading his mind, the animal shoved the half-eaten fruit into its mouth before scampering away on all of its hands.

Diamond chased.

The animal leaped right at the first door, vanishing.

Loudly this time, the boy called out, "Mother."

No one answered, and he turned where the animal turned.

The room was long and narrow with a second entrance at the far end. There was a high ceiling and multiple lights, but nothing about this space was large. Dead wood had been cut and fitted to make cabinets and shelves. There were dishes and old metal pots and every kind of utensil and bowl and plate. Broad metal boxes stood against opposite walls. One box had handles. The other was topped with iron grates, and above that box was an enormous tube painted black on the inside. Diamond smelled food. He smelled old fires and ashes and the stinking beginnings of rot. He assumed the animal had run out the far door, but a tiny noise came from overhead. That very small monster was on the highest shelf, perched on a space too small for its bulk and its energy. One misstep and it would tumble, yet it seemed utterly comfortable in that predicament.

Whatever the animal was, it had to know something about Mother. Diamond couldn't think any other way. And if he could trap it and talk to it, maybe he could learn what was happening. That's why the boy picked up a cooking pot by its handle, ready to threaten the animal with it, but the pot was filled with a cold sticky liquid that spilled over his arm and shirt. Diamond cried out in surprise, and seeing its chance, his opponent dropped to the counter beside him, ready to flee, the last of the fruit clamped in its greedy mouth.

Diamond swung the half-filled pot, smacking the animal in the head.

The luscious was dislodged, and the animal shrieked, and Diamond swung the pot again. But the animal was very quick. Jaws strong enough to shatter nuts pushed the long incisors into his hand, all the way to the bone, and Diamond yelled, in surprise and then pain. He dropped the pot. Standing on the counter, the animal opened its mouth and gave a hard long snarl. Diamond reached out. He had some idea about grabbing and shaking that furry head. But his enemy grabbed the boy's right wrist with its front hands and expertly pulled the smallest finger into its mouth, sharp teeth cutting through the first joint.

A piece of finger was gone.

Diamond jumped back, gazing at the damage.

The animal spat out the fingertip, and it cackled in a wild, careless fashion, letting the world know that it was a monster indeed.

Pulling his injured hand close, Diamond began to cry.

The animal retrieved the original prize. The luscious was mostly eaten and the meat had turned gray, but it would always be something worth savoring. Squatting on the counter, the animal took slow tiny bites, enjoying the wet sounds and the sweetness as it watched the boy bleeding. Its mouth didn't smile, but the black eyes did. Then nothing was left but the hard flesh around the pit, and the animal sucked on one end and then the other before tossing the pit to the floor, licking sticky lips and its own ten fingertips before those smiling eyes looked at Diamond, and it said, "Good."

"What?"

"Good," it repeated. Then it jumped to the floor and grabbed the handle on one metal box, opening a little door and reaching inside, and with an expert's precision it selected another delicious meal.

• • •

The fingertip was pale and dead to the eye.

Diamond knelt and picked it up. The skin was loose and sloppy between the fingers of his left hand, and the dead fingernail was long, and he could feel the little bit of bone in its center. For a few moments he stared at the glossy and slick and beautifully white joint. The living piece of his finger had stopped bleeding. A warm sensation was building, and he flexed his hand, feeling something that wasn't pain but wasn't pleasant either. Then because it seemed right and smart, he touched the severed fingertip to the stump, and within twenty breaths some kind of seal had joined him to what used to be him, and after twenty more breaths the fingertip was part of him again.

The monster ignored the marvel. A bowl of pickled cling-onions needed to be eaten, each with the same two-bite relish. When Diamond moved again, the monster looked up and lifted its fur, just enough for the warning to be understood. Then it belched and went back to its feast, and Diamond passed the rest of the way through the kitchen, moving into the next hallway.

For almost a thousand days he had listened to the voices inside this house, to the sounds people made as they moved. Every sound had been a clue, revealing shapes and proportions. Noise let a boy imagine the shape of this place. In that sense, Diamond already knew the general layout of the rooms and hallways. Yet he knew nothing. Nothing looked exactly or even close to what he expected, and nothing smelled right, and no place was as clean and pretty as he had imagined it to be.

Diamond walked slowly, calling to his mother. He watched for windows. He watched for the same window that he had seen before, making himself ready to give the world a long look. But the hallway insisted on taking him past nothing but tiny rooms and miniscule closets, plus one space that might have been inhabited once but was now jammed with young wood, golden and sticky to the touch.

His finger had healed. No mark showed on the smooth new skin, and the tip's feeling was fully restored. He might have been astonished, except nothing about the experience seemed extraordinary. Putting the finger to his tongue, he tasted tree sap. And then he called out again. "Father?" he said this time. "Papa? Are you home yet?"

In the kitchen, something substantial fell from a high shelf, and then the animal threw another high-pitched shriek at the world.

Diamond walked on.

Rooms had furnishings, closets did not. Most rooms wore doors that opened with the first push, while closets were hidden behind fabric curtains full of lines and color. No other door wore a lock, and the furnishings looked newer than his chairs and bed. Walls and ceilings were stained white, making the spaces bright. Yet every room was very crowded with belongings. A large bed nearly filled one space. Stepping inside, Diamond smelled his parents. A wide room was down the hall, perhaps half as large as his room but full of long chairs and tables hanging from the ceiling by ropes. There was room for ten or twelve adults to sit close together. When had his parents ever had so many visitors?

"Mother?" he asked the room.

Stepping back into the hallway, he called out, "Father?"

The air had grown brighter. Diamond followed the hallway around a sharp right turn, and then it straightened. Waiting on his right was a very large closet. He looked inside and gasped at the human bodies hanging high in the air. There were at least six bodies, none with feet or hands or heads. He took a full step back before realizing that these were only clothes—his father's special gray work uniforms—dangling from the ceiling, waiting to be needed. One massive shelf was filled with armored helmets and goggles and gloves, and on the floor was a row of reinforced boots battered by hard long use.

Just the idea of hanging bodies unnerved the boy. He didn't call for anybody now. He backed slowly out of the closet. Waiting farther down the hallway was a large window full of light. It was the same window he had seen that one day with his mother. When he thought about Mother, there was no space in his head for anyone else. He was focused and worried about her and distracted about everything else. One more door remained to be looked behind, and for no reason but hope, Diamond decided that she was waiting for him there.

The last door had a lock, but it had been left unlatched and partway open. Unlike other doors, it swung into the hallway. He stepped around it. A brief tunnel stood before him, cut through a different kind of wood—a dark dry fibrous wood—and at the tunnel's end was a glimmer of light and a heavy curtain with some kind of face embroidered into the fabric, staring at him.

Diamond walked forward and pushed at the curtain, a deluge of brilliant green light pouring up his arm and across his astonished face.

Then he pushed again, and that was how the boy finally stepped outdoors.

THREE

A flat solid surface lay under his feet. The world before him was built from motion and shifting mysterious sounds along with fixed shapes that could be anything. Daylight blinded. What he saw was blazing and relentless, every detail washed away by the fierce glare that had no source, no destination. Eyes squinted down to slits and still the light slashed into his skull, filling his head with scorching green-white fire. The boy sobbed—a sad little sound washed away by raucous noise rushing down on top of him. A million mouths were shouting, none human: rattling barks and wild long passionate hoots, melodies and brilliant shrieks. Then something overhead let loose a string of bright rhythmic chirps. He shouted, "Hello." The chirps stopped. Then he took his first breath, tasting water. But the rain was finished, why was the air wet? One blind step led to another. The floor beneath gave a patient creak, and he stopped. Beyond the voices, filling some distant space, was a rumbling roar. He heard it and felt it in his bones, and tipping his head to gauge its source, Diamond turned his nearly closed eyes toward the heart of the great sound, seeing nothing that made even the barest sense.

Fixing his hands beside his eyes helped stifle the glare. The flat smooth face of the landing reached out several more steps before ending with a high railing and open space, and slicing through the air beyond was a column of silver light, brighter than anything else in this baffling, wondrous place.

Diamond took another step.

"I know, I know," a voice called out.

He stopped walking.

From above, a girl shouted, "But I'm looking for my bracelet."

Then someone else spoke, a stern voice falling from a greater height, the sense of it drained by distance.

"I can't hear you," the girl shouted.

Diamond tipped his head, listening.

"Hey you. Do you see my bracelet?"

Her voice had grown louder.

"It's copper, with a face and blue shells," she said. "I dropped it last night. Look around. Maybe it hit your landing."

"A bracelet," Diamond said.

"Kid," she said. "I'm screaming at you. Do you see my bracelet?"

"I can't see anything," he said, dropping to his knees, eyes closed before he rubbed them with his knuckles.

The girl said something else, something quiet.

For several moments, nothing happened.

Then the curtain to his house moved. Diamond smelled the little monster. Stepping up beside him, the animal gave a hearty belch, and from someplace close, the girl asked, "Who's your ugly friend?"

Diamond opened his left eye, then his right. Pupils and the light-starved retinas were adapting to the piercing morning light. This time he could make out the wood slats of the landing and his hands and his feet. Wood railings stood on three sides, and behind him the same stranger's face that rode the other side of the curtain. The well-fed monster was near enough to touch, giving him a stern glare before looking up where the girl's voice had fallen from.

Diamond did the same.

The girl was floating in the air, bare feet and one arm dangling. Her other hand held a golden rope fixed to the wet brown bark. Nothing else kept her from falling. The rope stretched high overhead, vanishing into a milky mist. She might have been hanging there forever, judging by how easily she in the emptiness. She looked at Diamond and smiled. Then she looked up, shouting into the mist.

"Yeah," she said. "I'm coming straight home."

And then she looked down, giddy, effervescent laughter bubbling out of her wide mouth.

Diamond stood.

"Who are you?" she asked.

He didn't like her laugh. It was silly and loud and made him uneasy. But he started to answer anyway, ready to offer his name.

But the girl interrupted. "You're that boy," she said as her expression turned serious, chocolate eyes big and impressed. "You're the sick kid, aren't you?"

Once again, he tried to say, "Diamond."

She didn't hear him. Kicking the tree with both feet, she let go of the rope and he watched her fall, and she watched Diamond while she fell, hitting the landing with her legs bent and a smooth little pop at the end, jumping once before stopping beside him.

The little monster grunted and backed up.

"Go away," she told it.

Orange fur rose, trying to menace.

The girl made biting noises, pulling her long black hair over her head, mimicking the monster's gestures.

The animal retreated, leaping up on the railing before snarling at its tormentor.

She laughed at it. "Silly monkey."

Diamond watched both of them.

"How do you know him?" she asked.

"I don't know him."

"Well, he knows you." She stared at Diamond, fascinated. "He thinks you're going to protect him."

"We fought," Diamond confessed.

"When? Today?"

"He was inside my house. "

"You lost the battle, didn't you?"

He preferred not to say. "He was eating our food."

"You can't let monkeys indoors. Wasn't your house locked?"

"I guess not."

The girl was shorter than Diamond, but she had a longer body carrying strong arms and shoulders. Her mouth was wide but with little lips, and she had a fabulous long nose, and something about the spacing of her eyes and the shape of her cheekbones was pretty. Diamond watched her face and grew even more nervous.

Lifting the big curtain, she looked at the door. "It's open now."

"Yes."

She studied his eyes, his mouth. "You do live here, right?"

He nodded.

"Diamond?"

"Yes."

"That's your name. I remember. I've heard about you."

He felt shy and strange. Self-conscious about his tiny hands, he put them behind his back.

"Why are you outside?"

"I'm looking for someone."

"But you can get sick outside." Her voice became even quicker. "You were born weak. People say. What are you doing outside? You could catch some bug and die."

"I don't think I will," he said, halfway confident.

She didn't talk.

When he looked at her eyes, she said, "Elata."

"What?"

"My name is Elata."

He repeated that name.

"I like your voice, Diamond."

He didn't respond.

"Looking for who?"

"What?"

She didn't repeat the question. Putting her face closer, she said, "Everything about you. Those eyes, your whole body . . . it's all just a little different."

"Is it?"

"Don't you know?" Her hand jumped. As if it had its own mind, it grabbed him at the elbow, and he flinched and she let go again. "Shouldn't I? Was that bad?" Guilt and worry came bubbling out, but her curiosity remained undimmed. "Does that bother you, me touching you?"

"No."

"I don't want to hurt you, Diamond."

Nobody but his parents and the doctor were allowed to touch him. And he never saw the doctor anymore. "I'm fine."

"You're sure?"

"Yes."

"Well, I hope so." The big laugh returned. "I live just up there, by the way. I live with my mother." Her arm and a self-assured finger pointed the way. Each landing was a rounded platform supported by timbers. Dozens of landings were hanging beneath the mists. Exactly where she was pointing was a mystery, and then her arm dropped. "You haven't seen my bracelet, have you?"

"What is a bracelet?"

"It's copper and round, about this big." One hand drew a round shape around the other wrist.

"I don't think so, no."

"With an Emblem of Luck."

He shook his head.

"Somebody will find it. Don't worry." She kept watching him, laughing. "We moved here eighty days ago."

He said nothing.

"From the Baffle District. Near Suss-and-Hope."

He was waiting for words that made sense.

"I heard all about you," she said. "My first day, when the neighbors brought us gifts, people told us about you and your parents."

With a quiet, hopeful voice, Diamond asked, "Have you seen my mother?"

"No, she didn't come to our party."

He puckered his mouth, frustrated.

"Oh, you mean since then. Yeah, I've seen her. A few times, I think. I think."

That answer wasn't helpful either.

"How old are you?" Elata asked.

"Nine hundred and eighty-three."

"You seem older."

"I'm not."

"I'm twelve hundred and ninety-five days old."

He could think of nothing to say.

"I haven't seen your mother. Not for ten or twenty days." The broad shoulders went up and down. "Why? Don't you know where she is?"

He said, "No."

"She's not inside your house?"

"No."

The girl blinked and blinked again. "I don't understand. She's always here. She's the one who takes care of you."

He dipped his head.

"When did she leave, Diamond?"

"We talked last night, just before I went to sleep."

"Well, I bet she and my bracelet are lost in the same place." Elata started to laugh and then thought better of it. "Stay here," she said.

"Why?"

"Because I'll get my mother and come back. We'll figure out what's going on. Okay, Diamond?"

"Yes," he agreed.

The dangling rope was close enough to grab. The girl started to climb the magnificent tree, eating the distance with the long arms, vanishing onto one of the higher landings.

Diamond was crying again, just a little. He didn't know this girl, but now she was gone and he felt more alone than ever. So he looked at the monkey perched on the railing, watching its face grimace as it deftly and with great seriousness pooped into the open air.

• • •

Diamond kept forgetting what was happening, what was wrong. Stepping to the end of the landing, taking his first long look at the world, he foolishly began to ask his parents what he was seeing. His mother was beside him.

Father was behind them. He couldn't imagine those people being anywhere else. He wanted someone to answer the questions that kept rolling from his mouth: "What is that? And those? And that?"

But no one was here to explain.

The landing was built from long timbers once painted blue but now returning to bare blonde wood. The railing was head-high and flat, pegged into place on stout posts, dozens of thin vertical boards partway filling the gaps. But if he wasn't careful, a boy would fall through. Cautiously approaching the edge, Diamond grabbed the railing with both hands, standing on sandals and toes, his stunted chin resting on the weathered wood. Marduk was behind him. Huge expanses of air lay before him, and a bright silvery column full of motion and thunder stood in the distance. The column was water. The busy water had begun its plunge far overhead, from inside the persistent morning mist, and it rumbled and roared as it passed, kicking out breaths of vapor that swirled in the bright warm air while the heart of the column fell on, vanishing inside another band of mist and rain-born clouds.

Insects hung in the air, some alone, others dancing together. The largest swarms moved like great bodies, gathering up close to each other, turning dark before racing off again. A monster insect suddenly dropped from above, wings longer than Diamond's arms, the narrow body built from spheres and cylinders with the jointed black legs tucked beneath. Humming like a spring-powered toy, the monster used those bumpy bulging eyes to search the world for a feast worthy of its rapacious mouth.

"Hello," Diamond said softly.

The hunter pivoted and dove from sight.

A flock of usher birds arrived, coming from several directions to form a loud happy flock. Maybe a hundred colorful bodies swirled in a one-minded mass. Diamond watched them, trying to understand the manners of the flock, but just as he seemed to be anticipating what would happen next, the flock dissolved. The ushers flew away on a dozen important courses, leaving single birds and several pairs chattering even louder about some vital, left-behind matter.

"Hello," he repeated.

Unaccustomed to distances, his eyes were endlessly fooled. But he knew the ushers were tiny, and what flew beside the water and out in the open air had to be much, much larger. Birds were usually brilliantly colored, but the quickest birds were brownish green and difficult to see against the trees. And there were flyers that weren't birds or insects, their bodies covered with brown or black fur while the wings looked like leather. Every animal had its manner of flight. Some turned long elegant circles while others hovered, and some tucked their wings and dove, and he watched one of the brown-green birds turn tiny before colliding with a smaller flyer that exploded in a spray of golden feathers.

Birds had raucous, important voices, and Diamond understood nothing they said. By contrast, the skin-winged creatures were silent, and one of them was especially large. After a few moments of watching, the boy realized that the giant was gliding in a wide arc that was bringing it in his direction. Chin on the rail, he studied the creature's narrow face and the huge unblinking eyes. Even in the open air, the giant felt close, its body as big as a room yet tiny between the gigantic wings. But the leather was so thin that light passed through, revealing a lacework of skinny bones and veins like crooked ropes. Diamond had never imagined any creature so large, and being gigantic, that it would be so quiet. A soft swoosh of air was the only sound it made, each of its four black eyes constantly looking ahead, conspicuously ignoring the astonished boy who was cowering behind those little wood slats.

Suddenly a great pink mouth pulled wide, big enough to swallow boys and men, and that sleek long body steered into a cloud of tiny black insects, the entire cloud inhaled and then gone.

A thousand questions bubbled.

And Diamond remembered who wasn't there, suffering that wrenching loss all over again.

The giant had passed.

Diamond rose up on his toes again, watching.

The world was air, and the air was full of trees. This was something he had always known, something so deeply embedded in his parents' thinking that they couldn't keep the eternal forest secret. Diamond had imagined the scene endless times, but nothing from his mind matched what stood before him. The falling water was a marvel. Every sound was complicated and important. He couldn't count the animals, each intensely busy with its own great life. But even the largest creature was little more than a drop of blood and dab of meat beside the titanic pillars of living wood and pushing sap. How many trees? He called Marduk, "One," and counted quickly and carefully, turning in a half-circle. Twenty-three mature trees were visible, plus three pole-like saplings, and between any two trunks were other trees standing in the shimmering distance that might never end. This magnificent realm was just a sliver of the world's endless forest.

Trees made the world, feeding every mouth while supporting everything above and everything below. Four types of trees were closest. Most common were smooth brown cylinders like Marduk. Another variety bristled with stubby limbs tipped with dense clots of emerald-green leaves. A third tree sported tall ribs of bark running up and down the trunk, green growth clinging in the valleys, while the fourth species was deeply black save for half-domes of intense blue-green.

Mother had claimed that their home tree wasn't exceptionally large. Yet Marduk looked like a great flat wall, part of something too large to measure. The wall reached upwards forever, and the bark that seemed smooth from a distance was pocketed with cavities and odd ridges, and every place that wasn't perfectly vertical and slick was home to bunches of plants, exposed roots drinking from the air, birds roosting in the foliage, no substantial piece of this perfect tree left barren.

The next closest tree sported the same slick brown bark, and like Marduk, its body was sprinkled with little landings perched before curtained doors. Long walkways and brief walkways clung to the bark. There were hanging ropes like the one that Elata had climbed, while other ropes were moving. Moving ropes came in pairs, one lifting while its neighbor descended. Diamond didn't see people at first. Again, distance made him into a fool. Then the eyes caught something tiny, like a midge held at arm's length, except when he looked more carefully the anonymous bug turned into a grown woman.

Hands around his eyes, Diamond saw people walking across their landings, climbing the dangling ropes and sometimes riding the moving ropes up and down. One man came up quickly, and he was straight across from Diamond when he jumped to one side, his journey moving to a suspended walkway that led to the landing where the first woman waited.

The two people clung and kissed.

Diamond dropped his gaze, watching his feet and sandals.

Every time he looked at the world, new details begged to be noticed. He stared at his home with the face on the curtain and the one big window and the long hallway that led to his hidden room. Beside the window, a piece of the railing was missing. Diamond went to the gap, discovering a short rope ladder leading down to a narrow walkway. The walkway passed several more ladders leading up or down, and it ended with empty air and two thick ropes carrying people where they needed to be. Stout wooden platforms were fixed to the ropes, each big enough for two people to stand together, and there was a steady clatter as the ropes and platforms bumped against the tree's bark, wearing it smooth and pale, and people rode past him and away, and he watched each of them.

This was where his father would appear, coming home.

The monkey squatted nearby, holding the railing with every hand and its eyes closed. It was sleeping, and it was dreaming. Smacking its lips, once again the happy voice said, "Good."

The boy tried ignoring the animal. What mattered were the people coming into view. Each traveler caused his hope to build before it crashed, again and again, and after a while, when nobody was his father, Diamond began to watch for his mother too.

Where did she go, and why?

A familiar sick feeling took hold, his heart beating faster. He wanted to talk to someone. If he couldn't find the voices he wanted, he would accept another. That's why he approached the monkey, asking, "Did you see my mother?"

Lips smacked again.

He reached for the little monster.

"You don't want to do that," said a new voice.

The monkey woke with a jerk, growling at something above.

Diamond turned. A strange woman was hanging from the fixed rope. Elata was dangling above her. Despite the difference in ages and size, they looked like one another. That's what he noticed before anything.

"That critter will bite you," said the woman.

Diamond nodded, pulling his hand back.

"You're waiting for your mother?"

He nodded.

The monkey climbed outside the railing, hanging over the open air, a thousand escape routes waiting.

"Do you really live here?" the woman asked skeptically.

"Yes."

"I told you," Elata said.

The woman jumped. She wasn't as graceful as her daughter, but the motion was almost unconscious, bent legs and endless practice breaking her fall. Her daughter landed beside her, and they approached to within an arm's length. Quietly, the woman said, "You're not what I imagined."

Diamond couldn't think of a response.

"You say your mother left you here, alone?"

"He never, ever goes outside," said Elata. "You know that."

"Well, he's outside now," the woman said.

They stared at the conundrum while Diamond went back to watching the ropes. Another person was rising into view, and he pulled a new hope close enough to be a comfort. He was ready to be happy, but the person proved to be another stranger, a man who glanced at the odd boy while riding past, one hand lifting as a greeting, neighbor to neighbor.

The woman said, "Diamond."

He backed away from the railing.

"Before today, have you have ever been outside?"

"No."

"Never?" she asked.

He turned toward her, shaking his head.

"Oh my goodness goodness goodness." Perplexed, she frowned hard. Then her mood shifted, and suddenly she was nothing but thrilled. A nervous laugh leaked free, and watching the boy, she asked, "Well, what do you think?"

He didn't understand the question.

"Isn't it the world beautiful? Spectacular? Wondrous?" Then giving him an odd wink, she asked, "What are you thinking, Diamond?"

"I want my parents," he said. "That's what I'm thinking."

FOUR

Elata's mother made a thoughtful face. "Before anything else, we need to search the house."

"He already looked there," Elata said.

"Did he check every room? Are you sure?"

Diamond had returned to the railing, watching anonymous figures stroll along a distant walkway.

Touching his shoulder, the woman said, "I don't know your mother that well. She's an older woman, isn't she?"

Diamond looked at the hand until it was pulled back.

"What are you saying?" Elata asked.

"Well, I think she might be lying down somewhere. Maybe she's asleep or something."

Elata became angry. "Stop talking that way."

"What way?"

"Mother!"

Ignoring their argument was hard work.

Elata joined him at the railing. "Maybe your mother is visiting a friend."

Diamond didn't think so, but he shook his head agreeably.

"Or maybe she told a friend where she was going."

That also seemed unlikely, but he didn't know how to explain his doubts.

The girl offered several strange names.

Her mother drifted over to the curtain. "I should walk through the house, just to be sure."

Looking at the window, Diamond wished hard that his mother would appear behind the glass.

Elata said, "Rima."

He stopped her. "I've heard that name."

"You have?"

He nodded.

Elata's mother pushed at the curtain and watched it fall again. "You kids go to Rima's. See what she knows, and I'll be two leaps behind you."

Then she slipped behind the curtain, vanishing.

Elata smiled at him. For some reason she was suddenly happy, spinning and then climbing down onto the ladder.

Diamond looked at the rungs skeptically.

"You've never climbed," she realized.

"No."

"Well, it's easy. Do what I do."

She tried to move slowly, but that wasn't her natural pace. Partway down the ladder, she stopped to wait. Diamond was examining a round, hand-worn piece of wood sticking out of the railing. Noticing her gaze, he turned and grabbed hold of the handle, dropping one foot over the edge, reaching until he felt the rope rung against his sandal. From below, she said, "Good," and started down again. From much farther below, she asked, "Do you know what to do if you fall?"

"No."

"Aim for the tree. With your body and the air, steer your way toward a walkway or one of the landings. And if you can, let your feet lead."

He imagined all that. With a doubtful tone, he said, "All right."

"If you fall carelessly, bones get broken. But you'll survive."

Diamond said nothing, moving faster now. Then a foot slipped, and he dropped and grabbed the swinging ladder with both hands, dangling in space. His home landing was above him. Every supporting timber wore a tangle of green epiphytes, and nests shaped like baskets were defended by sitting birds, and straddling one of the main timbers, watching him with considerable interest, was the orange-faced monkey.

Diamond started down again.

"Good," said the monkey, as if encouraging him.

"Are you his?" Elata asked.

"What?"

She was waiting on the walkway. "Orange-heads don't make good pets. But sometimes, nobody knows why, they'll adopt one person. They make him into their pet."

Diamond jumped down the last little ways.

"Did he tell you his name?" she asked.

He looked up at the animal. " 'Good', I think it is."

Something deserved a long laugh, and she waved. "Come on. Rima and her boys live over there."

• • •

They walked under his landing. Wood slats and heavy rope created the walkway. The ropes were pegged into Marduk's dense bark. New slats were pale, and fresh ropes were tied into the old fraying pieces. The walkway creaked and sometimes shook underfoot. Diamond let his hand ride along on the rope railing, touching the posts that came every few steps. He watched the air beside him. Elata watched him. He slowed to stare at a cavity inside the bark, a tiny garden growing just out of reach. Plants sported strangely colored leaves, and a pair of tiny blue birds buzzed loudly while hovering overhead.

"Candy orbs are my first favorite," she said.

"What are candy orbs?"

"They're a kind of flower, and that's them."

He didn't reply.

"Do you know about flowers, Diamond?"

He started walking again. Questions were confusing and made him feel foolish.

"Do you know about birds?"

"I know usher birds," he volunteered.

"You've seen them before?"

"Yes. Yes, I have."

Elata watched his feet and legs. But when he looked at her, she blinked and stared out into the air. "Last night was amazing," she said. "I slept and slept and then I couldn't sleep anymore. Nobody remembers a longer, darker night. That's what my mother says."

Diamond remained silent, thinking about his mother.

"Inside your house . . . did you know it was night?"

He nodded.

"But nobody let you look out the window?"

He walked faster, saying nothing.

Elata slowed, watching the odd sandals crossing the creaking slats.

A new post was topped with rough wood, and one long golden splinter burrowed inside his thumb.

The pain hit. Diamond stopped and flinched.

She said, "Oh, my. I'm sorry."

He touched the splinter with the other thumb and forefinger. Elata swallowed before asking, "Do you want me to pull it?"

But he already had. Putting the wound to his mouth, he sucked as he turned, walking even faster now.

"That looked bad," she said. "How does it feel?"

Diamond broke into a steady run.

She sprinted to catch him, and laughing, grabbed his elbow and tugged until he stopped running. "Where did you get those legs?"

He had no words to offer.

"I've heard about kids born without legs, or feet with no toes. I even heard about a boy with two heads. But you're not like them."

Diamond dropped his gaze.

And she became self-conscious too. "I'm sorry. That was rude."

Bright air beckoned. He gazed out at the birds and plunging water and what looked like the same giant leatherwing hunting for insects.

"I talk when I should think," Elata said, passing him and turning before pointing at herself. "Teachers tell me that all the time. But if you didn't notice, my mother does that too. It's a family trait. We have loud blood. An idea pops into our heads, and we can't help ourselves."

The railing opened, revealing a new rope ladder that ended on a distant landing. Until then, Diamond was only a little bothered by heights. But the great tree seemed to sway under his feet, and looking at that impossible gulf, a sharp pain began to dig in his belly.

Standing beside him, Elata tried to see everything from his point of view. "It seems far, I know. But you won't fall."

"I might," he said.

"So I'll go first," she said. "If something goes wrong, I'll grab you."

"You would?"

"Or better, I'll jump and steer you to where you want to be."

Where he wanted to be was home, but he nodded and followed his best new friend, slowly working his way down the long trembling ladder.

• • •

Nobody fell and nobody jumped.

Diamond was never at ease, but his legs and hands soon knew what they were doing. He could even imagine some remote future where he wasn't scared. But today he was sweating and breathing hard, and standing on the new landing, he still felt the ladder's jerky sway.

What looked tiny from above was enormous. Jutting far out into the air, the landing was wide enough to hold a dozen chairs and giant boxes jammed with plants, plus one long rectangular basin lined with rubber and filled with water. Diamond approached the basin. Big beetles swum furiously to the far shore. The rubber was black, making the pool look deep. Beneath the surface, a long silver animal hovered on little wings, motionless until he touched the water, and then it was gone.

Elata stood beside a huge purple curtain. "Maybe your mother's here."

He didn't believe so, but that slim hope smiled at him.

Past the purple curtain was a short hallway ending with a massive, iron-encrusted door. An elegant silken rope hung from the ceiling. Elata gave it a hard yank, and bells began ringing indoors.

"These people are rich," she warned.

He couldn't guess what those words meant.

"Filthy, wicked rich," she said.

The door was unlatched, and a woman appeared. She didn't look dirty at all.

"Oh, Elata."

Diamond recognized the voice and the woman's eyes. This was the mother who was nice to him when he visited, using happy warm words, but she wasn't very pleasant this morning.

"You're too early," she complained. "He's not ready for school."

"I don't want Seldom. We're hunting Diamond's mother."

A first glance wasn't enough. The woman stepped into the hallway, staring at the odd, unexpected boy. Big eyes and startled gasp came before, "Oh my. Diamond? What are you doing here?"

"We're looking for his mother," Elata repeated. "We need to find her."

The woman nodded, finally understanding some part of this. "But Haddi isn't here."

Mother's name was Haddi.

"Do you know where she is?" Elata asked.

"I don't." The woman backed away, fascination slipping into worry. "Are you all right, leaving your room like this?"

"I'm fine."

"You're sure?"

He nodded with confidence.

But she wasn't convinced. "Come this way, you two. Into the greeting room, and sit." Then she put a hand on his forehead. "You feel hot."

"I'm all right."

"You're not well. Sit down and rest."

The room would have been spacious, except for the chairs and hanging tables. Broad tubes brought in the daylight. Diamond sat on a chair full of pillows. Elata dropped beside him, saying, "My mom's going to be here." Then with an odd tone, she added, "As soon as she's done searching his house."

Rima needed something useful to do. "Do you want anything, Diamond? A drink, maybe?"

He was thirsty, yes. "Water, please."

"Of course. And you, Elata?"

"Whatever Diamond wants. Thank you."

The woman left. But from somewhere close, she said, "No, stay with me. You don't need to go down there."

A deeper voice muttered a word or two.

Then with a louder voice, Elata said, "I mean it, Karlan. You're not bothering them."

Elata sat up straight and said, "Shit."

Diamond didn't know that word.

An older boy rounded the corner, smiling at the guests. Diamond recognized him instantly and felt uneasy. Elata was worse. She clapped her hands on her knees and twisted as if hurting. "Go away," she said. "Go."

The boy was taller than before. A man's body was forming under a child's face, and the bright dead smile grew bigger as he approached.

"Hello, monster," Karlan said.

Diamond didn't talk.

"You healed up, did you?" The boy laughed and dropped to his knees, putting his face too close. Then he straightened a long finger, stabbing Diamond in the stomach. "Got a scar there, do you?"

Walking into the room, Rima let out a bright sharp scream.

Everyone but Karlan jumped. He remained calm and happy, and feeling no reason to hurry, he slowly rose to his feet, smiling as he stared at the much smaller boy.

"Leave him alone," said a mother's voice. "I mean it."

A good deal of Rima's life was spent throwing warnings at her oldest boy, and better than anybody else, she knew how to fend off trouble. But she also understood that she couldn't push too hard or throw down mandates that couldn't be defended. Her big cheerless smile was important. Resting a hand against her son's back, she said, "It's nearly school time. Think of all the fun you can have somewhere else."

Karlan winked. "See you around, monster."

He left the room.

Rima handed two tall cups to her guests before sitting on the nearest chair. She didn't want to talk about past troubles, but every time she looked at Diamond, her resolve broke down a little more.

Elata sipped her water and put the cup aside.

Diamond drank half and left the cup in his lap, the water stained green by the morning light.

"You're definitely all right," Rima declared. "Definitely recovered."

Elata watched the two of them, trying to decipher what was being said.

"I'm just so happy," the woman said, nothing about her voice happy. "I was terrified afterwards. And I was so sorry for you, of course. But you did recuperate. No permanent harm, I heard."

Diamond watched his water shimmering.

"I don't know how many times I asked about you," said Rima. "I wanted to see you and tell you how sorry I was. But your mother explained that you were weak and recovering and I couldn't visit. And later, she said they were being very, very careful with you. They couldn't take any more chances."

Diamond was embarrassed and unsure why.

"What happened?" Elata asked.

"A mistake was made," Rima blurted. "An error in judgment, that's all. And we don't need to talk about this anymore."

Diamond focused on his cup and little hands.

"About your mother," Rima said, steering the conversation. "I think of Haddi as a friend. I do. But I don't see her much anymore. In fact, we barely speak. So no, I don't know where she might be." She squinted as she concentrated. "Now, of course, one of her cousins is a very good friend of mine. I suppose I could send you to him. But the last news that I heard was that even relatives aren't invited inside the house, and Haddi never visits anymore. The family only sees your father going to work or doing errands."

Elata turned to Diamond. "But your father's going to be home soon. Isn't that right?"

Diamond nodded, finding one good reason to smile.

"Well then," said Rima, relieved by the news. "I'm sure we'll find him, and all of these mysteries can be resolved."

The three of them sat quietly.

A throat was cleared, and Diamond looked up. Standing in the hallway was a boy no taller than him. He looked a little like Rima. Maybe he was Elata's age, maybe younger. A special gray suit made him look like a soldier. He smiled and jumped, muttering, "Oh, it's you. It is you."

Diamond sipped the cool water.

"Hi, Seldom. This is Diamond," said Elata.

"I know who he is." Entering the greeting room, the newcomer giggled and jumped again. "You're the mystery boy. I've heard stories."

"Be polite," his mother warned.

Elata patted Diamond on the knee. "Seldom is strange, but in the best ways. And don't be fooled by how stupid he looks. He really is smart."

How would a person look stupid?

"So you're waiting for your dad, huh?" Seldom came close enough to touch Diamond but didn't. He stared hard at the boy's face and hands. "You're in the open. Are you going to get sick?"

"Maybe," said Diamond.

"Oh, I hope not," Rima said.

Seldom bent down, his face level with Diamond's face. "Do you know where he's slaying?"

"What?"

With a slow, precise voice, he asked, "Do you know where your father is slaying today?"

Diamond knew very little about the world, yet this stranger expected him to know where his father was.

With different words, Seldom asked the question again. "Is he hunting the wilderness or near reef country?"

"I don't know."

"Doesn't he tell you where he's slaying?"

Diamond was nervous, wary.

Elata asked Diamond, "What's wrong?"

"I don't know that word," the boy admitted.

"What word?" the children asked.

" 'Slaying.' "

Surprised, Seldom looked at his mother.

Rima leaned close to Diamond. "What are you saying? You don't know what your father does for a living?"

He shook his head.

"Slayers are special hunters," the woman said. "And your father's very good at his job."

Diamond absorbed the words, but they refused to make sense. Dipping his head, he confessed, "We don't talk about those things."

Everybody stared at him, puzzled and mute.

Then Seldom jumped into the silence. Happy to be the smart voice, he said, "Your father hunts the coronas. And that makes our district rich, and it keeps the world safe, and I don't think there's a better job anywhere."

• • •

What was a corona?

Diamond knew the word and that perhaps a monster was attached to it. But if he said nothing else, nobody would realize just how foolish he was. That's what he was thinking, looking at Elata. A little smile broke out on her face, and she took a deep breath. Then she began to answer the unasked question.

"A corona is," she said.

Loud bells began ringing. The big house door was opening, and a familiar voice shouted, "Rima? Taff here. Where are you?"

"In the greeting room," Rima called out.

Elata's mother appeared. Her first chore was to give Diamond a careful stare. Then she told everybody, "I looked. Every room, every corner. I'm sorry, but I couldn't find his mother."

Diamond nodded, accepting what he already knew.

The woman approached and bent over. Every face wanted to be too close to his. With a serious voice, she said, "Your room is in the back, with the toy soldiers. Is that right?"

He nodded.

"You said before . . . that you've never been outside . . . ?"

"No."

"Until today."

With authority, he said, "Never."

She lowered her body, sitting on the floor. A long sigh was necessary. Then with a strong and quiet but distinctly furious voice, she asked, "What kinds of parents lock their child inside a big closet?"

She wasn't talking to him.

Turning to Rima, she asked, "Did you know about this?"

Seldom's mother straightened her back, hands on knees. "Yes," she began. Then with a defensive tone, she said, "But they had to take precautions. He's a very frail child."

Taff shook her head doubtfully.

Rima leaned forward. "You haven't lived here long, dear. You don't realize. Those old people love their boy, but he's so weak. The first time he got sick could be the last. So they did whatever they could to protect him."

"Locking him inside that old storage chamber."

"You make it sound horrible."

"It is."

"Good gracious, I visited this boy. Ask him, he'll tell you. We've talked. He and I had some nice conversations. Really, he's always seemed very happy, very bright. As good as any boy I know, and maybe better."

Diamond dropped his head, feeling miserable.

Taff stared at him until he looked at her eyes. "How do you feel, Diamond?"

"All right."

"Are you sick?"

He shook his head.

"Well, I'm sorry. If this is going to make you ill . . . "

"I'm all right," he insisted.

"Good."

Elata touched his hand with hers. "You do feel warm."

"I always am."

Her mother pushed her hand against his forehead. "Warm like this?"

"Yes."

Rima wanted any fresh topic. "We were just talking about Diamond's father. You wouldn't know where we could find him?"

"Between here and the sun," said Taff. "And you're right, I don't know these people. Not like you do."

Rima bristled.

Then Seldom laughed. "Guess what? Diamond doesn't even know that his father hunts coronas."

"Well, that is odd," Taff agreed.

Diamond wanted to leave.

Taff touched the stubbornly warm forehead again. "What do you know about the world?"

He shrugged and practiced making silence.

"And they never let you look outside," she whispered.

He said nothing.

Elata grabbed his hand again. "Leave him alone, Mother."

"But I want to help him."

"Everybody wants to help," Rima said.

Taff pulled Diamond's face to where their eyes met. "I stood inside your room. For a very long time, that's what I did. It's comfortable enough. I suppose. But it's so isolated. I couldn't hear the world outside. If I was child raised inside one dark room . . . well, I couldn't have grown up normal."

"Who's normal?" Elata asked.

Taff ignored her daughter. "When we were standing on your landing, Diamond . . . I saw how you looked at everything. Every bird and bug was amazing. I don't know if I've ever seen a person as impressed as you were. The most ordinary things in the world, but you couldn't stop staring. And now I know why."

Elata looked at Diamond's left hand. Then she reached across his lap and picked up his right hand, turning the thumb.

"Where's the cut?" she asked.

He pulled the hand to his stomach.

"You could get infected," she warned. "Maybe we should clean out that wound."

"What wound?" Rima asked.

"On our way here," Elata explained. "A fat splinter got into his thumb. I just don't see it now."

Diamond made fists, saying nothing.

Taff continued. "If you were my son, and if you really were frail and sickly, I'd make your room bright and full of color. I'd paint pictures of the world on your walls, and I would tell you about everything outside. And do you know why? The world is perfect. There's nothing but the Creation. The world is enormous and wonderful, and you can't be a person and not understand these things."

Rima started to speak but thought better of it.

Taff slowly stood. "I don't know your parents. That's certainly true. Maybe they have spectacular reasons for what they do and don't do. But I can't just stand by and not complain. That's not my way."

There was a long, painful silence.

Then Rima rose from her chair, lightly touching the boy's warm forehead before putting two fingers under his chin and lifting his eyes. "What do you know about the world, Diamond?"

"My parents love me."

She let go. To the children, she said, "Stay here. Wait here." Then to Taff, she said, "We need to talk to people, see what we can learn."

• • •

The women left. Diamond watched the smooth golden-brown floor in the hallway, holding his breath while listening. Rima and Taff were inside another room. He heard them whispering, and an odd hum came and went and returned again. Then Elata turned to Seldom, saying, "You have a line?"

"Yes."

"Our house has a line," she reported. "But we can't afford to connect it."

With a loud voice, Rima said, "Ivory Station, please."

There was a long pause, and then another voice answered. Diamond didn't recognize the man's crackling voice.

Elata was watching Diamond, not quite smiling. Then he looked at her, and she grabbed both of his hands, trying to turn them and open them up. He didn't let her. He held his fists closed, and she laughed, saying, "You're strong."

Feeling self-conscious, he relaxed his hands, letting her peel back every finger.

"We're looking for a slayer," Rima was saying. "Named Merit."

Merit was Father's name.

There was a quick pause before another new voice spoke, the words slurred and too soft to be understood.

"I don't see it," said Elata.

Diamond didn't react.

"What are you looking for?" Seldom asked.

"He cut himself," she said. "I saw a hole in his thumb, and blood."

"You made a mistake," Seldom said.

"Maybe," she said. Then with a defiant tone, she said, "No."

Somewhere down the hall, a door was closed and latched. Now even Rima's voice was muffled, unintelligible.

"Who are they talking to?" Elata asked.

Seldom shrugged.

"Go listen," she suggested.

"We're supposed to stay here," Seldom said.

Elata stood anyway. She stared at Diamond, as if committing him to memory. Then she walked into the hallway and vanished.

Diamond watched the floor again.

With a quiet, impressed voice, Seldom said, "You've never gone to school."

He shook his head.

"I go to school. I started when I was eight hundred, which is very early."

"Oh."

"I can read anything," Seldom boasted. "I learned how before I was nine hundred, in fact."

Diamond looked at the boy.

"I'm different," Seldom said, flashing a confident smile.

Diamond kept seeing Rima in that face. His color was darker than his mother's. He had smooth hair and wide ears that poked out of the hair, and his mouth was narrow and his golden teeth were crooked. But the eyes dominated his face. There was a gleam to them, to their blackness, that made them seem like the brightest objects in the room.

The boy took a breath and let it out slowly. "You know, Karlan told me what he did to you."

Diamond said nothing.

"He told me after he came home, after Mom was finished screaming." Seldom's voice fell away, and his eyes narrowed. "He said that he'd met you.

Karlan said you were tiny and odd looking and you didn't talk much. He said the knife was an accident. He was just trying to have some fun."

Diamond looked at the smooth, uncut thumb.

"My brother's different too. But not like me." The boy straightened and smiled again, sadness in his face. "Something's broken inside his head, his brain. That's what I think."

"What's broken?"

"I don't know. It's hard to describe." The boy didn't want to look at Diamond anymore. Staring at an overhead light was better. "Karlan told me that he wanted to make you scream. Just to scare everybody. He loves scaring people, kids and adults. Mom says that in that one little area, he's a genius."

"What's a genius?"

"Smart."

Diamond closed both of his hands.

"He stuck you. He told me about it. He expected you to shout out. But you didn't. The rest was an accident, pushing the knife that deep inside you. 'If that kid was a monkey, he'd be a dead monkey now,' he told me."

Someone was walking in the hallway, approaching slowly.

"My brother knows about killing monkeys," Seldom warned. "But Mom says that's better than the other choices."

Diamond wrapped his arms around his waist.

"Is the scar ugly?"

"What?"

Seldom was horrified but fascinated too. He couldn't stop himself. "Can I see the scar?"

Diamond said, "No."

The boy shrank back, embarrassed by what he had requested.

Then Elata returned, and looking at Seldom, she asked, "What's going on in here?"

"Nothing," Seldom said, sitting farther away. "We were just talking."

Elata entered the room and spoke to Diamond. "Seldom's mom is talking to your father's bosses. I heard pieces of that. Merit is still out on his hunt, they say. He hasn't passed through on his way home, which he always does. Then the boss said something about the big rain and maybe that's why he's been delayed."

Diamond concentrated, trying to make sense of the words.

The girl grew quieter, more serious. "And now my mother's talking to a police officer."

Seldom sat up. "Really? How come?"

Elata was quiet, her face tight and simple.

Nobody spoke.

Dropping beside Diamond, she stared at him until he returned her gaze. "Be honest. Until today, have you ever gone outside?"

"No."

"And you've always lived inside the same room?"

He nodded.

Elata looked at his hands again. Her mouth closed tight, teeth grinding. Then talking to the hands, she explained, "Sometimes parents have trouble with kids. My mom knows somebody, never mind who. But her parents tied her up when she was little, trying to keep her under control. Which is wrong and illegal, and if anybody had found out, her parents would have been huge trouble. And the girl would have been taken away from them."

"Who got tied up?" Seldom asked.

"Nobody."

"Somebody was," he said.

"Nobody you know."

Seldom put his hands under his legs, frowning.

"Anyway." She looked at Diamond again. "My mother is talking to the police, explaining what she found inside your house, about the mess in the kitchen and that dark little room of yours."

"The monkey made the mess," he said.

"I can believe that."

He had been scared for a good portion of this day, but this was worse. Diamond breathed in long sore gulps, and he wished that he could fly home to yesterday, starting everything over again.

Elata looked at Seldom. "My mom was talking, but then your mom took the receiver from her."

"Did she?" Something about that was worth a laugh.

She looked at Diamond again. "Rima's talking to the officer now. You're a sick kid, she says. You've got a fever."

"I don't."

"She says you need is a doctor, not the police. Otherwise you're going to get even sicker and die."

"I'm not sick," said Diamond.

Seldom jumped up. "Let me touch your head."

"No," Diamond said. "Don't."

Both studied him. Then with a grim voice, Elata said, "I don't know what's going to happen."

“Somebody’s going to get in trouble,” Seldom said with an expert tone. “That’s what’s going to happen.”

Diamond stood.

“What are you doing?” Seldom asked.

Elata jumped up. “I think he wants to go home.”

That was Diamond’s intention, yes. Nothing was more important than returning to his own room, to loyal and silent Mister Mister. He would wait there for his parents. This long awful morning had brought so many new faces and troubles, and he craved what he knew best. Police officers and new doctors should be met inside his walls. That’s what he was thinking as he left the greeting room, making for the main door.

Elata walked beside him.

From another room, Rima told someone, “Hurry, please.”

“I’ll help you,” Elata promised.

“We don’t want to be late for school,” Seldom said.

Elata didn’t react.

They passed through the iron-braced door. Slits of daylight sliced through gaps in the heavy purple curtain. Seldom was trailing, saying, “I want to go too.”

“You’ll be late for school,” Elata said.

With a big voice, he said, “Oh, I don’t care.”

Elata went through the curtain first, and once more she used that hard little word that Diamond didn’t know. Quietly and fiercely, she said, “Shit.”

• • •

Karlan was standing at the landing’s far end, his back to the curtain and feet apart, arms dangling at his sides. He was dressed in a brown school uniform like the one his brother wore, but the shirt was too small for his growing body, fabric straining across his broad back, sleeves squeezing his thick wrists. The air was filled with a new rumbling, harsher and closer than the falling water. A vast silvery ball was pushing past Marduk, fins and whirling blades stuck to its skin. Karlan might have been watching that ball, but he just as well could have been observing things nobody else could see. Either way, as Diamond stepped outside, the older boy turned, showing everyone his big odd smile.

The world didn’t seem as bright as before. Diamond had come through the curtain with eyes narrowed, but this time he barely blinked with the glare. Karlan looked at the two of them, eyes jumping back and forth. Then Seldom appeared, reading the situation in an instant.

"Let's go," he suggested. "Right now."

They hurried for the ladder, Elata leading.

Karlan laughed hard and then quit laughing. "Where are you going?" he shouted.

Elata broke into a shuffling trot.

Karlan laughed again, except nothing was funny. And when he shouted again, he sounded furious. "Hey, monster! Come here, I want to show you something."

The rope ladder reached almost to the landing. Elata made a little jump and grabbed the bottom rung, pulling herself up with quick arms. Diamond looked up, and Seldom touched him on the back. "Go on," he said.

Karlan was walking, not running. Diamond looked at him and then up at the ladder, and he jumped. He had never jumped this hard. Feeling clumsy and wrong, his hands shot past the first rung, and he fumbled with the second rung and one hand let go, and then he gripped tight with his left hand as his body began to drop. The hand clung to the stiff rope and he spun around as Karlan jogged up.

Karlan was furious, or he was pretending to be. "What are you doing?" he asked.

"We're taking him home," Seldom began.

"Yeah, but I've got something to show him."

Diamond grabbed the ladder with his other hand and started to climb. But somebody grunted and a big hand snagged his trailing ankle, jerking hard enough to bring him down.

He expected to hit the landing. But Karlan caught him and held him in both arms, and the expression that wasn't any smile grew worse. "You've never seen the world, have you?" He walked, cradling his catch. "I heard you and the mommies talking. Never left your prison until today. Well, it's a good morning and there's a million things to see, and I want to be the first to show you."

Diamond squirmed.

"Quit," Karlan told him.

He fought harder.

Then with both big arms, the boy tried to crush the fight in him.

Seldom was beside them. "What are you doing?" he asked his brother. Then with panic in the voice, he said, "Don't."

"Don't what?" Karlan asked.

Naming his fears seemed reckless; Seldom quit talking.

They reached the landing's end. "You should have seen that ship up close," said Karlan. "We don't get traffic like that here. Not usually. But the fancy people onboard can still see us. Go on now. Give them a friendly wave."

The machine was huge, dwarfing even the giant leatherwings. Whirling blades reminded Diamond of the pinwheel that he had until it broke. Six pinwheels were working hard, and the engines that powered them made steady warm noises, and there were rooms underneath and what might be people moving behind the rooms' windows.

Diamond forgot everything else.

"Put him down," said Elata. Standing back from the railing and Karlan, she was still panting from a long jump and quick run. But she was angry and brave because of it. Diamond looked helpless, and the girl despised anyone being helpless. It was important to shout her first words, and when that didn't do any good, she said, "Don't you dare, I mean it, I mean it."

Karlan laughed. "Dare what?"

"Throw him over. You can't."

The laughter stopped. The fake smile turned into a fake serious expression, and Karlan did nothing. Maybe he was thinking, or maybe this was for show. Either way, he finally said, "Throw him? I never thought of that."

Seldom muttered a few words.

"What's that, brother?"

"Nothing."

"Then be quiet." Karlan reached up with one hand, yanking Diamond's head to where it was staring straight at him. "Suppose I drop you. No, imagine I throw you. As far as I can, and then you fall. Do you know how to fall, little boy? Do you know how to save yourself and not get too beaten up when you crash?"

Elata cried out. There were no words in what she was saying, just raw furious noise that helped to push her past fear. She used fists on Karlan's back and kicked him twice in the back of his leg, and when that accomplished nothing, she jumped and punched him hard in the ear.

Diamond was dropped.

He was on the landing-side of the railing, if only barely. He hit the hard slats and felt nothing but the jarring, and he put his left hand on a railing post and turned in time to see his friend throw her fist at Karlan's stomach.

The boy deflected the blow with an arm. "Shit," he said as he used his other arm, an open hand slapping Elata in the face, just beside her chin.

She didn't simply fall. The impact lifted her off her feet, and her head snapped back, and the neck was twisted sideways, fighting to hold onto the dazed head. Elata landed and skidded and ended up limp. Too stunned to cry out, she slowly realized what had happened, and then she was too stubborn to make any noise. But when Karlan took one stepped toward her, Elata shrank down, instinctively protecting her face.

Seldom stared at his brother, wishing for some perfect, awful words to say. But all that came to mind was, "You're in trouble."

Diamond was standing. He didn't remember getting to his feet, and he wasn't certain when his fear and passivity evaporated. Something awful had been done, and he was caught up in anger. Somebody had to put an end to this trouble. His little hands closed, and then Karlan turned and read his face. Seeing everything clearly, the giant laughed. It was the largest, most terrible laugh of the day, and to make it worse, he said, "I showed you something. Show me your scar. I want to see how you healed up, little monster boy."

He reached for Diamond's shirt.

Diamond hit him in the face, in the long fleshy nose.

The impact startled. Just like with Elata, the head popped back and the neck absorbed the energy. Karlan wasn't knocked off his feet, but he hadn't expected that impact and needed a few moments to shake off the pain, dealing with embarrassment and the wet feel as blood flooded out of his aching nose.

With the back of a hand, he touched his blood.

"Damn you," he whispered.

Diamond straightened his back.

Again, Karlan touched the blood above his mouth, licking his mouth clean, and after a moment of deep reflection he reached with both hands, grabbing Diamond by the long shirt and yanking it high. Then he kicked the legs out from under the little boy and put him on his back, exposing that perfect pale and unscarred belly to the world.

"What is this?" Karlan asked.

Diamond slapped the hands away and pulled the shirt down.

"I gutted you." Karlan looked at the other two, wanting witnesses. "Where's the scar? Do you see a scar?"

The children stared at Diamond.

"Well, damn," Karlan said at last. "I've heard a lot of monster stories, but nothing like this. Nothing like you."

Then he grabbed hold of Diamond, and before the boy could manage any fight, he threw him as far into the air as possible.

FIVE

Alone in his room, Diamond would stand on the stool, dropping soldiers to watch them hurry to the floor while guessing how falling would feel. And what imagination told him wasn't very different from what he experienced now. Nothing was beneath his feet and hands, and the air was rushing past, and his body had no sense of control as he rolled those first few times. Yet this wasn't what he expected either. He knew that his body would speed up, but the acceleration was slower than he assumed. He was ready to feel terror, but the tension and surprise were washed away by giddy fascination. Moments ago, Diamond was part of the world, and now the world was something apart from him. The air was moving and Marduk was moving. The forest was streaming past his little body, as if a vast force were lifting the Creation higher, its ascent yanking up the air and the trees—everything but one boy desperate to go somewhere else.

Diamond didn't scream, but others did.

A voice followed him, and then another voice, and someone was laughing. Fighting to control his body, he managed to roll on his back and look up. One landing jutted farther into the air than any other. Three people peered over the railing. The faces were already too distant to wear names. More words were shouted, none making sense, and then one of the faces vanished and someone leaped into the air, arms flattened against the long body and the head down, leading the way.

Then the wind gusted, and Diamond began whirling again. A second large landing was under him, reaching up for him, and he tucked too late, one hand slapping the railing, two fingers shattering. That was when the fear took hold. Diamond rolled, flailing with his arms, his legs. He ended up on his belly, falling slower. Arms and legs were bent upwards. The shirt flapped and the trouser legs popped and his thick long curly hair rose up from his scalp. Tiny details offered themselves to his astonished eyes: three boys in brown uniforms racing along a walkway; an old lady wearing a tall red hat furiously sweeping a tiny landing; dangling pieces of metal ringing against one another in the same wind; and a solitary banner fixed to an empty piece of the tree, covered with words worn away by rain and sunlight, rendered too faint to read.

Perched on railing was one tall golden bird, and seeing the boy pass, the bird tucked and fell, narrow as a knife until it was close, and then the wings spread, cupping the air as the creature gracefully turned a half-circle, letting its curiosity gnaw at the helpless boy.

Diamond looked at the bird's black eyes.

"Careful," said the bird.

Except the bird said nothing. He thought it had, except it was gone suddenly and the voice remained.

"Diamond," she said.

He turned his head, and his body flipped again.

"Keep flat," Elata shouted. "Use your arms, your legs. Steer yourself, Diamond. And watch below for a landing place."

Head down, she was closing fast and screaming to be heard. Diamond foolishly looked up and again started to spin, and she yelled, "No, stop, no," and he got control of himself as she reached him.

One moment, she was vertical, arms flush to her sides. Then just before streaking into the lead, she flattened out and spread her arms and legs, pulling up, and suddenly both of them were motionless. Marduk was rising fast beside them. She coughed and then spoke. As much to herself as to Diamond, she said, "We're going to be all right."

He tried to talk but couldn't.

"But we're little enough to fall slow." Moving one arm, she pulled closer. "With dropsuits, this is easy."

"With what?" he muttered.

"I'm watching for a place," she said.

"What place?

"To land," she said.

He looked down too.

Her voice was inside one of his ears. "The public landing. See it?"

The morning mists were retreating, pulling down the tree trunk and exposing what looked like a long gray belt. From high above, there wasn't any target. If that was the landing, it seemed very narrow. But distances kept shrinking and everything far away became larger and more important, and the mists continued to drop, revealing more portions of a trunk that might never end.

"Be careful," she kept telling him.

He made agreeable sounds.

"At the last moment," she said, "put your feet down and roll forward. And leave your legs bent when you hit."

He didn't say anything.

A giant leatherwing slid past them, a high soft voice washing over them.

"Relax," Elata said.

And Diamond became more nervous, more self-conscious.

"I've fallen this far before," she insisted.

Their target had grown wide and complicated. The flat gray face was littered with objects that didn't move and objects that did. Diamond tried to gauge speed and direction. Then Elata said something else, and he couldn't understand.

"What?" he asked.

"Don't hit those people," she said. "Don't hurt anybody."

The moving objects were people.

"Are you ready, Diamond?"

Cupping his hands, he attempted to steer himself.

Then she grabbed one of his hands. "I see where. Relax, relax. And when I tuck, you tuck. Okay?"

But he pulled his hand away.

Elata grabbed him again.

Diamond didn't push hard, but suddenly there was air between them. They were pulling apart as he looked at her scared face and the long black hair blowing up, and she curled her fingers, as if clinging to the wind. Then another figure dropped down, flattening and hovering just overhead. Diamond assumed it was the golden bird, but then that bird shouted, "You're too close. Too close to the tree."

Seldom had caught them.

"Come back here," Elata begged.

But Diamond wasn't afraid. He didn't want to drop on top of anyone, and once he saw the answer, he felt better. There were a lot of good reasons to be scared, but not about the landing.

Arching his back, Diamond sent himself plunging forward. Marduk was a great brown wall, and there was nothing else in the world. Little pockets in the bark were full of epiphytes and angry birds, and the wind seemed louder, and he shut his eyes out of reflex, shut them tight.

The massive tree felt nothing when that tiny boy struck first with his face and then with his crumbling body.

• • •

Tumbling was followed by stillness and darkness. Then a voice found him. "Oh, gracious," a woman said. "My gracious, I can't look."

Someone else said, "What a waste."

Other voices buzzed in the distance.

Then an angry man said, “You shouldn’t have done that. What were you doing, you idiot?”

“Are you all right?” a woman asked.

Diamond tried to answer, but his jaw was broken.

“You’re hurt,” the sorrowful woman said.

“I’m fine,” Elata said. “Just sore.”

The angry man said, “You’re a very thoughtless girl.”

Elata said, “My friend fell. I had to help him.”

“And your friend is a fool,” the man continued. “That was the worst fall that I have ever, ever seen.”

“He’s your friend?” the woman asked.

“Yes.”

“Well, don’t look at the poor boy. Put your eyes somewhere else.”

People were moving closer and moving away, and then Elata whispered, “How are you, Diamond?”

Diamond tried to answer, but his mouth wasn’t working.

Seldom came close. “I shouldn’t have jumped,” he said.

“It’s against the law,” the angry man agreed.

“Look at him,” said Seldom. Then he was close, quietly asking an ear, “Are you alive, Diamond?”

Diamond tried to move an arm, but the bone was fractured.

Somebody touched him.

Several voices were talking about the police.

The sorrowful woman said, “Oh please, cover him up.”

“Stupid kids,” the angry man kept saying.

Elata said, “Thank you.” Something slick and cool was thrown over Diamond. A darker blackness was pulled across him.

Elata touched him and pulled her hand away.

“What?” asked Seldom.

“Feel this,” she said.

“No.”

“Touch him here.”

“I don’t want to touch him.”

Someone put a long hand on his shoulder and left it there, and Elata said, “Look,” and then a moment later, “Are you watching?”

“Yes,” Seldom whispered.

Once more, she said, “Touch him.”

Another hand fell on his shoulder.

Seldom said, "He's hot."

"Like fire," she agreed.

Both of their hands pulled away.

Again, she said, "Look."

"His face . . . "

"Do you see that?"

There was a long pause. Then with a soft, impressed voice, Seldom said, "This is amazing."

Diamond didn't feel feverish, but the wood beneath him was impossibly cold. His best arm moved his best hand and he touched himself, sticky fingers brushing against the gore that had been his face. There was no perceptible heat. His entire body was cooking itself to remake itself. Shredded flesh remembered its shape and found the most elegant route to return that earlier state. A fractured eye socket was rewoven and hardened in the space of thirty quick breaths. Then light returned to the world, sudden and too brilliant to endure. He tried to close his eyes, but the impact had ripped away one of his eyelids. Using the good arm, he covered the exposed eye. "Bright," he said with a mouth that felt borrowed.

"That tooth," Seldom said.

Cold fingertips touched his lip, his gum.

The eye and its lid were trying to finish. Diamond lowered his hand, touching Elata's hand, and she took hold of a finger and thumb.

The brightness dissolved into two figures kneeling beside him, big eyes dancing inside spellbound faces.

"His arm," said Seldom.

"What?" Elata asked.

Into her ear, he whispered, "It was broken. Wasn't it?"

"Quiet."

A borrowed poncho covered Diamond, save for his face. He was lying on his back, his battered head turned to the right, his two companions on their knees beside him, inadvertently helping to hide what was happening. The adults were nearby, watching what little they could. There was respectful worry and lingering scorn for what these three children had done. "It's nothing but dangerous, falling on top of people," said the angry man. "Innocents could have been hurt. I hope they get punished right."

"The authorities," a distant woman said. "Are they coming?"

"To nab that pair for detention," the man said. "And if he survives, the other criminal goes to the hospital."

"Don't say that," the sorrowful woman warned.

The man grunted. "Hey, I saw him hit. Face first, and hard."

"But—"

"That boy's never waking up," the man promised. "If he's lucky, he dies before he feels a damned thing."

Diamond took a long wet breath.

The crowd quieted.

Then the badly injured boy sat up, and everybody gasped.

Elata fell back.

Seldom blinked and stared, nervous laughter dribbling out.

Everybody could see Diamond. There was a lot of blood to absorb, and some people retreated from the gore. Others, inquisitive or tougher, stepped forward, trying to make sense of the phenomena.

The angry man was gray and heavy-set, and he didn't move. He could see fine from where he stood, and nothing he saw was pleasant. With a scowl, he asked, "What's going on here?"

"He doesn't look too bad," the sorrowful woman said.

Again, the man said, "I saw him hit. And I know that arm was busted."

Diamond lifted the arm. Rebuilt eyes watched his fingers open and wiggle and then close tight, the pressure of his grip making a small ache inside his freshly repaired wrist.

"What is going on here?" the man demanded.

Elata put her face to his ear. "Are you all right?"

Diamond nodded.

"How can you . . . ?" Her voice trailed away.

"It's not possible," Seldom said.

"You saw," she said.

Again, Seldom giggled anxiously.

"Why are you laughing?" the angry man asked.

Using both hands, Diamond examined his mouth, his entire face. Fractures in the lower jaw had healed, teeth finding their way home. The shattered nose was whole again, and when he blew air through it, something that wasn't blood or mucus slowly fell out of one nostril. A big yellowish glob of living tissue lay on the landing's gray wood, and the three of them stared at it, watching it change shape and begin to slowly, slowly crawl, trying to make its way back to Diamond.

Seldom scooted to the side in horror, and he cackled.

"What is that?" Elata began.

Diamond touched the living piece of himself, closing a hand tight around it. "Maybe it's my brain," he offered.

She laughed in a sobbing, desperate way.

The angry man now had a reason to step forward. Shaking his fist, he asked, "What's so damn funny here? Was this some stupid joke?"

From the back of the crowd, another man said, "I see the police. They're coming."

Seldom quit laughing. "I don't want to be in trouble."

"And I do?" Elata asked.

But it was Diamond who stood up first. "I want to go."

The other two got to their feet, both asking, "Where?"

"Home," said Diamond.

"You're not leaving," said the angry man, marching toward them. He had a shuffling gait and enormous hands that grabbed Seldom by the hair. "You faked this whole business, didn't you? A practical joke, was it?"

Seldom's head was jerked back. "Hey," he complained.

Elata looked at Diamond. Then she turned and told their audience, "He's fine. We're fine. It was a joke. That's all."

Glad to be proved right, the man let go of Seldom.

Except now every adult was angry. Nobody was thankful that this gravely injured boy was standing and seemed to be healthy. They had been fooled. Their emotions had been played with, empathy and pity wasted on some trick that nobody could explain. But what reasonable explanation was there except that this was a stupid prank?

Seldom rubbed his neck.

Elata looked to her left and then her right.

A small black blimp was descending. Two snarling horns sounded, alternating rapidly and with considerable importance.

"What's that?" Diamond asked.

"The police," said Seldom.

Diamond didn't understand what that meant, but his wasn't good. Irate adults had formed a semicircle around them. Marduk stood at their backs, and there was no place to go. The self-appointed ruler of this mob continued glaring at these awful wild children, complaining about the slide of morality and the decay of what used to be a good honest society.

Diamond stepped to one side.

"Stop there," the angry man warned.

Elata looked at Diamond, smiling in an odd fashion, and reaching with both hands, she grabbed his fist.

"Give that to me," she said.

He opened his hand.

Then she told both of them, "Go left, as fast as we can."

The slug-like piece of Diamond had to be ripped off his palm. Then she tossed it underhand, dropping it on the old man's face, and he grimaced and pulled it off, shouting obscenities as he flung the monstrosity down in disgust.

Elata ran, one leg limping.

Seldom was behind her, while Diamond was already in the lead.

• • •

"Where?" Diamond asked.

"Here," she said. "Turn in."

A long and very tall curtain had been pulled open. Cut into the living wood was a tunnel—a long public avenue full of shops and restaurants and people busy with their still-young day. The sight of three running children wasn't unusual. Someone warned they might be late for school, but nobody tried to stop them. They ran until Elata was sure nobody was following, and then she caught up to Diamond, using the last of her breath to say, "Stop now. Walk."

He nodded, slowed.

Seldom stopped and bent over. "Wait, please," he said.

The other two stopped.

"I can't believe we fell that far," he said. Then with a frightened, happy expression, he asked, "Did you see my landing? Not too bad, was it?"

"Better than mine," Elata said.

Shoppers were filing past. The air was fragrant and sweet with cooking odors and morning fires smoking inside big grills. Diamond was instantly hungry. He had never been this famished, the sensation making him ache.

Elata studied him.

Seldom began to catch his breath, growing more scared as he felt better. "Where are we going?" he asked.

"I don't know," Elata said.

The boys looked at each other.

"We need help," she said.

"My father," Diamond began. "He would help us."

"But we don't know where he is," she said.

"Well, we can't go back to my mother," Seldom said.

Elata didn't mention her mother, not even to push the possibility aside.

"I'm hungry," Diamond announced.

The others didn't notice.

The starving boy walked up to a vendor. Sticks of blackened meat and grilled fruit stood on a warming plate, begging to be eaten.

Diamond reached for a stick.

The vendor slapped the back of his hand, stopping a potential thief.

Elata saw the drama. "What's the matter?"

"I have to eat," Diamond admitted.

"You really need to?"

"Yes."

"How much?" she asked the vendor.

The man showed his fingers and thumb.

"I've got two," she said, reaching into her trouser pocket.

"Five," the man repeated.

"Help us," she told Seldom.

Her friend had a pocket full of coins. The five-spot was accepted, and Diamond grabbed up the stick, eating with big craving bites.

Thinking about what had gone wrong and could still go wrong, Seldom watched the crowd moving past them. And then his face changed and he was laughing. Standing taller, he took time to relish this little dose of pleasure. And then he said, "I know where to go."

Elata asked, "Where?"

He put his face close to hers. "School."

"Now?" Elata shook her head. "I'm not dressed, and what do about Diamond?"

"Master Nissim," Seldom said.

She took a moment, considering.

"If anybody," he began.

"Great. Let's go." Then she tugged at the strong, rebuilt arm. "We know somebody, Diamond. Somebody sure to help."

SIX

They ran past shops and dozens of strangers and through the bright constant rattle of unfamiliar voices discussing more strangers and senseless topics. Running wasn't work. Being swallowed up by oddities and puzzlements was work. Feeling weight on his shoulders and inside his heart, Diamond slowed his gait, and he tried to narrow his eyes, avoiding distractions. But the hallway's left wall was littered with side tunnels reaching deep inside the tree, and there were chambers cut into both walls and unexplained doors that could stand open or closed and mysterious cavities where wooden people stood on pedestals, wearing colorful clothes and paint on their handsome faces.

One side tunnel was marked with important numbers, and it obviously dove deep inside the tree.

Elata shouted, "Turn."

Diamond was exhausted. He was ready to sit in a corner, resting his mind. More than anything, he wanted quiet and closed eyes and his old friend Mister Mister to hug. But they ran down a long passageway, deeper into Marduk. The only lights hummed and flickered, like fire and not like fire, and the surrounding wood smelled different. Diamond pulled away from his friends. Then the wood smelled like before—a living wet smell—and a doorway appeared, revealing sunshine. He slowed and Elata said, "Go out," and Diamond led them onto the same broad public walkway they had already fled once.

He fell into a quick walk, watching for the angry man and the black blimp, but the blimp was gone and every face was new, and most of the people didn't waste time noticing the odd boy in their midst.

Elata and Seldom caught up to him.

The walkway was wider than before—a great plain of blue-painted wood reaching far into a different kind of air. No column of water tumbled from the sky. There were three blimps and different trees growing in the distance, while smoke and perfumes gave every breath strange tastes.

"Where are we?" he asked.

His friends were talking between themselves.

Diamond stopped and looked at them. "Where's Marduk?"

"It's here," Seldom said. "We came out the other side."

Diamond turned in a slow circle, finding new landmarks.

"We need to climb," Elata warned.

The great tree rose up into a morning mist that wasn't as thick as before. Hundreds of structures were fixed to the trunk and long mysterious structures reached far out into the bright busy air.

"Come on," said Seldom.

"I can't climb," Diamond said.

"It's all right," said Elata. "There's another way."

They approached a wide gap in the walkway, a narrow red safety rope marking the hole. Massive ropes were moving beside the tree, a dozen ropes rising and just as many falling. The smallest rope was thicker than any person's body, dull brown and creaking sharply. Several people stood beside the hole, waiting. An attendant released the safety rope. Then a broad platform dropped into view, different people and a few small boxes riding down the side of the tree. The platform never stopped, and most of the waiting people calmly stepped onboard, vanishing without fuss. Then the attendant looped the safety rope back into place, glancing up and then down before telling everyone, "Step away."

Diamond stood beside Elata. Seldom was behind them, watching the crowd and then watching his feet.

"Police," he said with a quiet, scared voice.

Two men in black uniforms and rounded black hats emerged from the hallway, studying faces, working their way toward Diamond.

Elata walked up to the safety rope.

The attendant was a small stout woman. Her uniform was gray with white stripes, and she wore a tall pointed hat. She looked important and sounded that way when she said, "Back now, girl. Freighter coming. Back."

Elata whispered to Seldom.

The boy winced and said nothing.

Diamond looked over the edge. The rising platform was covered with long boxes.

The important woman said, "Get back, son."

He didn't like that word from a stranger. "Son." But he backed up and dropped his face.

Elata took his hand. Her tug meant something.

"They see us," Seldom said.

The freight platform was close when Elata squatted and jumped under the rope, bringing Diamond with her. Seldom followed. The attendant cursed, but she had no interest in chasing them. Their fall was quick and ended with a noisy crash, landing on top of the largest box. Thick wooden planks were pegged to a heavy framework. Spaces between the planks allowed air to move in and out. Something directly under Diamond's feet made a rough noise, like the cough of a giant, and then a broad pink nose pushed close enough that he felt the wet breath warming the bare parts of his feet.

The platform rose past the walkway and the waiting people and the attendant who invested a few moments shaking her fist at them.

Diamond didn't see the police again.

Seldom kneeled, peering into the dark interior.

"What are you doing?" a voice shouted.

"We're late to school," Elata said.

A man was climbing up on their box. He had the same gray and white uniform, the same pointed hat. But his anger was different. The first attendant had seen one rule broken, but what could she do about it? On the other hand, these three hitchers were riding on this man's platform, which was nearly his own property. This was a very serious crime.

"So you're late," the man said. "But now you're doubly in trouble, because you don't belong here."

"Throw us off," Elata said.

"I should," he agreed.

Terrified, Seldom backed away.

Again, the beast inside the box gave Diamond a good hard sniff. Then a sour deep voice said, "Odd, odd, odd."

Diamond stepped back.

The nose followed him. And again, the creature's voice said, "Odd."

The attendant looked at the three of them, ending up with Diamond. A polished club was fixed to a heavy belt, and he pulled the club free, passing it from one hand to the other and back again. Seldom moaned, and Elata put her feet apart, ready to move. But then the man knelt and struck the box hard three times, shouting, "What's odd, growler?"

"Smell is."

"Whose smell?"

The nose looked halfway human, sniffing Diamond again, sniffing hard.

"That boy?" asked the man.

"No boy," the growler responded. Then it put its nose under Seldom, sniffed and said, "Nothing like this boy. Nothing this nose ever smelled ever."

The attendant rose, studying Diamond's face.

"What's a growler?" Diamond asked no one in particular.

"They do work," Elata explained. "They're big and strong, and smart enough to follow orders, if their trained right and willing."

“I am willing,” said the beast in the box. “I am a heroic worker.”

Except for the big nose, Diamond couldn’t see what was under his feet. Putting both arms around his chest, he gazed out into the air, at a tree even larger than Marduk that was laced with tunnels and houses and covered with big walkways, and maybe twenty blimps were tied to structures that reached out like arms, and beneath every walkway were other structures where still more people lived.

Not even at his dreamiest best had Diamond imagined so many people alive in the world.

The attendant approached, holding his club with both hands.

“What’s wrong with you, son?”

There was that word again. “Son.” Diamond took a deep breath and looked down at his silly feet, and then he looked up and frowned. “I’m sick,” he said. “I’m dying.”

He didn’t believe that story anymore, but he could offer the words with convincing despair.

The man said, “Oh,” and dropped his gaze.

Nobody spoke for a while.

Then Seldom said, “We’re close.”

A smaller walkway was directly above. Elata took Diamond’s hand again and tugged, smiling at him until he smiled back. She didn’t tell him that they would jump, but he knew what her face was saying. Then she turned forward, and he kept watching her profile—the smile swirling inside fatigue and fear and undiluted stubbornness. Real faces weren’t paint on wooden soldiers or wooden statues. A human face was much more complicated, and if you stared at any face, it showed you more and more that you hadn’t noticed before.

• • •

Wood sawed from other trees had been carried to this important place and pinned together to form rooms and hallways, windows and doors, and the entire building was painted a brilliant shade of blue that Diamond had never seen before. Like a giant hand, the school had grabbed hold of Marduk. Every room was lit by daylight. Students dropped to school on ropes and ladders, and they climbed up to it, and strung-out groups scampered along parallel walkways. There was endless motion, yet nobody seemed to hurry. Every day in the world began when it began, and every day lasted as long as it would last. Time was fluid. Starts and endings were never clearly defined. This was morning and not necessarily late in the morning, and it felt like the right time to begin school, and school would last to that vague, still distant point in the afternoon when minds grew too tired to function—student minds as well as those of the teachers.

Someone said, "Seldom."

The boy nodded vaguely, pushing on.

A girl approached, asking Elata, "Where's your uniform?"

"Laundry," she blurted, her excuse at the ready. "My mom forgot again."

"Who are you?" The girl was short and stocky, and she liked to touch what didn't make sense. She put both hands on Diamond's arms, saying, "I don't know you. Where are you from?"

"My old tree," Elata said.

The boys looked at her, surprised.

"He's visiting," she explained. "His family's thinking of moving to Marduk."

"The world's best tree," said the girl. And she ran off.

The three of them continued to walk. Then Seldom said, "I know better, but I almost believed you."

"Lying is my gift," she said, smiling.

The first few doors were avoided. Planks and a minimal railing created a rising staircase that nobody else used. Elata climbed and paused, waiting for Diamond. "This man we want to see," she began.

"Master Nissim," he remembered.

"There's a story about him," she said.

Seldom acted self-conscious and nervous, and that was why the teacher noticed him. Standing at the bottom of the stairs, she shouted, "What are you doing there, Seldom?"

He stopped, hands wrestling in front of him.

"Come down here," she demanded.

"We have an appointment," Elata called out.

The teacher hadn't noticed Elata or Diamond. "An appointment?" she asked skeptically.

"This boy is transferring to school."

"And where are his parents?"

"We're looking for them." Elata nodded with authority. "Have you seen two new adults, Master?"

The woman considered and said, "No, I don't think so."

"We'll keep looking, Master. Thank you."

Elata broke into a crisp run and the boys followed, reaching the next walkway and turning into the first doorway. A tunnel led inside the tree, and suddenly the world became wonderfully quiet.

"What is the story?" Diamond asked.

Elata paused. "What story?"

"About Master Nissim," he said.

"Oh, he isn't a teacher anymore." She showed him a wink and smile. "He used to be. I guess. But something happened long ago, something very bad, and you can never ask about that. Is that understood?"

He thought, *No.*

But he nodded and said nothing more.

• • •

Power saws and pneumatic chisels had carved an enormous room, apparently for no purpose but to be filled up with ash-stained vents and giant grills, cupboards taller than any person and ovens large enough to cook meals for hundreds of growing bodies. Smoke hung in the close damp air. Yesterday's garbage needed to be thrown out. Jammed into the aisles were block-like tables where food was prepared, each table holding a long rack filled with wooden spoons and huge pots scorched by hard use. Men and women wore uniforms that might have started the day white. Every apron was filthy with plant juices and blood. Everybody was talking, and as the three of them stepped into the kitchen, one woman in back shouted a few words that Diamond didn't recognize—funny words, judging by the laughter rolling toward them—and then another woman yelled the warning that everybody feared most. "Children," she called out.

The laughter didn't die immediately, and several adults repeated the new words. But then the place turned quiet enough that Diamond heard the ticking of ovens and a cauldron of water boiling with enthusiasm.

A different woman stepped forward. "Not now, he's busy," she told Seldom.

Seldom hesitated.

"Besides," the woman continued. "It's class time and you two aren't dressed."

Elata smiled pleasantly while nodding, as if ready to apologize and leave again. But then she told everybody, "This is Diamond. He's starting school today, and according to tests, he's even smarter than Seldom."

Seldom bristled with that news but kept quiet.

"We told Diamond who the smartest person in school is, but he doesn't believe us. He thinks it should be a teacher."

Everybody laughed in a head-shaking, cross-the-arms fashion. Then the woman who tried to coax them to leave personally escorted them into a second, much smaller room. White walls and the sudden chill signaled a very different place. The only person present stood at the farthest table. He was covered with blood, the apron soaked and red flecks on his face and the gloves soggy enough to drip blood when he gripped the big cleaver, both hands needed before he could take a whack at the gruesome remains of a long animal leg.

The woman waited for the cutting to stop. Then she said, "Nissim, hey," and gave Diamond a shove of encouragement. Then to the three of them, she said, "Not long. Or you'll eat double rations, as a lesson."

She left laughing.

Diamond had never seen a taller or stronger man. The school's butcher was younger than his father, but not by too many days. The forearms looked swollen with muscle. The long narrow face was never handsome and was usually forgotten by everyone who looked at him only once. What were memorable were his eyes, oversized and brilliant even though they were blacker than seemed natural. Master Nissim also had an easy, infectious smile and an agreeable voice that was deeper than expected—a smoldering low voice that could say anything and say it softly and still end up being noticed by everyone in earshot.

"Come here, boy," he said to Diamond. "And bring that nice odd face with you."

Diamond crept halfway to the table and stopped.

"I don't know you," the man decided.

Diamond looked at his own feet.

"There's a story here, isn't there?" Nissim set the cleaver into a coral sink and pulled the pieces of leg aside. Removing his filthy gloves, he kept his eyes fixed on Diamond. But he said, "Seldom. Tell me the story, please."

Elata tried to speak first.

"No," the man insisted. Up went a huge hand, one finger noticeably shorter than the others. "You can tell it next, dear. But I want to hear something closer to the truth, and you are an accomplished exaggerator."

Seldom took a cold breath and exhaled, vapor hanging before his thrilled face. Then with a rush of words, he repeated what he knew personally and what others had told him. A morning full of adventure was relived, and then he was left gasping for air, happy enough that his feet began to dance.

Nissim never stopped watching Diamond. "Your first time outside, he says. Is that the absolute truth, my boy?"

Diamond nodded.

"Amazing," said the butcher.

"Can I tell it now?" Elata asked.

"Oh, please. I've been waiting for this."

She began at the moment when she first saw Diamond standing on his landing, relating events in their approximate order. It was the same story, and it wasn't. Seldom said that his brother dropped the boy, and it might have been an accident. In Elata's telling, Karlan was bigger and meaner, flinging his victim into the open air and cackling as he tumbled out of sight. Seldom mentioned how the wounds healed quickly, but he was stubbornly unwilling to believe what he saw. Maybe Diamond wasn't hurt that badly, he allowed. But Elata was convinced, and for emphasis, she said that she was sure that Diamond died in the fall but came back to life again as easily as normal people woke at dawn, and she didn't know what to think about this odd wonderful boy who had spent his life in darkness, except that he seemed remarkably nice.

Diamond listened to every word, absorbing the drama, but it felt as if she was describing a stranger. Meanwhile he studied the cold room, the walls covered with white papery insulation, the work tables washed clean and the deep bins beside them, each filled with sorted bones and chunks of dark red meat, and in one sink, the intact head of some big animal with huge flat teeth and empty holes where the eyes should be. He went to look at the head, and then he spied a different sort of table and a small chair hiding in the back corner. Papers and books were stacked on shelves fixed to the white wall. Elata had finished her story. Diamond was approaching the desk when Nissim clucked his tongue and laughed quietly.

"You don't believe me," Elata complained.

"Believe you?" the butcher replied. "Oh, I believe everything I'm told. That's the human curse. People are gullible animals. That's why I've taught myself to step back and give a skeptical look at everything, particularly ordinary, commonsense thoughts. Which your story is most definitely not."

Diamond stood beside the desk, reading what little he could. Familiar words and strange words were written on the bindings. The books set on the highest shelf caught his attention, and he couldn't help but climb up on the desk, on his knees, grabbing the top volume from the stack.

Nissim was beside him and had been for a while.

A great cool hand touched the boy's back, and a matching voice asked, "What are your parents' names?"

"Haddi and Merit."

"Merit," the warm voice repeated.

Diamond opened the book. The binding was on the right, and every page was filled with swirling, senseless lines.

"Can you read this?" Nissim asked.

"No."

Seldom laughed, saying, "Of course not. People don't read papio."

Diamond set the book down.

"Except you, Master," Seldom added, deeply impressed.

"The papio are people too," Nissim warned.

"I know that. They're our cousins, I know." But Seldom smiled in a stubbornly doubtful way.

"Why did you select this book?" Nissim asked.

"I have some of these in my room," Diamond said.

"Really?" asked Nissim.

Diamond nodded.

The butcher's hands were rough and steady. He tilted the boy's face to let giant eyes hunt for wounds still healing. There was nothing to see. "Such a peculiar architecture," he began. "Merit the Slayer is your father. Yes?"

"Do you know him?" Elata asked.

"Not well. But we've spoken." Nissim paused. "Never for long, I'm afraid, and so I can't claim to know him. But I think I would recognize the fellow, given the chance."

Seldom cleared his throat. "Why would his father have papio books?"

"Well, I know his work takes him to the world's edges," Master Nissim pointed out. "But of course a lot of tree-walkers wander the reef country, and how many of those bring home these?" He set the book back where it belonged. "Merit had a child, I heard. But someone told me . . . I don't remember who . . . long ago told me the boy was weak and soon to die."

"That's me," Diamond allowed.

"Well, I was misinformed." Nissim pulled his lower lip into his mouth, sucking hard while he thought.

"We need to find his parents," Elata said.

"From what you've told me, Merit's hunting in the wilderness . . . "

His voice trailed away.

Diamond fidgeted.

Returning to the table, the butcher began to wipe clean his knives and cleavers. Smiling, a little embarrassed, he allowed, "I've got this awful urge, my boy. All these fine sharp implements, and I'm thinking about a little poke, a short slice. Something to test these rumors of healing."

Diamond held out his hand, waiting.

"No," the Master told him, folding his little fingers and pushed his hand back. "I am sure you've been cut enough for one day."

• • •

The three of them went into the kitchen to wait while Master Nissim cleaned and changed clothes. He had told them to keep out of the way, which meant standing together between a pair of enormous grills. Diamond watched the fierce blue flames and the frying meat resting in the bubbling oils.

"Have you ever seen fire?" Seldom asked.

"On candles."

Elata touched an arm. "Are you still hungry?"

He nodded.

She went to the woman who met them when they arrived. Three greasy cakes were found and wrapped in waxed paper and handed to them with little winks and warnings not to tell the other children. "Teacher cake," Elata explained. "Extra good."

She and Seldom ate half of theirs, giving the remnants to Diamond.

People stopped working, watching the sudden feast. By the time Diamond licked up every crumb, Nissim was emerging from the cold room. He wasn't wearing any uniform. Somebody made noise about tutoring, and he nodded and smiled, remarking, "These kids are going tutor me today. The meat's all cut. I'm sure you can survive without me." Then noticing the stares, he asked, "What's wrong?"

"That poor starving boy," said the woman, describing what she just witnessed.

Nissim put a hand on Diamond's forehead. "Are you always the big eater?"

"I don't know," he admitted. "I usually eat alone."

Nissim kneeled, placing his eyes directly before the boy's eyes. "Do your parents ever talk about the world outside?"

He shook his head.

"Did they tell you about the trees and canopy and the sun?"

"Sometimes we talk about Marduk."

"Have they shown you paintings of the world?"

"No. Just of the Creators."

"Who nobody has ever seen." Nissim smiled. "Do you know the world's shape?"

"I . . . I don't know . . . "

The Master nodded, ready to say something else. Important words waited in his mouth, and he did everything but say them. But in the end he stood and shook his head, leading them out of the kitchen. Then with a stern, irresistible voice, he told the other two children, "I want you to be quiet. I want to talk to Diamond, and you can't make a sound. Please.

"And I mean you, Seldom."

The boy rolled his eyes, trying to laugh.

They walked through the same doorway leading to the outdoors, back into the bright open air. Several little blimps were wandering past, and birds sang, and a pair of leatherwings fought in the air, snarling and spitting as they decided who was biggest and strongest.

Nissim said, "Stop."

The school was below them. Teachers were talking with loud voices and students were making lots of little noises, competing to be noticed.

"We're going to visit our District headquarters," Nissim explained. "They'll know your father's whereabouts, and we'll find him before long. Does that seem reasonable to you?"

Diamond nodded hopefully.

"But first," said the Master, kneeling again. "I want you to tell me something. If you don't know the answer, guess. Whatever idea pops into your head, I want to hear it."

Diamond nodded.

Seldom and Elata stood back, watching.

Nissim put up the hand with the short finger, reminding the others to be silent. "Where is the sun?" he asked.

"Pardon me?"

"The sun," he repeated. Then with a patient wide smile, he said, "Point to the sun, my boy. Right now."

Diamond straightened his index finger and pointed up.

Seldom laughed, and Elata struck his bony shoulder, saying, "Stop that, stop."

The Master was nodding. Emotions played across his plain face while both hands started to shake, and he took one deep breath that wasn't enough. So he took several more breaths and then stood again. One trembling hand wiped one eye and then the other. Then speaking to nobody but himself, he said, "I have read about this."

"What do you mean?" Elata asked.

"About people like Diamond?" asked Seldom.

But the man wouldn't answer. He took another long breath, and then with a serious sorry voice, he told the lost boy, "No, Diamond. No. The sun is and has always been beneath our feet."

SEVEN

The sun was beneath them, and why would it be anywhere else? Nobody had come to his room and pointed at the ceiling, telling him, "The day comes from above, my boy. The sun sits over our heads." And he had no reason to doubt what he was told just now. Yet Diamond shook his head skeptically, making Seldom laugh again. Squinting, he gave his toes a long skeptical stare, and Elata took hold of his elbow, saying, "You had no way to know. But now you do."

Except what did he know?

Very, very little, it seemed.

Without sharing his thoughts, Nissim walked on.

Still fighting, the leatherwings screeched and flapped hard and then pulled apart for a moment, gathering violence for the next collision. Teeth cut, insults battered. Then one animal shrieked and turned and flew away, fur and bright blood following it as the winner triumphantly took claim over the bright air beside the school.

Students, mostly boys, cheered from their classrooms.

The Master was climbing a long set of stairs, and the three of them hurried to catch up.

"Where are we going?" Seldom asked.

"Special occasions demand luxury," Nissim explained.

"We're riding," said Elata with a grin.

No, they were walking. The stairs were wide, room enough for three students to walk together without brushing elbows.

Seldom poked his new friend. "What about the rain?" he asked.

Diamond pretended not to hear him.

But the boy persisted. "Where do you think rain comes from? Above or below?"

Nissim looked back as he climbed, interested in the answer.

"I don't know," Diamond said. But one finger insisted on pointing up.

Seldom giggled.

Elata punched his shoulder again.

"It's a fair question," Seldom moaned.

Then with two fingers, Elata jabbed him in the ribs.

Nissim had stopped climbing. He looked at the mysterious boy, and then his eyes were pulled away. Quietly, with a curious tone, he said, “I wonder what the police are doing here.”

A large black blimp had risen into view, maneuvering to dock with the school.

“They’re chasing my brother,” Seldom guessed.

Nissim opened his mouth and breathed deeply. “That seems like an extraordinary number of officers to chase one boy.”

Then he turned and started climbing again.

“Let’s hurry,” said the man’s big voice, on arm pulling at the railing. “We don’t want to miss the next part of our day.”

• • •

A narrow landing reached far out into the air. Several adults were standing at the end, waiting beside a tall pole. Flags wearing assorted emblems were flapping on the pole. A white sock stuck out sideways, and as the winds shifted, it collapsed and then pointed in a fresh direction.

The four of them walked out on the landing, out where it began to wobble under Diamond’s feet, and he stopped and grabbed the railing, waiting for the pitching to stop.

The motions only grew worse.

Reaching deep into a pocket, Nissim retrieved square coins of glass and polished coral. A stubby silver blimp was falling towards them, one flag dangling from the mooring post jutting out from its bow. “There’s some luck,” the Master said. “Our ride arrives.”

The other people stared at the odd boy until he looked at them, and then everyone watched the blimp. The machine seemed small until it was close, and then Diamond felt tiny. The cockpit was just below the long mooring post. A long window was propped open, the wild-haired pilot watching everything. Big propellers roared and slowed and then roared again, pushing the blimp close. The blimp’s mooring post ended with mechanical fingers, and there was a stout iron ring clamped to the end of the landing, waiting to be grabbed. The fingers reached the ring, but the wind gusted unexpectedly, and with a bright useless clank they closed on empty air. The gigantic machine had to back away slowly before trying again, helped along by the pilot’s fierce cursing. This time the fingers grabbed the loop and the blimp rose over them. Its mooring post was like an arm bending like an elbow, and once the post was vertical, its base locked in place, allowing the blimp to turn in the wind without endangering itself or the people on the landing.

A flexible gangway was released from the belly, and out ran a pair of red monkeys. Big and powerful, the beasts jumped into the air with ropes fixed in their mouths, long falls ending when the hand-like feet grabbed hold of iron grommets. Then they dragged the gangway into position and started to tie it down, still making knots as the travelers put themselves in a line.

A second crewman appeared. His gray uniform was tight and too long in the arms, and he had a happy face that was just as put-on as his shirt. "Bound for the canopy," he shouted, throwing biscuits at the monkeys. "Marduk's final station, and then Rail and Hanner and Bliss. Welcome to all."

A well-to-do couple went first, displaying important pieces of paper.

Nissim offered coins.

The attendant counted them quickly and accurately. "Your family?" he asked.

"They are," Nissim said.

"Fine looking bunch," the attendant said, paying no attention to the dissimilar threesome.

Nissim led them up the gangway and then paused, looking back at the school.

Nobody was following.

"That's a different kind of monkey," Diamond guessed.

"Capables, they're called," Seldom said. "Although they have to be well-trained to be that way."

"Who doesn't?" Nissim joked.

A big horn sounded, and one capable untied the gangway while the other kicked the post's fingers, triggering them to release.

Diamond found himself in the back of a long narrow cabin. Tall-backed benches were set in rows, and Elata claimed an empty bench. She sat and patted the bare space beside her, and Diamond sat and then lifted up again, peering out the window.

"No, let's trade," she said. "I'll let you watch."

Nobody else looked outside. Every other person saw nothing remarkable or beautiful. This was just the world and not even an important portion of the world, and what mattered most to travelers were their private, often secret thoughts.

Whispering, Diamond asked, "Where does rain come from?"

"Below," Seldom said, waiting all this time to explain. "It flies upwards when the night ends. That's how every morning begins."

Nissim was sitting on the bench in front of them. He turned and smiled, one elbow perched on the wooden back, two fingers thoughtfully tapping his curled mouth.

"Rain doesn't fly," said Elata.

"Sprays," Seldom said. "That's what I meant."

Nissim said nothing, studying the boy that had unexpectedly wandered into his life.

Questions begged to be asked. Diamond wanted to know everything about rain, but he was also thinking about flying, and that brought the blimp to mind. "How do we stay in the air?" he asked Elata.

"Gas holds us up," she said.

"Hydrogen gas," Seldom added.

That first word meant nothing.

Sensing confusion, Nissim used a teacher's voice. "Air is made up of different species of gas. Some are common, others rare. And the lightest gas is hydrogen. Certain plants make quite a bit of hydrogen, and we harvest what we need. Have you ever seen wood float on water?"

Diamond nodded.

"That's what this aircraft is doing now. Floating."

"But we're falling," he pointed out.

"That's because the blimp always starts its run heavy. It begins up high and works its way down the tree. The air gets thicker as we drop. Do you feel your ears aching? Well, they might. Or might not, I don't know about you. But the blimp falls, picking up more passengers and cargo, increasing its weight which helps it fall faster, and then it drops a little ballast, lightening the load just enough, after which it runs above the canopy to the turnaround point."

"Ballast," Diamond repeated.

"Sawdust and water," said Seldom.

"Usually," said Nissim. Other people were watching the conversation. His face needed to be closer to Diamond, his voice lowered. "At the end of the run, the pilot drops most of the ballast, and our blimp jumps back to the top of the world."

Diamond stared out the window. The school and black blimp were far above; walkways and homes and elaborate buildings covered Marduk's endless trunk.

"What's at the top of the world?" Diamond asked.

"Not the sun," Seldom said.

Nissim placed one hand on Seldom's head, shaking him gently. Then in a whisper, he explained, "Not many go there, and nobody would want to live there. It's always dark, always night. But that's where Marduk and these other trees put up their roots. Against the world's ceiling, everything hangs."

The boy blinked and sighed. Hard thought brought another question, and he asked, "What is the world's shape?"

Seldom smiled smartly. "Guess."

Nissim frowned but didn't reprimand.

"You don't have to," Elata said.

But then Diamond put up his hands, fingers and cupped palms drawing a sphere. In his mind, the sphere was smooth and perfectly proportioned. And of course it was enormous. And when nobody corrected him, he described what was in his mind, stressing the enormity of this realm about which he knew almost nothing.

Then he felt finished, and nobody spoke.

Diamond readied himself for corrections and laughter. But Seldom spoke first, nothing but amazed. "That's it," he said. "That's what it is. The Creation is a perfect, perfect ball, and that's all there is."

• • •

The blimp and its floating gas kept falling. Diamond watched the world, and Nissim and Seldom and Elata took turns describing the world. It was as if the boy had two sets of eyes, one pair staring out from his skull while an even bigger pair was turned inwards, watching an imaginary ball filling with forest and people and the blazing, still unseen sun. The eternal sun lay at the bottom of the world. Hundreds of species of trees hung from the highest, flattest portions of the ceiling. The District of Districts was fixed to the top of the sphere, while Marduk was far out where the forests thinned and the wilderness began.

"Bloodwoods are much bigger than blackwoods," Seldom said. "Marduk is a twig next to them."

Diamond tried to imagine those impossible giants.

"The District of Districts is in charge," Elata said.

"What does 'in charge' mean?" he asked.

"They're the bosses," she said.

"Like parents?"

Something was funny. When the laughter stopped, the Master explained, "There are nine districts, but nearly half of the population lives in the District of Districts. In all things human, they have the largest say. They take money from us and steer the laws, and while every District has its own army, they control the biggest army that keeps us safe."

"My father was a soldier," he said.

"Many serve," Nissim said.

"What do they protect us from?"

"The papio," Seldom said.

Elata shook her head. "We don't fight the papio anymore."

"Because we have armies," the boy said.

She touched Diamond on the knee. "Mostly soldiers fight monsters. And other tree-walking people too."

"What people?"

"Bandits in the wilderness," she said.

"There's other bad people too," Seldom insisted.

Nissim looked around the cabin, his mouth shut.

The blimp was changing its pitch and velocity, propellers rumbling with purpose. Diamond pressed his face against the window glass, spying another landing jutting far out from Marduk.

"What's the wilderness?" he asked.

"Dangerous," Seldom said.

Elata said, "Beautiful."

Nissim agreed with both answers. "Different trees grow outside the districts," he said. "And there are different animals, creatures you would never see here. And once you move even farther out, out where the spherical world becomes vertical, another realm takes over." He pulled a slick white coin from his pocket, handing it to Diamond. "The reefs are coral. This is cut from a kind of coral. It's a hard, half-living material. What's alive is part plant, part animal. It feeds on sunlight and gnats and feces, and the reefs are older than any tree, and that's where the papio live."

"Papio," Diamond repeated.

One of the passengers was staring. She hadn't noticed the odd boy until now, and when Diamond glanced at her, she grew self-conscious, looking out her own window with sudden intensity.

The blimp was docking. Diamond saw men standing together, waiting to board, and the burly red capables pulled hard at the ropes, fighting a breeze to bring the gangway into position.

"The papio live on the reefs," Seldom explained.

"They look like people," Elata said.

"No they don't," said Seldom.

Nissim put his face close. "The papio are complicated. Let's leave it there for now."

Diamond remained silent, wondering how anybody could understand the endlessly complicated world.

Horns sounded, and again the blimp moved. Three men entered the cabin and stopped in the aisle, talking to each other with their eyes. Diamond watched them, trying not to stare. One man nodded and another moved to the front and sat. The nodding man and his companion said nothing, filling an empty bench in back.

Diamond looked out the window while he studied the new world inside his head. "How far down do they reach?" he asked.

"Do what reach?" Elata asked.

"The trees."

"Less than halfway," Seldom said.

With stubby fingers, Diamond made the sphere again. Trees dangled down from the top and something called a reef grew on the edges. Seldom put one finger into his round cage, swirling where the trees ended.

"The canopy is my favorite part of the world," Elata said. "That's where trees make branches that grow sideways and wrap together."

"Most of our food comes from the canopy," Seldom said.

Nissim wasn't talking, and he didn't seem to be listening anymore.

"Days are brighter in the canopy," Elata explained. "That's where most of the sunlight gets eaten by the trees and epiphytes."

"What are epiphytes?"

"Plants that hang from bigger plants," Seldom said.

The world was steadily rising around them. Maybe it was Elata's words, but the air did seem brighter than ever, and out from the last shreds of mist came a rich green floor that looked solid, impenetrable.

"There's thousands of species of plants," Seldom said.

"And tens of thousands of different bugs," Elata said.

"There's more than that," Seldom said. The topic was exciting, and he reached across Elata to grab Diamond's knee. "We don't know how many species of insects there are. Sometimes one species vanishes, and sometimes a scientist finds some little beetle or fly that nobody has ever seen before."

"Is that true?" Elata asked doubtfully.

"It is," Seldom insisted.

"Who told you that?"

The boy grinned and looked at the Master. "Isn't that true, sir?"

Nissim seemed to be watching them, but he didn't react, blinking several times before he returned from wherever his mind was.

"Is what true?" he asked.

"People are finding new insects," Seldom said.

"Yes."

The boy straightened his back, proud of himself.

"But it's very rare," the Master cautioned. "And we aren't certain why it happens. Some voices argue that new species are forming. But experts and every textbook will claim that the little things have managed to hide from us until now. They've been here since the Creation, and they always will be."

"That's what I think," said Elata. "Always, and always."

"I like the other idea," Seldom maintained.

Nissim sat sideways on his bench, watching the youngsters as well as the two men sharing the bench at the back of the cabin.

"Which story do you believe?" Elata asked the Master.

"I avoid opinions," Nissim said. "It's easier that way to accept both answers equally, and deny both of them at the same time. That's how I treat problems that I don't understand."

His answer confused everybody, and the subject was dropped.

The canopy was not simple or simply green. Fat brown branches emerged from Marduk—horizontal and thick, radiating straight out from the trunk—and every branch was covered with small branches and lush leaves and moving patches of color that were birds and machines. The closer they approached, the more confused and amazing the view became.

"What's below this?" Diamond asked.

Nissim put both of his hands on the boy's shoulders. He seemed ready to talk, but then he pulled his hands back, his mind still wandering.

Seldom spoke. "What's below the canopy, you mean?"

"Yes."

"Air," said Elata.

"And daylight," Seldom said. "Too bright for ordinary eyes, and kids aren't supposed to ever look it."

"The sun can blind you," Elata warned.

Diamond remembered the dark goggles in the closet back home and how his father's eyes were pale when his face was very brown.

"And what are the coronas?" he asked.

Elata sighed and Seldom twisted against the hard bench. Just the word "coronas" made them nervous and thrilled.

"They have their own place, and it's a very different place," Seldom said.

"Nothing like this," Elata added.

Once again, the blimp changed speed and direction. Propellers rolled hard and fast, and from somewhere on the canopy another horn sounded, thunderous notes rising up through the machine and through them.

Once again, Diamond made the spherical world with his hands, fingertips touching with his thumbs closest to his face.

Seldom reached between his palms, down low. "This is where the night grows. Between us and the sun."

"Night grows," Diamond repeated doubtfully.

"Sure," Elata said. "There's a second canopy down there, only the plants aren't anything we would recognize."

Suddenly the Master made a soft sound, lifting a finger.

The others fell silent.

Leaning close, the man put his face in front of Diamond's face. "Those three men who came onboard," he whispered.

Seldom started to turn his head.

Nissim dropped a hand on Seldom's shoulder. "Hold still. Look at me, please." Then he watched Diamond, saying, "One of them is sitting ahead of us. Do you know who I mean?"

"Yes."

"Do you know why he might know you?"

Diamond shook his head.

"What's wrong?" Elata asked.

"Those gentlemen are taking turns," Nissim explained. "One at a time, they're watching us. And they're mostly interested in Diamond. Which is reasonable, I suppose, since the boy is remarkable. But what worries me is that they don't strike me as being the inquisitive sort."

• • •

Once more, the great horn sounded, and the blimp finished making its majestic turn, aligning with the new landing.

Thinking about the three men, Seldom trembled. "What do we do?" he asked.

"Nothing," said Nissim.

The boy started to turn his head, trying to catch sight of the two men behind them.

"Stop," Nissim said.

Elata took Seldom by the hand. "We're all right. Nobody's going to hurt us."

Diamond felt cold and sorry.

Nissim touched his shoulder. "You need to go to the bathroom."

The boy started to say, "I don't."

"Come. I'm taking you." Then the man made a point of grabbing the others' hands, squeezing hard as he said, "Sit and wait. This won't take long."

Seldom started to ask questions but thought better of it.

"Let's go," Nissim said.

Diamond's legs were weak, and his breath came in quick shallow bursts. But he managed to stand, joining the Master in the aisle, a sure hand guiding him toward the front of the cabin. The strange man sitting in front was quiet, staring hard at the floor between his feet. But as the two of them passed, he turned and stared, brown eyes unblinking and his mouth clamped as tight as could be.

A long hallway ended with a staircase leading up to the cockpit. Diamond looked at the bank of controls and the pilot standing before the open window and her assistant sitting beside her. "Now," said the pilot, and the assistant pulled a long lever, deploying the gangway again.

Two narrow doors stood in the hallway, facing one another and each wearing a bowl-shaped emblem. Nissim knocked on one door and opened it, ushering the boy into a tiny room. The sink was dirty and the toilet smelled. Diamond felt a sudden need to urinate. Nissim closed the door and pulled a latch to lock it, and then he reached behind his back, saying, "If you have to go, go."

Diamond didn't need any more encouragement.

And from behind, Nissim removed a pair of knives wrapped in soft brown leather. He had carried them from the beginning.

"Three men," he began. "Somebody sent them, and I can't guess who. But it doesn't matter. The problem is that there's three of them. If somebody wanted us followed, he would send just one person, somebody we wouldn't notice. But three big boys strutting onboard like they did . . . no, that means they plan to take you. They know who you are, and I don't know how that can be. But I'm almost certain that they want to grab you up."

"Me," said Diamond. "Me?"

The butcher's knives were designed to cut stubborn meat off bones and carve away tendons. Nissim used the smaller knife, working on the window high on the outside wall. The window was already partway opened, supplying meager circulation to the stinking room. He jabbed the knife's point into a hinge, prying it away from an old wooden frame.

"Why me?" asked Diamond.

"A fine question and I wish we had time to talk. But we don't." Nissim stopped working on the hinge, rewrapping each knife in its own leather. Then he grabbed the window with both hands, and he waited.

Another horn sounded.

The blaring was enormous and close, and it covered up the sound of the big man twisting the window away from the rectangular opening. Without a false motion, Nissim set the glass on the sink and knelt down in front of the boy. "Who they are and why they want you—I don't know the answers. But there are three of them, and I'm responsible for the three of you. And I think this is our best chance to get away."

Diamond glanced at the window.

"This is a big landing, and we're floating over it right now," the man explained. "In a few moments, the gangway will be pulled back up. And you'll climb out through this hole and carefully, carefully jump down."

"But then what will I do?" he began.

"Listen," said Nissim, pushing a broad thumb against Diamond's mouth. "You'll have to run to the District office. The office is on the big blackwood tree called Hanner. When you get lost—and you will get lost—ask for directions. Find a nice woman. Tell her that you're meeting your father at the Ivory Station, and beg for help. You're a sweet odd boy, and she'll take pity on you. It's a trick that you could master, I think."

One last time, the horn sounded, and the gangway lifted as the blimp began to push forward again.

"This isn't fair, but this has to be," Nissim insisted. Then he picked up Diamond, aiming his legs for the hole in the wall.

Diamond straightened his arms, making himself small enough to fit.

"We'll be at the Station waiting," the Master promised. "Are you ready?"

The boy didn't have time to answer.

"Good," said the man, giving him one hard shove.

And for the second time in his life, Diamond was falling.

EIGHT

The blimp was fixed to the air while a broad sheet of wood moved beneath him. Diamond fell sideways toward the landing, letting out a bright shout to warn those not looking up.

People looked up, but nobody moved.

Legs bent, he crumbled and rolled. Nothing about his landing was graceful, but the wood was softer than expected and the only pain was from a bruised shoulder that immediately started to heal.

An old woman bent down. "What do you think you're accomplishing?"

Diamond sat up, watching the blimp push away.

"You nearly hit me," she said, even though he hadn't. "And why would you jump from an aircraft?"

She was holding a stick, and above her head was a round piece of fabric supported by smaller sticks.

Diamond stood, paying strict attention to his body. Something hard was pressing against his side, and reaching under his shirt, he found the small butcher's knife wrapped in soft warm leather.

"Answer me," the woman insisted.

"Where's Hanner?" he asked.

She fumed and stepped back. "Where it always is," she said, throwing a sloppy wave behind him.

"Thank you, ma'am." He turned and ran.

The landing narrowed, becoming a walkway. Diamond watched the flat planks of wood ahead of him, sliding left or right when feet and legs had to be avoided. People called out warnings. Other voices had nothing to do with him.

It was terrifying to know that three strange men were chasing him, but only to a point. This was a new fear that easily dissolved into the day's other horrors.

Diamond stopped running, breathing deeply.

Nobody was following. He touched the knife stuck into his waistband, and after a moment touched it again. The walkway was white and slick because it was dirty. Everybody except Diamond carried an umbrella. Soft popping sounds came from ahead and behind, and then a little fleck of something wet struck the top of his hand. He lifted the hand to his nose, finding an acrid, familiar odor. Eyes narrowed, he looked straight up. Blimps and birds and the enormous leatherwings were tiny in the air, and everything seemed to move slowly, and he wondered what happened when those huge animals relieved themselves.

Diamond dropped his face, wiping his hand against his trousers.

Ropes and posts created railings. The walkway was built on top of one of Marduk's enormous limbs—a massive, nearly straight column of wood that had seen healthier days. Bark was missing, wounds full of deep rot. Yet nothing about the limb seemed weak. Countless smaller branches erupted from it, some dropping into the canopy, out of sight, while others reached out to both sides, every branch ending with knobby leaves as big as people.

Diamond grabbed the rope railing, staring into the canopy. Leaves twisted in the breeze. Their topsides were a paler green and different in texture than the dark glossy almost black faces that pointed downward, aiming for the unseen sun. A face was gazing up at him. The green-gold monkey was balanced on a tiny branch, and with a spitting voice, it said, "Go, leave. Go."

The boy ran again. The walkway dropped, slowly and then steeply, and the limb it was riding grew narrower frailer. Every gust of wind caused planks and ropes to creak. A second walkway soon appeared, rising up from the deep canopy as it moved closer to his path. Stairs and ladders descended into other places, every destination hidden by the foliage. Then the two paths crossed, and reaching the intersection, Diamond slowed. A young woman was sitting on a long bench, protected from feces by a broad fixed canopy. Her hands and eyes were occupied with a toddler trying with all of his might to run away.

Diamond watched mother and son struggle.

Without looking up, the woman asked, "What do you want?"

"My father," said Diamond.

She still didn't look up. Leather straps fit around the boy's chest, and she grabbed her son from behind, yanking. He let loose a pitiful wail, and her instant reaction was laughter, telling him, "You're fine, silly nut. You couldn't be any better."

Diamond waited, and when the crying quit, he asked, "Where is Hanner, ma'am?"

She pointed up the new walkway. "Straight ahead."

"All right, ma'am. Thank you."

The mother rose, uncoiling a narrow rope. One end of the rope was looped and needed to ride her wrist, while the clip on the other end was fastened to the boy's leather halter. Having control of her son, she picked up a blue stick covered with bird feces, opening the spring-powered umbrella.

Diamond jumped back in surprise.

She looked at him. She hadn't paid attention to him before, but she became curious and then agitated. Surprised by his face, she asked, "Who are you?" Then before he could answer, she said, "You're too young to be out by yourself."

"I am," he agreed.

But one boy was enough of a burden. Tugging on her son, she said, "Come on, nut," and the two of them took the new walkway in the opposite direction, heading for the green shadows.

Diamond looked for chasing men. There weren't any. He looked over the edge and saw where Marduk's old limb had broken away. The ragged wood looked fresh and sappy, and the tip of the branch had tumbled into the canopy, smaller branches and thousands of leaves pulled down by the catastrophe. He was staring down into an enormous hole. It seemed like a new hole, perhaps torn out by the morning rain. The hole's sides and the bottom were rich green. Holding the railing, Diamond pushed out, staring down into a dense tangle of crisscrossing branches and epiphytes and odd bright birds, and he listened to the white buzz of animals talking, and his thoughts shifted and shifted until he came back to where he began the day.

"Father," he yelled to the canopy.

For an instant, the buzz diminished. A thousand voices hesitated, and then they started up again, screaming only what mattered to them.

• • •

Nissim took Diamond to the toilet.

Waiting as told, Elata sat beside Seldom, touching him and both of them nervous and neither one talking. Elata hated silence. She always had. Odd, awful thoughts kept burrowing into her head, and talking was how she coped whenever bad things were happening. Sitting on her hands was what she did at school when the teachers warned her to be quiet. She sat on her hands now, and Seldom noticed, chewing his bottom lip when she started to shake.

She wanted to jump up and shout at the strange man in front of them, telling him to leave them alone.

Seldom saw her staring at the man. "Don't," he whispered.

But she couldn't just sit and pretend nothing was wrong. The blimp had pulled away from the landing, pushing toward the next stop. Where was the Master? And Diamond? Sitting like a book on a shelf made her crazy, and she was sure that she wouldn't last another breath. Yet she did, and that surprised her as much as anything.

Seldom told her not to stare, but then he turned, looking at the other two men and making a sorry little sound.

"What?" she asked.

He jerked his head forward again. "They were talking."

"Talking how?"

"I don't know . . . but then one of them looked at me."

She started to turn.

"Don't," he said.

But she looked anyway. One man had stood, walking up the aisle now. She and Seldom both sat on their hands. The man passed them and bent low, saying a few words to the man in front—quiet words put inside an ear—and the sitting man shook his head, whispering and flapping his hand in the air.

The standing man nodded and returned to his seat, staring blankly at the children as he passed.

The blimp kept pushing. Elata watched the canopy. A gold-and-blue pashta bird was hovering above a bakebear, stealing ripe fruits with his long tongue. Rail was the next stop, Hanner after that, and what was Master Nissim doing? Was Diamond all right? The worst fear wasn't the fact that something had gone wrong, which was plainly true, but not knowing what that something was.

"Get up," she told Seldom.

He didn't want to move, and he didn't want to stay. The debate ended when the girl poked him the ribs.

They stood together, and she pushed him to the aisle and into the hallway. Both toilet doors were closed. She looked up into the cockpit, earning a bored glance from the pilot's assistant. Then with the flat of her hand, she knocked hard on one door, listening to silence and knocking again.

"Occupied," Nissim said.

Seldom put his face close to the door. "Are you all right, sir?"

There was no answer and no hint of motion, but then the door clicked and opened. Nissim was leaning against the sink. He looked as if he had been standing that way for a very long time. The window was closed but crooked after a rough repair. There was no corner where a second person could hide.

Nissim put three fingers over his mouth, wanting silence.

But Elata couldn't stop the words. "Where did he—?"

"No."

She opened the other toilet door. No Diamond.

A grim and peculiar smile filled the old face. The Master winked at them and in a whisper asked, "Where are they?"

Elata risked one hasty look. "In their seats, watching us."

"I bet they are," he said. Again he put his fingers to his mouth, a strange, scared expression blooming on his face.

They said nothing after that. They walked back to the open bench, and Elata sat where Diamond had been. She felt the propellers working and the slow swaying of the blimp, and for a few moments she forgot where she was. Suddenly she was a tiny girl, riding beside her dead father, enjoying her very first blimp ride.

The two men behind them were muttering.

Nissim shared the same bench, sitting beside the aisle, his shoulders held high.

One man went to the man sitting in front, and both of them continued into the hallway. Elata couldn't see them, but she heard one toilet door open, then the other, and never any courteous knock.

She sat like Nissim sat, straight and square.

The men didn't come back.

"What are they doing?" she asked.

Seldom tipped his head, trying to see.

"Probably talking to the pilot," Nissim said. "But they won't learn anything useful."

The men eventually returned, joining their friend in back. The three of them were muttering and cursing. People turned to watch. Passengers who hadn't noticed anything before now began to pay close attention.

The third man, the one who always sat in back, said, "Wait here."

Then he walked up to Master Nissim.

"Move over," he said.

The Master looked up, making a long odd sound, as if he felt sick. Then he pushed to the right, and Seldom shoved Elata against the window.

The man sat, staring straight ahead. He had a face that probably always looked annoyed. His mouth was tense, the eyes like slivers. A voice came out of someplace deep inside his chest, asking nobody in particular, "What happened to the boy?"

Nissim said nothing.

The man turned to glare at him. Then he stared at Elata and Seldom, measuring them. To Seldom, he said, "Where did your friend go?"

As if lashed by electricity, Seldom flinched and moaned.

"We don't know the boy," Nissim said.

"No?"

With that, the Master started telling a story that was much lie as truth. This very smart man, this one-time teacher, often talked about duty and integrity and being relentlessly honest. But he was suddenly weaving an elaborate tale about a strange boy showing up at school this morning. He claimed that he was a naturalist and these children were his students, and the three of them were on their way to the canopy to hunt for a rare species of ant. The strange boy had tagged along, which was a mistake. Master Nissim regretted that and hoped that nobody would get in trouble, particularly him. Then he introduced the children, except he used invented names, and he offered a palm to the annoyed man, claiming that his name was Master Shine.

Elata liked to lie, and she always had the talent. But she couldn't begin to keep all the details of this story straight.

Nissim was doing a grand job of wasting time, she realized.

Finally the annoyed man said, "Just shut up."

Nobody spoke.

Glancing over his shoulder, he nodded and one of his partners came forward, bending low while the annoyed man told him, "Search the cargo and search between the bladders. Make sure he's not onboard."

"Oh, the boy isn't here," Nissim said.

The annoyed man turned back, acting surprised to find him still here. "So where is the nameless one?"

"I was trying to explain," Nissim insisted with a tight, offended tone. "I wasn't comfortable having him with us, but then he said that he needed help with the toilet. So I took him. And when we got behind that door, the child looked at me with those pale sick eyes . . . he looked at me and said that he didn't very much like the world, and he was leaving."

The annoyed man didn't react.

"Leaving where?" Seldom asked.

Nissim sat back in the bench and shook his head. "I was standing beside him. And then a moment later, he was gone."

The man made a long wet sound, as if preparing to spit.

"But you obviously know something about the child," Nissim said. "And I can guess why you want to find him."

The man started to answer but thought better of it.

"That boy is magical." Master glanced at Elata, flashing a fine little smile. Then to everybody, with a teacher's best voice, he announced, "That peculiar little creature just melted into the air and was gone."

The nearby passengers had been listening, and they laughed nervously. The annoyed man got to his feet and started to curse, nobody able to tell just who was receiving the brunt of his rage. Then he went to the back bench again, and eventually his partners returned. The cargo hold and every cubby had been searched, and no odd boy was uncovered. Then a few moments later, the blimp arrived at Rail and the gangway deployed, and after a few hard words, two of the men disembarked.

"Now who's left?" Nissim asked.

Elata looked. "The leader is."

As if in misery, Seldom bent forward. "Did that really happen?"

Nobody answered.

"Did Diamond vanish?"

"No, of course not," said Elata.

"Good."

Then Nissim leaned close to them, quietly saying, "But there is magic about our friend. And probably more than any of us can know."

• • •

Diamond ran until too many people were sharing the walkway, and then he walked, quick feet taking little steps. He was always watching faces. Young men deserved special attention. The men who had scared Master Nissim could be somewhere close. With his mind's eyes, he studied their faces. If they appeared again, he would run. If cornered, he would fight. He wasn't sure how to fight, but he had the knife and healthy share of fear, and while he walked, Diamond imagined battles between him and those big dangerous men—noisy wild struggles full of blood and deep wounds.

The walkway grew wider, and the branches rose up to create a ceiling as he approached the next tree. People left their umbrellas closed. Enormous leaves absorbed the endless fall of wastes. The air inside the forest canopy was damp and surprisingly quiet, voices and bird songs smothered by the foliage. Women with babies were always happy to offer directions. All of them knew Ivory Station. One lady promised that it was close, but the next said that it was quite a walk for a little guy, and should he be alone like this? Diamond trotted on, weaving through the traffic. Doubts kept attacking. But this wasn't where he needed to be, and what was behind him wasn't where he wanted to stay.

A crossroads appeared. Three other walkways intersected with his route—a collision of people and motion demanding a huge circle of varnished wood, golden and shiny. Diamond hesitated. There were too many faces, too many judgments to make. He kept seeing the dangerous men shuffling along, and then he would look again, realizing they were strangers. The world was jammed with people, and how could a person hope to know everybody? Being surrounded by strangers forever seemed terrible, and at that point the boy found a bench at the edge of the circle, sat down and let tears come.

People noticed. An old woman took it upon herself to come over, inquiring if he was all right.

He stood again, wiping his eyes.

"Do you need help?" she asked.

He nodded, ready to ask once again for directions.

Then someone called out, "Diamond."

It was a man's voice, but not deep. Not like his father's or Master Nissim's voices. Diamond saw a man and woman walking toward him, holding each other's hands. They seemed utterly happy. Nothing else in the world mattered to them but each other, and certainly there was no reason to care about one small, odd boy.

"Well, what is your problem?" the old woman asked impatiently.

Diamond blinked and lied. "I'm fine," he said.

Grumbling, she set off in her own important direction.

The couple was leaning into each other, whispering and laughing. Turning with the circle, they moved out of Diamond's line of sight, and that was when he noticed the slender man sitting alone. A book was opened in the man's lap, but he was looking only at the boy. A broad smile filled his face. He seemed joyful. He didn't stand but he lifted his left arm and waved, and once again the high-pitched voice said, "Diamond."

Diamond stepped backwards, hope overruled by worries.

Then the man's expression turned serious, and he took the trouble to rise to his feet. "Your father sent me," the man called out. "Come here, please."

Hope won. Diamond started forward.

Nodding agreeably, the slender man sat again, closing the book and setting it on a tall stack of books and papers. He had a thin small mouth and a slender face that still looked boyish despite thousands of days of life. He was dressed in neat clothes with a dark jacket and some kind of elaborate rope dangling down his narrow chest. His shoes were black and glossy, open in front for the toes. He was working hard to appear relaxed, but one foot was crossed over the other, long toes wiggling.

Diamond stopped a few steps short of him.

Caution amused the man. He smiled and straightened his back, nothing about his manner changing. "Your father did a wonderful job describing you. Hello, Diamond. How are you?"

He didn't answer.

"I know. You're worried and scared." This man didn't worry. That's what he said with his confident grin and how he calmly sat back down again. Only his toes refused to relax. "This has been such a difficult day, I'm sure. For your parents as well as you, I know."

"Where is he?" Diamond asked.

"Your father's close. He's waiting at the Station, in fact, and he's very sorry for what happened. He heard about your adventures. He returned a little while ago and found messages from the police. Apparently you woke up this morning and found yourself alone. Of course you went looking for your parents. Two ladies got involved, and you had some adventure with neighbor children, and people reported seeing you after that. Nobody knows the whole story—except you, of course. But Merit is a smart man, and he guessed that you were trying find him at his office."

"Is Father all right?"

"Except for being so very sorry, yes. He is fine."

Diamond smiled.

"My name is List."

"List?"

"Oh, this has been one enormous string of mistakes." The man shook his head sadly. "That's why your father confided to me. He needed help finding you. That's why I came out here myself. I've always had a talent for understanding children. I suppose that's why I guessed where you might show up next."

"Where's my mother?"

List paused for a moment. "She's home again."

Another great hope was answered. Those words were accepted, embraced and believed. Diamond was still scared, but at least he could imagine Mother sitting in his dark deep room, crying to herself while clinging to poor Mister Mister. And Father was waiting up ahead somewhere. His parents felt awful for leaving him, and they should be miserable, and the boy was suddenly angry. And somehow that anger only made him happier.

The slender man waited patiently.

Then a woman emerged from the endless stream of people. She rushed over to him, saying, "Archon, my goodness. I didn't recognize you."

The man didn't want to take his eyes off the boy. But just before the woman stepped between them, he stood and took her offered hand. "Hello there. Yes, you are . . . one of the Oppal sisters, aren't you? Jam Oppal, right?"

"You're a genius for faces and names," the woman said.

He nodded agreeably, turning back to Diamond.

"And what brings you to the wilderness?" the woman asked.

"Oh, this isn't the wilderness," he said. Then he winked at the boy, adding, "I have many close friends out here."

"I'm one of them," she said.

He tried to laugh and then squeezed her hand again. "It is good to see you, Jam. Tell your sisters that they're all lovely, but you are the smartest."

Giggling, the woman left.

"Archon," said Diamond.

"Yes?"

"Is that also your name?"

"It's a title, and an office."

Diamond said nothing.

The Archon remained standing. "Your father wants to see you right away."

"How is my father?"

"He is very well," the man said.

"Did he kill a corona?"

The man blinked and said, "Yes. A giant corona, in fact."

"Is he happy about it?"

"Of course he's happy." With his toes, the Archon gripped the flat face of the wood. "Let's go see him now and make him happier than ever."

"All right."

The man turned to pick up the books and papers.

And Diamond ran away.

• • •

Long legs carried him to far side of the circle. Staying on the route he had been on before, Diamond ran next to the railing and then down the middle, weaving around people, racing past the young handholding couple. He saw a sign full of words and important arrows, but he couldn't read well enough to understand what the signs told him. Then a voice behind him shouted, "Diamond," and he ran faster than before.

The voice called to him a second time, then a third.

Diamond ran on his toes, startling people with his speed and his desperate face. Adults jumped out of his way and shouted after him, and then the following voice, suddenly close, said, "Slow down, Diamond."

He tried to run faster but couldn't.

"It's me," the voice called out. "Seldom."

Diamond stopped instantly, and Seldom rode the bicycle into his friend's leg, lost his balance and crashed. Passersby asked if the boys were all right, but when the only reaction was laughter, the adults insisted on telling the little thugs how irresponsible it was to do everything they had been doing today, and on public walkways too.

NINE

Bright blood had seeped through Diamond's trousers, but now the blood darkened and seeped back into his skin, leaving the fabric clean but slightly damp. Seldom's knee and the back of one hand were badly scraped. He wiped the hand against the leg of his school uniform, studying the resulting stain.

Both boys stood, and Diamond gave the bicycle's front wheel a hard spin, watching the wooden spokes blurring.

Then Seldom threw the stiff leg over the seat, remembering to say, "We have to hurry."

Diamond walked beside his friend, astonished to see him stand on the pedals, maintaining his fragile balance.

"Master Nissim's waiting," Seldom said.

Diamond started to jog. "How do you do that?"

"Do what?"

"Stay up."

The boy considered. "I don't know. I learned how, and I do it."

Hanner was straight ahead. The largest, most cherished tree in the District, its oldest surviving limb was beneath the broad golden walkway. Wooden buildings and long platforms were clustered along the way—a confusing mishmash of homes and businesses and gardens grown for food and for color. Epiphytes dangled from special pots, and the air was perfumed, and people were walking everywhere, and some of them were talking, one man shaking his hand at empty air, telling nothing, "I'm sorry I brought you."

Seldom pedaled and then coasted. When they were past the shouting man, he rolled his eyes, saying, "That one's crazy."

"What does that mean?"

"He can't trust his own thoughts."

Diamond looked back at the shouter. "What about those other men?" he asked.

"From the blimp?"

He nodded.

"I don't know where they are," the boy said, pedaling again.

Every nearby face was new to Diamond.

"When they realized you were gone, two of them left the ship," Seldom said. "The other man, the scariest one . . . he walked down the gangway behind us.

That wasn't long ago. Master Nissim told us to run ahead and hunt for you. He's going to find us later."

"Where's Elata?"

"Up ahead." Squeezing a clamp, Seldom made the back wheel squeak and slow down. "She doesn't know how to ride a two-wheeler. That's why I'm the one who borrowed it."

Diamond didn't react.

"I borrowed this machine," he repeated. "I don't steal."

"What does 'steal' mean?"

"Taking what isn't yours," Seldom said. "It's always wrong, unless of course you don't have any choice."

Twin white pillars stood on flanking sides of the walkway. They were still in the distance, tall and narrow objects curling toward each other up high and ending in points. Grand red flags were stuck on top, flapping in unison as breezes blew.

"Diamond," said Seldom, his voice quiet and nervous. Glancing at the boy trotting beside him, he asked, "What else can you do?"

"What do you mean?"

"Besides healing fast . . . what other magic do you know . . . ?"

"What's magic?"

Seldom was breathing quickly, deeply. "Master Nissim says you have powers. Rare powers, and it's not just that you heal when you get hurt. There's going to be other things you can do. You're special, he told us."

"No," Diamond said.

Seldom didn't hear him, or he didn't listen. "That's why those men want you. The Master doesn't know how they know, but they learned about you and they're desperate to catch you. You're that important."

Diamond glanced over his shoulder again.

"What other enchantments can you do?"

"None."

"You run fast," Seldom pointed out. "I've never seen any kid run this fast or for as long."

"I can't climb," Diamond pointed out. "Not ropes and barely ladders."

"I guess not. But you're stronger than you look."

"Adults are stronger than me."

The boy thought for a moment. "Maybe today. But what happens when you grow up? You'll do all sorts of magic, maybe."

"I don't know."

"Maybe you'll be a giant," Seldom suggested. "Powerful and bulletproof, and everybody will be afraid of you."

"I hope not."

"Or." Seldom hesitated, and then a brilliant smile filled his face. "Maybe you'll grow wings."

Diamond said nothing.

"Your parents must be remarkable people," Seldom said. "If they have a son like you, I mean."

"They are remarkable."

"I want to meet them," Seldom said.

Diamond smiled. "I see Elata."

"You do? Where?"

"She's on the right tower, watching for us."

Seldom didn't see her immediately. "You've got good eyes too."

"But I won't be a giant." The words were important. He slowed to a trot, and with a louder voice said, "And I won't grow wings either."

"Are you sure?" his friend called back to him.

"Yes."

"Too bad," Seldom said. "Wings would be a lot of fun."

• • •

Elata jumped down from the pillar and ran to meet them. She was thrilled to see both boys, but Diamond got the hug.

"Where's the Master?" Seldom asked.

"He's trying to lose that man." She said the words and then thought that was a funny way to talk, as if the dangerous fellow was a possession to be put into a box and forgotten. Hugging herself, she watched the people streaming past. People were watching them, watching Diamond. Keeping her voice low, she told Seldom, "We'll look for him now. Leave the bicycle here."

"We should take it back where we found it," he said.

He was such a nervous boy, nothing at all like his brother. "The owner finds it or doesn't," she insisted. "Either way, we'd waste time, and Master Nissim would have to wait for us."

Seldom left the machine propped against the railing. "It looks lonely," he said.

"I guess it does," she said.

They trotted ahead. Past the pillars, the walkway spread out into an enormous open plaza, silvery-white and famous across the world. Half a thousand citizens were moving in every possible direction, all of them busy. The tree trunk was covered with government buildings, elaborate wooden constructions soaring up and up, windows and staircases and ladders beyond number, every office marked by a banner hanging in the noisy air. The biggest banner was the highest, and it read, "Archon."

Diamond paused beside one white pillar, his hand playing across its surface.

"Come on," Elata said.

But he was fascinated, focused. The pillar was built from hundreds of teeth, each tooth long and slightly curved, each set snug against its neighbors. The razor edges were buried inside. Gaps in the mortar and a few stolen teeth afforded handholds for a determined girl, and that's how she had managed to climb to the top. Slick and very cold, the teeth felt as if they were alive. That's what she thought whenever she touched one. And nothing else in the world was as purely, perfectly white as what was slipping beneath her friend's quick little fingers.

"Where do these come from?" Diamond asked.

"The corona," she said.

He looked at her, touching his mouth, his teeth.

"I don't know who put them together," she said. "But these markers are older than any tree, and they always stand guard in front of the Corona District's headquarters."

Diamond stepped back and looked up, mouthing the letters on the flapping flag.

"The District of Corona Welcomes All," she read aloud.

Again, Diamond looked at her.

"The district is named for the animals," Elata told him.

"Why?"

"Because there's no better hunting in the world than here," she said.

She could have predicted it. "Why?" he asked again.

"I don't know why," she said. Then a nice thought jumped into her head, and she said it. "Ask your father when we find him."

Seldom was listening. He had his own big smile, and he said, "Look where I'm standing. These came off the coronas too."

Diamond stepped out on the plaza and knelt down, hands pressed against silvery-white surface. Thousands of scales covered the thick planks of wood. Each one was as big as a man's shirt, and they overlapped like they would have in life, fixed in place with special glues and pins.

"These weigh almost nothing," Seldom said, always happy to sound smart. "If you held one of them, it would feel like paper, except it's very strong, very tough. We use the scales to build machinery and armor and other important, expensive stuff."

Elata was watching for Nissim. She didn't want to admit it, not even to herself, but she was scared. Where did the Master go? When would they see him again? And what if they couldn't find him and he couldn't find them before the wrong men appeared again?

"Corona bones are stronger than ours," Seldom said. "We use their teeth to carve their skeletons into fancy shapes, and pieces of their bones end up inside whatever needs to be as tough as possible."

"Enough," Elata interrupted.

"I was just explaining," he said.

She hit him with her stare.

Seldom felt a little ashamed, if not certain why. Then he stood and started to watch faces, and right away he smiled and pointed. "Over there. Isn't that Master Nissim?"

• • •

Cowardice wore many faces, and none of those faces were shy.

The urge to flee kept shouting at Master Nissim, again and again and again. It warned him that nothing here was what it seemed to be, and he was nothing but a clumsy, foolish imbecile, lacking any good clues about what was true. The day wasn't halfway done, and it was already jammed full of impossibilities. Aiding a strange young boy seemed good and noble, but that illusion had vanished. Who was he helping? Nobody, obviously. The temptation was to leave now, take his next breath with him and walk away. He could be standing beside the familiar butcher's block before the day was finished. That's what the cowardice promised him. Nissim had a comfortable room where he slept well enough and waking habits that weren't unpleasant. Maybe his life was a touch dreary, even lowly, but that life didn't injure anybody. Nobody thought about him in any important, dangerous way. Yet that peace was finished, at least for the time being, and he ached in his guts and his heart beat like growler drum, and his remaining thoughts were consumed by one furious moment that shouldn't have happened.

There. That was the heart of the trouble.

Again and again, Nissim imagined a bloody leg on the block and the favorite cleaver in his hand, aimed and falling.

A man screamed in his mind, and then the man screamed once more, louder.

Nissim had to get out of this mess. He decided to hunt for the first person in authority, he didn't care who, and he would confess about the lost boy, explaining just enough while confessing to nothing. Then he would board the next blimp for home. That was the right plan—the only sane plan—and so sure was he that he took his first deep breath in what seemed like too long, enjoying the illusion of being certain about things that would never make sense.

But fear had endless faces, and a compelling new visage emerged.

Run away, even for the best reasons, and the guilt would easily chase him down. The butcher was sure about that much. And if anything ugly happened to one of those children, remorse would define every awful day until death finally claimed him.

The man was near shock, but despite his worst nature, he saw exactly what was at stake.

"Go find those kids," Nissim whispered to himself.

Then he told every fear but one, "Leave me alone."

Ugly shame was what pushed him up the stairs, up onto the busy broad plaza.

• • •

Diamond rose and saw the Master.

"What's wrong with him?" he asked.

The man was moving slowly, painfully. Once in the open, Nissim paused, eyes sweeping the plaza until he saw three children watching him. He tried to smile but managed only a painful grimace, and he took one enormous breath before walking again.

Elata ran toward him.

The boys followed, and then Elata stopped and they fell in beside her. The Master was pale and sad, but he managed to smile. The voice wasn't the same, too soft and too gray. But the words sounded optimistic, saying, "This worked out well enough. Everyone is all right, I see."

"Are you hurt?" Elata asked.

He didn't answer.

She stopped in front of him. "What happened to that man?"

Nissim sucked on his teeth, narrowing his eyes for a thoughtful moment. Then he said, "No. No, I'm not hurt."

She didn't believe him.

"What about the man?" asked Seldom. "Is he following us?"

"No." Nissim started toward the government buildings, telling no one in particular, "He won't be our problem anymore."

That sounded like good news, except Elata wasn't happy. She was still full of scared thoughts, and now she felt sick to her stomach, and her throat hurt.

Seldom looked sick too.

"Is that man dead now?" he asked.

Nissim took one step and another before he stopped and looked back at them. Then with a careful firm voice, he said, "Nobody has killed anybody. And nobody wants anybody dead."

• • •

Diamond stopped under the big doorway, trying to read the banner.

"That word is 'Slayer,' " Seldom explained. "And the word below is 'Agency.' "

"Boys, hurry," Nissim said.

Heavy curtains had been pulled away, revealing a bright room built for giants. One giant stood in the middle of the space, dressed in the slayer's uniform, heavy goggles dangling around his neck. One carved hand held a long rifle, some kind of spear fitted inside the rifle barrel, and the spear's tip was triangular and sharp to the eye, even though it was cut from blackwood. Diamond gazed at the wide strong face of the statue, and Seldom asked, "Is that your father?"

He shook his head.

Nissim stopped walking, reaching under his shirt to adjust the butcher's knife. Then he knelt and looked at Diamond's face. "Before we go on, I want to ask you again. Do you know who would want to grab you up?"

"Did those men really want him?" Seldom asked.

Nissim's eyes didn't leave Diamond. "They were following orders, I think. Somebody else is in charge."

Diamond looked down. "There was a man."

"A man."

"When I was coming here, he was sitting on a bench."

"Tell me."

Diamond rubbed his eyes. "He knew my name. He said he was waiting for me."

"You're certain?"

"He said my father was his friend. He said that Merit was waiting for me at the Ivory Station."

"And I suppose this gentleman wanted to take you to your father."

"But I didn't believe him."

Nissim nodded. "Those two who left the blimp at Rail . . . I bet they called their employer with the sorry news that they'd lost track of you. Other people were dispatched, and one of them happened to spot you."

"List," said Diamond.

"What?" asked Nissim.

"That was his name."

"A lot of people are named List," said Seldom.

"And there was a woman who walked by," Diamond said. "She knew the man, but she called him 'Archon.' "

The Master took a moment, the dry tongue licking dry lips.

Elata said, "Shit."

Nissim waved a finger, begging her to stay quiet. Then he got low and said, "Every District has its leader, Diamond. There is a boss, an elected civilian authority. Each one of them is known as the Archon."

"Ours is a woman," Elata said.

"She's nice," Seldom said, with great confidence.

"But what we're talking about here . . . this is very, very unlikely." And with that the Master leaned close, asking, "What did this man look like?"

With words, the boy drew what he saw perfectly—the thin face and its cold odd smile.

"Was his voice low and deep?"

"No." Diamond shook his head. "It was high, like a bird's voice."

Nissim said nothing, and for a little while he did nothing.

"What's wrong?" asked Elata.

"What Archon looks like that?" Seldom asked.

"How would I know?" she said.

The Master didn't answer. But he had to take some serious breaths, one after another. Then he stood tall again and wiped his mouth and stared at his feet, shaking his head slowly as he told the floor, "Let's not talk about Archons again. And we have to find your father. As soon as we can."

• • •

A woman sat behind a high table. She was smiling and laughing with the other people in the office, and then civilians came through the door and she turned into a different woman. She wasn't old and she wasn't young. A hard stare greeted the newcomers, and she glanced at the children before noticing the man walking with them. One boy earned a long gaze. She spoke to the tall man while eyeing Diamond, asking, "How can we help, sir?"

"We're looking for this boy's father," Nissim began.

"Which boy?" she asked.

Nissim put his hands on Diamond's shoulders. "The man works for your agency. From what I've heard, he's one of your best."

"I know everybody on our staff," she boasted.

"Merit," he said.

The name startled. Everyone in the room turned, people whispering while the woman behind the desk continued her examination of the unusual-looking boy.

"Do you know Merit?" Nissim asked.

"Oh, I do." The woman blinked and sighed, collecting her wits. "I'm just a little surprised. We've heard about his son . . . but . . . but . . . "

Diamond fidgeted.

She walked around her desk, wanting to touch him. But after lifting her hands, she stopped herself. "You're too sick to travel," she said.

"Is his father here?" Nissim pressed.

"No."

"We were told he killed a corona."

"I can't believe anybody knows that. Rain soaked our wires. We've been out of communication with the far stations since last night." But that didn't seem like enough of an answer, so she admitted, "Merit's late coming home, and that usually means success."

A couple co-workers gave preliminary cheers.

The woman couldn't resist any longer. She touched Diamond's warm forehead and ran the back of her other hand across his cheek and down his neck, admitting quietly, "You're not what I expected."

"I want to see my father," said Diamond.

"And I wouldn't be surprised if Merit stepped through this door by the middle of the afternoon."

From the back of the office, one man shouted, "He was hunting near Bright River."

"Unless he's gone somewhere else," the woman countered. "Coronas go where they want, and our people have to follow. The only certainty is that every day brings change."

Diamond backed away, escaping the caring hands.

The woman was offended. "And where's your mother today?"

"I don't know."

She blinked and sighed. Then she said, "Well," and looked at the other civilians.

"You can appreciate our dilemma," Nissim pointed out. "His mother disappeared last night or this morning. Nobody knows where she is, and that's why we're searching for Merit."

"Bright River Station," the man repeated.

The woman lifted a hand, demanding silence. Then from some secret reservoir came pity, more pity than anyone would have guessed she was capable of. Her old face softened and the eyes became bright and sad. After a painful sigh, she said, "I'll tell you what, my boy. I'll dispatch a fletch to find your father and bring him here. Would that be good enough?"

Diamond said, "No."

"Excuse me?"

"My mother's gone, and I need to see my father," he insisted.

"Well, we might . . . " She concentrated, piecing together the bureaucratic excuses necessary for this indulgence. Then another thought occurred to her. Turning to Nissim, she asked, "And who are you, sir?"

"The boy's bodyguard," he said.

Eyes narrowed, her mind wrestled with the unexpected.

"And we're his friends," Elata added.

The woman looked at Diamond again. "I suppose you want them going with you?"

Diamond said, "Yes."

And she shook her head in resignation. "I want you to understand. If your father were anybody else, I wouldn't do this. I wouldn't even wrestle with the thought of doing this. And I would probably laugh at all of you before I sent you on your way."

• • •

Official papers were yanked from an iron box, and the woman wrote important words on them and stamped them decisively, leaving evidence that each document carried the weight and authority of a very important office. Then she handed the stack to Nissim, giving directions to the hanger before adding, "If somebody wants to doubt you, come back here immediately."

"And we'll try something else?"

"Oh, no," she said, disgusted by the suggestion. "I'll burn the evidence and throw you out."

The four of them left the office. Diamond kept close to the Master, unsure about their destination but happy to be moving again. Distance was being covered. Surely Father was getting closer with every step.

"I can't believe we're going to Bright River," Seldom said.

"Inside a fletch," said Elata.

Diamond didn't know what a fletch was, or a river, and he wanted to ask. But then the hallway ended, and they had to climb inside a tiny room. An old man wearing a gray and white uniform stood against the back wall. He looked at them without noticing anything. "Destination?" he asked.

"The hanger," said Nissim.

"Shut the door yourself," said the man.

Nissim dragged down a wooden grating, and the man pulled a switch and pushed one blood-colored button, something about those various motions causing the entire room to leap upwards.

"Is this a fletch?" Diamond asked.

Seldom laughed. "No."

They started to rise faster, and Diamond felt his legs working. To Elata, he said, "I'm heavier."

"We're going up," she told him.

He knew their direction, but how this was tied to his weight was another mystery.

They passed a big room. People were standing on the far side of the grating, but they vanished before he could have a good look at them. Then he saw different floors, some with long hallways and others with big offices full of sitting people, and there were other offices where nobody was visible. The final stretch had nothing to see but smooth dark wood, and then the elevator shook hard and stopped beside the largest room of all, endless and noisy and smelling badly. Someone screamed a harsh, unfamiliar word. Other men laughed. The old man behind them said, "Hanger," and motioned for Nissim to raise the door.

A young man was sitting on a tall stool. Diamond recognized the soldier's uniform and the soldier's bearing—a wooden stiffness to his posture beneath a hard suspicious face that would fit on any toy warrior.

"Passes," the man demanded.

Nissim handed him every piece of paper.

The soldier flipped through the stack and wrote in one corner, and pointing with his free arm, he gave the papers back.

That arm had to be followed. Nissim walked fast, Diamond remaining close. The hanger was huge and full of busy men and curses and fumes and filthy tools and racks of clean tools that were older than any man. The ceiling was remote, and the far wall had giant doors, as many opened as closed. Full-sized blimps hung in the air outside, tethered to landings and one another. But more impressive were the little blimps that sat indoors—sleek, arrow-shaped machines with wings and elaborate tail fins and windows on the nose and propellers that seemed too large for their bodies.

"Those are fletches," Seldom said.

"Fast, fast, fast," Elata said.

But the ships were stationary, and some couldn't move now. Men in red uniforms were tearing apart engines and tinkering with fuel lines, and they were talking to one another with rough, familiar voices, and when the little parade walked past, they would stop working to watch. Some were curious why three children were here. The obvious answer was to supply entertainment, which was why one fellow showed them his back as they approached, and then for no obvious reason, screamed in agony.

Diamond jumped.

The mechanic turned towards him, holding his prosthetic arm with his surviving hand. Fake wooden fingers were clenched in a fist. His stump was short and hidden inside the floppy sleeve of his shirt. "Oh, damn. Creators, damn you! Look what you've done to me, bastards!"

Other mechanics laughed. Nissim shook his head, smiling but not smiling. "Come on," he told the children.

Seldom laughed and jumped. "I wasn't fooled."

"You were," Elata said.

"I wasn't."

Diamond stared at the fake limb. He wasn't smiling or upset, just curious. He stared until its owner took offense, stepping forward to tell him, "You are a funny looking critter."

The boy nodded.

"What's so interesting here?" the man asked.

Diamond tugged on the finger that was bitten off this morning. Then because he was curious, he asked, "Will it grow back?"

"Will what grow back?"

Diamond touched his own bicep.

"That's a damn stupid question," the man decided. Then a big grin filled his face, and he started swinging the fake arm over Diamond's head: once, and again, hard enough to make the air whistle, and then a third time, vainly trying to make that odd little boy flinch.

TEN

The fletch wore the name *Happenstance*, and painted above its name was a young woman dressed in feathers and gauze and nothing else. Diamond stared at the woman while Nissim spoke to the pilot. Official papers would need study, but that wouldn't be enough. The pilot insisted on knowing the real story. Crossing his arms, he waited for any excuse to refuse these unwelcome orders. Nissim put on a smile and pointed at Diamond, and with the first mention of the father's name, the pilot uncrossed his arms, blinking quickly. Nissim continued talking. Then the pilot waved him off and ran to Diamond, kneeling low, shoving his vast nose close to the boy's face.

With an astonished, well-meaning voice, he said, "You should be dead. You should be yesterday's rain. And do you know why you're not lost forever?"

Diamond shook his head.

"Thank me," the pilot said. "The day you were born, I sacrificed not one but two royal jazzings. Which nobody else did, and I did that because I think that much of your good father. Do you understand me?"

Diamond nodded, understanding nothing.

"And look at you now. Always the runt, but I can tell you're a sturdy runt, which isn't a bad way to be. That's what I was when I was a half-done."

The pilot was smaller than most men, and despite thousands of days of life, he still seemed boyish. Up he jumped, and clapping his hands, he shouted to his crew, "Time to fly. File the route to Bright River."

His men seemed rather less enthusiastic. But they moved when prodded, and since they knew what to do, the result was inevitable. The ship's two bladders were topped off with gaseous hydrogen, alcohol was poured into the main fuel tank, and the engines were adjusted to match the midday level of oxygen. Before long, Diamond and the others were sitting inside a little cabin tucked inside the ship's belly. Everything about the *Happenstance* was lightweight and sleek. The chairs were stiff rubber frames and little else. The walls were fabric, windows taut sheets of transparent rubber. But the engines sounded massive, igniting with purposeful roars that shook everything and everyone. Seldom squealed his approval. Elata tugged at Diamond's arm and leaned close, shouting, "I've never ridden in a fletch before." The pilot walked around the outside of the ship, studying the propellers and fabric and the roaring racket. Then he came through the cabin, taking the trouble to yell a few words to the Master.

"We've got a leak in the right bladder. Somewhere. We can't find it, but there's stink mixed in the gas, and if something smells foul, you come get me."

"Maybe you should make a sacrifice to fix it," said Nissim.

But the pilot wouldn't play along. "Sacrifices don't work with machinery," he shouted. "Only with people, and then, only if you're lucky."

• • •

The *Happenstance*'s belly dragged against the slick hanger floor before passing through the nearest open doorway, and then it began to fall, gaining speed as the engines roared even louder.

"I feel lighter now," said Diamond.

Elata sat beside him. "That's because we're falling," she said, explaining nothing. Seldom giggled as the world moved fast around them. Nissim sat in front of Elata, and he turned to watch Diamond. It was as if he had never looked at the boy before. He was ready to say something or ask some fresh important question. But conversation was impossible. The engines were louder than ever, the air seemingly tearing apart as the fletch finally earned enough lift above its wings, beginning its quick muscular climb over the green canopy.

Giant trees slid past, each adorned with walkways and homes and tiny, tiny people who sometimes looked at the noisy aircraft but mostly ignored it, marching through their own magnificent day. Species changed—different bark and different trunks hanging from the sky—but it was easy to believe that this incredible forest had no end. In no time at all, the fletch had carried Diamond farther than he had wandered during his entire life. That obvious idea startled him, and he laughed, just a little bit. But more surprising was his reaction: he didn't look for his parents now, ready to share his astonishment. They weren't here, not even in the corner of his eyes, and for the first time today he found himself wondering what would happen if he never saw them again.

Guilt grabbed hold. His mother and father were a little bit dead to him, and he had already adjusted to that hard fact. Bending forward, he shut his eyes, fighting that one simple idea. He could be an orphan, but accepting that possibility seemed treacherous. Wrong. Palms to his eyes, he concentrated on his breathing and his heart, and after a long while a big hand that he knew came down on his head, tousling his curly hair.

Nissim shouted his name and pulled back the hand, saying, "We've crossed. We're in the wilderness. Do you want to see?"

Diamond sat up, wiping at the eyes once more. Sunlight was bright and close and a little less green. The dense old canopy had been replaced by smaller branches that were above as well as below, and the trees were smaller and far more numerous, and even when he searched hard he couldn't find any trace of homes or human beings. This was a very different forest. The fletch was slowing, changing course every few moments to avoid limbs. One giant leatherwing insisted on flying beside them, flapping hard and then tucking its wings, slipping between twin trees before returning to tease the fletch with its grace and fearlessness.

The engines ran slower and slower. Nothing was quiet, but it was easier to talk, and that was what Nissim wanted. Leaning across his seat, he waited for Diamond to meet his eyes. "Once in my life, I was a teacher," he began. "Maybe somebody mentioned that to you. There were days when I held a high post at the Grand University in the District of Districts. But there was trouble, and I lost my post and my credentials and my home. I ended up living in the Corona District, needing work. My father was a butcher so I already knew the trade. And that's how I earned my post at the local school."

His voice wanted to sound steady but wasn't. His face was self-conscious and indignant, big eyes staring into the distance, and the Master needed a few moments to shape his next words.

"What I just told you is what students and their parents hear about me," he continued. "It's a simple story. There aren't any details, and more than most stories, it happens to be true. I was a professor. There was a kind of scandal. And now I cut up animal parts every day, without complaint. I've worked in that school for three thousand and eleven days. Of course people have to look at me and wonder. Rumors aren't usually kind to a former Master. But I didn't do anything horrible. I don't wear manacles or prison tattoos, and the authorities don't seem especially worried that I'm close to children. So how awful was my crime? It couldn't have been too terrible. At least that's what charitable parents like to say to one another when they think that they're out of earshot.

"But believe me, my crimes were appalling. What I did was unimaginable and wicked, and that's why I was tried in a secret court and stripped of my degrees, my fancy titles. It has been thousands of days since I told anybody what I did. Not since I came to Corona and met with the local police. Not since long before any of you were born."

Squirming in his seat, Diamond glanced at the passing branches, details smeared by the rubber window and their fantastic speed.

The Master said his name.

The boy blinked and looked at those great black eyes.

"We count our days," Nissim continued. "From the beginning of time, humans have used the days to measure time. Everybody knows this. But most people don't realize that there are a few scholars, very unusual researchers, who spend their lives doing nothing but trying to make a fair full count of the world's days and nights. An honest number would tell us quite a lot. That's the logic, at least. Knowing when the world was born would give us a huge number, and wouldn't that be fine evidence of the world's greatness?"

"How many days are there?" Elata asked.

Nissim smiled grimly and lifted his hand, clamping it over Seldom's mouth.

"You don't know," he said to the boy. "And don't bother guessing."

Seldom shrank back and stayed quiet.

Nissim said, "Various counts exist. Scholars are divided into important factions—warring tribes, really—and nobody agrees. Nobody can ever agree. Each answer has a different path behind it, and long gray reaches of history compromise every number. There have been wars: tree-walkers against papio; civil insurrections. Governments have fallen into the sun, and chaos has ruled for generations, and nobody knows how many times our records were burnt or left to rot.

"Now most authorities believe the world was born at least one million days ago, and some claim it was more than ten million days ago. I've known smart men and smart women who invest all of their intelligence in one number and then convince themselves that it's not just right, but inevitable and beautiful and theirs. But there are a few of us, always just a few, who are interested in finding a new means of counting.

"Which brings me to me."

He paused. The fletch dove suddenly and then just as suddenly jumped higher, and someone from up in the cockpit screamed—a boyish wail of approval at the airborne dance.

"The edge of the world is marked with the living coral." Nissim was looking at a point behind Diamond's head. "The coral grows from where existence begins, and it creates a strange terrain. This is where the other people live, the papio. They live in villages and giant towns, and except for all of their differences, they're exactly like us. They fight each other and sometimes they pick fights with us. The papio are intense and very intelligent and they like to be silent when they're with us, but they have their own language and their own wonderful alphabet, and like us, they have scholars who keep count of the days."

Nissim paused, licking his lips.

"The coral grows," he said. "Every day, it lays down a tiny layer of new coral along the reef's belly. What lives is as blue as it is green, and every night that coral rests. Nights leave behind faint dark lines in the ground. When I was a young student, I read that it was possible to take a core sample from the coral and count the daily rings, measuring the passage of time. As a scholar, I decided to make that my life's work. The deepest and presumably oldest coral happens to be there." He pointed forward. "That's why I passed through the District of Corona on my way to visit the papio. I needed to learn their customs and language before receiving permission to drill, which took effort and time and a good deal of luck. And even with those accomplishments, everything remained difficult.

"I had to hire papio engineers to design the drilling apparatus. Cutting into deep old coral isn't easy work, and I don't know how many times wise people from both species warned me that I was attempting the impossible.

"And to a degree, those doubters were correct.

"The first drill went into the old blue-green stone on top. It cut deep and then wore out, and I pulled a core sample and the second drill cut even farther. Eventually I had the deepest hole in the world. But the youngest coral is far tougher than the grandfatherly stuff, and after nine drills, the stone was too young and too deep, and I was only halfway to the bottom of the ancient reef.

"Still, I had my lines to count. I was young and proud, and that's why I boasted too much. The papio were offended. One old papio man, dead now for thousands of days, looked at this little tree-scrambling human with his wasted learning and his stacks of cylindrical rock. 'Come with me,' he said. 'Something needs to be seen by ignorant you.'

"Few know about this place. Even the papio don't know about it. High on the reef country, beyond where even the papio live, there is one tiny patch of existence on which nothing grows. There is no coral and no soil, and not even the woeful-vines take root there. It is a different part of the world than anything I've seen anywhere—a place no larger than a large man's arms can stretch across. The surface is smooth and gray and perfect, except for the words embossed in the middle."

The fletch shuddered and dove again. Nothing changed outside the window. The same twisted branches raced past, little dashes of color showing a flock of scattering birds. The day was older, but the sunlight insisted on growing even brighter.

"Were those papio words?" Seldom asked.

"And what did they mean?" Elata pressed.

"Oh, the language was a mystery to me and to my guide too," Nissim confessed. "But there were similarities to parts of archaic human language, and I saw hints of papio in the lettering. So I made an exact copy. I brought the words back to the District of Districts, and I brought my core samples too. For a thousand days, I buried myself inside the University library. The oldest surviving books in the world are stored in a special room, in the driest possible air, and I studied there until my sinuses were full of dust, and I learned as much or more about old languages than anyone else in the world. And only then did I try to translate that mysterious emblem."

Nissim stopped talking. Suddenly he resembled an old man wrung empty of breath and stamina. He shook his head slowly and narrowed the eyes that refused to let go of what he had seen, and he dipped his head, watching the back of one hand as he began reciting the words.

" 'We are boys and we are girls,' " he said, " 'and we have come to this fruit of perfection, this utopia, to live as good people must. Every temptation has been left behind. We bring nothing but pure thoughts. In this great realm, we will build a society of fairness and modesty, or we shall fail and suffer the doom that failed souls must suffer. Then we will die, and the great fire will consume us, and nothing will remain of our good dream but the eternal promise that always and forever draws creatures of courage, pulling us onward.' "

His voice stopped and he lifted his hand, watching it close and then open again. "To the best of my ability, that is the full text."

Diamond closed his eyes, absorbing each word. But nothing made sense, and he felt foolish.

"I don't understand," said Seldom.

"What does that mean?" Elata asked.

Again, the Master placed his hand on Diamond's head

The boy opened his eyes.

Nissim was showing him a wary smile and hard unblinking gaze.

"These words likely mean more than I realize," the man said. "And I won't pretend to understand the people who wrote them. But the phrase that destroyed my life, the piece of this puzzle that utterly fascinated me . . . it is where they wrote, 'We have come to this fruit of perfection.'

"Now 'fruit' is the simplest translation. On the one hand, that just means the edible seed of any plant. It might be the only fruit in one grand Creation. But the ancient word means quite a lot more: it was used to describe a great tree covered with countless branches, each branch heavy with fruit. Just one of those sweet treats is the world where we happen to live. That's what I realized. Sitting alone inside that library, close to the perfect center of the perfect world, I began to understand that what we think of as the Creation is what those lost authors called 'this great small realm.'

"It presses against one's sanity, I know. But regardless what people are taught and regardless what we'd love to believe, this world is not everything. There are other fruits suspended on many branches, and perhaps we aren't the only people. That was my revelation. My great scholarly paper was focused on that premise, outlining a set of fantastic, inevitable conclusions and proving every point as well as I could.

"I wasn't an idiot. I did expect doubts. There are people who are terrified by any idea, and I accepted that. But I didn't appreciate the pride and power of our rulers. If vast realms are set beyond the walls of the world, then our great men and women are tiny. And if the fruit tree is vast, then we are next to nothing.

"That idea is what made them furious. That's why I was tried and convicted of heresy—an ancient crime rarely invoked but always in the books, always waiting its day. And that's why I lost my life's work. And that's why my papers were burned. And while I watched, my precious cylinders of ancient coral were taken to the bottom of the University Tree, and one after another, they were thrown off into the scorching, cleansing sun."

• • •

The Master turned away, wiping at tears.

Diamond looked out the window, embarrassed and sorry, waiting for his thoughts to make sense. How could anything be larger than this enormous world? But even as he denied that impossible idea, dream-like images swirled in front of his mind's eye. Suddenly he had too many fantasies to count and none felt real, and he believed each one of these impossibilities. In despair, he covered his face with his hands. A thin breathless cry leaked out. Then some little word was whispered. Who spoke? Diamond dropped his hands, looking at Seldom and at Elata. They were trading whispers while watching him—that sense of being spellbound never more obvious.

Master Nissim took a deep breath, ready to speak again.

Two quick explosions shook the *Happenstance*. The left engine screamed, and startled, Diamond stood up, face against the window. The propeller was still spinning, pushing dense black smoke behind them. Dirty red flames flickered inside a shell made of iron and corona scales. Elata and Seldom were beside him, laughing nervously. Then Nissim pulled them away from the window, and the engine coughed, and the rattling slowed to a hard steady pounding as the smoke kept rushing out and the propeller seized up. Long white blades were frozen in place, each one cut from a corona bone, each carved into an elegant, lovely airfoil.

The pilot ran into the cabin cursing. "Back, back," he warned everyone but himself, picking Diamond up by the shoulders and pushing him away. Someone in the cockpit yelled a question, and the pilot flung himself against the rubber window, muttering an answer that couldn't be heard even by the boy standing behind him.

"Is it off?" shouted the cockpit voice.

The pilot backed away. "It's done."

"Fire?"

"Seen worse, but it's burning," was the expert assessment. "Throttle back starboard. Half power."

The remaining engine quieted substantially.

With total faith in the window's strength, the pilot pressed against the flexible material, pushing out into the air as he gazed at the ship's body. After careful study, he said, "No punctures. No secondary fire. Good."

"What happened?" Elata asked.

"The engine exploded," Seldom answered.

The boy's answer brought a hard long laugh. Hands on his hips, the pilot looked at his little audience. "My good loyal trustworthy engine, and it blows. Think of the odds. But the ship is mostly right, and we're not ridiculously far from our destination. Not close either, mind you, but let's just count our fortunes and limp in the rest of the way. Nice and slow, and hope that we don't blow the other engine too."

On that grim note, he left again.

Nobody felt like sitting. Standing was easy when the fletch was cruising at a lazy pace, and there were plenty of reasons to feel fortunate. Diamond returned to the left side of the cabin. The sun was brighter than ever. Nothing lay below except twisting limbs and enormous leaves. Some leaves were dark green, others almost transparent. Some grew from the surrounding trees, while parasites and epiphytes clung to every worthy surface. Colored birds and drab birds and enormous, machine-like insects flew everywhere. The air had grown heavy and definitely warmer. Diamond was sweating, and he wasn't moving, breathing slower than ever, holding one good breath deep and then slowly letting it out again.

Sitting on a wide tree branch was a human, a man calmly watching the ship pass. Feet dangling and the face curious, he stared at the gasbag and the smoky dead engine, and then he noticed the boy leaning against the window.

Diamond waved at the man.

The man lifted his arm and then thought better of it.

Master Nissim said, "That's a forester, probably. There's a lot of good wood to be pruned from these trees."

"Or a bandit," Seldom said.

Nissim didn't believe so. He clucked his tongue while patting Diamond on his side, feeling where the little knife still rode against his hip.

They didn't mention the knife or any ordinary dangers.

"Do you think it's true, Master?" Elata asked. "Is there another world?"

"No," Seldom said.

Nissim responded with a long pause and then his own question. "And why do you believe there isn't, Seldom?"

"The world is all there is. What more can there be?"

"That's the faith for you and every other old man," Nissim kidded. " 'There can't be anything else because this is everything we need, now and forever.' "

Seldom shrank down, thinking.

Branches started closing in from every side, and the surviving engine throttled up in response, buying speed and a fresh trajectory.

"Suppose there was another world," said Seldom. "Suppose it was filled with people like us or people like the papio. Or somebody else, maybe. Wouldn't they sometimes come visit us? And couldn't we fly to their homes and see them for ourselves?"

Elata grabbed up Diamond's hand.

"Wouldn't the strangers be everywhere?" asked Seldom.

"But," Elata began.

The Master looked at her. "Yes?"

"Every house has hollow places," she said. "There's always little holes in the wall that nobody sees, nobody cares about."

"But I know what I know, and I'm right," Seldom said.

Elata glanced at Diamond, ready to say something more.

But then the ship slowed abruptly, everyone stumbling toward the bow. A screeching roar came from every side, long branches shoving against the hull and engines and wings. The pilot was steering them into a tangle of snags. But the limbs were young and pliable, and fletches were woven from the flesh and tough bladders of supple young coronas. Nothing was punctured, nothing hooked. The *Happenstance* slowed again and then surged, emerging into a wide empty cylinder hacked from the forest—a vertical avenue made with axes and power saws—and Diamond found himself floating inside a river of light that carried the sun's brilliance into the highest reaches of this perfect, seemingly endless world.

ELEVEN

Two engines were pushing the ship, each possessed by rhythms and harmonics familiar to ears that missed very little. She recognized the ship by its sounds and saw it plainly in her mind, and from the changing pitch and volume she could envision its future. The fletch would come close but not very close and then swiftly move away. On a normal day, she would remain where she was and how she was, changing nothing needing. But then the steadier engine gained an odd rattle, banging once and again, and the fire inside its belly suddenly jumped free.

The explosion was thunderous, persistent. The entire forest was frightened. Pretty shells retrieved their insects and hollows sucked up their monkeys, while various wings picked up their bodies and fled. She watched the wings rush away. She listened to the ship slowing, its surviving engine growing soft and careful. Moments like this were rare. Fletches liked to fly as if moments were precious and distance was cheap. Yet despite being crippled, the ship stubbornly maintained its original course, giving her the luscious chance to enjoy a good close look at something different.

Yet every action wears costs. Motion meant burning energy as well as a piece of the day. No matter the precautions, there also was the insidious risk of being seen by the wrong eyes, and she never wanted to be seen. And of course this could be a trap designed for outlaws, or as unlikely as it seemed, for her. But the worst risk was that nothing bad would happen, or worse, that this little adventure would end well. Sweet-tasting indulgences had their way of building tendencies, and she appreciated how tendencies became habit. Render the joy from one good experience and the mind was ready to accept that same risk again; survive ten thousand happy risks and the ten thousandth and first would look harmless, regardless of the looming dangers.

How many wise creatures stepped on the wrong branch before falling to their deaths?

Too many to count, she reminded herself.

The forest calmed itself, and she made ready. Traps could be waiting. Studying her surroundings, she sniffed deeply and listened to the fletch and to everything else, and then once more she looked at the world, using fresher eyes. Only then did she feel secure enough to slip out from the protective shadows, changing colors to match the green glare of the day, running lightly along the nodding limbs.

Animals noticed her passage. She wore camouflage and worked for silence, but there was no perfect way to be invisible. Indeed, she learned long ago not to try too hard to vanish. Startle a bird, and it would screech and fly away, drawing eyes in inconvenient directions. No, it was better to give birds little warnings that she was coming, convincing them that she was nothing. Monkeys were worse hazards, since they often shouted words that tree-walkers and reef-humans understood. That's why she chose to look like a harmless creature or some peculiar gust of wind and leaf. Appearing suddenly in front of a large troop could bring a cacophony, which she never wanted. The entire forest had to accept her as mannerly and simple, and most of all, harmless. Chasing the same logic, she made herself appear smaller than she was while making comforting noises and calls of peace. But perhaps her finest trick was leaking odors that any nose would find reassuring. She could dance past jazzings and chokers and all of the nervous monkeys in the world, and every beast caught a whiff of something that was pleasant, and every mind smiled in its fashion. And only when no animal noticed—as she filled the world with happy noise and happy stink—would she risk nabbing a body or two for a meal.

But today she ate nothing. The crippled ship continued pushing ahead, and she ran parallel to its course and then glided even nearer, finding a fine perch where she could hesitate, watching her surroundings once more. Every tree wore a name given by her, and she knew the major branches and most of the little ones. Nothing was out of place. Yet she turned nonetheless, turned and ran away from the rumbling engine, testing every hunter's patience.

Nobody followed; nothing cared.

And she attacked a crooked trunk, climbing higher, making herself bigger and far stronger as she scampered through the shadows above the midday canopy. The forest lived inside the world and inside her mind. Better than its human pilot, she knew where a fletch would fly and the tangles it should avoid while heading out of the canopy. She did a fine job guessing which limb would supply her with concealment as well as an excellent vantage point. She placed herself ahead of the ship, and nobody saw her when she hid where she had never stood before. With every eye, she watched the *Happenstance* approaching, growing loud and huge, and then it steadily slid past again. Human bodies stood and sat behind the clear rubber windows. Human faces stared at the ship's controls and at one another, and they talked to one another and to themselves, and then finally she saw the little faces of children looking out at the dense forest.

One boy glanced at her with intensity.

She did nothing and his eyes saw nothing, suddenly jumping to other empty patches of green.

Only at the end did she notice the second boy. Except this was no boy, but instead a creature wearing the strangest hair and pale wrong eyes, and she realized too late that he was deeply strange in his features, in his build, born as something peculiar and probably sick and maybe destined to die soon.

The *Happenstance* was gone when she realized that in some fashion the strange boy was familiar.

That mad idea took hold and squeezed.

The boy himself wasn't familiar, no. She had no memory of seeing him on any other day. But there was something about that odd face and his bearing that was utterly recognizable, and long after the fletch had vanished into the sun's glare, she sat wondering what to think—to think about everything that had happened and everything that had not.

"My name is Quest," she said to herself.

Then to the world, she asked, "What is yours?"

• • •

Valves turned and whistling came from overhead, measured doses of hydrogen released from the twin bladders. The ship responded by falling, slowly and then faster. Ailerons on the wings swung while the surviving engine turned on its mountings, and they began a slow stately descent with the cylinder's wall sliding past on the right. Leaves were plastered on top of leaves as the brilliant white light came from below, growing steadily brighter. There was nothing else to see. Eyes squinted and watered. Everyone but Diamond soon turned away from the sunlight. "There should be goggles," Nissim said, and as if that was a signal, the pilot reappeared.

"This will be a short day," he predicted. His face was covered with a sheet of black glass, and he carried a wooden box full of battered old goggles, none small enough for children. But everybody put them on, and the men tightened the cracked rubber straps until every face ached. Then the pilot said, "We're at midday, judging by the signs. But if the glare's too much, pull the blinds from the ceiling."

"How much longer?" Nissim asked.

"To the station? Oh, I'll say three hundred recitations, but you might expect four." The pilot kneeled beside Diamond and lifted his face shield, one boy winking at the other. "We'll get you to your father. But without engine power, we don't want to bleed too much hydrogen, and even free of the forest, we'll have to limp our way to the hard country."

The mask came down again. Diamond saw his own dark reflection on the shield.

When the pilot left, Diamond asked, "What is a recitation?"

With a shared voice, Elata and Seldom spoke the same words. Humanity and the beauty of the world was praised, and good citizens served the creation of the gods, and they were promising to be the best citizens they could be today, and should they live until tomorrow, they would again make this solemn pledge.

Their voices were flat and fast. When she was finished, Elata said, "Every school day starts that way."

"Sometimes faster," Seldom admitted.

"It's a rough unit of time," Nissim explained, placing a hand against Diamond's back. "Come. The two of us need to talk more."

They moved to the back of the cabin. Master Nissim sat and smiled, waiting for the boy to look at him. But Diamond felt shy and wary. His hands wrestled each other as he settled on the neighboring chair, watching the unbroken wall of leaves, the rich green turned almost black by the goggles. He smelled the rubber straps and his own perspiration. He looked at his nervous hands. As he leaned back in his seat, Nissim said, "You must miss your room very much."

Diamond nodded.

"And you miss your parents."

His hands went still.

"Describe them to me."

"Describe what?"

"The room and your family."

Picking one parent before another might betray a favorite. So Diamond began with the room—a space that now seemed tiny and simple next to this great bright busy world. Yet even the simplest chamber requires many words to make it real. He talked and talked, and sometimes it felt as if he was another person listening to a stranger. The room was a real place inside a tree left far behind, but it was also real inside his mind. He saw the walls and floor as he spoke. He saw the woven bed and old furniture and the shelves and toys, and that made him miss everything. He didn't cry, but tears were gathering. He was sick and sorry for so much, and to feel better again, he focused on the old wooden soldiers, each name followed by descriptions of their faces and uniforms armaments, halfway through his army when Nissim touched him lightly on the shoulder, saying, "I know what your father looks like."

"You've talked to him. I remember."

"You remember quite a lot."

Diamond felt the praise, but it didn't mean much. He nodded, waiting for whatever came next.

"So that I know her when we find her," said the man, "would you please describe your mother to me?"

Diamond tried. He opened his mouth, waiting for smart words, but he discovered that someone so important couldn't be rendered easily. His mother was too large, and every detail felt important. Finally, almost in despair, the boy spoke about her hair, conveying how she wore it long but tied it back quite a lot, and it was white and it was black but when the light was poor it was mostly silver and very pretty. He loved his mother's hair and her worn fine face and how she smelled when she had been cooking and how those cool hands felt when she touch his forehead and face. It was one of her many habits, measuring his endless, unimportant fever.

"My parents used to worry about everything," he said. "I was going to get sicker and die. Every day would be my last."

"Why did they think that?"

"The doctor told them."

"What doctor?"

"The man who came to check on me," Diamond said.

"Because you were too hot," Nissim said. "And you were small and looked wrong. So they found a physician. Of course they did."

Diamond waited.

"Your father," Nissim said. "Describe him now."

"But you know him."

"I want to see what you know, Diamond."

His father's hair wasn't as gray and old as his mother's hair, but his face had more wrinkles and lines, and there were many important scars. Diamond described the big scar on the face that he was going to see again, hopefully in a little while. He imagined hugging his father and being hugged by him, and he smiled as he cataloged the smaller scars and other marks on his hands and forearms.

Nissim listened. Goggled eyes looked out the window, but he only saw his next question.

"And he has another scar on his left hand, here," Diamond said, turning his own hand to map the location. "It curves and it's very small and new. And then farther up on the wrist, up here . . . "

"Diamond," Nissim interrupted, turning toward him.

The boy fell silent.

"I'm not the smartest person in the world," the Master allowed. "But I have never met any person with a better memory than mine. And to save my life, I can't remember every scar on my own hands."

The boy watched the big hands open and then close.

"You don't have scars," Nissim said. "Your friends tell me you heal that fast and that well. But I think your mind is much more impressive. Just naming and knowing each of your little soldiers . . . well, I don't care how isolated you've been. Nobody should be able to recall so much."

Diamond head dipped. "Last night," he began. But he felt shy again, and he couldn't talk.

"What about last night?"

"My mother asked where my mind was. Was it in my head, or was it somewhere else?"

"She said that?"

He nodded.

"That's interesting," the Master said. "Tell me about life with your parents. Whatever you think of, no matter how unimportant it sounds."

But nothing was unimportant. He described meals long digested and conversations about very little and the dead usher bird and then that one time when he left his room and Mother found him. But he didn't mention hitting her, even if he was supposed to tell everything. Even if it was an accident, he felt ashamed again, and that's why he looked out the window and changed topics, falling back to some the oldest memories of his parents—masked faces smiling down at him while he lay in the little second-hand crib that he slept inside before he had a real bed.

Maybe the day was half-done. Maybe this wasn't the pure light of dawn anymore. But the hole in the canopy had grown wider, and the brilliance was astonishing. Leaves were a pale watery green, letting much of the sunlight push through them without being absorbed. Diamond talked about his life, but at the same time he marveled at how the trees looked like the sweet clear green-tinted gelatin that his mother fed him on special occasions. Somewhere inside his mysterious mind, he tasted the gelatin again, and he smiled and stopped talking, and then the *Happenstance* let out some ballast. Sprayed water made rainbows, and he stared at those endless, unexpected colors. Then they stopped descending, picking one direction and heading straight on.

"I'm hungry," he said.

The Master called to Elata. "Ask the pilot, would you? Is there any food onboard?"

Elata left, and Seldom followed.

Nissim picked up one of the small perfect hands. "Who else came into your room? Besides your parents and your doctor, I mean."

Diamond listed everybody, finishing with Seldom's mother and Karlan.

"And your doctor," Nissim repeated.

"Yes."

"Who examined you from time to time."

Diamond shifted his weight. "Yes."

Nissim had a suspicious face. "Yesterday," he said. "Tell me about yesterday. I want to hear every noise in the house, every word your mother said to you and everyone else. Tell me what you saw or might have seen in her face. That's what I want to know about."

"Why?" Diamond asked.

Nissim nearly smiled, but an unwelcome thought stole that expression away. Leaning close, he placed his hand on the head that might or might hold the boy's mind, and with the voice that people use when they share secrets, he said, "This probably is going to be a short day, and already quite a lot has happened. Either there has been one big collision of random, remarkable events, or there is a single simple explanation for everything."

Diamond nodded, but he didn't understand.

"And a lot more will happen to you soon," Nissim warned. "Tell me about yesterday, Diamond. And don't stop talking, not until we step off this gas bag."

• • •

Diamond talked until Seldom arrived with a paper box of full of biscuits and dried meat. Elata followed with bottled water and an apology from the pilot for the food's miserable charms. A quiet quick meal broke out, Diamond eating the most, and then the others retreated again and the boy went on describing yesterday. He expected his mouth to stop. The words would stop coming at any moment. But a steady flow of tiny details were waiting to be remembered, each event knowing exactly where it stood in what had been the most ordinary of days. He described meals eaten and games played and passing thoughts and morning conversations with his mother, all of it normal. But nothing had been normal. He realized that now. Like Nissim, he listened to the voice pouring out of him, trying to find the true clue, that soft signal that *here* was something important. But nothing appeared exceptional. Nobody visited the house, even for a quick, "Hello." Bells sounded when a call arrived, which wasn't all that remarkable. The call came before dinner, and he didn't hear his mother talking to anybody, and she didn't mention anyone after that. She brought his last dinner and left him to eat alone, which was a little peculiar. Then she returned to put him to bed, and everything had changed. She was angry with the mess in his room, but she wasn't angry. Maybe she was sad, and she was definitely worried. Yet she was fine before that, which was baffling, and that was the moment when the Master dropped one finger on Diamond's mouth and bent down, interrupting the words to say, "While you were enjoying dinner, she used the house line. She knew that you had good ears, and so she spoke quietly to somebody. And whatever was said left her terrified."

"What was said?" he asked.

"I don't know. We'll ask her, as soon as we find her."

The conversation paused. The Master fell into his own thoughts while the Happenstance continued threading its way through the lowest, thinnest reaches of the wilderness forest. Every leaf looked shriveled, spent. Skeletal branches wore silvery epiphytes that grew nowhere else. Birds were scarce and each bird had slits for eyes, and the insects wore mirrors on their shells. The sun was something to be endured. It scorched flesh and peeled bark, and the reflected glare made Diamond's eyes ache even when covered with the goggles. Nobody else looked out the windows. But Diamond could stare into the distance, and the discomfort was bearable. He felt the fletch bleed gas and drop still lower. This big fine machine was nothing but a speck inside a great room filled with golden air, and all of the world's trees were above them—a ceiling of burnt yellow and black-green that seemed small compared to this vastness of wind and light.

Far to his left, something moved.

Something fell.

A long slender shape was spinning, distance making it tiny. Diamond squinted and laid his hands under his eyes, fighting the glare. The object was a large branch or whole tree, something ripped free of the ceiling and plunging into places even brighter and hotter. The event was enormous and soundless, without any sense of violence. A tiny stick tumbled and grew tinier, and he watched the stick vanish, swallowed by the sun's magnificent glare.

Then with a big jovial voice, the pilot shouted down from the cockpit. "Reef coming," he said.

Diamond pressed his face into the window, looking ahead.

What was empty air just moments ago was changing. Emerging from brilliance was something dark, weightless and massive in the same glance.

He couldn't piece together details. He thought the object was just ahead, but distances confused him. Falling leaves and tumbling bugs and monkey poop and the endless drip of rainwater made for cluttered air, and rising sunlight made a mist from the falling debris, hiding what was too far or too small.

The dark object gradually spread sideways. A distinct line divided the mystery into a top and bottom. Below was bright blackness, like the glass in his goggles, and above it was a different species of darkness. Then Diamond closed his eyes and opened them, and that's when he realized that the reef was like a shelf hung on a wall. The shelf blocked the light from below, and he was seeing shadow on top. With too many questions wanting to be asked, he did nothing but stare, the one side of his face pressed against rubber that was hot to touch and growing hotter.

And the *Happenstance* let out a huge blaring roar. Everyone in the cabin jumped. The Master laughed without really laughing, and with a fond slow voice said, "The Bright River station. We're almost there."

• • •

The ship passed over the shelf's lip, and the sun softened. One moment the full glare of it was everywhere, and then the fringes of shadow washed over them. Seldom took his hands off his eyes, looking at Diamond before clamping them shut again. "He can see outside," he told Elata.

"Of course he can," said Elata, not bothering to look.

Again, the horn gave out its warning. Diamond couldn't make sense of what was under him. Turquoise shades predominated, but there were odd greens and radiant blues and cold blues and golden splotches that refused to come into focus. This was a place visited in dreams, not in life. Pushing deeper into shadow that was still well-lit, the terrain turned into a series of mounds and holes and faces of exposed coral cliffs and stands of odd upright plants, nothing in this place resembling any of the wonders he had already seen today.

His friends dropped their hands and joined him, gazing out and down.

"And this is the reef's wasteland," Seldom said. "This coral is old, drained of its nutrients."

On the poor ground beneath them was a big animal, thick and strong with long jaws and a fleshy sail down its back. Rising up on its hind legs, it greeted the ship with a solid, high-pitched wailing.

"A burnish-hound," Seldom said.

The children pushed their shoulders against Diamond.

"Do you see any papio?" Elata asked.

Seldom looked everywhere, admitting, "I wish I did, but no."

Elata shoved her face against the flexible window, pushing to look ahead, pushing as if she wanted to split the rubber and fall free. "I see the station," she said. Then after a pause and one abrupt deep breath, she said, "Oh my, my! I think that's . . . it is has to be . . . I can't believe it . . . !"

"The papio?" Seldom asked.

"A corona," she said.

"Dead?" he said.

She laughed. "If it was alive, I'd be screaming. Wouldn't I?"

Horns sounded from below, modulated, rich with meaning. The *Happenstance* turned away from the corona. Diamond caught a glimpse of something long and pale, but then it vanished behind a tall knob of blue-green coral. The station was a sprawling, thinly populated collection of industrial buildings and bunkhouses, and on the outskirts were circles of ground stripped of foliage and roughly smoothed out, pylons standing in the middle of each circle, waiting for ships to be tied against them. A small busy man waved red flags, and the *Happenstance* paused above him, bleeding just enough hydrogen to begin a slow, graceful fall. Then a troop of capable monkeys galloped out of a bunkhouse, grabbing the lines cast off from the ship, and they climbed the pylon, each weaving its own slipknot before falling into boisterous arguments about which knot was best.

The pilot was first down the gangway, cursing to the one human about his miserable luck and his extraordinary good fortune. "That engine flew to pieces, but did we catch fire? Did we puncture? Did we fall into the sun? I don't know whether to moan or cheer, so I'll do both. How about that?"

The man with the flags nodded absently, watching three children and one older man approaching.

"Merit," said Nissim. "We're looking for him, sir. It's very important."

The man was short and strong and perhaps a little simple. But he liked being called, "Sir," and talking about the famous corona hunter always brought a smile to his filthy, unshaven face.

"I don't know where Merit is," he said. "But steer for the carcass. The man brought us a half-giant this morning. A beauty. I'm sure he's there now, kneeling in its shadow, begging for forgiveness."

Everything was amazing, and Seldom laughed at everything. "Do you know who this fellow is? This is Merit's son."

The flag man was pleasant but not terribly impressed. "Well, it's a pleasure to meet you," he told Diamond. Then voicing some old, well-rehearsed joke, he added, "You certainly got lucky, my boy. You don't look at all like your father."

Seldom and the flag man laughed together, for different reasons.

Diamond's head dipped and he walked on.

The *Happenstance*'s pilot remained behind, steering the conversation back to what mattered: the condition of his broken engine and how soon could he roundup the mechanics to help him and his crew make repairs.

The Master dropped his goggles down around his neck, and the others did what he did, following him along a broad trail covered with pulverized, closely packed coral. With a teacher's voice, Nissim said, "The reef is rough and we don't have adequate shoes. So walk the established paths. And please, whatever you do, stay close to me. This isn't safe country for the prepared, and we aren't even that."

"I know," Seldom said.

"We'll be careful," Elata said agreeably.

"And I have one command," Nissim said. "From now on, nobody mentions fathers and sons. I think we need the habit of keeping certain kinds of knowledge private."

Seldom asked, "Why?"

"For a flock of reasons," the man said. "And I'll just leave my warning at that."

The native ground was bluish-gray, full of holes and crevices, and wherever there was a dab of soil, plants thrived. Leaves were thick and fleshy, holding tight to their water as they faced the scattered sunlight. The trail rose up onto the big knob of coral and flattened out. Walking beside Diamond, the Master said, "If a boy wanted, he could walk all the way around the world."

Turning his head, Diamond began the journey in his mind.

"The reef is a circle growing on the world's waist," Nissim said. "The underside is what lives, and like trees, it grows toward the sun but only so far. Like the trees, size and weight limits how far the coral can reach. Rain and plant roots break up the coral, and like old glass, every little crack builds into large fissures. And when the edges are weak, the edges fall free."

"Avalanches," Seldom said with relish.

Nissim nodded. "Little landslides are common. But someday everything we're walking on is going to shatter, sliding down to where the coronas live. Then new coral will grow in the gaping hole, and the slow majestic business of building the reef starting over again."

"But not today," said Elata.

"Most likely not," said the Master.

Diamond looked away from the sunlight.

"You're watching for the papio," Seldom guessed.

"No," Diamond said. The human forest was vast in one fashion, but this country was just as enormous, marvelous and limitless. The coral never quit rising as it approached the world's edge, growing dark with shadow and the old, black-leafed forests that thrived in shadow. What was he searching for? Diamond forgot to walk, stopping on the trail while hunting for the words, and after a few moments of feeling lost, he ran to catch up with the others.

The trail crossed a weathered ridge before descending into a short broad valley. The ground was gravel and sand and easily walked. Several small fletches drifted at temporary moorings, forming a semicircle, and a small town of tents had been erected in the last little while. Rumbling generators and tiny two-man airships were scattered across the open ground. Seven spherical balloons were partly deflated, barely able to hang in the air, each tethered to a long flattened silver-white shape. Diamond's first impression was that a peculiar airship had crashed in this remote place, and the balloons were ready to lift the wreckage back into the sky where it belonged. But Elata and Seldom said, "Corona." They said the word together, with the same quietly astonished voice. And Diamond looked again, fresh eyes working the mysterious shape.

Nothing looked like a head; there were no visible eyes or mouth or nostrils. The body had some shape while it lived, or many shapes, but in death it was a vast bulk of flesh that had been dragged across the valley's abrasive floor, balloons and fletch engines yanking the corpse until came to rest here. It seemed unnaturally long and too narrow at the same time. Where the skin was stretched most, scales were pulled apart, revealing milky skin. Even at a distance, the monster was huge. And then they walked closer and still hadn't gotten close, and the corona was too enormous to absorb in one long glance. Diamond's heart hurried and his breath deepened. There were no feathers, no leather, just silvery scales on the white skin that had already been dried by death. For no obvious reason, one portion of the body was buoyant, as if a great bubble was trapped inside, or better, an inflated balloon had been swallowed and was trying to lift the carcass free. That seemed like such a reasonable explanation that Diamond mentioned it to the others, and Elata began by saying, "Be nice, Seldom."

Seldom walked with his hands woven together, riding on top of his head. "No, that's just a corona bladder that's still inflated."

"With hydrogen," Diamond guessed.

"No, with a vacuum."

"What's that?"

"Nothingness," Elata said. "Which is lighter than any gas, if the corona's alive and the bladder is intact."

Master Nissim steered them to the far side, in case the bladder suddenly imploded. When Seldom edged closer, Nissim said, "Don't." But then he stopped to stare at the carcass, admitting, "I've always wanted to see a corona, but I gave up wishing for it a long time ago."

Thinking of his father, Diamond kept walking.

Elata called to him.

His legs started to run.

Huge as the corona seemed, its body still looked deflated, slightly shriveled. A wide slit was visible between the folds of meat, propped open by timbers, power cables strung deep into the wound. The air turned warm suddenly. Giant fans were pushing out heat and moisture, and Diamond smelled the rich oils and alien perfumes that clung to a man's hair despite repeated washings. Sprinting, he called out for his father. The boy who couldn't forget anything didn't know when he began to run. Nissim was yelling. The others were chasing. The corona's body rose up like a hill beside him, scales as big as tabletops still shiny and unscratched, but the exposed flesh between them shredded from being dragged over the raw coral. And then the body suddenly ended, becoming a forest of tangled necks that must have followed the creature while it was alive. Each neck was long and narrow, boneless but strengthened with interlocking fibers and muscle and nerves and a metabolism as hot as an iron forge. Every neck ended with a head sporting three triangular eyes and three triangular jaws, and every jaw was adorned with curved white teeth exactly like those the boy touched at the Ivory Station. This corona had fifty large heads, and every mouth was open, rasping tongues lying in the dirt, the bright long teeth slashing at the light.

A dozen necks and heads had been lifted high with portable scaffolding. Workers stood at a safe distance, dressed in the heavy gray suits necessary for the next essential job. Oftentimes other slayer crews would arrive to help, but no other ships were close today. They would have to work through the night and probably most of tomorrow before help arrived, and that helped set the serious, deeply focused mood. Cutting tools were propped behind the crew—long blades and powered saws and hand saws and lengths of priceless copper wiring. They were staring at something important inside the corona. Nobody was nervous, but there was determination to their faces—professionals engaged in the kind of work where one mistake or the tiniest failure of luck ensured disaster.

In the distance, the Master shouted, "Diamond."

And the crew turned, finally noticing the boy charging toward them.

Men lifted long arms.

Someone shouted, "Back, back. Get away, boy!"

None were his father. But Diamond knew Father was close and kept running, even as the men waved and ran toward him. Except they didn't run in a straight line because they were steering clear of the corona's heads. They knew better and he knew nothing, and three dead eyes detected movement and the nearest neck dragged itself from the scaffolding and opened the jaws even wider, teeth sharper than the best metal slicing Diamond's foot off at the ankle.

He crumbled, crying out.

Ten burly men descended, but then as a group pulled up short. This youngster was in misery and crippled for life, and they felt a little responsible or deeply responsible. Ashamed and horrified and sorry, several of them openly wept while a couple of young fellows restrained the neck with ropes and spikes, and then the biggest man stepped forward, using a pry bar and hard words to wrench open the dead jaws.

An odd little foot and its matching sandal fell to the sand.

The corona head was dragged back, and in frustration, the big man began beating it with the iron bar.

Diamond watched blood pushing from the stump of his leg. Another man called out for a towel or shirt—anything clean enough to press on the wound—but long before suitable rags were found, the bleeding had stopped.

By then, the Master and his friends were standing beside Diamond. Elata cried and Seldom threw his hands over his face. Diamond looked at the pale foot and the sandal that his father made for him. "Give it to me," he said.

Nobody reacted.

Then with a loud voice—an impatient defiant voice—he shouted at the world, "Give me my foot please."

• • •

Another man appeared.

A corona's necks and its heads were not real necks and heads, but instead were more like toothy fingers that carried the beast's eyes. Those swift jaws could kill any prey, and those precious teeth shredded the flesh and shoved the bits to the true mouth—a giant maw that had been wrenched open with three blackwood timbers. Walking slowly out from the dead corona's mouth, the new man was barely dressed, wearing a thin shirt and shorts, his face browned by the sun but the rest of his flesh pale. He was sweating hard. Gray hair was plastered against his scalp. The breeze felt good, but the man was surprised not to find his crew waiting for him. Each one of those men was trusted and reliable, yet all of them had wandered off at the worst possible moment. Merit paused. He heard worried voices. Then he turned slowly, safely, discovering the missing crew standing in a closely packed circle.

A stranger was among them, taller than the others, and older. Merit knew the face but couldn't remember from where. Two children were beside the familiar man, and it was the crying girl who picked something off the ground—cradling a little object with both hands. Merit saw the sandal and then the bloody foot. What a mess! Freshly killed coronas were treacherous. Dead reflexes were still capable of violence, and every head carried a small, furious brain. He had seen this tragedy too many times, and what in the Creators' good world would tree-walking children be doing in this wasteland?

He stepped carefully among the dead heads, avoiding their gaze while watching the girl carry that severed foot into that circle of men.

Another child sat on the ground. He didn't act injured. He was uncomfortable perhaps, but he sat upright and never cried out. The boy was familiar, but Merit had no expectations of finding his son. The idea that Diamond would be anywhere in the world but inside his room, safe and secret, was beyond his reach. One his sturdiest men turned away and vomited on the sand. But the boy didn't throw up or faint or show any signs of shock. He simply held his lost foot in both hands, and he looked at the fresh stump, and then he tried to put the foot back in place. And in the middle of that madness, what was most surprising was the poise he showed—as if this was any day, and this was any little chore.

One fellow was beating the guilty head, accomplishing nothing. But when he looked up, seeing the boss, he said, "We don't know who they are, how they got here. We aren't to blame, Merit. Regardless how this looks."

Hearing that name, the boy looked up.

And still, it took a moment to recognize his son. The context was wrong. No reasonable story could put him on this ground, not today or any other day. Merit assumed that he was sleeping or dying. Dreams and hallucinations were far better explanations for what sat on the bloody ground. But just to be sure, he called out, "Diamond?"

"Father."

Merit ran. Better than anyone, he knew the risks, but he couldn't stop himself. Exhaustion was forgotten. Old knees were healed. He covered the ground in a sprint and dropped beside his boy. The crew were stunned. Was this really the famous never-seen son? Merit touched the hot forehead and said Diamond's name several times, quietly and doubtfully, ready to ask questions that came to him and were forgotten in the next instant.

"Mother left home," the boy said, no prompting necessary. "She went last night or this morning and didn't come back. I went outside looking for her. And I looked for you. Then I found Elata and Seldom." He pointed at the other children. "And they took me to Master—"

"Nissim," said Merit, looking at the tall man. "Of course, I remember you now, sir."

The butcher nodded.

All that while, Diamond held the clean white bone of his foot against the fresh stump.

"What are you doing?" Seldom asked.

"I think it's working," Diamond said. Then with a calm voice and a fetching little smile, he added, "I did this with my finger today."

"Did what?" his father asked.

"There was a monkey inside our house. He bit off my finger."

Merit stared at his son's uninjured hands. Then looking at the foot and leg, he realized they were not two separate objects anymore. The flesh on both was turning soft and strange, tendons emerging to kiss and then join together.

"And how did you get here?" Merit asked.

"Inside the *Happenstance*," the boy said happily.

Merit looked at Nissim.

With a quick clear voice, the Master replayed the journey to the Ivory Station and the strange men following them and how he did what he could to protect Diamond and the other children. There was an unfortunate incident after the blimp. Nissim was cornered and had no choice but use his knife.

"You killed that man," Seldom said. "I knew you did."

Nissim sighed and rubbed his empty hands. "No," he said. "I just crippled him."

Nobody spoke for a moment.

Then Nissim told how Merit's son, alone and entirely out of his element, had found his way to the Ivory Station. Diamond even managed to avoid a stranger who knew his name . . . a high-voiced man who might have been Archon from the District of Districts.

"What's that?"

Nissim described the encounter, adding, "But your son has better recall. Diamond has a fabulous memory for details."

"He does," his father agreed.

Gray toes were turning pink, and the foot wasn't dead anymore.

To Merit, Master Nissim said, "I have some private matters to discuss, if we can speak alone."

Merit rose again. His knees were old again, cracking like dried twigs. His gray work clothes were waiting to be worn again. Dressing, he said, "Someone needs to speak to the delegate, warn her that our work has found a big delay."

The man who vomited had his chance to escape.

Joyous but baffled, the other men stared at the wiggling toes.

"Leave us," Merit told his crew. "Go anywhere else, and I don't care what you do with yourselves."

The men laughed good-naturedly, but they took their time retreating.

Elata was jumping up and down, hugging herself.

Seldom said, "This is magic. It's like nothing ever, ever, ever."

But what impressed Merit more than anything was the calm, stoic face on his only child.

Nissim stepped close to the slayer. "Other people know about the boy." That was worth saying twice, and with a whisper, he added, "I think I know what happened. I'm guessing, but someone called your home yesterday. Someone knows too much and threatened to tell about your son, and your wife left the boy alone to meet with the caller. To plead with him or bribe him."

"Except we don't have money," said Merit. "And believe me, Haddi isn't the kind to beg."

Nissim sighed. "I don't know the full story. But whoever is responsible, it's fair to say that Diamond was lucky to escape and find help, and we were extremely fortunate to find our way to you."

"I'm going to stand up," said Diamond.

The other children offered hands to the wounded boy. But he flexed both feet and stood up on his own.

From a distance, ten grown men stared blank-faced at the impossible, and then a moment later, in unison, they let out a shout of approval.

"That's one explanation for what's happened, yes," said Merit. Then he took a deep breath, thinking hard about everything.

Seldom knelt down, conjuring enough courage to touch one toe. "Do you feel that, Diamond?"

"Mostly."

"Leave him alone," Elata said.

Then three of them began to laugh, hands touching.

"Thank you," said Merit. "For my wife and for me, thank you so much."

The butcher smiled, relieved to be at the end of his trial.

But Merit looked down the valley, gazing up at the wilderness and the heavy green canopy leading into the shrouded distance, staring at home first and then the District of Districts. He didn't know what he was searching for, but his eyes narrowed. Then he quietly mentioned, "There is one problem with your story, however."

"Where is your wife?" Nissim asked.

"No, I think I know where she is," Merit said, looking at the world's center. "But I have to think like a hunter, you see. I know how to chase, and I understand how to build a workable trap. And I think that if the Archon or whoever wanted to steal my son, he would have been stolen by now.

"No," said the corona slayer. "Our enemies, whoever they are, were consciously, carefully driving you."

A sorry little sigh came out of Nissim.

"I'm afraid," Merit said, and then his voice stopped. He turned and looked at the children, saying, "Someone feels very confident. The trap is inescapable, they think, and they want the boy here. For good reasons, for their reasons. Whichever. They want Diamond here."

"Do you know why?" Nissim asked.

"Well," Merit said. "A story comes to mind, yes."

TWELVE

Diamond tried jumping on his two feet, measuring the aches and his body and discovering that the pain had become very small.

"You're shorter," Seldom said.

Diamond agreed. "My hurt leg got shorter. And I think the other one did too, maybe."

"To keep you balanced," Elata guessed, giving him a rough hug.

Father had been talking to Master Nissim. But now he turned away and with a big voice called to his crew. The men had just reached the tents, and now they were coming back. Except for one person who Diamond hadn't noticed before—a woman who wasn't part of Father's crew.

Something was wrong with the woman. She had a very long face and a peculiar stance, pitched forward on her overlong arms, big eyes staring out from her heavy, misshapen head.

When Seldom saw her, he made an odd little sound.

With a doubting tone, Elata asked, "Is that a papio?"

Seldom nodded and his feet ran in place.

The strange woman said a few words, and one of his father's crew paused, laughing nervously when he pointed at his own foot.

The papio kept staring at Diamond.

Father walked out to meet his men, and they gathered close around him, letting him speak quietly for a little while. Everybody listened intently. They watched him as if nothing else mattered. Then they started to move away, alone and in pairs. Some broke into shuffling runs. Father called to one man by name and brought him back again, putting a hand on his shoulder, giving him encouragement along with extra orders.

"Oh, the papio's leaving," said Seldom, disappointed.

The woman had a different gait than people. She walked easily on two strong squat legs, but pitched forwards slightly, and where the ground rose she used her arms to help climb across the raw, slashing coral.

The last man was sprinting for the farthest tents.

Father returned, watching the ground as he approached Diamond. His face looked tired and thoughtful and very serious, but then he brought up a smile and a sudden wink.

"That was a papio," Seldom said smartly.

"She's our official delegate," Father explained, looking only at his son. "This is their realm. We pay them to use their ground as an abattoir, where we can safely butcher the coronas."

"Like your butcher block at school," Elata said to Nissim.

"On a Creator's scale, yes," the Master said.

"But we're very sloppy butchers," Father said. "Normally this carcass would be hacked to pieces, organs and scales and flesh and skin mixed however seems best, and then we make five roughly equal piles as the delegate watches everything, coming forward afterwards to choose two piles for her people. The first pile is to pay the papio for using their land, while the other pile is our gift or our tribute, depending on how you read the history books."

The running man came out of a tent, one long object in each hand.

Seldom asked, "Can we watch you butcher the monster?"

Father didn't seem to hear the boy. He looked at the ground again, one hand wiping at his mouth, one of the fingers absently following the raised ridge of the long handsome scar. "No," he said at last. "No, you may not."

Then turning back to Diamond, saying, "Son. I have something to tell you."

• • •

Father walked away from the corona and the tents, following the valley's slope while Diamond walked beside him, as close as possible. Then his father stopped and called back to the others. "This isn't a private conversation. Believe me, everybody deserves to know."

Five of them walked the valley together. The ground was gravel and pulverized coral boulders and short deep crevices jammed full of vegetation and raspy-voiced insects. This was the eroded, depleted top of the reef, and the valley ended with a sharp line and empty air, and Diamond was thinking how easy it would be for a person to walk to that edge and with one more step plunge into whatever amazement lay below.

"What's under us?" he asked.

"The true world is," Father said.

"What does that mean?" Seldom asked.

"Quiet," said Elata.

"Quiet," said the Master.

"Oh, I'm just making noise," said Father, starting to laugh. "Don't listen to me."

They walked for a recitation. Nobody spoke.

"It's just the way slayers think," he explained. "Our world, with its forests and rain and birds, is a cold and very simple place. Each day lets the trees grow a little bit, making the air fresher. Then come nights that last a little while or a long time. But every dawn finds the same forest hanging at the top of the world. A few tree-walkers have died, others have been born, and it's the same for the reef and the papio too."

Father quit talking.

Seldom began to talk, but Nissim put a hand over his mouth.

Father asked, "Have you learned much about the coronas, son?"

"No."

The Master cleared his throat. "I might have unleashed a lecture on the boy. But I'm not the expert on the subject."

Nodding, Father looked at his son. "I assumed your mother might have mentioned the coronas."

"Almost never, sir."

"No? But she did teach you to read, didn't she?" He didn't wait for answers. Dropping a hand on Diamond's shoulder, he said, "I've been gone too much. But that doesn't mean that I don't know a thing or three."

Diamond said nothing.

Father extended the other arm, holding the hand flat. "Up here, in our realm, the air is pleasant and cool. Perfect for humans, and that's how it has always been." And he lowered the hand. "But below us is something else. The something else requires an entirely different kind of air. And between the realms is a barrier. Think of a floor, flat and perfectly smooth, resting below the lowest branches and underneath the reef. We call it the 'demon floor' for some reason or another, and everybody knows that barrier is there, yet like any respectable demon, it can be very hard to see.

"In a sense, the Creation is one house enclosing two enormous rooms. Ride a fletch to the bottom of this world and you can throw out a handful of coral dust, and the dust scatters across the demon floor. That's a good trick to discover exactly where the barrier begins. The heaviest grit sinks out of sight first, followed by the dust. Thankfully the ingredients in our air are too light or too small to make the passage. But if you drop anything heavier than grit—a coral boulder or a man, or the fletch and its crew—those objects easily fall into the room below us. And at night, when the air is especially calm, your fletch can hover just above the demons and their floor, nothing to see but a faint endless glimmer stretching to the ends of the world. On that kind of night, a young slayer can reach out the ship's window with a torch and pitcher, sacrificing his beer by pouring it onto floor, watching it flow sideways before sifting through, and if his eyes are sharp and his torch is strong, he can see his good drink drop a very slight distance before instantly turning to steam."

Diamond nodded uncertainly.

"Now I suppose this would seem strange," said Father. "If I knew as much as our scientists know, that is. I've been told that the magic baffles them and probably always will. Some deep thinkers actually claim that real demons inhabit the barrier, too many to count, and each demon spends its existence sending the heat down and the cold up while keeping the two atmospheres apart. But I'm a person who doesn't need imaginary creatures. My mind is happy to accept the barrier as being just another beautiful mystery in a world full of nothing else."

He paused, taking a deep breath.

"If you haven't guessed, the coronas live in the lower half of the world. In their realm, the air is denser than water and fiercely hot. Take a ball—a hollow ball of our finest steel—and tie it to a steel cable. Then hover low and drop the ball through. Do you know what happens next?"

"It gets squashed," Seldom said.

"And to retrieve the squashed ball, we have to drop ballast and use the fletch's engines at full throttle," Father said. "Which is another intriguing mystery: why is the barrier a lot more stubborn moving in one direction over another?"

The valley was finished, except it didn't end where Diamond expected. The ground simply dropped into a lower valley that hung over the open air. They were still standing in shadow, the sun hiding behind the reef's edge. But the day was far enough along that Diamond could stare down at what looked like yellow mist, smooth and bright. He didn't blink, and his eyes didn't ache. Glancing up at his father, he discovered that the man was gazing up, not down.

"Dawn is the brightest time," Father said. "That's because when day begins, very little grows between us and the sun. But that transparency doesn't last. Minutes after the rain rises, new plants begin growing. The coronas' realm is full of spores and seeds, and little creatures that swim in that dense air, and before your first meal sits happy in your stomach, a new forest is thriving below us. By midday, the forest is thick enough that the sun is noticeably weaker. By dusk, that air is choked with bladder plants and new generations of odd birds, and the coronas are feasting. The sun vanishes for us, but it never weakens, and for that matter, it never grows brighter. Night comes to us because all of the sunlight is trapped by that hot young forest. Likewise, just before dawn is the blackest moment, and sometimes it feels as if the world will never feel day again."

The running man finally caught up to them, breathing hard and quick to apologize for being late. "Baby-Tam gave me a message. We can't call Ivory Station now."

Father nodded. "The line is broken."

The man was carrying dark tubes tipped with glass disks. Handing them to Father, he said, "Yeah, and how did you know?"

"I'm a pessimist. And thanks for bringing these."

Father handed one tube to Diamond, and then he walked a few steps back with the other man, giving fresh commands.

Diamond turned the tube between his hands.

"Do you know what that is?" asked Seldom.

"You do," he guessed.

"Oh, it's just a telescope," Elata said. And she pulled at one end, the tube becoming four linked tubes. "Look through the little end."

Diamond put an eye to the glass and stared at the valley below.

Father returned and opened the second telescope, but he looked up and out with his bare eyes. "I don't quite trust these toys," he said. "They narrow your vision down to one tiny, spellbinding spot."

Diamond lowered his telescope.

"Can I?" asked Seldom.

He handed it over.

"Night," said Father again. "It happens here, and in a different fashion, it happens below us. The corona forest keeps growing where it can, but only close to the sun. The farther places, like underneath the reef, fall into their own darkness. And remember. One night can seem long to us, but for those hot fast-living plants, darkness is death. They spread seeds and spores as they die, and the animals lay eggs, and the forest closest to the sun thrives to the end, but the end finds some way to happen. Ends always do. Vapor that was part of the morning air is now tied into the new wood and meat. The dense hot air makes fire inevitable. Sparks happen. You're never sure where the blaze starts, but it spreads quickly, and the day-old forest explodes. Except this is nothing like our little fires. There are no ashes. No smoke. This is an explosion, an explosion so vast that even the stubborn demons stop doing their work. Steam and thunder rise through the floor, and by the time the steam reaches our old slow trees, it has cooled to where it doesn't cook us, and slow cold life can grow a little more."

Father paused, staring at the same point for a long moment. Then he put the telescope to his eye, focusing by turning the littlest tube. What he saw brought silence and then a soft sigh, and then he lowered the telescope, closing it back into one tube.

Seldom aimed in the same direction.

"What do you see?" Elata asked.

"Nothing," he said. Then he laughed nervously and said, "No, there's a big airship. Near the canopy, pointed this way."

The two men glanced at each other. Father handed the telescope to the Master as he began talking again.

"The forest explodes," he said. "Seeds and spores and the tough eggs can withstand the steam. The only living creatures that survive are the coronas. At least nothing that I've seen, and I've watched that realm longer than anyone else alive, I'd guess.

"I know coronas. And by 'know,' I mean I'm a little better than most when it comes to guessing where they'll be tomorrow and which one is the easiest to stalk and how to make my kill without killing myself. Which is why an old man can do a young man's job."

He gave his son another smile and wink. "I'm sure your mother has mentioned how much I enjoy being a slayer."

"You hate it," Diamond said.

"The killing and carving up of these big magnificent beasts, each one older than me and sometimes ancient. But there is one blessing that found me only because I spent my life going out into the sky and killing giants."

He took his son under his arm and said nothing.

"What?" Diamond asked.

"I want you to know why," Father said. "Why your mother and I feel so fortunate to know you, whatever you are."

• • •

Lowering the telescope, the Master made a sorry sound.

"What?" Elata asked. "What did you see?"

Nissim shook his head and touched Father on the shoulder, the two men exchanging slow significant nods.

With one finger, Father touched Diamond on his tiny, tiny nose. "The coronas like to visit our world. And do you know why?"

The boy shook his head.

"I don't know why either. But I know how they do it. Each one of these creatures is full of bladders. It inhales the hot dense air and compresses the air even more than before, and when the bladders open, a roaring jet comes out of their central mouths. That's what throws it past the stubborn demons. And then the corona's black muscle inflate the same bladders, making them round and swollen but with nothing inside. Nothingness is lighter than hydrogen. The vacuum buoys the creature up into what has to feel frigid and dry."

"They come to feed," Seldom said.

"Sometimes," Father said. "I've seen them hunting for meat at the bottom of the canopy, which means they're hungry, maybe. But they're more likely to ignore easy meals. If they were humans, I'd describe them as being curious wanderers, but they aren't human and 'curious' might mean nothing to them. Usually they travel alone, and I don't know why. My sense is that they're not loners by nature. In fact, I'd wager quite a lot that they're intensely, obsessively social creatures. Even alone, they are constantly, constantly talking to one another. One of their voices is deep and loud, bladder spitting out words that shake our world. And they also leak stinks that make other coronas happy or angry, and they have special organs hidden under every scale. They'll lift those scales and produce brilliant light. The color of that light can change instantly. Color has meaning. Certain patterns are exceptionally important, and I've deciphered a few words and concepts, but really I know nothing. Nothing. And nobody else understands the coronas. But I'll tell you what most of the slayers believe; the real reason they rise into the high thin empty air is the same reason why people stand on a stage when they have important opinions to share: from high, they can broadcast their brilliance down to their entire world."

Father paused, wiping his mouth with the back of a hand.

"What we usually see here are the younger, immature coronas," he said. "Most of them are smaller than the poor lady behind us."

"A lady?" Elata asked.

"They're always a mixture," Father said. "Slayers are supposed to count the glands and leave good records, and this one is three parts female to two parts male. And I don't know why. But we know quite a bit about their ages and movements because we keep careful records. Every harpoon wears its slayer's code, and the files are kept at Ivory Station. Now I wouldn't be surprised if we found several old harpoons buried in this body, which gives us dates and places and descriptions about when she was last seen. My guess? She's eighty thousand days old, maybe older. Which seems like a long time but isn't. There are older and much larger coronas, giants that rise up through the demon floor only under the most special circumstances, and those behemoths are astonishingly ancient."

Father paused, looking down. "How's the foot?"

"It's fine." Diamond lifted the other leg, testing the ankle. "Good."

What wasn't quite a smile appeared, and Father looked at the demon floor and the yellowish light. "Coronas usually surface near the reefs. For some reason our district sees more activity than most, which is why we have a proud history of chasing them. But more than a thousand days ago, a genuine marvel—a creature at least twice as big as the normal behemoth—appeared near the middle of the world. It was a huge dark unexpected beast that pushed its way through the floor, managing to make one long lazy circle before vanishing again.

"It rose up late in the day, and I couldn't have seen it if I wanted. Slayers hunt the margins, not the middle. Of course we were sorry to have missed the spectacle, but nobody expected a second sighting. Coronas don't fall in love with patterns. We assumed this was a fluke, a one-time experience. But less than thirty days later, the giant showed again. That time it was early morning. She emerged from the same point and made the same slow journey. I heard later that she was so enormous and so distended by her vacuum-swollen bladders that she cast a shadow across the District of Districts, causing a modest panic."

Hugging himself, Seldom said, "Wow."

Diamond watched his toes and the gritty ground.

"The third appearance was at night," his father said. "The old lady was seen only because people had figured out her schedule, and everybody was watching for her. As I told you, coronas make their own light—most of it purple and colors beyond purple. But 'Help' is a plea made with a golden fire. Our mystery corona emerged that night and flashed a yellow cry in all directions. Normally it would have been brilliant, a searing light visible across the world. But despite its size, the beast had a feeble glow. Only at night would the plea be visible. And the fourth time it appeared, another twenty-nine nights later, she repeated her cry for help, but even weaker than before.

"So there was a pattern to her appearances, and it was precise. People made graphs and looked into the future, deciding it would be midday when the behemoth emerged again. And we were ready. Every healthy, sober slayer in the world was hovering above that location, and exactly when it was predicted, a long dark shape emerged from the superheated soup."

Quietly, Nissim said, "Oh yes. I remember."

"We were worried about an awful fight," Father said. "Old slayers appreciate just how smart the coronas are, and it occurred to us that this could be a trap. Maybe our quarry were tired of being hunted. Maybe they were teasing us with one of their own, and their entire population was hiding below, ready to rise up through the demon floor and slay their foes.

"But it wasn't a trap. The old-timers were wrong and glad. Of course the young slayers were hoping for a big battle from the giant—something grand and noble, worthy of epic boasts—but they were wrong too. The old lady didn't so much as take a nip at any of us. In fact, as soon as she saw us descending, those weak yellow flashes stopped begging. No more cries for help. She just let her bladders lift her away from her world, and sometimes her mouth spat out jets to keep her cruising straight and slow. The harpoons punched deep, and she did nothing. Those old dark scales were fragile, like rotted wood. Coronas are full of organs. Many of the organs and glands are mysteries, but we know the vital few. The harpoons reached the weakest tissues, and a dozen fletches pumped electricity down into the central brain, and we had our monster. The kill took three recitations, but I think one slayer and one crew could have done the same in a single recitation. We got in each other's way, and I never even got off a shot, and I can't remember an easier or stranger kill. We were putting an end to something older than we could ever measure, and I'm wondering to myself if that's what she was chasing all along—her merciful quick death."

Father stopped talking, lifting one hand, flat beneath his eyes to cut the reflected glare. Out in the distance was a long silver aircraft. Diamond watched the ship because his father watched it, and in his mind, he watched a giant corona surrounded by dozens of little fletches.

Father continued. "I didn't make any shot, but I helped secure the carcass. In the end, that was epic in this story. We sank barbed hooks into her round body, hitting the ribs but avoiding her bladders, and then balloons were deployed to supply lift. That dead lady behind us took seven balloons to carry. But the giant, the wonder, was more than twice as wide and ten times heavier. Seventy balloons were barely enough. We were so far from the reef that we couldn't even see our destination, and we spent the rest of that day and all night and the full long day that followed taking her where she had to be.

"Harvesting any corona requires tools and skills, but most importantly, you need a solid surface capable of holding great weight. There is no suitable abattoir in the forest, and besides, we have treaties with the papio. Sharing is mandated, by treaty and by custom. So we towed the old girl in the best direction. Unfortunately some young slayer failed to secure several balloons, and when they popped free in the night, our prize started drifting toward the floor. Then several more balloons ripped free of the old meat, and it was big rush just to deploy and secure enough lift to pull her back up to the minimal altitude. Even then we barely dragged her over the edge of the reef. The valley where she was to be butchered isn't far from here. A determined papio could walk there before night. And it was almost night when we finally had the giant body secured, waiting to be honored, waiting to be chopped into pieces."

Father pointed sideways but kept looking forwards. "We were in this flat little bowl, in the gloom. I led the honor ceremony, and despite a lot of complaining, I didn't hurry. Something greater than me was dead, and when that happens, you have to beg for forgiveness, if only so your little soul can sleep when it has the chance. But there wouldn't be sleep soon. The best dozen crews were ready to set to work, including these boys with me today. And despite darkness and despite the remote location, we had an audience. The papio arrived in force—all of the locals and delegates from different cities, all gathered to watch the spectacle, waiting for the five piles to be finished and their chance to choose.

"There were human dignitaries too. Our local Archon came to wish us well. A fair and practical leader, I've always thought. But that day, she proved to me she had a heart. Her name is Prima, and she took the time to speak to my crew and to me. She was the only Archon to ask about the creature's age. I made inadequate guesses, and not only did the lady say she was sad for the corona, but she looked sad. And that was before any of us realized how little value there was inside that enormous corpse.

"Those scales were dark as soot, but soot is sturdier. I had never seen so many necks and heads on one body, but half of the heads were damaged and several more missing. The skeleton was even weaker than the scales. Bones were fractured and healed, others fractured and unhealed. Important glands were half-dead. There were cysts and odd cancers and scars lain over scars. Even the muscle and blood were poor quality. A barrel of meat usually yields ten different metals, including enough iron to build one strong tool. But that woman was anemic—anemic to the point where a strong torch could shine through a thick steak—and with all of that illness inside one beast, it makes the mind wonder what kind of misery she was suffering at the end.

"Seven harpoons were found inside that meat. Three wore legible marks, but no one found any record of the slayers who had shot them. The other four harpoons had different designs than anything used today or even in the oldest history books. Some said that the corona was as old at the world, which is another reason to be impressed and feel sick to your stomach. At the beginning of time, that creature thrived, touched by the Creators and now killed by a troop of fancy monkeys.

"Without question, the District of Districts sent a full delegation, led by the Archon of Archons. I had never seen the man before. Never seeing him again would make me happy. I was standing in the gore, up to my knees in greasy gray livers, and that's when the Archon and his various assistants walked up to congratulate me. His name's List, and he didn't wait for me to talk. With that scratchy voice, he told me that the corona was impressive and he was glad that he had seen it, but in the end it wasn't much of a prize, and where would the investment be recovered? He struck me then as the kind of man who always sounds half-smart, particularly when the topic is unimportant. When he spoke, what mattered was to make me appreciate that huge quantities of manpower and fuel and capital and hope had been invested in this adventure, and nothing of real substance would come of it, and then he turned to one of his aides, and with a voice meant to remind me who was in charge of the world, he said, 'We can't afford bonuses. Tell the other Archons that nothing will be paid from the common pool.'

"And with that bomb thrown, he left us, retreating to his personal airship and comfortable bed.

"My crew spent the next dozen recitations cursing. And then our Archon returned. Prima told us not to worry. She didn't exactly insult List. She's too charming and too shrewd for that. But she promised to pay what she could from the smaller local fund, and she reminded us how proud she was of us, yes, and of every other slayer crew from the Corona District.

"By then the papio numbered in the hundreds. This is the end of the world to them, a place beyond every better place, but delegates and citizens, soldiers and even children had gathered. They were curious and remarkably talkative. Plus there were other human dignitaries, and slayers crews waiting to spell us when we got tired, and there were rich individuals who had hired fletches to come here for no reason other than to see something that would never be seen again.

"A different crew finally sliced open the corona's stomach.

"It was the darkest part of the night, and my boys were exhausted. I went looking for relief, for fresh willing backs and hands, and I happened to see the stomach's juices spilling across the coral. Those juices are highly, highly acidic. The coral was fizzing and popping as the mess spread and sank underground. Nobody was paying attention to the interior, at least not then. Even after being dead for so long, there was a lot of residual heat. I don't know why I swung my torch at the hole. But I had a good angle to see far inside, and I had to be the first person to spot something moving. The object was large, larger than me by a long ways. I held up my torch and caught a round shape wiggling at its edges. Then I climbed inside that hot gutted stomach, avoiding the dangerous last puddles, and I put a gloved hand on the big odd moving object, and what looked like a hand started to emerge, apparently trying to touch me.

"I ran back outside, startled.

"Another crew noticed, and they took the trouble to yell some abuse my way. What kind of slayer got scared like a little boy? I laughed off the jokes, and when they returned to their work, I began to study the stomach and intestines. Corona guts are usually a nice round ring, simple and tidy. But not inside her. There were turns I'd never seen before. There was a giant pocket full of acid and bad stinks and I don't know how many kinds of filth. The mystery object was tucked inside that pocket, and beside it were three odd shapes, each quite a bit smaller than the one that I saw first. I don't know why, but I picked up the tiniest specimen. It was round and warm and very hard on the outside, like callused skin, and it smelled wicked as can be. Nobody was watching me. I stripped off my shirt and wrapped the object inside it before walking outside and over the next ridge, then down into a gully where nobody was watching, where coral sands made a soft flat space.

"That's where I put down what I had taken. What wasn't mine. Not even slayers are allowed to claim any part of the corona without permission, but I was angry about the bonuses, and I was very, very curious. That simple chunk of meat was something that the corona had eaten but never digested, which was bizarre, and I had never seen such a thing, and I had never heard of such of thing, and I wanted one good long look before I surrendered the prize."

Father hesitated, and he sighed. The approaching ship was too big to be a blimp. It had a framework made of corona bones, and it was big enough to seem big though it was still a long ways off. Steady strong engine sounds gave the air a slight and very pleasant hum.

"What happened?" Seldom asked.

"Yeah, what?" Elata asked.

Father used a voice that would never stop being amazed. "I knelt down in the dark and watched that little blob," he said, staring at Diamond. "I saw its shape change. The transformation took time. There didn't seem to be any sense to what I was watching. But there were differences in its appearance, and new shapes emerged, and I touched the object on one end and felt what could have been bone where twenty recitations earlier there was nothing. Then the little arms pulled free, and legs that were bent back and newly born straightened out suddenly and this sweet, half-formed face looked up at me. And then you coughed—a hard big cough that threw stinking liquids over my face—and as soon as your lungs cleared, you said words to me. Words I've never heard before, or since."

Diamond kept watching his toes. Pieces of this story seemed familiar, or his imagination was painting pictures.

"Night ended," his father said. "The corona forest that grew in a day turned to steam and burst through the demon floor. Warm water rose over the reef and me, and over you, and I sheltered you with my body. When the worst of the rain passed, you looked like a two-hundred-day old baby—oddly shaped but healthy enough to smile at me—and I hid you under my coat again and walked past the remains of the corona. The stomach was still exposed, but those other three mysteries were gone. I never found out who took them. I emptied my toolbox and set you inside, wrapped in a towel, and you were quiet enough to scare me on the journey home. But nobody noticed how I carried that old box, carefully and with both hands. I carried it all the way to our house, and I stepped through the curtain you saw today for the first time, and your mother looked at me and knew something was happening. The first words that I said were, 'You aren't going outside for a few days.'

" 'Why not?' she asked.

" 'You're pregnant. Not far along, and you're going to give birth early.'

"She stared at the toolbox, and I opened it. And there you lay, smiling and patient and peculiar beyond belief. This was nine hundred and eighty-three days ago. And when your mother looked at me again, I knew. I just knew. You were ours, and we belonged to you, and we would never surrender one another. Certainly not without waging a war, I would think."

THIRTEEN

Diamond memorized each word and the shifting sounds of his father's steady urgent voice, and he saw the keen amazement of the other faces hearing the same story. There was deep importance in what had just been told but he understood very little. This day was already full of complications and the unexpected, and no matter how bright he might be, this was too much. Yes, his father discovered him inside a corona's stomach. That seemed incredible to others but felt utterly reasonable to him. Seldom might have nodded smartly and said such things happen every day, and Diamond would have believed him. "I could never, ever have dreamed this," said Master Nissim. Yet the miracle boy had no doubts, no complaints. This was just another ingredient to a world too big to comprehend. It didn't even occur to Diamond that Father wasn't his true father. No story could diminish the man's importance in his life. "You were ours, and we belonged to you, and we would never surrender one another." Mother was just as real, just as vital, and he was thinking only about her when the long silver airship let loose a shrill wail, announcing its momentous arrival.

"Come on," Father said, leading them back up the valley.

Nobody else spoke. Faces thoughtful and looking at the ground, no one ready to look Diamond in the eyes. He stared at the spent, badly eroded coral. He couldn't remember walking here before. And he had no memory of riding inside the closed toolbox, much less being trapped in the belly of a monster. But he saw his mother's face hovering, and Father kneeling beside her, and it was possible to believe that he could feel the cold metal against his bare feet and baby hands. Maybe it wasn't a genuine memory but it felt authentic, and he clung the image, convincing himself that it was his birth, or at least his beginning.

The airship passed directly overhead, the air drumming and the ground shaking as the vast engines throttled down.

The men from Father's crew were running away from the dead corona, running straight at them.

The horn sounded once again, followed by an explosion and bright flash. A steel anchor was catapulted at the ground, slicing into the coral and biting hard, and then a thick steel rope fell after it, building a gray pile taller than any man.

The running men dropped their heads and ran faster. Father waved and shouted a warning as two more anchors were launched, one from the bow and one from close to the stern.

The ground to their right exploded—dust and gravel lifting high and falling down on them.

Then the propellers reversed, screaming with a different voice as they killed the last of the momentum.

Father cursed and looked up.

His men came close, and he told them, "They just want us scared."

"We are scared," one man said.

The others laughed.

Father kept looking up.

"We're done with the chores," said the first man. He was oldest and seemed in charge of everyone but Father. "What's next?"

A few breaths of hydrogen were vented and the metal ropes were winched tight, killing the slack and testing the anchors before the ship was yanked low enough to deploy the gangway.

"Where do you want the glands?" the man asked.

Father looked at them, considering.

The men smiled at him and at Diamond, every one of them did, and the youngest face said, "Show us that foot again."

Diamond lifted his leg, drawing circles with his toes.

"What a thing," the young man said.

Father raised his hand.

The faces returned to him.

"I'm ordering you to do nothing," he said. "You can't imagine how much trouble this is going to cause, and you've done too much already. So leave the glands under Little Rilly and walk anywhere else. That's my order."

"Yeah, but what do you want done?" asked the first man.

"Seven hundred days ago," Father said. "That trick we used to save the Bascher crew."

Nobody acted surprised.

"You want Little Rilly rigged up," the first man.

"I'm telling you not to," Father said. "I'll do that work myself."

"No offense, sir," said the young man. "But we'll do it better than you can and do it a damned lot faster."

Everybody nodded, satisfied with that response.

Father opened the telescope, ignoring the blimp to look at the tents. "The papio are back," he said. "And this time, in strength."

Squinting, Diamond counted a dozen big bodies standing in a ragged line, watching the ship and watching them. They were sitting back on their haunches, several pressing telescopes against their long strange faces.

"You're off-duty," Father told his men. "The day is yours. Do whatever you want, or do nothing."

The men gave one another some friendly shoves, hurrying back toward the dead corona.

One last time, the ship blew its warning horn. And before the bright echoes faded, Father knelt beside his son and said, "Listen to me. This is what will happen, and this is what we are going to do."

• • •

"That's the *Ruler of the Wind*," Seldom told Diamond. "It's the biggest machine in Creation."

The airship was too vast to absorb with one look. The *Ruler* was a separate landscape, like a silver hill that just happened to be above their heads. Countless objects were lashed to its body—smaller airships and cavernous vents and the engines falling quiet and the propellers smoothly slowing until they stopped turning altogether. Turrets clung to the belly and sides, each bristling with big guns pointing out at nothing. Tall windows revealed rooms spacious enough for hundreds of people, but nobody was visible, giving the machine an incurious temperament to everything else. The reef and the papio were nothing, and this little group of people were nobody, and the hill would continue to float where it was for reasons that were no one else's business.

A bright hiss of air ended that mood. The main gangway was deployed—a long reach of pounded metal and cable that unfolded from the ship's bow, the lower end settling on the ground before them.

Nobody appeared. They stared up into a giant cavity, and for a long while it was possible to believe that the ship was empty, a derelict brought here by unfortunate winds.

Master Nissim turned to Father, saying, "It has to be a skeleton crew."

"Flying light and fast," Father agreed.

Then a man emerged. He seemed small at a distance and got tinier as he came close. It was his posture that shrank him. He was nervous, fearful, one hand riding the railing and the shoulders sagging while the face tilting backward, as if trying to keep his eyes from staring at the three children and two older men.

"Just as I guessed," Father said.

The doctor stopped before reaching the ground.

"Where is she?" Father called out.

"Just behind me," the doctor said. Then he needed a deep breath, giving him the strength to make a thin unconvincing smile. "I didn't tell anybody about the boy," he said. "I kept my promises to you."

"Yet here you are," Master Nissim said.

The doctor glanced at him and then back at Father. "The Archon came to my office yesterday. He knew everything. I don't know how. He explained this would be a wonderful opportunity. You were going to be gone for the night, and he told me to contact your wife and threaten to tell people about the boy. He ordered me to arrange a meeting away from the house, which is what I did, and that's all I did."

"Show me Haddi," Father said.

"I told you. She's with us."

"And what will the Archon pay you?"

"I didn't ask about money," the doctor said.

"Because you're a noble, honest man."

The doctor said nothing.

"Helping kidnap a man's child," Father said, dropping his hand on Diamond's shoulder.

The little man said nothing.

"This is all wrong," Master Nissim said. "The Archon doesn't make law. No matter how powerful he thinks he is, he doesn't have that right."

The doctor sighed wearily. "You won't believe me, I know. You can't. But the man doesn't want anybody hurt. Bringing your wife is proof of that. And besides, the boy isn't yours, Merit. Not by blood or by any law. So I don't think you gentlemen should talk too hard about legalities and a parent's noble rights."

"Fine," Father said. "We'll march to court and make our claims."

The doctor clung to the railing.

"Or you can come here," Father added. "Let me dance your face into the ground a few times."

The doctor winced and looked over his shoulder. "I told you," he shouted. "I knew he'd be difficult."

And the Archon stepped into view.

It was the same man Diamond saw at the crossroads. He was no bigger than the doctor, but nothing about him was small. Erect and confident, he stood at the high end of the gangway, his smile secure. A sharp, unhurried laugh was offered. One hand made an important gesture, and another. Then he offered a few words to somebody out of view, and Mother appeared, her left arm held tightly by one of the men who had followed them this morning.

She called to Diamond. With a scared tight voice, she said, "You don't want to get on this ship. Run now, go."

The man pulled at her arm, and she winced.

Diamond was sick and he was angry. Reaching behind his back, he once again touched the butcher knife.

Two more men appeared. One was limping, his left leg covered with a long white bandage, his face twisted in pain. The other man started down the gangway, and with a loud high voice, the Archon told him, "This doesn't need to be ugly."

"It won't be," the walking man promised.

The limping man followed, glaring at Nissim with each miserable step.

With help coming, the doctor turned courageous. Shaking his head and wagging a finger, he asked, "What did you think, Merit? That you could keep this creature secret all of his life?"

A soft, sorry noise leaked out of Seldom.

Master Nissim brought out his long knife, holding it with the practiced hand.

Then Elata grabbed Diamond by the shoulder and shook him hard, as if trying to yank him to pieces.

"Don't let them have you," she cried out.

Then Father looked squarely at his eyes. "Run now," he said. "Run, run, run, run!"

• • •

High quiet places were the best places to sit, watching the days pass while listening to the voices inside.

The sun never found the back of this wide, weather-battered crevasse.

Hiding was easy here.

Even better, the dark air was reliably, deliciously cool, which meant that the body was comfortable. That great bundle of life sat on a thick mat of dash-and-ash fibers that had been stretched across the powdery old coral, and there was fresh water and there was ample food in easy reach, and every piece of that gigantic shape was happy enough. Good familiar smells waited to be inhaled. The rugged beautiful reef fell away before it, while behind and above were woeful-vines and deadeyes and other odd growths that carpeted the darkest portions of the reef, rising up to the edge of existence. But best of all, nobody was keeping the body company just now. Others were supposed to be here. The body had several dozen attendants—children dedicated to seeing to its occasional needs. It was honorable work, helping this gift from the Creators. But honor was something that could be found every day. Honor was a routine, rather boring business. But today the tree-walkers were visiting the butchering ground, and a large dead corona had been dropped into the valley directly below, and one of today's visitors happened to be a famous old slayer who had killed the corona with his harpoon and a lightning bolt: each one of those reasons was a good enough excuse for children to leave the body where it was, secure and safely out of sight.

All that happened long before the injured fletch ship arrived; and an interesting day suddenly grew into something quite a bit better.

There was no debate inside the body, no battles of doubts and desires. Huge eyes focused on the visiting machine, seeing its name and the homely monkey woman riding the ship's bow, and inside the same moment, every voice said, "*Happenstance.*"

In all, there were eight voices, and in the next moment, most of the voices began to tell old stories about that particular ship.

Tree-walkers were smaller than papio which was why they preferred to ride inside enormous bags of gas. At least that was an explanation often heard in this realm. They were tiny and scared monkeys, but the blimps and fletches and big airships inflated with explosive gas made them feel a little larger and just a little less fearful.

Eight voices inhabited the body hiding inside the old crevasse. They shared the same long mouth, the same bowl-like ears, while twin black and gold eyes stared at the magnificent world.

Over more than nine hundred days of life, each voice had watched the gas ships come from the distant forest and then return again. With identical memories, unerring and apparently effortless, they learned the names of important ships and the special monkeys, just as they absorbed each of the faces and names and life histories and peculiar talents of those deemed worthy of looking into their great face. On several occasions, they saw the monkey ships destroyed. Ships had accidentally caught fire and fallen apart, corona skins and motors and dying bodies plummeting through the floor of the sky. And coronas had destroyed other ships that came too far out from the forest.

The *Happenstance* triggered all of those stories, and no two voices agreed on anything but the details. These eyes were equal windows, yet some of the voices were thrilled, even amused by these disasters. Others were nothing but sad. Each voice was balanced on a soul, and souls were notoriously independent. Reactions varied according to their natures, but there were deeper variations too. Each told its stories in its own manner. They shared senses and experiences, and they shared a massive home of odd bones and mismatched meat; but some different part of what had happened before had to be accented. Different details were pulled out of a perfect memory. Every voice clung to its version of the same tragic incidents, marking the death of creatures that had done nothing wrong to them, and for that matter, nothing right either.

The damaged fletch arrived, and the Eight talked and talked and talked.

Except one of the voices didn't tell any stories.

Something here seemed odd or important. But she wasn't sure what she was thinking, which was a good reason to say nothing. She watched the tree-walkers come out of the fletch. Some to them might never have stood on real ground before. They talked to one another and talked to the man who waved flags, and then the newcomers walked from one low spot to the next, coming a little closer, and she stared at their walks, noticing more by the moment.

Every voice had its name.

The silent voice preferred to be called Divers.

Nobody else noticed what Divers noticed. Monkey children were unusual and interesting, and she studied them closely in the corners of the eyes, noticing the deep oddities holding tight to one of those tiny bodies.

And still she said nothing.

Another voice finally mentioned the children, in passing, and then another wondered what they were doing on the reef.

Still, no one else seemed to notice what was most strange.

In many ways, this shared body looked like a papio, except built on a gigantic scale. But it had always been clumsy to the brink of crippled, which was why caretakers were essential. Each voice had a small or large role in tightening muscles and relaxing muscles while keeping the entire structure in rough balance. Too many times to count, there had been mistakes. The Eight had fallen down jagged slopes, crushing fingers and gouging eyes. Entire limbs had been lost for no reason but simple clumsiness. Yet none of the wounds lasted for long, which caused some to suggest that the Creators were wise in their hearts, and despite evidence to the contrary, they were kind, fashioning a creature that couldn't hurt itself for very long.

Perhaps, and perhaps.

But Divers' voice had the largest role in shaping the body's growth and then making it move. And as the others spoke endlessly about memories and odd conjectures, telling the same but different stories about events long passed, she took hold of every muscle that she could, and with one titanic urge, caused their body to rise up from the comfortable mat, one leg and then its mate driving it forward onto the crumbled, desiccated coral.

Seven voices shouted their fierce disapproval.

Divers said, "Quiet," and then she said, "You blind fools."

That earned more comments, insults and several reflexive attempts to stop their forward motion.

Coral grit slid down the slope, kicking clouds of dust into the weak glare of the day.

The odd boy heard something, or maybe he felt the Eight's presence. Or it could have been chance that turned his head, making him look up at their hiding place.

In unison, the great body froze where it was, muscles rigid, clamping down on the breath trapped inside its various lungs.

The boy paused, and they felt seen.

But then he walked on.

With every step, his oddness became more obvious.

Giant eyes grew dry, and tears flowed. But each voice fought the urge to blink, for fear of missing anything.

They watched the boy leave the others, running beside the corona, which was so very dangerous.

"Whatever he is," said one voice, "he has to be as stupid as a bellringer bird."

Then the dead neck leaped, and the foot was chopped off.

Every voice gave its opinion—scorn or pity, and sometimes both.

Then the foot was recovered, and the boy returned it to his leg, and the famous slayer stood before this magical creature. Sensitive as the big ears were, no words were heard. But there was a sense about what was happening before them, and what the slayer and boy were to each other.

Every voice had opinions.

Not one of them spoke, watching spellbound.

The boy stood on his dead foot, which wasn't dead. Then some of the monkeys walked with him down into the valley, and they became even tinier as they stood next to the empty air.

"He is like us," the voices whispered.

Which begged the old question: what exactly were "us"?

Then the *Ruler of the Wind* appeared, bringing the Archon of Archons to the lands of the papio. But the giant airship wasn't important, and List was just another monkey from the trees, and the arrival was like the false calm that comes to a story when it loses its way.

• • •

"Run, run, run, run," Father said.

Diamond did just that.

Voices chased after him, shrill and close and then not so close. Suddenly there was nothing to hear but his quick breathing and the bite of sandals into the rough coral dirt. He didn't look back. He felt as if all he had to do now was run forever. Forever might be possible. A boy who could reattach his severed foot should be able to run day and night, eating what he could grab and sleeping in those little bites of time while both of his feet were in the air, free of duties. Running forever wasn't what Father had wanted. It was Diamond's plan, nobody else's, and he promised himself that he wouldn't stop until he was halfway around the world, and only then he would pause long enough to glance over his shoulder—days and days between him and his pursuers.

The tent village was stretched out before him, and those very strange people were standing on the flat, foot-packed ground. Papio faces sported long, strong jaws and teeth bigger than human teeth, or his. They had pink hair on their scalps and some men had long red beards, and there were colorful, intricate tattoos wherever the brown skin showed. Eyes were bright and gold, staring out at Diamond from deep holes. Neat, durable clothes ended with bare broad toes on the long feet and bony hands curled up, knuckles touching the ground when the papio were doing nothing but standing. Knives and pistols rode on several of the belts. They didn't stand any taller than humans, but they were massive with muscle and bone. Golden eyes stared at the running boy. The faces seemed very different from human faces, but the same emotions made their expressions flow in important ways. Then one of the papio, the delegate woman from the beginning, pointed her eyes and arm at something behind the running boy, and then she hollered a few sharp, senseless words.

One of Father's men emerged from a tent, each hand holding a long toolbox. Seeing Diamond, he began to laugh. He couldn't act happier. Then he looked past the boy, and the laughter drained away into a low mutter while he lifted the boxes in front of him, as if to use them as a shield.

Diamond slowed to look back.

Papio bodies were a little strange, but what was chasing him was far more peculiar. The body was covered with yellowish plates of armor, bright spikes on the elbows and knees and around the crest of the head, and the creature's legs were at least as tall as Diamond's legs, and if the gait wasn't the same as Diamond's running stride, it was because that armored suit covered the entire creature, including a nightmarish mask that couldn't be the face.

Diamond slowed to a trot, measuring the threat.

The creature was taller than him, and it was broader, and maybe it wasn't as fast but the body relentless pushed forward. "Someone like me is inside," Diamond thought, giving himself time to invite happiness. What a great day this would be, finding another person with his shape and perhaps even the same face. But it occurred to him that the armor wasn't worn. Those spikes and plates looked as if they grew from the body, and the eyes staring out from the mask were strangely shaped and too green to be real, and where one mouth should be enough there were two big openings, one on top of the other. The top mouth began to shout at him. A voice neither human nor papio asked, "Have you ever seen anything so beautiful as me, you cowardly monkey?"

Diamond ran again, sprinted, cutting through the back of the tent village.

A broad, heavily used trail attacked the slope leading out of the valley. Two white-haired papio were coming down the trail together. One was an old man who was careful in his manner, while the other papio was an even older woman and—a once-powerful creature reduced to a frail wisp, holding her companion's offered hand while grinning at the odd fellow who was desperately climbing towards them.

Diamond jumped sideways, and his sandal clipped the gnarled dead stump of a tree, dropping him, and then the ground tore through his trousers, coral stripping the flesh from one knee.

The old woman stood over him for a moment. The wrinkled face was tattooed with faded vines and half of her teeth were missing, and she whistled when she offered a single human word. "Careful."

The boy sat up, and then a callused knuckle touched him on the forehead, tapping him twice.

Catching Diamond's gaze, the male papio told him, "Blessings of the Creators upon you."

He leaped up and ran on.

The trail was slick and the steep pitch of the hill became steeper as he reached the summit. Nothing was as easy as before. Fatigue grabbed the backs of his legs, warming the muscles. The harder he ran, the heavier and duller he felt. One moment he was thinking about nothing, and then a tangle of ideas came to him in hard, confused bursts. He was running forever, except he couldn't. There was a plan at work. But what was the plan? Then his father's voice found him, repeating everything in one breathless rush, and the boy listened to that memory. He was going to be caught. For everyone's sake, he couldn't get away. But that didn't seem fair or right, certainly not this soon, and that was why Diamond gathered himself, pushing to the top.

Behind him, the old papio man cried out.

Diamond finished the climb. Generations of feet had built the trail, cutting into the hill's crest, and he stopped where it flattened and turned. The armored creature had just pushed the two papio aside. The old woman began to scramble across the loose rock and the man lost his grip, and with a clatter of dry gravel and soft dust, she tumbled forward, rolling limp and quick to the bottom of the hill.

Her misery deserved one backward glance from the armored beast, and nothing more. Then it looked forwards again, the talking mouth taking a huge wet breath, and what could have been a laugh erupted from it.

"Ugly stupid monsters," he said.

The old woman gingerly picked herself off the ground.

"This is beauty you see," boasted the creature. Then the other mouth spat at the ground. "Come with me, little monster," the talking mouth shouted. "Surrender and nobody else is crushed."

Streams of dust flowed down the slope, and voices called out, and Diamond heard birds speaking fiercely and the wind blowing in the distance, and then he felt the wind rush warm across his damp dusted face.

"I know you," he said.

The strange face changed expressions.

A smile, was it?

"You came out of the corona too," Diamond shouted. "We were inside her stomach, sleeping together."

"You don't know me," the creature said.

"We're like brothers," said Diamond.

The other mouth spat out a gob of golden juice, and eyes that weren't like any others stared at some point above his head. Calculations were made, and the creature increased its pace, charging up the sheer slope. Save for shorts and a belt, its powerful body wore nothing but the armor. Spikes and brass-colored scales made it seem bigger than it was, and the voice was fearless in every way but its speed. Maybe the species always breathed fast. But as it moved closer to the boy, it breathed in hard deep gasps, muttering, "We're nothing like brothers and you belong to me and try to fight me, please, you cannot win, you shit."

They were four strides apart when the creature pitched forwards, exhausted, and Diamond spun around and tore down the hill's backside.

This was new ground, a new landscape. This portion of the reef was shrouded in low thick foliage. Plants didn't fall from the sky but instead rose up out of the weathered coral, which somehow seemed more reasonable, more proper. The bark was like leather and the leaves were dark green and thickly built, each shining as if waxed by careful hands, and the talking birds were loud and urgent, and the air buzzed with myriad insects. Little animal bodies moved down runways hidden beneath the hip-high canopy. Diamond listened to them and the heavy feet chasing after him, and looking down to the next valley, he wished for Father's voice to come tell him what to do now.

No one spoke to him, not even his enemy.

The new valley was smaller and wetter than the valleys behind them. The first, trees stood as tall as a grown man, and they looked a little like blackwoods. A small papio was scampering with her hands and head down, and then she heard him and looked up in time to move aside, hiding long incisors behind bright pink lips.

The armored creature was running fast again, closing the gap.

A sharp ugly spat came out of the bottom mouth.

The papio let the creature pass, and then she pulled a deep long meaningful scream out of her chest.

The little forest was shocked into silence.

Diamond sped up again. The trail flattened and broadened before coming to an abrupt end. One long patch of ground had been thoroughly stripped of trees and smoothed like a floor before a thick coat of blackened pitch was laid across the pulverized coral. The surface was rubbery and a little soft. Various machines stood in the open, no two identical but each following the same logic. Each machine carried little rooms up high and closed doors, and they stood on big wheels that came in pairs and foursomes. The wheels were made of rubber and wood, and the rooms rested on metal skeletons that must have been shiny once but had turned rusty red. Three papio were climbing down from one machine. They saw Diamond and stared, and then they saw the other creature. One of the papio turned to the others. Senseless words sounded like a question. Her companions considered the matter and gave different answers, and they ended up doing nothing as the two monsters ran by.

Diamond turned away from the sun, staying in the open, following the rubbery ground deeper into the reef.

Stout buildings were gathered up ahead, each fashioned from massive coral blocks. The buildings had no windows, just narrow high slots, and every door was built from heavy timbers and iron hinges, closed and sealed tight. Diamond had built ten thousand forts with blocks, and forts didn't look too different from these structures. He slowed when they were beside him, and after glancing over his shoulder, he slowed again, trying to clear his mind.

The creature was closing again.

Diamond reached behind his back. The knife was still wrapped inside the worn leather, and he pulled it out and unwrapped it as he spun hard, slashing the air with the bright blade.

The creature dipped its head, out of reflex.

Diamond tried another swing.

Up came an arm, the motion too quick to follow. There were little spikes on the fist that smashed into Diamond's wrist, bones shattering as the hand went numb and weak. The knife that he had carried across the world fell to the ground, skipping back the way they had run. Any fear or caution inside the armored creature was finished. It laughed at the human. It laughed and walked away and kneeled, not even bothering to watch Diamond slump over, holding his damaged arm close to his belly. The silly knife needed to be snatched up by the blade, and the breathing mouth said, "You don't know how to fight."

"I don't," Diamond agreed.

"My father says, 'He is an innocent, and we don't need innocents. Teach him what you know, King.' "

"What's King?"

"My name," said the creature.

The hand holding the butcher's blade had six fingers, matching thumbs on opposite sides of a broad hard palm.

"What does that mean?" Diamond asked.

"What does what mean?"

"King," he said.

The spitting mouth had bright teeth, sharp teeth leading back to flat ones. The talking mouth took a long breath. "The king is that great man who sits on the world's largest chair. It is an empty chair today, unclaimed and lonely. But my destiny is to fill the king's chair and make this world my own."

Diamond considered using his good hand and arm, striking that very strange face.

But King read his face, his body. Laughing loudly, he said, "Try fighting and I'll beat you to death."

Diamond did nothing.

"I'll beat you so dead you won't wake again for a day."

The boy took a little step backwards, then a larger one.

"Here," King said. "Take your toy."

The odd hand turned the knife, offering the white bone hilt to Diamond.

"Take it and hurt me now." Then with a soft, almost tender voice, King said, "Please."

Diamond shook his head. He said, "No," and turned away from the creature, walking slowly in the same direction that he ran before. The fortified buildings were behind him and the valley ended with the steep face of a cliff—except at least one deep cave was cut into the cliff. He hadn't seen the cave while running, obscured by curtains of fabric and webs of string colored to look like pink coral and deep shadow.

King suddenly knocked him forwards.

The half-healed wrist broke again.

Diamond stayed on his knees, panting. "Do you see it?" he asked.

"See what?"

"That strange machine," Diamond said.

"I see plenty of machines," King replied.

"No, the big one that's hiding." Then he got his feet under him and stood. "Maybe your eyes aren't very good."

"My eyes are spectacular."

"Behind those curtains," Diamond said, pointing with his working arm.

King stepped past him. Perhaps his vision wasn't great, or maybe he wasn't in the mood for this game. Either way, it took the creature a moment before he stopped seeing only the camouflage. That's when he discovered a long sleek contraption that dwarfed the wheeled vehicles behind them. Curiosity dragged him a few steps closer and then he paused, intrigued but not wanting to be. Finally King forced a laugh. He sounded human and he sounded otherwise, and he looked back at the little creature that he had already broken twice.

"That's a papio wing," he said.

"What is a papio wing?"

"It's a machine that flies. Except it can't stay up for long, and these shitty beasts don't have half enough to courage to launch them."

The wing looked like a fletch ship, except the ship had been squeezed to a tiny dense body. Maybe it swelled up when it was filled with hydrogen gas, or maybe not. But Diamond was impressed with its sleek contours and the bright corona scales fixed over its skin and that a hungry toothless mouth below with a single glass eye above. There wasn't room for more than one papio onboard the wing, and just looking at the marvel caused a hundred new questions bubble out of his tired head.

"Impressive," he said.

"You want to be impressed," King said. "Let me amaze you."

Diamond turned.

And King grabbed the Master's knife by the hilt, driving the keen steel blade up underneath one of the big scales on his chest. Flesh and bone put up a hard struggle, but the arm was powerful enough to push past the resistance. Then the creature released the knife, the hilt hanging in the air, and he laughed and the lower mouth spat up bright purple blood. "Clipped an artery, by the way this feels," he said.

Voices called out from a distance.

Diamond turned away from his tormentor.

The old papio couple was walking towards one of the wheeled machines. The old woman appeared even frailer than before, but she managed a steady pace as her companion held her closely, lovingly. They were talking, but those weren't the voices that Diamond could hear.

He broke into a slow, slow trot.

A string of humans emerged from the stunted forest. The Archon was with two of his men, and there was the Master and Seldom and Elata. Father was trailing, holding Mother by her hand while he dipped his head, speaking quietly while she stared at her son.

Diamond ran faster.

King jogged up beside him, spitting purple blood at the boy's feet.

Diamond stopped.

"Don't run away from me," said King. "Because if you run again, I'll grow bored chasing, and somebody will abuse those old people of yours."

"No," Diamond said weakly.

"Believe me," said King. "It would take very little to rip the arms out of that slayer's shoulders."

With his good hand, Diamond grabbed the exposed hilt and yanked the knife free.

"Are you ready to cut me?" King asked.

Diamond said nothing, cleaning the wet blade against his trousers and wrapping it inside the old leather. Then he put it under his shirt again, this time on the right hip, and he trotted close to the two papio.

King was relaxed, victorious and happy. The contest had gone perfectly, and he was the champion of the world, and running beside Diamond, he certainly didn't expect the defeated boy to shove him from the side, shoving him high while pushing hard with both legs.

The creature fell onto the runway's surface.

"What was that?" King asked, laughing. "That was nothing."

But then the old papio woman shuffled close to him. Once again, she said the word, "Careful." And then those old jaws opened wide, and she calmly bit King hard in the face.

FOURTEEN

Mother couldn't look happier or sadder. Diamond came close, and she pulled herself out of Father's hands, starting to run, long arms raised high even before she reached her son.

Sobbing, gasping, every fatigue showed in her face. She hadn't slept for two moments since the night before last, and her features were worn and thrilled and sick with worry, and they were beautiful. The best arms in the world grabbed hold of his shoulders, shaking him. "Why didn't you stay home?" she asked.

Her voice was furious, but she smiled as she berated him.

She took hold of his broken arm, asking, "Does it hurt?"

"No," he began.

But she interrupted, asking, "Do you know what kind of risk you took, coming out of your room, looking for us?"

Diamond smiled at her smile.

"But I found you," he pointed out.

She hugged him and wept, burying her face in the crook of his neck.

Father stopped short. The Master stood beside him, and they glanced at one another, saying nothing.

Elata and Seldom eased past the two men.

"Stay here," Nissim warned.

Seldom stopped, but Elata took one more step.

"It caught you," Seldom said.

Elata reached back, poking Seldom with a finger.

Then the Archon arrived, flanked by two bodyguards wearing pistols. A grim, important sneer defined his face as he walked past Diamond and past the two papio. Speaking to King was the first task—angry and quiet words, almost inaudible, were delivered in one breath—and King did nothing. He remained motionless. Then the human grabbed one of the spikes and tried to shake his son, and King still did nothing, standing rigid, never moving, resembling a statue carved from some bright golden species of coral.

Exhausted by their trials, the old papio continued on.

The little doctor had just emerged from the trees, standing in the distance, dancing on nervous feet.

The Archon turned, walking back toward Diamond.

"I have a confession," he said with that singsong voice. "I never imagined you'd travel this far or fast on your own. My sense of these things was that you wouldn't find the courage to come out of that room until afternoon."

"You unlocked the door," Diamond said.

"An assistant did." The man clucked his tongue. "No, you aren't as timid as promised. And who would have guessed that you'd find a butcher with time and the inclination to help an orphan?"

"What does 'orphan' mean?" asked Diamond.

"It's a boy who has been cast aside," the Archon said. "By Fate or design, his parents have been lost forever."

Mother straightened her back. "He is not an orphan, sir."

"He is and King is." The Archon was close enough to touch her and Diamond, and one of his hands rose, as if considering doing just that. But then it dropped again, and he said, "Madam, you were the boy's guardian. But to my mind, the dead Creators were solely responsible for this child. They built this miracle when they built the world, but there wasn't any place for him. Until now. His immortal body floated beside the sun, which is the beginning of all life, and a corona ingested him but could never make him into a meal."

"What is this?" the Master asked. "I don't know that legend."

Diamond took a step backward, and then another.

The Archon offered him a wink. "There's no way to know how long you floated inside that awful gut, waiting to be found. Waiting for the Fates to place where you needed to be. But I credit *Happenstance* and the other Fates for everything. For King, for you. For every blessing, including making such an enormous journey on your first day in the world."

Then with his reaching hand, Archon motioned to King, and the statue turned into an armored boy again, coming forward to stand beside his foster father.

"I've heard rumors," the Archon continued. "Tales about other children being cast from the belly of that enormous beast. I'm not a fool, my boy. What happens once can always happen again, and I know when a man is being blessed, and I am not a soul who ignores opportunities."

Kneeling, he waved his hand.

"Come here, Diamond."

Diamond didn't obey and he didn't retreat.

Something was a little bit funny, and the Archon let himself laugh. Then he winked again, saying, "Ask your parents. Ask them what the average person would think, if something as strange as you were put into their grasp."

Father shook his head and sighed, and Mother stared at the ground.

"If any other ruler came upon creatures as different as you are, creatures with no obvious place in the world . . . then that important person would be entirely within his rights to call you abominations. You'd be judged threats against the norms of good society and what is permitted. If your friend the butcher were honest, he would have warned you: the average Archon would wish you dead. Yes, yes, yes. He and his citizens would sleep well knowing that an infestation of monsters had been destroyed—monsters that shouldn't have been alive in the first place. Your great fortune, my boy . . . what you must appreciate first and always . . . is that in some ways I am as unique as you are. In the realm of Archons, I am one of a kind. No one else has both the power and wisdom to treat you and your brethren with the proper respect."

Again, the Archon said, "Come here."

And again, Diamond did nothing.

His stubbornness wasn't humorous anymore. The Archon rose and motioned to King, and King grabbed Diamond beneath the arms, carrying him where he had to be.

To the Archon, King said, "He's carrying a knife."

"But he won't hurt me," the Archon said. "Nobody needs to be injured. I'm sure everyone has learned that lesson by now. And as long as you behave, these other people won't suffer in the slightest."

Diamond looked at his parents first, and then he glanced at Elata and Seldom, and Master Nissim too.

Every face was scared.

"What happens now?" Diamond asked.

"First, naturally, we return to the *Ruler of the Wind*, and as my guest, you enjoy a quick flight to the District of Districts. King should tell you about his grand home. Frankly, it's a wonderful place for children who never break. You'll have a hundred rooms to explore and the best tutors, and as time passes, we'll all come to appreciate your significance, your potentials."

Again, Diamond looked at his mother, his father.

"Merit and Haddi are allowed to reclaim their lives," said the Archon, anticipating the question. "If they really want what's best for you, they'll keep the secrets and abide as they did before you arrived. I won't even prosecute the corona slayer for stealing what never belonged to him."

"Me," Diamond said.

"Coronas are public property. You don't belong to this man, and it's only taken a thousand days to bring you back to where you should be."

Master Nissim made an angry sound.

The Archon looked at him. "Yes?"

"That's a narrow interpretation of law," said the Master.

The Archon's smile was stern, sharp. "An assistant of mine was hamstrung today. The criminal responsible deserves five thousand days in the penitence house, locked inside our tiniest cell, with nothing to read and no one to listen to his educated wind. I suspect that sentence would destroy the man. But I don't want to throw anyone into such miserable circumstances. So I'm cultivating a gracious, charitable mood. I'll interpret those laws so that Diamond's friend remains free for now, and for as long as there is cooperation."

Diamond said nothing.

"Walk," the Archon insisted.

Diamond found a slow, even pace, and the humans formed a tidy line that marched up the wooded hillside. The old papio were out of sight. The doctor was in the lead, looking backwards as much as he looked ahead. The rest of the papio were waiting over the crest of the hill. Where the ground was still falling, they stood in two neat lines, watching the odd parade pass between. King was worth close study and a few comments, but it was the slayer's son who was fascinating. One and then another papio chopped at a leg, describing the miracle about the foot that rejoined the body and healed, and they spoke to him in their language and with guttural human words.

"Are you smart?" one asked.

"Are you grown?" asked another.

Then a third whispered some papio words, and others barred their incisors, someone saying, "Quiet, you. Quiet."

Then the Archon was surrounded by the papio, and that conversation ended, big golden eyes turned on him and that relentless, unnerving smile.

"List," several of the papio said.

At the bottom of the hill, the Archon stopped suddenly and turned.

"Come here," he said. Then he waved, attempting the same words in their language.

His bodyguards were flustered. One whispered some little warning, and the Archon laughed, giving the air a dismissive sweep of the hand.

The papio formed a half-circle above them.

"I have something to tell you," List began. "Something important, something you need to tell all others."

The smallest papio was larger than any human male. Men and women were the same size. Those strong mouths and thick arms were remarkable. Every face was decorated with elaborate, beautiful tattoos. Guns and knives were carried in plain view. Every head had the same bright pink hair, and the men often sported dense blood-colored beards while the women fancied soft beards hiding shyly under their chins. One woman made a low growling sound before wrapping her mouth around the words, "Talk to us."

"These two children are marvels," said the Archon. "And you might remind yourselves that they're only just beginning to grow into men. Think what they'll mean to my species, to humanity. Which is why on this momentous day, I want to graciously offer the papio some enlightened advice."

The woman broke into a wild, quick laugh, asking scornfully, "What advice?"

"Take these boys from me," the Archon said. "You should do that now. Immediately, no hesitations."

The world fell silent, every face watching him.

"Kill me," he said. "Murder me and steal these two treasures. That brings war, I'm sure. Assassinate the political leader of humanity, and you have to expect outrage and a terrible long fight. But if you can hold onto these warriors, and if you use them effectively in the future, your descendants will celebrate your bravery and vision. That's my advice for the papio species. Start one awful war today and win the world. Or do nothing, let us walk away, and the world is lost."

The hair on the woman's scalp lifted. "Why make such stupid noise?" she asked.

"Because I know you," the Archon replied. "This is a proven fact: creatures that live on solid ground are slow, unimaginative thinkers. Climbers adapt and change every moment of our lives. It's a great lesson, knowing we can't trust a branch to be here tomorrow. Meanwhile you live as you always have, and every tomorrow is the same as yesterday, and it's impossible for you to believe that anything changes or that there is any better existence for your dusty kind."

The papio stared at him, teeth bared, eyes blazing inside those deep sockets.

Then the tree-walker laughed and swept the air with his hand before he turned and walked away. The doctor was far ahead. The other humans followed the Archon. Diamond and King followed. They walked between the tents and past the dead corona. The chase had lasted for a long while. Scales had been yanked away from the carcass. Ugly holes were hacked from the flesh beneath. But the men who had done that quick work had already vanished, and nobody seemed curious where.

Master Nissim walked past Diamond, touching the boy's head. He looked at him sadly before calling ahead. "Is this why you wanted to come here?" he asked the Archon. "So you could parade what you have in front the papio?"

The Archon stopped and turned.

"Oh, I have nothing," he said. "The boys are blessings from the Creators, and they belong to all of us."

Nobody spoke.

The narrow face was satisfied, smug. "I know the full story," the Archon continued. "Four gifts were inside that ancient corona. Two of them are ours now, and two more remain missing. But big as it is, this world doesn't hide anything for very long."

"And you want to capture the others," the Master said.

"I want what's best for our species."

"Which is what?"

But the Archon didn't respond. He shook his head and turned, spending a long moment admiring the view from this rough little valley: the vastness of air and the hanging forest and the coronas' scalding realm and that thin yellowing light of a sun that no human had ever truly seen.

• • •

The doctor hurried up the gangway, happy to vanish.

The crippled man stood at the bottom, carried by his last good leg. Holding a long rifle, he glared at Master Nissim, lifting the barrel and lowering it again while cursing quietly.

"Have you seen anyone else?" the Archon asked.

"A couple of the slayer's gang," the man reported. "Gawking at the ship, a little too curious for my mood, so I sent them on their way."

"Good."

Father and Mother dropped to their knees, and Mother pressed her thumb against her son's wet cheek.

She said, "Honey."

Diamond wasn't sure when his tears started flowing.

"There has to be another way," she said.

Then Father touched Diamond on the shoulder, saying, "About our plan."

Mother looked at Father.

"King is a complication," Father said. "I might have guessed something like this . . . but I couldn't . . . "

His voice faded away.

"You have a plan?" Mother asked.

"Something risky," Father said. "And that was before we knew about the other boy."

She looked at both of them, and then she looked at the ground, saying, "You have to save our son."

"I know, and I will."

Diamond's face was wet and sore, and his body shook, and looking up the gangway, he was nothing but weak. Too exhausted to move, much less climb any distance, he found hope. Maybe he was finally sick. Too much had happened too quickly, and his strength was gone, and the often-promised illness was going to push him into a scorching fever, destroying the powers that he never wanted in the first place.

Was that something to wish for?

The Archon whispered to the crippled man and then started up the gangway, looking back just once.

"King," he called out.

Diamond's brother hurried to catch the Archon, walking beside the human and out of sight.

Again, the long gun lifted.

"Hugs and kisses," the man said. "Hurry up."

Mother sobbed, grabbing hold of her son, squeezing until her joints cracked. Father put his arms around both of them, leaving his eyes open. He looked up at the airship until the man again said, "Hurry up."

"We have to go," Father told Mother.

His parents walked away. Diamond was dreadfully weak, but he didn't collapse. Another bodyguard came close and motioned for him to follow, and Diamond took one little step and a long step. Then he stopped and turned, looking at Elata and Seldom.

"Thank you," he told them.

Surprised, Seldom asked, "For what?"

"For buying me that food," he said. "And everything else."

The children nodded, faces dipping.

Elata said, "Good bye."

"Yeah," said Seldom, sniffing. "Bye."

Diamond walked up to the Master. "And thank you, sir," he said.

"I wish this had gone better," Nissim said.

The boy nodded in agreement, and the bodyguard gave him a nudge.

Reaching under his shirt, Diamond pulled out the knife and sheath, handing them to the Master. "These are yours. I don't need them anymore."

"All right then." The missing fingertip helped grab the hilt, and smart eyes winked at him, one eye and then the other.

Diamond passed the crippled man, starting up the gangway. What seemed like weakness had turned into something else. The lightness in his body came from boundless energy, nervous and relentless. He had never been this awake, this alert. Every detail in the world was obvious. Time was slowing. Without trying, Diamond pulled ahead of the three men who had followed him this morning. Then he paused, looking back at the sad people standing close together.

"Seldom," he called out.

The boy swallowed and said, "What?"

"Wings," Diamond said.

"What?"

"I can feel them," he said. "I feel them growing."

FIFTEEN

Humans were easy to scare, and they remained afraid afterwards. Yet they hated that emotion, so much so that they would do any mad thing to get free of the fear that made their hearts hurry and their soft, fragile hands shake.

King wasn't at all like humans.

King was always afraid, and he was happy because of it.

There were days when the boy believed otherwise. It was easy to imagine the creatures surrounding him were right and smart while he was plainly wrong inside. Humans didn't measure every face as a potential threat or a temporary ally. King did. They didn't consider every shadow and closed door as hiding places for enemies. But the boy's deep nature was to do exactly that. Even in the presence of well-known enemies, humans could relax enough to keep their breathing slow, their manner easy. A man like King's father—a leader who had accumulated status and great power—could allow himself be surrounded by his worst foes. King would be too alarmed and pensive to ever do that, at least not for long. Yet those wicked people would smile at his father, and the Archon would show his teeth to them, and it seemed deeply unnatural that nobody would ever make fists, much less start to batter each other's face.

But as King grew older, more experienced and quite a lot smarter, he began to understand what was true and what was weak.

Fear had more than one shape, more than a single definition. Human fear was a small wild shambles, tiny when set beside King's magnificent fear. Among his tutors were retired soldiers who had won medals by battling bandits and wild beasts. They were proud bold men, but when they spoke to one another, usually with drinks in hand, they eventually confessed that their fears had to be controlled with training and iron resolve and more training. In their experience, the finest warriors could fight only so long before the terror became an enemy, making them physically ill. Sometimes they discussed the great old wars against the papio and how soldiers came home afterwards but never truly came home, how they couldn't sleep a normal night again and cried often and drank too much. Some of those broken men even did the unthinkable, climbing to the bottom of the canopy, insulting the Creators by falling into the air, letting the coronas and the sun claim their defeated selves.

The humans were cursed, and they were cursed because their emotions were too small and untrustworthy.

King was nothing like a human.

He was unique and significant and blessed.

Even the simple task of standing was a different experience for King. Humans didn't care about the floor under them, or the tree branch, or the dusty patch of coral. One place was as good as another, in their eyes. But King always knew what was beneath him and what was nearby. Everybody was a threat. Even the most familiar, benign face had to be measured for its intentions, and the body below that face had to be weighed for weaknesses and blind spots. Everyone scared King, without fail. Even his father—no, particularly his father—had to do very little to worry the orphaned boy. Was he going to punish King today? Or worse, was he going to spoil him? Or maybe this would be the terrible moment when the powerful Archon decided that the armored boy had become too much trouble, or he showed too little promise, and the good in King's life was about to be stripped away.

Every space that he occupied had to be defended or surrendered.

There was no third choice.

Whenever the fright was its largest—paranoia running wild with every bad dream—the boy would be treated to a keen rush of blood and oxygen, and his hearts felt happy, and his thoughts were slick and sudden, and the great world looked richer and more colorful and small enough to hold in either hand.

If the space beneath him was especially precious, or if he was in a certain mood, King felt gigantic, invulnerable.

Yes, his physical power was a benefit, and so were the armored body and his durability and the endless quick memory. But fear was the richest tool woven through his nature, and that was the emotion that he nourished now.

Today, inside this one recitation, King was straddling the entire world.

Everything was at risk.

Panic, muscular rich panic, made him ready.

His great life had been lived to reach this moment, and how very wonderful it felt to be so afraid.

• • •

Stopping at the top of the gangway, Diamond waited for the bodyguards. The longest hallway in the world ended with a tall metal door. Voices came from behind the door, from inside the bridge—men and women making ready to drop anchors and fly away. Then the Archon spoke, and everyone else fell silent. "When do we get home? Before night, or after?"

"As night rises, sir," said a man.

"I want to see the palace sooner," the Archon said.

And a different man shouted, "Engines. On."

The entire ship trembled and began to sway. The crippled bodyguard finished his long miserable climb, slamming a sweaty hand on an important red button, and the gangway hissed and began to rise. Standing on his toes, Diamond caught a last glimpse of his friends and the Master looking up at him, and his Mother mouthed a few words as she waved her hand.

Father was missing.

"Where do we put him?" another bodyguard asked.

"Second suite," the crippled man said. "You stay with him, always. You? Stand watch outside."

"Easy work," the first man joked.

The crippled man stared at him, hard. "You said that this morning. 'This is baby snaring.' "

The floor was vibrating and the walls too. Explosive thuds ripped the anchors from their cables, and water ballast was dropped from a dozen reservoirs, and the long airship began its lazy ascent. Diamond was flanked by two guards, walking in the middle of the long hallway, moving away from the bridge. The ship's engines grew louder, and he looked up at the faces in profile, and when one man looked down at him, Diamond told him, "You should leave."

"What?"

"If you can get off this ship, you should."

"Why are you saying that?"

"I don't want you to die," the boy replied.

The men blinked and fell into the same hard laughter.

Every room along the hallway wore a heavy blue door. The first door on the left was marked, "Archon," and after that was, "Two." Across the hall was another suite wearing a handwritten sign over its number. "King," the sign read. The first man unlocked and opened the door to Suite Two and walked inside. The doctor emerged from behind a smaller door farther down the hallway. Hands in his pockets, he called out, "All this is for the best, son."

Diamond didn't react.

The guard showed the boy a smile. "Aren't you going to warn him to jump clear?"

Diamond shook his head. "No."

Nothing could be funnier. Both men laughed as Diamond walked through the open door, and then the man who came inside with him shut the blue door, turning two locks. Diamond examined the enormous room, the heavy furniture and big bowls of fancy glass, corona bones and scales embellishing everything. Dark dead wood had been carved by trained hands. The tanned hides of special animals had been stretched across pieces of open floor. He couldn't imagine the wealth poured into this space, and the prestige was beyond his imagination. But the high ceiling was impressive, as was the entire outer wall made from glass windows, thick and sealed.

He walked toward the windows but stopped short.

Something was wrong.

The inside man was standing beside the locked door with his arms at his side, watching nothing but that odd little boy who couldn't be worth half this trouble.

"Who else is here?" Diamond asked.

"Nobody."

Diamond tipped his head, listening. But the huge engines were roaring, accelerating them into a long turn that would carry them farther over the reef before they could start for home. He heard nothing but the rumbling, and maybe he was wrong. Maybe. But a deep breath caught a familiar scent, and stepping toward the man, Diamond asked, "Where's King?"

"Sitting in his big chair," the guard said, grinning. Then he looked from side to side, asking, "Why?"

Several closed doors led to smaller rooms. One door exploded to slivers, and already running, King ran straight for the guard. No sound accompanied the creature. Two long strides and he lifted his arm, and the guard turned, reaching for the locks on the suite door. He barely touched one knob when King reached him, and the man started to yell, dipping his head while putting up his other hand to protect what couldn't be protected. The armored fist struck him at the back of the skull, and King's other hand came up under the chin and yanked back hard, and a man who was bigger and trained to fight was suddenly limp and empty-eyed, lying on a fancy carpet made from the weavings of a spider that lived only in the darkness at the top of the world.

"Is he dead?" Diamond asked.

"Or alive," said King. "Either way, he won't help you."

Diamond looked at the alien face. It wasn't as strange as before. He expected two mouths and the odd eyes and that living armor shrouding what wasn't at all human.

The airship was finishing its turn, the engines no longer pushing hard.

King approached.

Diamond didn't move.

"They'll discover that I'm missing," King said. "And my father's going to know where I went."

The human boy put his feet apart. "The Archon is your father?"

"Sure."

Diamond nodded.

"But you're not his son," King said.

The human kept nodding.

"Do you know what I'm telling you? Can you understand me?"

Diamond was barely listening. He was full of questions, and the first question to jump out was, "Do you remember things from before?"

"Before what?"

What did he mean exactly?

"You mean back when we sitting inside that monster?"

Diamond shook his head. "No. Before the corona. Do you remember any of that earlier life?"

The armored boy stared at him. The eating mouth spat, and then the other mouth said, "You're crazy."

"Maybe I am. How would I know?"

"What do you remember?"

"A woman, a human woman. And there was a man too. They were like me, and there were a lot of people like me."

"You recall this?" King said doubtfully.

"I think so." Diamond nodded, looking at his feet.

"There is no 'before,' " King said. "Do you know what we are?"

"No."

"Then I'll tell you."

"All right," said Diamond.

"Build anything—put together a ship or house or anything—and there's always pieces left behind," King said. "That's what you and I are. Leftovers. The Creators made us along with the world, and we were extra pieces. They let our bodies fall down near the sun where we got eaten, and we've been waiting all of this time, waiting for our chance."

"Who says that?"

"My father knows it."

Diamond studied the scaled chest and broad arms and then a face that was more familiar each time he looked at it. "I don't think the Archon's right."

With a quick trained motion, King punched with his left fist. Diamond felt the blow and dropped to the floor, the breath beaten from behind his ribs.

"My father is very, very smart," King said.

Diamond couldn't speak.

What may or may not have been a laugh emerged and failed. Then King gave him one little kick before saying, "But I'm even smarter than him. And you're probably a lot smarter than your parents too."

Diamond found just enough breath to say, "I feel stupid."

The light changed abruptly. Emerging from the reef's shadow, The *Ruler of the Wind* found the late sun blazing up from below. Some kind of minor magic turned the glass windows dark. The room grew only a little brighter, and Diamond looked at the feet in front of him. He studied his feet and King's, and then King said, "My brain is incredible. Nothing is like it, except maybe yours."

"Why is it incredible?"

"The first man that had me was a slayer, like Merit. He didn't know what I was until he got home, and then he got scared. Scared and so he got drunk and tried to kill me. I was a monster, he decided. He used knives on me. He cut into my chest and tore out my hearts, but I grew new hearts and my chest healed. Then he chopped off my little legs and my arms and new ones came out of the stumps, which made him angrier and more scared, and humans don't do well when they're scared."

"What happened next?" Diamond asked.

"Oh, he got even drunker, and he fell asleep."

Diamond didn't know what it meant to be drunk.

"That's awful," he said.

"Don't talk," King said. "I'm telling the story."

The boy nodded, letting time run along.

"Anyway, the slayer had a woman friend. I don't know why, but the woman felt sorry for me. So she fed me milk and nuts, and I grew big again. The slayer slept for a long time, and then I was mostly back where I was before. And when the slayer woke and figured out what happened, he beat her hard and kicked her outside and went back to trying to kill me.

"I was an abomination. We're both abominations, and the man knew that he'd get in trouble for all kinds of reasons. So he put my head into a vice, face down so he didn't have to look at these eyes. I was a baby, and he fixed me down good and used a big power drill and fat steel bits to cut a fat round hole in the back of my skull. He cut faster than I could heal and got through the bone after breaking the first three bits, and then he took his hardest, best bit and tried to force it down inside my brain."

Diamond touched the back of his own head.

"Human brains are soft and wet and gooey. Did you know that?"

"No."

"Shake their heads hard, and they forget who they are." King bent his knees, putting his face close to Diamond's face. "My brain isn't gooey. This body is strong, but it isn't half as tough as the brain inside my skull. That stupid man tried to kill me. He used that spinning piece of hard steel to cut at something that can't be cut. He burned up the bit and all the others, and his drill overheated and died, and he shot me in the head with every bullet in the house, and he even used one of the big slayer harpoons. I was this baby with my skull ripped open, and he was ready to put a fourth harpoon into his target. Three others had already busted. But he was drunk again and angry and trying to aim, and that's when the girlfriend brought the police to his house, and that's how my father found out about me. The police told the Archon. And my father has kept me safe ever since."

Diamond watched the alien face—the little flicks that the eyes made and how each mouth moved in its own fashion.

"I bet your brain is the same as mine," King said.

"Maybe it is."

"Pretend it is," King said. "That means nothing can kill it. But that doesn't protect you from everything. What if some sharp knife with muscle behind it were to rip that head off your shoulders, and what if that head and your body were cut into little, little pieces, and your brain and everything else was dropped out of an airship running fast over a place where no person can go? What if you were thrown away and swallowed by a thousand coronas? Do you believe anybody would ever find enough of your bits to make you live again?"

A day of fear and the unexpected had reached this place, this monstrous moment. Diamond was terrified and cold and angry in ways that he didn't recognize. He stared at the inhuman face, managing one worthwhile breath before saying, "Your father doesn't want this."

"My father," said King. "My father wants many things. And so long as I'm the only son, no one else is in his dreams."

• • •

Diamond started to shout.

King grabbed the boy's throat and shook him until he was limp. Then he stood up, just the one arm lifting Diamond off his feet. They stared at each other's faces. A rude wet sound came from the eating mouth, and the breathing mouth said, "I am not cruel. I promise, I'll cut off the head, and you won't feel anything again."

Diamond was limp, and then he moved. The dangling right foot started to kick, and King pushed back his hips, another curse leaking out of the eating mouth. That's when Diamond struck with his right fist. Endless practice wouldn't have made him able to hit harder. Terror and rage gave him power. He aimed at the high mouth, the breathing mouth, but King started to jerk his head back. The tiny fist hit the eating mouth before the lips could clench, and the knuckles hit teeth, and then the hand vanished and a hard long tongue retreated deep into the body, recoiling against the alien taste.

King bit.

Diamond drove his left thumb into a glassy green eye.

Eyelids encased in scales shut, but too late. King cursed and shook his head, and he bit hard enough to shred flesh to the bone. But wounds meant blood, and the salty crimson blood ran fast across the tongue and down the throat. There was a choking sound followed by red bubbles full of stomach gases that burst, making the air foul. King let go of Diamond's neck and bit harder, and he punched the human head with alternating fists. But that changed nothing except to slice open the boy's face ten different ways, and it was Diamond who tried to laugh, talking through gore, saying, "Give up. Give up. Give up."

The breathing mouth yelled, "No."

Diamond shoved his left hand into the soft wet hole, grabbing a tongue that was as delicate and soft as anything on that armored body. Then he yanked and kicked, and King tried backing away. He dragged the boy until one heel caught the leg of a chair, and he tumbled with a thud to the floor.

Diamond found himself on top.

He shoved his right knee into the neck, but the overlapping plates were harder than steel. King kept chewing and throwing blows at Diamond's face and chest, and Diamond put the pain aside, watching the face, studying the emotions rolling across it.

King started battering the arm inside his breathing mouth.

Diamond drove his forearm deeper, cutting off King's airflow.

And King panicked. He swung and swung with the fists, wasting oxygen by beating what was already mutilated. Then he picked his rump off the floor, and with hands and feet dragged both of them toward the windows. A long chair faced the window, offering passengers a comfortable seat while watching the perfect world pass by. A neat stack of tools was waiting on the carpet: two saws and a long sword and boning knives just like the Master's, only newer. This was where King had planned to butcher Diamond. An empty cloth sack was waiting to hold all of the living pieces.

Suffocating and desperate, King pulled them toward the sharpened steel. Diamond climbed forward and pushed down hard at the head, trying to slow their progress. But he was too weak and much too small, and this fight wasn't buying more than a few extra moments.

Through the window and through the walls came the urgent piercing sound of a horn wailing.

The airship's engines began to throttle up again.

King's motions slowed, and the throat around Diamond's left hand began to relax.

Again the horn let loose a long scream, followed by the rapid hard thuds of a single cannon firing into some great distance.

The big armored body kept moving its arms and legs, but there was little progress. King was half-choked and nearly limp. White smoke came into the eyes, and armored plates relaxed as they would in death, affording little gaps where a blade could enter and cut at tissues no stronger than Diamond's. The boy looked at the sword and that keen ready edge of the blade, and it occurred to him that he could chop off that monstrous head and toss it into oblivion.

He could do what his enemy wanted to do to him.

And that's when he recoiled—an image of violence and justice; a turn that would leave no retreat—and all the miseries of the day were nothing compared to the horrible thought that he would do that and do it happily.

Diamond eased his hand out of the breathing mouth.

King gasped, and the teeth and tongue in the other mouth started to chew until that sorry mess of a hand was yanked free.

King managed another deep breath and started lifting his arms.

Diamond picked up one long knife, and before the battle could start again, he pushed the tip into the gap that had already been stabbed once, pushing to the healed artery and twisting the blade until a heart was shredded, leaving his brother temporarily dead.

• • •

The cannon fired quickly and then quit firing. Some of the engines slowed while others held their terrific pace. The ship was attempting one hard turn, but the *Ruler* was enormous and stubborn and nothing changed quickly. Somebody shouted in the hallway, the words tangled together, making no sense. Then a big male voice came through a tube in the ceiling, calling everyone to battle stations, and that's when hands began pounding at the locked door.

Diamond stood and let go of the knife, taking the sword with his better hand, lifting the hilt but not the heavy blade.

Keys rattled.

The Archon called out, "King. Have you seen him?"

King reacted to his name. Legs kicked, and he grabbed blindly at the knife in his chest, pulling and pulling again, finally yanking it free. Purple blood rose from the gash, forming a bright persistent bubble. Then he managed a pair of deep soggy breaths, finding the strength to whisper, "Here."

Locks yielded, and the man on guard outside kicked the door open. His partner was limp on the floor and the human boy had a sword in hand, but the guard couldn't see King behind the furniture. He cursed and came close and then thought better of it. What kinds of powers did this little creature possess? Stopping a few steps back, he pulled a heavy pistol from under his shirt, and with a hard voice, he said, "Come in."

The Archon eased his way into the room. Nothing about him seemed formidable or special. Staring at Diamond, he yelled angrily for his son, but the voice was shrill and almost too soft over the droning engines.

"Here," King repeated.

Keeping his distance, the Archon walked around the long chair. "What is this?" he asked neither boy. Talking to the bloody floor, he said, "This is not what we wanted."

He asked, "What is this? What's happening here?"

The airship had just started making its turn and now the engines changed again, struggling to push them in another direction. It was as if the steering hands didn't know which line to follow. Another big gun began firing, this time beneath them, the furniture and the windows rattling hard. Diamond looked at the heavy glass and then at the sword, and once again, he tried and failed to lift the massive blade.

Out in the hallway, one of the ship's crew shouted for the Archon.

"In here!"

The crewman entered. He was wearing a fine blue uniform and a tilted hat, and his jacket was soaked with perspiration, and the hat fell to the floor when he tried to salute.

"What's the count?" the Archon asked.

"Three coronas, but dozens are rising, sir." The crewman scooped up his hat and twisted it in his hands. "The captains says we've got maybe five recitations before those first few reach us."

The news was an irritation. More important was his bloodied, helpless son. Eyes fixed on King, he said, "As I told you and everybody else. Shoot the slayer's damned ship."

"It's very maneuverable, sir. And we're short of gunners."

"It's no warship," the Archon said. "Kill it, and the coronas forget about us."

The crewman nodded, saluted, and ran out the door with his hat.

Diamond's chewed hand was half-healed. He grabbed the hilt of the sword with both hands, lifting the tip off the floor.

The cannon under them fired again, seven fast rounds followed by nothing. None of the *Ruler*'s guns were firing, and the captain had given up trying to maneuver, the engines running hard and straight now.

The Archon decided this was good news. He smiled and let himself breathe deeply, some of the original smugness shaping his face. Looking at Diamond, he said, "I suppose Merit was trying to lure the coronas out of their house."

"He is," Diamond said. "Father told me his plan."

"What exactly did he tell you?"

Diamond looked at the strong blade and the bright sharp edge. "While you were chasing me, my father's men chopped the special lights out of the dead corona and tied them to a slayer ship. I don't know how, but those dead lights can be made to shine again."

The Archon nodded, and then he began to speak again.

And Diamond swung the sword. He didn't think that he could, but he got the blade into the air and turned his entire body around once before the tip dropped again.

The Archon and bodyguard reflexively jumped back.

Diamond swung a second time, driving the hard steel into the middle of the tall darkened pane.

But the glass was thick and far too strong to break.

"Except Merit's scheme is finished," the Archon told him, finding a good sharp smile. "Drop your weapon, son."

"I'm not," Diamond said.

"What's that?"

"Your son," he said.

Then the cannon beneath them fired twice, and after a pause, it threw one more shell into the air.

Several voices shouted from the ceiling tube at once, no word making sense.

Suddenly the Archon felt less certain about everything.

The bodyguard was standing beside the injured man. Relieved, he said, "Just a blow to the head, by the looks. I think he's coming around."

"This boy is what matters," said the Archon.

The guard came around the chair. He finally saw King lying on his back, fighting to breathe, and the man opened his mouth and said nothing and closed his mouth again.

Boots ran in the hallway. A uniformed crewman appeared in the open door, his scared face visible in profile.

"Status?" said the Archon.

But the crewman was racing for the stern.

"Status!" the Archon shouted.

The third bodyguard appeared. He was sweating too, pain more than any terror responsible. He came into the doorway and tipped himself against the jamb, blood seeping through his bandages and his face pale as milk.

"That little fletch is too close," he said.

"What does that mean?" asked the Archon.

"It means that the asshole is near enough to kiss," said the crippled man. "Fire again, and we'll cut our own guide wires and likely puncture our bladders too."

"This is madness," the Archon said.

Nobody else spoke.

"Why would the man put the boy at risk?" He looked at Diamond and tried a smile. "What else is planned?"

Again, Diamond swung at the window.

The glass shook but held, and the Archon watched him. Recognition came into that narrow plain face, bringing doubt and amazement and a sturdy capacity to do nothing, not quite believing what he knew to be true.

Several cannons started firing from the ship's stern.

The healthy guard thought that was good news. "Merit's getting punched now," he said.

But the crippled man just shook his head. "Those are long shots. Don't you know anything? We're shooting at the coronas, now that they're nipping at our tail feathers."

"Both of you, shut up," the Archon said.

The men fell silent.

Turning to the healthy guard, he said, "Grab the child. Now. We're going to the hanger, to the escape ship."

The guard took a wary step toward Diamond, and then he paused.

Talking to the crippled man, the Archon said, "Stay here with King. When he's strong enough, come join us."

"I can carry your son now," the healthy guard volunteered.

"No, he has to save himself . . . after trying this crap . . . "

King laid still, armored eyes closed tight.

Looking at his new hand and the long steel blade, Diamond marshaled his strength for one more swing.

The guard took another step toward him.

"I told you to grab him," the Archon said.

"But he's got that sword."

"You think the baby's dangerous?"

"He put your son down. That's some kind of power."

Furious, the Archon said, "You have a gun. Shoot him. A bullet in the chest and you carry him like a sack."

The guard looked down at his pistol, apparently surprised to find it waiting in his hand.

Diamond lifted the sword and spun, ready to try another desperate whack at the window. But he didn't have time. The guard lifted the pistol. King was still flat on the floor. Then the guard started to aim, and King moved. Furious and swift and nearly silent, he reached for the guard's hand and the gun. Diamond hit the window once more, accomplishing nothing. The guard's wrist shattered with a hard crack, and the man crumbled and screamed, and King was standing over him, the pistol inside his strange hand.

The Archon shouted, "No."

He told the guard in the doorway, "Shoot both of them."

"I could try doing that," the crippled man replied. "Or I could do nothing and finish out this damned awful day."

King turned to Diamond, and the one mouth asked, "So what's the rest of your father's plan?"

"I jump and he catches me."

"What if he misses?"

"A corona eats me, and Father spends the rest of his life hunting for that corona and for me."

King's mouths made different little sounds, and then he turned to stare at the Archon, saying nothing. For a long moment he was as still as any statue.

Then he said, "Save myself," and the pistol lifted. King aimed carefully and pulled the trigger and six bullets struck the glass, ricocheting wildly across the suite. But the seventh bullet pierced the pane, cracks spreading out from the center.

Once again, Diamond swung the sword, and this time shards of heavy glass tumbled free of the airship, and the sword followed the glass downwards, spinning fast as one boy leaped into that chaos, plunging toward the late day sun.

SIXTEEN

Diamond was on his back, flattened against the roaring air, waiting to be scared. He promised himself to act brave when the terror grabbed him, crying a little maybe but with the stiff-faced resolve of a wooden soldier. Except he wasn't scared. Not so much. He felt safer while falling than when he was standing with King and the Archon. And what surprised him even more, he was comfortable. A warm wind blew up into him, and nothing was touching him, and the airship was slowly growing smaller while the little fletch flew just beneath it. The fletch's belly looked as if it was burning, bright purple flames flowing around stubborn patches of blackness. Diamond's skin seemed to be dipped in the same rich purple. Both ships were pressing ahead, desperate to leave him behind, but they still felt close. Only a few moments had passed since he jumped free. And now the flames weakened and then dissolved, save for one stubborn blotch that meant nothing. Diamond's father had taught him today: to coronas, significances were carried by a light's patterns and rhythms, and even more so, by the intricate darkness between.

A tiny figure came out from the slayer's ship.

Diamond moved when he shouldn't, flipping and spinning before ending on his belly, gazing down at a great forest that had grown old inside one brief day. He wasn't truly scared. This was so much easier than fighting his brother. But a dread had started to claim him. He contemplated falling for a very long time and then vanishing, maybe forever, and this shouldn't happen, not in this way, and what shook him was the powerful sense that he was failing to meet some great old promise.

Silver disks moved above the demon floor. From high overhead, the coronas looked delicate and slow and lovely. They looked simple. Human eyes wouldn't be able to count them in a glance, but Diamond could. He found sixty-one of the giants, and then he counted again, discovering five less. Then the largest individual changed shape, compressing its body as it turned, and once it was narrow like a spear, it dropped. It plunged. The demon floor absorbed the impact, and a splash of golden vapor welcomed the animal back into its world.

Seven more coronas followed while others continued to circle, not one of them working to climb this high. The fletch wasn't calling to them anymore. The raging, insulting voice was finished. But three coronas had been threatening the airship. He hadn't seen them. Were they gone too? And almost too late, Diamond rolled onto his back again.

The heat fell over him. It struck hard and there was a terrific wild irresistible motion. His flesh felt ready to burn as the creature passed just above him, no warning that it was close, and then it was past, and he felt its scorching body and the slipstream that rolled him and spun him and left him tumbling on a new course.

Feet down, he fell faster.

The corona was smaller than the one Father killed, and it was enormous, and graceful, and spectacularly alive. The great body was as fluid as it was solid, silver with glimmers of color washed away by sunlight. Diamond thought of umbrellas. He thought of certain mushrooms and wide bowls filled with sweet oils. A giant round mouth buried in the creature's flatter side, surrounded by a tangle of necks sporting jaws and teeth and eyes. A jet of furnace air roared from that mouth. Then the jet quit. Sharp percussive blasts shook Creation. Bladders were made huge and empty in an instant, and the body was enlarged, swollen and buoyant, matching his pace of falling, the trailing necks and heads catching up to the body and flowing into it as the beast twisted around, deftly starting back toward him again.

That gaping central mouth swallowed air, compressing each breath, making its jets ready to fire again.

A brave pair of necks stretched far away from the body, supplying the eyes that stared at this tiny apparition, this human-like creature that fell from above perhaps to feed a great soul.

Diamond flattened again.

The corona fell a little ways beneath him before swelling more. Diamond flipped and flipped, trying to flee, but the vacuums balancing its weight. Infinitely more graceful, his companion deftly matched each of the boy's desperate moves. A single neck extended, triple jaws opening and tongues emerging, and Diamond rolled and kicked, but a tongue touched his foot and pulled back and the head retreated a moment later.

The corona had wanted nothing but a taste.

In the roaring wind, a voice shouted.

Diamond didn't understand words or guess directions. It was possible to believe that one of the corona's heads had called to him—not the most incredible notion in a day filled with impossibilities.

"Leave me alone," he shouted at the head. "Go away."

Then a man screamed, telling someone, "Leave him alone."

Father.

Diamond turned onto his back again. The fletch had pulled away from the airship, a final few glands still leaking purple. One of the two remaining coronas was clinging to the slayer's ship, jaws biting into the skin and struts as the long necks twisted, wrenching free whatever was weakest.

Father plunged toward Diamond. His trajectory was close but wrong, and sweeping past the boy, he flattened out, arms and legs supporting fabric wings that rattled and popped as the wind swept past.

He waved, beckoning.

Diamond tipped his head and fell faster, and the corona fell beside both of them. A dozen heads studied them; none bit. Not yet. Diamond pulled closer but slipped past his father, and the man stretched and reached and touched a hand but couldn't hold on. Then Merit changed the angle of his body and wrenched his old back far enough after that finally, after such a very long fall, he managed to collide with the little boy, sweeping him up with his arms.

Father was wearing a drop suit and a bulky pack, and around his waist was a wide leather belt. "The bottle on my belt," he shouted. "Pull its plug."

The rubber stopper was topped with a shiny ring. While his father held tight, Diamond yanked at the ring. A cold thin fluid exploded out into the wind. What was inside was sweet and thick and alien, and Diamond buried his nose in his father's chest while the man kept clinging to him, as the corona got a first awful whiff.

Blistering air came from the mouth, and the giant fled.

Father laughed.

"I got you," he said, congratulating both of them.

"What was in the bottle?" Diamond asked. "It stinks."

"You can smell that?"

"Yes."

"It's a year's worth of corona musk." Then Father admitted, "I never met someone who can smell it."

His unhuman son had to be moved to a better position. When they were facing the same direction, bellies down, they wrapped an extra belt around Diamond and fastened it and cinched it tight before Merit shouted, "Wings."

Diamond clung to one arm. His father reached behind with his other arm, pulling a handle, and the big pack exploded into fabric and cord that leaped up behind him, catching the air.

There a staggering jerk, as if a hand caught them, and then the screaming air was gone and they were falling gently beneath a grand umbrella shaped like a wing. It was as if they had been pulled into another, more peaceful world. Diamond held the arm but didn't need to, relaxed and happy even though he couldn't imagine where they would touch down.

"Look," Father said.

Up, he meant. Diamond threw back his head. The third corona was bigger than the first two combined, and it had deftly woven its necks across the ship's bow, covering the bridge, assuring that the Archon's cannons couldn't fire at any part of it. Yet nothing about its actions looked violent or even mischievous. For all of the movement it made, the creature might have been resting.

"There's a favorite old trick," said Father. "Wait."

The great airship was tilting. The bow was no longer buoyant enough to remain trim, and the corona added to the catastrophe by collapsing its bladders one after another, and blowing with its jet, nudging the bow lower still.

"The captain should know better," Father said. "But he can't imagine the monster being his master."

Water and sawdust were falling free, lightening the load enough to bring the ship back where it should be.

And then with no warning, the corona let go of the *Ruler*, calmly falling away.

The airship's bridge leapt up, dragging the great long body with it.

"And now the captain's going to panic," Father explained, his voice excited but also sorry. "But he can't let too much out. In the afternoon air, with all the free oxygen, he's inviting a fire."

"What will happen?"

"The pride and heart of the tree-walker's fleet is going to crash into the canopy, where it'll be snagged and useless."

"Will people get hurt?"

"I hope not. I didn't want this. But I never imagined so much incompetence either."

The catastrophe continued to unfold slowly and with great majesty, the *Ruler* driving into the thin, sun-blistered branches.

Then Father told him, "Look down."

Between them and the demon floor was an object moving slowly, working to hold a useful position. Their target seemed tiny even when they were close. Father put on goggles and jerked hard at the parachute's ropes, gliding them into a better course, and inside another two recitations Diamond saw the woman painted on the side of the *Happenstance*, and he heard a bright horn blowing in celebration.

"We'll land on top," Father promised.

"Can we?" Diamond asked doubtfully.

"I don't know," he said, laughing. "This is a first for both of us."

• • •

The *Happenstance* remained trim and nearly motionless beneath them, and they turned and dropped over the bow, Father starting to run before his feet reached the hull's taut skin. Then a stray gust of wind gave the umbrella new life. The fabric thudded as it filled with warm damp air, and they lifted as he yanked at the straps, once and again, and they dropped together. Diamond was down with Merit kneeling over him, both of them watching that great wing soaring, pressing fast into the bright distance.

"You should know," Father said, gasping. "I thought this crazy plan would work. I couldn't have believed in it more. Right up until you were inside the big ship, out of my sight, and then all the things that could go wrong showed themselves, and in my heart, just as sure as before, I knew you were lost."

The gust failed and the lost parachute collapsed, falling fast. Diamond squinted against the glare, watching it shrink.

"I flew up and you didn't jump. I assumed they'd wrapped you up in chains, or worse. So I made another plan. I was going to board that ship and search every room to bring you out. That's what I was getting ready to do when you jumped. And with that idiot scheme, I was confident all over again."

Father was laughing, releasing Diamond's belt.

"Consider this a warning, son. When your mind tells you a story, you have no choice but to believe in it. Unreasonable stupid or mad as any fantasy might be, you'll embrace it, cling to it, and do your best to let it enslave you."

A top hatch opened. Out came the smiling face of the little pilot. "Those two jazzings are still paying dividends," he boasted. "Let's get below, and I'll rush us all back to Ivory Station."

Diamond hesitated.

Father pulled at him. "Come on now."

The boy shook his head. "No."

"We don't have any choice, little man," said the pilot. "A lot of explaining needs to be done, and delaying won't help anybody here."

The parachute was a crumpled wad below them, and then it spread wide, the demon floor slowing its fall, the fabric spreading out, as if hands were pulling a sheet across a tidy bed. Then it slipped through the magic barrier, turning to fire, to ash and nothingness.

Father pulled, but the boy slipped under his hand and stepped away.

With a rare sternness, Father said, "Diamond."

The pilot laughed grimly. "Yeah, their big ship is foundering. Oh, this is going to be one expensive day."

Diamond said, "I don't want to go the Station. I want to be home."

The slayer touched his own face, fingertips running along the scar.

The pilot climbed onto the hull. Watching the boy, he noticed the injured hand, the last hints of damage quickly becoming the smoothest, most perfect skin. Under his breath, the little man offered a simple prayer, and then he looked at Merit, ready to ask some obvious question.

Father spoke first.

"All right," he said, pointing into the distance. A tiny shape had appeared—another fletch carrying his crew. "Are they close enough to signal?"

"Soon if not now," the pilot responded.

"My orders," Father said. "Tell them to sprint to the Station and explain what they can. If they get the chance, meet with Prima. Tell our Archon that I think she is a wonderful leader and smart and that I have delivered to her more misery and danger than she would ever wish to bear. But she needs to come to my home and meet my son."

Diamond was crying, and he was giggling.

"Then you'll fly us to our front door," Father ordered. "I think this boy deserves that much consideration. Don't you?"

• • •

The sun and the day weren't brilliant anymore. Seldom was standing in the passenger cabin, standing beside the windows, pressing old binoculars against his bare eyes. Spellbound, he caught glimpses of Diamond falling free from the *Ruler* and the corona dancing beside his friend for what seemed like ages, and then Merit caught his son and where was the corona now? Gone and the parachute had opened, Merit and Diamond falling in a looping course while the *Happenstance* slowed its engines, wishing them to a safe landing.

Nobody spoke. Elata and Master Nissim and Seldom watched the parachute until it vanish somewhere above the ship. Haddi was standing above, in the crowded bridge. Then the engines turned them back into the wind and slowed. The old woman screamed from the bridge, which had to be bad news; Seldom had never felt so scared. And the pilot sounded scared when he started to shout, except the words were good.

"They're down, we got them," he screamed. "Damn we got them."

Elata was beside Seldom, crying and jumping. And the Master was behind them, quietly saying the same word again and again.

"Remarkable," he said.

But then the parachute was blown off the *Happenstance*, falling past Seldom's windows. He was brave enough for one squinting glance, and he saw what he feared, shutting his eyes and pushing the binoculars hard against his sorry stomach. The pilot had warned them how the air was still near the demon floor, how they had to fly low to intercept their people, no room for second chances. And now their friend was going to be a cinder, and Merit was sure to die.

Seldom wasn't ashamed to cry.

"What's wrong?" Elata asked.

What was right? Nothing was.

And deciphering the tears, she laughed at him.

Anger made the eyes open. The parachute was a floppy mess, nobody riding it to their doom, and the loud little pilot was climbing stairs somewhere above them, shouting instructions to his people. Then Diamond's mother came into the cabin, smiling warily. Seldom wiped his face with the sleeve of his school uniform and the Master patted his shoulders.

"Just remarkable," he said.

In that instant, Seldom went from miserable to joyous. Pushing the binoculars against wet eyes, he watched the *Ruler of the Wind* continue to break open and fall to pieces. But the little airships that it had carried were free and racing off. Maybe the crew and everybody had been saved. That's what Seldom wanted, but he didn't want that very much. He hoped the *Ruler* would catch fire, which would be spectacular, and that's exactly what happened next: hydrogen was leaking where the corona skin was ripped open—more hydrogen than any fire retardant could fight—and touched by a spark, the gas exploded. The blaze was blue on the edges and invisible inside its fierce heart, and the nearby canopy began to burn, and the ship's cabins and fuel tanks and every giant engine too.

Seldom was so thrilled that he felt weak, almost sick. His mind started jumping, as it was known to do, and he suddenly remembered how Nissim had talked about worlds other than this world. The boy hadn't believed the Master. Of all the things that happened today, that possibility had bothered him more than any. Yet now, wearing this seamless, effortless joy, Seldom could believe impossible ideas. Of course there were worlds past theirs, just as there were other creatures like Diamond, and not only did he embrace what a moment ago seemed ugly and impossible, but Seldom found himself half-fearing, half-wishing that somehow he could visit one of these worlds.

Wouldn't that be a wonderful journey?

• • •

Diamond walked into the little cabin with its lightweight chairs and flexible windows and the big flanking engines, repaired and roaring. Elata gave him a sturdy hug and the Master clasped his hand.

Seldom was standing at the window with binoculars in his hands. "What happened on the *Ruler*?" he asked.

Diamond didn't want to talk about the fights.

"I thought I could see you," Seldom said, waving the binoculars. "You had a sword. Then the glass broke, and out you jumped out."

"Seldom," said the Master. "Leave our friend alone, please."

Diamond wiped at his dirty face.

"Sit," the Master suggested.

"I'm hungry," Diamond confessed.

Seldom dropped the binoculars and both children ran off on a food hunt.

Mother was sitting in the middle of the cabin. She looked pale but happy, waving to him. "Here. Please, keep me company."

He sat, and she held his hands.

The Master sat elsewhere, Father joining him. The two men spoke quietly, every word serious and every gesture careful. They were talking about laws and the codes of the slayer and political matters that shouldn't matter to normal boys.

Diamond leaned into the old woman, and she leaned into him.

"I'm tired," she said.

He nodded.

"Are you tired?"

He said, "Maybe."

"Weak?"

He thought for a moment, one hand grabbing the other wrist. Both were healed, and he said, "I'm back to the same."

She felt the arm. "You are."

They sat together for a few recitations, saying nothing.

Elata returned with two ancient meals wrapped in clear rubber, plus a flask of warm water. "This is all, so far. Seldom's chasing rumors about a lost lunch. But nobody remembered to load food at the reef, what with the engine and the excitement."

"Thank you," Mother said, using a smile to coax the girl to leave.

Then to her son, she said, "Eat it all."

The meals were dry and nearly tasteless, and he wasn't sure what the food had been when it was fresh. But he was famished, and she watched him for a little while before saying, "Diamond."

"What?"

"Your name. I want you to know where it came from."

His mouth stopped chewing, and he looked at her.

She motioned at Father. "He told me you understand, you know where he found you and how he brought you home."

"Yes," said the boy.

"Afterwards, I pretended to be pregnant," she said. "At my age, that seemed unlikely. But we announced that you were coming and I didn't let myself get seen without wearing a pillow under my shirt. Then we announced that you were born at home and sickly. Maybe we shouldn't have. It might have been smarter to run off to the wilderness and live like bandits. But your father had his work, and wild country has its dangers, and so we kept up this lie until too many people were asking to see you, wanting to help.

"Friends found the doctor for us, and the doctor convinced himself of your afflictions, at least for a little while. You were one bug away from death, and in one fashion or another, we believed our own lie."

Diamond listened intently.

"I used to watch you lying inside your crib," Mother said. "Your father was working, and I didn't have anything half as important as studying you. Such a little baby, you were. So sweet you seemed, but odd. Sometimes you'd gaze at me and smile and make me weep, I was so happy. But there were spells when I would do everything I could to win a grin, and you did nothing but stare at the darkest piece of your room, watching nothing. As if you were hypnotized by the darkness. And then sometimes, without warning, you laughed for no reason, and you smiled like you smiled at me, only better. A radiant smile, and that's when I realized you were remembering your real mother. Whoever she was, whatever she was. Ages spent in the belly of a corona, yet you still hadn't forgotten this other life that I can't begin to imagine."

"I don't remember anybody else," said Diamond. But the words felt forced, and when he fell silent, he could almost see another face.

Sipping stale water, he waited.

"Your father and I fought," Mother said. "We argued about what to teach you about the world and yourself. In the end, I won. I said you were happy as you were. I reminded him that I was responsible for you, day after night after day, and if you knew too much about the world—if you ever decided to leave—I wouldn't be strong enough to keep a creature like you in one place.

"That's not a worthy reason for everything. I feel terrible. I deserve to hurt. But that's one reason you were locked away, so a weak old woman didn't have to make impossible choices."

Diamond wasn't sure how to react.

Seldom returned from his search, empty hands held high.

"My name," Diamond said.

"What?"

"You were going to explain my name."

"I'm sorry. I distracted myself." Mother made herself laugh, just to prove she could. "When I was a girl, about the age of your friends, I was a student at the Marduk school. There was one very long day, and my class traveled to a special place where ancient artifacts are kept safe. We were shown one rare, exceptional marvel. It was a rock. The rock was tiny, like the tip of the tip of your finger, but it was bright and glittery in the special light they shone on it. The story that I was told was that there are only so many of these tiny rocks in the world, and the gems were stronger than everything but the shell of the world. They're called diamonds. According to legend, when the first humans in the world were married to one another, the man and the woman each wore a ring encrusted with these exceptional gemstones. That's the way the Creators made us. People died, but diamonds are the everlasting symbol of love. But there are very few diamonds left in the world, and thousands of days later, I was gazing at a baby who had come across an unimaginable route, enduring untold miseries to find me, and it seemed to me that the world would be better—a stronger, more enduring place—with one more diamond among us."

SEVENTEEN

Every course has its benefits. Flying beneath the wilderness canopy, the *Happenstance* pushed ahead as fast as the repaired engine allowed, following the straightest possible line back to the Corona District. And every course had its risks. Any moment, some wild branch might drop or an entire tree could tumble free on top of them. And if the other engine exploded and punctured a bladder, they would start a long horrible fall without any snags to stop them. Flight meant calculations, and their course was the best imperfect choice. But at least the sun was so weak that nobody wore goggles, and Diamond could sit at the window with his new friends, everybody watching a vista that few had seen before.

Mother and Father were sitting with Master Nissim, talking in whispers.

Seldom started to laugh.

"What's funny?" Elata asked.

"School," he said. "When we go back tomorrow, what are we going to tell people?"

"The truth," she said.

"They'll say we're lying," Seldom said, laughing harder.

Elata was laughing. She patted Diamond on the knee and smiled at him, and when he looked at her face, she said, "When I talked to you that first time, when you were standing on your landing . . . do you know what I thought . . . ?"

"No."

"You were boring."

Diamond nodded slowly.

"Oh, I knew he was fascinating," Seldom said. "Right away, the first time I looked at you."

"You did not," said Elata.

"I did."

"You're lying," she said.

"Maybe," Seldom agreed. Then something was so funny that he couldn't speak, shaking his head as he giggled and snorted.

The reef country had vanished into the late-day haze. Between the *Happenstance* and where they had been, an entire tree suddenly ripped free, plunging from the canopy without sound or apparent haste, twisting until the heavy base of the trunk was leading the way. Diamond watched it grow small, and then came the demon floor, heat and pressure claiming their prize, and he thought about the monkeys trapped on that doomed wood.

His friends kept laughing, and he was sad.

"After school," Seldom said.

Diamond blinked. "What?"

"I could come to your home. I'll bring my two-wheeler and teach you how to ride."

"Maybe." Diamond looked at his parents. "I don't know."

"Riding is easy, if you try."

Balancing on two spinning wheels didn't sound easy. But Diamond wanted to sound positive, saying, "Okay," while pulling up a smile.

The overhead wilderness was changing. Corona blackwoods pushed out from the paler green limbs, and a single blimp moved sluggishly from one destination to another. Diamond watched the blimp and the dense canopy adorned with cultivated epiphytes and fancy flowers, and suddenly they passed close to a suspended platform where long green blades hung off the bottom—like hair, except that it was some kind of plant.

A word came to him, and he spoke it.

Nobody understood him.

The word brought a brief image, real as any dream, of green vegetation standing tall and the sun overhead and an impossibly beautiful woman watching over him.

Diamond shut his eyes, clinging to the image.

Master Nissim came over and sat among the three of them, and after a while the man said his name.

Diamond looked at him.

"I've been talking to your parents. About quite a lot, and all of it wrapped around you, of course."

The boy nodded, waiting.

"Do you know what a tutor is?"

"No."

Seldom knew. His cheeks blew up big, and guessing the rest, he said, "You're going to tutor Diamond."

"That's the plan of the moment, yes."

Seldom leaned close. "This is great. You're so lucky."

Diamond said nothing.

The Master watched him until their eyes met, and then he laughed quietly and a little sadly. "I don't believe in luck. I never have. 'Good fortune is the sweat of good acts,' says the proverb. But if ever there was a creature smiled upon by Fate, it has to be you, my boy."

"I don't feel lucky," Diamond admitted.

His tutor leaned close, nodding. "Which is perhaps the best part of the blessing."

• • •

The canopy gave them a suitable gap, and dropping water, the *Happenstance* rose toward a place that Diamond already knew. Marduk welcomed him and welcomed everyone with its enduring trunk, with the landings and shops and the now-empty school that looked small against that great wall of bark. A vessel designed for speed had to coast and crawl its way around to the far side. Some features were familiar. Elata pointed to the public walkway where Diamond had crashed and healed again. He looked the other way. Where was the falling water? But the runoff always dried by afternoon, Seldom explained. There was no mist, the air dry and clear, and the green sunlight was on the brink of being extinguished. Hearing big engines, people came out from their homes to watch the first fletch ship they had ever seen in this space. They waved with exaggerated motions. Elata and Seldom waved back. Father left to help guide the pilot, and the engine that hadn't been broken before started leaking smoke, making the air stink. Then the *Happenstance* got into position, its nose pointed at Marduk, and the engines were throttled back and more water was dropped, and Diamond felt the world falling around them.

Nearly forty people were sharing one large landing. Seldom pointed and hollered. "My mother. Your mother too. Do you see her, Elata?"

"Yeah, I do."

Karlan was alone at the railing, standing almost exactly where he had been when he tossed Diamond over the edge. He was still wearing the school uniform. He looked as if he hadn't moved all day, waiting for this moment, and now it had arrived and he wasn't happy or sad or anything. He just stared at the spectacle and at Diamond, and then Diamond waved to him and Karlan's face flushed and he pretended to be fascinated by the smoking engine.

Every landing was crowded with people, save one. The pilot nudged them ahead, and the little gangway was dropped and secured to the weather-stripped wood. Citizens were hanging on the various ropes above, and they jammed the walkways. But only three people occupied the landing. Two of the strangers remained near the ladder. A woman was standing alone in front of the curtain, two women's faces watching the world, and as his parents walked Diamond down the gangway, each said, "This is our Archon."

Their voices were the same, quiet and respectful.

Prima was smaller than Diamond imagined, and younger. She stared at him as if one hard look would answer every mystery. But nothing was answered, so she turned to the face that she knew best. "Merit," said the Archon. "We haven't seen each other since when? The Festival of Lasts, wasn't it?"

"Something in that order. Yes, madam."

"And it's been too long, Haddi. How are you holding up?"

"Well enough," Mother said.

The short woman bent lower. An adult who had no children, she was both too formal and too eager to be a friend. Her smile was brilliant. She spoke with a voice accustomed to being listened to. "So. So you are the famous Diamond."

"Yes, ma'am."

A buzz of voices fell from above.

Diamond looked up at the staring faces, and his Archon dropped to a knee, saying, "It's been a storm of rumors, I'm afraid. Your father's crew talked, and my staff said too much, and now every call line in the District is busy. And do you know what people are saying? The kinder voices, I mean. They are saying that you are some great gift from the Creators, and today you bested the big Archon, and you have magical powers, and by the way, you turned the flagship into torn cloth and scrap metal."

Diamond didn't know how to react.

"A quiet boy," she judged. Then she stood, waving for her assistants to approach.

The Master and other children joined the group.

"There are some weighty legal questions," Prima told everyone. "But the best course, from what I can see, is that my office and my good word grant you asylum from other claims. So long as you stay inside the Corona District, you are my guest. You are protected and free, and let's let the lawyers fight the rest of the battles for us. Does that sound like a reasonable strategy?"

Diamond didn't know whether to nod or not. He decided to turn to his mother, asking, "May I go inside? I'm tired."

His parents laughed, their exhaustion easy to see.

The Archon made the decision. Backing away, she told everyone, "Diamond wants to finish his journey home. Let's allow him, please."

Diamond walked.

His parents and Nissim stayed behind, discussing abstract matters of state and law and simple decency.

Seldom and Elata fell in beside the boy, each asking if he or she could see him tomorrow.

"Maybe," he started to say.

A rough voice interrupted. From his perch on the railing, the orange-headed monkey shouted, "Good."

One of the assistants took it as his duty to shoo the animal away. But Diamond said, "No, please, leave him alone."

"He's yours?" the man asked doubtfully.

"I'm his," Diamond answered. He gave Good the finger that was bit off once, and the monkey looked at it and at him and then cackled wildly. Then both walked to the curtain, and Diamond turned, telling Seldom and Elata, "Come by after school."

They nodded and giggled.

Good and then Diamond entered the otherwise empty house, walking the hall by the long way around, passing rooms that the boy had never entered and slipping through a kitchen that desperately needed to be cleaned. The side hallway to his open door seemed far too short, and his room was too small for either of them. Diamond left the door open. The monkey casually shoved the papio books off their high shelf and started to build a nest with shredded pieces of an old blanket, looking nothing but happy.

Diamond left him to his work. Shoving Mister Mister under his arm, he crawled to the tiny chamber with its locked drawers and rounded walls. He didn't expect to find a secret door waiting. But he was ready to find that door wherever he looked, and in the end that might be what his day meant.

Diamond was ready, and he always needed be.

BOOK TWO

THE CORONA'S CHILDREN

PROLOGUE

Every soldier is born from wood—the finely grained wood of a tantalize tree carved and polished until the faces and strong arms and an array of dangerous weapons have been revealed. Every soldier wears paint and time. Each stands where he is set, a willing part of the colorful army that obeys every command. The soldiers never suffer fear, never know doubt, and despite similarities in appearance, each wears a unique name that serves as the trusted root from which one great life dangles.

The boy gave the wood their names and life stories. One glance, even a slow touch, is enough to recognize each good soldier.

The boy always knows where his army waits—on high shelves or inside their special box. Of course the soldiers aren't waiting. Toys are objects, and objects are too simple to hold souls. But playing with the wooden men is more fun because it means nothing. Almost every day of his life holds games like these. His fierce legion battles bigger toys and pretend monsters. Each piece of painted wood is awarded its turn as hero. Then as the boy grows older and a little smarter about the world, he makes larger wars, and his voice is louder, filling his very big room with fury and brutality until sometimes the game goes too well and he makes himself afraid.

Like other children, he climbs to school to learn and tries to be normal, and then he climbs home again and plays games.

The warriors lie scattered across the floor, on their backs and bellies, yet they are beautifully unable to concede defeat.

Wood cannot breathe, cannot weep, cannot stand back from the carnage and wonder where the battle went wrong.

"It's your game," says Mother. "If you don't like the results, pick up the pieces and start again."

"But these are the dead." He tries to be patient, except that he doesn't sound patient. Pointing to the casualties, he explains, "They have to rest all night to be alive again. Those are the rules."

Every game has rules. Life and the Creation have rules. Maybe there are agents somewhere that don't obey the hard codes, but thinking that way invites a different kind of fear into the mind.

"It's time for your early dinner," his mother says, trying to make him stop.

Dinner isn't ready. But he sets the dead inside their anglewood box, waiting to live, and the survivors stand on the shelves with a view of the green outdoors, helping watch for Father. The boy moves to the kitchen, sitting on the counter while his mother cooks and cools the various parts of the meal. Eating is a great pleasure. Nobody in their household eats like him. He loves sitting with his long legs dangling, talking about school and friends and what special things happened in the day, and when Father isn't home, the boy always asks when he will be.

Father used to be gone overnight, but that has changed.

Quite a lot is different now.

Mother laughs as she cooks. Vents pull the odors outside, and an orange-headed monkey is drawn by the smells, walking past the front curtain and through the house door, ready to eat.

The monkey owns the boy.

That is the way the world looks to the monkey. His name is Good, and he is smarter and nicer than most orange-heads. But he isn't *much* nicer. Jumping up on the counter, he tells the boy, "Move."

The boy slides a very short distance.

"Food," the monkey says.

There are indoor rules. Good cannot open drawers or the cooler and certainly not the oven, even if the fires are off. He has his own plate and cup, and he can eat his share of the day's first and last meals. But he isn't allowed to bite anyone, even the boy. And if he curses, which happens too often, Good is sent outdoors again, sometimes for the entire night.

Animals sleep outside.

Good is not an animal. He says so when he behaves himself, proving every other monkey inferior.

He loves his boy, even if he comes across as an irritable beast, giving orders with his muscular body and the crisp, fierce language. They sleep together in the boy's big bed. Every night Good makes a fresh nest out of torn paper and clean rags, and he always uses the room's chamber pot or house toilet to relieve himself, and there haven't been any important mistakes for two hundred days. But Mother still doesn't approve of Good. "Who else in the world invites an orange-head to her dinner table?" she asks.

"Nobody," the monkey says, happy for the easy meat and sweet cold fruit.

A long table stands in a special room beyond the kitchen. The boy has the important job of setting plates and utensils in their places, which doesn't take long, and then he and Good may go outside to wait. Father usually arrives when the sunlight looks tired and the faraway trees fade to sloppy, ill-defined greens and browns. People across the world are coming home. Marduk is a great ancient and very important tree. The only door to the outside leads to a new curtain wearing a giant corona, and past the corona is a new landing that looks like no other: its railing is tall and every wooden slat stands close to its neighbor, like soldiers ready to march, barely any room for a sideways hand to reach through. A great net is suspended overhead, every thin rope close to its neighbors and more ropes pulling the net outwards to create a lovely high dome. There is only one gate where people can come through. Monkeys can slip past the largest gaps but nothing larger. Birds and young leatherwings sometimes fall in through the same holes, and sometimes they can't get away, flying about panicked and helpless, and the boy never likes that.

Three people are always on duty at the gate. Two inside and one beyond the landing. They are usually men and each is a guard, which is a kind of soldier, though they don't wear uniforms and their guns are kept hidden.

Each guard has several names and a full long life that the boy didn't invent. He knows their faces and pieces of their stories, and some of them are friendly and some prefer to act like wood, tough and immune to whatever happens in the world. No matter who they are, the boy calls to them by their names, and sometimes Good teases the guards, knowing just how bad to be without finding real trouble.

As a rule, guards curse easily and with great skill.

Night is coming into the world now, darkness rising out from the cool shadows, and then Father arrives with his own guard walking before him.

There are reasons for these precautions.

"Fear is the main reason," Father has said. "Most of the fears aren't even real, except when they live between the ears."

The gate is unlocked for Father.

He enters and bends over, grabbing at the boy who barely looks human, what with the long legs and wrong feet and arms that are stronger than they appear but never gain the meat that even a runty girl would possess. But he loves this boy utterly, and they hug, and locking the gate behind him, an inside guard might say, "Good evening, Merit."

His parents are Merit and Haddi, and those aren't uncommon names.

But only one creature in the world is named Diamond, and he kisses his father's scarred old face while Good hurries into the lead, already tasting dinner with a monkey's keen imagination.

• • •

After guarding the gate, these retired soldiers have forms to fill with careful words describing their uneventful shifts. Once the forms are filed, they are required to train hard at one portion of their unique job—marksmanship or risk-rating or hand-to-hand combat. Then they are free to stamp out and go home to their mates and children, if there are any, and they will end up in whatever bed is best, and they usually sleep hard for as long as possible. But whenever they awaken, day or night, their first duty is to fill out another set of forms describing their dreams and any second thoughts about the previous shift.

Parts of what they do make sense to them.

They assume what feels silly is really smart, but they don't waste the effort trying to piece together the obscure logic.

These strong men and very strong women are the result of a long, careful search. Each was born and raised in the Corona District, although their parents might have been born elsewhere. They have unblemished service records and no secrets left to uncover, and by most standards, they are neither political nor religious people. But the most important quality shared by each is a supreme, nearly superhuman capacity to avoid opinions about that one strange boy.

The guards' identities are supposed to be confidential, but the District isn't large enough for anonymity, particularly when the subject proves so fascinating. Every guard faces moments when a cousin or childhood buddy or that pretty woman on the stool beside him asks questions.

Simple questions are easy to deflect, and rare.

Everybody knows quite a lot about the boy already. Four magical creatures were rescued from the belly of the ancient corona, but despite his odd proportions and the curly hair and a nose that looks tiny against his very peculiar face, Diamond seems to be some kind of person. He certainly looks more like the guards than he looks like the papio. But his unique birth and curious appearance aren't half as fascinating as his freakish, unnatural capacity to heal.

That's what people ask about when they think they have permission.

"How fast does he heal?" they want to know.

"Have you ever seen him badly injured?" they inquire, hoping for stories of carnage and rebirth.

"Is it true?" they ask. "Can the creature cut off his own hand and then push it back on the wrist, and the hand reattaches in one or two recitations?"

No guard earns his pay by answering the wrong people's questions. But if they told the truth, their audiences would be disappointed, probably dismissing the answers as lies. Diamond rarely suffers anything worse than scrapes or splinters. Four hundred days of shadowing the child has produced remarkably few tales about weathering injuries or other mayhem. And there haven't been a dozen incidents where somebody had to brandish a pistol or wrestle some troublemaker to the floor.

Maybe the guards aren't necessary. It's possible that there aren't any dangers looming over Diamond. But every person likes to believe that he or she is doing important work, and that's why the guards see their own work as being instrumental, nobody else doing half as much to keep the client safe.

"And who are you protecting him from?" civilians might ask.

But everyone knows the answers. The world is the upper half of the Creation, and there can be nothing else. Old faiths are the most enduring, and every old faith, human or papio, claim that the walls of this world are its ends. Certain people whisper and grumble. They say that these strange entities—the four children of the corona—are abominations. Guards know that whispers often turn into action. Except this boy acts nicer than most boys, and he seems utterly harmless. Inside his home district, Diamond's presence is usually taken as a blessing, and maybe he is a great blessing, just as their Archon says.

Trapped inside the corona's stomach, the children weren't dead and they weren't alive. Rumors claim that the papio took possession of the biggest prize, but rumors are liquid, hard to hold and never the same shape twice. No authoritative eye has witnessed anything that casts a shadow. Of course it can be assumed that the papio are plotting to steal the most human child. But complicating the problems is a different mess of rumors about a secretive monster that lives in the wilderness, hiding between the old forests and the reef. If that monster exists, then one has to wonder if it will slip into the District some day or some night, aiming to steal away its one-time sibling. What the guards can't dismiss, they have to believe. And then there's Diamond's famous brother who lives at the very center of the world, in the palace with the Archon of Archons. Except for having arms and legs and one head set on top of a giant body, that monster barely resembles humans or the boy or even the biggest papio. That powerful creature is covered with armored scales and bright sharp spikes, and he has two mouths and a burly temper, and he happily wears the name King, which is an ominous old word.

Every guard appreciates that List, the Archon of Archons, is ambitious and unnaturally shrewd, cultivating the talents of his adoptive son while no doubt wishing to steal Diamond away, earning him a special place on the chart of worries.

No matter how much is known, a great deal is mystery. No opinion should feel like steel. But Diamond has been tested by doctors and scientists.

Blood and hair and his skin have been studied with every available tool, and according to the smartest gossip, he is surely the most human among the four.

This intrigues the average citizen more than anything else.

Yes, the boy seems indestructible. But his magic blood looks and tastes like ordinary blood. Under a microscope, his skin is indistinguishable from human flesh. Tree-walkers and the papio have very similar bones, varying a little in shape in shape and size, and it's the same with Diamond. Every human is assembled according to the same orderly rules. What's more, Diamond's voice and most of his manners are familiar enough, and if you didn't see his odd face, you might think that you were talking to any child.

Unknown beasts and the armored King can make the public marvel only to a point. Similarities are what make Diamond the biggest wonder among the corona's children, giving rise to dreams and endless and nearly crazy speculations.

Guards should never discuss their duties or observations with the world outside. But in their own realm, when two or five or ten of them are together in the same private room, they'll trade stories about the boy and his odd ways and the monkey nobody likes and the school where Diamond pretends to be normal. Drinks help the guards share frank opinions about the boy's friends and his teacher and those old people who pretend to be his parents. Then one of the guards, usually someone who has been off-duty for a few days, will turn to the others, and with a quiet, careful voice, he or she will ask what matters beyond everything else:

"Are his whiskers coming in?

"Is he losing that little kid voice?

"Any sign, anywhere, that his seeds are trying to move?"

• • •

Diamond's parents work to immerse their son inside a happy, half-normal life. The boy has friends and routines that include attending the local school with only minimal precautions in place. Bright children deserve the best teachers, and the boy has a genuine Master named Nissim—a one-time butcher and scientific scholar brought to the Corona District through some fusion of fate and odd opinions.

In principle, Diamond is free to travel anywhere inside the local District, but always accompanied by his guards. Calibrated intrigues try to deflect the uncounted, mostly invisible enemies. Meanwhile, important people have traveled across the world just to shake his hot hand and match his white smile. List has visited the boy several times, usually for important civic events, bringing that odd shrill voice to make apologies for deeds that might be regretted and disasters that were misunderstood. He even brought his monster son for the last visit, which meant that ten guards were stationed in the same room, each hoping for the excuse to shoot King, leaving him temporarily dead. But the armored creature said nothing except polite words, and King left without challenging his brother, not with either mouth or a single one of his armored fingers.

The local Archon has always been the boy's great champion. Prima was adored long before this wonder-child fell into her lap. No other Archon could have handled her citizens with the same graceful ease.

The other Archons are considered the same as generals and scientists. They can't visit the boy at home. Home remains a sanctuary clad in nets and guards and sensible rules. Prima is the sole exception. She is welcome to walk through the corona-adorned curtain, and portions of her staff can come along. But nobody will argue if the parents say, "No." Nobody dares. Master Nissim is also welcome, and certain trusted neighbors have attended occasional feasts held on the big new landing, and every happy boy deserves to have good friends.

For four hundred days, public opinion has held steady as an old blackwood: the boy is a prize leftover from the Creation, and he could well be a treasure too. If the big Archon wants to steal Diamond away from them, then Diamond certainly must be a creature worth knowing.

Hundreds of children attend the Marduk school, but barely a dozen are allowed inside Diamond's home gate. After classes, once every three or four days, a group gathers on the landing. Ancient contests like tag and spider-scramble lead to new games invented for the occasion, using whatever props and moods are on hand. Diamond isn't a natural climber. His arms are short, his instincts slow. Everybody else finishes before their friend climbs to the top of the net and back down again. But the boy runs faster than anyone on the flat wood, and he rides a bicycle built to fit his long legs, and when the current game ignores him, he quietly settles down to do nothing while his friends play, sitting next to the stoic guards while gazing at the net overhead, screams and laughter filling the space, right up until Haddi steps outside, arms waving as she chases away the chaos.

Exactly two children are special enough to be invited into the boy's room.

Seldom is a slight but growing boy, and Elata is still a sharp-tongued girl with a strong build and very little fear.

A team of workmen bearing hammers and chisels enlarged the old room, with the compliments of the local Archon. An oval hole has been cut through the thick brown bark, and two sheets of transparent coral glass have been set inside the new window, tiny bars of the best steel lending strength to that very expensive indulgence.

The three children play near the window. Seldom likes board games with complicated rules that he knows better than anyone else. Elata is fond of puzzles and reading stories. "No better friends could exist," Haddi often tells him. Diamond understands comfort and happiness when just the three of them are sharing his fine new room. He likes his classmates and always tries to be pleasant, getting along with them and everyone else too. But sometimes Diamond's hand makes a foolish move before letting go of the wooden disc or the coral warship. His turn is over and those are the rules, except he hears himself asking Seldom for a second chance. He'll claim that he didn't mean to do what he did or he doesn't understand the rules yet. His complaining doesn't sound like complaining, and he has a big smile, and if Seldom ever says, "No," then the matter will end. But Seldom never tells Diamond, "No. Now it's my turn." He always lets his friend pull the piece back, and sometimes he even coaches by throwing his eyes in an important direction.

Seldom never gives Elata second chances, and noticing as much, she sits on her hands, saying nothing.

Sometimes Diamond complains while playing with the girl's puzzles, using a tone that isn't angry but isn't nice either, convincing Elata maybe half of the time to give him what he wants.

Games are wrapped inside games, and Diamond wages these little battles just to win thin, unnamed prizes.

His attitudes are less subtle when a big group shares the landing. Bodies run and climb, balls flying and the guards standing safely to one side. Diamond invents a new flourish to the current game—something he can do better than anyone else. Explaining himself in a few words, he usually wins allies and believers. But sometimes the other children don't want to play that way. One or two of them might even insult their host, claiming he isn't being fair. There have been days when this good boy with his strange life and his various mysteries will walk up to the guards and ask politely that so-and-so be sent home now, and if they can't learn how to play nicely, maybe that name should be sliced off the friends-list.

Small moments like these are always noticed.

Children and the guards see them. It's possible to find an alarming trend at work. Or maybe underneath the oddness, he is an ordinary, immature boy.

But people are watching.

Marduk is one tree hanging inside a vast forest. Every tree is covered with apartments and windows, and there are people wielding telescopes, staring at this one house with the corona on the curtain and the boy that nobody can explain. Even indoors, playing with his two great friends, several sets of eyes are fixed Diamond, reading lips and guessing his thoughts. Then night rises and the household falls asleep, and peering into the darkness, magnifying the last glows of lights and candles, these same watchers study the prize as it settles into sleep and dreams.

• • •

Every soldier wears a name and a rich life full of exploits that the boy can summon at will. Every soldier has died multiple times, always as a hero, and Diamond sits on the varnished blackwood floor with those gangly legs trying to make a knot, stunted toes curling as he talks, replaying the killing blows from swords and bullets and arrows and gigantic bombs. He doesn't remember every game played—his mind isn't that relentless. But death should be memorable and tens of thousands of good deaths beg to be shared, and it is easy to forget that even best friends don't have feelings for chips of wood and these elaborate stories.

Elata bores first, and she's first to complain.

"Let's do something more, anything else," she says. "Or we can do nothing, maybe. Nothing can be fun too, if you do it right."

Seldom wants to be patient, and where he can, he wants to uncover whatever proves fun. Nobody in the world has such a friend, and sitting in this one room, feeling bored, is an honor that can't just be thrown away. So he listens to the soldiers' names and the battle names. Seldom is smart but doesn't wield this kind of memory. When he concentrates, the play-fight becomes crisp loud images living inside his head, and with a boy's instinct for violence and heroism, he listens as Diamond moves hundreds of men across a complicated landscape that doesn't resemble any part of the world.

Nobody else has the honor to be bored and mesmerized in exactly this way.

One day, listening to the history of a pretend war fought five hundred days ago, a good new thought finds Seldom:

Diamond is a puzzle.

Their friend is huge and intricate and maybe without answers, and those various puzzle parts are set inside a human-shaped box.

They are talking to a box, and the box talks to them.

Except now Elata and Seldom and the box are snacking on finger-dabs, and thirty-seven soldiers have been charged with defending a fortress built from armor and white light.

The enemy is a monstrous giant marching its way up the long hill.

"What does that mean?" asks Elata. "What is a hill?"

She is interested, but only a little bit.

Diamond stops talking. He doesn't want to stop, but he can't let the question go unanswered. " 'Hill' is a papio word. The ground of the world rises to one high point."

But that's not quite how the papio use it.

Elata squints. "What, like on the reef? At the edge of the world?"

Diamond pauses, considering.

"That's where this is, on the reef," says Seldom, and he bends forward, wanting the story to continue.

But Diamond says, "No, it isn't on the reef. I'm talking about a different hill."

Seldom is wrong, which makes him uncomfortable.

Diamond uses hands and words to describe what he imagines—a cone resting on a flat surface. There are few trees in this place and they grow in the wrong direction, rising up instead of dangling down. And the cone is a tall important place on this impossible terrain, and so it must be defended to the last man.

"I don't understand," Elata complains.

Seldom doesn't understand either. But he won't say it.

"Did you imagine this after our visit to the reef?" Elata asks.

Diamond shakes his head. "This game was from before. This is one of the first big battles that I ever thought up."

"It's just a game," Seldom says.

Elata shakes her head. "I don't know."

The three of them sit quietly, each working with the problem.

"I've asked this already," says Elata. "But what do you remember from before? Before you were living with your folks and us, I mean."

The boy closes his eyes.

"Nothing," he says.

"Inside the corona," she says.

Diamond shakes his head.

Then Seldom sees what has always wanted to be noticed. Leaning forward, he says, "The cone and fort . . . maybe they're leftover from your life before . . . "

Diamond thinks for a moment. "Maybe," is all he can say.

"Maybe you were a soldier once," Elata says, "and you battled the monsters in the same way."

"I don't think so," Diamond says.

The day is getting old. The evening meal is coming, and two of them will have to hurry home.

"But your memory is so good," Seldom says. "How can you forget everything from before?"

"Maybe there wasn't any 'before,' " Elata says.

"I don't know how long I was inside the corona," Diamond says.

The finger-dabs have made Seldom hungry. He stands and waits for Elata to stand, ready to walk out together.

But she doesn't get up.

"I don't think you were a soldier either," she says.

"You said he was," Seldom says.

"I was wrong," she says. "He was just a baby, and the game came with him from somewhere else."

She gets up, and Seldom moves toward the door.

"Monsters," she says.

The boys look at her, each with a serious face.

"I hope your monsters don't come here looking for you," she says.

Then both friends hurry out the room's door and the house's door, past the waiting guards, running hard and not just because their stomachs are complaining.

• • •

Dream has a longer reach than memory.

The boy sleeps, putting him in a realm where the ordinary dances with the fantastic. This is the nature of dream. But there are faces that he sees while he sleeps—reliable, familiar faces—that look so much like his face. The same few voices whisper to him and sing to him in a dense quick language that has never been heard in this Creation. Yet Diamond understands every word. He must understand them because when they talk, he laughs, and then they talk again and he cries. Those known faces are smiling and weeping as they deliver some vital last instruction—shaking him to help him remember—and he tries hard to remember, pulling his limp body out of the sleep, back into the room that he knows better than any other.

Diamond is awake, and what did the dreams tell him?

Quite a lot, but all he remembers is the warm touch of familiar hands.

Good sleeps at his feet, chirping as his dreaming legs twitch. The boy sits up in bed, measuring the darkness, deciding that the night is in no mood to leave. Slipping out from under the sheets, he tiptoes through the bedroom and past the kitchen, entering the tiny closet where a polished coral bowl waits for his urine.

His pee smells different from other people's pee.

Finished with the chore, he continues touring home, passing his parents' bedroom where a curtain hangs and two different chests breathe and growl, his mother muttering wet words about being quick and careful.

It seems that everybody is caught up in dreams tonight.

The next turn delivers him to the front of the house. His father's gray work clothes used to hang inside the one large closet there, but he doesn't hunt coronas anymore. As a testament to his age and skill, or maybe because his son misses him when he is gone, Merit has been made into a teacher. He works at the Ivory Station on Hanner, when he works. His clothes are normal now. Only one uniform remains—armored fabric closer to white than black and dark goggles and boots designed to protect careless feet—and those items hang at the back of the closet, clean enough to appear new and barely smelling of corona blood and guts.

Diamond likes to stare at the uniform, letting his mind be fooled into seeing a person dangling against the black wall.

The outside door is always locked at night. Steel and choice woods are stronger than the tree. On the other side of that door, on this side of the curtain, sits one of the guards. His stool is tall and easy to tip. The guard is never supposed to sleep. That's why Diamond uses knuckles to hit the door, and he steps back and counts the moments before his protector thumps at the wood with an elbow, saying hello.

Then the boy returns to his room.

Good stirs long enough to lift his fierce head, staring at the half-naked shape that approaches his nest.

"Sleep," says Diamond.

"Sleep," the monkey agrees, curling into a fetal tuck and lost again.

But the other inhabitant is too alert to climb back into bed, much less try to rest. Instead he picks soldiers from the shelves and arranges them in a half-circle, every blind face pointing at their owner, their general.

Nothing about the moment feels special.

Many nights stretch too long, and the boy often wakes early and sits near one of the night lights, playing quietly, waiting for fatigue to claim him.

If he is patient, sometimes the dreams reveal themselves.

But this is not one of those nights.

Diamond moves the soldiers into a perfect circle, every face looking outwards, and he leaves them, walking to the window. A greater richer darkness sits beyond the reinforced panes. The landing juts far out into the air, and the net is a popular perch for the glowing insects and buzzing insects that don't exist in the day. With an ear to the glass, he listens to the rasping, chittering songs. Sitting to his right is a second guard, barely in view, feet up and eyes plainly closed and the boy wondering what he could throw at the window that would scare the man.

A heavy rubber ball sits inside a toy box, waiting to be used.

Diamond follows his memory to the box and opens the lid, reaching inside with his free hand, memory closing his fingers. The ball is black, but everything is black in the darkness. Remembering the wooden soldiers, Diamond crosses the room again, passing the ball to the other hand and back again, never looking where his bare feet touch.

One of the soldiers isn't where he expects it to be.

The boy has never been bigger, never heavier, and the heel of his left foot pushes hard against the bayonet and then the helmeted head.

Pain is quick, but he is too distracted to notice.

The soldier fights bravely, jabbing the fake blade into the giant's foot, but the pressure is enormous and an ancient flaw in the wood reveals itself with a bright sharp crack that makes a monkey jump to his feet.

Diamond drops the ball and then his body. The sharpest piece of tantalize wood is buried inside him, and it hurts no worse than a nuisance. Mostly he is angry and sorry, unsure how the toy was somewhere it didn't belonged. Two pieces of the body are on the floor, and he yanks the third from his heel, the blood already retreating inside the torn skin while the entire foot warms even more than normal.

The soldier might be repaired.

If Diamond asks, Father will do that.

But the questions of glue and craftsmanship fall away. The burly monkey stands at the edge of the bed, his head cocked to one side while the black eyes gaze at nothing. Maybe he can hear something. That's why Diamond listens, following Good's example. And maybe he hears something too. But when it happens and even afterwards, the sensation isn't so much like a voice or any other sound. No. It is as if the little sounds of the world cease. The endless play of tree trunks bending and winds drifting, insects celebrating the dark while fifty million souls mutter in their collective sleep—all of these noises suddenly fall away.

Silence finds Diamond.

And the silence has shape and color, and it has meanings as deep and true as any word, and this misplaced boy suddenly hears what can only be a warning.

"Be wary," says the presence, the Other.

Diamond isn't breathing, and he might never breathe again.

"Danger is everywhere," it says.

In the quietest fashion, Diamond whispers, "Monsters."

"There are no monsters," says the voice.

Diamond fumbles with words, with concepts. Then to the invisible agent, he says, "But there are evil ones."

"No."

"What do you mean?"

"There is no evil," the voice warns. "Everything is good, and that is the ruin of All . . . !"

ONE

Wind came before the sun.

Nothing changed and nothing changed, night holding tight to the world, and then wet hot masses of angry air rose in a thousand places, suddenly punching their way through the demon floor far below the vast tree canopy.

Shifting pressures were felt. Every ear heard portentous rumblings from below. Leaves twisted in response, ready to let the wind pass, while nocturnal insects found hiding places and sleeping birds instinctively clung to prized perches. The empty air between the demon floor and canopy was crossed in a few recitations. The first impacts lifted small limbs while broad strong branches creaked and moaned but refused to bend, fighting the rising wind until the atmosphere turned furious, and then the entire canopy groaned with wrenching voices, the first touch of the day driving itself up where the great trees hung from the roof of the world.

Hundreds of thousands of nights had ended exactly this way, and Marduk had endured each of those mornings. Strong dead heartwood and the vigorous sapwood formed a single column encased inside bark and walkways and landings and homes. Every airship was in its berth, securely tethered. Bright electric lights blazed in the gloom, along with luminescent panels and forgotten candles. Rope lifts and elevators were shut down, and the few people who found themselves outdoors felt the tree shiver and heard the wind's roar pressing close, and buttoning down whatever raingear was in reach, they either dropped low and grabbed hold of any likely handle, or they took a different measure of the danger, walking to the edge of a landing, watching the gale come straight up into their grinning faces.

Good and Diamond were awake and maybe they had been for a little while. Each yawned, and the boy sat up in bed as the first spray of rain swept across the window, and the monkey jumped to the floor and shuffled over to the old chamber pot, efficiently doing his business.

On the floor beneath the bed was a fancy metronome—a recent gift from his Archon, from Prima. Diamond pulled it out. Eight hundred recitations was the count—a short night. But he had guessed twelve hundred, judging by how hard he slept and how rested he felt and no residue of dreams.

Good helped himself to the bakebear fruit left from last night. Picking up the chamber pot, Diamond walked down the hallway, dumping the pot and using the toilet and then washing his hands with the hard soap that smelled like bride-witch flowers. By the time he returned to his room, the wind was screaming and there was as much water as there was air outside. The monkey was back on the bed, napping on Diamond's warm pillow. Diamond pushed his face against the reinforced glass. An electric security light rocked above the locked gate. Two guards were huddled beside the gate, one inside and one out, each wearing a rubber poncho blacker than the rest of the world, resembling lumpy globs of corona fat, faceless and unwilling to move. But the third guard had abandoned his post at the house doorway, standing at the far end of the landing instead. Wearing a long poncho, the figure was perched on the brink of the open air, both hands on the railing and the feet apart, short strong legs and the stronger shoulders able to fend off the gusts and the sprays of water and every reasonable urge to stay safe and dry.

Short nights usually brought small rains and quick bright dawns.

Diamond put on yesterday's play trousers and shirt, and then he sat beside the monkey, thinking about nothing, about everything, his mind following no particular direction while the first trace of the sun began to emerge.

Good woke and grunted at him.

The boy put two of his fingers inside the monkey's mouth, on top of the very wet tongue.

"No," Good said, spitting him out.

Nobody liked to be teased.

The ruddy glow was strongest near the trees, while out in the distance, where the water was thickest, the storm pushed like hot fingers high into the forest.

Diamond slid off the bed again.

"Stay," said Good.

"You stay," he said.

"No."

One led the other to the locked house door, and Diamond threw the steel bolt and pushed against the pressurized air. The storm slipped through the gaps and around their feet, and then the bright keening sound fell away, leaving the home quiet again.

Good went as far as the curtain, where he planted his feet, saying, "I tell. I tell I am good, you are bad."

"All right," the boy said, pushing through the heavy curtain.

The first touch of rain always felt chilled, which was peculiar because it was warm enough to be bathwater. His clothes were drenched in an instant. Bare feet slid across the face of the landing, and noticing him, the sitting guards yelled at each other. The man inside the gate fought his way to his feet, but he plainly didn't want to bother with this craziness.

Diamond broke into a slow run.

The original landing had been small, old, and in poor repair, and on her own authority, the Archon decided to have it torn away, replacing the structure with more wood and a fine eye on security. In principle, there was no way for Diamond to be hurt. The worst storm might throw him around, but the net and high railing wouldn't let him fall. Freak winds sometimes broke necks, but his neck would heal, and this happened to be a weak dawn already past its most dangerous prime.

The one guard shuffled after him, shouting with all of his authority, words scrubbed by the wind until nothing remained except anger mixed with a great heap of outrage: his slight comfort had been disturbed by a boy's impulse.

The third guard was still standing at the rail. Hearing the shouts, the broad back straightened, and leaving one hand holding tight, he turned and knelt down, putting his face even with the boy's. But it wasn't any face that Diamond expected. He knew every guard, and this was somebody else. Pulling up short, he gave a little jump, and the man shouted, "Your mother is going to be angry with you."

"With both of us," Diamond said.

"Probably so," Father said.

"Where's the other guard?"

"He went home sick. I volunteered to take over."

The unexpected always made the boy laugh.

Then Father swung his free hand, as if clearing a space beside him. "You can't get any wetter, I suppose. So come here and have a good look, before we pay your mother's price."

• • •

But Mother was in an agreeable mood. She had to give both of them her cutting gaze, shaking her head in supreme disappointment, but there wasn't a word about her son being drenched or her husband pretending to be a dangerous young man. She reminded them where to find clean towels. She promised a rack of heart-melons if her boys would pull them from the oven in ten, no, nine recitations. Then she opened the house line and began calling women-friends, organizing her day.

Diamond and his father ate the roasted melons and dipped yesterday's baby loafs in sweet oil, and Good consumed his share before hurrying outdoors, ready to defend his territory and perhaps have fun with his girlfriends. There was still time for a second meal before school. School occupied only the long middle of each day, save for holidays and vacations and illness. Except Diamond never became sick. A stomach virus once made half of his class throw up, but not him. Germs were no more dangerous than the air to him. Yet people talked about feeling better after vomiting, and on the principle that he might feel better than he was, he sometimes used a finger, vainly trying to take part in this ritual of purging and renewal.

Diamond's class was built on its busy formalities. There were friends and the friendly-enough others, plus Master Nissim loomed at the front of the room, and the boy liked much of it. But the great joy of his spectacular new life was wearing the school's deep brown uniform and a pair of leather boots designed specifically for his odd feet.

After the last baby loaf, Diamond cleaned his white teeth and washed the most important pieces of his body, and then he went to his room to dress.

New guards were on station. A tall man stood beside the window, dressed as any office worker, golden trousers pressed and the black dress shirt tied around the waist with two purple cords. His name was Tar`ro, and he looked rather sleepy, which was normal enough. But he spotted the boy immediately, and after offering a little nod, he pointed his half-open gaze forwards again, studying the mists and falling waters as they were polished by the day's new sunshine.

Tar`ro was perhaps Diamond's favorite. He had a strong, memorable voice, and he seemed to notice everything, and unlike most of his colleagues, the man would bend rules, chatting amiably with his client.

Diamond tapped at the heavy glass.

Without turning around, Tar`ro said, "Bits and Sophia."

Bits was a stocky little man, and Sophia was one of the few women guards. They were on morning duty too.

Yesterday's school uniform was dirty, but three others hung in the cupboard, waiting their turn. They were cut for his body; nobody else in the world could happily wear these clothes. Diamond put on the trousers and shirt and then tied both belts with the official knots, and then he set his boots by the door before propping the stepladder next to a wall covered with shelves. Soldiers stood at attention, waiting for orders. "Do nothing," he said, reaching past them. A big book begged to be read, and he brought it down and sat on the edge of his bed, smelling the slow rot of ancient bindings and tired paper as he pulled open the plain gray cover.

The papio book sat the wrong way in his lap, no letter or little mark resembling anything found in a schoolbook.

Diamond read carefully, and every word was remembered. There were drawings in the book, and every drawing lived inside his head afterwards. Remembering where he stopped was easy. Understanding the familiar words was usually easy, although meanings could shift in odd, misleading ways. There was an entry about what humans called "woeful-vines"—poisonous plants that grew only at the edges of the creation. Their sap blistered skin, and their black leaves were full of acidic chemicals, and despite living only in deep shadow, they grew quickly, spreading by runners and sometimes producing toxic orange fruits that had never once displayed any interest in sprouting. Diamond was looking at a colored picture of the fruits when Father came into the room, and without looking up, the boy asked about a strange word.

"It means, 'Liar.' "

Diamond looked up. His father was dressed for his work. "I'm reading about woeful vines."

" 'Lying mock-snakes' is the rough translation."

The book was an encyclopedia meant for papio children. Diamond could remember quite a lot, but he struggled making his voice match what was written down. Several more words had tested him, and Father asked to see. Pages were turned and two of those odd words made sense, but the other three remained mysteries to both of them.

Father was wearing a green suit, still new and very elegant.

"Are you teaching?" his son asked.

"No, my day is nothing but meetings."

Merit didn't like meetings, but he preferred sitting in a room with anybody over hunting coronas with harpoons and explosives.

"In fact, I should be leaving," Father said. "So I'll see you tonight or maybe sooner, if I can slip away early."

Diamond closed the encyclopedia.

"Your mother is going out too," Father said.

The boy slid off his bed and followed him out of the room. In the hallway, just short of the front door, Merit bent to kiss his son's head, burying his lips into the thick and twisted brown hair, and Diamond kissed the last part of his father to leave, which was the back of one hand.

Mother was in his parent's bedroom. The small woman was sitting on a tall stool, working with her reflection in a mirror. Diamond had seen her wear those clothes twice before, always on special days. The tunic was gold with white flowers that weren't quite like any of the world's flowers. Her slacks were the kind of black that looked purple in a strong light. Haddi saw him watching, and guessing what question would come next, she said, "I'm going shopping with my cousins. You handle your next meal and get to school on time."

"Tar`ro will make sure I do," he said.

She looked at him. Old women usually weren't as pretty as she was. Her hair was still long and thick, white as sun-washed mist and now carefully combed and braided. Haddi's trousers had thick legs and the tunic reached down near her knees. Powder painted her face and jeweled clips rode the tops of her ears, one pink and the other pinker, and she was smiling even when she told her son, "Don't."

"Don't what?"

"These men are here for a purpose, and it's not to be servants, much less act like extra fathers."

"Sophia is here too."

Mother looked at the pale coral rings on her fingers. Again she said, "Don't."

"Don't want?"

"Deflect my very good point."

Was he doing that? Maybe, and he felt a little bit clever.

She said, "Darling," and looked at him. "You have your own responsibilities. And your father and I expect you to carry them out like any boy of your age."

"How old am I?"

For a third time, she said, "Don't."

Diamond remained silent.

"Normal lives. That's what we want. For the three of us, we want some existence that can be confused for ordinary."

She stood and worked on a single wrinkle on the blouse that refused to obey the sweep of her long hands.

He studied her wardrobe and face, as always.

"Do I look all right?"

"Yes."

She glanced at him.

"You look spectacular," he said, mimicking what Father offered at moments not unlike this.

Then she laughed softly and kissed him on the tiny, tiny nose. "Have a good day at school, son."

"I will."

She left the room, left their home.

Except of course Mother was still standing inside his mind, and for as long as he lived, there she would be.

• • •

No new day wanted to repeat the rhythms of its ancestors. Each morning found its pace and its perfect length, and the most unremarkable child was expert in reading signs, knowing when one thing had to end and another begin. But not Diamond: left alone, he arrived early to most events and ridiculously late for everything else. Metronomes counted recitations, but they only helped find rough answers. That's why the boy relied on friends and the endlessly competent guards, and that's why he was busily setting up a wooden army when he should have been leaving for school.

Tar`ro kicked the window with the heel of his boot, warning him that this morning was growing shabby.

Diamond gave his soldiers one last study and then ran for the front door.

The tall guard looked as if he had just been roused from an unhappy nap. But his voice was alert and pleasant. "Your monkey and I just had a nice chat. Did you know? I'm very stupid and he is very smart, and he has ten girlfriends for my ugly one, and that's why he pities me."

"Is that what Good said?"

Tar`ro grinned. "The message was implied."

No other guard talked this way, and Diamond was always interested in their game and how his own face tingled and grew warm.

Pulling the door curtain back into place, Diamond touched two of the heads of the painted corona, wishing for its protection.

Then Tar`ro led the boy to the gate.

Switches had to be turned, alerting unseen people about the client's movement. Two locks needed different keys. Sophia was stationed inside, Bits outside, and they worked together with neat, efficient motions.

The morning mists had disappeared. Following a weak rain, waters escaping from the high ponds and swollen bladders were barely able to hold together in one thin ribbon of tumbling water. Ten thousand winged creatures crisscrossed inside the bright air while endless voices screamed. The great old forest was vertical pillars of wood, none close to its neighbors, all hanging from the invisible roof of Creation. Diamond knew the names of every tree and how to recognize the various species. The canopy below was a dense dark green carpet, thousands of people and millions of animals living inside that tangle of branches and huts and farms and little factories. Diamond had often visited the canopy, and his father and Master Nissim twice took him to the highest portions of the District, showing him that odd realm never touched by daylight. And of course he once flew through the wilderness and walked on the reef country. Almost no one was able to walk with the papio. Yet despite his experiences and the flawless memory, Diamond knew almost nothing about the people that he saw every day—those scurrying figures moving up and down the various home trees.

The gate opened with a sharp whine. Beyond was a small platform ending with a strong ladder leading only downwards. Bits took the lead, grabbing the ropes with hands and the insides of his boots, dropping neatly out of view.

From overhead, a voice called out, "Diamond."

"Your girlfriend," Sophia teased.

Elata.

"Go," Tar`ro told him.

That was the rule. Three guards had to stay close while he was outdoors, and Diamond knew that Bits would turn to vinegar if he were told to climb back up and wait for the neighbor girl.

Elata was standing on the walkway far above.

"Catch up," Diamond called.

"Don't tell her that," Tar`ro said.

Bare ropes used to dangle between there and here. They were a security risk and cut away, but that didn't keep a bold girl from climbing over the railing, jumping with limbs stretching out and her belly down.

Tar`ro cursed quietly, without heat, and again, he said, "Go."

Diamond took the ladder with one hand, but he moved slowly, watching Elata dive onto the highest portion of the net. Supporting ropes creaked, absorbing the impact. Laughing, she rolled down across the fine-meshed netting, reaching him in a few moments. Her trick was well-practiced, as was the guards' outrage. Some high boss had decided that the net would protect Diamond, and maybe it did, but not when it came to keeping one young girl away.

"Good morning, Diamond."

"Hello."

Elata loved falling. She was fearless and pretty and big in the shoulders, which were stronger shoulders than most people her age could muster, girl or boy. Her wide mouth suited her, as did the golden teeth, and her long straight hair always wanted to be tied into elaborate braids. Her uniforms were usually clean but sometimes thin in the elbows and knees. She had taught her friend how to climb, and she had watched him heal when he made mistakes and fell. But Elata never mentioned what both of them understood: Diamond would never be her match when it came to scampering up and down.

"I'm first," Elata said, slipping past him on the ladder.

Tar`ro cursed again, but he was laughing too.

These were daily games.

Diamond followed. From above, his new landing seemed large yet normal enough, but from below it was far more impressive. Great timbers of bloodwood had been brought from the District of Districts, bolted to Marduk to lend unusual strength to the supporting framework. Within the timbers was a protected berth where a police blimp could be tethered safely out of the elements. Different blimps rotated through, each one black as ink. Some crew was always on duty, and as the subject of all of this interest dropped onto the lower walkway, today's blimp kicked its engines awake and pulled out into the open air, ready to make the escort complete.

Sophia was following Diamond.

Above them, Tar`ro relocked the gate, wrapping a seal around the bars to prove to the next guards that nobody had slipped inside unseen. Then the blimp let loose an important roar of its horn, announcing that it had cleared its berth.

Tar`ro was starting down when another newcomer approached.

"You're late," Seldom said.

Nobody disagreed.

For Seldom, there was comfort in rules and codes and any law that was full of important knots. The boy was growing fast, but it was a gangly growth that fit the graceless stride he used as they marched along.

The group strode out from under the landing.

A scream arrived, then a body.

Even knowing what was coming, everybody was startled. The monkey thumped down hard in front of his boy, and Good laughed as he joined the others. Two of the guards complained, but not Bits. Working at the lead, the stocky man glanced over the railing and then back at them, smiling as he always smiled. He wasn't a happy or joyful soul, but he was often grinning. Diamond noticed the shining teeth and shining eyes, and he thought about the guard for a full half-moment. Then his brain skipped to ten other subjects of infinitely greater importance, and the Creation and this child were another breath older.

• • •

No other student looked like the boy-creature. The rest of the school didn't have funny bones and funny hair and that weird neat way of walking on those little-toed feet. Nobody else needed bodyguards carrying hidden pistols. Surely no child in history had ever been allowed to bring his orange-headed monkey to class. But just as impressive, the local Archon had never visited this school until Diamond arrived, and now she had come here fourteen times in four hundred days.

"I'll earn my diploma soon," she joked during the last tour.

But Diamond's oddness was far bigger than that.

Everybody knew how the boy could be cut and bruised and even burned, but those wounds always healed in a few recitations. Lucky people had seen that miracle a few times. Hurting the newcomer was a common game among children, and during those first days at school, Diamond was knocked down plenty and poked with his own fork. Everybody wanted to see a gouge that would seep blood for a moment or two, then scab over and vanish. Even teachers were fascinated by the tame carnage. Of course the guards put an end to that chaos. The worst children were sent home; parents were publicly insulted. Two of the Archon's early visits were for no purpose but to assure everybody that she was proud of this school, and she reminded these decent people that they were deeply decent, and without using names, that warm and very tough little woman warned that charges would be filed and fat fines would be paid if this crap didn't end.

But accidents couldn't be outlawed. Diamond wasn't graceful, and the school's big playroom was full of climbing bars and ropes—places where mistakes found ways to be made. It was loud news that day when he slipped and broke an arm. Everybody was shouting. Everyone wanted to push close and watch. Being in the front row was an honor, teachers outnumbering students two-to-one. It meant quite a lot being able to talk later about that short strange arm, how the wrist was fractured and the little hand that was riding at the wrong angle. The celebrity boy appeared uncomfortable but not in true pain, squirming as he looked at his countless new friends, and then he smiled as if embarrassed, tugging on his hand to set the bone, the entire wrist growing hot and the bone knitting, already half-done before the angry guards pushed their way through the spellbound crowd.

But one schoolboy had tried even harder to hurt the boy.

Karlan was huge and famously mean, feared by everyone, including teachers. The world knew that Karlan used a knife to gut Diamond as a toddler and later threw him off a landing. As Karlan's little brother, Seldom would admit to those ugly incidents. But the young brother also swore that Diamond was never hurt for long, and that was long ago, and Karlan had learned some kind of lesson, because he never went near the boy anymore.

Of course Diamond stood in the shadows of his bodyguards, and the guards had guns in deep holsters, and while Karlan enjoyed quite a few foul ideas, he was also undeniably smart.

Ordinary troubles didn't concern the guards. Since the Creation, bullies had been shaking coins out of little pockets. But every guard had also served as a soldier for the District, defending the borders from wilderness bandits and the hypothetical foes on the reef. Soldiers appreciated order, and with at least one black blimp moored to the school, the police were on hand. Incidents happened every few days. Sometimes Karlan was involved, and sometimes it just seemed like a good idea to bring the big fellow into the chief teacher's office for a chat. One bodyguard would collect a couple of policemen, the three of them pulling Karlan aside. That was standard. That's how much they respected his power and menace, even when the young man never fought with them. Sharper guards noted Karlan didn't care about the stolen money or the general misery. Those little dramas were meant to give his day spice, and the spice came with armed men, always nervous, always ready, someone putting his bravest hand around the giant forearm, finding a steady voice before muttering, "Come with us. Please."

Diamond rarely saw his former tormentor, but that didn't matter. Everybody in the school was safer because of the guards, and Diamond brought the guards every day, and that's how the boy helped keep every student secure.

A chain of easy thoughts had made him into a hero.

That's one reason why children watched for the blimp's arrival, and that's why several dozen of them always gathered on the walkway Diamond normally used. Being close to the famous boy was the goal. They hoped to bump elbows with him, to look close at that perfect skin, and if very lucky, trade a few words that could be added to a big story where the teller broiled at the center of attention.

The guards didn't like groups, but little kids weren't much trouble.

The orange-headed monkey had bigger fears, and that's why Good always leaped onto Diamond's left shoulder, not snarling and certainly not biting but looking quite ready to do both if this chaos grew any worse.

Master Nissim's classroom was a local landmark. Most people remembered when the man was only the school's butcher. His finger remembered too, its tip missing. He had a good deep teacher's voice and odd ideas about many subjects that no reasonable head could follow, and he was the perfect tutor for an odd, odd boy.

That morning, nineteen students escorted the celebrity into the bright blue schoolhouse, straight to the Nissim's room. Diamond usually made a point of thanking them, although there wasn't much life in his voice. Manners were a chore, as every young boy understands. But even when his mind was wandering, Diamond remembered each face and every name, and he used their names while wishing each a very good day.

That was another piece of magic from the creature. It was impossible not to smile when you heard your name from that strange mouth.

Customs had evolved over several hundred days. But not every custom was understood, which was why a very young girl pushed close, handing Diamond a piece of jewelry that she had made without help—a clumsy colorful mess of icebeetle carapaces fused together with common white glue.

Looking at the carnage, Diamond said nothing.

Elata closed his hand, and speaking for her friend, she said, "Thank you, thank you."

"It's for his mother," the girl said.

"It's very pretty," Elata lied.

"My name's Prue."

Diamond knew that already. The girl's classroom was down the hall. She was barely a thousand days old, probably not reading yet, but she smiled at him as if he meant everything. He couldn't help but feel good about that smile.

A giant horn blared, urging everybody to class.

Prue didn't want to turn away.

"Thank you," Diamond finally said.

The little girl stood up taller, and she looked ready to cry.

Tar`ro and Bits were ushering the others towards their classes—not the noblest work, pretending to be teachers.

"It's for your mom," the girl repeated.

Diamond said, "Yes."

"My mother wanted me to do this," said Prue.

Diamond nodded.

Then she made a glad smile to show how amiable she was. "My mother wants us to get married," she confessed. "But I'm not old enough. I will be, but not today."

• • •

Laughter led the way into the classroom.

Master Nissim was standing behind an old bark-and-heart desk that he rescued from the school's trash. Every drawer had its own way of sticking, and one leg had been repaired by a sloppy carpenter, leaving a distinctive tilt. But their teacher claimed to like the gouges and mysterious pale stains decorating the desk's historic top, and in particular, he liked the slick bright face of its caramel-colored wood. Selected books stood in neat stacks, flanking a tablet of lined paper. There was also a broad coral bowl full of pens and charcoal sticks and—kept as ornaments—a corona's broken tooth and an intact corona's scale, plus the pickled chrysalis from a giant green thunderfly.

Nissim was tall, almost a giant, sporting a butcher's forearms and big hands. A plain face was wrapped around bright black eyes, and inside the man was a smile that could fill the room. But the smile was hiding. A stern voice, deep and disapproving, asked, "Now what is so funny, my boy?"

Everybody was laughing, but the Master was staring at Diamond.

Dipping his head, Diamond said, "I'm sorry, sir."

"Maybe you should be. But I want to know why you were giggling."

Why was he?

"Because that girl wants to marry him," Seldom offered.

"I am sorry, Seldom. I was speaking to Diamond."

Nissim had a warm nature, and in different circumstances he would be everyone's favorite uncle, the jokester in the middle of the fun and the storyteller who went last because nobody would willingly follow him. But he ran his classroom as if this was the Grand University in the District of Districts. Manners and tone were as important as facts and calculations. Every student existed inside a ring that defined what was proper, and if the most important pupil stepped out of the ring, he would suffer a well-deserved dressing down.

Diamond was self-conscious, wary. "I don't know why I was laughing, sir."

"Well, I think I do," the Master said.

Everybody paused. Even the guards seemed curious. Only Good ignored the coming lesson, jumping off the boy's shoulder to scramble onto the windowsill.

But just as the tensions rose, Nissim said, "Later. We'll talk this through later."

Six students were already sitting at their desks, books open and lessons begun. Invitations to join this class came only from the Master, and nobody was certain about his reasons. Intelligence was rewarded, and he was a champion of imagination, but there were smarter, more artistic students sitting bored and unappreciated in the ordinary classrooms. These six were bright enough, but all of them were older than Diamond, and as a rule, each of them tended to be suspicious and sometimes hostile towards him.

"Humans are social beasts," Nissim liked to say. "You need to learn how to get along with them."

"I feel human," Diamond would respond.

"And you're putting the emphasis on the wrong word, my beast."

Three empty desks waited beside the open window. Their classroom was perched just under the highest roof. The police blimp had already locked its anchor arm with the overhead iron loop, and now it was floating close to the window but not too close. A black-clad officer was linking the blimp's call-lines to the school's lines and the world's, and the growling engines began throttling down, preparing for the day's sleep.

Seldom sat in front of Diamond, always, and Elata was directly behind him. The classroom was meant for twice as many students, but the extra floor space had been consumed by tools and distractions. Reinforced bookcases held a library as big as the school's, drawn from Nissim's stocks as well as donated by the local Archon. Heavy, historic tables held scientific equipment, including microscopes and dissection kits and growth chambers and fancy corpses floating inside thick-walled jars. Cages controlled what was small enough and tough enough to survive captivity. The final three desks were dedicated to the guards. Tar`ro usually claimed the desk beside the door, while today Bits took the back wall and Sophia sat facing the classroom from the window-side front corner, looking like a second teacher ready to leap in should Nissim lose his way.

Bits was in charge of both receivers—the school call-line and the secure line to the Ivory Station. Regulations required waving to the blimp, letting them know that they were in place, and then he lifted the line to the Station, informing Prima's office that they had arrived and everything was normal.

Diamond often spent the first recitation staring out the window. The window was a long rectangle protected at night by heavy shutters that were lowered and stowed after the rain. Living higher up on Marduk and on the opposite side, he normally faced smaller trees and the distant wilderness. This vista was dominated by Rail and Hanner—enormous blackwoods, thicker and even older than their home tree. Each giant was surrounded by huge reaches of empty air. There was always blimp traffic that wanted to be watched, and there were birds and leatherwings, and certain species of insects preferred flying in the damp brilliance of morning, and even after endless practice, Diamond couldn't keep track of which creature made what music, squawk or shrill whistle or weightless trill.

Nissim was giving the newcomers instructions.

Seldom opened the right book and found the proper page.

"Which page?" Elata asked.

Diamond knew. He wasn't consciously listening but still knew, except that he didn't offer any help today. He had already disappointed the Master, and silence seemed to be the best course.

With a yelling whisper, Seldom told her the page number.

Thin netting covered the otherwise open window, keeping wildlife outside. Good was leaning against the screen, in a place dented by hundreds of past naps, contentedly closing his eyes.

Beneath the sill, stacked in neat heaps, were cloth sacks painted red and needing no further explanations.

Diamond opened the textbook.

" 'There are colors of light that humans cannot see,' " the Master read aloud, " 'and we rely on our machines to define them. But what if there are shades and tones and even nations of color that our best devices cannot define? What if we are so blind that we don't know how to put a measure to our blindness?' "

Silly questions deserved abuse, and Tar`ro laughed.

Too polite to do the same, Sophia showed a smile and nothing more.

The guards often believed that the Master's ideas were idiotic. They kept every opinion secret in the beginning, but familiarity put an end to that sanction. And besides, the teacher welcomed their scoffing attitudes.

"They are the voice of the world," Nissim would say with force.

Lessons wrapped in lessons: that was the ex-butcher's way.

Once again, the Master said, "Blindness."

Everybody was sitting up straight.

"Let's discuss the idea," he said.

Everybody had the opportunity, and they knew it.

Diamond kept his arm from lifting. Three of the older students had the first say, and then Seldom, and Diamond listened to every word even as his eyes watched blimps dropping toward the canopy and lifting when they made the return route. Then the school call-line came alive, its distinctive buzz ending when Bits lifted the receiver.

"Yeah?" the guard said.

Sometimes Diamond heard the voice on the other end, but not today.

Bits offered a hard curse.

Seldom's ideas were finished, or maybe he had merely stopped talking. Either way, everybody else had turned in their desk, watching the man who was sitting erect against the back wall.

The handset had to be returned to its cradle, and Bits looked at everyone, the usual smile missing.

Tar`ro had the highest rank. He leaned forward, asking, "What's wrong?"

"Karlan," said Bits.

Seldom spun and sat straighter. "What did my brother do?"

"Just slugged two teachers." The guard sucked air between his teeth. "And he's battling a couple others right now. He's too damned big to bring down."

Tar`ro cursed.

But it was Sophia who stood up. "I'll go help, I guess."

"Not you," said Tar`ro. "Where is the bastard?"

Bits named a classroom four stories below.

Tar`ro got up, and talking to himself, he said, "No." One possibility had been thrown aside without being discussed. Then to Sophia and Bits, he said, "Stay here. Both of you stay. I won't be long."

He left.

Whenever Karlan's name was mentioned, Sophia's eyes grew big. But her fear triggered a sense of duty, the need to help take care of this problem.

Bits watched his colleague standing at the front of the room.

She looked down at her little desk.

"Go," said Bits.

She thought about sitting, and she thought about following.

"I can handle this crew myself," Bits said.

The police blimp was huge but not close. The morning breezes always pushed it as far out into the air as possible. Only one young officer was watching the classroom, plainly untroubled by whatever he was hearing and seeing. Meanwhile the Master and every student had fallen silent, each watching the tiny drama play out. Nobody was moving, except for Seldom, who squirmed in pain while he imagined what his fierce brother must be doing and what it would mean to his family.

"No, I'll go," Bits said. "That kid's a terror. You stay here."

Diamond focused on Elata's book, the printed page begging to be read.

Then Sophia muttered, "No, I'm going," and the woman's feet slipped across the smooth planks of the floor, carrying her out of the room.

Normalcy tried to return.

Diamond looked at the police blimp and then turned his eyes forwards. The Master smiled at no one in particular, and then glancing at Diamond, he said, "Remind us. What were we just talking about?"

The boy repeated phrases and sentences, pointing at each speaker in turn.

The monkey was dreaming, one cheek pressed against the dished-out screen.

Two recitations and part of a third had passed since Sophia left, and that's when what might have been nothing was felt. Everyone in the room noticed what wasn't very large. There was no movement but there was the possibility of movement, subtle and then gone in the next moment. And then suddenly, instantly, the outdoor air was jammed with desperate birds, and insects boiled out of every crack and wormhole on the tree, and Good screamed as he woke, giving the room one wild glare before jumping on his boy, biting Diamond hard on his little nose.

TWO

One forest filled the top of the world, while a smaller, simpler forest thrived inside the relentless mind, and stretched tight between those two realms—the real and the imagined—was a creature named Quest.

Quest was flesh, liquid, and ever changing. She was invention and potential and the utter absence of play. She was emotion, joy, and wild wonder buoying the flesh upwards while metal-clad fears constantly threatened to drag her off her perch. But this morning hadn't been especially fearful. She rode the light winds and drank the rain before eating a city of beggar bees, and then swollen by the bodies and their honey, she pulled herself into the shape and feel of a mature sap-thief.

Her roost was high in the wilderness, on the fringes of the Corona District. She came here as often as she went anywhere. A human boy lived in the District, except the boy wasn't human, and she saw him by chance once but the next eleven events were done by design.

The boy remained a mystery to her, and a marvel, and like any object of fascination, he was a hazard best left alone.

But there was another way to seek him out: sap-thieves were enormous and she let herself grow, and when her liquid flesh was large enough and mature enough, she sprouted hidden eyes and deep nostrils and too many ears to count. Those eyes absorbed great swaths of the world, and she could test the winds for any hint of scent, and even better were the forests of flowery ears tied into a mind that could pull the important whisper out from the roaring music of the world.

This was what Quest was doing today.

Today the boy was too distant to be seen or heard, and his distinctive farts would die before drifting this far. But tree-walkers were the loudest, most careless monkeys. Thousands of people had seen him with their own little eyes, or they knew people who claimed to know him. Diamond was rumor and story, the outlines of his life as clear as Quest's own. She had learned quite a lot about his parents and two best friends, his various champions and the humans that he should fear. Just by listening, Quest could measure the relentless, ever-shifting flow of opinion. To some the boy was a wonder. Others considered him a monster, though many of his enemies considered him to be a marvelous monster. There was a second, far more frightening creature living in the District of Districts. Tales about King made Diamond appear small and weak. The local Archon liked to travel throughout her home, singing about this gift, this baby destined to be found by the best people, and within the hoots and proud postures of every citizen were a few simple rules:

Humans were supreme in the Creation.

Tree-walkers were superior to the papio, and the Corona District was blessed by the honor of having Diamond while the other Districts surely were jealous.

Of course the fierce papio had to be watched every moment and without trust. Every average citizen in the forest knew that their close cousins were envious and crafty, and being dangerous brutes, they would do whatever was necessary to serve their interests.

That toxic noise was always in the air.

Quest was thankful for being invisible. Alone, she could move where she wished, relying on nothing but her unparalleled talents, and regardless what rumors swirled around her existence, she felt safe enough and powerful enough to withstand assaults from either one of these half-smart monkeys.

In that fashion, Quest was utterly different from her two famous siblings.

Yet on that particular morning, when the air was damp but clear—when an angry man's voice might carry a long ways—she heard nothing worrisome.

The tree-walkers seemed unusually happy.

From her hiding perch, Quest sewed together the chattering and the jokes, people fighting about tiny matters and celebrating tiny victories. Meanwhile a troop of magic sloths was climbing unaware down the branch of an old dobdob tree, and she couldn't ignore them. She was very close to shucking off pieces of her great new body, pulling what lived into a fresh invisible form and racing after this easy meal.

But that's when a single voice found her.

She felt the voice as much as she heard it. Washed within the ordinary mayhem was a shrill and distant scream, male and very loud. "Now now now," the man yelled. "We have to get out of here now!"

The screamer didn't offer any reasons, and the forest took no notice of his warning. Birds and monkeys, always ready for any excuse to panic, remained at peace, and Quest thought that this was a little peculiar, and that's why she remained where she was. She was curious, hundreds of ears turning slowly toward the mouth that had caught her attentions.

Moments later, a nearer, louder voice found her.

The woman sounded big—a creature of meat and wind—and she was screeching at other people, telling them to hurry and leave those damned things, to get themselves into the air now.

"There's no more time," she swore.

Quest tried to guess why time was done, and then a blimp engine roared, wiping away the woman's voice.

Quest began hunting for a third voice.

There might have been dozens of heart-seared warnings. She never heard them. But with her attention fixed on everything nearby and everything above, Quest noticed a few hard noises almost washed out of existence by distance and the intervening trees. Far overhead, in places where few creatures went, machines of a particular size and character were at work. Maybe they had been at work for a little while, and she hadn't noticed. Generators were coughed as they fired along, and capacitors hummed with a high keening noise. Measuring directions, estimating distances, Quest made careful counts until she was certain from where each sound was falling. But she still didn't understand. Experience hadn't prepared her for this puzzle. Only fear had. The fear that never stopped tugging at Quest was suddenly a vast weight, malicious and sharp, eager to yank her into the oblivion below.

She couldn't imagine what was happening, and neither could the forest.

The magic sloths continued dancing along their branch, and human babies complained with tears, and a few more aircraft than usual were flying quickly. Then each of the capacitors gave a tone, loud and almost pretty, signaling to someone that they were fully charged. And since fear was a good enough reason, Quest spawned a thousand new arms, grabbing hold of her dobdob branch.

The first explosion was enormous.

But the next detonations made that first blast seem like the dry pop of a cricket rubbing his favorite legs together.

The forest outside her skin was changing its shape.

And the forest inside her terror-stricken mind could only struggle to keep pace.

• • •

The monkey bit down on Diamond's nose, bringing blood, and then Good slapped the boy's cheek, shouting, "Leave go fast go."

Every bird in Creation was flying. Save for the frantic beating of wings, there was no sound. The world had turned furious and silent. Every insect, from speck to thunderfly, was flinging itself into the open air. Wild monkeys and bark rats and broad little ribbon snakes abandoned their homes, giving up nests and treasured hiding places, eggs and babies. Thought was left behind. Speech too. Breath fed muscle, nothing else. Consideration and fear were abandoned. What mattered was an instinct riding on thousands of surviving generations—leaping into the air before Doom won.

Having given his warning, Good jumped back to the window, desperately kicking at the screen. The children stared at him. An instant passed when nobody moved. Then the classroom floor began to slowly tilt, the well-loved tree swinging just enough that even stupid humans had to notice.

Diamond was sitting at his desk, bleeding.

Seldom rose slowly, and Elata was already on her feet.

"No," said Seldom, staring at his feet. As if arguing with the floor, he said it again. "No."

The other students were finding their feet.

But Master Nissim remained behind his desk. He looked strangely passive—affected but unresponsive. Just from his expression, it was possible to believe that this was an elaborate drill and he already knew about it and he had stubbornly decided not to play along. His hands were spread on top of his desk, flanking the opened book. The Master's eyes were fixed on the green thunderfly chrysalis. He looked ready to speak to somebody, to give directions or small encouragements. But he said nothing. Then in a subtle way, the man appeared almost angry. That was Diamond's next thought. Nissim's morning lesson had been interrupted, and someone would have to be reprimanded.

The boy grabbed hold of his shredded nose, pressing the bloody edges close, trying to make his mind believe that this was nothing but a foolish training exercise.

Above the classroom door was a bell, and the bell began to rattle.

Bits was on his feet, walking rapidly while shouting, "Calm calm calm. We know what to do."

Good was attacking the screen, trying to reach the open air. His little hands were bleeding, sliced by torn wires, and using incisors, he started yanking at the edges of a tiny useless hole.

The screen had an emergency latch. Seldom grabbed the latch, but his hands forgot what to do.

Elata was beside him. The other children began pushing behind them. With two fingers, Elata neatly freed the screen, and then she thought to grab Good by an arm. The monkey started to fall and came back again. Springs drove the screen away from the window frame, out where the next breeze ripped it loose—a rectangle of dark wire and bright air tumbling from view, and gone.

The school's emergency bells could rattle in different ways. This was the very worst sound, very loud and faster than a racing heart.

"Today is no exercise," said the bells.

Bits was standing beside Diamond. The big hand felt warmer than the boy expected, and the man's voice was quick and sure of itself. "Let's stand back," he said. "Let the others pull out the drop-suits."

"We don't need suits," Seldom said.

There was a horn perched on the bow of the small black blimp, and it had a different voice. That horn sounded once, the clear shrill roar of it tearing at the air, at the exposed ears. Its warning fell and rose again, fell and rose quickly, and the blimp's two engines coughed and came awake, propellers carved from corona bones beginning to spin.

"We won't jump," Seldom said. "We have the blimp."

The Master still sat behind his desk. His hands were out of sight. He was working with something, using both hands as he looked at everybody, dragging his tongue across his lower lip.

His tongue stopped. His hands stopped.

Then Nissim called out, "But others might need our suits. Get them ready, children. Get busy."

The red sacks were easy to yank open. Bright clothes spilled out in folded heaps, each size wearing its special color. Every student knew how to put on a drop-suit. On his second day in class, a school-wide drill was held on Diamond's behalf, and he learned which suit to wear and how to jump through the open window. The drills were universally enjoyed—the one time when students were required to be fearless. The little fabric wings under the arms helped steer them to safer air. Of course inhabited trees never fell, not that anyone could remember. The likeliest danger was fire. Schools were full of dried wood and careless people. Everybody knew that Marduk was strong, healthy and sound. Classmates told the new boy not to worry, that the great tree would outlive them and their children's great-grandchildren too.

But despite every promise, the tree was suffering. The massive trunk swung like the slow pendulum inside a gigantic metronome, relentless stresses shifting and the bark shredding while the heartwood screeched in misery. Storms made Marduk sway, but this was no storm. Violent blows were coming from above, not below. Diamond felt each impact. One blow and another and then two more pummelings rolled down from the darkness where gigantic roots clung to the roof of the Creation.

The blimp's engines were running strong, propellers becoming blurred white discs, and the machine pulled out and then bounced back again, still firmly moored to the school and the tree.

Bits yanked at Diamond's shoulder.

"Step back more," he said.

Almost no time had passed since Good went wild. Every event happened inside the same recitation, and even Diamond had trouble following the rapid, overlapping actions.

The monkey was perching on the windowsill, cursing with his voice and fingers. The moorings kept the blimp from moving. Four policemen were crowded together in the nose, pushing a flexible walkway toward the window, but the morning breeze was putting up a fight. Every bird had vanished, but the tiny insects were thick as a fog. Alarms were screaming up and down the school, and sometimes a young voice shouted louder than all the others, and sometimes people laughed with a weird joyless sound, out of nerves, and then suddenly quick legs were running in the hallway, coming their way.

Diamond thought of Sophia and Tar`ro.

Bits must have thought the same. He turned, looking at the open doorway. But the person was a teacher, and she ran past their door, racing for her own classroom.

Diamond watched the back of the teacher's head, and then he glanced down, discovering the gun that filled Bits' right hand.

Drop-suits lay in heaps. Two older students made it their job to sort the suits according to size. There were always more suits than people. Nobody would be left behind. The blimp was tiny, barely enough room available for this class, but if the worst happened and Marduk fell, other children and teachers could slide into these suits and leap, throwing open their arms and legs while gliding away from the trunk.

Various adults had explained that emergency plan with brash confidence. But his parents didn't share their faith, and neither did Nissim. The Master admitted that falling trees loved to spin and often tumbled end over end. Lucky people existed. Some avoided every hazard and broke only bones when they finally struck the canopy dangling from the neighboring tree. A few landed on an airship floating nearby, or on rare occasions, they grabbed a dangling net or rope. There were even cases where people fell past the canopy, and then ignoring the long odds, they were plucked from the air before dropping into the superheated realm where the corona ruled.

Diamond had made that long fall, saved by his father. But he didn't need his father because the blimp was outside the window. Four black-clad police officers had turned into six, and they were making another attempt to shove the obstinate walkway into the window, aiming for nobody but Diamond.

Master Nissim was still sitting.

Diamond stood beside his guard, which was what he was supposed to do. But they kept backing away from the open window, which wasn't expected.

Good had a special name for the police.

"Go go go turd-men!" he shouted.

Elata spun around. She wanted to say something to Diamond, and it surprised her to see him standing in front of the animal cages.

She put a hand beside her open mouth.

Then a single shout began. People across the school were screaming. So many voices poured from every classroom that the emergency bells and the blimp horn seemed to grow quieter.

Elata turned back to the window, looking outside.

The Master was holding a tiny knife in his hand. The large green chrysalis was in the middle of desk, pulled open at the seam, gray fluids slowly seeping across clean paper and old books, and the Master didn't notice the mess, looking at Bits and at Diamond and then back at Bits.

Every other student in the class was standing beside the open window, staring into the distance. Seldom's face was twisted, eyes crying and the mouth shouting, "No it can't be no no . . . !"

Diamond followed those eyes.

The next nearest tree was Rail. Rail was half-again larger than Marduk and exceptionally strong.

But Rail seemed to be moving.

How could that be?

For no fathomable reason, that great ancient tree was plunging towards the floor of the world.

• • •

Two dozen guards had been chosen to protect Diamond. Brave talk said that the special unit was pulled from a thousand eligible candidates, but Nissim never believed in large, easily rounded numbers. There were only so many retired soldiers with the training, the clearances, enough youth, and open-minded attitudes. What's more, every guard had to be local, loyal to the Corona District and to its Archon, with a family history that didn't cross its pollen with the wrong kinds of humans.

Papio, in other words.

There were probably less than a hundred potential bodies to fill out questionnaires and endure the tedious interviews and endless background checks, and a surprising portion of them had made it through the gauntlet.

But knowing your own soul was impossible enough. What about people dedicated to protect a half-human child? That's why the duty rosters were intentionally complicated and sometimes blatantly random. Each shift varied in length, and schedules could be replaced without warning, and individual guards couldn't be certain that they would work tomorrow. Since trust wasn't tested until there was an attack, no guard was ever permanently teamed up with colleagues. Sometimes an armed man sat inside Nissim's classroom and then outside the boy's home, and then he wasn't seen again. Twenty days later, Nissim mentioned the missing guard. He tried to sound glancingly curious, as if the matter was barely worth the breath. Of course nobody explained anything to him. But a person could learn a lot from the way stern faces wouldn't quite look at him, dismissively telling the empty air, "You're just the teacher. This is a personnel matter. Don't ask."

In those early, learn-as-you-go days, guards came to school in pairs. Two guns seemed like plenty with the police floating outside and nothing but children and rule-hungry adults inside. But the job was evolving. Rumors of threats and rumors of spies kept finding their way to Nissim. The papio had spies everywhere and ten different plans to steal the boy. And the District of the Districts wanted him in their giant hands too. And meanwhile, a hundred little tribes of scared people were talking about abominations and what must be done to save this sorry wicked world.

One day someone inside the Archon's office decided that three guards was the superior number, which puzzled the Master until he gave it a little thought.

Picking his moment and his target, he said, "I want to ask a question."

"I won't talk about the job," said the guard, flat out.

"I wouldn't dream of trying," Nissim said.

Tar`ro was sitting near classroom's front door. The other guards were at their stations, beside the window and in the back. The students and one monkey were standing and kneeling in front of the biggest cage. A young fire spider was being fed, except Nissim had already fed it, in secret. A terrified scurry-champ was running away from its fears, but the hairy blue spider showed little interest in this uncooperative second meal.

"You wouldn't dream, huh?"

They were sitting close, talking quietly. Tar`ro had a narrow mouth and chin but bulging cheek bones, making it appear as if two dissimilar faces had been glued together. A master at the art of looking everywhere and seeing just enough, Tar`ro was usually the first guard to notice when something new was brought into the classroom or when an artifact had been taken away. And sometimes he showed lesser talents, like traces of sarcasm, and even better, a tiny capacity for doubt.

"Tell me your question," he said.

Nissim asked, "How many legs does it take to build a stool?"

Tar`ro saw the point immediately. "You want me to say, 'Two isn't good enough.' Is that right?"

"But two is enough. It requires balance, but balance is possible."

"Until you quit paying attention, and then you fall over." Tar`ro liked the game enough to grin. "Three legs make the stool stable. That's what you want me to say."

"Except four legs work even better."

The guard shrugged. "Which means more wood and more precision, what with getting each piece to be the same length. Look at your old desk, standing crooked on the floor."

"I like my desk," the teacher said.

"Good for you," said the guard. "But talking about stools, let's say that maybe we're already at the bottom of our inventory when it comes to working legs. Ever think in those terms?"

"Never," Nissim said.

The grin came again, and Tar`ro looked at him, hard. "I know all about you."

"I'm sure you do."

"You're the professor who got fired. Then you were the butcher who got old inside the freezer. But now you lucked into this easy job because that boy likes you and his folks want you here. Merit and Haddi demanded you, in fact. And you happen to be a damn smart man who makes every other teacher in this place feel like an idiot."

"You don't know that."

"You're right. I haven't tested all of your colleagues." Looking into the back of the classroom, Tar`ro said, "Here's something else I know: this school's teachers and administrators don't relish the idea of an ex-butcher and crazy man working with their most precious student."

"Crazy man," Nissim repeated.

"You. You hold some peculiar ideas. Not that you bring them out and let them dance every day. You're trying to be careful. But despite appearances,

I'm not altogether stupid. Little pieces of what you call 'thinking' keep slipping inside my head."

"Which pieces?"

"The Creation isn't everything. In fact, the Creation isn't even the first thing. People and the papio came from the same stock, which is why we can crossbreed on rare, beer-inspired occasions. And you also think our peculiar, unbreakable boy might be even more remarkable than we can guess."

The students' faces were pressed against the cage wall, watching the unhungry fire spider lazily pursue the frantic rodent.

Diamond's face was in the middle, enthralled.

"What do you think the boy means?" asked Nissim.

"I don't think. Thinking is a civilian job."

"And you're a soldier."

"And soldiers believe nothing but the clear clean ideas that they're ordered to believe."

"You are an exceptionally fortunate fellow."

Tar`ro shrugged, ignoring sarcasm and any personal doubts. "I believe what our Archon says: the child is leftover from the Creation. That King beast is another leftover. And there were two more creatures trapped inside the corona's stomach. But like I was told, our boy is the one who matters. He matters because despite the differences, he is so much like us."

"There are similarities," Nissim agreed.

The guard put his hand to his face, pretending to find itches that needed attention. "You know, it would make this school happy to get rid of you."

"Some people like me," said Nissim.

"Don't be confused, sir. You're too smart for that. People are nice to your face, but that's because you're important today. And, 'Today is always half-done,' as they say. You don't believe what everybody else believes. In fact, you prefer to think crazy crap, and if your rank happened to be stripped away tomorrow, your friendliest colleagues would run away rather than share your air."

At long last, the spider was gaining momentum. The children hooted, and Nissim had more questions to ask.

But Tar`ro surprised him. "Let's talk about stools," he said.

"I'd like that."

"There might be situations, special circumstances, where four legs would work better than three."

"I can imagine that," Nissim said.

"You can? Well, then you are a brilliant man." Tar`ro glanced out into the hallway, making certain it was empty. And again he whispered under his scratching hand, saying, “Three people are allowed to carry guns inside this school.”

“That’s a reasonable regulation.”

“But maybe an old butcher could slip a small knife or two inside his pockets.”

“Knives aren’t worth much in a fight.”

“No? I’ve heard that you had good results with your butcher tools, one time or another.”

Nissim responded with chill silence.

Then the spider struck, and the children broke into cheers—except for the boy in the middle, who acted rather sorry to see the scurrier’s pink insides.

“You’re the science teacher,” Tar`ro said. “To me, science is a bag of magic tricks. Nothing else. But I’m guessing there’s some good trick that will let you hide something small, but something that has punch.”

Nissim sighed and looked out the long window. “You and your colleagues like to search my classroom for hazards.”

“But those are routine searches,” Tar`ro said. “And here I’m going to share one very big secret. Show us something that we can see easily. Set it in an obvious place. The most amazing things will vanish when we never stop staring at them.”

• • •

The neighboring tree was falling.

Rail was falling.

Children yelled, and adrenalin made them jump. Arms lifted, hands to the head. Simple words were repeated. “No can’t never be never no!” Screams were too loud to carry anger. This was not possible. How could this be real? But the great tree was clearly sliding downward, clearly gaining velocity, and everybody at the window realized it and their voices died away in another moment, mouths and brains struck dumb by the enormity of what couldn’t be conceived.

Desperate to watch, Diamond started toward the window.

Bits’ empty hand grabbed the boy around his neck. “Stay with me, now, stay close.”

Diamond stopped and looked over his shoulder.

The slick gray pistol filled the guard’s other hand, aimed at the empty floor but moving, drawing circles with the wide barrel.

"Stay," Bits repeated.

In all of this, what was most striking—the odd detail that Diamond would never forget—was how the man's face suddenly became handsome. Bits was engaged, serious and focused. This great noble work depended entirely on him, and it transformed him in the eyes of a lost child. He was the same man, but the grand nose and those scar-pitted cheeks were suddenly being drawn with a different, more supremely talented set of brushes.

Diamond leaned closer to his guard, feeling glad for nothing but the touch of that rough certain hand.

Then the Master spoke.

"I'm stupid," Nissim said.

Diamond looked at him.

Odd beyond measure, the Master was still sitting on his chair. Rail was dying and Marduk was shaking hard, yet he remained behind his desk, glancing at the window and then at Diamond, disgusted when he said, "I'm an idiot."

Bits tugged at the boy, pulling him a step closer to the cages.

"Stealing the boy," Nissim said. "That's what I assumed somebody would try."

Bits glanced at the doorway and hallway, pulling the pistol a little closer to his side.

"But what if they wanted to kill Diamond," Nissim said.

The boy stared at his teacher.

"Destroy him while murdering all of us too," the Master said. "I never imagined . . . not seriously, no . . . "

A hard sound came out of Bits. It wasn't laughter, though it sounded like laughter. There was pain to the noise, and fury, and then he said, "Shut up."

Marduk was being shaken hard from above, but now a second strong vibration was driving upwards from the canopy. Rail's long branches were yanking loose from Marduk's canopy. The twin insults met in the wood surrounding them, causing the floor to rise up and then drop again, and cages tried to leap off their stands, and the biggest tank of rainwater sloshed and then pitched sideways, shattering against the floor as the room tilted sharply towards the open window.

Bits managed one quick glance at everything, and then his eyes turned to the open door.

"To kill one child," the Master called out. "Why all this?"

Bits opened his mouth and stopped his voice.

The floor rolled and Nissim remained seated. Both of his hands were under the desk, arms moving as if the fingers were very busy. That coral bowl with its favorite pens had slid up to the desk's edge, and Diamond suffered the odd urge to run over and rescue the bowl before it fell.

Then he realized what was missing from the desk.

The chrysalis was. Maybe it fell and rolled where he couldn't see it, and that made him weirdly sorry. He liked that rich green sack full of salted juices and the half-finished fly, huge wings folded down, black in appearance because the colors were piled on top of each other, and if countless other things hadn't been happening during those few breaths, Diamond might have asked the Master where the ornament went.

"Just kill him and be done with it," Nissim said.

Peculiar, disturbing words.

"Cut off the head and throw everything back to the coronas," said the Master. "But why murder thousands along with him?"

Again, louder this time, Bits said, "Shut up."

Then the guard's gun jumped, seemingly on its own, and the free hand yanked at the boy, dragging him back to where the floor was slick with water and the open doorway was close, and Bits squatted, as if trying to hide in Diamond's feeble shadow.

"I know why," said the Master.

The teacher's arms weren't busy now. He sat motionless, as still as if fixed inside a painting, staring only at the boy. He was plainly, painfully terrified, which couldn't have been more sensible, except of course his fears had an added dimension. When he finally spoke, his voice was loud enough to be heard over the splintering wood and the crying children and the drumming engines of the blimp. "This is a warning, isn't it?" he shouted. "The corona's children are abominations, and all of us are guilty when it comes to ending this scourge.

"Am I right, Bits?"

The gray pistol came up, punching Diamond on his right ear. Then the man told the boy, "Do what I tell you. Do it. Or I'll shoot your friends."

Rail was falling fast. The broad black trunk was plunging, nearly vertical, gaining speed by the instant as the brilliant morning sunshine flooded up through the shredded canopy. Light filled the air outside and inside their room, quicker than even Diamond's eyes could follow, as if the sun was always here and hiding, eager for its chance to blaze.

Everybody blinked.

The walkway from the blimp was almost to the window, but it rose again, seemingly buoyed up by the brilliance.

Seldom was weeping, staring at the Master.

Elata's infuriated mouth was closed, and she stared at the gun and Diamond as her hands lifted and found one another, fingers meshing.

Diamond squirmed.

A reasonable, nearly calm voice came from some hidden place. Bits said, "Stay with me, and they get away." He shook the boy's shoulder. "Trouble and everybody dies with you."

Diamond remained perfectly motionless.

Nissim was still sitting and Bits was still squatting, and the pistol's steel barrel was brushing against the boy's ear when Sophia ran into the room, starting to yell some important words.

Bits turned and shot her in the jaw, shot her from down low, and the woman's skull was demolished with the brains and frightening red blood mixing into a fountain of shattered bone.

The screams began again.

Children dropped to their knees, throwing hands over their faces, while Nissim remained on his chair. For no apparent reason, one of the teacher's hands was shoved inside that beautiful chrysalis, bright slick embryonic fluids pouring free. The chrysalis was pointed at Diamond, and Nissim looked sorry and maybe he started to offer an apologetic sound, but then he fired three quick shots.

Two bullets of polished black coral burrowed their way inside the boy.

Bits was turning, still hunkered down, trying to aim for the teacher.

But Nissim's third shot clipped the boy's sturdy collar bone, bouncing and spinning sloppily upwards, and another fragile brain was instantly ripped free of its home.

• • •

The floor was wet and twin holes had been ripped through Diamond's chest. He was conscious, miserably aware of everything. He knew who shouted what and who could do nothing but weep and how every person in the classroom acted once the bullets quit flying.

Elata didn't cry. Standing motionless, hands wrapped together and her pretty face hardened, she let some deep reflex scrape away her emotions and throw them aside.

Seldom was tears and action, rushing toward Diamond, putting his face close when he asked, "Can you hear me?"

Easily, but Diamond seemed empty of words.

Master Nissim shook his arm and the chrysalis fell away, revealing a stubby pistol built from rare woods and coral. His face was even stiffer than Elata's. Eyes looked at the dead while the pistol nearly vanished inside the big hand, and the students shouted around him, and the walkway finally, finally pushed through the wind, spring-loaded hooks grabbing hold of the window's sill.

Making no sound, Good jumped high and landed on the teacher's arm, big jaws crunching down on the gun and fingers.

Nissim cried out sharply.

Diamond tried to shout, "Stop." But some thick hot and slightly bitter syrup had filled his mouth.

The gun that shot him was dropped, and the Master saved his hand, and the monkey brought the gun straight to Diamond.

The boy coughed up blood mixed with nameless secretions.

Good carefully set the gun in his hand.

Then an adult appeared in the doorway, attached to another gray pistol. Tar`ro looked at the two bodies lying close to each other. His weapon moved like a nose, as if sniffing the air. Then the surviving guard saw Nissim pressing hard at his bloodied hand, fighting to staunch the flow, and he walked around Diamond, staring at the wounds that were already beginning to heal and the coral gun in his hand and the orange-headed monkey that kept every hair erect, ready to battle anyone who threatened what was his.

Diamond saw that much. But his wounds and what passed for adrenalin pulled most of his focus to places inside him. Ribs were shattered and his flesh was shredded, his heart opened wide and both lungs choking, and one of those fat rock bullets had burrowed into his spine. But those injuries weren't dangerous. He was certain to survive. Every damaged organ had calmly put itself to sleep, and every essential function was replaced by hidden talents, by secret reserves. He couldn't remember being any way but alive, yet this was a different kind of life. Breath was unnecessary. Blood was just another kind of clothing, and without a heart, he could be naked while the blood was washed. He felt like a fancy new battery fresh from its box, full of sparks, and maybe this was why he ate so much every day. Invisible motors filled his tiniest places, eager for their chance to help. Those motors gave him strength. Even with twin chest wounds, he felt as if he could pick himself off the floor, running to the window and the walkway, escaping this wicked place.

But he remained sitting on the slick floor.

Another teacher had entered the room—a woman followed by the youngest, littlest children.

And beside her was a huge muscled fellow dressed in brown.

Karlan stared at the gore, impressed and maybe fascinated, and compared to everyone else, utterly calm.

Someone shouted from the world outside.

Three of Diamond's classmates were already on the walkway, crawling forward, while a furious policeman waded over them, offering up a string of curses when he wasn't telling the others not to come.

"The boy first, the boy now!" he said.

Something about the classroom was changing.

What was different?

Tar`ro knelt close to Diamond and looked at the monkey, but he was speaking to Seldom. He told the crying boy, "Help me lift your friend come on hurry."

Marduk had changed. Stillness had claimed the long trunk. It had just happened, and Diamond accepted that as very good news. Whatever force or monster had cut Rail away at its roots had failed with Marduk. Diamond's tree was too strong to die, and Diamond had known that all along. Joy took hold. Joy caressed him, and now he weighed nothing. Seldom didn't need to help lift him from the floor. Suddenly everybody was as light and insubstantial as gnats, and the walkway was arched high in the middle, and the blimp had decided to yank itself into a very unlikely angle, as if it were trying to cling to the school's roof.

The policeman guarding the walkway tried to shout directions or curse again, or maybe he just wanted a deep breath before doing whatever was to come. But his next step was clumsy, and the black uniform flapped hard as everybody in the room started to fly.

The policeman lifted off the walkway, and then he was gone, so quickly that it seemed as if he had never been.

Marduk had just wrenched itself loose from the world.

Everybody would die. Every unsecured body and piece of furniture were flung against the ceiling. Diamond hit hard and lay on his back looking at a floor swept clear of desks and books, but not blood. People were bleeding and hurt, pinned to the ceiling, and nobody had the energy to cry out. Tar`ro was still beside to him, shouting something about waiting, and Good clung to his boy, and Diamond started turning his head, trying to find the Master.

Tar`ro said, "Wait."

Far below, Marduk's branches pushed into the canopy that still held it on three sides, and then the largest limbs were grabbed by the surviving neighbors, and the tree's plunge suddenly slowed.

Bodies and desks rained down on the floor again.

Diamond stood. He wasn't sure when he stood or how, but the half-repaired body knew what to do. Seldom was beside him, stunned and limp. Diamond dropped the coral gun and picked the boy up and ran to the window, and he shoved Seldom onto the walkway and then did the same with Elata.

The police blimp was dropping back into view, both engines running full.

Tar`ro got behind Diamond, put a hand on him to shove him onto the walkway, but Diamond slipped sideways and ran to the big desk. The desk was again where it belonged, and Nissim was behind it, on his knees and bloody hands, fighting with his legs to stand.

Marduk hadn't stopped falling. Branches exploded beneath them and the big limbs dropped to new perches where they would slow again, and each time the floor fell out from under them for a moment and then jumped up again.

Diamond tried to help the Master stand, but the boy wasn't strong enough and they helped each other find their feet and run.

Tar`ro grabbed Diamond and threw him onto the walkway.

"When we break, grab hold," he shouted.

Those words meant something, but he didn't know what.

A web of soft rope and handholds was laid over a skeleton of boards, and the walkway was covered with scrambling bodies. But there were people still left in the room. They were classmates and little kids and a few adults, and Karlan. Not one day of Diamond's life would pass without those faces and those voices coming back to him, calling to nobody but him, hands rising to where they always seemed within reach—some days thousands of hands wanting this single boy to rescue them—and his sorrow and the fierce anger would always make him fall quiet, if only for an instant.

Diamond crawled out onto the walkway.

The blimp started to lift higher, engines screaming, as if the machine was gamely attempting to hold Marduk still in the air.

Then Nissim and Tar`ro were behind Diamond, kneeling, fighting with the release mechanisms. The pressure was relentless. Worse, Tar`ro wouldn't drop his gun and Nissim's bloody hand had to be weak. Nobody could get past the two men, and nobody on the walkway could help. Pulling free was all that mattered. Ropes creaked sharply and the great tree picked up its velocity and then slowed once more, for the last time, and then somebody yelled, "Catch her," as a tiny girl flew up at the two kneeling men.

In reflex, Nissim grabbed Prue before she fell into the open air.

Then Karlan emerged from the crowd, slapping the gun out of Tar`ro's hand and pushing all three of them back up the walkway. That nearly grown man was huge and dangerously powerful, and he had no trouble winning a patch of terrain where he could turn, reaching down with both hands, one grand tug finally causing the releases to trip, saving all of them.

Then the walkway broke free, hooks and the blue school and the doomed tree left behind, and the man who had saved everybody looked up the walkway, smiling at them, shouting, "Hold tight you shits! Hold tight!"

THREE

Only powerful noises could reach across the Creation.

King's father was a ripe example. Nothing about that human was physically impressive. His skeleton was a collection of narrow bones draped with weak pink muscle. Small eyes and small teeth and a youthful, inconsequential face made for a forgettable presence. His brown hair held no special tone. His skin was pale enough to look sickly. On social scales, the man was neither charming nor energetic, and despite a life spent in public realms, he had never told one joke worth its breath. Father's most famous feature was a high-pitched voice, like a bird's cackle pushed through some boy's wet throat. When he laughed, he giggled. He would use the smartest, most reasonable words when addressing an audience, yet everything they heard sounded small, nearly weightless. On those very rare occasions when the Archon shouted, the voice had a nasty habit of shattering in embarrassing ways, threats emerging as sharp, silly daggers that left his enemies grinning, ready to mock him as soon as they were out of earshot.

Father had many, many enemies.

"Which is a mark of strength," he often told his adopted son, using the quiet voice that both of them preferred.

Powerful noises didn't need to be loud. One smart whisper delivered by the right mouth, inside the proper moment, would make the entire world shiver, and that whisper could only come from his father:

A frail, tiny creature named List.

Father's enemies were King's enemies. Each was a coward hiding in some other room, preferably straddling a distant tree. Their foes teased Father for how he sounded and for everything that he said. They mocked him by calling him a bureaucrat, or worse, a lowly clerk, and even more insulting, they claimed that every success in his father's life was earned by stupid good luck. Yet no enemy ever dared speak that way directly to List, and that held true long before he had a monster for a son.

One day, King told his father, "I can always hear them talking about you."

Smiling, the Archon said, "Your ears are better than mine."

"And there's more of them," said his son.

"I was making a joke," Father said.

"And you aren't a funny man. That's what everyone claims."

King had studied many topics, including human politics. There were nine Districts with outlier communities haunting the surrounding wilderness, and each district had its strengths and its own Archon. An Archon rose to his office or her office through angry contests called elections, and sometimes luck was involved, but most victories came from careful hard and nearly invisible work.

The District of Districts hung above the world's center. Bloodwoods were the ruling trees. Giants compared to all others, they were vast pillars wearing short stocky branches and spear-like blackish-green leaves. Bloodwoods weighed surprisingly little for their volume, yet they were strong enough to reach far deeper than the world's lesser forests. The heaviest rains washed over them with the morning, and the strongest sunlight made them creak and roar as they grew. The bark was thick and as dark as the leaves, while the flesh inside had many colors. The "blood" in the name came from the countless splinters, huge as well as miniscule, each one sharp enough to pierce the heaviest leather. Every finished bloodwood plank was said to carry at least a few ruddy drops—traces of the foresters and millers and carpenters who sacrificed flesh to make their livelihoods.

King lived at the Archon's palace, inside giant rooms made from corona parts and polished, heavily waxed bloodwood.

Alone in the world, his armored body had nothing to fear from sharp lumber.

In this world, King was a species of one.

Strong and tall and still growing, the Archon's adopted son had always appreciated his nature, each day offering up new lessons underscoring how special he was.

Humans had only two ears, while King had ten.

Humans were immune to most sounds, but King could hear the highest notes inside a bird's song, and even more impressive, he could listen to the clattering clicks of the tiniest leatherwings—the flying rats that came out only in the night, filling the forest with their bug-hunting voices.

Physicians and other specialists had examined the Archon's son. Every portion of King had been measured and imaged, and pieces of him were cut loose and then reattached again, sometimes in novel locations. Expert faces watched spellbound as the finger or several plates of armor silently rejoin the host body. A few surgeons were allowed to cut into his deepest parts, and that was how King learned that in addition to odd-shaped guts and nameless organs, he had eight ears hiding inside his purple blood and his purple meat, absorbing not just the world's high-pitched squeals, but also the deep low throbs that only a few scientists knew about.

The Archon of Archons was proud of his son, and he was scared of him.

Fear was completely reasonable. On that score, father and son were in full agreement.

In the same way, King and List appreciated how badly things had gone when Diamond stepped into the world. Father had decided to flush the boy from his home and his old life, and the boy went farther in less time than he had imagined. But seeing a chance to teach the papio lessons in real power and real strength, both of them had seriously overstepped, and the lessons ended up being theirs to learn.

"I tried too much, which spoiled the prize," said Father. "And of course I didn't take your feelings to heart, did I?"

King had multiple hearts and mouths and eyes, and he ate like ten healthy men, growing every day.

"I was crazy with rage," King admitted.

"And you tried to do too much."

"But I learned, just like you learned."

Send Diamond back to the coronas: that's what King wanted, and he nearly succeeded. But he was hundreds of days wiser now, and unlike humans, he wasn't so crippled by pride that he couldn't see the good fortune in his failures. Life changed after that very bad day with Diamond, for the better. The human-like boy remained tiny compared to him, and weak, condemned to a small life in an isolated District. What's more, King was no longer a surprise waiting to be seen. He was free to wander where he wished inside the Archon's palace. Allies and opponents came visit the world's most powerful man, and after being introduced as the famous son, King would select a piece of floor to defend through the evening, using those hidden ears to absorb every awful word being whispered about the host. He was also free to travel with his father, walking among the small and the poor. These were the people who appreciated their Archon. Freed of pretensions about power and wealth, they could love the world's ruler, offering hands to be touched and happy words, even as they wisely kept their distance from the monster standing silently to one side.

Father and son had a shrewd difficult love for each other, with respect built from past misunderstandings and threats that neither would forget. Perhaps they looked bizarre, walking together in public. But when it was just the two of them, and when they were talking quietly, the best parts of their relationship came into view. King would give his impressions of the day, sometimes quoting whole speeches from the admirers, and then Father sucked air through his little teeth before giving advice about leadership and the fickleness of human nature.

Humans rarely impressed King.

One night his father said, "You hear quite a lot, and that might have value. Or maybe that's a distraction. But I do know that you're missing the spine in these perfectly rendered words."

"What do you mean?" asked King, the plates on his shoulder lifting slightly.

"Those people don't adore me," the Archon said. "They show teeth and use the right words, but they don't actually worship anybody except themselves. And that's the way my species has always been."

More plates rose, but his son said nothing.

"Next time, ignore the noise but watch their honest eyes. What these people enjoy are my policies, although they know almost nothing about my decisions and my laws. They heartily approve of my tone, which reassures them without making them spend much effort. Decisions carried out in my name are what make me real. Where I take no stand, they don't see me. And even my richest, most learned supporters don't often think about me. The wealthy and the comfortable relish my tax codes. They love my commitment to order and one particular species of fairness, the one that blesses them. They worship the eternal supremacy of the District of Districts. Bright as they might be, the very best place they can imagine is the place where they happen to live today. The world they see is the world they want. That's what their eyes are seeing when they sing about whoever is in charge, and that fortunate soul is temporarily me."

King wasn't easily amazed. Yet inside that one conversation, after the boy's armor had laid flat and he stared at the message itself, he discovered that people weren't as simple as he had envisioned, and the Archon was the best among them—a subtle creature wielding an array of talents that his young son had still not begun to understand.

That was why King was at his desk, conscientiously reading his daily lessons.

It was morning in the world, and he was hard at his studies, just like every other morning and through most of every day too. Eventually King would take charge of the world. His name and nature had settled that matter long ago. But first, before that great day, he had to learn quite a lot about these red-meat creatures, their honest eyes and their fluid, fickle affections.

King preferred to stand while studying, and his tutor stood nearby, about to ask one of her nagging questions. This morning's book was ancient—a government text about the weights of ordinary objects—and she would want her pupil's interpretation about the language or the hand that wrote the words, or maybe she would use the document as evidence that jooton nuts were exactly the same size now as they were five hundred generations ago, only they were called ooloo nuts by the dead souls that ate them for breakfast.

King felt ready for any question.

But when she finally cleared her throat and spoke, he didn't hear her voice. He didn't hear any words or the hint of meaning wrapped around this exceptionally dull lesson.

A low sound had washed into the room.

His buried ears heard the intrusion, and he felt the vibrations with his bones, and some part of his rapid, ill-mapped mind recognized what he was hearing. Yet he had never experienced any sound so enormous or deep in the register. This happened on occasion—the unexpected would arrive along with a potent sense of the familiar. Ancient memories teased him while he spread one hand across the time-worn page, both thumbs extended. She spoke and the moments passed, and he ignored everything but the distant rumbling, trying to decipher distance, trying to guess a direction. But the vibration ended too soon, forcing him to wait, holding his breath and focus against the pressure of an old woman's words.

Then another deep rumbling arrived, followed by several more woven over one another. Suddenly five recitations had passed with the same spent breath inside him, and the tutor was watching her singular student with a guarded expression. What was happening? Was the monster angry, and if so, was she going to suffer now? King's talents were gradually improving when it came to reading faces, and he remembered one very good lesson:

The proper noise could make any human happy.

King abandoned his desk, intentionally towering over her. "I don't mean to be rude, Master. But something awful is happening in the Corona District."

The woman was relieved first and then startled, that wrinkled, spent face believing him. But she insisted on asking, "How would you know?"

There was no time for responses, polite or crude. Alarms were already sounding inside a distant room, and people were running in the hallways outside, familiar voices saying something about test and false reports, begging that this was nothing but a security trial, please.

King broke into a hard, breathless sprint.

Father's favorite office was at the end of a long hall. The room was no larger than any other, but it offered wide windows looking across the District. There were no canopies in bloodwood country. Trees grew towards the morning's brilliance, branches covering the trunks from their broad foundations almost to the pointed tips. Branches never reached far into the air. The sun was welcomed, able to rise up to the highest portions of this forest, which was only one reason why this District was the ruler of the others—the reliable fire from below washed away shadow and the other species of darkness, letting a multitude of crops grow and grow.

The boy found his father standing before a long table. Ornate receivers were clasped in both hands, and more receivers were on the tables behind him, pulled from their cradles. Dozens of voices were shouting from the outlying districts, each voice sputtering, distorted by the long reaches of wire. King heard the words and understood what they were describing, but what did more than impress him—what shook his unbreakable mind—was the utter terror filling the only face that he had ever loved.

• • •

"Hold tight you shits. Hold tight."

The walkway dangled from the blimp like an exhausted arm. Boards and rope and assorted bodies were being dragged backwards through the roaring air. Big hands and long toes clung to the webbing. Diamond's tiny hands fought to keep their grip. The blimp was dropping every drip of ballast water and two emergency slugs of black iron, and the twin engines pressed past full-throttle, threatening to explode as the aircraft fought for speed, for altitude, for any unlikely blessing.

The holes inside Diamond's chest were healing, and he was breathing again, the new heart pushing pristine blood. The boy made himself look up the walkway. Seldom and Elata were stretched out on their bellies before him, side by side, faces hidden. Brown uniforms and blowing hair carpeted the walkway all the way to the blimp's opened nose. Three police officers were standing inside the nose. One man was desperately trying to grab the nearest boy, cursing him when he wouldn't reach out. Another man did nothing but point empty eyes at the tree in front of him, at Marduk. The third officer was flushed in the face, cheeks ballooned outward to create an odd expression, and a moment later he tipped forward, leaning with poise, even grace, as he threw up a breakfast of berries and curdled milk.

With every breath, the sun grew more brilliant.

Buried inside the screech of engines, Diamond was certain he heard people wailing. But only people in the distance and only behind him. Nobody trapped on the walkway wasted their strength making noise.

Good was squatting beside his boy, four hands locked in place, and he tilted the long head sideways, broad black eyes unblinking and amazed.

Diamond shoved his left arm under and then over the tight webbing, as if his short limb was a needle and he was sewing with it. Forcing his arm into a position at once painful and secure, he grabbed the webbing with his left hand and let go with his right and both clumsy boots, allowing his weight to hang from the shoulder.

That was how he spun around, eyes pointing at what the monkey could see.

Marduk was plunging, straight and fast.

Home was on the far side of the tree. But even knowing this, Diamond couldn't stop hunting for what the mind knew best. A relentless, machine-like agent inside him paid strict attention to the walkways and each distinctive landing and the curtains of hundreds of strange homes. No detail seemed familiar enough. For a breath or two, he was convinced that this wasn't Marduk at all and the blimp had been flung somewhere else. But that was a crazy, desperate idea, and he was ashamed to think it. The canopy was clear of the forest. The colossal brown trunk was roaring downwards. Diamond's father was working at the Ivory Station, which was on Hanner and Hanner hadn't fallen, had it? What was important was to remember that Father was safe. And Mother had gone shopping, which left so many ways to be spared. But the piece of Diamond that insisted on finding hope was also relentlessly searching for the big new landing of his home, and the painted corona on the door curtain, and in particular the wide window that would let him peer into his room, at the soldiers and Mister Mister and the rest of a left-behind life.

But the window was lost. Those familiar rooms were already below him, gone. In that tangle of endless detail, he saw people jumping. Some wore drop-suits, many did not. Figures ran and flung themselves off the walkways and the ends of landings, fighting for distance as the stubborn, hard-swirling air grabbed them. But often some larger structure would rush down from above. The proud landings of the richest neighbors swatted at everyone below. The tree refused to set them free. Marduk continued to accelerate, and other strangers did nothing but stand where they happened to have their feet, a thousand people holding tight to railings and each other as they watched a small black blimp pull away.

The bravest and the most fearful had leapt with the tree's first shudder.

Those wearing drop-suits had glided a long ways, and several of them arrived like a sudden flock. Each body was tied to screams. One fierce yell descended on Diamond, followed closely by a barefoot man who struck just above the boy and above the monkey, grabbing at the webbing and missing, sliding down to where he could cling to the boy's free arm and waist.

Good cursed, ready to bite any hand that came close.

Diamond didn't know the man's face. Gripping with his left hand, he watched the stranger fight to find better handholds, any toehold. Only when the man felt as if he had stopped falling did he look at the boy beside him, and he blinked, finding something wrong about that face . . . and if there was any doubt who this was, it was dispelled when he noticed a monkey that was nearly as famous as the corona's boy.

With a quiet exhausted tone, the man cursed, and he took a deep breath, and without trying to act too abruptly or too carelessly, he grabbed Diamond's left arm, attempting to yank it free.

Diamond seized the webbing with his right hand too, and he kicked with his school boots, striking nothing.

Tar`ro was directly below them. Master Nissim was holding the little girl close, and Karlan was at the bottom, watching the tree fall. Only the bodyguard saw what was happening, and when he started to climb, the man kicked Tar`ro, kicked his face as hard as he could with his bare heel, and Diamond's right hand tightened its grip.

The man had a rough strong voice.

Furious, he said, "You." He looked at Diamond and said, "You," once again. Then he found a better grip and grabbed the boy, jerking with most of his weight, dislocating the small shoulder.

With one swift bite, Good claimed the man's right ear.

Tar`ro grabbed a bare foot and pulled hard, accomplishing little.

Then Diamond let his right hand relax, fingers slipping out of the webbing, and with the nails of two fingers, he pushed into the soft wet centers of the stranger's eyes.

The man cursed the Creators and every monster as the pressure built, turning his head to shake off the miserable pain. Then Good reached into the man's mouth and yanked the broad pink tongue, bringing it out where it was bitten off and spat out.

Blind and mute, the stranger let go of Diamond and the walkway, and then Tar`ro managed to punch him once as he spun past, vanishing inside the dazzling wash of sunlight.

Marduk was just above the demon floor. Below that floor was heat beyond all measure and the coronas swimming in air so dense that it acted like water. The lowest, most sun-bleached branches of the tree struck the floor, punching past and igniting, and within moments the entire canopy was swallowed and burning. Then the tree's descent began to slow, which was normal. Diamond had never seen a tree fall under him, but he had read accounts left by shaking hands. The tree slowed, and tiny factors caused it to tilt slightly, and then it tilted quite a lot, the highest portions of the trunk beginning to swing towards the blimp.

Diamond made himself look up.

The highest portions of the trunk had no homes and few signs of human activity—a broad brownish-black pillar polished smooth by time and darkness. Following behind were the broad branch-like roots covered with bladders and bowls meant to catch the dawn rain. Two roots were close. The blimp's pilot saw them dropping, and he abruptly shifted course. Diamond was yanked sideways as one engine slowed while guide wires twisted the tail fins, but the descending roots refused to follow any line as they fell, seemingly eager for the chance to smash this tiny black bug.

They were going to be hit and killed.

Diamond knew it and believed nothing else, even as the nearest root missed them by a long ways. Rainwater was spilling from the tipped bowls. Gouges had been cut in the bladders. A tiny cool rain fell over them as the blimp shuddered in the shifting air, feeling the wood race past but surviving unharmed.

Most of the high roots were missing, left behind in the topmost reaches of the Creation. But what remained was burning. Irresistible forces had wrenched apart living wood, setting fire whatever refused to break. The final roots were long and jagged, as if a great hand had yanked so hard that most of their bulk had been forsaken, and the remnants dragged black smoke after them.

The blimp jerked and twisted, finding a new trajectory, and then another, and finally, one straight quick line.

"Maybe," Tar`ro shouted.

Diamond's shoulder was healing. Marduk was half-swallowed by the world beneath their world, its canopy lost and a ring of flame encircling the trunk. The trunk looked like a brown finger shoved into filthy water. The coronas' realm was dark with smoke and wild sparks of light. Diamond cried out, and then Tar`ro said something else. Tar`ro was looking up at him. A wild smile came to his face, and the man shouted, "They don't practice this. Pilots don't."

The guard let out a great sorry laugh.

Roots would catch them, or a burning ember would set the blimp on fire. Or maybe the swirling air would be enough to pull the overloaded machine into oblivion, everyone but Diamond dead.

The room below the human room was Diamond's first home.

With that odd thought, he shut his eyes, and Good gave a wild howl as scorching heat swept across their faces, and then the air twisted and the walkway gave a wild kick, like the end of a whip, and he opened his eyes to find everybody still clinging tight. Even Karlan at the bottom of the whip had kept hold. The blazing root was below, and the smoky choking air stilled, growing hot as an oven, the heat of the fire and the heat from the ripped-open floor welling up, and the blimp continued pressing backwards, climbing higher while the police officers riding in the nose found enough hope, at last, to begin helping the refugees climb on board, one crying person after another.

• • •

The black corona meat was infused with every metal, including so much iron that the blisteringly hot muscles shone black and smelled like engine parts. Corona scales and bones weighed little yet outlasted the best steel, while no knife was as sharp as a young milk-colored tooth. And each of the creature's exceptional organs filled some essential role, whether in industry or the military, which was why so much wealth was wrapped inside their greasy black guts.

Each District had its slayers and their famous ships, but every history of the subject agreed: the richest hunting and finest crews always worked beneath the present-day Ivory Station.

Commerce meant merchants and markets, laws and professional codes. Civilization would be impossible without that one dull person sitting before a stack of ledgers. Yet the corona traders were often regarded as selfish mercenaries and thieves, and because they also dealt with the papio, some voices regarded the traders as being conspirators against their own kind. Yet Prima's parents had always avoided the traditional controversies. Famous for integrity and a tenacious need to make their customers happy, her mother and father were never in the top tier of their profession, but buyers knew that her family didn't lie about wares, and they paid their bills in a timely fashion, and the only people who needed to fear them were the selfish and the foolish who had tried to cheat them or their sterling names.

Prima was raised to appreciate honesty and expect decency, and among her siblings, she was the one who took those lessons deepest into her heart.

Born in comfort, every venture was open to the young girl. Politics was never her first choice as a career, and she could imagine it being her last. But cancer had killed the previous Archon, and she agreed to fill out the final hundred days of his uneventful term. Friends as well as enemies warned Prima that she wouldn't like the job. The Archon's desk meant corruption of the spirit, dilution of the soul. List was everyone's favorite example. Once a fine little fellow, bright and deeply competent, he probably would have stayed decent and basically harmless, if only for a loss or two at the polls. But he won every contest, and now he was a power, a guiding force of nature. His District held half of the world's humans and two-thirds of its wealth—a circumstance reaching back for as long as any history could see. And if that wasn't awful enough, the one-time bureaucrat had acquired the King creature, monstrous and allegedly brilliant—a weapon of unmeasured power walking about free and half-tamed.

But Prima had a tougher nature than anyone expected, including Prima. She didn't corrupt, and she didn't dilute easily. After one hundred days at the desk, her citizens demanded another thousand days, and by the end of the term she had mastered the office and its limitations. No serious candidate faced her in the following election. Prosperity followed, and every scandal was small. Understanding traders and the corona markets, she was able to deftly avoid even the odor of impropriety. The world concluded that the woman couldn't be compromised, fouled or seriously tested. And that's why the Corona District worshipped their small lady, most of the citizens nourishing some deep personal reason for these remarkable feelings.

Energy and focus were her strengths.

She was charming, and her memory was tenacious, and she never stopped surprising her staff as well as the public when it came to threading solutions through tangled problems and little disasters.

In reflective moments—a rare commodity for any Archon—Prima recalled her father sitting inside his tiny, paper-choked office. A good friend was near death, and she was about to take the Archon's desk. Her logic felt sound, but emotion carried her words, and she spoke about her plans and half-born policies until the heavy warm voice interrupted her speech.

"You know, my dear," said Father. "I always imagined you as the next trader sitting in my chair. But since that future isn't great enough for you . . . "

"This is a temporary job," she insisted.

"Lie to someone else," he said.

Hearing that, Prima's first thought was that she needed to improve her skills weaving the truth.

"Let's discuss the future," Father continued. "Starting now, I want you to aim for twenty thousand days from now. That's my only advice, daughter. Picture the historian sitting at her dusty little desk, a cup of tea at the elbow, and now watch her write her seminal account of your life. 'Earn a hundred good acts for every bad.' That cliché is not a bad way to judge any life, particularly your own."

She was thinking that just then, the heavy knowing voice shamelessly tugging at her pink human heart.

And that's when an aide behind her said, "The fletch is still waiting, madam."

She said nothing.

"Madam Archon?"

Her aide was named Bealeen. He was young and had a duty, and he also had a hope that was nicely aligned with his duty. He was trying to coax one stubborn woman to a safer place, which would have the benefit of saving him too.

For emphasis, Bealeen repeated, "Madam."

"Enough," Prima said, lifting a finger, tapping the man on his lips. "If they attack again, I'll flee. But not until then."

They were sharing a remarkable room where only maintenance crews and new Archons were typically allowed. Tens of thousands of days had passed since important noise had occupied this space. But the command post was now full of talk and busy bodies. Every chair was claimed, and more people crowded beside the various reinforced windows. The sitting people called to one another when they weren't focused on crackling, wire-born voices. News was being gathered and shared. Those on their feet knew to whisper when they spoke, keeping the noise to manageable rumble. For people without jobs, the windows were the main attractions, and everybody had to defend their portion of the glass, staring out at what had swiftly become emptiness: a panorama of sun-pierced air that made eyes blink and tear, the occasional blimp or fletch gliding between the smoky bits of wreckage still tumbling from the highest reaches.

Bealeen moved closer. "But madam. For all we know, Hanner's high trunk is burning."

A stout woman filled the nearest chair. She was wearing a drab grayish-green militia uniform, half a dozen unplugged call-lines stuck between her fingers and two headsets pressed against her ears.

The Archon touched a broad shoulder. "Any word from the scouts?"

"Anytime," the woman said.

That same answer was offered ten recitations ago. Since the elevators rising to the Hanner's roots were waiting for repairs, one small fletch had been dispatched to investigate the blast zone. On the Archon's explicit orders, every other available aircraft was saving people, or at least patrolling at the ready for survivors. Of course that scout might have been destroyed by falling debris, or the damage to Hanner proved hard to measure, and even if the mission went well, the crew would need a secure line that was still intact, leading back down the trunk to her.

Once again, the Archon asked, "Which trees?"

The sitting woman was tough as anyone, her adult life spent in the District's small army and then the reserves. But the voice cracked when she said, "Rail."

Rail was her home. Her sister and two nephews missing. Watching that tree fall into the sun, everybody assumed Hanner and the Ivory Station were next. This was the nerve center to the District; every enemy wanted it destroyed. But the explosions and subsequent fires had fanned out in the opposite direction.

"Marduk and Yali," she said. "Hartton and Cast and Shandlehome."

Then the bombs had finished, but the morning's weak rains had left the forest ceiling as dry as possible. A dozen smaller, younger trees were still burning, still collapsing, following a widening, endlessly brutal arc.

Contemplating fire, the people at the windows looked up. But roots and the remnants of the severed trunks continued to smolder, and smoke always loved to gather in the highest reaches, hiding everything.

What kind of weapon could inflict so much horror?

And which enemy would be stupid enough to use it?

The suspects were few, and everybody understood who they were—so few that spare fingers would be left on the counting hand. But nothing was certain, including who should be cursed.

Prima gave the woman a comforting pat on a shoulder.

The nagging aide had given up on Prima. Moving down the window, he offered his sage advice to the very worst person.

"She needs to be safe," said Bealeen. "If you insist, she'll take the fletch that's fueled and ready."

"No," said the anguished man. "I'm waiting with her."

"But the *Happenstance* is waiting," the young man said. "Think about it. The two of you could fly to safe places, hunting for your son from there."

"Kill that notion," Merit said.

But the aide believed that he had the rank as well as the urgency to tell the old man, "You aren't in a position to dictate."

Too late, the Archon considered interceding.

But Merit turned to stare at this busy runt. The poor man looked ancient, that scar on his face deeper than ever, blood making his cheeks glow. It was hard to imagine how someone so plainly miserable could muster the energy to remain on his feet. Yet the big eyes were full of scorn and conviction, and a matching voice said, "One little ship can't do anything, hunting all of this space. The survivors are everywhere, and we're here. If Diamond and Haddi are alive, they know to come here. Here. This is where the world can reach us and we can talk to the world, and this the best awful choice that I have."

Instinct told Prima to do nothing.

Devoid of good sense, Bealeen said, "I am sorry, sir. But you surely know that your family is most likely dead."

Merit understood quite a lot. The awful words had no effect. How could he suffer more than he was two moments ago, before this babe came by to pester him?

"My son is not dead," he said.

That earned silence and a stiffened back.

"Diamond falls through, and I'll go find him again," said the slayer. "And if I don't cut him from the belly of some corona, then someone else will do that job, in a thousand days or ten million."

The crowded room had fallen quiet.

The aide found himself inside a box, and he didn't like boxes. Feeling the pressure of eyes, he saw one last gambit. Very quietly, but with rage building, he said, "Well, but of course your son is the reason . . . "

His voice fell away.

"Bealeen," the Archon called out.

"The reason," Merit said. "What do you mean by that?"

The young man couldn't have stood taller. "This happened because of him," he said, his voice fierce and shrill.

And again, the Archon called to him. Nobody could ignore what her tone meant.

The aide turned. "Yes, madam."

"Go," she said.

"Yes, madam?"

"Immediately," she said.

"I'll wait onboard the *Happenstance*," he said hopefully.

"No, you'll go home," she said. "Or you'll run to any other tree in the world. Or for all I care, you can leap out this window. I don't want your company again. Do you understand me?"

The man waited to be sad or angry, but his emotions never rose to that level. This was his chance to escape, and Bealeen said, "Yes, madam," before hurrying away.

Everyone else was staring at Merit. The room was thinking about nothing but the magical son.

Then the Archon walked over to the grief-stricken father and husband. "May I stand with you for now, sir?" she asked.

He said, "Of course."

She raised a hand, resting her palm against his shoulder. Then with a voice that everyone would hear, she said, "I can't promise much, sir. But I know this: one way or another, we'll see the boy home again."

• • •

Every school uniform started out too big for Karlan, but that never lasted long. There were larger men in the world, and perhaps some were naturally stronger, but the near-man had other gifts: he was the masterful bully, an expert in violence and the artful threat of violence. Students gave him money and he gave them peace, and certain teachers found it was easiest to bribe the giant, gaining ease of mind while winning tranquility in whatever classroom in which he sat. But despite the terrors, he had never been expelled from school or arrested for any crime. Investigated, yes, but not arrested.

Karlan wasn't as smart as his little brother, but he was shrewder than ten Seldoms and a genius reading the signals displayed on any face. Long ago, he saw what was different about Diamond, calling him a monster before gutting him with a knife. That history was something that Tar`ro and the other guards never forgot. But since Diamond came to school, there hadn't been any hostilities between them. Karlan knew better. The little creature didn't matter anymore. Doing just enough to keep his reputation airborne, Karlan had capably kept himself in a place where he felt comfortable, and by his measures, in total control.

Diamond was watching Karlan.

The survivors had been ushered inside a never-big cabin in the blimp's belly. Every seat had been heaved overboard—for weight and for room. But there wasn't one piece of empty floor bigger than a handprint. People sat hip-to-hip, limbs often woven together. Little daggers of light came through the gaps in the curtains. One dagger kept catching the biggest face, round and imposing and drenched with tears. Like everybody else, the tyrant was weeping.

Karlan made no sound when he cried, Diamond noticed.

Seldom sat in front of his brother, tall but still tiny between the giant legs. Deep sobs ended with sniffles and panting breaths, and then after regaining his strength, Seldom would let the sobs begin all over again.

The big face looked at Diamond, and Diamond looked away. Then the face looked at the Master and finally at Tar`ro, and one of his hands attacked the tears on Seldom's face, not his own, wiping them away as his sturdy voice said, "Yeah, this is shit. Shit, shit."

Tar`ro sat with his back straight, wet eyes watching everyone. Or maybe his training kept him in that pose, letting him pretend to be alert even when his mind was lost in its private miseries.

Master Nissim seemed shrunken, ill. One arm was thrown over Diamond, as if trying to lend comfort. But as much as anything, he was leaning on the boy, inviting the warmth of that body into places cold and dark.

Good was curled up in Diamond's lap.

Elata and Prue clung to each other, talking.

"I want my mommy," said the little girl.

"I want mine," said Elata.

Seldom took a long breath, rebuilding his strength. "Do you think our mom got away?" he asked.

"Quiet," Elata said.

"Karlan," said Seldom. "What do you think?"

"That you need to shut up," said his brother, the voice flat and hard, but not angry, not strained.

The blimp's engines were running fast. They were climbing slowly and making sharp turns, the daggers of sunlight constantly shifting positions.

Tar`ro was staring at Karlan.

Diamond was paying close attention to both of their faces.

Prue kept saying, "Mommy."

There were moments when Diamond stopped thinking about his mother. But those were aberrations, coming when his brain was too full with too much and something had to be shoved aside. Suddenly Mother wasn't sitting behind him or floating over him or wishing him a very good day. He was busy reliving the gunfight and clinging to the walkway, and children with faces and names were dying all over again, and with perfect clarity, he saw trees dropping out of this world again. Each tree was severed at the top and burning, and every person trapped on the branches and inside the trunk was turned to fire. Even those riding inside airships weren't safe. How many blimps and fletches had been torn to scrap by falling debris? Diamond counted those he had witnessed. There was no way to forget what he knew, and no thought remained lost for long. Shutting his eyes, the boy willed his mother to appear, and Haddi was standing over him just as she had when he was little, cool fingers gingerly touching the forehead that always felt as if it had just come out of the oven.

Forgetting his mother was a failure, perhaps even a crime.

Each time he forgot, Diamond bent forward, focusing every thought on the woman, forcing her to seem as real as ever, which put him in a mood where he was certain that the old woman had survived. A creature that vivid, that rich, must have jumped free of Marduk, or maybe she was shopping on Rail but ran to Hanner in time, or she fell a little ways but then grabbed hold of one of the commuter airships that survived. Each of those unlikely scenes was equally plausible, and in those moments, doubting nothing, the only worry in him was the idea that his poor mother was sick worrying about him.

Diamond was alive, and Father, and Mother too.

In secret, the boy smiled, and that was when his thoughts turned wild again.

Tar`ro continued watching Karlan.

After another two recitations of silence, the giant returned the man's gaze. "Staring is impolite," he said.

"I'm curious," Tar`ro said.

"Good for you," said Karlan.

"About this morning," the guard said.

Karlan shifted his weight, and after the silence built, he used a hand to wipe his own face, making it a little drier.

"You weren't doing anything, were you?"

"In class? No."

"But we got that call asking for help," Tar`ro said. "Bits said you were beating up teachers."

"Was I?"

"No."

"Well," said Karlan. "Bits was a liar."

"Except the call-line did ring." Tar`ro shifted his legs. "Even if you're innocent, someone made that happen."

"I'm sitting in the back of the room, pretending to read," Karlan said. "Then you come flying in, and you give me how much of a look? Barely any. What I remember, you blinked and turned to Miss Ulla and started to ask her . . . I don't know what, probably what was the trouble or if I had been bad . . . and that's when Marduk started shaking . . . "

"You don't know anything," Tar`ro said.

"That's what I do at school," Karlan said. "I sit and know nothing."

Tar`ro cursed.

"But I followed you back," said Karlan.

Most of the survivors watched Karlan, but Nissim and then Diamond stared at the guard, studying his face and the one hand that was out of sight, holding the butt of his little reserve pistol.

"The tree was breaking, and sure I chased you," Karlan said. "Why the hell wouldn't I? This bag was my best hope to get out of school alive."

Tar`ro sighed.

"I saw your partners' brains," Karlan said.

The engines throbbed and the blimp started climbing again.

Karlan made a laughing face. "Which one made you the fool?"

Tar`ro said, "Quiet."

"Because you're an idiot," Karlan said.

Tar`ro breathed deeply through his nose, his hand still massaging the unseen gun.

Karlan held still, ready for whatever happened next.

What happened next was a door opening and a policeman shouting down into the darkness.

"Ivory Station is open for business," he called out. "And the Archon herself is waiting for us."

FOUR

No district was eternal. Borders and names found ways to shift, as did the allegiances between seats of power. But the coronas had always lived beneath these trees, and Father knew every guess why: the creatures congregated below them out of habit or superstition, or this was where they preferred to hunt, or there was no better place to breed and raise their young. Or perhaps these were just the weakest members pushed out of an overpopulated realm. But even as he offered those possibilities, the retired slayer reminded his son that hunting and killing the coronas had taught him only how little he knew. It didn't matter why the bravest or weakest or the most foolish coronas rose out of their realm, up into the cold whispery-thin air. They came to this world and both species of humanity thrived, and lucky slayers grew old enough to sit at their dinner table, explaining their ignorance to their sons.

There had always been an Ivory Station, regardless of its name or precise location. Today's Station was a complex of buildings, fletch hangers, and critical offices fitted to together like blocks against Hanner's giant trunk. A wide platform lay at its base, paved with silver corona scales, and twin pillars had always stood at the landing's main entranceway. The pillars were built from corona teeth, predating Hanner as well as several long-dead trees. After the attack, brave souls took upon themselves to save those treasures, using power saws to cut them free of the wooden planks below. One of them was already on its side, ready to be shoved into a rude sling that would be carried off by the first available blimp. But the would-be heroes were noticed, reprimanded and ordered to more valuable posts. Later the police blimp appeared, towlines dangling, the spent, overheated engines leaking black fumes. Diamond was standing in the nose. Amplified voices and a set of bright flags ordered the blimp to one end of the landing, and a dozen big men grabbed the lines and tied them down. An audience had gathered near the tree trunk—soldiers and government workers, and the Archon, and standing beside Prima, one retired slayer.

"Father," said the boy.

Tar`ro stood on one side, Nissim the other. It was the teacher who put a strong hand on Diamond's shoulder, squeezing as he said, "We'll be down in another recitation, don't worry."

Perched on his boy's head, Good clucked softly.

"Why aren't we at the hangers?" Elata asked.

"They want us where we can take off fast," Seldom said.

"Why would we take off?"

"Hanner might fall," Seldom guessed, making everyone uneasy, including the boy who made the claim.

But Tar`ro said, "No, the tree's strong enough. They don't want this little balloon in one of their berths."

"I suppose they wouldn't," said Nissim.

"Why not?" asked Elata.

The adults pretended not to hear. But from the back, Karlan said, "They're saving space for the warships. District reserves are going to fuel up and arm up, and then we'll launch the counterattack."

There was a pause.

Then his brother asked, "Who will we attack?"

"Whoever we want," Karlan said, buoyant enough to laugh. "Anyone who gives us reason gets smashed and burned."

That's when Diamond and Good leaped out the doorway.

Falling through the sunshine was a pleasure. Falling had a beginning and some inevitable end, but there was the great middle where a mind could concentrate, drawing out details and slowing time until it felt as if there was nothing in Creation but the busy sound of wind in the ears and wind against the clothes, hands twisting like tiny wings, dancing with the air that was trying its best to make the plunge last forever.

Legs bent, the boy struck the landing with as much luck as grace.

The crowd immediately pressed towards him.

Then the monkey landed and bounced, ending up on Diamond's right shoulder, showing the world how bravery looked with its orange fur fluffed wide and every tooth shining.

Diamond ran for Father, and Father ran before falling back into a quick shuffle, arms crossing on his chest, squeezing once before the hands lifted, wiping at his miserable, joyous face.

The two called to each other.

Good shouted, "Merit."

Tar`ro's colleagues formed a protective ring around the boy.

Father was allowed through, smothering his son with shaking arms, and the same as when he was falling, his son struggled to make the next breaths last forever.

Good hissed at the unknown faces.

Standing at a polite distance, the Archon spoke to a younger woman. With an urgent voice, the aide said, "The scout ship's reporting."

"Reporting what?" Prima asked.

"I wish I knew, madam. The captain wants to speak to you, alone."

The Archon nodded, eyes fixed on Diamond.

And just like that, time charged ahead, and the boy could do nothing but watch the world doing everything at once.

"For the time being, you're me," Prima told the aide. "Welcome each survivor, make everybody comfortable, and make certain, please, that Diamond and his people remain together. Understood?"

"Yes, madam."

The little woman walked away.

Diamond didn't want to speak, and he wished that he could stop thinking. But he heard himself ask, "Where's Mother?"

Dripping eyes looked at him. Fingertips touched the bullet holes in the school uniform's chest, and Merit said nothing. His face seemed weak, and then his face changed. Diamond couldn't name what changed. But Father had stopped crying, gazing out at the emptiness and inviting his son to do the same. Hanner was solid enough to trust, but many of the named branches had been sheered away by Rail's collapse. A dozen mature trees had been lost, fires roaring far above and one giant hole ripped into the forest, and the sun-washed air couldn't seem more vacant or anymore dead, reaching for a fantastic distance until the trees began all over again.

• • •

Three old men wearing green silk uniforms and fur busbies stood at attention, speaking about their competence and their innocence, and with blood shining beneath naked faces, single mouths cursed the enormous evil that had brought this day's treachery.

King listened from a distance, and sitting much closer, Father listened.

Father used nods and little winks, assuring his generals that he understood their words and respected them deeply. Indeed, he was walking with them down this very ugly branch.

That subterfuge made the old warriors courageous.

Of course the generals had to promise their Archon that the bloodwood forest was secure. Scouts and assorted fortifications saw no evidence of intrusions, much less sabotage, and no full-scale attacks were in the offing. What happened in the distant Corona District could never happen here.

"Besides, our trees are stronger," said Father.

"And far less flammable," said the general of generals, rocking slightly as his legs weakened. "Blackwoods and fire like each other far too well."

His colleagues said nothing, nodding in ways that might mean anything.

"What did our allies do wrong?" Father asked.

Possibilities were offered, and they came too quickly. Quickness signaled reflexes at work, which was different from level, rational thought. These military creatures knew what was expected, and their speculations chased the premise that the Corona District was ruled by incompetents and possibly worse.

"You think they have traitors in their ranks," said Father, speaking from behind his large bloodwood desk.

The three generals were in sad agreement; that awful possibility was very much in play.

"Traitors who want Diamond dead," said Father, glancing at King. "Or at least they'd like to put him out of our reach again, I suppose."

"But the boy has survived," one general reminded everyone.

"And so the Creators have blessed us again." Father nodded. "Now I have another foolish question. Blackwood burns, you say. That seems like a critical detail."

Three faces nodded agreeably.

"But I know those trees. I've seen Marduk for myself. It isn't a bloodwood . . . it wasn't . . . but that trunk was massive, a proven survivor. Yet you seem to claim that an ordinary fire can tear a pillar of wood out of the world's ceiling."

"This was no natural fire," said the youngest general. "That kind of blaze requires special explosives, very powerful, with almost supernatural heat."

The general of generals nodded enthusiastically, happy to finally say the words everyone was thinking: "The papio are certainly involved."

Father shrugged. "I don't know much about bombs. My apologies."

The ranking officer was happy to teach. "Our enemy has stockpiled many kinds of weapons, and destroying our trees would be one of their immediate goals."

"And we have nothing like this?"

The generals hesitated.

"If I recall, there are some enormous, coral-shattering weapons in our armories," said Father, flashing a proud smile. "You showed me those stockpiles once, right after I won this office. I remember rockets as long as this room, and you explained how those corona-bone tips would let them burrow deep inside the reef before detonating."

The other humans exchanged glances, deciding who would reply.

Finally, the youngest old man said, "Coral-splitters, yes. But they wouldn't be any use in tearing down a forest."

"What would be?"

"We don't make a habit of discussing the issue, but our District does maintain a small number of bombs designed to cut wood, not coral. They can demolish any tree trunk, and we keep them in case an outlying area has troubles."

The human was describing civil war.

Father put on a satisfied expression. "But you're sure that our great enemy, the papio, attacked us. Yes?"

The generals were happy with that conjecture.

"The papio in conjunction with traitors," Father said. "They must have infiltrated the Corona District with allies."

Each man relaxed his arms, in one way or another saying, "Yes."

"But we don't have any traitors."

The middle general blinked. "We?"

"The District of Districts," Father said. "None of our citizens want that young boy dropped into oblivion."

"There are probably a few wicked sorts," his superior said. "But not many, and nobody of consequence, I would think."

"Why would you think that?" Father asked.

Again, the responses came too quickly—stated and then followed by more clinical evidence that looked sewn onto the reflexive mess. Basically, the men inhabiting those silk uniforms were convinced that they knew everybody of worth and had measured each of their souls without error.

King hadn't moved since before this meeting began. He was supposed to keep his distance, pulling lessons from this slow, polite interrogation. But then the Archon of Archons now gave him the quickest glance possible followed by a subtle nod, which was his signal to step forward—a tall armored creature with fierce green eyes and two determined mouths.

Generals preferred the company of generals. They tolerated civilian leaders but preferred not to notice the leader's child. Standing at attention, they faced List while explaining what they knew that was certain and what they could surmise without too much imagination. Conspirators inside the Corona District had used the papio, unless the treachery flew the other way. Terrible weapons had been smuggled into the highest portion of the forest, and while evidence would be uncovered quite a lot might be learned in future days, the generals thought it vital to warn the civilian at his desk that the whole story might never be known.

"Oh, I agree with that," Father said.

Faces grinned, not relaxed but not scared either. These were creatures with long careers, honors earned without once fighting a serious battle. These were masters in the realms of public speaking and sure, solid words delivered with authority, particularly during practiced meetings. Father would end their careers today. He had explained his plan to King before the men were let into his office. With his voice high and sharp, he had confided, "These are not the men to lead the fleet tomorrow."

"Where are we going tomorrow?" King had asked.

"Indeed," his father had replied cryptically. "That's my point exactly."

Now King approached the four humans, stopping only when the generals nervously glanced his way.

Father pretended to be irritated by the boy's presence. He pretended to look at a stack of useless papers. Then he focused on the doomed soldiers, saying, "Perhaps you should explain this papio bomb to me. Exactly how big is it, able to drop all of those trees?"

Tired backs needed adjustments.

"I assumed it was a single weapon. Am I wrong?"

The generals had a lesson to deliver. The youngest said, "There weren't any reports of papio aircraft. So more likely, our enemies would use a series of demolition charges. Materials could be smuggled through the wilderness in small quantities, presumably over many days and nights."

"I suppose that is more reasonable," said Father.

Again, the generals glanced at the peculiar creature standing still as a statue near his tiny parent.

With a sigh, Father said, "Well, at least the Diamond boy survives."

Everybody but King nodded happily, that lone bit of good news worth repeating again and again.

"So," Father began.

Nobody spoke.

"Some secretive group planted explosives inside several trees—explosives brewed by our eternal enemies—and then the trees came down, killing tens of thousands of citizens."

The men said nothing, perhaps hoping silence would help their circumstances.

"Early reports are sketchy," Father continued. "But I was speaking to Prima just before you arrived. She claims that one of Diamond's bodyguards tried to trap him on Marduk, assuring his death."

"Well, a huge plot like this," the middle general began.

Then he hesitated.

Father called to him by name, not rank.

The man swallowed. "The Corona District is utterly incompetent when it comes to security. As I have said more than once . . . "

"They are not incompetent," Father said.

The general of generals scoffed at that statement.

"Shut up," Father said, leaning across his desk, one stick-like finger stabbing the air. "For the last four hundred days, my office and my good people have worked hard to place agents inside Prima's security apparatus, and the results have been lousy, more often than not."

His audience wasn't happy with that revelation.

"Espionage," said the middle general.

"Why wasn't I informed?" asked the top general. "What are we talking about? Intelligence missions against an ally?"

"The work happily wears any name you give it," said Father.

The general of generals was outraged. "Plots of this sort aren't supposed to be hatched and nourished by the civilian element."

"Yet they were," said the Archon of Archons. "I'm an ambitious, conniving man with thousands on my staff, and I managed to launch a dozen operations under your oblivious noses. Does that adequately define the situation?"

Silence.

"And now you're so desperate for explanations that you'll claim that a few treacherous people managed to carry out a grand attack, and a security network that made my life difficult was just as ignorant as you three."

Generals looked silly when their shoulders slumped, when their busbies tilted and their uniforms seemed to deflate.

King laughed with his insulting mouth.

"There are other possibilities," said the youngest old man.

"I'm well aware of that," said Father.

"If Prima is culpable," said the general.

"Let's assume that my colleague and dear friend is innocent," Father said.

"Then the papio are in charge," the general of generals allowed. "With their military skills and key agents in Prima's staff, everything is possible."

Father used the hardest voice he could muster. "Be careful what you believe. Our peace has held for generations. We must be exceptionally cautious when we start blaming one old enemy."

"The papio helped," the general maintained.

"Everybody is a suspect," the Archon declared, finally rising to his feet.

The generals offered weak shows of teeth.

"Of course we'll mobilize," said Father. "The Districts have rules, have protocols. My office has called a worldwide alert. Every military resource will be readied. I intend to follow our primary plan for a large-scale attack on an outer district. Half of our fleet must be ready by tomorrow, and because I want to sleep tonight, I insist that each of you resigns before offering yourself to military court, in preparation for a lengthy examination of records and motivations."

Soft human faces grew softer. Nothing should have been a surprise, yet twice in the same day, these creatures were astonished by a surprise attack.

Father waited for some trembling voice to ask, "Why?"

Two of them sputtered the question, and he said, "I don't believe any of your stories. We don't have any substantive evidence, and indeed, as you warned, we might never have a respectable picture of the truth. But you also told me that we have comparable weapons, if only in small stocks. And if there is a conspiracy at work inside my District, my three ranking officers are staggering incompetents who can't appreciate their deep weaknesses."

Each general angrily professed his innocence.

But Father was never moved by innocence. And he didn't care about guilt on this score. He had already explained his thinking to King. War was not equations on a long page. War was brutal and real and urgent, and what mattered was putting younger men in charge of the human fleets. And that was the only reason why the Archon presented the old men with their replacements' names, waiting for signatures and stamps.

"I know very little about military matters," Father continued, "but I'm going to ride with our fleet tomorrow, out to give Prima whatever help she deserves."

"And I'll go with you," King said.

Father let a grin show. "But what if I tell you to stay here and study?"

"I won't."

"What if I send a hundred soldiers to restrain you?"

Father and son had planned this game, this loud show. But the generals weren't paying attention to the family drama, and they weren't looking at the papers in their hands. All that mattered were their personal miseries, standing inside the bud-green silks and their wrinkled flesh, wet eyes close to leaking tears.

That was why King picked up his father's massive desk.

The Archon wanted people to be impressed with his son. He wanted his generals to talk about the child's warrior spirit. But this was too loud, too bold. With a glance, List told King to quit. But Father's papers had slid free and the desk hung in space, needing somewhere to go. So with his total strength and a contrived flash of rage, King flung the lump of bloodwood partway across the spacious office, watching its flight and then the hard landing that shattered every seam.

"Send a thousand soldiers to sit on me," he told those cowering old men. "Do it. Please do it. But we'll go to war a thousand soldiers weaker."

• • •

That young boy generated every possible reaction in people.

Prima was no exception.

Diamond revealed empathy inside the coldest soul, amazement in the most banal. What he meant to the world might leave twenty passionate, conflicting opinions inside the same average head. Some citizens couldn't sleep with their worries. A mad few claimed to feel his presence—a black chill or a blazing second sun transforming everyone and everything. Even in his presence, the boy was a conundrum. Sometimes he was the wondrous child, charming and sweet and reassuringly ordinary. But then suddenly he became an odd face and a smile that meant nothing. A rational person had to wonder if every appearance was camouflage, an exterior worn by a crafty monster biding its time, waiting for the world to lose its focus, its strength.

Compassion and suspicion lived inside Prima. Seeing Diamond that first time, she wanted to take care of him, marshaling the powers of her office and District in his defense. Yet she also feared him in the deepest worst ways. There were nights without sleep and more nights infected with wild dreams, and odd as it seemed, the only reliable cure for the doubts was to board the hub elevator early in the morning, standing beside a stern, silent gentleman dressed in a stern, silent gray and white uniform, the two of them rising to the highest reaches of the forest.

There was no darker, more oppressive place in the world.

In normal times, barely a whisper of sunlight reached that bleak terrain, and then only noticeable to eyes accustomed to the night.

Yet the world's roof was plastered with life. Not the trees, no. Named trees and tiny nameless trees weren't the end of the Creation. Roots snaked only part way inside the fleshy black sky-reef. Learned scientists described that reef as lichen, but instead of being green with algae it was full of organisms that consumed the long-light that no human eye could resolve. Rising from the sun, that portion of the spectrum was relentless, passing through wood and every human body, and the spherical shape of the world served to focus these energies against higher regions, up where the oil-infused reef was deep enough for the gigantic bloodwoods to cling with their greedy, oversized roots.

Prima had climbed the high, half-lit reaches above the District of Districts, but she preferred her home with its blackness and the shallower roots, and in particular the spongy bladders filled with phloem, dangling heavy and rich in the morning gloom. She loved the great dish-shaped basins that hung from trees like intricate shelves, one beside the next in close order, each gathering up the highest drops of rain. Strange creatures thrived where light was rare. She particularly liked the bizarre little animals that flew through the trapped water, fins and pink gills flapping. In that realm, an Archon could find the time to remove her shoes and stockings, sitting on the brink of a favorite basin where the trail was maintained and ropes were strung across the gaps. Then the toes went into the chill water. Many of the water-flyers lacked eyes, but they seemed to taste her flesh in the currents, and when they felt especially brave, they would dart forward, enjoying little nibbles of human skin.

Worries about the boy brought Prima to the world's ceiling.

And so did the King monster living in List's house, and the rumors of two more mysteries, whatever they might be.

Just the idea of these creatures was a lure, a nectar perhaps, or perhaps the bait in a trap. Prima could never be as close to the ends of the Creation as she was there, and it was possible to sit in the dark, feeling bony mouths chewing harmlessly at her toes. And in the dark, as alone as any Archon could be, she was able to consider each impossibility.

"Madam," said a man's rough voice. "You wouldn't recognize this place now."

Prima was standing alone in her office, the call-line pressed hard against her ear and her mouth. "Tell me," she said.

"There's smoke everywhere, and sunlight," said the fletch's captain

"Of course," she said.

The line crackled for a few moments, threatening to break. But the voice returned in mid-sentence, telling her, " . . . but the ignition failed or they didn't finish the setup."

"What are we talking about?" she asked.

"The bladders, madam. Somebody pumped fuel into Hanner's oldest bladders. We're guessing by the smell, but the alcohol's been spiked with explosives. That would make the blast hotter and much quicker."

"Inside the bladders?"

"Yes, madam."

"Which was brought there how?" she shouted.

"In drops and dribbles, I'd guess." The captain paused, and the roar on an engine sounded. "If I seeded this entire area—what exploded and what didn't—then we'd be talking about a hundred loads of high-quality papio fuel and explosives."

"Papio," she repeated.

"That's what I'm guessing, madam. And the detonators are definitely papio. Which makes it double-lucky that Hanner didn't come down too. The papio have great detonators."

Did the man know how he sounded, praising the murderers?

"But are we safe now?" she asked.

"Your tree?" The voice became quieter, as if he were holding the call-line away from his mouth. "Hanner will survive the day, madam. And we can drain this bomb out without too much risk. But the fuel is toxic and the explosives have some ugly chemicals. This mess has already seeped through the bladder walls, poisoning the wood for a hundred paces in every direction. Long-term, we're talking about abandoning Hanner before she dies and drops on her own."

Prima straightened her back, narrowed her eyes. "Thank you."

"But we think, we hope, the fires are done burning," he continued. "So at least the damage won't spread farther."

Plainly, the captain wasn't seeing what she saw. The first fire might be done, but a far worse blaze was beginning.

"Madam?"

The Archon said nothing.

"Can you hear me, madam?"

But she had nothing to say. Standing alone and feeling alone, she thought about the mouths that had lived inside those dark basins of rainwater. Did the attached minds—those little white drops of brain—ever ask if there were better places in existence?

Did they believe in brighter realms?

And would that be a comfort, knowing it was so?

FIVE

The woman never pretended to be their mother, not when she did her duties and not inside their minds. Explaining her place, she told the other papio that she was a door between the Eight and the world. Her deep voice and uncompromising attitude colored everything. Some of the Eight always loved her, while others felt that way only afterwards. One or another might ask to know her feelings. Did she love them, and if so, in what order did she love them? These weren't fair questions, and she told them so. But then she would answer the question, claiming to love each of them equally, even though that was untrue. She also assured them they shared a wonderful body, a beautiful body, and everyone wanted to believe those words even more than the promises of love: this contrivance of flesh and imagination was the Eight, and it was lovely, and the woman rightfully saw magnificence standing before her.

She was tiny beside them.

Every papio as small, and the clever monkeys scrambling through trees were smaller still.

The woman first visited the outpost soon after the Eight were discovered. She was one body among the government dignitaries and important scientists—the quiet assistant to a high-ranking doctor. That man didn't like the Eight. He saw an abomination and the need for hard measures, and that's why he was quickly sent away. The initial examination was hers, and with important people watching, she worked with her eyes and fingers, then razors and swords and a sequence of increasingly elaborate machines, exploring the conundrum that the Creators had bestowed on humanity.

Eight creatures lived inside a bag of sloppy, ill-ordered flesh. Maybe they were together at the beginning of everything, or maybe they merged inside the corona's stomach. There was no way to know. Piercing the skin with sound and metal, the doctor identified each enduring mind as well as the different flavors of meat. In those days, the Eight had a few sloppy eyes and ears, temporary limbs and no working stomach. They were close to helpless when the doctor bathed them with sugar water and injected pulverized meat inside them. Despite that miserable diet, they managed to grow, gaining insights and little talents as the body became huge. Their first good hands were tendrils. They made holes that pretended to be mouths. Then through the force of clumsy shared wills, they created muscle and various stomachs, and a kind of bone appeared inside that knotted confused flesh, defining arms and legs and ribs and the interlocking disks that joined into one broad backbone wrapped around eight distinct spines, each springing from a mind with its own voice.

The tendrils vanished and the holes healed. A skull formed around two giant golden eyes. Several hundreds of days passed before their body appeared finished. That was the body that the doctor admired—a looming papio-inspired frame from which came an avalanche of a voice.

Selected people came to stand before the Eight, and in one fashion or another, every visitor begged to know what the Eight knew.

What the Eight understood was confusion and a gnawing sense of loss. But words didn't have bones. Words were difficult to tame, and nothing they said emerged in the proper ways.

"What is your oldest memory?" the papio asked.

No memory felt true. They might have been trapped inside the corona for ten days or ten million days. And before that they could have been sitting on the laps of the Creators, giving advice about the building of the world. The bitter truth was that the Eight could make any claim, sing any wild brag, but they wouldn't know enough even to guess if they were lying.

Vagueness and mystery were reliable ways to make the papio unhappy.

Patience grew even thinner when the Diamond boy emerged from his room. The doctor happened to be gone that day, having some distant errand to walk. Diamond boy came straight to this place, as if searching for the Eight. But he wanted only his father, and King followed him. King and Diamond were individuals, not alloys. Each had one voice and a single personality, and they could run fast in a straight line, and they didn't waste any time with riddles, and they didn't fall silent because the voices inside them were fighting to control the world's largest tongue.

King and Diamond were gone before the doctor returned.

Important people came with her. Leaders and old thinkers squatted before the giant Eight, arms crossed, tough feet set against the reef. "You're gifts from the Creators," they said. "That much is undeniable. And belonging to the Creators means that you once stood in their presence, even if that was ten billion billion days ago."

A thread of logic lay in those words, narrow and seductive.

The Eight stared at the papio. Each face showed terror and amazement, resignation and despair, while incoherent rages hunted for any worthwhile target. The audience was a multitude, and they were disorganized, and nobody dared call the papio insane.

The leader among the leaders stepped forward.

"The children who tend to you like to boast about you," she began. "They claim that each of your minds is bottomless, that everything you see is etched in hard coral. So tell us what you remember. Tell us about Those Who Made Everything?"

Emotions ran hot inside the Eight. Urgent words and the staring faces triggered old thoughts and utter nonsense. Too many answers offered themselves. Eight fierce, terrified wills battled for the giant mouth, and what emerged was dense, passionate, and convoluted—much of it wrapped inside eight vanished languages.

During earlier days, visitors like these might pull out a few words that seemed familiar. There was illumination and comfort in the Eight's nonsense—any sound that might prove a tiny personal concern. Or people would hear nothing but a mess and then return home. In those days, patience was in charge. Inertia was the pilot. Nothing needed to be different tomorrow; nothing needed to be changed. But now the tree-walkers had a warrior in the making, and they had a human-like creature with his own magic, and what if the clever monkeys also found the missing child, that ghostly phantom that wandered the wilderness?

But that was before. Every past moment was different. What happened now could not have been more important, which was why the Eight focused remarkably well, agreeing on one clear answer, if only for a few breaths.

In the papio tongue, they proclaimed, "The Creators are dead."

"But we know this already," said the leader, rocking forward on hands as well as her toes.

"And the Creators looked like you," said the Eight.

"Why would they look any other way?" the woman asked in return. "Why make this world and not put your face on its rulers?"

"But they created nothing," said the Eight.

"Who created nothing?"

"The ones you keep misnaming," they said. "If they deserve a name, you should call them 'The Destroyers.' "

Nobody understood. Each word was known, but the implications were too strange, too enormous. Even the Eight were as lost and foolish as everyone else, listening helplessly as the words bubbled out of the long graceless mouth.

The mouth stopped working again.

A few of the papio said, "Blasphemers."

They were the ones who hurried to their wheeled vehicles and drove away, wanting to be as far from this madness as possible.

The other papio walked slowly to their vehicles, but they didn't leave. With their backs to the Eight, quiet voices spoke about possibilities and plans. Twice the doctor woman came close to those people, attempting to join the conversation. Twice she was told to step away and not approach her patient either. Then the government people finished, a bargain finally struck, and they called to the doctor and gave her explicit instructions, causing her face to turn stiff and sorry.

She came up the face of the reef, up into the shadows where the corona's child liked to sit, a dash-and-ash mat underfoot and the entire world stretched out before their two enormous golden eyes.

"Did you hear them?" she asked.

They had only two ears, but those ears were huge and sensitive, pulling in sounds from everywhere.

"We heard nothing," said the clumsy voice.

She laughed at them.

"Liars," she said.

Better than any other adult, she understood them. Tired from the climb, she sat at the edge of the mat. A pair of young boys was approaching, carrying dried rockworms and soggy tomalots. She turned and said, "Leave the baskets and go. Wait for me below."

Boys never liked to be told what to do. This was something the Eight had noticed. But the children respected the woman. In fact, they liked to boast to the giant that she was the best doctor in the papio world, which meant the entire world. Tree-walkers were stupid little monkeys, said those boys, and of course their monkey doctors were idiots.

"Go now," she snapped at the boys.

They grudgingly set their baskets on the mat and galloped off.

To her patient, the doctor said, "I have quite a lot to tell you."

"We heard every word," they said.

"I know what you heard, and that's why I won't repeat their idiot noise. They want me to spell out the possibilities, but I don't need to spell anything. You understand their plans. Their plans look awful to the nine of us, yes. But my impressions and my frustrations aren't worth much at all."

The Eight waited, and the woman said nothing.

Then the long mouth opened, each of them trying to move the huge pink tongue.

She saw the struggle, and she laughed sadly.

They stopped moving, still as the coral beneath them.

"First of all," she said. "You must, must, must change. I know your circumstances are difficult. I can't imagine how it would feel, sharing my skull with seven brilliant souls. But this is not a natural arrangement. I told you that long ago and every day since. I think each of you were eaten by the corona but not killed. That stomach was an acidic oven, but you survived. I can't guess how you managed, but you survived as one body, round as a green nut, and after so much time in that awful state, under pressure, in the worst hell, you were joined. And even after all of my work, I still can't count how many ways in which you are fused into One.

"But you aren't One.

"Being many might be wonderful, but I don't see the wonderful standing before me. And you plainly need to be reminded that we aren't lying inside a hot acid bath. The trap around you is far worse than any corona's stomach. From this moment on, your existence will be in question, and that assumes just one of you takes charge of the body and your voice."

"But that can't be done," one of the Eight said, and another said, and then several more. "We've tried and failed and failed again. Quit demanding the impossible."

They spoke the same words, but the tongue and mouth created only a gush of angry, slurring words.

"I don't care which one of you leads," the doctor claimed, even though they suspected who was her favorite.

The giant body slumped down on the mat, each soul defending its pieces.

"And that isn't all of my news," said the doctor.

None of them wanted to listen. They were sick of papios and their noises. But the doctor's admonishments were followed by silence and a hard stern stare that caught everyone by surprise.

The giant head rose.

One mind asked, "What do you have to tell?"

"I am like you now," she said.

"Like us how?"

"I'm more than one." The woman put her weight on her feet, hands lifting, lifting away the clothes around her chest. "A second entity lives inside me. It's vigorous and enduring. By all evidence, it took root inside my left breast before spreading to other places, and it should outlive me by a moment or two. Or if someone takes these cells and cultivates them, my companion can live forever."

They didn't have words or any useful thoughts.

"Cancer," she said, exposing the rib-rich chest and the surviving breast and the mutilations masked by padding and vanity. "The cancer is killing me."

In that instant, each one of them loved her.

"I'm going home soon to die, and you'll be left here inside the world, and the world is a monster's stomach too."

A long slow noise leaked out of them.

"And no," she continued, "I won't tell you who should rule that body of yours. But if you keep acting like a crazy beast squatting in the shadows, then my people will have no choice but action."

She covered her wounds, weeping quietly.

"Believing there's no choice is the same as having no choice," she warned. "Can any one of you see that?"

• • •

The Archon was elsewhere. Diamond asked when she would return, but nobody seemed to know. Good was riding on Diamond's left shoulder, growling out of habit. Tar`ro had placed himself beside the boy, growling with purpose. When one of his armed colleagues approached, presumably to help protect their charge, Tar`ro said, "You'll want to give me distance."

The other guard didn't understand.

"Bits," said Tar`ro. "You were friendly with Bits, weren't you?"

"Pretty much."

"Then get out of my sight." Tar`ro waved at the other guards, saying, "Believe nothing and watch each other. Agreed?"

Prima had left her aide in charge. Excited by the responsibility, the young woman led the refugees across the landing and into the atrium. The giant room was filled with sunlight and sorry voices. The blackwood statue of a slayer remained in the room's center, and when they walked past, habit took charge. Diamond stopped and stared up at that magnificent figure.

The aide had a specific destination. She paused to wave. "Hurry up now please," she said.

"No, we can wait here," Tar`ro said.

She shook a finger. "Why here? We're exposed here."

"Yeah, but I probably won't feel safe inside any little room." Tar`ro gave the space a quick, thorough study. "We can see everybody here, and we've got escape routes. So this is where we are going to live for next few recitations. Understood?"

The aide was in charge one moment, and then she wasn't. Her face turned sour, and a matching voice said, "All right, but not for long."

Merit and Master Nissim were at the back of the group, talking quietly.

People were walking past Diamond. Some of the people were strangers, but plenty of faces were familiar. Some people looked straight ahead, thinking dark important thoughts. Some noticed the boy, staring at him until they felt self-conscious, and then their eyes jumped away. People were holding books and folders and critical sheets of paper. Empty hands often made fists. Nervous perspiration made everyone smell. Office clothes were wrinkled and dark with sweat, and there were green-gray militia uniforms not quite buttoned up, and four uniforms made of fancy green silk were walking together, worn by officers in the District Regulars.

The soldiers approached the famous statue and a tangle of lost kids, paying attention only to each other.

"So it was the papio," one officer said.

"Evidence says," another said.

The third officer offered up curses, nothing else.

Then the man at the lead said, "I don't believe it's them."

Others didn't agree, but nobody dared argue the point.

The ranking officer wore corona teeth on his shoulders and a hat made from fancy red fur. "This was a bee bite. This was nothing. If I were the papio, I'd have hit us a hundred times harder, while I had surprise working for me."

Then the soldiers were past, out of earshot.

Again, Diamond looked at the slayer's statue. Up close, there wasn't any face. The blackwood had been attacked with chisels, leaving a lumpy surface that didn't look like any human being. Only from a distance did the eyes appear, and that stern smart mouth, and the long noble nose worn by every hero in the history books.

Schoolmates stood close to one another. The littlest girl was watching faces. Her expression was very serious, very hopeful.

Diamond stepped close and said, "Prue."

She didn't look at Diamond. "Do you see her?" she asked.

"See who?"

"My mother. Don't let me miss my mother."

Good had grown heavy. Diamond poked him in the ribs, and he jumped to the floor, pushing between his boy's school boots.

Elata was behind Diamond. She was crying again, and Seldom stood beside her, looking as if he was going to be sick. Karlan was in the background, his face flat and dry, lips pressed into a scar-colored line, both fists drumming on his thighs.

"Do you see Mommy?" Prue asked.

There was no name to put to his feelings. Diamond was miserable before he talked to Prue, and this was just a different, newer misery. Looking out at the people, his stomach felt as if it had been cut open, and that's when a piece of him turned curious, wondering if he would throw up and what that would feel like.

"But why would your mother be here?" he asked.

"There are so many people," the girl said, sounding nothing but reasonable. "She's going to be one of these people."

Diamond backed away. Master Nissim was talking to his other students. Even on his knees, the man was taller than anyone from the class. Holding two boys by their shoulders, he looked at all of them when he said, "Hope for the best, because it happens. The best happens." He nodded hard, trying to convince. "Someone is coming to help, and you'll get to where you need to be."

The oldest girl asked, "Are you leaving us?"

Nissim made his mouth tiny, and he glanced at Merit.

Father put himself beside his son again, one hand on his shoulder.

"I don't want you to leave us," the girl said.

But then one of the boys shook free of the Master's hand, and he said, "No, we want to get away from him."

The boy pointed at Diamond.

Diamond's soldiers had burned to nothing. He was suddenly thinking how those toys had names, but real people were so much bigger than any piece of paint and carved wood. He had sat with these other children for hundreds of days, and he knew their names and quite a few details about their lives, although he didn't know very much at all. Yet with his memory, he could replay each of their days together, if he ever wanted.

If it was ever important, that is.

Then the pitch and pace of voices changed. The Archon had suddenly emerged in the deepest part of the atrium, back where the elevators waited.

The aide saw Prima, and relieved, she turned to Diamond. "This way," she said to him and only him.

The boy began walking, but not fast.

Good leapt up on his left shoulder again.

"What about my other students?" Nissim asked, rising stiffly. "Do they come with us?"

"No, we have people to help them," the aide said.

She wasn't looking at anyone. People who lied often hid their eyes.

Diamond stopped and turned.

Elata was standing beside Prue, looking at Diamond. She said a word or two to the little girl. Then she ran over to her friend to say, "I don't know."

"Know what?"

She didn't answer. She didn't look at Diamond. "Seldom, come on right now," she shouted.

Seldom walked with his arms tight around his waist.

Karlan began to follow, and Tar`ro stared at him.

"I saved your boy," Karlan pointed out. "Without me, we'd have all gone down with the damn tree."

"So you're a hero," Tar`ro said.

"Oh, don't worry," the giant boy said. "You can be hero someday too."

Nobody's face was calmer than the Archon's face. Nothing about her could be confused for happy or relaxed, yet the day's horrors hadn't damaged her normal self. Problems here wanted to be solved, and there were opportunities ready to be found, and just the way she carried herself was a testament to poise and strength and an infectious will that almost everyone wanted to feel.

When the woman looked at Diamond, she smiled, compassion dancing beside a thousand subtle considerations.

When she and her aide met, Prima held the young woman by an elbow, saying, "Thank you," before whispering a few private words.

The aide blinked and stepped back. "I thought we were going to protect him in the Station," she said.

"Except our security is lousy," the Archon said. "We've got more than a thousand people in this building, plus refugees, and if we think we can trust everybody, then we're vulnerable to the next surprise."

"Yeah, we're a mess," Tar`ro said.

The group was standing close together again.

The Archon looked at Tar`ro. "Did you know that guard well? The man named Bits?"

"Obviously not, madam."

Father and Nissim were whispering back and forth again.

"All right," the Archon said to the surviving guard. "If you're making decisions, what would you do? How would you protect the boy from this point on?"

Tar`ro had thought the problem through. "I'd find a fast fletch and wait for darkness. Then we'd run away."

The Archon nodded. "The *Happenstance* is fueled and ready."

"I like that ship," Diamond said.

She nodded, playing with a weak smile. "And where would you take the boy, if that's what we decide to do?"

"I don't think I'd tell anybody, madam."

"That is a wonderful answer," the Archon said, turning to her aide once more, ready to deliver orders.

Father came forward.

He didn't hurry, and he certainly didn't push anyone. But the man put himself in front before he said, "Prima," with a warm voice.

"Yes, Merit."

"For a lot of reasons, I need to talk to my son in private. Is there any way that would be possible?"

She barely had to think. "Of course. I understand. In fact, you can use my office, and in the meantime, we'll make arrangements with the *Happenstance*."

"Wonderful, madam. Thank you."

They were walking again, but the Archon stayed behind to deliver more orders. Father pressed the pace. They went into a long hallway, discovering a familiar old man and his old gray-and-white uniform leaning against the blond paneling of his elevator.

Diamond looked back.

The bodyguards had nobody to watch but each other. Elata was approaching, and Seldom, with Karlan following everybody else. Diamond had to step out to look past that enormous body, but the hallway curved slightly. He couldn't see into the atrium anymore. The rest of his class had been left behind, and Prue too. Diamond felt uneasy thinking about strangers walking past the students, nobody noticing them, and in another few moments he might have suggested that someone return to check on the little girl. But then Father ushered him inside the elevator, and the rest of the group followed, doors rattling shut and everyone standing quiet and still as the world dropped fast around them.

• • •

The forest should never stop falling. There was always a limb snapping free, slipping out from beneath the dense canopy. There always had to be dead birds blown from their last perches and desperate monkeys that couldn't make one long leap, and whole insects and pieces of insects and animal wastes, solid and wet, made a filthy rain, pungent and endless, and the tree-walkers never quit throwing their trash into the open air, pencil stubs and jeweled bracelets and worn-out shoes tumbling down to where the demon floor waited, and after that, oblivion.

But then the explosions came, and following the blasts were fires that ate their way towards the wilderness. Quest had never seen any collapse of this magnitude. For one horrible moment, the world looked ready to turn black and die. But after the last few trees ripped free of the world, the flames were choked out by their own smoke. That's when the stillness came. Every weak branch had already fallen. Scared animals didn't eat or willingly climb anywhere, and nothing in the world was relaxed enough to shit. Suddenly it seemed as if no living creature would ever move again, as if the forest had been trapped inside some invisible glass, clear but unforgivingly rigid, and what if this moment of perfect stillness continued forever?

Quest was terrified in new ways.

And then a breeze stirred, twenty little branches falling, and the creature secretly rejoiced.

Quest had never been so large. Throughout the morning, flocks and swarms of displaced animals had fled to her dobdob tree, too panicked to notice her swollen, barely camouflaged body. She had eaten beyond her fill, beyond any sensible need, using cheap flesh to weave more eyes and more ears and enough nostrils to grab the quietest, most distant scent. Old cautions had been set aside, and while she had no plans to remain this huge, she had to wonder how much larger she could grow before the dobdob branches would split and fall.

The breeze grew stronger, offering a rich mass of odors and new sounds.

A thousand human voices were close enough to be heard. Quest listened to citizens on the District's wild border, and she eavesdropped on foresters and hunters perched in closer places. Every one of them was agitated, angry, and terrified, and they couldn't reveal their deepest feelings quickly enough.

Half of those voices talked about the papio.

Half of that half saw no reason to give the enemy warning or measured decency. The counterattack had to be immediate, without limits. Justice demanded murder on a matching scale, which was ten or twenty or fifty thousand dead, and they wanted nothing else and many wanted to help with the killing.

"Damn all of the papio," they said.

That was when Quest finally twisted a portion of her eyes and ears, fixing them on the distant reef.

Watching the tree-walkers was always easier than studying the papio. The wilderness trees grew thin and high at its margins, and the reef-humans had better eyes than their cousins had. Worse still, Quest could see very little besides limbs and leaves, and she expected to hear nothing but wilderness sounds. That's what came to her at first. A hundred thousand trees were calmly swaying in the wind. But then a whisper arrived, strained through wood and cricket song, and she pivoted almost all of her ears, aiming for the inhabited coral.

A rough rattling noise emerged, like a giant insect shivering itself warm.

Then a second rattle found her.

And suddenly she counted five rattles, with vaguer sounds coming from up and down the reef. Powerful jet engines were laboring but not moving. Fuel was being spent for reasons she couldn't imagine, and she waited for the papio wings to launch. But some invisible signal was given or an established timetable was being followed. Inside the same moment, every engine dropped into silence.

Clinging to her fragile perch, Quest wondered how fast she could strip away her new flesh, and where she could hide before night.

SIX

Father closed the office door while Good claimed the top of the Archon's desk. A wealth of important papers stood in a stack, ready to be shredded into a workable nest, but the monkey squatted at the desk's edge, defecating into the round trash basket, and then he closed his eyes as if deep in sleep.

Diamond thought he should put the mess somewhere else.

But he did nothing.

Father slowly lowered himself into one of the guest chairs, and Diamond sat beside him. The Archon's chair was behind the desk, very tall and made from black leather, steady use leaving the faint impression of the woman's shoulders and head.

Father took a deep breath.

The boy studied the empty chair.

"I never imagined this," said Father. "That anyone would want to do this . . . whatever this is . . . "

The Archon wasn't with them, yet Diamond could see her plainly.

That was important.

Why was it important?

"Look at me, Diamond."

The boy didn't want to be seen. He was waiting for his face to find a worthy expression—some sorrowful grin or wild grief or simple crazy terror. Any expression would be better than the rigid, unfeeling mask plastered over his features now. But too many feelings were roiling inside him, too many wounds. Maybe the invulnerable brain had been injured and needed to heal. But the brain was harder than his flesh and his bone, and maybe the wounds would never heal. That's what Diamond was hoping, because awful days like these should leave scars that never went away.

Father put a hand on his hand.

Diamond turned toward him.

The soft old face was wet under the eyes. The scar seemed to be the biggest wrinkle. Father sighed, and with another man's voice, he said, "I want you to know."

The voice was too high, too thin.

Diamond smelled fresh turds and his father's sweat and his own sweat, which was saltier than anyone else's. A full recitation passed before he asked, "What do you want me to know?"

"How thrilled I am that you're alive."

A set of broad windows looked across a slice of forest that hadn't fallen yet. The air was teeming with screeching homeless birds. Commuter blimps and private airships were coming from far-flung parts of the District, wanting to help or at least hoping to measure the catastrophe. A much larger airship maneuvered in the distance—an elegant long machine woven around a skeleton of corona bones, made silver from the many corona scales fixed to its hull.

Father kept talking. "That's what your mother would want," he said. "First in her mind would be your survival."

Diamond looked at the chair and the left-behind impressions again.

"Mother isn't gone," he said.

"Maybe not," Father said. "It's early. Ships and refugees are scattered. We can't say anything for certain."

Diamond meant something else, but he did a poor job saying so.

Suddenly, with both hands, someone struck the closed door.

The boy jumped, but not Father.

"Yes," Merit said without turning. "What is it?"

Tar`ro looked in. "The *Happenstance* is ready."

"All right."

"We can climb on board whenever we're ready."

"Thank you, my friend."

The guard nodded, watching both faces. Then he said, "It looks like a very short day. The sun's dimming fast."

A lot of trees had fallen and burned, and the coronas' realm always thrived when that fierce air was seasoned with ash.

"We won't be much longer," Father said.

Tar`ro nodded, left.

The military airship had dropped from view. Diamond watched the birds, except he wasn't seeing them. His eyes were open yet in some odd fashion blind. He closed his eyes and rubbed them, softly and then hard, and opening them again, he found his father sitting in the Archon's tall chair, hiding every trace of the little woman.

"I was counting on them putting us inside somebody's office," Father said.

Diamond looked at the walls. Each was adorned with pictures and plaques and certificates full of words that he didn't have the patience to read.

"They'd leave me with a working call-line," the man added.

Prima enjoyed five working lines to the world, which was a huge number. Maybe only the Archon of Archons had more. Father lifted the receiver and touched several glowing buttons. A ring ended with a buzzing voice, and when the voice quit, Father said, "This is Merit. Now I want you to listen to me."

• • •

Older children had always helped care for the youngsters.

That was the human way.

Adults weren't suited to the demands of little ones. Somebody needed to feed the creatures, and they had to be bathed and clothed. Small transgressions demanded punishment. Someone needed to act as a diplomat when young friendships were tested. But there was a subtle, far greater blessing in this tedium. The caretakers had no choice but talk to these tiny, uncivilized beings. Every day, instructions and clear warnings had to be given, moral laws invoked, and the same laws had to be defended from evil and doubt and lazy blood. Old stories were recited from memory, and even if the little ones were filthy loud brats with the attention spans of roaches, old stories had a habit of coming alive for the speakers. Suddenly these weren't strings of memorized words, but they were Truth and Authority, and this was why noses were wiped and asses were spanked every day: the partly grown caretakers were making themselves human.

Papio children had always helped raise the Eight.

At first local boys and girls were gathered up and sworn to secrecy. They helped feed the odd mouths and clean up the nasty messes while the doctor and various experts failed to make contact with the Eight.

But one caretaker made it his mission to stand before the swollen, helpless monster. Day after day, he would hold up a simple object or body part, showing it to whatever looked most like an eye. He named the object, repeating the word a thousand times, and then he listened to the best mouth, ignoring the mutters and groans, waiting for that clumsy first word.

"Hand," was what the Eight said first.

"Hand hand hand hand . . . hand hand . . . "

One word grew into a toddler's vocabulary, and the Eight begged for more children to help it learn and grow.

The papio searched their world for bright patient youngsters. A secret village was built underground, and to help maintain security, none of the helpers were allowed to return home again.

Soon the Eight grew one mouth and four clumsy limbs, and each mind learned to speak. Names were given to the Eight. The doctor had her favorite, and every child had his or hers. Hundreds of busy days passed; nothing substantial changed. The Eight remained divided and chaotic. The Eight spoke in riddles and nonsense, although the children were adept at guessing moods, and better than any adult, they could separate their favorite's words from the mayhem.

The oldest children became adults. They were thanked and replaced, and with nervous anticipation, they began to dress in adult lives. But the old rules remained in force. Each had to remain in the vicinity, working where they could, and in one case marrying one another. It seemed inevitable that their future children would eventually take up this great work, and their grandchildren.

But then Diamond came to the reef, and King, both running wild among the furious, horrified papio.

After that, nothing was the same. King went back to the middle of the world, living inside his father's giant house of wood and sap. The strange human child was sleeping in his old room, pretending to be a happy normal tree-walker rich with friends, school, and peace. And there were whispers about some magical beast with no shape and no weight, living free in the wilderness between the two human worlds.

Suddenly the Eight seemed like the weakest child. Powerful voices regretted their patience, and meanwhile, the old doctor who had studied them and protected them returned home, and as promised, she and her cancer died.

New doctors assembled in a distant city, making plans.

Throughout those troubles, the children kept vigil, bringing food and drink, news and rumors. And sometimes one of the Eight would take charge of the mouth, speaking to a favorite child with a clear voice, or washing all of them with bent little riddles.

King and Diamond had been home for forty days. The oldest child—the same young boy who taught the monster to talk—was now a young soldier serving in the local militia. One afternoon he left his post to run up into the reef's shadows, nothing in his hands but still full of news. The doctors had arrived, bringing tools and odd machines. They wouldn't discuss their plans, but it was obvious what was coming, perhaps as early as the day after tomorrow.

One voice took the mouth long enough to say, "I want a basher nut. Bring me one basher nut."

Moments later, the Eight collapsed on the favorite dash-and-ash mat, eyes blind and the mouth wide.

Each entity was at war with its siblings.

King and Diamond had strong little bodies. But the Eight was a giant, divided and useless so long as each of them ruled just a few pieces. War was inevitable, and silent. Blood was the weapon of necessity, and their blood came in eight distinct shades. Three were red: smoky red or bright pink or red like a man. Two forms were violet, while one was black and another a cold blue. And the final blood was a scalding, flame-worthy orange. Each had its taste and temperature, its consistency and limits. Each carried cells that might have once fought diseases but now battled foreign organs. Some were strongest in the day, others at night. The bloods flowed where they could, and when every course was blocked, they would pool inside friendly hearts and livers, gathering energy, waiting to attack whatever new weakness was revealed.

Blood could change its color, pretended to be another.

On occasions the blood scattered until it was too thin to notice. What was invisible slipped past barriers, attacking like poison, like cancer, killing the enemy from within.

Fouling the siblings' meat was a common tactic.

Cutting nerves and food to the enemies were equally valid.

Through the night and during the following long day, the giant body was wracked by endless violence. Children brought food that wasn't eaten and water that wasn't sipped, and they sat on the coral dusts, watching nothing change. Meanwhile the new doctors approached cautiously, taking temperatures and samples of flesh, scribbling elaborate notes while ignoring what the children told them. The Eight were fighting for control and all the doctors needed to do was to wait for someone to win the last battle. But as a group, those smart doctors decided that war wasn't the smart conclusion. The corona's largest child had fallen ill. The eight creatures had lost their equilibrium. Yes, the body was in turmoil, and it was hard to see which part belonged to which creature. But the eight brains were distinct, and doctors understood knives and surgery. To people like them, only one plan made any sense.

Divers had the reddest blood, and her muscle was red and her bones were white, and Diver's cells and tissue resembled human cells and human tissue.

The old woman doctor had commented on the similarities several times. But even once would have been too often. Divers' siblings saw the implications. The papio were imagining a human cousin floating between the monstrous Seven. What would be their value once another Diamond was hacked free of her prison?

And there was a second advantage that Divers held—innate talents for managing her organs and blood, and for manipulating the complex, chaotic nervous system strung between each of her siblings. She was the strongest when war began. But everybody else saw the value in stomping on Divers, making her feeble. As the second night arrived, she was the seventh strongest power—her brain pushed to the top of the skull while her surviving body was a ribbon of red meat running down the body's long back.

But what is small can be strong, in the right circumstances.

Night arrived, and the doctors had made their decision. Long knives and cauterizing loops were laid out on the adjacent mat. By every measure, the giant body was helpless, eyes shut and the breathing fitful. One last battery of tests had to be carried out. A thousand bits of flesh were taken from everywhere, and the Eight's body was painted as the doctors worked, each patch of skin given an owner and rough borders.

Just then, five caretakers appeared.

Two of the children were nearly adults, while the others belonged to the youngest class. Each shouldered a covered basket or polished gray jar. Sober, serious faces went unnoticed. Children normally chattered with one another, but not this group. The doctors mapping the body reacted by waving at the air, telling them that they were needed anywhere but here. Yet the caretakers claimed orders and duties. Reaching the edge of the Eight's mat, they set down the baskets and tall jars, and instead of leaving, they stood shoulder to shoulder, pulling guns out from the baskets and jars.

The finest surgeons in the world were told to sit on their hands and do nothing, and they did just that.

Then the oldest children grabbed the long razor-edged surgical blades, and following the brightly colored ink lines, they opened twin gouges down the Eight's long back.

Divers was tiny because her plan was to be tiny.

Losing every battle, she had retreated purposefully until she was as small as Diamond and easy to reach.

The plan—her simple brutal perfect plan—began long ago. Through riddles and codes, she spoke to her favorite papio children. She explained just enough to make them understand what she wanted. Then she gave the signal, the code words, "Basher nut," and the one young soldier went back to the armory to collect weapons and make ready.

Surgical blades slashed deep into the hot rainbow blood. A war-torn body tried in vain to heal, but there was too much weakness, too much damage. With the skull suddenly exposed, the biggest child yanked an iron hammer out of his water jar and swung hard ten times before exposing the brains. Each brain was remarkably similar. They had the same size and a similar elongated shape, covered with tiny hairs that had infiltrated every other brain. They wore the same glossy gray color of something that wasn't metal or stone, that couldn't be shattered by human force and that was alive without belonging to the living world.

Divers' brain was on top, attached to a long armful of ruddy wet meat.

And Divers had won.

Her siblings felt it, knew it. Another pair of cuts, graceless and savage, and she would have popped free from the body, torn loose from her siblings' minds. But the children with the knives did nothing more. Obeying instructions, they stepped aside while the wounds struggled to heal, and that was the moment when Divers said to her sisters and brothers, "No, I won't leave you."

No one else spoke, not with any kind of voice.

The minds had always known how to talk silently to their neighbors, and that was the voice she used then.

"We'll stay as one and die as one," she promised.

Decisions were made in those next quiet moments.

Then after more healing, Divers took hold of the mouth, the long tongue, announcing, "We are done."

The children put down the knives and guns. By the time soldiers arrived, the ravaged body was halfway recovered. An event resembling an election or chemical reaction had run its course. One soul was granted full control over the mouth and motor functions as well as the largest share when it came to decisions and plans. And that soul lifted the gouged body off the mat, telling the papio, "We are finished."

The doctors were too flustered to think clearly. But all of the children smiled—even those temporarily wearing chains.

"I'm in total charge," said the new voice, lucid and strong. "But if you should ever try to harm any of us, now or tomorrow—if you raise a blade against us for any reason—none of us will help you again. Do you understand what I'm telling you?"

The doctors claimed to understand, and so did the various leaders who arrived over the next days, paying their respects to the reborn child.

And for hundreds of long days, Divers had walked about the world with a measure of freedom, and Divers spoke to whomever she wished, and life became such a pleasure that the Seven inside her began to love everything that they shared.

• • •

The man's words were being dragged through long reaches of secure copper, making his voice even less impressive than usual. Sounding like a shrill boy reading a script, the Archon of Archons told her, "My condolences for you and for your suffering people."

"Thank you," she said.

Then aiming for a caring tone, he said, "Prima."

She bristled whenever the ambitious little man used her given name.

"This is a grave tragedy, a supreme crime," List continued. "You know I'm not a man given to idle promises, but I swear, there will be justice, Prima."

Prima was standing at the back of the command center. What was it that made a simple sound into your name, and why did you hate your opponents mangling your identity with their unworthy lips?

"Thank you," she repeated.

"What have you heard from the other Districts?" he asked.

"Every Archon is promising every resource. And their offices and mine are coordinating our united response."

"Wonderful." List didn't ask for specifics. No sane leader could spell out what "united" meant.

"Every District is on full alert," she said.

"Naturally," he said, papers shuffling near his microphone. "In fact, Baffle District has front-line ships patrolling the fringe of papio airspace."

Prima hadn't heard that news. With two curling fingers, she caught the attention of a young lieutenant, bringing him close.

"I only wish we had our forces stationed in your District," he continued.

"They'll arrive soon enough," she said.

What might have been a click of the tongue came into the earpiece. "This is the not the time for doubts. But if you'd allowed us to base a portion of our forces inside your territory—"

"Destroying precedents older than any tree," she said, invoking that hoary cliché.

"A mixed force, a balanced force. Every District would have a picked contingent."

But Baffle District and the Mists, Bluetear and the rest of her allies would send only an elderly scout ship or two. Only the District of Districts had the resources and buffer zones to station forces outside their home berths. List was making noise for its own sake, and Prima had her own fine reasons to say nothing, jotting a question down on privacy paper, folding it and sealing it before handing the slip to the waiting officer.

The lieutenant nodded, put the slip into a pocket and left.

"How many wings have you seen?" asked List.

"Three wings patrolling near the reef," she said. "Other machines were running on their landings. But they've been put back to bed again."

"And the papio," he began.

"Yes?"

"Have you had been in contact with them?"

Prima threw her gaze out the long windows, but all she saw was a small man made sick with ambition.

"Just tell me," she said. "What are you hunting here?"

Laughter was the response, or the wires invented that noise out of the random vibrations. Either way, List seemed to enjoy himself. "The coral-shitters are making outrageous claims. They're innocent, they are blameless, and we're fools for thinking whatever it is we're thinking."

The tone was peculiarly aggressive, and important.

"Our local consulate sent everybody to my door," Prima admitted. "Maybe they're lying, but these diplomats seem terrified. The same as you, they claim to be helpless spectators to this ugliness."

"Of course," List said.

"I insisted on their help. I want to understand who would gut my district, brutally murdering so many, all in the useless attempt to kill one of my citizens."

"How did the papio respond?" List asked.

"They showed incisors and claimed my best allies were responsible."

The hiss of the wire ended with a curt, "Nonsense."

"Of course I told them that they were mistaken," said Prima. "Our allies and our friends of convenience have no motivation here. But the papio assured me that my species is afraid of the boy, that certain old notions don't relish what he represents. And that's why they want him burnt up and lost to our world."

Suddenly loud, seemingly close, the Archon of Archons said, "That's not my wish, madam. Not in the least."

"I understand that. Believe me, I do."

"You know my feelings. The boy's a treasure, and I've always thought he would be safe and happy living with me."

"You can't say anything else," she said. "Not and remain believable."

List sighed.

A second voice intruded, shouting with that hard distinct bark. "Is the little fellow safe?"

King was yelling.

"Diamond's quite safe," she said.

"The one blessing in this very miserable day," said List.

Sad to think, she had doubts about this supposed blessing. Without the boy, the future would become more predictable. Not that anything in the world would ever find its way back to normal again, but the human mind kept searching for the expected and the boring—that's where most of life's blessings were waiting.

With a careful tone, List said, "Madam."

A blackwood cabinet stood near Prima, sporting rows of important lights. A few lights were beginning to flicker.

"Where's the boy now, if I might ask?"

"Sitting across from me," she lied. "His father and his teacher are here, and his monkey is asleep on his lap."

"I am glad to hear that," he said.

"And what about your son?"

"King is well, thank you."

"And safe, I trust?"

"As safe as anyone on this day."

"Indeed," said Prima.

Then the Archon of Archons ended their difficult conversation with remarkable honesty: "Give that young man your very best, Prima. Because I doubt he would ever accept mine."

"I will do that," she said gladly.

"And we'll see one another soon," he said.

The line went quiet before she could offer a polite response, her ear filled with static. Setting the receiver on the desk, she thought about King. Just hearing the voice in the background triggered memories, few of them pleasant. Each time she met the creature, he was noticeably bigger and more powerful. But what mattered more than strength or the hideous appearance was the slow transformation in the creature's character. King could still yell like a monster and pout like a little boy, but he was learning how to stand in one place and carry on a civil conversation. The brute was maturing, or he pretended to be older and wiser while his nature remained the same. How could she judge? He was a puzzle. The armored face with its two ugly mouths and hard black eyes gave away nothing about his real thoughts. Politicians read emotions, but when that creature wanted, he could make himself into a statue, spitting out canned phrases along with silence.

List was vile, but he was a man. She accepted the Archon's shrewdness and the craving for power, but Prima never doubted that she could piece together what was honest inside the fabrications, and where the big smile meant nothing but one mouth full of bright teeth.

The lieutenant had returned with a fresh slip of privacy paper.

Prima broke the seal. The sloppy hand of a fletch captain had written, "*Happenstance* fully loaded, at the ready."

She nodded and dropped the note into a fire tank.

The lieutenant waited.

"Your name is Sondaw," she said.

"Yes, madam."

Sondaw was a member of the Regulars. The youngster had a pleasant face, a man's features drawn over a boy's bones, nothing behind the eyes but nervous energy and an instinctive need to please his superiors.

She said, "When I was little, your grandfather visited our home for dinner."

"My father's father. Yes, madam."

"He was the great general charged with rebuilding our fleet, and needing the best materials, he was building good relations with my parents."

The lieutenant was thrilled for the attention, but he still chewed at a lip, unsure where this moment would lead.

"I want to use you, Sondaw."

"How, madam?"

"I need certain files," she explained. "Start with our Intelligence Department. Tell Lady Rankle that the merchant's daughter wants to see everything she has about the King entity. I want observations and speculations, and if there are any prophetic dreams, leave them at the bottom of the stack, please."

The officer was willing but puzzled.

To focus his attentions, Prima added, "This is your only priority."

Sondaw nodded and then walked away, and seeing an opportunity, other officers and aides converged on their boss. Prima dealt with refugees and power outages, and she looked at fuel stocks and ammunition manifests. Then she started to address the ongoing problems with Hanner and the tree's slow death, her mind making the inevitable turn, praying to the Creators that this endless awful day would end.

That was when the blackwood cabinet began to buzz.

She heard the warning before noticing that half of the red lights were flashing slowly and then faster. There wasn't much room left inside her for fear, but there was still enough curiosity to make her heart skip. She approached the cabinet and the lights. Suddenly two colonels pushed past her, their fears soaring.

Hundreds of days ago, these same men had explained this machine to their new Archon, mixing expert words with rigid poise. Details were lost, but Prima retained the image of microphones set in far places, scattered across the wilderness between her District and the reef. Each sensor sent home the most common forest noises. Only the loudest, shrillest tones caused the lights to come alive, and then only when a fletch passed nearby, or maybe a single papio wing making a reconnaissance sweep. But even the loudest roar normally produced just one or two slow flashes from adjacent bulbs. But these flashes were rapid, which was significant, and the officers were plugging headsets into the portals under the busiest lights, numbly listening to noises beyond their experience.

Prima stepped past the box, using her rank to find space at the window, and she stared at a day that was rapidly drawing to a close.

Behind her, panic danced closely with duty and training.

The poise that had served her in public life was surviving. The Archon stared at the empty air and the occasional airship heavy with survivors, shaking her head slowly. A smart voice behind her—not one of the colonels with headsets—was laughing at everyone. "It's a malfunction, a surge," he said. "This is nothing, forget it."

The logic had its charms.

Of course this was a malfunction. If the papio were coming in large numbers, she would hear the sounds of those engines for herself.

With fingertips, the Archon gently touched the reinforced window.

Vibrations played with the glass.

"Quiet," Prima shouted.

And the command center fell into a forced calm, and everyone listened to a hundred horrible roars washing across them, still distant but already loud, and in another few moments, the papio had arrived.

• • •

The *Happenstance* had served its District for a long while, suffering few failures while enjoying no celebrated distinctions. But then Merit and Haddi produced their sickly baby, and wishing to help that good man, the fletch's captain sacrificed a pair of royal jazzings. Some voices claimed that the baby wasn't sick at all, but that didn't stop the captain from openly taking credit for the child's survival. Why should any decency remain secret? And as if to prove him right, almost a thousand days later Diamond arrived at the captain's berth, searching for quick transport to find his father.

The *Happenstance* and Diamond were lashed together in the public mind.

What had been a minor fletch enjoyed its celebrity, and the superstitious captain was judged either an agent of history or the idiot recipient of the worst kind of luck—depending on what those jazzings had bestowed to the world.

The ficklest of the Destinies, *Happenstance* was a beautiful and treacherous lady spirit. She saw to it that when Rail fell and Marduk fell, her fletch was on duty at the Ivory Station. There was scared talk about abandoning Hanner, and that's why the ship's tank was full of alcohol, her corona bladders bulging with hydrogen gas. The crew worked hard throughout that awful day, keeping their vessel ready to fly at a breath's notice. Eventually the boy's bodyguard delivered a flight plan that was to remain sealed until night. Tar`ro met privately with the captain, and a little later the captain emptied the hanger's berth before herding his worn-out crew to their fletch's bridge, warning them that secret passengers were coming onboard and they needed to keep their eyes on each other, not below.

Of course the boy had to be one of their passengers. Cover the cabin's rubber windows and demand secrecy, but some truths were apparent. To keep the ship trim and ready, the hiding people's weight had to be share. Diamond and his friends and the one guard and his teacher, plus Merit, were onboard. There was also one very large second guard. So the secret wasn't secret, and nobody meant harm when the day was growing old and one or two of the crew mentioned "the famous boy" to the mechanics working on the ship, and to the soldiers protecting them, and maybe a spy or two were standing in their midst.

The papio attacked before darkness. They came exactly as they were supposed to come: a rapid bruising strike with those winged machines that both amused and terrified every fletch captain. Big wings flew beneath the trees, burning fabulous volumes of alcohol even before they climbed toward Danner and the Station. Local airships and tree-mounted gun turrets fired at the blurring targets, and the papio pilots spun and evaded the worst of the gunfire, targeting the worthiest, easiest targets. Fortunes of metal and polished coral were sent flying. Holes were punched through even the toughest corona scales. Late day battles were always the worst. The atmosphere's high oxygen content meant that fuel tanks ignited with the first spark, while bladders filled with hydrogen gas were bombs waiting for any excuse. Wings shattered and dropped. Airships turned to clouds of flame, their bones littering the open air beneath. But the *Happenstance*'s captain had his youngest, sharpest-eared crewman listening to the winds, and he launched with the first rumbling of jets, diving into the thickest portion of Danner's surviving canopy.

Ship and captain roared between branches, shredding leaves and a lot of birds as they fought for distance and invisibility and one last dose of luck.

Then the first mate tore open the sealed flight plan.

"Dirth-home," she read aloud.

That was a small surprise. They were being ordered toward a keenwood growing on the edge of the District of Districts. It wasn't an obscure place, but on a table of useful destinations, Dirth-home dangled near the trash can.

"Do we have any followers?" the captain asked.

No papio were visible, thankfully.

The superstitious man had little faith in their prospects. He gave orders about direction and speed, yet he refused to sacrifice the resident baddilick—a golden rat kept for desperate occasions.

"Leave him alone," the captain said, forcing his crew to shove the angry animal back into its cage.

"But blood could help," said the first mate. "And it certainly wouldn't hurt."

The captain meant to respond. Another moment or two, and he would have explained how their good luck would be someone else's curse. But a papio flex-wing spied them, diving low and turning its jets to hover long enough to afford two clean shots, and their unarmored engines were instantly turned to scrap.

Twin fires were quenched with smothering gases and foam, but meanwhile the *Happenstance* drifted into a great old branch, and one of its bladders was punctured, bleeding a fountain of hydrogen.

Of course Diamond could be burned alive and live regardless. Isn't that what the rumors claimed? The boy was the target, the prize, and that's why the first wing fell back and fired off flares, signaling its companions. Suddenly three more roaring machines found stretches of bark and walkways where they could set down. Turning to his crew, the captain gave one order, and he meant it, and when nobody reacted, he cursed them and grabbed up the baddilick, throwing the live animal out an open window.

Again, he screamed at his people, "Get out of here."

But the papio had already reached them. Males and females were the same size, each as heavy as two normal men. They wore the same coral-colored blue-black uniforms. Forcing open both hatches as well as the service entrance, they boarded with the precision that comes only after considerable practice, conquering the crippled ship before another recitation passed.

The top papio was a powerful male with a long rifle and brass pins buried in his ugly face. He looked like a man ready for a fight, the papio mouth proving adept at the human language.

"You will walk me to the cabin," he told the captain. "You will lead."

In his life, the captain had never been braver. He was a prisoner, and his ship was crippled, the stink that rode with the hydrogen souring every breath. The carbon dioxide tanks were drained. Any little spark or ill-aimed bullet would ignite that deflating bladder. The little man had every right to feel doomed, and he was pleased to make it halfway to the cabin without collapsing. But his courage felt spent after that, and legs that he had trusted all of his life turned to noodles. He stumbled twice before the soldier picked him up with one hand, shaking him like a monkey, saying, "We want nothing but the boy."

The captain managed to stand, discovering his voice again. "Why do you want him?"

The rifle barrel jabbed him between the shoulders

He recovered his stride. Navigating the stairs, he asked, "Why do you want Diamond?"

"Because you don't deserve him," said the papio.

The cabin door was locked, and the captain spent moments patting his pockets, hunting for a key left behind on the bridge.

Sensing duplicity, the papio reached past him, punched the lock and forced the door inwards.

Brutish faces stared out at the two of them. Royal jazzings were the miniature, half-domesticated versions of the murderous wild jazzings. They had short jaws wrapped inside muscle, their green eyes furious and terrified, each trying to yank loose from the ropes that kept them helpless.

"Where's the boy?" asked the soldier.

"Where *Happenstance* wants him to be," the captain said.

The papio thought of shooting everything, but he wasn't a fool. So he carefully set down his rifle and used his hands, breaking the monkey's neck, making no sparks at all as he reached down for the gun again.

What caused the fire would never be known.

The boarding party burned, and the crew burned, and five more jazzings were sacrificed, each with a charm reading "Diamond" fixed to its blazing chest.

SEVEN

Father spoke about finding sleep. He led them to the cabins and one at a time put them inside, closing doors while instructing them to rest. Every cabin had its rubber floor and one tiny window set high, black shades drawn. The spaces were narrow with single narrow cots claiming one of the long walls. Diamond's cabin was last. The linen was stiff and white, crackling as Diamond sat on the edge of the cot. Father looked at him from the hallway. Then Father looked at the floor, attempting to smile. "Rest," he said. "You need to," he said. Perhaps he was talking to himself when he pushed the door closed.

Diamond promised himself dreams. Mother was dead or she was alive. Either way, the boy was certain that she would find his sleeping mind and tell him important somethings with her own voice. That would be a tiny, much wanted happiness. But Diamond couldn't sleep. He could barely close his eyes, lying on his back in the darkness, his right hand open on his stomach while his left hand made a fist that wasn't happy anywhere. The fist dug into the sheets and into his hip and sometimes it reached down, banging against the cool rubber floor.

The big ship was trying to be quiet. No engine was running. The crew spoke rarely, never louder than a whisper. But there was a tiny metronome living inside the cabin, flywheels and gears counting the recitations. Diamond listened to that busy machine and to the outside air blowing through the cooling darkness. Tied to heavy branches, the ship continued to move, its frame creaking in a few reliable places. Sometimes rumblings and roaring engines came from distant places, but most of the world was resting. Good was asleep in the safest part of the cabin, under the built-in desk and chair. Seldom was inside the adjacent cabin and Elata was down the hall. His friends cried in their sleep, and they cried while awake, and the crew did some quiet work in the shop and up on the bridge, and Diamond listened to everything before shutting his eyes as an experiment.

A hundred recitations were misplaced.

Some tiny sound woke him. His body and hands hadn't moved. Diamond slowly opened his eyes, but the perfect darkness left him blind. Where were the dreams? None offered themselves. Maybe he forgot them. Real people usually misplaced their dreams, and that might be the same for Diamond.

His relentless brain might be living another fifty lives while asleep, but if he forgot those dreams, there was no way to know about them, and that odd notion made him more hopeful than sorry.

The urge to sleep was lost. Diamond made his left hand stop being a fist, and he reached over his head for a lamp remembered well enough to be turned on with the first blind attempt.

The metronome had measured his sleep. Diamond studied its numbers until he believed them, and then he sat up.

Yesterday there had been talk about fresh clothes, but Diamond was still dressed in the brown school uniform. That might not change for days and days. When they were sitting in the Archon's office, Father used the call-lines and his name, building a new plan, and then he hurriedly took a select few people up to the highest berth at the Station. Secrecy was everything. The Archon wasn't told about the new scheme. Tar`ro left the other guards sitting outside the wrong room, and nobody wasted time finding clothes that would fit children. The big hunter-ship was already fueled and inflated, but only so that it could get out of the way of the warships that were coming from across the District. Their ship escaped long before the papio attacked, slipping into the wilderness once night was done taking charge.

Bountiful was an honorable old name, attached to a big corona hunter so new that Father had never even flown inside it. But he knew the crew, by name and by story, thousands of days shared in the air with these people.

Diamond slid to the end of the cot, feet finding the waiting boots.

The monkey lifted his head, eyes open but seeing very little. Then he settled again, and Diamond slipped away.

Sitting on the hallway floor, Tar`ro was letting his chin rest between his knees. But he shook himself when the cabin door opened, telling the boy, "Stay put."

Saying nothing, Diamond stepped over the man's feet.

"Wait for me," Tar`ro said grudgingly.

Diamond waited.

They walked together, the boy leading them past the empty galley. The hallway ended with a wide door propped open, a great volume of darkness waiting along with the abrupt silence of a conversation interrupted.

Diamond paused at the edge of a room.

From the darkness, Father said, "Here, son. Come over here."

But the boy didn't steer toward the voice. This was the machine shop and flying dock where the smaller hunter-ships could be refueled and repaired. Every light had been extinguished—affording a little more security—but one of the three service doors had been lifted high, the soft glimmers and luminescence of wilderness life drifting inside.

Diamond stopped three steps back from the empty air, standing high on his toes while peering out.

The world's ceiling wasn't far above them. Wilderness trees were shorter and much thinner than blackwoods, each adorned with twisting branches that usually battled with their neighbors for light and for rain. The wilderness was a tangle. *Bountiful* was floating inside a confused, ever-changing maze. This realm was shared by multitudes of creatures using colored light to proclaim their assorted majesties. Other animals screamed with their legs or sang with their mouths. The dry night air carried odors that meant nothing to a human nose or to Diamond's, but each scent belonged to its own language, intense and presumably ancient. Night-flying leatherwings were already heavy with insect meats and bird meats and sips of nectar given by night-blooming flowers. One more step forward and Diamond peered over the floor's lip, at the living maze, marveling at how *Bountiful* had burrowed deep into the canopy, hiding where even sharp papio eyes would have trouble spying it.

Two steps and a leap, and he could fall out of this world.

The idea didn't surprise Diamond. It came to him so clearly and suddenly that he had to wonder if it was a thought that had been dwelling inside him for a long time.

Is that what his forgotten dreams were about?

A half-step more, and he squatted.

Father came up behind, each knee cracking with its distinct voice as he knelt, the cool legs on both sides of his son.

"Are you done sleeping?" Father asked.

Diamond assumed so. Yet now, surrounded by the familiar body, he felt ready to close his eyes to everything.

Master Nissim approached, sitting on their right.

Tar`ro claimed a portion of the floor to the left.

Several recitations passed.

Reluctantly, Father asked, "Did you hear us talking?"

"Yes," said Diamond. "But I wasn't listening."

Father and Nissim didn't believe him. They said so with silence, and he noticed how they shifted their bodies, as if their bones weren't comfortable.

Diamond let his mind guess. Then he spoke quietly, though not as sadly as he expected. "They killed all those people, but not me."

"Not you," said Father.

"But if they wanted me gone, why didn't Bits just shoot me when we were alone? Shoot me and tie a weight on my body and drop me through the demon floor?"

Nissim and Father rocked back and forth, saying nothing.

"Well, that's got a simple answer," said Tar`ro. "Our enemies, whoever they are, consider the Corona District guilty of an enormous crime. We rescued an abomination. We should have murdered you as soon as you were in our hands. That's why we deserve to be thrown into oblivion too."

"He's not an abomination," said Father, with heat.

"In their minds, this creature threatens everything they trust. And they'll try to kill King as well, if they get the chance."

"My brother's more dangerous than me," said Diamond.

"Not in their minds," said the bodyguard. "King terrifies, but he doesn't make these people sick to their stomachs."

The other two men said nothing.

"That doesn't make sense," Diamond said.

Then the Master straightened his back, and with a careful tone, he said, "Merit. You should tell him."

"I know."

Diamond back leaned into his father.

Yet Father seemed to change the subject. "This machine is a marvel," he began. "We can't build a better hunter-ship than *Bountiful.* Not for any sum of money, not for all of the corona scales and skins and bones in the world. These engines couldn't be any stronger for their size, or faster, and there's not many military ships that enjoy the redundancies we have onboard. Even the crew is the finest you can assemble from among millions of living people."

Diamond leaned harder against him. "I don't understand."

"Yes, you do," said Father.

Maybe.

Then the man wrapped a long arm around his son, asking, "Now what if somebody thought up something new? Let's say it's that bright friend of yours. Seldom. Seldom grows up and imagines a revolutionary kind of airship. His design looks like *Bountiful*, except it floats without hydrogen gas, and it flies faster than our ships or even the papio wings, and best of all, you can crash his ship or set it on fire—any disaster that the Fates and Destinies inflict—but the machine rebuilds itself out of the pieces on hand, making itself stronger in the process."

Tar`ro laughed dourly. "Listen to him, kid."

"Me," said Diamond. "He's talking about me."

"And I'm talking about King and the ghost in the wilderness, and whatever creature that the papio might be hiding." Father held him tight and found a louder voice. "We don't know anything for certain. But it looks as if there's a huge, huge difference between you and the other three. King's nothing like human beings, and nothing like you has been seen in the wilderness or on the reef. You are unique, Diamond. You are special because in so many ways, you're human."

The boy fidgeted, and then he said, "But I'm not."

The men said nothing.

"I'm different," Diamond said. But he knew exactly what was being said.

"Your body's more durable, and your brain can't be broken," Master Nissim said. "But remember your tenth day in my class. I had your blood and Seldom's blood on two slides, and what did the other students learn?"

"They couldn't tell which was which."

"And doctors have had their looks," Tar`ro said. "Believe me, the Archon gets every report plopped down on her desk."

Prue came to mind, expecting to marry him. And just like that, Diamond felt angry toward the little orphan girl.

Father shook him gently. "What are you thinking?"

"Nothing," the boy lied.

"Everybody's waiting for you to get old enough," Tar`ro said.

"Old enough," Diamond whispered.

"I know you have inklings of this," Father said. "But you have to see it plainly now. Everybody—the Archons and the papio too—look at you as a potential father. If you can grow up and have children, and if your family inherits your powers—"

"Which might not happen," Nissim interrupted. "Hybridization is a complex, knot-rich process."

Tar`ro laughed again. "But what if he can? A thousand women marry him, and his kids get just a portion of his tricks mixed in with that ordinary blood . . . and the world is remade for all time . . . "

The other men shifted their rumps, saying nothing.

Tar`ro's voice brightened, hardened. "What's the matter, gentlemen? You think I should sit in a classroom or stand on that landing, suffering boredom, suffering rain, and for no good reason but to keep one odd kid out of trouble? No, no. I've always seen the big true picture."

"I don't like the tone," Father said.

"And neither of you appreciate the scope of things."

"Perhaps you should describe what you see," Nissim said.

Diamond stood, stepping out of his father's reach. The shop's floor ended with a raised lip, and reaching the edge, he gazed into blackness spoiled by swirling dots and blobs of busy light.

Scorn in his voice, Tar`ro said, "You dear gentlemen are too smart to see anything clearly. We're not fighting a war. Wars are a string of battles that end when anybody starts to cry. No, what's happening now is far worse than anything in history books. This is everybody fighting over one clear, spectacular prize. This is two species ready to risk everything, and this is each District doing battle with every other District, and every person tonight is trying to make sense of his thoughts. Now that the world has been stirred up, everything gets ugly, and there's not going be any good place to go for a long time to come.

"That's what I think," he said.

Every man was suddenly talking at once. Angry, sloppy whispers mixed in the air. Diamond was left free to bend until he felt as if he were floating over the lights of a million insects. Something about this scene was eerily, deliciously familiar, and ready to remember, he felt happy enough to smile.

Then the bickering and the talk of violence became loud, and an ancient memory fled back inside the boy's tiny, enormous mind.

• • •

Sleep had never been her nature. Fatigue had done its damage in the past, nipping at her flesh, playing games with her thoughts, but Quest had endured enough weariness to believe that sleep could never claim her. Except yesterday morning was relentless and sorry and wicked. Exhaustion arrived before she shucked off most of her body, letting the temporary flesh die in plain sight while the rest of her scrambled to a higher position. Abandoning organs and limbs demanded hard concentration. Climbing fast without being seen was always best done when she was rested. She wasn't rested. The last of her legs were trembling when she found a new perch—a marginal hiding place on the edge of the District—and that was when the papio attacked.

Quest was already taking wild chances. Just lingering near the settled forest was a gnawing risk, and that was before full war broke out. She saw the papio wings flying into the forest's wound, shooting at shadows, and the tree-walkers flung slugs and darts and swift little bombs, almost every shot missing its mark. Quest should have left immediately. She knew it. Yet there she remained, ignoring every wise impulse, eating more lost birds and using their meat to cook fresh eyes and great funnel-shaped ears, aiming the new organs everywhere but at the ongoing battle.

Was this a symptom of deep fatigue, turning blind to a thousand dangers?

She didn't know, couldn't guess. But the boy kept churning her thoughts. Instinct and every drop of new blood accepted his importance, yet she had no idea where he was or how awful his circumstances were. That's why she shucked off most of those new senses and slipped out of her hiding place, abandoning the wilderness. Exhaustion brought madness. Insanity made her leap and scamper, even as those scrawny high branches shook from cannon fire, and suddenly she discovered herself clinging to a bare trunk still warm from the morning's fire, gazing down into the raw gouge of open air and late sun and war.

The Ivory Station was on the far side of the gouge.

Her final eyes watched little else.

The battle was at its frenzied worst: rapid and vicious, and clumsy. Presumably both sides had intricate battle plans, but nobody seemed to remember them. Armored airships maneuvered clumsily beside the Ivory Station, and the wings slashed past, sometimes spinning their jets to hover long enough for two targets to fix every weapon on one another. Corona bladders and scales were extremely tough, weathering astonishing rains of gunfire. But even the strongest materials failed eventually. Airships turned to flame. Wings shattered and tumbled toward the demon floor. There was an instant when exhaustion would annihilate both armies, but then the final airships retreated into the forest, and as night rose, a flock of larger, slower wings arrived, delivering hundreds of papio soldiers to the wide landing at the bottom of the Ivory Station.

Night bloomed faster than normal. The papio launched flares as messages, and the tree-walkers launched flares to confuse their enemies. Small guns took over the fight. Eerily beautiful clusters of light were born from explosions. The Station burned in darkness. Hanner's trunk and battered canopy burned. Spellbound, Quest never noticed the pair of wings coming up her side of the gouge, and then they slashed past, near enough that their jets warmed her flesh.

She dropped that flesh and fled.

An agile little wing pursued her through the forest's highest reaches. Or it was hunting other quarry, and it just happened to fix its bright spotlights on her body. The glare made her flesh turn real, a small cowardly shadow lurking beneath. Burning precious fuel, the wing hovered. Quest was perched on a dead hard-willow branch. The pilot stared at her with a puzzled, halfway-irritated expression. "You are something and you are important," the woman probably thought. "But you aren't what I want tonight."

Quest let the branch slip away.

The papio fired her guns in response, splintering rotted wood.

Quest made herself narrow, falling as fast as possible. Wilderness was beckoning, familiar and dense, unconquered by either human species. Then she pushed much of what remained into long leatherwings, and she flew, flat at first and then higher, deep into places that nobody but her had ever named, her final eyes drinking the available light.

She had never felt as tired as she did then.

For the first time in her life, closing her eyes and mind seemed possible.

But time moved, and she moved through time, and there always seemed to be another point where she was sicker and weaker than before. No creature could live long in this state, not even her. Each stroke of the wings found misery. Muscles born just that day were spent, poisoned by their exertions, and she had to summon enough will to keep her mouth from hunting. The wilderness was jammed with creatures fleeing lost places, out of their territories and easy to kill. But she wasn't safe and maybe she never would be safe again. That grim possibility carried her high, up near the ceiling where the only sunlight came after the rain, and that's where she found a nest of daylight leatherwings—great beasts driven mad by explosions and the stench of burnt life.

She killed several and ate the pregnant female first.

She grew a few eyes and many more ears before grabbing tight to a lingerblossom trunk, dangling, passing into a state that wasn't sleep and never would be.

Her rest might have lasted a long while.

But words found her. These weren't human words. Every species of monkey had its language, and Quest knew all of them. Sleepless, paranoid jasmine monkeys were talking about an airship. They didn't name the vessel or any of the people onboard, but the animals counted the cables that moored the big dark gasbag in one place, and hungry enough to ache, the troop was plotting to walk across the cables, slipping inside that big open door at the bottom. There was food inside. They could smell feasts. But the main stink was unfamiliar and wrong, which was the only reason that they didn't attack.

"What is that stinky shit?" monkeys asked monkeys.

Quest grew nostrils.

Dry dark night air rose into what passed for her face, and she drank huge amounts of air before catching the musky odor of coronas and their odd, alien blood.

Only a hunter-ship would carry that stink.

Only someone wanting to hide would bring an open-air vessel deep into this labyrinth of trees.

Diamond was a faint, half-born possibility, but Quest couldn't dismiss this opportunity.

Should she rest or move?

Motion claimed her, fingers letting go of the bark, every fatigue and ache and tiny cancerous doubt left behind with the hiding place.

• • •

The galley was small and polished. Corona scales covered every tabletop, and the plates were bright white ovals cut from corona bone, and every utensil was quality steel decanted from the monsters' blood. Breakfast was hot and it was cold, each kind of food filling its own platter set on the first table. But most of the crew had been called away for a critical meeting. Three children and the monkey shared that table. Karlan sat alone in the back. The cook remained on his feet. Orders had been delivered, and the man wasn't shy about playing with the handgun in his apron pocket. The giant boy did some good yesterday, but he had a reputation for causing trouble. Stopping trouble was the cook's responsibility, and for what seemed like a very long while, he had been nervously imagining the circumstances that would make him shoot the young fellow in a leg or the shoulder, or maybe through the heart.

Everybody was hungry, but only Good was eating. There were no windows in the galley, but they heard the rain beating against *Bountiful* and everybody felt the rising winds, the red breath of the day combing the tangled wilderness.

Elata sat at the end of the table. She was a thousand days older than yesterday. Diamond thought the girl looked like her mother, and he nearly said so. His mouth opened, and noticing his eyes, she asked, "What's wrong?"

Seldom said, "Everything's wrong."

"I was talking to Diamond," she said.

"I know," Seldom said.

Seldom looked younger than yesterday. He looked smaller too, and he couldn't stop crying.

"Stupid," Elata said, picking up a bright fork.

"Who's stupid?" Seldom asked, sniffing quietly.

"Me," the girl said. "I keep thinking she's waiting for me. My mother. She's sitting at home, in her favorite chair, and she's not happy."

Nobody else talked.

"I didn't come home. I must have run off. Or she's angry about something else that I did or didn't do. Somehow I've pissed her off, and that's the only way that I can think about her. Cursing me."

She paused, and Diamond stared at his plate.

"But there's a weirder part," she said. "Do you know what it is?"

The boys glanced at each other.

From across the room, Karlan said, "You want to go home and get yelled at."

She nodded. "I do. But that's not it."

Diamond asked, "What's weird?"

"My father is sitting there too," she said. "And he's been dead for most of my life, it seems."

The rain spoke. Nothing else.

Then Elata sat up straighter, her features aging even more. She hadn't cried this morning. Her face was dry and stiff as if carved from coral. Out from her clamped mouth came her tongue, wetting her fingertips, and then she picked up a jar full of sugar, pouring half of it onto the clean plate in front of her. With two fingers, Elata began pulling the glittery brown sugar into her mouth, three tastes managed before she said, "This got me in trouble, every time."

The boys slowly dished food to their plates, and Diamond ate.

Karlan had claimed a platter of smoked amiables, and now he picked up the top slice. But he ate in nibbles, and slowly. His face looked carved, but it was different than Elata's face. Diamond couldn't decide if he saw strength or anger, or if something that he couldn't name was running under the skin.

With a spoon, Seldom pushed a half-egg to the edge of his plate. He looked as if he was crying but his voice was steady. "I keep thinking this is yesterday," he said. "It's dawn and everything's normal, everything's starting again. But this time I know what is going to happen. This time I can do something about it."

"What are you going to do?" Karlan asked, his tone was more curious than cross.

Seldom dropped his spoon. "I'll tell Mommy and Papa."

Karlan's face didn't change. "And they'll explain to you that you're an idiot, and Mom would tell you to go to school anyway."

Diamond put a boiled half-egg into his mouth, tasting the yellow.

"No, I'd stop everything from happening," Seldom said with conviction. "I'd call the Archon from our house and warn her, and Bits would be arrested, and the bombs above would be disarmed. Then I'd go to school like normal, and everything would be what it should be."

"Except you'd be the hero," said Karlan.

Seldom nodded, wishing for all of it.

"A hero who could see the future," said his brother.

"I guess."

"And what would the Archon do, after you saved the world?" Karlan had found enough reason to smile, and he took a big bite of meat, chewing as he spoke. "If you think she's interested in that critter beside you, then what would she get out of a beast who sees tomorrow and maybe a long ways farther than that?"

Good was finished eating. Jumping down, he said, "Shit."

Diamond pointed.

The monkey trotted past Karlan. The two exchanged glances, the human finding reasons for a long soft laugh.

Good laughed in his shrill way.

"Corona-boy," Karlan said. "What are you thinking about?"

Diamond was thinking about eggs, how the whiteness was one thing and the yolk was entirely different. He was thinking about various mothers and how fifty-eight days ago Elata's mother had invited Seldom's mother and Haddi inside her modest home, along with the two boys. Everybody sat in a nice little room. Adults and children played a game that nobody enjoyed. But everyone's best manners were on display, and Elata's mother—Taff—seemed thrilled with pieces of her little party. The woman particularly enjoyed watching her daughter talking to Diamond. Elata was funny that day, happy and quick to laugh, and her mother couldn't stop smiling at both of them.

Taff's expression seemed strange then. In some way, he knew what she was thinking, but after what he had heard last night, there was no ignoring the meanings.

"You aren't answering me," Karlan said.

"I've got a lot of thoughts," he said.

"Tell me one," said the giant boy, his voice low and abrasive.

"No," said Elata. "Just ignore him."

Seldom rocked slowly from side to side, matching the wind-born motions of the ship.

Karlan rose to his feet fast enough that the cook shoved his right hand into the deep pocket, aiming with his eyes.

But that's when Good came out from the toilet, and glancing at Karlan, he sensed nothing wrong. Nothing was dangerous. Unperturbed, the monkey jumped up on the table and claimed Seldom's half-egg for himself, consuming it with one bold slurp.

Diamond whispered, "I can see the future."

"What's that?" Karlan asked.

"I know what's going to happen," he said. "Not about tomorrow, but with the bigger things."

Everybody but Good stared at him. Even the cook was interested.

But Diamond was just talking. Words came out of his mouth, except they weren't his words. He didn't think before saying, "Fire."

"What about fire?" Karlan interrupted.

"Nothing," said the boy, wishing he had stayed quiet.

Elata stared at him, almost smiling.

The cook leaned forward. "There's fire in our future? Is that what you see coming?"

Then Seldom was giggling and groaning, saying, "Well, really. Really? Who doesn't see that?"

• • •

Flesh believed in time.

What was alive, no matter how simple, held deep confidence in the rhythmic changes of light and water, the passage of days and the inevitability of night. Time informed existence, defined its promise and framed every limitation. Complex, self-aware life went so far as to stare into the future, imagining what might be, and occasionally planning for events that wouldn't occur for one day or a thousand, or more likely, would never happen at all.

Great events were sweeping the world, but old schedules remained intact, and the papio were perhaps the most methodical creatures—serving the metronome, the calendar, and their deep need for the illusion for order.

That morning, a new child was given to the Eight.

"Tradition put you here," Divers instructed. "You've been granted the honor of serving the Corona's largest, most helpless child. Except we aren't helpless, and all you need to do is to stay close but stay out of our way too."

"Yes, I know," said a tiny voice.

"Don't bow to us, and don't ever strut in front of us," she continued. "Just come forward now and give us your name. And if you want, ask questions. Regardless what you ask, we'll pretend these are wise questions, fresh as the coral blossom sprays, and they'll be answered however we choose."

The child was a little larger than most for his age, and instead of red or pink hair, his scalp was covered with the darkest brown tangle of twisting hairs. In their life, the Eight had never moved from this isolated, thinly populated terrain, but they understood the reef through books and the stories told by others.

Judging by appearances, this boy came from the world's farthest ends.

"Zakk," he called himself.

The Eight and the boy were standing inside an empty hanger. The resident wing was destroyed during the raid on the Ivory Station. Its replacement would fly its mission today before dropping onto the tarmac outside, and that wouldn't happen for a long while. The hanger's doors had been left open. Vast golden eyes were turned forwards. Those eyes wore a papio face, strong and feminine and agreeably handsome. The hair was dense and pink, though up close it looked more like frizzy rope mixed with peculiar silks and spider webs and pale red worms wriggling slowly in the flesh. Half-trousers and a half-halter and new sandals were the only clothes. No tattoo ink or piercing could take hold in the brown flesh, and there was no way to build scars. Smooth flesh and huge eyes made the Eight resemble a toddler—a toddler built on a fantastic scale. But the toddler's clumsiness was gone. Balance was effortless, and speed mattered, and Divers insisted that the Eight were ready to move faster than anybody expected. To that end, during the night, when untrusted eyes weren't watching, she would force this body to climb steep slopes and sprint down the craggy backsides of the ridges.

The Eight leaned back, each hand holding a telescope, twin black tubes raised to the eyes. Both tubes were moving, sweeping the scene for anything interesting, and hopefully important.

Something about the scene made the new boy uneasy. His feet were moving, and the yellow eyes kept dancing, watching the open air.

"You're safe," said Divers.

"Am I?"

"Absolutely." She smiled, telling him, "We're dressed in shadow, Zakk. Even if the enemy noticed us, and they can't, we're shielded by coral and the hanger's iron walls."

"A lost bullet could kill me," said the boy.

"It won't. We promise."

Support crews and soldiers were working in the depths of the hanger, loud, brash voices suddenly rising. Their noise drew the boy's gaze.

Divers pulled his attentions back where they belonged, which was outside. "You're from the City of Round Roads, we think."

"Yes," said Zakk.

"Your parents belong to the League, and one of them, probably your father, is a member in high standing with the government there."

Zakk blinked. "You must have read about me."

"No, we're just guessing," Divers confessed.

"But I'm not here because of my father. I'm qualified on my own." The boy's feet squirmed against the rubberized floor, and he stared at the giant papio body—at the long hair and the child's face and the brown flesh that was entirely one color and one flavor. And in particular, the boy watched those long, quick-moving telescopes.

"Ask questions, Zakk."

The boy nodded. "I think it's interesting. You can see in two directions at once."

"It's easy, if you have multiple minds."

"Those are huge telescopes," said Zakk.

"We don't hear a question."

"Are you Divers?"

There was no point denying it. "You'll never talk to anyone else. Other voices lead to confusion."

"That's too bad."

"Is it, Zakk?"

The boy said, "I've read about all of you."

"Wonderful."

He began to name each important name.

"They gave you the standard briefing," Divers said, interrupting.

"And Tritian," Zakk said. "I read all I could about him."

There were reasons to avoid this subject, but Divers decided on straightforward questions. "Did somebody steer you toward that subject?"

"No."

"Studying my brother was your idea?"

"His blood is orange," the boy said, as if that was ample reason. Then he added, "I saw a sample inside the doctor's book. It was just a little dried spot, but I thought it looked very pretty. And then I read about Tritian, and he seems wonderfully strange."

"Stranger than Divers?"

Happy with the subject, the boy grinned. "I only meant that he's very different from the rest of you."

"In some ways," she allowed.

"In many ways," the boy said.

The crews and soldiers had finished their work, and when they fell silent, Divers looked back at them. The creatures were resting on their haunches while staring at the Eight. Several smiled until Divers looked directly at them, and then they stood tall and silent for a moment, making themselves feel brave before they retreated into the darkness.

Others emerged from a doorway—a few high officers and government people had come out to greet the morning, gathering beyond the hanger's iron door. They were conversing with mouths and long arms. Divers found the subject interesting. This would be a fine moment to approach, offering to help with their difficult day.

Zakk followed closely, chattering about Tritian's blistering hot acidic blood and the orange muscles that also worked like hearts and the other organs—muscles that could live outside the body for days. One silent brother absorbed to the unexpected praise. The other six ignored that half-informed noise. Their voices were what mattered, and they spoke to one another—one busy shared murmur discussing possibilities and practicalities about important matters that this boy would never understand.

The officers were still angry about yesterday's disasters. Government people saw nothing but ugly ramifications. Both sides agreed that war wasn't their goal or anyone's policy. The policy seemed to be rage, every papio face betraying a combustive mood.

The ranking general gestured at the two vast telescopes, asking, "Have you seen anything new?"

"Nothing," said Divers, walking out from under the hanger's roof.

"Stay inside," said the general.

"But I can't see as much that way," she said.

She had better eyes than anyone else, and she had the telescopes and endless practice watching the world from here. But the world could see her when she was in the open—another difficult-to-measure risk resting on a great pile of hazards. The important people were no doubt asking themselves if they should try to coax the Eight into the dark. But odds were that Divers would ignore them, which was disagreeable enough when you were standing alone. They weren't alone. The other important people would see the brave one fail, and that's why nobody tried to argue with her, every face nervous, lips curling while the hands built anxious fists.

The Eight walked out into the open, and Zakk followed. The safest position for the boy was inside their shadow, letting the enormous invulnerable body absorb any lost bullets. Yet without warning, the newcomer suddenly turned fearless, hurrying far out onto the rubber tarmac. Without a worry in his world, he dropped down on his haunches, a tiny pair of what looked like toy binoculars coming out of his deepest pocket.

Divers laughed gently, gazing up at the sprawling wilderness.

Talk among the officers fell back to the usual obsessions. Who had orchestrated that first attack? Was it the tree-walkers, some element in the papio ranks, or a marriage that straddled the reef and forest? Counts had been made. No weapons or fuel were missing from the local stocks, which was wonderful news. But you didn't become important by trusting the first report, and the ranking general demanded fresh counts. Then a government woman asked for the latest target assessments, which meant Diamond. The intelligence officer claimed that the boy had survived the onslaught. But was that believable? Everyone was talking at once. Nobody held real evidence. Diamond could be anywhere in the Creation, including beneath the demon floor. Beneath the floor meant that he could be lost for the next million days. And even if he was alive and still somewhere the Corona District, how much were the papio willing to do, trying to gather up this prize before the tree-fools succeeded in destroying that half-grown gift?

The Eight settled on their haunches, eyes watching the wilderness.

Divers didn't miss any word or the smallest breath.

A lesser general described the enemy's overnight attacks. Two distant Districts, working together, had attacked fortifications of the reef's lip, as many as one hundred dead and dying.

At that point, a government voice mentioned retribution.

The ranking general gave an unhappy sigh. "Our assault killed hundreds of our cousins yesterday," he said.

"Cousins" was the most polite word for tree-walkers.

"But they didn't have to fight us," the woman said. "We were carrying out a rescue mission. We haven't declared war. We were trying to extract our consulate personnel, and without provocation—"

"They'd endured one attack already," the general said contemptuously. "Do you really think they wouldn't try to slaughter the lot of us?"

Once again, various voices dismissed every blame, government people being the loudest and least secure.

"Anyone can build that kind of bomb," said the ranking civilian.

"And what reason would we have to attack?" her aide asked, trying to support a superior.

"None," said the woman, with feeling. "And besides, if war was our policy, then our first strike would have been fifty times more savage."

No general would argue with that blunt opinion. Divers put down the telescopes and glanced over a shoulder, finding looks that were uncomfortable and slippery, ready for any excuse to change subjects.

Every voice inside the Eight had fallen silent.

Then Zakk put down his tiny binoculars. He said, "The wilderness is prettier here than at home."

Divers lifted just one telescope, pressing it to the left eye. "Why does it seem prettier?"

"Because it's different," Zakk said.

Then inside the Eight, a voice said, "Watch this one. I don't like him."

Tritian.

The others told him to be quiet.

Divers didn't need to reprimand her brother. She rarely had to police her siblings. The great accomplishment of her brief life was to convince the Seven to obey her directions. They were free to offer opinions, and didn't she often bow to their shared will? But they understood what Divers had always known: each of them was tiny—a speck of flotsam riding the same Time together, hundreds of days and millions of little voices bringing them to this very dangerous brink.

• • •

Foresters sold wood for money. Foresters were better climbers than most tree-walkers, although many had papio blood in their deep past. But appearances didn't matter; they regarded both of their civilized cousins as being separate from them. Papio coins were the same as District coins, which made every species equally contemptible in any forester's eyes.

A colossal burr-tree had been recently carved into lucrative planks, leaving behind a void filled with quiet empty air. The void was where the hunter-ship had taken refuge. To hide from the coronas, its skin was painted a mottled green, and that's why the ship was hard to see against the trees. But once noticed, it looked out of place, preposterous, probably misplaced. Hunter-ships wanted the open air. Only skilled or drunken pilots dared punch their way through gaps and unbroken walls of foliage, reaching such a remote location. But there it was: corona bladders and bones, human machines and human bodies and human mind—all of that wrapped inside a carefully balanced entity, ten strong mooring lines holding it in place.

If not for its smell and her eyes, and also the endless tiny sounds raining out of it, Quest might well have flown past *Bountiful*, missing it entirely.

Quest was considerably harder to see than the airship. No unnatural scent leaked from her body, and every sound that she made belonged to the wilderness. Her shrunken form was transparent in places, richly green in others. She was breath and a dream, and maybe a flick of motion in the corner of the most observant, inadequate eye. Three times she had changed positions, gazing into windows and that one open doorway. She once even straddled a mooring line, contemplating making the short climb before slipping inside a space where hiding would be next to impossible.

The urge was resisted, and she retreated.

And then in the next moment, she imagined seven new ways to see what she wanted to see.

The decision was made. The adjacent burr-tree was a scrawnier, light-starved child of the original giant. She spread out along one of its branches and changed her flesh again. Sugar was a treasure to all kinds of mouths, and she made herself look like the sweetest plant in the forest—a rare epiphyte known as the sweetheart. The trickery took time, but she didn't need perfection. Long before she was finished, ten species of birds and swarms of insects were arriving, greedily feasting on the easy nectars.

The birds celebrated the prize, and people noticed their singing.

A tall man looked down from his cabin's window. His face was tired and forlorn, but when he stared at the sudden garden, he wiped his mouth and eyes and then his mouth once more.

Then he vanished.

A huge room claimed much of the ship's belly. That was where the one wide door was propped open, letting motor sounds and voices escape. Suddenly two men came out of the room. They were straddling a small airship, and the airship growled and climbed towards Quest and then slipped past her.

One of the men was the old slayer, Merit.

She watched Merit until he was gone, and then she watched him again in her memory. Meanwhile the large man had returned to the cabin window, opening its glass, talking with a voice that was both soft and loud.

"I want to tell you something," he said.

Diamond approached the window. He was crying without crying. His face was dry, those pale eyes free of tears, but everything about the boy looked miserable, worn and sorry and weak.

That pain shook Quest.

"What, Master?" asked Diamond.

Quest had seen the tall man long ago, riding with the boy inside the *Happenstance*. She found that memory and subsequent mentions of the boy's teacher, which meant that this must be Master Nissim.

"What do you want to tell me?"

"That I'm sorry, for you and for your family," said Nissim.

Diamond leaned against the cabin wall. His curly hair felt the breeze, lifting and twisting.

"For everyone, this is brutal," said Nissim.

The boy gave a slight nod, starting to agree with his teacher. But he said nothing, and wanting to be anywhere else, he looked outside. And that's when he suddenly found himself staring at the newborn sweetheart.

"Look," he said.

"What's that?" Nissim asked.

"Out there. Do you see it, on the branch?"

The man stood behind, following Diamond's gaze.

Lying, the man said, "Now that you point it out to me, yes."

"What is it?"

"A blooming sweetheart."

Diamond was miserable, but his face was changing.

"Anyway," said the Master. "What I wanted was to apologize."

"For what?"

"I was slow yesterday. I should have seen Bits for what he was."

Diamond watched the garden, the gathering birds. Fifty gold-throats made the air sing with their intense wing beats, and then from a high perch, a wild orange-headed monkey proclaimed his dominion over the distant prize.

The boy's monkey appeared at the window, shouting a competing claim.

Diamond said, "Quiet."

Perched on the windowsill, his monkey contemplated routes along mooring lines and the zigzagging branches. He didn't want to be quiet, but there was no easy route to his goal, and the trees were filled with strange monkeys. That's why the animal curled his upper lip, glowering in silence.

Quest quenched the flow of fake nectars.

"And things might be better now if I'd shot that man as soon as I knew. But I kept forgetting who you are, and I couldn't shoot."

The boy was listening, but he was watching the flowers too.

"So I am sorry," the Master continued. "I am and always will be. But as one of my Masters warned me when I was young, 'All of us are doing our best and our worst, and it happens at the same time.' "

Diamond turned and looked at his teacher, waiting.

Nissim's face began to cry.

" 'Our best and our worst,' " the boy said.

"In the face of evil, we can only do so much."

Diamond nodded solemnly, and then with a quiet, steady voice, he said, "There is no evil, sir."

"What's that?"

"Evil doesn't exist," he said.

"No," Nissim muttered. "What are saying? No."

"But that's how it is," the boy said emphatically.

His teacher was puzzled, dubious. Moving toward anger.

"All of us are good," Diamond said, his words washing across the dying garden. "Everything and everywhere is good too."

Nissim didn't like what he just heard. "After yesterday, why do you believe there's no such thing as evil?"

"I have to think that."

"Why?"

"A voice told me," he said.

"Whose voice?"

An odd smile tried to break the boy's face in two.

"I don't know," Diamond said. "But I've heard the voice several times, and it only finds me when I'm alone."

• • •

Until two hundred days ago, foresters filled the sprawling camp, but then the trees began to complain. At least that was the public legend: the brave men and women who harvested the wood could also hear the wood, and after so much cutting and carving, the wood had begged for rest. That's why the foresters packed up their power saws and their shrines, moving to a different portion of the wilderness. One camp was pushed into hibernation while another was brought back into service. Merit knew some of these people. Peculiar, independent souls living between the two human realms, they traded with both species and smuggled for all when the payoff was rich enough. Some of these people were nothing but admirable. But Merit had always suspected that the wood didn't talk to anyone. Money was what made these communities leap from camp to camp. If easy trees grew scarce, if it took too much work to cut another crop, one region was abandoned in place of another, more profitable site. And the foresters' spiritual noise was just another way that those who held the saws proved to the world they were special.

Yet that skepticism was easily forgotten. Moving through the empty camp, Merit felt the presence of its vanished owners, and listening to the silences, he accepted that at any moment the first voice from a tree would find him.

His companion held a less superstitious attitude.

"I found the room," Fret shouted from the far side of the lodge. "The copper river's here."

Startled birds broke into flight.

"Wait for help," Merit shouted, and not for the first time.

But then came the cold clank of iron, rusting hinges squeaking. "Too late," the youngster replied. And then, "All clear."

Barely three thousand days old, Fret was an idiot about many matters, including the need for caution. But there was no telling the state of this machinery, and *Bountiful*'s captain had nobody better suited to bring an old call-line back to life.

Moving carefully along the walkway, Merit watched for booby-traps left to ward off copper thieves. But there were no trip-wires, and the small room seemed safe enough. Fret was lucky, or he was blessed with sharp instincts. Either way, not so much as a dirty needle was ready to hurt them.

The prudent old slayer was in no mood to dress down anybody.

"It doesn't look too awful," Fret said, bare hands tugging at rubber-clad wires.

"The owners haven't been gone long," said Merit.

"But idiots left the service hatch open." There was a gap in the floor that allowed the rain to jump inside. "Another hundred dawns, and rust will start eating out the housings back here."

Call-lines were expensive to build, particularly in the wilderness. Long wires had to carry voices and codes all the way back to the Districts. The primary generators were always underpowered. And worse, there weren't any secondary generators on the wire waiting to boost the signals. Both men wore broad tool belts, and both carried alcohol in tall red cans. Fret pulled out his biggest wrench, and without the slightest concern, he straddled the hole in the floor.

Foresters liked their long views. The forest below had been cut and hacked until it there was only half of a normal healthy canopy. Brilliant sunlight was everywhere. Standing at the brink, Merit spent a few moments watching for coronas; the lifetime habit couldn't be set aside, even today. Then he took a breath and stepped back again, thinking of ways in which this one simple job could go wrong.

Fret's wrench was shiny and almost new—too expensive to be purchased by a youngster, perhaps given as a gift by parents ecstatic that their careless boy was entering a profitable trade. Corona meat had been cooked and refined to pull out the valuable iron, and the carbon came from the blackest old timbers, while methods older than human memory had built a simple, changeless device that could accomplish a multitude of tasks.

That very expensive wrench became a hammer.

Fret smacked the line below the floor, where it was suspended in plain view. With precision, he dented the insulation, and then he set the wrench on the floor beside one foot, nothing beneath him but bright air, and with a professor's voice, he explained, "You can tell a lot by the spring in the rubber."

"Be careful," said Merit.

"Oh, I didn't hit it hard," the youngster said, misunderstanding the warning. "But the insulation looks good. No sense wasting fuel if there's zero chance of our shouts getting through."

The generator's tank had been drained. Merit opened its cap and began to pour in the contents of the first can.

"I know these machines," Fret said. "I know everything about circuits and currents, all of that. But you know what? Nobody's ever explained to me what really happens inside the copper."

Merit was too tired to pour neatly. The fuel slipped free, building streaks on the tank's dirty red body.

Words flowed out of the youngster. "Sure, I studied negative charges, and the positives, and how they fly along the wire. And magnetism builds invisible clouds, fields or whatever you call them. But I had one teacher try to convince me that the world is full of lights that we can't see, colors that our eyes can't find, and invisible clouds that we're never going to feel. He said that those colors are here all of the time. Even in the darkest night, those nothings are busy. That's why we bury our wires inside these big sleeves. Because raw wire is full of noise, all of it senseless, and there's no room left for even one of our voices."

Fret was full of noise.

Drained, the first can felt weightless. There was no reason to use the second can. Their business would be finished soon, provided the generator worked and the line was intact, and provided they could contact Prima without delays or too many risks.

"Have you heard about these invisible lights?" Fret asked.

Setting down the empty can, Merit said, "Yes."

A moment ago he was exceptionally tired, but the stink of fuel or simple nerves had done something to his head, clear thoughts on the move again.

"Maybe people should wear rubber around their heads," the slayer thought, half-seriously. "Maybe our currents would flow better then."

Fret left the hole, walking to the line's endpoint—a wooden box wearing sawdust and one durable black receiver. Brandishing a small wrench and a heavy old screwdriver, he gave one mighty shrug. "Let's give the generator its chance."

The pull cord was on the other side of the chamber, and the quickest route was an easy jump over the hole in the floor. Merit felt light, almost relaxed, except he was neither. He was tired and so very sad at the same time, but those sensations had vanished. In the company of this young man, he felt renewed, and the illusion lasted until he was jumping over the opening in the floor—suspended above the oblivion, suddenly wondering if the exhausted legs had given him enough of a push.

They had.

But something was wrong, something that a piece of him understood before his conscious shriveled mind saw what was obvious.

"Sir," said a tight, angry voice.

Merit blinked, staring at Fret's furious expression.

"Stupid sir," said the boy. "You just kicked my wrench out the damned hole."

• • •

Zakk was watching the world with tiny eyes, with the tiny binoculars. He could see very little, but the view seemed to impress him nonetheless.

Meanwhile Divers and the other Seven saw enormous swaths of wilderness and busy air, and they felt nearly blind. Flocks of powerful wings flew fast under the canopy, avoiding enemy fire, and the airship fleet from the District of Districts was still in the remote distance—giant gasbags looking like a swarm of flies only now reaching the edge of the Corona District. But there had been no battles today. Each side seemed to be trying to avoid enraging the other. The great prize was still missing. Diamond was lost. The important souls were cursing beside the hanger, demanding answers that nobody could give, and a moment later, a lowly colonel came running on hands and feet.

He was a local man. Divers knew him.

"They're sending us our new wing," said the officer. "Everybody needs to be out of its way."

Zakk appeared eager to run into the trees above the tarmac.

Divers knew better. The aircraft in question was a slip of darkness on the edge of what he could see, and there was ample time. She dropped both of her telescopes and then showed the officer her canines, each as long as the man's tired arms.

The colonel summoned the courage not to back away.

Nothing happened. Nothing changed. Then without a word, Divers looked back into the hanger, into the gloom, noting that heavy wagons were rolling clear of the deepest bunkers, new weapons filling the cradles.

Yesterday meant little bombs and simple guns.

Somebody was getting ready for bigger battles today.

"Can we watch from above?" Zakk asked the colonel. "If we find a safe hole, I mean."

The colonel usually ruled this facility, but not with so many generals underfoot. Lacking the authority to answer, he instantly told the child, "No."

The Seven discussed the matter and took a vote.

There was no point in making trouble now, Divers agreed. Waving a telescope, she said, "We'll go inside with our new friend."

Zakk summoned a huge smile.

Inside the hanger, the soldiers were wrapping heavy ropes around one of the bombs, the streamlined iron body wearing a papio skull and poisonous spiders. Divers counted the bombs and then forced the eyes upwards one last time. As if holding binoculars, she set both of the giant telescopes against the vast eyes, making one final sweep before vanishing underground.

A sharp piece of sunlight was moving against the wilderness.

She saw the object, saw that it was spinning as it fell, and all of the Eight realized that this was a wrench. An enormous, rapid, and nearly useless discussion began, the voices trying to decide how someone's prized tool might have been dropped.

The other Seven talked while Divers thought.

She never spoke.

And then Tritian said, "Look higher."

What?

"In that pocket, that clearing," said that shriveled twist of burning orange flesh. "Do you see what I see?"

EIGHT

Panoply Night wasn't the largest airship in the Corona fleet. Its guns were minimal, the main engines underpowered, and wide-open throttles meant draining the tiny fuel tanks. Yet *Panoply Night* deserved to be the fleet's flagship. Secondary engines gave it the grace of a thunderfly. There were enough quarters onboard to house an Archon's staff, and there were call-lines waiting to be plugged into the world, plus several protected chambers where secrets could be discovered or discussed. But what made the ship most impressive, even unique, was the huge quantity of corona parts that went into its construction: bladders were stuffed inside bladders, layers keeping the hydrogen gas safe. Scales were fixed upon scales upon more scales, and the machine's skeleton was corona bone secured with silk rope and black-ivy glues. And in the event of a midair battle, uniquely trained pilots would watch the world through the world's most elaborate periscopes, making their ship bounce through the air like a crazed ball.

"All right, madam."

Prima was standing beside a tiny window. Armored shutters were open, and she had no idea where she was. Mooring lines held *Panoply* in its hiding place, while a cluster of call-lines ran off into the canopy. A never-used receiver was held tight in one hand. Behind her waited the small desk that she claimed last evening, and the office that came with the desk, along with the young lieutenant who had already proved himself as being endearingly, gorgeously competent.

"He's waiting, madam."

Sondaw had been a commissioned officer for just nine days.

Pressing the receiver to her ear, Prima said, "Yes."

A man asked, "Is this the Archon?"

She intended to say, "Yes," again. But the static exploded, pops and whistles generated somewhere along the copper.

Then the static was gone, and from the sudden calm, the man asked, "Are you Prima?"

"I'm Prima. Merit?"

"Yes."

Another surge of noise attacked the line. The call was coming from the District of Mists, but that wasn't why the sound was so lousy. Sondaw had explained that the voice could be coming from anywhere, but the caller had an ally in the Mists, and at least two long lines had been stitched together.

When the static dissolved, she shouted, "Are you safe?"

"Safer than you," he said.

Even from a distance, Merit looked to be in agony—a man who had lost his wife and whose only child was in peril.

"Don't tell me where you are," she said.

He laughed at that, or the interference sounded like laughter.

"We're trying to find the traitor," she said.

"You've got multiple leaks," he said.

"We don't know that," she began, but the static surged again.

Then the line quieted, and Merit was already talking. " . . . but the papio wouldn't want the trees dropped. They want Diamond. They'd love having my son for themselves . . . "

A bright surge of electricity left her ear aching.

Merit's voice chased the surge. "You can't protect my son."

"We can protect him and you," she said, unsure whether she believed those words.

There was no response.

Had the connection broken?

No. By pure chance, the interfering racket subsided. Merit could have been standing inside the room beside her. Very clearly, he shouted, "Explain the situation. What's going on at your end?"

Prima flinched.

"Do you hear me?" he shouted.

"Yes," she whispered.

Lt. Sondaw stood before the closed office door, hands behind his back, maintaining the image of the faithful soldier. Yesterday's young face was lost. The handsome mouth was tense, eyes swollen and red.

"There was a full assault on the Ivory Station," said Prima. "Wings and shock troops. We were lucky to pull the government before everything burned."

A little quieter, Merit asked, "Did they hawk you?" *Chased*, he meant.

"The wings followed us for a time, yes."

"And then they let you get away."

She nodded, speaking to herself as much as to the slayer. "They knew, I think. That we didn't have what they wanted."

"What about the *Happenstance*?"

"It escaped the Station, yes."

"And the papio went looking for it," he guessed.

"The *Happenstance* was captured, yes. Then destroyed."

Merit cursed. "What about its crew?"

"Lost."

Cut by the news, he said nothing.

Prima looked at the little desk. Nothing was on top but a broad stack of folders rescued from the Ivory Station, the top packet marked: CONFIDENTIAL, THE KING SYNOPSIS.

"You were smart, Merit," she said. "Making your own plans."

"Where's List's fleet?" he asked.

"I'd rather not say."

He rephrased, asking, "Are the big ships protecting the bloodwoods, or are they pushing your way?"

The fleet's motions couldn't be concealed. Merit's hiding place didn't offer a view, or maybe he was pretending to be blind, intentionally misleading anybody who might be eavesdropping on the line.

Or the spies haunting her shadow.

Prima offered the nebulous truth. "Our allies are giving us helping hands."

The slayer breathed once, deeply. "My wife?"

"Haddi's still missing."

Merit began to talk again, asking something else . . . but the static returned with his first syllable, frustrating both of them.

She put a hand on top of the King files, waiting.

Then the sputtering teased her, pretending to fade, and she said, "By nightrise, this will be the most secure District in the world. I'll send out heavily armed patrols, and they can bring you in . . . "

But Merit was speaking into the same electronic storm. " . . . is most important to me," he said. "And you appreciate that, I'm sure."

She stopped talking.

He paused as well, and then with a careful tone said, "Madam. Did you hear me?"

"Your son is the most important part of this. Yes, of course he is."

Through the curtain of white noise, the man shouted, "But do you understand why I would even consider this? Can you see my point of view?"

"What are we talking about?"

The noise worsened.

Then the line quieted at long last, and she said, "I couldn't hear you. Please, tell me everything again."

"Ten thousand ships can't protect Diamond," said Merit. "One maniac pointing one cannon decides to shoot *Bountiful*, whatever the reason, and my son burns and falls through the demon floor."

She bristled, but there was no fighting the logic.

"I intend to go where I need to go. Protecting my boy is everything."

A revelation squeezed her heart. "I understand," she said.

"Do you?"

She saw the context and his thinking, yes. But what was lucid and reasonable to one desperate person made her weak.

"You're thinking of going to the papio," she said.

"Give me a better target," he said.

"For now, hide," she said. "Move when you have to move, and call me on a fresh line tonight, tomorrow. I'll work through the day and make everything safe."

Merit said nothing.

She waited.

Then once again, he said, "Traitors."

"We have several suspects," she admitted.

"Who—?" he began.

But that overly long thread of copper and electricity finally failed, and nothing was left to hear but the steady whisper that inhabited every empty call-line—a voice that never breathed or used words; the voice from which a determined ear could pull free anything that it wanted to hear.

• • •

Diamond was sitting at the back of the machine shop, the monkey at his side.

The crew walked past the pair, looking at the boy in quite distinct ways. They were interested in him and they smiled at him, but they were suspicious too. They were scared of quite a lot today, perhaps including him, and maybe they weren't angry but there was always a raw, furious quality to the faces. Each man used every one of those expressions, sometimes within the same few strides. And sensing these shifting, combustive moods, it was easy to believe that one of them was his enemy. Father had offered a thousand assurances about the loyalty and honor of these people, but those faces showed Diamond too much. Nothing but time stood between now and the moment when somebody else would try to kill him.

The idea was vivid and deep, and then the idea turned into belief. Belief was as good as fact. Belief felt like truth and became nothing else. But that grim truth wasn't as terrible as he would have guessed. Some mechanic or harpooner would show the boy a mysterious grin, and his heart quickened. Or *Bountiful*'s captain would toss a little wink his way, and tiny places inside Diamond—tissues and talents without names—began to ready themselves for trouble.

"Are you all right?" Elata asked.

"I guess."

Not believing him, she glanced at the Master.

"Are you sure?" asked Nissim.

Even Good studied him.

Diamond shook his head. He wasn't certain about his wellbeing, no.

Tar`ro looked at the boy, chewing on his tongue as he made his appraisal.

"Yeah, what's wrong?" Seldom asked.

Too many answers begged to be offered. Diamond refused all of them, pointing across the huge room. "Something's happening over there."

The winking captain had just walked past them. Two crewmen were standing before the open door. *Bountiful*'s top harpooner had been bolting one of the air-powered guns into its proper cradle. Five spears rested nearby, each fat with explosives and timers, and a mechanic was working on a sixth spear, rebuilding it to kill machines instead of coronas. Except he wasn't working as much as he was glancing outside, looking down at some odd thing. The harpooner was doing the same. And Diamond could think of nothing but his father's return.

The captain approached the two men, and the harpooner stepped close, their faces near enough to kiss.

Diamond watched the man and woman talk.

The captain didn't look outside. She studied the eyes in front of her, and then she stepped back and pretended to examine the heavy gun, holding its handles while aiming at the open air.

Smiling, the mechanic said a few words.

Everybody laughed with their faces, their voices. But serious eyes kept giving the world hard study. Then the captain stepped away from the edge, and the three of them stood with their backs to the doorway, hands over mouths, each taking his and her turn in the conversation.

"Something is happening," Tar`ro agreed.

"They hear your father," the Master guessed.

Saying so made it a little bit true. But not enough.

"Father isn't coming," Diamond said.

"You don't know that," Elata said.

Just the same, the boy got to his feet. Sitting was awful. His legs were desperate to walk.

"Stay," Tar`ro said.

But Diamond was already running on the hard black rubber floor, leaping over tied-down machines and a neat stack of deflated bladders. The captain was a short woman, stocky to the brink of fat, and she had a deeper voice than some men. The voice said his name. One arm lifted, and Diamond let himself be caught short of the doorway. Then she squeezed his shoulder, saying, "Please, stay with me."

"Where's my father?"

As if expecting the question, she said, "He isn't late. But we need to leave this place at once."

"No."

"Quiet," she said.

He didn't think that he had been yelling.

"Look at me, Diamond."

She had been a pretty woman before she got old, and she was always talented, and more than once, Father had mentioned how rare it was for any woman to give her life to killing coronas.

Diamond yanked her hand and skipped sideways.

Shaking what hurt, she told him, "We had another weak rain this morning. The canopy below was already thin, but now it's thirsty, and someone could easily see us from below."

"The papio might," the mechanic said.

"Anybody might," said the harpooner, sucking air through his golden teeth.

"So we're preparing to cut loose and move," the captain said. "But don't worry. Your father knew this was possible and told us where we'll go next. He might well beat us there, honestly."

A broad leatherwing came from under the ship, slow lazy strokes beating at the bright air. A flock of millguts swirled high above. From inside the canopy, in those places where shadows joined ranks, a single big jasmine monkey proclaimed dominion over the best part of Creation.

"But there's something else," said the captain. And with that she put her bulk in front of him.

Good jumped up on Diamond's shoulder, and the others walked up after him.

Tar`ro asked Seldom, "Do you see your brother?"

"Not now."

But Elata nodded, saying, "There."

Karlan was helping drag heavy machinery. Working on the far side of the shop, he was a huge figure beside the crew, and even at a distance, he looked as close to happy as any of these miserable people could be.

Diamond wasn't worried about Karlan. The crew scared him, but not the boy who tried to kill him.

Was that foolish?

The captain touched Diamond with her sore hand, lightly.

"Listen," she said.

He focused on her face, her open mouth.

"Stories," she said. "Out here, all of the stories get told. People think they see things and they believe they hear things, but nothing's ever certain. Except that four creatures were trapped inside that old corona."

Diamond saw where the words were pointing. Harpooners had great eyes; the boy couldn't count the times people had said so in his presence. Once again, he slipped past the captain, two leaps putting him at the floor's end, a lip of bone and featherwood pressed against the toes of his boots.

"Where's the ghost?" he asked.

"Nowhere," said the harpooner, an exceptionally strong hand dropping on the boy's shoulder.

Diamond remembered to be scared of the man.

"It's that burr-tree that worries us," the harpooner said. Then the hand moved, pulling Diamond back from the emptiness. "I was counting branches, which everyone should do. You know, to keep your faculties sharp. And somewhere in the last five recitations, while I was looking everywhere else, one of those very big branches decided to melt and then vanish."

• • •

The fleet had come from the District of Districts—one hundred and seventy-three giant machines serving as backbone to humanity's combined fleet. Each airship was dressed in the name of a hero or famous battle, or some vivid emotion, or moral concepts that even the wicked enemies would appreciate. There was the *Fire at Night*, the *Wettle*, the *Passion*, the *Honest*, *Raging Fist*, the *Marqlet*, *Vengeance*, *Shattered Wings*, the *Chew*, and the venerable *Destiny*, older than any living man but holding its hydrogen as well as any of its mates. Every ship was held aloft by the best corona bladders, tough as steel and a fraction the weight. Each had a skeleton of corona bone draped with skins and scales pulled from a thousand dead monsters. The fleet moved together, like a mishmash of dissimilar birds forced into one long flight. Some of the ships were little fletches, bird-shaped and lightly armored to allow for speed and endless grace. There were bigger fletches with banks of engines, a few towing complacent, balloon-like panoplies. There were warrior-class spears and battle-class behemoths, and a dozen fast-freighters carried stockpiles of fuel and food and munitions. And the fleet was bearing quite a lot more—a stew of orders and guidelines, ranks and egos, thousands of soldiers who had never walked on coral, and one overriding command ruling all others:

Protect the flagship.

Nestled in the armada's heart, the *Ruler of the Storm* was both safe and magnificent. The younger sibling to the *Ruler of the Wind*, the machine was only two-thirds finished when her sister was destroyed. But a useful bureaucratic panic allowed the construction to be finished in record time. The *Wind*'s crew was dropped like gears into their old tasks, minus the original captain who was given a public trial leading to a loud plea of guilt by incompetence. Then the Archon of Archons spoke to a select audience, telling supporters that while old Merit played a role in the disaster, he appreciated the slayer's motivation. He was also a father, and however wrong the methods and however shameful that day, the Archon used his office to grant the hero a full pardon for that enormous crime as well as for any and all failures of character during the last thousand days.

"Remember the pardon, son?"

Every word returned to King, as well as his father's burning humiliation.

"No," said King. "It's lost to me."

Smiling, List said, "We know better than that."

The past was usually a prologue to some little lesson.

"Now what if I'd accepted everyone's wise advice? Put our most famous slayer on trial, the man standing for a cause that nobody had ever imagined possible. I would have won an effective verdict. Our allies in the outer Districts would be warned. No one would doubt that I was in total command. But that's all I would have won—a lone judgment underscoring what everyone already appreciated. Words riding soft white leather, framed in my office and worth nothing.

"The boy was going to remain inside the Corona District. Prima would make certain of that. Diamond is hers, and contesting her ownership would have been a massive waste of time and resources."

And here was the lesson, King knew.

"I win and the rest of history plays out as it has. Merit languishes in jail, while his son runs free in this District, despising me. Then the evil and the idiotic try to murder Diamond just the same. And what's my position in that scenario? My fleet goes where it wishes. Nobody can stop us. But look at the people above us. Better and better, you know how to read our moods, our fears. Study those faces. Find one face isn't thrilled to see us, threatening our common enemies with quick brutal law."

King and his father were sharing one of the observatory blisters, riding on the *Ruler*'s top spine.

"Are you looking at the faces, son?"

"I'm watching your face, sir."

Smiles were never simple. Father's grin was smug but cautious.

"Well, yes," said the little man. "Take my word for it. If I'd listened to my shrewd advisors, we'd be looked upon as invaders. Even as it stands, I'm sure that a few of our supposed allies think we're responsible for this miserable mess."

King asked, "But why would you want to kill the boy?"

"Your brother," said Father.

King stared at the changing smile.

"I can't say this enough: we're emotional beasts, quick to judge and stubborn when it comes to defending our opinions." Father paused, eyes turned upwards. "But worse, we are an exceptionally, shamelessly lazy species. If people look at me as their enemy—if I bring rage to their bellies, their hearts—then I must have been the agent who ordered bombs exploded on the top of the world. I'm the one who killed thousands in hopes of murdering one soul. And why hold that wicked notion? Because smart opinions involve quite a lot of tedious, unthankful work, and we are too busy to bother."

King made a rough wet noise with his eating mouth, and with his breathing mouth, he said, "Lazy and stupid too."

He was provoking Father, but the man was clever enough to see it.

"If only we were stupid," said List. "No, we carry big brains. Not unbreakable like yours. But I've never met the man whose head was filled up in one lifetime. And the smartest of us, if he wants, can feed that lard so many carefully picked, well-pickled facts. We're lazy and instinctive, and we find it so easy to believe what's unlikely, and we fight for what pleases us while ignoring most everything that's hard, and what genius we have builds elaborate lies that have no good function except to put us at the center of this glorious, eternal world."

King finally looked up. The fleet had reached the point where the overhead canopy suddenly grew thin, great old branches missing their ends and then absent entirely. The *Ruler*'s engines changed pitch and speed as the airship slid beneath the tree called Hanner. These were little blackwood trees, barely sticks compared to the giants of home, and ballast was being dropped—

thousands of buckets of water released into the midday light—and suspended on rainbows, the flagship began its ascent into the enormous gouge that had been hacked into the forest.

King was thoroughly impressed.

What he saw and what wasn't seen captivated him.

Verbal accounts weren't adequate. The sheer volume of lost trees took him by surprise, and so did the blackened carcasses of buildings clinging to Hanner's fire-ravaged trunk. Crude new gun emplacements had replaced those destroyed last evening. Hundreds of little civilian blimps had been brought from everywhere, apparently to do nothing but look tiny against the carnage. Banners hung on the surviving trees, names asking other names to come and find them. Countless survivors sat on the brinks of landings and sheered-off limbs. They were watching the *Ruler of the Storm* climb towards them. The *Ruler* bristled with cannons and armor, and the front battleworks brandished rockets bigger than any papio wing, each tipped with the Creation's most powerful explosives. Yet King couldn't see the promised relief or pride or even the scornful stares of hatred. Father was wrong. The greatest ship in the world, and the most that it earned was weary curiosity from fat brains already too full with too much.

King imagined the slaughter of the falling trees. The mind gave fire and misery to thousands of nameless bodies, and his hearts began to race, and the armored plates rose from his body. His rage was as pure and sharp as it had been in a very long while, and he was at least as crazed towards every enemy as any human could be.

An elegantly uniformed officer had appeared inside the blister.

"Find us a working line," Father said, pointing at the ruins of the Ivory Station. "I want a conversation with Prima."

"Communications are problematic," the officer pointed out.

"I beg to differ." The Archon of Archons walked up to his son, reaching high with both hands, starting to push. Other fathers might straighten their children's unruly hair, but List risked slicing fingers, trying to make the plates lie flat. "The greatest military force in the world is under my colleague's feet. I'm quite certain that she knows that I'm here."

The plates began to drop under the little fingers.

Father winked knowingly. "But this idea is always warm in your mind, isn't it, son? Conversation is really the least impressive way to deliver your message."

• • •

Bountiful dropped little streams of water meant to evaporate before being noticed, and tanks of pressurized hydrogen were milked for a few moments, giving the bladders more lift. Then the tethers were released, anchors left buried in the trees. Smoothly and quietly, the smallest two engines nudged the ship ahead, pushing it through the first gap and into a crooked airborne tunnel that would carry them up to places where the big machine would never be seen.

Father hadn't returned.

Good sat beside Diamond, both watching the open doorway. "Merit where?" asked the monkey.

"Coming," Diamond said.

Good stood on his four hands, considering his boy.

Diamond had promised the captain that he wouldn't approach the open air again. But he could tell his monkey, "Watch for him. Go on now."

A slow gait carried Good across the shop floor. Everybody in the crew had a job, a task, some consuming chore that kept him distracted. The harpooner's chore was to stand beside the long gun, an explosive round sleeping in the breech. The man was counting branches, and then he looked at the monkey, unhappy about something. And Good tried to smile—a peeling back of lips to reveal yellow canines and pink gums—and as he did on rare occasions, he rose up on his hind legs, clumsily shuffling forwards like a shriveled old human man.

The harpooner said a word.

The little man beside him said several words.

And together, the two of them watched the world steadily descend around them.

Elata and Seldom sat on the floor with Diamond. Tar`ro and Nissim filled matching chairs. Both men had made cups with their right hands, chins against their palms as bleary eyes lost the war against sleep.

"I don't want to be here," said Elata

The boys squirmed silently.

"I know, I know," she said. "There's nowhere else to be."

The day was as short as any could be. The high parts of the world had never warmed properly and now they were growing black. The ship's little engines rumbled, easing *Bountiful* inside shadows. Disturbed, a young leatherwing rose from below, wings beating hard to match the ship's motion, four lidless eyes peering inside the shop before the creature pivoted and spun away.

Master Nissim snored softly.

"But what am I doing here?" Elata asked.

"Sitting," said Seldom. Then he made himself laugh.

Diamond looked at the girl's hand, and in his mind, he took hold of it. But when he tried to do that in life, she pulled her arm away. "I didn't ask," she said.

"What do you mean?"

"Did I say, 'Let me ride along'?"

Diamond felt his stomach and his heart, but he wasn't sure why.

"We're here with our friend," Seldom said.

"I know where we are. But I don't see why."

When he concentrated, Seldom squinted. The long squint ended with a firm voice claiming, "We're here to help Diamond."

Elata looked at Diamond. Her eyes and face had never worn that expression, mistrustful and sad and very nearly desperate. Then she looked out the open door, saying, "He doesn't need us. He has the Master and his bodyguard, and everybody else."

Crossing his arms, squeezing his chest, Seldom said, "Diamond is our friend."

"I know."

"Diamond's my best friend," he said.

"Not mine," she said.

The air had changed temperature. Diamond couldn't tell if it was colder or warmer, but there was a difference.

She said, "You're my best friend, Seldom. Diamond is second."

The boy had to smile, but he didn't seem to like the happiness.

Diamond wanted to talk, and so he said, "Maybe."

His friends looked at him, waiting.

"Maybe you're here so I can take care of you," he said.

Elata made a scornful face, considering those words.

"Maybe," said Seldom, without conviction.

Yet if that were true, then Diamond should accomplish some good act. But nothing could be done or said that seemed beneficial, and those thoughts put him back into a gray sorry place.

Then Good let loose with a wild celebratory hoot.

Out in the wilderness, myriad monkeys returned the call.

Dropping to all fours, Good sprinted back to the children, saying, "Old man back."

The little airship climbed into view, chasing them through the trees.

Nissim was awake again.

The children stood.

The little airship revved its engine and then slowed again, aiming for *Bountiful*'s door. Mr. Fret nearly clipped his right wing as he slid onboard.

Father was out and walking before the airship was restrained. It was important to give his son a smile and nod, and then he asked a pair of mechanics, "Why aren't you gone? These woods are clear as glass."

Nobody answered. A captain's decisions didn't need defending.

Tar`ro got to his feet, but the Master remained seated. From the chair, he asked, "What did Prima say?"

Blood lit up Father's face. He intended to answer, or perhaps he had a different subject in mind. Diamond never learned what words would come next.

The man hesitated.

His head tipped on its side, eyes nearly closed. "Cut your engine, Fret," he shouted.

The engine was rattling and spitting stink, and then it was quieter, the propeller taking its time spinning down.

Bountiful's engines continued pushing, but a sharper second noise was closing.

Tar`ro stared at the floor, and getting to his feet, Nissim looked at the ceiling, nodding without comment.

The crew began racing each other around the shop.

Holding his gun by its handles, the harpooner was taking aim at something that nobody else could see, something that was moving.

"Tell the captain," Merit yelled.

But the captain already knew. *Bountiful*'s main engines came awake, driving as hard as possible, and the floor was rising beneath them, pushing at Diamond's legs as various alarms began to screech. Yet those noises were nothing compared to the burly wrenching roar that lifted another ship into view. Narrow through its body and bristling with propellers set at odd angles, the newcomer looked like strange bird—a giant bird with a glass body and a belly full of papio.

The papio looked through the *Bountiful*'s open door, staring at the tree-walkers. Their faces were made from long jaws and long yellow teeth with candy-bright red gums, and their smiles were very much like Good's smile. And everything in view seemed to make them exceptionally happy.

• • •

" 'A wind moves all leaves but one,' " her father liked to quote. " 'And which leaf does the eye notice?' "

Prima was the motionless leaf, and the forest was being thrashed by the gale.

"The central fleet's gathering inside the Hole, madam," said Sondaw.

"The Hole" was the District's gaping wound, and everyone had embraced that grossly inadequate name.

"They found a working call-line," the Lieutenant continued. "Your colleague's at the other end, and he wants to speak to you, madam."

"Is it secure?"

"The line is civilian," the young man said.

"Not secure, in other words."

Sondaw saw the problem in its simplest terms. "Two people can discuss quite a lot, if they know and accept that limitation. If neither of you mentions troop displacements or timetables, of course."

The little office was crowded with uniforms. Every high-ranking soldier made approving noise about the lieutenant's assessment.

She cut off discussion with a slash of her hand.

When every eye was fixed on her, she said, "You don't understand. List is not our priority. Our priority is to make ready for what comes next."

Seeing her opportunity, another officer stepped forward. "Madam Archon. You wanted our resources and dispersals."

"Show me."

The young woman offered a thin stack of papers. Most of the Corona fleet was hiding in the nearby forest. "The District mobilization is complete," she said. "Including ships lost in the attacks and the reservists who are presumed to have died before, we're short eighteen percent of our total forces."

"And we have our allies," Prima said. "From other Districts, but not counting the behemoths inside the Hole."

A second, far smaller stack was laid on top of the first.

The Archon nodded while reading. Two friendly Archons had sent important airships, particularly the neighboring District of Mists. The other five outliers had handed over control of certain commercial freighters. The Coronas had their own commercial fleet, plus the corona hunters, and those were just the easiest ways to milk promise out of these numbers and impressive names.

The audience stood at attention, but focuses were wavering.

She ignored them. The rest of the world had to vanish, nothing existing but an army of calculations battling for dominance.

The still leaf suddenly wasn't quite still; her right hand began to tremble.

Noticing, Sondaw said, "Madam."

"I need air," she said. "I want to walk."

People emptied into the narrow hallway. Critical orders had been promised, but the Archon was still not relinquishing details, much less goals.

Did she have any plans yet?

Prima walked beside the woman officer. "We sent two fletches after Merit," she began.

"Yes, madam?"

"Not enough. Send another pair."

In one fashion or another, every face was concerned.

Only one general was onboard, and he willingly rose to the bait. "I can't help but notice, madam. You're playing a very active role in these matters."

"I am," she said.

He said, "We are here to help you, Madam Archon."

"And I'm not shy about asking for advice." A massive locked door led into the *Panoply*'s belly. Looking back at her audience, she used a flat stern voice to ask, "Have we declared war?"

"No, madam," the general allowed.

"Have the papio declared?"

The man sighed. "No."

"Peacetime means that civilian leaders hold the first and last word in matters of defense. This is a good smart policy, perhaps. Or it's a lousy, clumsy tradition that makes us slow and stupid. Either way, this is what every District does. Ours and List's too, judging by my colleague's prominent status in his fleet."

Nobody spoke.

Looking at the woman officer, she said, "Send two more fletches from our ranks. And there's a fast freighter, courtesy of the Bluetear District. It carries oversized fuel tanks, am I right? Load it up and send it too, as support for the mission."

"Yes, madam," the woman said.

"We need to find our friends," she said.

"Of course, madam."

"And we will find them, yes, madam," the general muttered by instinct.

Once again, Prima looked at the papers in her hand. She knew every ship by its name and designation, its manpower and munitions, and that was a surprise. The fatigue that she expected hadn't arrived. Yet the calm leaf didn't want to read another word. That's why she handed the papers to Sondaw. Then to no one in particular, she said, "We can't allow Diamond to be delivered to the papio. Not much is certain, but that is. They don't get the boy. And no cost is too great."

People nodded, trying to agree with her foggy platitude.

"Come with me," she told Sondaw. "The rest of you, make the fleet ready to embark. Soon."

"To meet up with Archon List and the main fleet," the general guessed, concerned but hopeful.

"One way or another, of course."

She struck the steel door. A soldier on the other side looked through the tiny window, slowly twisting the locks.

Prima and her lieutenant entered, and the door was locked again as they walked downstairs. Every interrogation room was occupied, but the quality of prisoners was generally poor. Two papio pilots wore chains strong enough to restrain giants. Neither had offered anything but curses and the desire to rescue one helpless boy. Several office workers had always lived beyond their means. They were now sharing the same cell, but besides selling a few harmless secrets to the enemies, they seemed to be blind little nothings living inside moldy wood. Merit was right about one bitter fact: this nightmare wasn't about the papio government or papio intrigues. The reef-humans didn't want to fling Diamond back to where he came from, and they certainly wouldn't bring down trees and lives, risking total war to make their point.

A different beast had killed the trees. Criminals from both species working together seemed most likely. They seemed like a deep wicked enemy, evil beyond measure, and that's why a handful of foresters and occasional smugglers had been shoved inside the biggest cell. These were the people who could carry the fuel and explosives from the reef to Rail and to Marduk and the rest of their targets. But more credible suspects had vanished, including an explosives expert and the bodyguard dispatcher who placed Bits where he needed to be yesterday morning. Were they dead innocents or enemies in hiding? And how many papio knew, condoning or at least ignoring the plot's horrible progress?

Time and patience would normally wring out clues. But time and patience were luxuries. Worse still, the Ivory Station had burned, destroying all kinds of records. From birth, Prima was taught to believe in good ends waiting after the greatest tragedies. She couldn't stop imagining sanity and stability, both kinds of humanity sitting at the traditional Table of Accord: polished coral and polished wood in equal measure. One day, perhaps in her lifetime, the scope of this wicked conspiracy would become apparent. Maybe not the full details and not every guilty name, but the Creation was built on true principles, and nothing as horrific as yesterday could fully vanish.

She could only do what she could imagine doing, today and tomorrow and no farther than that.

Protecting her species was what mattered. Saving the world was the only priority, and that's why she came down to this place. Prima wanted the room behind the final wire door. A hard stool was standing in the hallway outside, and sitting on the stool was a specialist who was talking to the prisoner. A powerfully built man of no particular age, the interrogator was bland in appearance and manners. As the Archon approached, he stood up. His right hand was scraped. Someone else's blood gave his white trousers their color. Reading her face, he stepped back from his post, saying, "I could stand a break, if you'd like to keep watch for me."

"Thank you, we will," said Prima.

He left, and she touched the wire door. Sondaw was standing on her right. Both looked into the little room. A steel cot once stood in the back, but that indulgence had been wrenched loose and stolen away. There was a tiny bucket for shit and an electric light that was too powerful for the overhead fixture. The prisoner had no place to sit but the floor, but heating coils had been woven inside the bone tiles, keeping the surface too hot for exposed skin. The man's left arm was hanging at an unnatural angle. He had two bare feet and nothing for clothes except oversized underwear, intentionally filthy, and he stood on one foot for a long moment before rocking to the other, and after the pain built too much, he returned to the first foot.

"His statement," she said. "Show it to me again."

The lieutenant handed her an important piece of paper.

The trees just begun falling when an old woman in the dispatch office announced that one very suspicious man once stood at her counter. Was it twenty days ago, or thirty? She described the suspect to her colleagues. They didn't remember him. She claimed that they weren't paying attention to their jobs, and why didn't anyone else see that he was evil? But the woman had developed a sloppy memory, the sort of mind where yesterday was lost while the deep past was vivid and close. There might have been a suspicious visitor once. Who knew? But the woman was close to retirement, and her colleagues liked her well enough to help her search the recent files, and that's why the recent permission form was discovered—a thoroughly routine document allowing one survey team and one airship to fly through the highest, darkest reaches of the forest, coring out samples of the living trees to determine their health. That was a routine project. But the flight was happening ahead of the published schedule, and the airship wasn't only several times larger than necessary, but it was last stationed in the wilderness, working for foresters living on the brink of papio air.

The prisoner's signature lay at the bottom of that form.

The barefoot man confessed to writing his name on the appropriate line. How could he deny it? But he also claimed no special knowledge or evil design. The form was a duty. As a member of the Archon's staff, his duty was to tend to hundreds of forms that slid over his desk every day. Making official business happen: that was what he did, and that's all that he had ever done.

The prisoner was brought here and the interrogation commenced. Again, Prima read the bold words and studied the eerily neat signature. The confession didn't take long, and it admitted to very little. The man was guilty of nothing but a rank principle, an ugly belief. This young man told his interrogator that the Diamond creature was no child, and it wasn't human either. He claimed that the Archon and her government were coddling a soulless beast that was only pretending to be human, and as such, the corona's spawn was even more dangerous and vile than the armored King.

Bealeen was the prisoner.

Her one-time aide had admitted to nothing but hatred, pure and rich.

About the surveying airship, he knew nothing. But Bealeen did mention that if he were given the chance and half a measure of courage, he would have done exactly what others had tried to do. On that ordinary stationary, he wrote that ten thousand dead was no great loss when the world and Creation were at stake, and he was proud. His loathing was majestic and it was just, and against some long odds, he had kept his thoughts hidden from foolish eyes.

The Archon put her fingers through the wires, watching her prisoner.

She didn't know this man. This Bealeen was silent, eerily composed. He hadn't made any noise since she arrived, his face damp from sweat but genuinely impassive—despite the arm hanging from the shoulder, out of joint, the collarbone presumably shattered.

It was the stare that she came to see. She studied those hard fixed eyes and the face carved from unfeeling wood, and the man's silent rage. There was enough rage to spread thick across time, making the next twenty generations ache.

The one leaf had recovered, standing still in the blowing forest.

Prima dropped the confession, watching the useless page twist and curl on its way to the floor. And then to her lieutenant, she said, "He knows a lot more than we realize, I think."

"Madam," Sondaw said.

"I can see it in him," she said.

The officer stared at the same face, seeing very little.

"There must be ways," she said. "On a day like this, with so much at stake, we have to take every measure."

Bealeen made a raw little sound.

"I am no expert," Prima continued. "But I can't help but notice that our suspect has that second arm, his writing arm, still sitting happy in its socket."

• • •

In little places, where boughs and foliage made tangles, there lived pretty little creatures named whiffbirds. The papio aircraft was named after them. Like their namesake, the machine was ferociously hungry, able to fly only brief distances before gulping down more fuel. Diamond had read about them. He remembered a big book and the specific page. This whiffbird's body was tilting, long bone propellers carrying it closer to the corona-hunter, and three papio soldiers filled its open hatch, guns pointed at the machine shop and the crew inside.

None of the crew moved now, everybody staring at the apparition. Diamond was staring. The soldiers were big papio, two women and a man. In the last moments their smiles had become something else, more toothy and much more serious. They wore identical uniforms, blotchy gray fabrics and tall boots and glass masks over their long-jawed faces. Rubber cords kept their bodies pinned to the cabin floor. Every soldier was shouting. They were shouting in a language they barely knew. *Bountiful* was still rising and the odd craft was keeping pace, propellers screaming in the air, and Father shouted something to someone—an order, maybe—as the whiffbird slipped around an overhanging limb and then moved closer, offering the harpooner one perfect shot.

The long spear leapt out of the barrel, out through the open air. The papio had no time to react. They screamed commands that couldn't be heard over the roar of engines, and the world felt thick and slow, and Father was turning, turning fast and shouting, "Don't fight don't fight," as one hand started to wave at his son.

The steel shaft plunged into the cabin. A fourth papio soldier was standing back from the hatches, and then he was gutted and dying, and the bright razor nose of the harpoon dug into the hull behind him, that jarring impact detonating a charge meant to kill one gigantic creature.

The whiffbird's backside was shredded.

Diamond watched the force of the blast shove the doomed machine towards them. It seemed as if the whiffbird might get shoved against the airship's body. But *Bountiful* kept rising while the other ship began to fall, its tail dropping fastest while the propeller on the nose tilted until it was nearly vertical.

That propeller had four blades of carefully shaped bone, mounted on a metal hub and spinning toward the opened doorway.

Merit was running for Diamond.

The boy knew what would happen. In perfect detail, he saw everybody being sliced apart. His legs made the decision. On instinct, in panic, he turned and started to run, maybe to do nothing but save himself. Except he couldn't die, not this way, and that simple thought pushed away the ugly rest in what he was thinking.

Tar`ro had his pistol out.

Master Nissim was standing beside Tar'ro, reaching for the running boy. But the butcher's hand had already missed.

Elata was standing with Seldom. They weren't moving. His friends looked as if they were posing for a fancy picture, the kind of image taken with cameras and expensive chemicals, with sunlight focused on the children while tense invisible parents begged them to surrender their feelings and smile.

The propeller struck the open doorway and the rubberized floor, its hub shattering with a hard sharp crash. Each blade had been carved to cut at the air, and now every shard flew across the shop.

Diamond managed several full strides, arms outstretched.

Too late, his friends began reacting to the catastrophe.

The racket was enormous and much too complicated to decipher. The only good fortune was how the blades smashed into the floor and ceiling and back into the floor again, losing momentum. The ceiling was armored. The shop was built to contain accidental explosions. Bone and fancy alloyed metal exploded, and Diamond collided with Elata and grabbed Seldom, shoving them down hard on the floor as a bright white piece of corona spun through the air, perfectly aimed to cut off every head but too slow, missing all of them in the end.

Diamond was on top of Elata, and then big hands pulled him up.

Father had grabbed him.

"You're all right," said Diamond.

Father cursed. He looked tearful, touching himself, sure that he would find blood. Except he was fine, and Tar`ro was on the floor, alive, and so was Master Nissim. But the harpooner was in two big pieces, and part of his head was missing. Two other crewmen were dead, another man had one leg, while the young man who flew with Father was cut through the middle and noisily bleeding to death.

Fret called out to somebody.

"You saved us," Seldom said weakly.

Diamond needed to walk. His legs wanted to walk.

Elata came up to him. She was hunting for words, but she saw Fret on his back with his pink insides sliding out, blood coming faster each time his heart pumped. Then she backed away again.

Karlan ran from somewhere. Stepping in front of Diamond, he carried a long crowbar in both hands. The giant seemed unsure who needed to be hit, but he was angry. He was wild and furious and ready for any good battle. Maybe he considered battering the corona's little boy, but there wouldn't be any satisfaction there. So he settled on striking Diamond on the shoulder, just enough to make him ache, saying, "Stay behind me. I'll protect you, you little shit."

A second whiffbird had appeared, hovering just beyond the shop door.

More papio shouted in at them, demanding that every gun was tossed to their wood-loving feet.

Master Nissim stood beside Karlan.

Tar`ro stepped in front of both of them, his pistol held high, as if ready to shoot the ceiling. Then to Karlan, he said, "If you think you can drop that ship with a piece of iron, do it. Go on."

"I might," Karlan said, almost laughing.

"Drop the bar or I'll shoot you here," Tar`ro said. "Otherwise, they'll kill everybody and let one of us heal."

"Yeah," said the giant boy. "That's what they should have done to begin with."

Father was kneeling, holding Fret's pale hand.

The crowbar hit the floor, and then with an underhand motion, Tar`ro tossed his gun toward the open air.

Bountiful had stopped climbing. Diamond felt it hovering, and after a few moments it began to drop, another pair of whiffbirds settling on top of its frame.

Fret said, "This."

Father asked, "What?"

Diamond stepped around the blood. The man ate fruit today, chewed pieces showing inside the opened stomach. Fret looked sick but calm, weak but not quite uncomfortable. Life meant pain, but he was gone from life in too many ways, and Diamond studied his face and the open mouth, waiting for his father to tell him to not look, to back away.

Father did nothing of the kind.

The two of them kneeled, keeping their knees out of the gore, and then Diamond said, "I wonder if I could help. If I gave him my blood, or something."

Father didn't react.

The body beside them managed one good breath, and then death was everywhere inside a piece of something that wasn't Fret.

"They tried that," Father said.

"Tried what?" Diamond asked.

"Your blood." Father's face was pale, his eyes red and sorry. "The samples from your last physicals. Remember them?"

Teams of doctors had given Diamond a day full of tests, stealing away huge vials of blood.

"I agreed to those experiments," Father confessed. "We thought . . . your mother and I decided . . . that if your blood could restore life or cure illnesses, it would just be another blessing for having you . . . "

"Did it help?" the boy asked.

"Not even a little, no."

Papio were everywhere else in the ship. They had come through the bridge's hatch, and now they were filling the hallway, walking upright with guns cradled in their big arms, each one shouting orders. Diamond had never seen papio soldiers. As promised, they were huge men and women, each trained until the muscles bulged, but what Diamond didn't expect were voices even bigger than those magnificent bodies.

"We are great," they roared. "And you must be good."

Father stood and offered Diamond his hand.

The boy took hold.

And then Father confessed something else.

"We were greedy with your blood," he said, smiling shyly as his voice broke. "We wanted more, as if one marvel wasn't enough."

• • •

Every day began with rain and misty brilliance, and every day faded at its own pace, approaching that moment when the sun had to be strangled.

Watching the night build was a trustworthy pleasure.

Standing at the front of the *Ruler*'s bridge, King stared out through the pilot's window. Lights came alive in the surrounding trees. Several quick vessels were passing under the fleet—fletches scouting the territory past the Hole, probably. Father was talking to his new generals. Those men were still wary of Father. But they were soldiers and natural fighters, and they didn't let themselves stay quiet when they didn't agree. They warned the civilian that merging their giant fleet with the Corona's forces was a huge undertaking, cumbersome yet essential. And Father told them that he didn't want any part of the military work, but since they were new to their posts, they had to appreciate the goals and what missteps were completely unacceptable.

King could twist his head farther than any human could. He could watch the world outside and enjoy whatever was happening behind him.

"We're going to win tomorrow," said Father.

Faces nodded out of reflex.

"And we are going to lose," he said.

Nobody else understood. Chests came forward, and someone said, "We never lose our wars."

" 'Our wars,' " Father repeated. "Is this 'our war'?"

They sensed a trap, and the generals assumed it was the only trap. One of them took it upon himself to say, "Humans have been slaughtered. Even if the papio had no role in the first crime, they came out of their sanctuary to kill hundreds more of our brothers. We must, must push ahead in force, with full resolve. We have no choice but make them bleed, or more trees will die."

Standing in one neat line, the military men were nodding in unison.

"I agree," said Father.

His audience expected to hear as much.

"But what happens if we're too successful?"

They didn't understand.

"Vengeance is always sloppy," Father said. "Our enemies won't just stand on their hands, counting their dead until the tallies are just about even. They'll claim their turn, counterattacking us, and we will lose expensive ships and soldiers who were your friends, and then it isn't tomorrow. It's the day after, war is declared. Then it's twenty days later, and you're standing on this bridge, trying to win a struggle with half your fleet and no ammunition, and I'm a political beast working out of sight, desperately trying to bring us back to a place where some ugly peace holds."

The generals looked sour, ill-at-ease.

King glanced into the gloom outside. The scout fletches had vanished, but now the little local fleet was arriving, armed airships and commercial vehicles and several corona-hunters converging beneath the Hole. They were following a timetable agreed on a hundred recitations ago. The woman Archon remained stubbornly out of reach, but Father and his generals had come to this decision: they would marshal here for the night, and in the morning, after the rain, the combined fleet would fly en masse to the nearest portion of the reef.

"I am a politician," Father continued. "I'll never be a soldier, and don't let me pretend to be. But this situation is political and it is very complex. You have no choice but believe me. Winning tomorrow is not a matter of bombs and death. Losing might be, but not winning."

"What are you talking about?" one officer asked.

"I know something," said Father. "Small events and patience have given me insights, and I won't explain myself. Don't ask. But we have a rare opportunity here. We can come home richer than when we left, and at least in their public eye, the papio will think that they have won a good small war of their own."

"Which war is that?" another asked.

"Our fleet will provide cover for the righteous people," said Father. "The Corona forces are free to blow up all of the bunkers and hangers they can find, and they can even land troops and try a running war on the sharp coral."

"They'll get chopped down," the ranking general warned.

Father said nothing, and he said it in a certain way.

Finally, the soldiers understood some part of this plan. They found themselves agreeing with the little man, at least enough that they could narrow their eyes, peering into the future with cold smirks and knowing clicks of the tongues.

The meeting ended when a military session began in a distant room.

Father joined King at the window.

His son was counting the little ships, and then another one of the endless aides announced, "Sir, you have a visitor."

Father turned away, immediately saying an unfamiliar name.

King found an old man standing on weak legs.

"I'm very busy," Father said.

"So I see," the old man replied with a sharp tone.

"Where's your daughter?" Father asked.

King saw a familiar face inside the new face. This was Prima's father—a retired trader in corona guts and skins.

"She's directly below you," the man answered.

"And the boy, our friend Diamond . . . where is he?"

That amused the trader. "I haven't been told. Which makes me think, sir, that you probably know more than I do."

The Archon of Archons nodded thoughtfully, and he looked down from the bridge. Then with a tight slow voice, he said, "We have berths here for every ship. Tell your daughter to dock beside me, and we can meet."

"No, sir."

"What's that?"

"There are no call-lines in mid-air. That's why she asked me to come and deliver this message to you personally. She wants you to know her intentions."

"Her intentions," Father said.

The plates on King's body lifted.

"My daughter and her armada are ready, and they intend to embark now, without delay. This is a night journey. Speed matters. But she wants me to tell you that you are welcome to push free of your hiding places and follow at your convenience."

"My convenience?"

"Or stay where you are. She would never presume to feed orders to any Archon."

Father's eyes grew big. "And where is she going?"

The old man laughed quietly.

"Really, List," he said. "Are you begging me to paint you a map?"

NINE

She was a burr-tree branch and then a ghost, and then she returned again as a leatherwing watching *Bountiful* with four superior eyes. She kept tabs on the Diamond boy and the humans, learning that the airship was about to slip away to a fresh hiding place. A sleek leatherwing could match the ship's pace, but someone would notice her. Quest didn't want anyone noticing her. She wanted to run the branches, biding her time. But then she heard papio wings on patrol and the whiffbirds rising, and that was why she turned into a ghost again, sloughing off her clumsiest pieces and everything that was remotely visible.

She hadn't been so tiny in a very long while.

Bountiful passed near the ghost's hiding place, but she couldn't see Diamond. She wanted to see him again but she was above the airship and the shop was in its belly, and the whiffbirds were coming fast, and she was so tiny and so invisible that it didn't feel like bravery when she fell like a leaf.

Any other time, someone would have heard the odd thump or felt the tiny change in buoyancy. But *Bountiful* was maneuvering and the whiffbirds were arriving, leaving her free to scamper where she wished, clinging to ship's steepest face.

Every camouflage was in play. Quest's overlapping shells bent light and delayed light, and what remained would look and feel identical to the ship's skin, complete to the textures and vagaries of the green dye. Every sound that she made was either killed or transformed into harmless noise. Any odiferous molecule that might leak free was destroyed before it could betray her. Her legs were minimal and silent, and most importantly, her toes were eager to cling to any surface. The entire body served as one adequate eye, and because she was so silent and free of scent, powerful little ears and nostrils missed nothing and nothing could sneak up on her.

One whiffbird died, but the roaring stinking machines were everywhere, landing on top to drop off the soldiers and ropes, and once those ropes were secured, the soldiers climbed down the ship's body, aiming for hatches and doorways and the open shop.

Quest clung to the ship's skin and to her courage.

The simple weight of the whiffbirds took hold of *Bountiful*, dragging it down. Three papio passed within reach of her, and the bridge was boarded.

Then the new captain bellowed orders in papio, and a new pilot dropped ballast while turning the ship's bow. A fresh course was attacked. Engines pushed them toward the reef, following the straightest possible line. Speed mattered. But darkness was more important, and it was coming soon. With her abrasive dense language, the papio captain spoke across the intercom, explaining what she wanted and what her superiors wanted and what her species deserved to gain from the next little while.

The ship's skin was slick and vertical and then it was past vertical.

Quest was walking beneath the bladders, listening past the engine sounds and footfalls, hunting for the name.

"Diamond," said a papio mouth.

Another mouth asked, "What?"

"I'm honored to meet you, Diamond," said the papio.

The reef-human sounded young but grown.

Quest had her best ears pushed against the ship's skin, and she crept down to where she was level with the crew's cabins. Each cabin had a little window wearing shades. All of the shades were closed. She made no sound as she moved, voices growing louder with each short careful stride.

"We've already met," Diamond said. "When I visited the reef, you were there. I remember you."

"You remember my face?"

"The Archon of Archons walked past you," said the boy. "You watched him while he was talking, telling the papio what they should do."

"I remember that."

" 'Murder me and steal these two treasures,' he said. He was talking about King and me."

"Your memory is remarkable," said the man.

A new sound arrived. Metal banged against metal. Quest was near enough to hear Diamond take a deep breath, as if ready to talk again.

But he said nothing.

Quest wanted to listen to the boy. But it was more than just wanting. Quest longed to hear the mind tied to that voice. She wanted words and the quiet breaths that meant nothing and the face too. No moment in her life was filled with such deep wrenching hope. She was tiny and too exposed already, and she didn't have a mouth on this body, much less any voice that her brother would comprehend. But she wanted to see him inside the cabin, talking to the man that he remembered and that she had probably seen from an enormous distance.

Diamond made a small anguished sound.

"Don't worry," the papio said.

Quest was clinging outside Diamond's cabin. But the shade was pulled tight and secured, and she didn't dare cut through the window or the wall. Much as she wanted to look inside, there was nothing to do but cling to the ship and listen.

A new voice came, loud and close.

"No," said a monkey.

The papio man said, "Hold him for me. Please."

"Why?" Diamond asked.

"Because he's your friend and you don't want him hurt."

Objects were hitting the cabin floor, and Diamond said, "Are you putting Good in that sack?"

"No, Diamond. You are."

The monkey said, "Bad. Bad, shitty bad."

Noises built a picture. Quest listened to a battle that ended with one loud bite, and what might have been bone snapped. But then the monkey was inside the sack, cursing and sobbing at the same time.

"Show me," said the papio.

"No."

The man laughed. "I've seen that kind of marvel before. You'll have a fine new thumb soon enough."

The boy didn't talk.

Metal objects were moved.

"What is that?" Diamond asked.

"A cooler."

"What's inside it?"

"Dry ice."

"Why?"

"Trousers," said the man.

"What?"

"Let your trousers fall."

"No."

There was a pause, brief and tense. Then the man asked, "Do you think that I want to do this? I don't. I don't at all. But I have orders. We need pieces of you for study. I'll take them and place them carefully in this cooler, and everything will grow back quickly enough, I promise."

"No," Diamond said.

The man tried to laugh. Then he tried to sound angry disapproving. "It won't hurt any worse than your thumb hurt. And how bad was that?"

Diamond was breathing quickly.

"Or maybe I should settle for taking your thumb," said the man. "Here. Let me kill the monkey and cut him open."

"No."

"What I want looks a little bit like a thumb, doesn't it?"

"Don't," said the boy.

"Trousers," the man said.

Silence.

The man said, "Now."

"All right," said Diamond.

Quickly, without a sloppy step, Quest ran. She was a quiver of light racing across the ship's skin, hurrying toward the shop. Every big door had been closed and secured, but there were hatches for emergencies and vents to push fumes out of the close spaces. She slipped inside the first vent. Fear didn't exist. Without hesitation and very little caution, she slipped into a big noisy room smelling of tree-walkers and the papio. Only the papio were visible. Three whiffbirds were being refueled, and that's what she needed. Quest wanted energy and mass, and the odors of the living couldn't hide the sweet fragrances of dead meat.

A storage closet was closed but not locked.

Nobody noticed the door open briefly. Inside that small dark space, dead tree-walkers had been stacked on the floor. They were in pieces. Quest looked for living faces and found none, and then she eased her way down to the carnage, ready to battle any kind of revulsion for what was to come next.

But there was no revulsion.

She dissolved one of her shells and made a mouth.

Two bites told her what she had always suspected: humans tasted exactly like monkeys.

• • •

"I don't feel good," Seldom said.

"Are you throwing up?" Elata asked.

"Not yet."

The prisoners were jammed inside the galley. *Bountiful*'s crew sat in the back, shoulder to shoulder. Only the pilot and captain were missing, presumably helping the papio fly their stolen ship through the night-bound wilderness. The first table was half-empty, reserved for the children and Master Nissim, for Tar`ro and Merit. The galley wasn't built for papio. A giant woman was squatting in front of the door, and three glowering males were jammed inside the kitchen, guns behind the long counter.

"Are you ill, or are you scared?" asked the papio woman.

"He's scared," said Karlan.

"You shouldn't be," she said. "Nobody lifts a hand, unless you give us cause."

"I won't," Seldom promised.

"Then you are spectacularly safe."

Seldom was sitting between his brother and Elata, arms wrapped around his aching belly, his back to the guards. He was a stick next to Karlan, but there was no denying the resemblance in their faces, in the eyes and noses and the shape of their mouths. They had never looked more like brothers.

Karlan was the only prisoner whose hands were tied. He liked that. There was an honor in the caution, and he picked up his thick wrists, studying the sharp brown cords that were already cutting into the flesh.

"So you're taking us to the reef," said Tar`ro.

The guards said nothing.

Nissim and Tar`ro were facing the children, facing the kitchen. Merit had been told to sit alone at the far end at the table, closest to the woman soldier.

"I've never walked the reef," Tar`ro said.

"I have," Seldom said, and then he smiled at the memory, momentarily forgetting his bellyache.

"Flying the canopy at night," Merit said. "That's a tough game."

The ship's crew made concurring sounds.

"I hope we don't snag a sneaky branch," he said.

The male papio didn't know the language, and they didn't approve of any noise. One of them said something harsh to the woman, and showing her canines, she said a papio phrase to him.

"What did she say?" Elata asked Nissim.

The Master and Merit glanced at each other, neither answering.

The papio woman had a quiet, careful laugh. "Wanting this and wanting that don't matter, I said. Orders have been given, and we are walking the path."

Elata squirmed against the steel seat. "But why take all of us? If you want Diamond, put him inside a whiffbird and fly home."

Merit knew why but decided to keep quiet.

"Whiffbirds can't fly far," Seldom said.

Karlan snorted. "But they can refuel from *Bountiful*'s tanks. They're probably doing that right now."

His tiny brother squinted at nothing. "Yeah, I forgot."

The woman papio shifted, letting her weight find a little more comfort.

"I'm brave," she said, "but I wouldn't risk such a trip. Night inside a little craft is too dangerous. A rotor clips one branch, and the mission ends. And if we sit still and wait for daylight before launching, then your people would enthusiastically shoot down the whiffbird before it's home, and that would be a terrible loss for the world."

Nobody spoke.

"You see, we believe the boy is precious," she said. "And we aren't like you, killing ourselves while trying to murder him."

Seldom let loose a moan.

"Let me take him to the toilet," said Elata.

"No," said the woman. Then she spoke to the other guards, and a cooking pot was found under the counter. One guard handed it to her, wanting nothing to do with the prisoners, and she kicked it along the floor, putting it under his seat. "Heave into that bucket."

"Throw up in front of people?" he asked unhappily.

"Do it," she said.

Always agreeable, Seldom bent down, and his last two meals spilled out into the bright steel pot.

Elata patted her friend on the back.

To nobody in particular, Tar`ro said, "Thunderflies."

The Master nodded.

"Know of any chrysalises sitting around in easy reach?" Tar`ro asked.

Merit looked at the two men, curious now.

"Not so far," said Nissim. "How about you?"

"No. But I'll keep hunting."

The papio understood none of that. But the woman was suspicious enough to say, "Be quiet now."

"Sorry," Tar`ro said.

Merit took a breath, and then against the rules, he stood.

"Sit down," said the woman.

In papio, Merit said, "No, I will not."

"Sit down," she repeated, in papio.

He shook his head. "Shoot me."

The male guards were willing. The woman studied the old tree-walker, planning where she would slap him and what would break if she used force.

A solitary thud came from some distant part of the ship.

Nobody inside the galley noticed.

"My son won't be safe with your people either," Merit said, shifting back to the prisoners' language.

Inside her mind, the woman beat him.

"Your weapons dropped our trees," he said. "I'm sure of that much. My people helped you, but the blame rests mostly on you."

"None of us," she said.

Merit rocked slowly from side to side, thinking.

A door opened and closed in the hallway, and papio feet walked past the galley, making no effort for speed.

Once again, the woman said, "Sit down."

"Are you certain?" Merit asked.

"Certain?"

"That they're trustworthy," he said, gesturing at the papio soldiers who couldn't piece together any of this noise.

The woman looked at the three faces.

Another thud was followed by shouting, not close but loud enough to seem loud. A papio had yelled a few words.

"What did that mean?" Elata asked.

Merit hadn't heard enough.

Nissim had, and he gave Tar`ro a careful glance.

Somewhere in the back of the ship, somewhere past the shop, gunfire suddenly broke out, intense and swift and then gone again.

Echoes and the memory of gunfire lingered. The imprisoned crew jumped to their feet, and the four papio shouted orders at them and each other, waving their automatic weapons. But then nothing else seemed to happen. Normal sounds of engines and life drifted into the galley, lasting long enough that the mind could almost wonder if nothing was wrong. The slayer crew began to sit again. Nobody relaxed, but most of the room was ready to stop breathing fast.

Then another voice shouted, closer than the first.

"Enemy," a woman called out, in papio.

Gunfire erupted again, and wild shouts, and this time the mayhem didn't melt into doubt.

• • •

Three guns were firing. Soldiers were fighting inside the machine shop, and then they were climbing and shooting. Diamond was almost glad for the distraction. He counted the guns and listened to voices, imagining a single brave crewman who had managed to remain free. He pictured Tar`ro running with his pistol in hand, and then Karlan swinging a huge steel bar. But he didn't imagine Master Nissim, and he never used Father. Even in his head, those two men weren't allowed to be heroic.

Eventually the gunfire slowed and then was gone. Shrill papio words wandered through *Bountiful*. Someone yelled for someone to be careful about the bladders. Corona flesh was strong, but bullets were stupid. If a bullet found weakness and the hydrogen jetted free, they could be screwed. That's what the papio were shouting in both languages. "Screwed screwed screwed."

The cabin door had been left slightly ajar, allowing the guarding soldier to keep watch over Diamond. The guard filled the hallway. The boy was lying on the narrow bed, wearing his school trousers again, watching his new thumb emerge. Good was sitting in the cabin's safest corner, his back to the walls. The hated sack needed to be torn to ribbons. Still furious for being shoved inside that blackness, the monkey punched holes in the sack with his incisors, and he tugged with his arms and with curses, creating long ribbons of canvas.

"Bad evil bad wrong," he told the growing stack of rags.

Diamond watched his thumb, but he wasn't thinking about his thumb.

Then a single shot rang out, as far from the cabin as possible.

One very big body ran up to the door and the soldier. An officer looked inside the cabin, staring at the chewed-up hand, and without a word, the newcomer shut the door and used a small key to work the lock.

It was dark inside the tiny room.

The soldier in the hallway said several papio words, including, "Why?"

The officer responded with orders. Listening to papio was different than reading it. Diamond didn't understand, but the tone and breathless speed of the words made the orders important. Then the officer named the enemy with a word that was the very much the same in both languages.

"Jazzing," he heard.

"Angry angry angry," said Good, staring at him.

"I'm sorry," Diamond said. But he didn't feel sorry. He had saved the monkey's life and was bitten for his trouble.

Good had never been this furious with his boy. "Angry mad pissed," he said.

"They're chasing a jazzing," Diamond said.

The monkey's eyes understood before the rest of him. The eyes grew bigger and scared all over again.

"One of the wild jazzings got onboard," Diamond guessed.

No monkey was ignorant about jazzings, even if he lived far from the wilderness. Good looked past Diamond, and his arms quit ripping the canvas.

Full-grown jazzings were powerful killers, and huge. But the giant predator wouldn't be able to climb between the bladders, which was why this jazzing had to be a lost youngster.

Diamond felt sorry for the imaginary animal.

He felt very sorry for himself.

He had been working for a long while, trying to push aside certain awful moments. But his mind was too perfect to cooperate.

A distant shot reverberated.

Then the echo was gone, and a new noise found him. The tapping was light and very quick. Good heard the tapping. Something was striking the cabin's little window, and the talk of wild jazzings was too much of a coincidence. The monkey jumped up, staring at the shades before deciding to crawl under the cot.

Diamond imagined a fingernail striking glass.

The tapping stopped.

Bountiful was still pushing towards the reef. Branches might have clipped the ship as they passed, although they would never sound so clean and neat, so rhythmic.

Again, the tapping began.

The cabin wasn't as dark as before. Diamond's eyes had adapted. His thumb looked too pale but otherwise felt and acted normal. The other wounds needed more healing. What wasn't pain told him the state of affairs. His brown trousers still had loose buttons, but he didn't want to touch himself there. He would finish dressing when he wasn't thinking about the knives or the papio man bent over his exposed body, and maybe then he would be healed.

The tapping became complicated, swift and full of patterns. By the sound of it, twenty fingertips were working the glass.

Diamond stood, the trousers drooping without falling.

From under the cot, Good offered a quiet growl.

The shades were black and heavy, ready to help an exhausted crewman sleep through the middle of the brightest morning. Diamond touched the outer corner of one shade, and the tapping continued. Then a single shot—a loud closer shot—startled him as well as whatever was outside.

Nothing was outside. Clinging to the ship's skin wasn't possible.

The tapping had stopped completely.

"Because it wasn't real," the boy whispered. And then he grabbed both shades by the touching corners, and he yanked them open.

A face was plastered flush against the flat glass.

Diamond took a step backward.

The face wasn't human, and it wasn't a monkey or bird or anything else normal. And it didn't resemble King either. The only creature that wore any face like this was an insect. A long jointed mouth and various antennae were wrapped around the bulging eyes that covered a substantial portion of the head. But insect eyes were built from hundreds of little eyes. What was staring at Diamond was were smooth domes, clear like glass, and nothing in the world resembled them. Even the coronas were not half as strange as this creature.

Stepping up to the window, Diamond said, "Ghost."

The glass eyes couldn't blink, or they wouldn't.

"It's you," the boy said.

And then the face was gone.

• • •

The ambush came between pages. Prima was studying the tense account of a dinner with List's supporters and King's explosive reaction to some perceived insult. That dinner was three hundred and nineteen days earlier. That King was smaller and angrier than the creature she last saw. How long ago was that encounter? Thirty days. What these files revealed, time and again, was that he was changing. The fiery vindictive King was absent from the later accounts, but Prima doubted that he was hidden very deep under those spines and proper manners.

For the last hundred recitations, Prima had done nothing but peel back one report to reveal the next, gaining tiny insights into a species that was utterly familiar at the core.

Then the woman dipped her head, just for a moment, her forehead kissing the desk as she fell into deep sleep.

The ambush came with dreams.

She woke shouting. She was sitting upright with her face sweat-drenched and Sondaw standing before her.

"Madam, are you all right?"

Hardly, and she never would be again.

"You were yelling," he said. "About Rail."

"Because it was falling and wanted to pull us down with it."

The lieutenant nodded soberly, understanding the image too well.

"I'm all right," she lied.

He looked at the files, the sweat and upside down words.

"What are our loyal allies doing now?" she asked.

"Chasing us and signaling us," he said. "It took those big ships a long time to leave their berths."

She knew that would happen.

Sondaw said, "Madam." He had questions, but the youngster was too polite or lowly to give them words.

Prima turned the pages, letting both of them learn from the incident. King had battled the human witness with insults as well as spit thrown from the ugly tooth-jammed mouth. Even when List took exception to the behavior, the monster boy continued to berate what had been a wealthy, powerful individual.

"Are these records helpful?" Sondaw asked.

"There's a scheming monster at work," she said. "Vain and charmless, prepared to cheat and mislead governments and an army of opponents to get his way."

The lieutenant nodded, believing that he understood.

"I mean List," she said, correcting the misapprehension. "Every Archon has heard the stories. Believe me, each of us has scars. Even List's supporters—particularly his supporters—understand that he has few principles, except for earning the greatest profit possible for his office, for the District of the Bloodwoods, and for those who can stomach watching him slice apart every political threat."

The young man flipped back through the rest of the files, finding the brief, inadequate account of Diamond battling with King.

"Somehow our child won," he said doubtfully.

Prima didn't hear the comment. "Yet List does seem to be civilizing his son," she continued. "An armored beast roaming Creation, yet the boy ate dinner with me at the last festival . . . .a young man who stayed calm and in control. It's hard to believe, but he seemed ten times more appealing that his adopted father."

"Yes, madam," Sondaw said.

"Which makes King even more dangerous," she said.

Suddenly her aide was tense enough to tremble.

She didn't understand his thoughts.

"You think that King is responsible," he said.

"Responsible?"

"For the attack on Rail and Marduk," the lieutenant said. "The monster found allies to help him try and kill the boy again. That's what you're thinking."

"Honestly, no," she said.

Not until that very minute, at least.

• • •

The Ghost's face was gone, replaced with brilliant green light.

Diamond saw blackwoods and other trees that didn't belong with the wilderness. Beyond that little window, daylight had returned. He blinked and his heart leapt as he stepped closer, nose to the glass. This was some kind of picture, and parts of the picture were moving. Branches swayed. Airships climbed and fell while winged creatures beat at the bright air. One male hairyheart elf came close enough to show its bright face, except the colorings were wrong. Rings were etched inside the purple plumage on the breast, but Diamond knew that bird didn't have rings. That was a wrong detail, until he remembered how Master Nissim once said in class, "We have our light, what our eyes enjoy. But blossoms and feathers sometimes have details that we can't see. They hide past violet, and without special tools, we're as bad as blind."

Two fingers and the new thumb touched the glass.

The picture ceased moving.

Stubborn latches held the window closed, but Diamond managed to open them and pull the glass into the cabin far enough that his head and neck could fit into the gap. Then the picture began to move again. Birds had voices and the nearest airships moved with engine sounds, but far more impressive, Diamond found his nose full of rich flowery stinks and rain smells and an aroma that was like an animal, only it wasn't.

Diamond eased his healed hand through the opening.

Out from the bright air, an insect's limb emerged—jointed shells ending with a collection of hard dry fingers.

Those fingers reached for his hand.

Diamond pulled back.

Then the Ghost touched him on the face, so lightly and so carefully that the sensation seemed to fall short of being real. And the creature had a soft quick voice, not human or anything else.

"Quest," it said.

"What?"

"My name is Quest."

Diamond asked, "Why?"

"The word suits me," it said.

The boy wasn't sure what to think, and he tried to empty his head.

"Do you remember before?" Quest asked.

"Before?"

"Before this world."

"Maybe," said Diamond. Then he pushed his hand and arm deeper into the picture of the Corona District. Fingertips found a curved surface, warm and dry. The insides of a huge empty snail shell felt this way.

"I like to watch you," said Quest.

Diamond's hand returned to the cabin.

"I make eyes like you make hair," said Quest. "I watch Creation."

"If I could grow more eyes, I would," said the boy.

There were clicking noises that sounded happy, or it was just clicking.

"We're brothers," Diamond ventured.

"I'm female," said Quest, her insect hand retreating.

"Oh."

"You and King are male."

Diamond was surrounded by Quest, and the air was growing stale. He pulled his head back inside but left the window open.

"I watch everything," his companion repeated.

One question begged to be asked, but Diamond didn't speak quickly enough.

"You were taken from the corona before I was," Quest said.

"Who took you?"

"A tree-walker," she said.

"Which one?"

The scene dissolved into gray light, and then a simple image was drawn on the grayness. One man's face appeared, sturdy and unfamiliar. It would take some thought, but Diamond said his first impression. "I don't know your father."

"He's not my father," she said.

He started to ask.

"He's a thief," she said. "Thieves like to steal from the corona kills. He was dressed like a slayer when he stepped inside the stomach. Three of us were still there. The man saw your father take you, and then he went inside. He picked up King first and could have taken him. He wished that he would have. But I was the smallest, the easiest to hide, and he carried me to his home."

"Where is that?"

"He lives in the wilderness."

"When did you leave him?"

"I can't leave him," she said.

"I don't understand," Diamond said.

"I shared his house for three hundred and fifty-seven days," said Quest. "Every sight remains seen, every moment keeps living. What is part of me cannot be left behind."

Diamond was exhausted, baffled. Meanwhile Good remained under the cot, and the papio were still shouting in distant parts of the ship. *Bountiful* was pushing toward some important destination, and night might hold tight for a very long while. More questions begged to be asked but the boy said nothing, carefully remembering each one of his questions.

"I lived inside a strong cage made of steel and corona parts," Quest said. "The thief fed me good foods, and some bad foods, and he gave me water. I learned to how to shape myself while I grew, and then I stopped growing. He wanted me to be large and important. So I stayed small and ugly."

"But you got out of his cage," said Diamond.

Quest made a clicking noise, perhaps agreeing.

"Before," said the boy. "What were you showing me before?"

The thief's face melted back into the gray, and the gray became trees again. The trickery was extraordinary, almost frightening. Diamond looked out at the scene, feeling small, and in ways he had never imagined, he felt foolish.

This was two days ago, he guessed.

The bird sounds melted away. The airships turned silent, and not so much as a whisper of wind could be heard. Then a distant voice, human and unfamiliar, came from deep inside the Corona District.

"Now now now," the faraway man shouted. "We have to get out of here!"

Diamond had no weight, and he wasn't breathing anymore.

Then the explosions came, muted to keep the papio from hearing them. The trees fell exactly as they did before, and Diamond wrapped his arms tight around his chest, waiting to feel sick and miserable. But the strongest emotion was anger, slippery and chaotic. He wasn't certain where the rage was pointed, but the next words jabbed in an unexpected direction.

"I hate that man who stole you," Diamond said.

The grayness came again, and silence.

"You're hiding from the thief now," he guessed.

The voice became more female, and it sounded young. "I cannot hide, and he cannot find me."

"Because you're a ghost," Diamond guessed.

"Because he is the ghost," she said. "The moment I escaped from the cage, I said his name. I said it nicely, and when he looked at me, I killed him."

Diamond's arms dropped.

"I am killing him now and always will be," Quest said. "But I never ate any portion of his body. I would have enjoyed crunching one of his fists or a foot. But in my life, I have done nothing smarter than killing that brutal man and then flying away from the urge to eat him whole."

• • •

A papio was hurrying down the hallway. Merit felt the floor dip under the soldier's weight, and then the soldier stopped, calling a name through the door.

The woman soldier wore that name. She looked alert until she stood up, and then fatigue took hold. Her thin pink beard was holding crumbs from the last rations, and the tattoo on the forehead—a blood-and-bone whiffbird—needed to be washed.

The papio said a second name.

"Deserve" was a poor papio translation for Merit's name.

"I need him. Let him out," the man said.

The disruption was a bother. *Bountiful* had finally fallen quiet. The prisoners had dropped their heads on the tables, sleeping or pretending to sleep. But now the faces were lifting, secretive conversations beginning all over again. Merit rose with the first prompting. The woman put a hand on her steel-and-coral pistol, opening the galley door with the other hand. To somebody, Merit or her colleagues or maybe herself, she said, "Long long night."

The papio waiting in the hallway didn't know Merit, but he was under strict orders to treat the boy's father with dignity. "I would be honored if you would help us," he said, the half-learned words dribbling out. "A problem requires an expert."

"What have you done to our ship?" Merit asked.

"An accident needs a repairman," said the papio. "You may pick which one."

Merit looked back into the room.

"Fret," he said.

Unease and pain didn't need translation. The dead man's name caused the crew to look at the tabletops and their own hands, and then an older man got to his feet. Dressed in blue, he clicked his heels, saying, "Fret reporting."

"Come with me," said Merit.

The mechanic joined them in the hallway, and the galley door was closed again.

"A bladder is leaking," said the papio.

In reflex, the tree-walkers took deep breaths.

"I don't smell anything," the mechanic said.

"It's a small leak, far above. And maybe our noses are more sensitive to the stink you give the hydrogen."

Two of them started to walk.

Merit didn't move.

The papio turned. "What?" he began.

"My son," the slayer said. "Before anything, you'll show me Diamond."

"Afterwards," said the officer.

Merit sniffed the air again.

"The boy first, and then I'll help you," the mechanic said.

"Very well."

A young soldier was blocking the hallway. He didn't wake until the officer kicked him, and then he rose and fumbled with the door.

Merit reached past him, claiming the handle. As the door opened inwards, as he stepped inside, he knew that something was wrong.

The boy was sitting on his cot, his back straight and both feet on the floor.

Diamond never sat that way.

Merit looked around the tiny cabin.

Good came out from underneath the cot. "Good sorry," he said.

"What did you do?" asked Merit.

"Bit best finger."

Merit couldn't count the times he had walked into a room to look at his boy, and he couldn't shake the strong, chilling sense that something was amiss.

"Show me your thumbs, son."

The boy pointed two healthy thumbs at the ceiling.

"Is there something else?" he asked.

An odd expression broke on the boy's face. The little nose crinkled, and Diamond began to comb the curly brown hair with one hand. Tugging hard, he said, "Nothing else," and then he started to fiercely chew his bottom lip.

Merit turned to the monkey. "Why did you bite your boy?"

"Angry."

Behind him, the papio officer said, "We need to go."

Instincts screamed. Everything was wrong, and Merit didn't want to leave. But whatever had happened was finished, and he was powerless, and the papio could well have made a bullet hole while chasing whatever it was that had scared them so badly.

This puzzle had to wait.

"I'm sorry, Diamond," said Merit. "It's my fault we were caught."

"No," the boy said.

"I dropped a wrench, and they saw it," he confessed.

"This is bad," Diamond said. "But it's also wonderful."

"Why wonderful?"

White teeth shone, and the boy realized that he was smiling. Dipping his head, he said, "Never mind."

The situation kept growing heavier. But Merit forced himself to shut the door, and the sleepy soldier once again sat in front of the cabin. Walking back to the shop to collect tools, Merit noticed as much as he could. He counted soldiers and whiffbirds. A narrow door was open. What was that room? The dead men and pieces of men had been dragged there for safekeeping. But now the papio's mission leader was filling that tiny space, looking out the door with yellow eyes narrowed, as if she was waiting for enlightenment or the punchline of an intricate joke.

Merit fell in beside the escorting papio.

Behind them, the mechanic said, "I smell it now."

The stink was rich and unforgettable. Pulled from blossoms of a bug-eating plant, it was the wickedest rot in the world, adored by flies and cadaver bugs. Noses said that this was a bad leak, and Merit regretted wasting time talking to his son.

The officer was ready to accompany them, but he had no anti-static clothes. The mechanic pulled down two pairs of boots and jerseys. Nothing here would fit the papio, but they needed to know the stakes.

"One spark and we burn," Merit explained, in papio.

The officer looked at the slick rubber clothes, reconsidering his orders.

"I don't want us to burn," Merit said. "So yes, you can trust me to go up and patch the hole and come back again."

"Yes," the officer agreed. Then turning to the mechanic, he said, "Good luck, Fret."

The mechanic sighed and walked on.

Bountiful was huge, and every surface was new. Black rubber stairs led to black rubber-draped gangways illuminated by jars of luminescent yogurts. The corona bladders had a milky whiteness that came from being stretched, holding back the hydrogen. But they were young and strong, and nothing besides a huge rifle or small cannon could rip any hole in this material. Several papio filled the gangways, nervous enough to spin around when prisoners approached. Merit told them that their bosses were below, where it was safe. He asked the last soldier what she was hunting. She touched her tattoo of a whiffbird, presumably for luck. "It was nothing, a little wild animal," she said. "But it's gone. Are you going above?"

"Shouldn't we?" asked the mechanic.

"If you can save our lives, go above. Go." Then she retreated with the rest of her troop.

Rope ladders carried them to platforms too tiny to hold even a small papio. They climbed and sniffed, walked on horizontal ropes and pushed at the rigid bladders with their slick boots. Tanks of compressed carbon dioxide gas were fitted into the gaps, waiting for any excuse to flood the air and kill combustion. But there wasn't any fire to fight. And with every few steps, the smell continued to strengthen.

"This feels wrong," the mechanic said. "This high, surrounded by hydrogen, we should feel light in the head."

Merit nodded, counting more senseless details.

"You know," the mechanic said. "If we had the proper attitude, we could split some bladder and vent a little gas out the top of *Bountiful*, and then by accident, light it."

"A signal, you mean."

"Visible at night and hot enough to burn the passing leaves, leaving Prima a nice bright trail to chase."

"Except our hosts would notice the fire," Merit said.

"Maybe not for a while. Wings and jets aren't flying, they're just ballistics. They're way too fast."

Another tiny platform waited in front of them.

"I want to try signals," the old fellow said.

"Except," Merit said. "The last time I spoke to our Archon, I might have threatened to take my son to the papio and safety."

The mechanic used a few quiet, rich words.

Merit absorbed the abuse.

And then nobody was speaking. The platform was the last flat surface, and a body was sprawled across it, limbs dangling on three sides. They approached until they were baffled, and then they knelt on the rope, Merit in front, holding the railing with one hand while he played with two days of whiskers.

"It's a jazzing," said the mechanic. "A young dead jazzing."

Merit eased forward, pulling a torch from the tool belt.

"Don't spark," his companion warned.

"The bladders aren't leaking," Merit said. "This is the stink's source, and I don't think it ever was a jazzing."

The body had been shot several times. Odd flesh had been torn apart, and a sticky black fluid had leaked from the holes, not coagulating so much as simply drying out in the open air. There were eyes that were little more than the pits on a coral viper. No mouth existed because no mouth was needed. The limbs were powerful before they died, and he touched the nearest foot, discovering that the jazzing-style claws were as soft as warm rubber.

"Smell this," Merit said, waving his fingers under the mechanic's nose.

"That's our stink," the man said with a grimace.

Merit stood. "We drop this body out the nearest vent and climb down like heroes."

The plan was accepted with a soft laugh. Then the mechanic added, "But what is this creature? It's nothing like any beauty in my school books."

"I think the school books need updating," said Merit.

"And the rest of us could use some youth too," joked his companion.

• • •

Once again, Diamond stepped back from the window.

Grayness came again, and the girlish voice. "I won't be seen. Before dawn, I'll hide again."

"Where?"

"In the best place, and I haven't decided."

Good was sleeping on the floor, on a nest made from sack pieces and scrap paper. The monkey smacked his lips at some imagined food, and then he gave a long loud fart that changed the cabin air.

Something was funny. Diamond caught himself laughing.

"Dawn's coming," Quest warned. "I see signs, and I only have a few eyes."

The creature was plastered to *Bountiful*'s hull, a fake window on her backside. She didn't want a passing ship, any kind of ship, to spy her. She had explained some of her tricks to her brother, including how she played with light and odors. But Diamond had the impression—a quiet, growing impression—that the girl had no real explanations for what she did.

"How big can you grow?" he asked.

"I don't know," she said.

"How much can you eat at once?"

"More than I ever have, I think."

"Good is my friend," he said. "Don't eat him."

"I won't."

Diamond sorted questions on a list that never grew shorter.

Then she said, "You interest me."

"You interest me."

"Do you know why I'm fascinated?"

"The same reason that you want to know about King," he said. "We're your brothers, in a fashion."

"We are, and no."

"Why then?"

"I heard you talking to your teacher. I was outside the window yesterday, and you told your teacher that nothing is evil. A voice said that to you."

"I don't know whose voice," he said.

"But that interests me. Very much."

Outside, the big engines were beginning to throttle back.

"They'll tie down the ship before dawn," Quest said.

Diamond needed sleep, and he feared closing his eyes. "Do you know the voice I'm talking about?" he asked.

Quest said nothing, and the grayness in the window held steady.

"Does some little voice push between all of those ears?" asked Diamond.

"I can have a thousand ears," Quest said. "I weave them until they are huge and sensitive, and nothing escapes them. But I've never heard the voice you are talking about. It's a stranger to me."

Once again, Diamond put his face against the glass.

"That's part of why you are fascinating," she said.

And the boy said, "If you see so much, maybe you look in the other direction."

"Do I watch the reef?"

"You do."

"I never get close, because of the danger."

"But you can't stop watching for the other one. Can you?"

"You want to see what I know."

"Everything," Diamond said. "But we don't have time. You pick for my eyes, sister. Please."

TEN

King didn't believe in demons or in nailing myth and human words against what refused to be understood. But he understood and accepted that every sphere had its center, and the Creation was the largest, most perfect sphere that could exist. Humans ruled what mattered, and the District of Districts was the center of what mattered, and his homeland had always rightfully dominated this wonderful rich world.

There had always been a Grand University clinging to the bloodwoods, and the University typically kept a powerful telescope lashed to its great trees. Forever pointing downwards, the giant tube and crystalline lenses had one target, one subject. When night was young—when ordinary souls saw nothing beneath but ink and the senseless glimmer of the demon floor—a Master's eye, ruined by a life of hard reading, would be set against a round disk of glass, gaining the best possible view of the sun.

There were other methods of study. Any fire could be safely cast onto screens or trapped inside sealed boxes where its rich, complicated light might be carved into myriad flavors. Yet that flawless, perfect circle let itself be seen plainly only for brief times. That was when its qualities had been calculated. Lying at the bottom of Creation's sphere, its size had proven to be changeless, its brightness fixed and eternal. Night was the shadow cast by the corona jungle. The jungle grew thick in a day and thicker through the night. Every night, the blackness won, alien weeds pressing against the brilliance until even young eyes with their lenses could see nothing but velvety blackness marred only by the coronas—a scattering of tiny brilliances thriving inside that fiery sodden alien realm.

King's eyes were only a little sharper than human eyes.

But his vision was invincible.

Very late one night, the Archon's son visited the telescope. Using his most polite voice, he begged the Masters for the honor to peer through their fancy glass. How could they refuse? Playing the curious boy, King linked his hands behind his back and bent low. The sun was invisible behind the forest. There was nothing below but ink and twenty thousand tiny glimmers. He counted the coronas. He asked old questions about light and demons and how the coronas managed to thrive in those depths. The Masters told him what they knew, and because they were paid to be smart, they spoke too much. Invincible problems always led to conflicting theories, and every theory had flaws that were patched with guesses. Calm, reasoned conversation ended with two old men falling into a much-loved argument about how much pressure the demon floor absorbed before it let the dawn rise. The other Masters stood back, enjoying these dried-out passions. Only King noticed when the corona jungle suddenly turned to flame, and he instantly wrapped both hands around the eyepiece, locking his grip on the tube, the right eye staring down at a blaze indistinguishable from a vast explosion.

Father was standing in an adjacent room. He was watching the arguing men when the first red flicker of dawn came through a distant window.

Instinct always rules over knowledge.

That was particularly true with humans.

The Archon yelled a warning and wave his arms, making a fool of himself before he remembered. And then every Master panicked. Those very smart men forgot what King was, or maybe they never understood. The new day washed over the world, finding a dozen weary bodies tugging and cursing at a child who couldn't be moved, who had no intention of turning away from this marvel. Inner eyelids helped kill the glare. What a view, what a raw fine gorgeous spectacle! Then that eye was burnt and dead, and King calmly moved his face, placing the left eye against warm glass, watching one of the genuine marvels of Creation.

King was reliving that moment of sunshine, as he often did before rising. The soldier's cot was too small for his body. Every eyelid was closed, armored hands folded across his bare belly, and his quick thoughts slipped from the sun to Father and Father to Diamond before leaping to the papio living on their coral ring.

Then the bedroom door opened, someone standing close.

"We caught her," said the voice.

King wasn't asleep or awake. But he sat up instantly, eyes still closed.

"Her little fleet is tied to the canopy, waiting for rain," Father said.

Smiles could be worn outside, but he had to force both mouths to put on human smiles. Nobody appreciated how much work that took. He had to dress like a young man, even though his hard body was more impressive than any wardrobe. Talking with his eating mouth was rude—a rule that felt instinctively true to everyone, including King. With his polite mouth, he used polite words. "Thank you for telling me, Father."

The little man remained beside the cot.

King opened his eyes.

The human face was looking up at him, and its expression was talking.

"What's wrong, Father?"

"Very little, I hope."

This day deserved the best clothes. Father's tailors had used the toughest fabrics and thickest leather, and thirty days ago they built trousers and a shirt, boots and a wide belt, every article too big for the boy. But their target was a future child, today's boy, and King acted happy with the clothes and he genuinely liked the heavy leather belt decorated with the heavy copper circles. Putting on the useless boots, he asked, "Is the crazy woman talking to us?"

Father grinned. "And she's being clever."

King wiggled the six toes inside their prison. "You said she'd be clever."

"We've pulled up beside her ship, the *Panoply Night*," Father said. "She's invited me to cross over and meet with her."

"This is your fleet," the boy said.

Father stepped back. "It is mine," he said.

This was a test. King liked this kind of test. He said, "You should order her to come over here."

"Perhaps I already have."

An idea teased. King smiled, asking, "How soon will the rain come?"

"We have five recitations, perhaps less."

Dawn and the ruddy first light were rising. King smiled so that his teeth shone. "Make her cross in the rain. Make her wet and soggy."

"She won't," Father said. "I insisted, but she instantly refused me."

"You're the Archon of Archons."

The man lifted a hand, checking the lay of the bright bronze scales on his son's magnificent chest. "Prima has her excuse," he said.

This was a fun test. "Is it a good one?"

"The very best. She says she has a prisoner, a young aide from her office. The man is a traitor, and after some hard interrogations, he has unveiled a string of names and various intrigues. She has a clear picture about who organized the first attack and what we should do once morning arrives."

"You should see this prisoner for yourself," King said.

"Indeed, I should."

"Tell her to wrap him in chains and drag him to your bridge."

"Except there's a risk," said Father. "Her prisoner has survived this long inside the *Panoply*, which means that he must be safe there. But the traitor has powerful allies, and she isn't convinced that he would survive the walk."

Both mouths snarled. "The woman wants you to cross to her ground, on her terms."

"And I should have already gone."

"What about me?"

Father looked at his eyes, the mouths.

"She doesn't want me with you," King said.

"Prima said a few words about you, and my sense here . . . yes, she'd prefer me to leave you in bed, asleep."

Father's narrow face smiled, tiny teeth showing.

"You can't leave me behind," said King.

"If I thought otherwise, I'd have left you dreaming." Father opened the door, walking into the suite's main room. "And since the gangway is uncovered and I don't want to arrive at this meeting dressed in a drippy rubber poncho, I think we should leave immediately."

But King had made one decision about himself. He kicked off the first boot, and with a few hard jerks of the arms, he tore away the new trousers and the shirt. Short trousers made from growler hide was perfect for this kind of day, and he kept the belt on and left his feet bare, and in case Father had doubts about his uniform, King got fine smiles ready with both mouths, plus flattering words about being the good son happily standing at a great man's side.

• • •

Eyes open, standing on the long tarmac while waiting for dawn, sleep took hold of her and she was dreaming.

Nothing about the moment was surprising or sudden. Maybe she had been dreaming a long while but didn't realize it. Every mind kept secrets, particularly from itself. Whatever the circumstance, Divers found herself feeling warm inside a special old dream, the dream where she was tiny again. She was a frail voice inside other voices that were scared like her and lost like her. The hand doesn't name its fingers and thumbs. None of the Eight wore names. Yet each voice was unique, and they were forgotten and frightened together, nothing outside the rounded shared body but darkness and heat, stomach acids and the roaring of a beast that carried them back and forth.

The nameless Divers couldn't move. She couldn't envision being mobile. Trapped and miniscule, she had nothing to do with her thoughts but share them, and the others shared what they thought, and nothing changed outside. Nothing was new. But the unrelenting sameness drove them to invent fresh notions, injecting what was new into a conversation that had gone on for thousands and millions of days.

"I belong here," she thought.

With seamless ease, she thought, "I am happy."

Happiness was what shook her, alerted her. The attack had begun, and there might have been a moment when inroads were possible. But Divers saw the truth and roused herself, discovering that the giant body had taken only two full strides without her being aware.

Divers was standing in the middle of the long smooth tarmac, in the final blackness of night. The hanger's long door had been closed since the sun vanished, but a smaller access hatch was propped open, revealing lights and the shadows riding on the lights, and she heard the bright hard whine of a corona-tooth drill cutting a precise hole through some fresh piece of corona bone.

The Eight were alone, nobody watching them.

Divers studied the rising slopes of the reef on her left and her right, dark and a little cool after the brief night. This was the world's quiet time. No nocturnal animal wanted to walk in the open, exposed at dawn. Without orders or some deep personal need, no sane human would risk the storm.

Aloud, she said, "Tritian."

Inside her, Tritian's voice said, "Yes."

"You tried," she said with her mouth.

"I tried very little," he whispered.

"You wanted to scare me, did you?"

"Are you scared?"

"Not even a little."

"Then the game's a miserable failure," Tritian said.

She agreed but said nothing.

Other voices began to flow, and recognizing each speaker and the connotations, Divers hunted for codes in the ordinary words and any implications and the hints of emotion that should worry her or make her happy.

Tritian had sympathizers. Yet Divers had allies and genuine power, inside the body and across the world without.

"Attacking me now," she said. "Is this the best time to seed chaos? Everything at stake and you launch an assault?"

"That accomplished nothing," said her enemy.

Diver's eyes—their eyes—were gazing down the long black runway. Where the pavement ended the reef fell away, and beyond the reef was open air and the first hints of red light. A giant fire was blazing under the demon floor, turning alien plants into volatile steam, and she intended to stand here, motionless as coral, allowing the hot first waves of rain to wash across the long potent body.

A child said her name.

Zakk said, "Divers."

And she woke again.

The Eight were standing where she imagined the body to be, and the scene in her dream was the same as reality—the hanger behind her, full of noise and frantic shadows, the sleeping reef and the tarmac, and the air and fire beyond, great waves of water poised to rise like a wave over the world. The trick of the dream had been masterful. But the mastery was wasted; the body was hers and hers alone.

The boy called to her again, asking, "Is something wrong?"

"You aren't sleeping," she said.

"I couldn't. I'm excited."

"Did you ever meet the other children?" Divers waved at the village hiding higher up on the reef.

"Not yet. I was watching mechanics repairing the wing."

"That is fun," she agreed.

"I'll meet the other children today," he said.

She couldn't care any less. What mattered was the gnawing urge to be suspicious of everything.

"I have an errand for you," Divers said.

"Good," Zakk said.

"In the hanger, ask someone for a mid-length pry bar. Find one with a sharpened end and bring it straight to me."

The boy broke into a nervous laugh.

"Are you going to hit me with it?" he asked.

"Maybe that too," said Divers. "But no, my plan is to stab myself. The bar is a tool, and pain is an even better tool. You see, I could be lying in a hole, sleeping and stupid. But more likely, I'm trapped in a sleepwalking state, which is an even worse prospect."

Zakk had the largest eyes that she had ever seen on such a tiny, young face. He stared at Divers and at all of them, and then he said, "Yes," as he turned, running quickly for the open hatch.

Something about that boy was wrong. In subtle, persistent ways, he made no sense, and she couldn't decide why, and she watched him until he vanished and then turned to look at the brightening glare.

Little time passed before feet came back across the landing, aiming for her.

She pivoted, ready to compliment Zakk on his speed.

But it was a local soldier—an officer and one of the Eight's first caretakers—and he had news that might already be too late.

"*Bountiful*," he said.

The name meant something. But three other voices remembered the corona-hunting ship before Divers could.

"They found *Bountiful* hiding in the wilderness, and Diamond hiding inside her," the young man said. Then a smile burst loose, and he added, "They've also found an open lane through the trees and signaled ahead, just a little while ago. As soon as the rain quits, *Bountiful* drops below the trees and sprints to the reef."

"Putting the boy where?" she asked. "Here?"

But that was too much to hope for. "No, they're going to the far side of Bright River, to the installations at High Coral Merry."

That was a long distance. Covering the rough ground would take speed and focus, but she had both in abundance.

But what if this was a dream?

The officer—one of the allies who lived outside her body—was very much interested in whatever Divers said next.

"That boy," she said. "I sent him for a tool."

"We don't trust him," the man confessed. "We sent him chasing nonsense."

"Very good," she said.

"Should we do something more than mislead him?"

"Whatever you think reasonable."

The officer nodded, saying nothing.

"Thank you for this news," she said.

Her ally smiled, rocking side to side, watching in amazement as Divers began to run away at an amazing pace.

Stopping beside the first slope, she picked up a great chunk of hard blue coral. Then the left hand struck the right hand, crushing two fingers and a thumb.

Pain drew a map of her body. Yes, she was awake. She was certain that she was awake. Then the first drops of rain found her—the cool brave rain that always preceded the hot and helpless—and Divers started to gallop, hands helping the feet climb, the first sharp ridge soon behind her and nothing ahead but hazards and doubts and little voices whispering too loudly while floating through their own dreams.

• • •

Towlines lashed *Panoply Night* to a big fletch, and a hundred straps secured both vessels to the overhead canopy. A long gangway had been erected between

Night's stern and the *Ruler of the Storm*. Soldiers in bright parade uniforms walked before the Archon of Archons and soldiers in green militia garb met them in the middle, protocol and routine duties delaying their progress. The ranking Corona officer insisted that the honor guard retreat to their ship. But the man who mattered had no patience for clumsy tactics, and pushing to the front, List said, "Enough concessions. My people are coming with me, and with my son."

King stepped up, letting the pests have one long glance at him. Then because it was so easy, so tempting, he planted an arm on the biggest shoulder and drove that fellow to his knees.

Bright uniforms took the lead.

And the wind rose, making a keening, sorrowful music with the tightening straps. But then the gusts softened just as quickly, and the world had a calm quiet moment before the first gouts of rain hammered at the gangway's belly.

Father made it inside before being soaked—one tiny victory.

Prima was waiting indoors. She looked like every tired, furious human. King assumed that her rage was going to be pointed at Father or maybe at him. His armor reflexively tilted, ready to impress. But Prima ignored King, and she barely nodded at the Archon. The eyes were bright fiery and distinctly crazed, fixed on those left behind on the gangway. She was dressed for no purpose but comfort, her clothes ordinary, even bland. "I'm sorry, that was stupid," she screamed across the taller heads, apparently addressing the drenching gale. "Give me a moment, sir. Please."

The next recitation was amusing, educational, and thoroughly bizarre. King would have known that just from his father's expression or anyone else left standing inside the *Panoply*'s entranceway. Every face watched the Archon stride straight into the storm. Neither of her hands used the railing as the extended, increasingly strained gangway was buffeted in several directions at once. A few trailing men had to be ignored if not exactly pushed aside. It would be simple to call the woman fearless or brave—two very different natures—yet she was neither. Mostly she was transfixed by one matter that was so simple, narrow and vital and pure, that it would take more than a gale of bathwater-hot rain to make her rational heart throb at all.

The officer who had led her reception committee needed to be reprimanded. Not two recitations from now, but now. In the rain, with everyone watching, a creature half of that man's size pushed him against the railing and shoved a finger against the tightly clamped mouth, screaming nothing that could be heard over the storm's roar, yet leaving the fellow in such a state that he squirmed, acting as if he might jump over the railing just to end his withering shame.

And then with no warning, Prima swung about and came back again.

This time she used the railings, bouncing from one to the other. Suddenly she was a slender woman past her physical prime. The strain of the last two days was etched in the thin face. The drenched shirt stuck tight to her body, and she stumbled as she came into the ship, two aides making the mistake of trying to catch her.

Their hands were batted away.

Staring at the wet hallway floor, she said nothing.

King watched her small chest fill with air, and then her cheeks inflated, blowing out the spent gas. There were children who were taller and stronger than this woman, and any shred of poise that she might have carried had been spent. But what impressed King was not her appearance but how the others around her, particularly her own people, treated her. Prima took a half-step forward, and important people suddenly backed away, keeping out of her reach. Prima took three long strides forward, and then she looked at her fellow Archon with a serious, sane intent, telling him, "You have no idea."

With that, she walked deeper into the *Panoply Night*.

Father didn't want to hurry after her. He was too poised for this game. And it was a game: King regarded everything as a pageant, guessing what would happen next and what wouldn't happen. The woman wanted the monster rattled, out of balance and unmoored. Father had mentioned the possibility. For their mutual benefit, Father had laid out the possible strategies of a person with few weapons of her own. And while he didn't warn about wild theatrics, at least he remained unaffected enough that he could maintain a leisurely pace, reaching out to tug at his son's hand, that gesture helping share his considerable amusement.

Their hostess paused before a locked door. Then she looked back at List, just List, asking, "Why did you come here?"

Father paused, blinked.

"The prisoner is one of my people," she continued. "He was one of my trusted, my stalwarts. Except he's a spectacular coward and a full-blooded traitor and everything about the plot is coming out now."

She stopped talking, and Father said, "Good."

"But I want to know from you, sir," she said. "Why do you want to meet him?"

Father's face flushed. "I want to hear the story, of course."

"That too," said Prima. "But be honest. You came here because you have every advantage. You want me to accept your dominance. And for a lot of strong reasons, you want to take my prisoner home with you. He's going to be a prize, a trophy. He is a useful picture of evil to drag before people everywhere."

When he was furious, Father had a very small mouth.

"I'm tired," she said. "The games, the political dance . . . if it doesn't make a person sick, she must not have a soul."

Father started to disagree with some or all of that speech.

"Just you," she interrupted, pointing at Father.

King stepped up.

"This is no place for boys," she said.

King killed the urge to use his eating mouth, but he let his shoulder plates rise until everyone else backed away.

"I hate this," she said.

But then she turned to a young lieutenant, poking his chest with two fingers. "All right, both of them. And you, Sondaw. Stay at my side."

"Yes, madam," the lieutenant muttered.

The locked door was opened. The prison stairs felt small under King's feet, and he made a fine racket as he followed three humans to the lower floor. Every prisoner had to be terrified, hearing his approach over the storm's rumbling. He stomped a few times at the bottom of the stairs, for emphasis, causing Father to look back at him with a wary expression, and then, a guarded smile.

Was he being childish?

Maybe so, and maybe he didn't care.

The interrogation cells were small and locked but only lightly guarded. Every door was heavy wire, and King looked through the wire, watching scared faces. Their destination was at the end of the longest hallway, back where the air was stinking of fresh blood and dried blood and human feces. Two large soldiers flanked a solid steel door, windowless and still warm where its hinges had just been welded to the frame. The soldiers stared at King. He ignored them, stomping where he paused in that fashion that drove everybody mad and always left him stronger. It was the lieutenant who had the key. Sondaw had just that one key, pulling it out of his uniform pocket with his left hand and passing it to his right, his nervous face glancing back at the others.

This was a trap.

King understood that much before the lock came open. Yet what kind of trap would anyone dare use? Hurting him was impossible. Killing or trapping his father was easy enough, but where would the gain find room to stand?

Prima and her people were surrounded by a massive fleet that was sworn to serve the state. The state wasn't his father, but humans loved faces and List's face was what would rally them. No, King thought. Only a madwoman would attempt something rash, and beloved as she might be, Prima's staff would never let insanity rule their fates.

The door opened outwards, as any prison door should.

A disheveled young man was sitting on the floor. Various chains had been worn and then discarded as his body broke down. One ankle looked as if it had been pulled out of joint and then shoved back together again. Neither shoulder appeared useable. The man had been crying. Seeing them, he cried again. The smell of urine became stronger, and with a voice shredded of dignity and most of its life, he said, "What more . . . is there . . . no . . . "

The four of them entered the stinking room.

Prima said nothing. But she looked at her lieutenant with clear hard eyes, and she nodded, and the young man stepped forward quickly and dropped low, picking up the prisoner as if he were a broken child.

The prisoner moaned.

"Easy," Sondaw said.

Father said, "What. Is. This."

The words sounded like a question.

"Perhaps I exaggerated," said Prima, her voice flat and a little loud. "This prisoner hasn't offered much enlightenment at all. We know he hates Diamond and your boy too, and he's not altogether fond of me, either. But if he had a role in any plot, it's a mystery to everybody. Including him."

The lieutenant was through the door. One guard looked in at the remaining three people, and then he smirked and winked, throwing the cell door closed and slamming the lock shut.

"No," said Father, his voice thick and low.

There was a simple, easy response. A few driving kicks would destroy the lock or the entire wall.

Unprompted, he approached the blank steel slab.

Some small noise came from behind, barely audible over the gusting winds and furious rainwater.

Expecting nothing, King glanced back.

Standing with his arms crossed on his chest, Father wore a stunned, confused expression. He acted like a man who was sick in his lungs, his heart. Sweat poured from his flesh, and his face was exceptionally red, and the voice that people everywhere mocked without end was shriller than ever.

"Why did you do that?" he asked.

Prima had punched him, and she looked ready to strike the man again. But instead of swinging, she laughed and grabbed her rain-soaked shirt, tugging from the bottom.

"The law gives us a choice," she said quickly, with minimal breaths. "In times of peace, we can have a council of the Archons, and we vote on a single leader. And you always win. You have more than half of the world's citizens and far more than half of our soldiers, and the rest of us couldn't legally stand against you. But I'm sure you remember the full law, that the forest doesn't have to be ruled by the District of Districts. In crisis but before war is declared, the leading Archon can dispense his power however he sees fit, and in another few moments that's what you are going to do for me."

Father was mute.

The woman had pulled off her shirt and the clothing under it. She was not young, and as King understood these matters, she wasn't more than passingly attractive. But he was curious nonetheless, watching the trousers fall next, and the clothing beneath them. A long horizontal scar defined her belly. She stank of energy and salt as she kicked off her shoes and all of the clothes, and naked now, standing in front of Father, she claimed the pose that King knew in his blood.

It was his posture, facing any enemy.

Instinct older than his flesh took hold. King stood against the door and the wall, watching that little woman approach a man with more strength and more mass. But Father couldn't muster the will to lift either fist higher than his aching chest, and the stick-like arms began to pummel him with long slow blows.

"No," Father said.

The man couldn't believe what was happening.

"Stop," he said.

She speeded up the swings.

Already bloodied, List turned to his son.

"Help me," he begged.

Crush the woman with one swing, and the fight would be finished. But this was Father's ground to defend, not King's, and far more important, nothing in this boy's life had ever been as fascinating or enlightening as watching a sterile old woman bring her fists down on the beaten man's face.

• • •

The cabin door swung open.

The window was a window again. Diamond was watching what was outside, unless of course this was another one of his sister's memories turned into light and noise. He couldn't tell, couldn't ask. But what he saw was interesting in its fashion, built from simple shapes and a few noises repeated without end. Dark rain broke against *Bountiful*'s skin. What might be the long tree limb was twisting in the gale. There were only two distances in that world, near and not-near, and that was a peculiarly fascinating thought.

Diamond pulled his head out from under the curtains.

A soldier filled the open door and part of the hallway. Motioning at the boy, he repeated a word that he had just learned. "Eat," he said.

Good sat on the cot, growling.

Diamond straightened the curtains. "Stay here," he said.

"Yes," the monkey agreed.

"I'll bring you food," he said.

"Hate you, thank you," Good replied.

The soldier closed the door behind him and then sat in the hallway again. A woman soldier was waiting outside the galley. She watched Diamond's walk. More curious than caring, she asked, "How do you feel?"

"Hungry," he said.

"I believe you," she said.

The galley was crowded, the air thick with sweat and cold food. People stopped eating to look at the boy. Some of them made faces. Some were glad to see him. Elata smiled and Seldom called to him by name, while Karlan saw something funny in his arrival, laughing loudly before he attacked his meal again.

"Your father's working," Master Nissim said.

"He'll be back soon," Tar`ro said. "Get a plate, sit with us."

Platters of cold meats and boiled eggs and greasy bread waited on the countertop. Diamond filled two white bone plates, and he might have tried holding a third. But that would be too much, too blatant and bold. Sitting beside the Master, he began with the eggs, one at a time.

"Have you slept?" Seldom asked.

Every question had its traps. Diamond lied, saying, "Yes."

Elata watched the eggs vanish. Then she put her hands on the table and studied her fingers, asking, "Will we ever go home, ever?"

Diamond stopped eating.

"What do you mean?" asked the Master.

"When Diamond reaches the reef . . . will the rest of us go free . . . ?"

Every little sound in the galley vanished. Nobody was eating. The only noise was the storm, and it had already spent the worst of its fury.

Nissim put a hand on Elata's hands. "We don't know," he said.

Elata looked at the woman soldier. "Can I go back to the trees?"

The papio had warmer eyes than Diamond had guessed. But she decided to say nothing.

"I'm staying with you," Nissim told Diamond.

Seldom looked at the Master and then Elata. "I don't think they'll give us a choice," he said.

Seldom didn't want to choose.

The urge to eat had vanished, but Diamond kept working with his hands, his mouth. One plate was bare when a mechanic came through the door, followed by Father.

"Come here," his father said.

Diamond was already on his feet.

"Is that yours?" Father asked.

He meant the last plate.

"Bring it here," he said. "And I'll get one for me."

They sat close to one another, as far from the other prisoners as possible. But the woman soldier was close enough to touch them, and she didn't care if she stared, listening to every word.

Father had filled his own plate, but he barely ate.

"Where were you?" asked the boy.

"Above. Our guests shot a hole in one of the bladders."

"What were they fighting?"

"A shadow, apparently."

Diamond looked at the papio, and then he stared at the long strips of cured pink meat. "Good wants some of this," he said.

"I bet."

They didn't talk, and they didn't eat quickly. Sometimes Diamond looked at his father's red, wet eyes.

"She's dead," Diamond said at last.

Father didn't ask who he meant. He just nodded, saying, "Yes."

"But that's all right," said the boy.

Merit kept his mouth closed.

"I've been thinking about the Creation," Diamond said.

"Thinking what?"

"It never ends," he said.

Father glanced at Nissim. Then to his son, speaking softly, he said, "I don't know about that."

"I know."

Father looked at Nissim again.

"This isn't one of the Master's lessons," Diamond said.

"All right. What do you know?"

"If the world does go on forever, if we can't count all of the days, then everybody has to come back again. If we're born once, we can always be born. Every trillion trillion days, each of us gets to live, and it always feels like the first time."

Merit said nothing.

The woman soldier glared at the boy, lips taut, long teeth showing.

"You figured that out," said Father doubtfully.

"I think I did."

"And Haddi gets to live again," Father said slowly, with care and some misery.

Diamond nodded.

"To live with us?"

"No," he said. Then he said, "Maybe. Each time, we get different lives."

The man's mouth opened and then closed.

Diamond believed his own words, so much so that he couldn't escape from them. But what was beautiful and obvious in his mind made the papio woman angry, and Father looked sick and no happier than before.

His plate was still half-covered with food. Diamond rose and picked it up, reporting, "Good is hungry."

Without sound or fuss, Father wept. But he stood regardless and picked up his mostly untouched breakfast, and then he told the papio, "I want to walk my boy back to his cabin."

The papio didn't want Diamond to remain here. "Go," she said.

Away from the galley, Father said, "Tell me."

Diamond didn't respond.

"There's something else. Tell me."

"Nothing," the boy lied.

Father didn't believe him. Shaking his head, he quietly said, "When we were above, high between the bladders, we found something. A strange something. Does that surprise you?"

Diamond remained silent.

"You say you're starving?"

"I am."

"And your monkey?"

He nodded.

The soldier before them rose and opened the cabin door, and Father said, "Here, hand me yours."

Diamond willingly gave him the plate.

Father walked to the middle of the little room and spilled both his breakfast and Diamond's on the floor, and then he cursed with a sharp, believable voice.

The soldier glared at the mess.

"I'll get you another helping," Father said.

Good suspiciously picked up a pair of dirty eggs.

Diamond lifted one shade, watching the simple rain. "Two more helpings would be nice, if they'll let you," he said.

Father wiped at his wet face, nodding. "I don't know what's stranger," he said. "Your endless appetite, or each of us spending eternity eating eggs."

• • •

The story raced ahead of Prima. At least some clipped inadequate version of what happened onboard *Panoply Night* passed like fire through the entire fleet. Her species had a new leader. The woman Archon was temporarily in charge of the fleet. When Prima arrived on the *Ruler*'s bridge, she was going to be met with cold stares and cold silence. She expected nothing else. And as she explained to Sondaw, there were reasons to be thankful for that blind, hateful response.

"What I have is a title," she said. "A barely legal status is folded up in my pocket. Not one of List's people is going to give me more than sporadic help, except when they go out of their way to offer bad advice, and that's going to bring a lot of silence and anger for as long as it takes them to build their rebellion."

"And why are we thankful?" Sondaw asked.

"List's people are going to ignore the realities, and meanwhile, my people will be able to accomplish two or three worthy deeds. I hope."

They were standing inside her office. Prima had put on clean dry clothes, and picked up the papers that needed to accompany her to the flagship. But most importantly, she wanted her bleeding to stop. In the end, driven to panic, a man who had probably never in his life struck another person had punched her on the chin, his knuckles sharp as razors. Her bottom lip was cut and the entire jaw ached. Yet compared to her opponent, she was virtually unscathed.

"I hope I can depend on you," she said.

"Of course, madam."

"Because I will."

He nodded.

She handed her aide a thick folder.

"I still don't understand," he said. "Why would you take such a risk?"

Ready for the question, she said, "Believe me, I know the man. List is self-absorbed and bloodless and shrewd, and worst of all, he perpetually thinks too much about himself."

The young man nodded gamely, but he didn't understand.

"Four hundred days ago, when the Archon followed Diamond to the reef, the man pranced in front of the papio. He told the papio to steal Diamond. He advised them that they should kill the Archon of Archons and start a great war with the tree-walkers because the boy was that important, that precious. His tone, that corrosive attitude, didn't help then, and it won't work today. And I think you agree with me. Today, everything depends on the face that we send against our enemies."

She picked up a sack full of intelligence reports and papio rosters. Everything else would be brought by others.

Prima carried the sack, walking quickly.

"And the Archon of Archons agreed to this change," the lieutenant said cautiously.

"Yes."

"Because you hit him a few times," he muttered.

Nobody was as important as this one young officer, and that's why she stopped and looked at Sondaw, staring until he grew uneasy enough to throw his gaze at an empty wall.

"I struck him in front of his son."

"Yes, madam."

"I don't know what King is. I can't say that he's a new species or something that the Creators forgot in their ovens. But ritual violence is King's breath. A one-sided fight would accomplish considerable good. That's what King believes, in his blood and spines. List was ashamed to be on the floor, and his adopted son was horrified by his father's lousy showing, and because I had every advantage, at least for a few moments, the fleet is ours."

"As long as we aren't at war," Sondaw said.

"We'll be at peace tomorrow," she said, walking again.

From two steps behind, her aide said, "But the Archon won't let this stand."

"He won't," she agreed.

"Madam," he said. "I know how a beaten man thinks."

She slowed. "From experience?"

"Every man knows," he said.

Women knew it too, but she let that declaration pass. "The risks are smaller this way," she insisted. "List is pushed aside temporarily. And as you pointed out to me, thank you, King might well have played a role in the various treacheries. Minimizing him is another blessing."

"Yes, madam."

She slowed, and the lieutenant had no choice but catch her. Glancing over her shoulder, she saw no one else. "I can trust you, can't I?"

Flustered, he said, "Of course, madam."

"Three days ago, you didn't exist. Not in my world. But here you are, helping your mother carry home the groceries."

The lieutenant glanced at the folder in his hands.

"The rain's nearly finished," she said. "Come with me."

The man took one step and stopped.

"Now what's wrong?" she asked.

Sondaw surprised her. With a hard gaze and stern tone, he said, "I don't believe this. List wouldn't simply hand over his fleet."

"Yet he did."

"No."

They stood alone in the hallway.

"What do you think happened?" she asked.

"You struck him, and in front of his son, you knocked him down. But that wasn't enough."

"No?"

"In the end, I think you made a deal with the man."

"A deal," she repeated.

"You come from a trading family. Traders know how to make agreements, and that's why you gave him something, and I think you gave him more than that one chance to hit you in the face."

"What could I possibly offer the Archon?"

Sondaw's face flushed, and he said, "Diamond."

Prima placed two fingers across the young man's mouth. "This is the trader's secret, Lieutenant: I would have done that anyway. Really, after the carnage at home, after so much death, how can we pretend to anybody that our little District might ever keep that boy safe again?"

ELEVEN

High-hands rode on top of warrior-class fletches. Selected for their sharp vision and sure reflexes, they were the key protectors on any ship. Nothing outflew the papio wings. But wings were expensive and lacked endurance, and one man riding astride a well-calibrated autocannon, if he had the necessary gifts, should be able to kill a wing before it finished its first attack. And that was why the papio would run out of wings, and that's why they were sure to lose the next war.

High-hands deserved to be the elite among their ranks.

Of course wars only lived in history books and wherever confident generals played their intricate, well-practiced games. For a very long while, the military had fought only skirmishes with the papio, and the *Jugular* had never done even that. A middle-aged fletch, in fine repair and with a well-trained crew, it had made a thousand patrols without delivering any killing shots. Three high-hands were riding on top, each inside a gun bubble. Quyte had earned the primary seat over the bow. His eyes were first to spot *Bountiful*. That long forest-colored machine was emerging from the wilderness, pushing hard toward the reef. Calling down to the captain, Quyte gave the target's position and apparent speed, and while he spoke, his hands reflexively checked his weapon, making certain that the first explosive round was ready in the breech.

Then he had finished talking and finished loading, and that's when Quyte realized he was gasping, and the rapid, rattling of his heart made his entire chest ache.

The young man had never been political or subject to religious passions. In temperament, he was considered, if anything, too mild for his critical post. There was no pattern to his friendships, except that he was close to almost everybody on the roster. He had no great failings of character. While he knew what the old books said about the Creators and perfection, he didn't think much about the lessons of faith and humanity's place in the world. What was important was that he had great respect for Prima and for the military. As it happened, Quyte had seen Diamond many times in the past. The boy lived close to Shandlehome—a buckwood tree where Quyte's family to live. Quyte's father had spent a portion of his savings to acquire the same fine quality telescope that high-hands used in their bubbles. Every time the high-hand visited the old home, he spent some moments looking at the landing that wore a big net and that big window where Diamond could be seen playing children's games, or playing with his monkey, or doing nothing but sleep.

Shandlehome fell two days ago. Quyte's parents were presumed dead, along with both his sisters and their husbands and a newborn nephew.

In that, the high-hand was the same as many others.

Everybody had suffered. Almost every citizen in the District and onboard the *Jugular* had spent the last two days wishing miseries for their enemies. Of course some of that hatred had to be aimed at the boy. Diamond was the target of this attack, and there was always extra rage that needed someplace to gather, and why not throw obscenities at the creature that brought this rain of carnage and waste? Yet Quyte never mentioned any of those deep feelings, assuming that everyone was the same. What's more, the gunner had fine reasons to honor his uniform and his District. He was married to a beauty he had known since school, and his wife was still alive, living near the *Jugular*'s primary dock, which was as far from the mayhem as possible. Also, she was fifty days pregnant. The future had become a very dangerous tangle, and it was important for Quyte to play the role of the loving, reliable husband. Two days ago, he promised his sobbing wife that he would be careful and smart, and he promised that nobody wanted war, and he meant those words when he spoke them and he believed them as well as he could believe anything. But the gunner's nature was to have very little faith in great callings, and he was even less introspective than most of his peers, and perhaps those were reasons why he was vulnerable to wild, unpredictable shifts of mood.

Quyte saw the corona-hunter and called to the fletch's captain, and he made his cannon ready for things that wouldn't happen.

Then his hands weren't busy anymore, and they started to shake. His entire body trembled. Time was empty, leaving him with all sorts of vivid thoughts, and he rolled into the next moment and the next, and ideas kept bubbling up, leaving him nowhere to escape.

The *Jugular*'s captain had clear orders.

Finding and intercepting *Bountiful* was his primary mission, and if that was accomplished, then the Archon wanted that every power short of brute force should be employed in bring the missing ship home again.

The captain, who had a well-deserved reputation for simple clear talk, had explained the mission to his disciplined crew.

Quyte understood his ship's role and his personal responsibilities.

Three others fletches were patrolling in the formation, all to their right. *Bountiful* was on their left, and while signaling with flashing lights and important horns, the *Jugular* pushed to full speed, dropping water and climbing to intercept the runaway airship.

Quyte was watching *Bountiful* when the first wings appeared.

From behind him, a high-hand shouted, "Two hawkspurs under the canopy's toes."

He should have seen the wings earlier, and he turned surly. An instant later the papio were on top of them, using those roaring wasteland engines to slice at the air and try to ruin his courage. But unexpectedly, the intruders were a welcome change. They made the situation vivid and immediate. Quyte was a gunner again, nailed to a tough worthy job. The newfound sense of duty rode with him all the way to *Bountiful*. The papio were brazenly supplying cover for the corona-hunter. Whether they controlled it or not was a question for others. His duty was to watch everything, protect the men riding with him, and protect his world to the best of his ability—and every moment of training seemed to matter as he held the gun with both hands, tracking one wing and then the other until the *Jugular* reached a point just ahead of the corona-hunter.

Their captain ordered a full stop, and the slick triangular airship reversed engines to block the way.

Bountiful sounded its collision horn, but the captain or its pilot weren't taking chances, dropping ballast before passing overhead, aiming for the next substantial gap in the canopy.

More papio wings appeared, three and then another pair buzzing about the scene without getting close to branches or those tough slow-moving targets.

Bountiful was climbing fast, but a second fletch had closed the gap, pushing overhead and then barring the escape route.

Again, the collision horn blew.

The third fletch pulled ahead and spun around, her nose facing *Bountiful*, her speed and grace matching every movement that the corona-hunter could manage.

Following protocols, the *Jugular* eased close to *Bountiful*, blocking another one of the available retreats.

The fourth fletch still had air to cross, but once it arrived, that big airship wouldn't have anywhere to escape. Long before the harpooners and slayers and that one odd boy could make it to the reef, *Bountiful* would be surrounded and boarded, and that's how the peace would be saved.

Quyte had very little to watch now. The hawkspurs couldn't approach the canopy, and there was nothing to see among the branches. So he watched the notorious ship, and in particular the open doorway and its airborne dock.

Their natural enemies were standing inside that huge room, pretending to own the place, which answered one critical question. The papio had been chasing the boy for two days, and now they had him. Quyte and the other high-hands watched the whiffbird propellers start to turn and the papio soldiers standing near the open door with weapons in hand, and then Quyte put his telescope to his right eye, discovering humans in the shadows, standing along the back wall in a neat short line.

The boy was there.

His proportions were weak and wrong, and Quyte recognized the tightly wound hair and the sickly face. Then he saw what might have been a smile, those peculiar white teeth catching the little bit of morning light that made it to the back of the room.

Quyte was certain that he saw a smile.

If someone could have talked to the young high-hand a day or two later—if Quyte was given the chance and enough encouragement to explain his actions—he would have had very little to say. He was no deep believer in any custom or tradition, particularly his own. He thought that Creators and the meanings of humanity were other people's interests. His personal losses from the attack were huge, yet he had the wife and unborn child too. He was trained. By every measure, he was disciplined and proud of his uniform. Maybe he had heard other soldiers talking with conspiratorial tones, plotting this or implying that. But the gunner had never felt interest in treachery. His sole crime was to not mention the dangerous chatter to his thoroughly indifferent superiors. Indeed, Quyte looked like the best man to put inside that blister. But then he peered through the telescope and saw the boy smiling, and he watched the papio working quickly to launch their whiffbirds, and the peace and apparent stability of that scene made this young soldier think in a startling new way.

Two days ago, trees died and people died so that one creature had this chance to move from the trees to the reef. That was the truth dangling in plain view. Maybe the boy asked to live with the papio. Maybe he even planned for it, or he was an innocent moved by some greater evil. Details didn't matter. The core of the story was impenetrable to reason and evidence and every fear of being wrong. What mattered was that vast forces had unleashed the explosions as a cover or as punishment, and it only seemed as if the boy had been lucky enough to escape.

But Diamond had to survive Marduk's fall.

That always was the plan.

And that had to be why the creature was standing where he was, the monstrous smile filling a wicked alien face. Those sick white teeth were what caused the gun to move, and only the faint, faint possibility of innocence kept the high-hand from shooting Diamond with the first shell, aiming instead for a place that was higher and far more frail.

• • •

"Women are rarely stronger than men," Crock's mother used to joke. "But women are never, ever as weak as the strongest man."

Crock was strong by every measure.

Becoming a soldier wasn't easy work, but after two days on that path, her vocation was set. Others failed in their training, and good soldiers could complain. But not Crock. Physical challenges were weathered without complaint. She liked to run. She loved to carry and climb. Shooting was a fine challenge wrapped around geometry, and following orders, even the dumb orders, proved easier than the headstrong girl had imagined. Once trained, she would never stop being a soldier. It was the blunt polished certainty of her existence that made her happiest, and because there hadn't been any war for generations, it seemed self-evident that her running and shooting were good reasons for fun, and following dumb orders was the cost to having a uniform and abundant food as well as a pension once it was time to retire.

Six hundred days ago, Crock was posted to the roughest, poorest slice of the world, and soon after that she volunteered to fly inside whiffbirds. Whiffbirds were risky duty, even in peace. But the pay was better, and she had new skills to learn, including new words and fresh curses. She endured bruising training sessions where crews were taught to protect something that was very special, very secret. Something that they were forbidden to know about. But soldiers had always been bold and young, and no secret was safe with those kinds of people. Smart voices talked about the Eight, and later Crock heard about an armored child and a half-human child who had come out of the trees for a visit. And once during a very long day, she was standing alone in the wilderness, inside a blind, practicing her stealth skills when a creature with no clear shape walked on the branch in front of her. And just like that, she was one of the few people who knowingly saw the beast that could dress itself in dream.

Soon after that the Eight became One, and that was Divers.

Every day more soldiers were stationed nearby, as bodyguards and mechanics, pilots and simple soldiers.

One night, a colleague asked Crock if she wanted an audience with Divers.

But she had been ordered to avoid the creature, which was what she intended to do until ordered otherwise.

Then came whispers about whispers, and rumors wilder than any tale about old coronas coughing up unlikely beasts. And soon after that the tree-walkers decided to slaughter each other in a mad, idiot attempt to murder one boy. Crock found herself in briefings about situations that had already changed in the field. Three times, she sat onboard her whiffbird, instructing her team about a new destination but always with the same goal—to grab up that miracle boy. But those important missions were aborted twice, and the third attempt was called off when an orange flare was sent past their bird's nose. Only the fourth mission mattered. That briefing came en route. Crock read from papers so important that they had to be burned afterwards. Like any assignment devoid of planning and good sense, there were needless casualties on both sides. But there weren't as many dead as she feared, and *Bountiful* was theirs, and the boy was theirs again. He was stolen from a corona set on their land, after all. And if all of that wasn't historic enough, Crock was told to take her three best men to the galley and sit on everybody but the boy.

Soldiers are consummate experts at sitting. Crock's prisoners were slender short creatures, except for the boy named Karlan. They smelled odd but not sour, and it took time to grow accustomed to their wispy, unserious voices. Because she knew their language, at least to a point, she found herself interacting with them, and liking them for good reasons, and not liking them for different good reasons.

Just once, Diamond came into the galley to eat and speak to his father.

She watched the boy and listened carefully to whatever he said. Diamond loved his father, that old man Merit. Merit knew the papio and respected them, and she could see his love for the boy. But oddly, Diamond didn't generate emotions inside her. He spoke words that she understood about subjects that didn't exist, and he seemed out of place in more ways that she could count, and then he had left the galley for his cabin again and she was glad of it.

Later, after the storm broke and night was finished, *Bountiful* was spotted by the fletches. The mission commander sent orders that one soldier was to guard the former crew while the rest of the prisoners were brought to the machine shop and lined up in plain view. Tree-walkers liked to ride inside gas bags. Their quickest bags were approaching in a hurry, and their captains needed to be reminded who was at risk if real fighting should break out.

Crock considered leaving the big boy behind. Karlan was the only prisoner who worried her, and because of that, she liked him. She saw good qualities in his walk and manner and how he wore his little miseries, and that's why she put Karlan beside her. To help the image of peaceful coexistence, she cut away the bindings around his wrists, and then she told him that if anything felt wrong, with him or the world, he would die first.

"Good to know," the boy said, winking at her.

Then the Diamond boy was brought to the dock. Three fletches had already caught them, and the papio commander called down from the bridge with orders to get every whiffbird ready. Smart leaders wanted options in case of trouble, and the first option was to throw their prize into one of the birds and then flee into the tangled canopy overhead.

Karlan was standing on Crock's left, and the big room was jammed full of engine sounds. Diamond stood to Karlan's left, flanked by his father and his teacher while that tiny monkey perched on his shoulder. Two other papio soldiers were on her right, while past them were the disarmed bodyguard and two other children.

Every face looked tense and brutally tired.

Every face but Diamond's, she realized. He was still smiling. Standing in that line, helpless as anyone in the world, yet that pale-eyed creature looked as if he was somewhere else entirely.

One fletch was visible, its flat top rising even with the shop floor. Crock hated the bouncy wrong feel beneath her. Hard coral, rough and honest, was what she wanted to walk across. Soon, she thought. Then she found herself looking at Karlan. Why was that? A lot of thoughts had been swirling inside her, and just then, willing herself to use fresh eyes, she finally saw what should have been apparent from the very first glance.

Over the roaring whiffbirds, she shouted, "You're a little bit papio."

Karlan turned. He was huge and bold and full of natural bluster, but her words left him mute. This was a revelation.

"It happens," she said. "It doesn't happen much, but the species cross. Our blood and bones get mixed with yours. Fifty generations pass, but the bodies remember their nature as they wander. Two tree-walkers meet and mate, and the old blood suddenly shows up in the big arms and legs and the strength that never sleeps. Which is the papio inside you."

Hearing every word, Karlan was too stunned to react.

And others heard it too. Diamond noticed and turned to look at Crock, something in those words worthy of a near-giggle. Then the strange boy looked forwards again, and Crock saw the fletch hanging close outside and the whiffbirds looked eager to fly—although launching would be a tough trick with so many aircraft bunched together—and that was the moment when Karlan started to respond.

She heard the curse and the first shards of pain coming with his words, and she started to turn back toward the giant boy, wondering if she had made a mess of things, telling him what he didn't want to know.

That was when an autocannon began to fire.

Every other sound in the world became soft, thin and weak.

The cannon fired three rounds and paused, and then three more. The fletch's front gunner was aiming high, aiming at one point, trying to punch a big hole through the ship's hull and first bladder. Crock was running before she gave her legs the order. She sprinted to the edge of the floor and shouldered her rifle, pinning her sight to a young man, and her first shot passed through the bubble and through his face.

Of course she fired. Fletches were flown by soldiers and soldiers had plans, and this had to be somebody's plan. That's why she swung her gun to the right, fixing the sight on the next gunner inside his little bubble. He was sitting. He was watching, his expression perplexed and a little irritated by what hadn't been deciphered by his head, and she managed a fine piece of shooting that left that bubble shattered, its interior painted with blood and brain.

The third gunner was moving.

Crock got her sight pinned him.

But hydrogen was leaking out of *Bountiful*, and the ship was tipping severely as the engines began to accelerate. She missed her shot and missed again, and meanwhile the final gunner managed to sweep the dock with cannon fire, shells bursting through the walls and closed doors and the one open door, a fat round coming into Crock's chest and out the backside before it turned into a hammer that pushed her dead body out into the bright rain-washed air.

• • •

With the first bark of the cannon, Merit put his eyes and one hand on Tar`ro, shaking him when he yelled, "Keep Diamond safe."

As if the man needed encouragement.

Tar`ro slipped closer to the boy, hunting for weapons. Papio guns were big and hard to maneuver. He wanted a piece of steel, preferably something sharp. But who would he fight? That perfectly fine question asked itself, and the man wasted another moment trying to piece together some strategy that wouldn't be impossible two breaths after it began.

The cannon stopped firing, and the papio woman was standing in the open door, firing at fresh targets.

Merit had run to the closest com-line, the receiver to his ear while he screamed to the bridge, "Right center bladders hit. Bleed their gas, drop ballast, open carbon dioxide tanks above."

It was morning. There was a little less oxygen in the morning air, which helped reduced the threat of fire.

There wasn't any sign of fire, was there?

There wasn't, and that jolt of optimism helped Tar`ro think.

The awful monkey was screaming. Soldiers guarding the boy were very serious about their duties. Golden eyes squinted when Tar`ro approached, so the tree-walker pretended to care about the damned pet. Kneeling, he shouted, "You're fine, I'm here. Bite my hand, you brat."

The soldier's interest moved across the room.

The nearest whiffbird was a busy loud machine ready to lift off the floor. Two of its crewmembers were shouting. One seemed to be waving Diamond closer, while the other, the pilot, just as surely signaled for everyone to get away.

The floor had been tilting for several moments.

The woman papio was still firing.

Tar`ro grabbed Diamond by an arm, and Good clamped down on the Tar`ro's wrist, and then the whiffbird was punched by a cannon blast that broke its windows and set its interior ablaze.

Tar`ro remembered a fat round button painted red.

He punched Good and turned away, trying to recall where the fire-suppression switch was waiting. But Merit was already there, holding it down as alarms sounded and *Bountiful* listed and various fires were burning around the dock. And then, just as people and the papio began to lose their feet, heavy carbon dioxide poured out of vents built for no other purpose.

Diamond pulled loose of the bleeding hand.

The soldiers weren't with them anymore. They were running and sliding their way down the rubber floor, stopping where the woman soldier had been. A couple other soldiers were already there, firing fast. The woman soldier was gone. The big fletch filled the long open doorway, dressed in strong scales, engines roaring as it prepared to accelerate. It looked like a beast deciding on the best way to run. Then a new roar arrived, louder still and probably fiercely hot, shaking the air and the floor and every person. The world shuddered as a wing slashed past *Bountiful*, next to no space between the two machines.

The wing was gone, and the fletch decided on its direction, pulling away.

Fires were burning across the dock, but not so brightly now. Choking gases made smoke and smolder, and Merit shouted something about holding your breath, except it was too late. Tar`ro had lungs full of carbon dioxide, and while he might not burn to death, he was beginning to wobble from a lack of oxygen.

Bountiful kept bleeding through its wounds and out the emergency shunts. Every water tank was opened. Heavy blackwood timbers set onboard when the ship was built were sent tumbling. Then the unrestrained machinery began to slide and fall free. A second door in the dock was opened, soldiers tossing out tools and furniture and several dead bodies followed by pieces of the shattered whiffbird. The airship struggled to remain buoyant, but that wasn't possible. How could it fly when the central bladders were gutted? The ship was plunging for the demon floor, and that black thought gave Tar`ro encouragement enough to cough hard and find a fresh good breath of real air before looking around the room again.

Diamond had pulled free of his grip. He and the monkey were crawling uphill. The floor had about a two-thirds pitch, and the other prisoners were clinging to anything bolted to the floor as well as each other. Nissim had Elata beside him, and she clung to him. Karlan grabbed his brother in a haphazard grip. Merit was trying to move along the wall above them, the receiver dangling on its wire. The slayer shouted orders to whoever might be on the end of the line. "Leave us crooked, don't bleed extra. And straight. Push straight for the reef, fast!"

Tar`ro climbed after the boy.

From outside, in the distance and then very close, came the sharp roars of more wings and the hard sputter of guns.

An explosion followed, huge and lingering.

Catching the boy, Tar`ro said, "Stay with me."

"No."

"Your father's orders," he said.

Diamond looked at his bodyguard. What was different about his face was apparent, and it was nameless.

"No, I have to find Quest," the boy said. "She's somewhere close."

"Who?"

"She's somewhere close," he said, climbing toward the hallway.

The remaining whiffbirds were sliding, crashing into the wall and the final closed door. Every rotor was shattered. Nothing else could fly. But ten thousand generations of corona hunters had helped build a machine ready for almost any disaster, even ones nobody could imagine. Merit hit important buttons, and the doors didn't just open, springs flung them free, and the whiffbirds tumbled away, and living papio followed, and the brilliant wash of sunshine came through the new openings, every surface and face and the soft black of the floor shining its fashion.

Good hollered a vile, immortal curse.

The boy had nearly left his monkey behind. He was showing a lot of pluck for being a miserable climber.

Tar`ro decided to give him a good chase.

The floor was no steeper than before, but it wasn't any better either. Holes ready to hold straps gave his hands perches, and he worked closer and the monkey did the same, and both of them cursed and said, "Slow down."

Diamond stopped just short of the hallway, breathing hard.

"What are you chasing?" Tar`ro asked.

Diamond was looking up, and he was listening. The ship's bones were groaning as weight shifted, and the punctured bladders collapsed into a useless state while the remaining bladders expanded, filled with hydrogen reserves that caused the corona flesh to distort, pushing at the skeleton and the outer skin.

Again, Tar`ro shouted, "What are you chasing?"

"My sister," the boy said, still looking ahead. "She's here, she's close."

Sister?

The word generated too many answers, and Tar`ro had no time. No patience. The other humans were clinging to little perches, safe only by the easiest scale. Merit was holding the wall and the receiver, shouting at the invisible bridge. Then he noticed his son climbing into danger. But Diamond had a problem—a long stretch of tilted empty floor without holds of any kind—and that should have stopped him. Moving again would be stupid for anyone. But the boy had already kicked off his school boots, and with the tiny toes gripping, every finger digging at the rubber, he tried hard to do what couldn't be done. And he slipped. And he caught himself for a moment and then dropped again, and Good stayed where he was, safe and screaming.

Tar`ro wasn't directly below Diamond, but clinging onto the last tie-hole, he swung his legs into the air, the boy grabbing one ankle and holding on.

"Get up here," Tar`ro ordered.

Merit had seen the fall. He was shouting and starting to climb out into the open again.

"Come on," Tar`ro coaxed.

The boy crawled over him, and Merit had scrambled down close enough to stretch out his long frame, offering his hand to his son.

Diamond grabbed and held tight.

Father and son were climbing together, and Tar`ro started after them. He had handholds. There were no obstacles. He had no idea why he let go. Maybe *Bountiful* shuddered, or maybe he was tired and still weak from the carbon dioxide. Or ten lucky handholds didn't mean that the eleventh would work, which was probably the simple ugly reason why he and the floor released one another.

Tar`ro flung his arms, blindly stabbing for holes that didn't want to be found.

But this wouldn't be too bad, the man reasoned. The doorways were only so long, and there were plenty of walls happy to catch him. That was a fine enduring thought that gave him hope, and then he was past the walls and spinning in the open air without a scratch on his body, tumbling three times before pointing his stomach up, arms and legs stretching out to keep his speed as slow as possible.

Bountiful filled the air above him. The corona-hunter wasn't flying, and it wasn't quite falling; the craft existed between those states. But it wasn't burning either. Two fletches were burning against the thin trees of the canopy, and a third fletch—the one that had started the attack—was part way through a hard turn, bladders punctured, blue fires making the corona scales glow.

Maybe another fletch was directly below him.

Just that one unlikely possibility gave Tar`ro enough confidence to roll over. Sure enough, there were several ships below, each driving hard toward him. He saw fletches from his District and ships from the main fleet and in the distance were the giant vessels, including the *Ruler of the Storm*.

What a sight, and all for him . . . Tar`ro thought . . . and then he remembered that he was a realist, cold and tough, and a lifetime of practice threw him back into that familiar, reliable state.

He was dead.

The wilderness canopy was high and sparse, and Tar`ro was still far above the reef's level. A man could fall for a very long time in this realm. He didn't want any of this, but this was how it was. He thought about watching *Bountiful*'s progress, seeing if the ship could somehow make the reef, or he could study the battle that was taking shape in the air around him. But instead he ignored his surroundings, thinking about his former colleague, about Bits. Not often but a few times the two men had sat together in a tavern popular among the boy's bodyguards, and they drank too much and talked too freely about various subjects. They were never friends but were always friendly, and Tar`ro had insisted on believing that he had a clear sense of the man.

But he hadn't, no.

Then Sophia got into his head. One little plan of Tar`ro's was to ask her out for drinks, just the two of them. He had some other ideas that dangled nicely from that one event. But she was dead and he was dead, and if there was something after living, he only hoped there was hardened wine involved.

Tar`ro thought about wine.

He thought about women, real and otherwise.

And he felt as if he hadn't moved. The demon floor was remote, almost unreal. He considered putting his head down and driving hard. But this wasn't that bad, falling slow and easy.

Then he remembered Diamond saying something about a sister.

What craziness was that?

Sitting in the classroom or standing outside that big window, the bodyguard sometimes glanced at the boy, just for a moment, and out of nowhere he'd find himself thinking about the enormous things that could hide inside even a little brain. And on those occasions, whenever Tar`ro forgot that he was a cold realist, he usually became sick with his self-induced terror.

Here he was, falling and falling, and he didn't feel half so scared as he was thinking about a crazy kid.

Now what could be more peculiar than that?

• • •

Zakk sat on a nob of sourlip coral, using his binoculars to watch the battle.

Once he realized that Divers had run toward High Coral Merry, the young man started to chase her. Of course it was ridiculous to believe that he would catch her. His little body couldn't cope with the rough, unforgiving ground. The same knee was skinned twice, as well as both elbows. It wasn't long before he was too exhausted to move, and even now, after sitting for ten recitations, he was still breathing hard, sweating and tasting blood in his mouth.

This was nobody's plan. This was never what he had imagined. But against long odds, he insisted on believing even now that there was hope, that whatever happened next would afford him the chance to talk and charm, eventually wriggling out of whatever trap was about the descend on him.

Hadn't he done that for his entire life?

Of course coming here had to be the ultimate trap. The man in charge of the operation had made quite a lot of noise about limited risks and eventual rescue. But really, how could any rational person believe that escape was likely?

"And if I don't come home," he said to the man. "What about my mother?"

"Your payment becomes her payment. And if the mission is successful, she gets your full bonus too."

Mother was a big plain lady with a secret bit of papio in her family history. As soon as her son was old enough to understand, she confessed that his father had been a diplomat stationed in the District of Districts—a smallish papio living far from home, living with a significant drinking problem and a habit of abusing local women. Her only child looked papio at birth and every day since. That's why he was raised in a special school for the handful like him. He was taught his father's language and the coral-bound customs, and then he was fully grown, as big as he would ever be but still wearing a child's voice and proportions. That's why he was selected ahead of everyone else. Alone among his peers, he could pretend to be a special boy, inserted into another child's life for a few critical days.

Someone special was living near Bright River. The man in charge told him that secret, and suddenly he was Zakk. That was his new name, the same as a papio boy who was going to be sent to that remote place, ready to serve as a caretaker for that exceptionally odd creature.

One day the Archon of Archons came to visit the school. That was a great honor; nobody needed to tell him so. The Archon called him a hero and examined his body, and then he explained how the papio kept their secrets. Zakk would learn nothing of substance until he arrived at the secret site. Caretakers were allowed to call home, but since every call-line was monitored at both ends, he had to speak to the real Zakk's parents . A vocabulary of code words had been built from ordinary words. One relay station along the reef had friendly ears, and every important meaning would be transmitted straight home. But the Archon promised that the mission wouldn't be a success until Zakk was home, and then the two of them could sit inside the palace, calmly discussing everything that he had seen and every impression that he had earned.

The boy who wasn't a boy nodded. "I'll be talking to the real Zakk's mother and father," he said.

"You sound more than a little like him," the Archon promised. "With the distance and interference in the lines, they won't know the difference."

"And nobody else will see the trick?"

The little man puckered his lips before saying, "Not immediately. We have a sturdy network in place, something that I inherited with my office. Records and your credentials will make everyone happy, for a few days at least."

The papio-shaped man was happy enough to smile.

"This is an enormous opportunity," the Archon said. "For you and for the world."

The new Zakk kept nodding and smiling.

"This is a very special creature that they're holding," the Archon began.

"Like your son?"

A smile blossomed. "A gift from the corona, yes."

"And like Diamond."

"One of a kind." Then the Archon reached out, squeezing the young man's shoulder. "But the papio are different than we are. We are good to our children, but they're torturing theirs. We have evidence, strong evidence, that they have savaged him once and probably will again."

He knew about the papio. They were drunks and rapists, and often worse, yes.

"What happens to the real Zakk?" the spy asked. "Where will that boy be?"

The Archon's smile changed, but it stayed a smile. "Oh, he's going to be sidelined for a little while. But don't worry. No harm comes to him, or anybody else."

"I'm not worried," the new Zakk said.

Then their conversation paused. The Archon surveyed the classroom, eyes focusing on the cages filled with animals and corals from the papio realm. The man was struggling to find some comforting words to add to the pile.

The new Zakk said, "Diamond."

"What about him?"

"I'd like to meet him, once I get home again."

"And you will," the Archon said immediately, with too much energy. "That I promise. In fact, I see a lot of strong reasons why you two should be good friends."

And then it was many days later, and sitting on the sourlip coral, Zakk repeated those delicious words.

"You two should be good friends," he muttered.

Jet engines growled and the cannons barked. Armored fletches were pressing forward, and the papio wings were crisscrossing while firing and taking fire. But at this distance, the battle remained muted, every contestant small. The noise was so minimal that Zakk could make out the distinct crunches of boots grinding into the coral dust behind him, and then the boots stopped and he heard the voice of the soldier.

"Your hands," the soldier said. "Drop the binoculars and lift both hands where I can see them."

Zakk did what he was told. When did he ever struggle against authority?

The soldier stepped and stepped, and then he stopped again. He had been running, but his breathing was already as slow as Zakk's. Soldiers were marvelously fit. When he got home, Zakk would start to train like a papio soldier. Diamond was supposed to be fast on his feet. Maybe they could train with each other, and when they weren't training, they would share stories about being alone and odd in the world.

"What are doing here?" asked the soldier.

"I was looking for Divers. Do you know where she is?"

"No."

"She was going to meet *Bountiful* when it lands," he said.

"Who told you about *Bountiful*?" the soldier asked.

Zakk told the truth, naming another soldier.

The feet behind him shifted, growing comfortable with their stance.

"Which ship is *Bountiful*?" asked Zakk.

The soldier didn't answer.

Nobody else had joined them, but it was easy to imagine other soldiers spotting the two of them sharing this high ground, quickly converging on tiny, dangerous him.

What else could he do?

"It's the green blimp," the soldier said abruptly.

"I don't see it."

"Lower. Look lower." The voice was tight, just short of angry.

"What's wrong with that ship?" asked Zakk.

"It's been damaged. Severely, by the looks."

Bountiful was a green bag that was falling as quickly as it pushed ahead. Instead of being long and trim, it was sagging, particularly in the middle. And in those next moments, even with bare eyes, Zakk noticed a flicker of piercing blue flame near the stern—the first traces of a fire that would only grow worse.

Concerned, the soldier said, "I don't know if she'll feel the reef."

"I think she will," Zakk said.

The soldier waited for a moment, and then he asked, "Who are you?"

Zakk started to answer.

"No, really," said the papio. "Tell me something true."

An unexpected thought came to Zakk. That happened quite a lot, and maybe it was because he was a mixture of bloods. Hybrid animals often had greater powers than their parents. Whatever the reason, the idea arrived fully formed, and he liked it enough that he had to smile. The entire world was descending into war, and an armed man was standing behind him, certainly holding a gun at his skull . . . yet he felt relaxed enough to turn his head to one side, showing his expression to the soldier.

"Why are you grinning?" the papio asked.

"I'm just wondering if we're like Divers. Like Diamond. Maybe all of us are the same as them."

"What do you mean?"

Zakk said nothing.

The hammer on a big pistol was cocked.

Not caring if this was a mistake, Zakk set the binoculars against his wet eyes. Fletches were burning. *Bountiful* looked ill and sorry. And at the last, with a quiet voice, he said, "Maybe we're also children of the corona. Have you ever wondered about that?"

• • •

What was amazing was the absolute lack of amazement. The boy was talking wildly about the sister that he had just met and the other sister, or whatever she was, lurking in the high shadows of the reef. Nothing else seemed to matter to Diamond. *Bountiful* was wounded, plunging out the sky. Its human crew had been let out of confinement, the surviving soldiers giving tree-walkers permission and helping hands to buy the ship more speed and more lift. Yet inside all of that chaos and purpose, what mattered was the quick crazed voice telling Merit about the creature that had clung outside the cabin window, and the other creature that Quest had seen just a few times, at extreme distance—an entity that the papio now and again mentioned inside their whispered conversations.

"Divers," he said. "That's my other sister's name."

"Where's Quest now?" Seldom asked.

The other children were listening too.

"I don't know where she is," Diamond said. "She promised to stay close, but she was hungry . . . and that was before the attack."

Bountiful had recovered most of its trim. People who couldn't work were sitting on the shop floor. A couple of the crew members were digging into one of the storerooms, working to assemble and inflate one of the little airships.

Merit yelled at them, and he tried to stand.

"Don't," Nissim said. "Let the leg rest."

Somewhere in the mayhem, his left knee had been wrenched. Even with adrenalin quickening his blood, Merit had trouble coping with the pain.

Pointing at the storeroom, he said, "There isn't time for cleverness. Tell them."

"Okay," Nissim said. "But what good can we do?"

"Deploy crash chairs. And find a working receiver, get an open line to the bridge."

The Master nodded, and in a moment of genius, he kicked Karlan.

"Get up and help me," he said.

Karlan cursed. But a moment later, with the weariest of groans, he stood and started walking.

Diamond had stopped talking about sisters, but he hadn't quit thinking about them. One glance at his big eyes said as much.

"And what does Quest look like?" Elata asked.

"Anything she wants," Diamond said, delighted. "She shapes the body she needs, or she peels away everything to become small."

"What about Divers?" asked Seldom.

A different siren began to sound, spreading through the ship with a rhythm that Merit knew too well.

"Fire suits," he shouted to Nissim and Karlan. "Unpack all of them, now."

The crew from the storeroom came running, throwing themselves into the task. And the three children continued to sit on the floor, not calm and not even a little relaxed; but they acted as if time didn't matter, as if their conversation could be cut off anywhere and resumed at some later, better moment.

Good was sitting between Diamond's legs, and he dropped his head whenever he heard the wings approaching, as if that would make the machines miss. Suddenly he lowered his head farther than ever, and the children and even Merit did the same. A pair of wings roared past, probably embarking from High Coral Merry on their way out to shoot at List's fleet.

"Divers," said Seldom, holding to the topic.

"She's like a giant papio," Diamond said. "Quest doesn't dare get close to the reef. The wilderness is too thin and high, and she might be seen. But from a distance, once, she saw Divers all alone."

"You're sure it was her," said Elata.

"She's huge. As big as a big room," Diamond said. "And she had hurt herself on the coral. That's what Quest saw, and that's what she showed me."

The other children nodded.

"I saw her bleeding, and then it was healed. Like me, and like King too."

"Quest is the same as you two?" asked Seldom.

"But she's even more powerful than us."

Diamond looked giddy and sick, joyous and ready to collapse. A father knew how to read his son's face, and Merit had only a little trouble piecing together the clues. Putting an arm around the boy, he said, "Maybe we should stop talking. Save our strength."

But the boy had to tell him one last wonder. "Her blood was red. I saw that. It was red and shiny just like mine."

Nissim dragged up shiny fire suits, looking like flattened bodies. Karlan was standing at the edge of the shop floor, one giant arm holding a strap so that the big body could lean into the open, affording him a better view of the world.

Merit fought his leg until he was standing.

The suits came in various sizes, few able to fit anybody properly. Diamond found the smallest two and gave them to his friends, and while Elata dressed, Seldom said, "You can't let yourself burn. Even if you healed, that would be awful."

"I'll wear something big and share it with Good."

Good jumped when he heard his name.

The crash chairs were built into the long back wall, and everyone would sit with the wall on their right, backs to the bridge. It took several recitations to dress and get into position. Merit wished he could help more, and he was glad not to be tempted. He claimed a chair behind his son, and Diamond turned and looked back at him. But the face was working to smile, the last of the genuine joy being spent.

As promised, the oversized suit had room for a monkey. But the animal had his own plan, climbing into a high cupboard filled with tools that were quickly flung across the shop, leaving an empty volume that was dark and cool when the door was secured behind him.

Outside, coming too slowly and too late, were a squadron of whiffbirds. But the at least wings had stopped flying close, making the world quieter when the final siren came to life—a bright screeching roar warning of an imminent collision.

Karlan was last to claim a crash seat, but he didn't bother with the undersized suits.

Nissim was behind Merit, struggling with the clips on his various belts.

Bountiful's engines screamed, begging for speed. Then they suddenly fell silent, and Elata asked, "What's that mean?"

"We're going into reverse," Karlan shouted. "Kill some momentum before we smash into the reef and die."

The airship jumped, passing from the open air into the confused breezes above the coral. Merit looked out the missing doors, glad for the pressure of the belts and sitting close enough to his son to touch him, waiting for smart words to come to mind—a last thought before everybody but Diamond was cooked to death.

That's all that seemed possible just then.

And then a papio appeared, galloping down the hallway and into the shop. The man was using an arm and both legs to run, and under the other arm was an insulated box bound tight with cords covered with various pillows pulled from various beds. The stranger ignored everybody else, sprinting to the first missing door and grabbing the same strap that Karlan had held, eyeing distances and speed before very carefully flinging the box into the open air.

Merit looked ahead, checking on Diamond.

His son had dipped his head, and his father couldn't be certain, but Diamond looked as if he was crying.

Then the old slayer looked at the open door and the papio standing with the strap in hand, and suddenly the papio was off the floor and rising, caught up in some fantastic gust of wind that was visible for a moment. It looked like a quivering mass of hard gray smoke, and whatever it was carried the papio up the side of the ship, out of sight, so suddenly that it seemed as if the man had been imagined, had never been.

Bountiful's engines coughed and returned, propellers aiming for a hard reverse.

The great ship slowed noticeably, and it plunged harder.

Merit hoped for a valley, flat-bottomed and relatively safe. But then he saw a ridge of coral edging towards them, lifting higher as they dropped . . . and to his son, to everybody, he shouted, "Wait for us to stop, then run!"

The collision was abrupt, and it was softer than he had any right to expect. Grinding roars ended with a merciless jerk of corona bones and lightweight alloys. In an instant, the bottom section was torn free of the half-deflated bladders. The shop and hallway, cabins and galley were lodged inside a long crevice, and they stopped moving while the rest of the ship found itself lighter again, leaping high before shredding and collapsing, the engines igniting a wealth of hydrogen in a scorching blaze that even at a distance felt like the world had been shoved inside a hot angry oven.

Screams came from everyone, and then silence.

Merit couldn't say when he got to his feet or if there was pain. But he was mobile enough to run, and what he did first was unfasten Diamond's belts and then the other children's. The knee didn't complain until they were out on the barren, eroded coral, and he was counting every head, not believing the number but still thinking that this was so much better than he dared guess. Karlan's hair was burnt, and maybe some flesh. And Nissim had gotten only one belt fastened, and now he was bent double and looking sick. *Bountiful*'s bridge and upper quarters were destroyed, the wreckage scattered along the higher portions of the ridge. The various fires were awful but growing weaker, and Merit wished the crew were alive, and he was thinking about Fret . . . and that's when Seldom asked somebody, "Did you see him die?"

See who die? Merit thought of Good, but the monkey was here too.

"Something grabbed him and took him," Seldom shouted.

"That's what I saw," Elata said. "Was it real?"

"What was real?" Diamond asked, stepping out of his fire suit.

"That papio man," Seldom explained. "When we got over the reef, he threw that box out the door. And then . . . "

"Your sister picked him up," said Elata.

"It had to be Quest," Seldom said.

"She was going to eat him," Elata said.

"No, I don't think so," Seldom said, shaking his head. Those kinds of thoughts troubled him.

"Where did you see Quest?" Diamond asked.

"I didn't," Seldom said.

"She was higher on the ship, riding on the bags." Elata said the words and then believed them, pointing up the long slope.

Diamond turned, and after a moment of saying nothing, he began to run toward the brilliant blue fires.

Merit tried to follow. The knee fought him, but the man refused pain and weakness and his own gathering age. He wanted nothing but to take care of the last shred of his family, and that's why he managed to sprint for a fair distance. Nobody followed. He discovered that he was alone, limping along the ridge's crest. Then he stepped wrong on the weak leg, tilting and recovering. But as the pain escalated, his strong leg slipped out from under him. He fell hard and spun down the far side of the ridge, and his cheek shattered and one wrist snapped before he came to a rest inside a wide bowl where rainwater clung to the sandy coral grit.

Merit lay on his back.

Machines were flying, approaching from every direction.

For a moment, he could hear Diamond calling for him. Or he imagined the familiar, wondrous voice. Either way, Merit sat up and remained sitting upright, and a creature that was scampering up that same slope spotted him and turned its course, approaching close enough that there was nothing in the world but the coral beneath and the titanic beast that overwhelmed—a papio's shape but enlarged, juvenile in the face but powerful and sure-footed, strange pink hair that wasn't hair, and lungs like bellows breathing hard after a very long run.

"Divers," said Merit.

"And you are?" a booming voice asked, in papio.

He said his name both ways. "Merit," and then, "Deserve."

"I know you," said the creature. "Yes, I know all about you."

Then Divers reached down with both of those huge hands, one set of fingers carefully cradling the injured body while other fingers closed together, and that was the hand that pulled, removing the man's tiny head.

TWELVE

The life inside him had never been so full and rich.

But the life outside, what Diamond carried on his shoulders and soul, was nearly lost. Home and that wonderful room were lost. The wooden soldiers were ashes, and so was Mother. Mother was lost everywhere but inside his mind, and he didn't have time or the resolve to make those memories even passingly real. Not thinking about his mother, Diamond felt ashamed. His good brief life was in ruins. Besides the tattered school uniform, he owned nothing physical. There was nothing to carry but thoughts and shifting urges, memories on the surface and memories buried and ideas that didn't deserve being called plans and emotions that scalded and brightened, too quick and far too restless to be tamed. Diamond had to shoulder his misery. Huge and relentless, the sense of grievous loss made his body tremble while roiling, bitter sensations kept finding ways to share the agony, the despair. A perfect indestructible mind could never leave any notion behind. The boy was convinced that he would never stop suffering, and indeed, he would have argued and maybe fought with any voice claiming that one day, with time, these horrific losses would stop slicing him down the middle.

But even now, more than devastation lived inside him.

That bizarre, wonderful sister emerged from hiding long enough to give him glimpses of the world she saw, which was different from the world Diamond knew. Quest was wondrous, and if she wasn't blessing enough, in those last moments together, Quest gave Diamond their second sister—another splendid creature, but this one more similar to him than different.

Even at its worst, the immortal Creation was inventive. What might happen was inevitable, and every event and circumstance and loving face would find ways to repeat itself. That great odd thought meant that if nothing ever ended, and Diamond realized that if the world could live on and on, with him or without him, then every good soul would come around again.

Woven through his misery: beauty.

Sitting inside the little cabin, he asked the walls and Good, "Where did that thought come from?"

No voice had spoken to him from outside. Plainly, this notion grew out of some secret piece of his mind.

But the beauty proved unreliable. *Bountiful* was about to crash, and

Diamond was begging with the Creators for everyone's survival, and that's when the papio man ran into the machine shop. He was the man with the knives. The padded box was under his arm. Suddenly the world was nothing but stark and sick and horrible. Old pains returned. Scalding embarrassment stole his breath. What had been cut away from him was aching again, and the boy instantly dropped his gaze, closing his eyes and making new wishes. Then the box was thrown overboard, and the man who cut him had vanished. Diamond presumed that he fell or jumped when *Bountiful* began to shake. That made it seem as if one wish had been answered, which gave those next moments a rich sense of magic . . . and what was magic if not the finest beauty . . . ?

As the airship crashed, Diamond focused hard on a single thought: everybody who died now would ultimately emerge again from the trees and sunlight, from the rain that washed every dawn and the ashes of the dead mixed into that rain.

That seemed a pretty, perfect thought.

And after the crash, it was possible to believe that everybody survived because of Diamond's thinking. He must have cast some spell, yes. Clambering barefoot out onto the dusty coral, the boy felt miraculous. All of his people were alive. They emerged from the wreckage hurt but whole, and Good was equally blessed. Diamond didn't think about the human crew or papio soldiers that he hadn't saved. He was a gruesomely tired boy who didn't have time or the urge to imagine the suffering of unseen faces. The bare soles of his feet were bleeding against the rough coral, growing hot while healing. Then Elata and Seldom began talking about the papio man, about the half-invisible shape that had yanked him upwards. Quest had to be responsible—they said it and Diamond believed it—and all at once he was running, sprinting on toes already healing as thick leathery callus.

Nothing was as important as this dash through smoke and across the wasteland; Diamond had to find his sister in the fiery ruins.

With its belly sheared free, *Bountiful*'s gas bags and bridge had jumped higher into the air, avoiding a long stretch of the rising ridge. The crash site wasn't as close as it appeared. Diamond's first surge took him into a wall of smoke that suddenly lifted, revealing coral boulders stacked haphazardly, lifting toward a faraway tangle of corona parts and fire. An irregular *pop-pop-pop* warned that ammunition was detonating. The smoke left behind the good odor of burnt wood and the sick flavor of cooked flesh. Diamond hesitated, eyes hunting for the quickest route. Then came more *pop-pops* from behind and overhead, and he stopped to turn and look, discovering whiffbirds descending, and beyond them, a pair of swift fletches flying the bloodwood banners of the District of Districts.

He managed one deep breath.

Then some little motion drew his gaze. He saw his father. Father was coming, struggling along the sharp uneven blade of this awful ridge, looking miserable, and Diamond had never felt more love. Father's eyes were looking down. Every stride had to be measured before it was taken. The sore knee had to endure one step and then brace for the next step, and the next. The man barely glanced up, and he never looked at Diamond, and then one bad step caused him to wobble, wobble and then catch himself before he tumbled, instantly lost to view.

Diamond ran back down the slope, calling to his father.

Overhead, one of the fletches fired a big cannon, and the most distant whiffbird exploded, haphazard pieces falling past the reef's last lip.

The boy paused on a knoll of sparkling blue coral, and one last time, he screamed, "Father."

Then he didn't as much run as he leapt, one knoll to the next, bouncing down the ridge and down the far bank, reaching a place where he finally saw the man alive and well enough to sit upright. And that was the last moment for a very long time when Diamond could find anything inside him that felt remotely like happiness.

• • •

The allegiance of outsiders let Divers win over the Seven, and that great success left her free to entertain the seductive, nearly respectable notion that dominion didn't have borders, that control didn't have to end with her skin.

No soul would be as close to her as the Seven. Yet there were different ways to belong and endless avenues when it came to possession. Divers had allies among the papio, and she was shrewd enough or lucky enough to choose the right champions. For several hundred days, she asked for favors that were just large enough or wrong enough to test their resolve. None mentioned her little crimes to the higher powers. Researchers and the military didn't seem to watch her anymore carefully than before. Then one day—a decidedly ordinary day—she casually asked a few trusted soldiers and former caretakers if there might be an easy way, a clean way, to get rid of the Diamond boy.

More than she had hoped, her suggestion was embraced. Plans were drawn up and thrown into fire pits when they proved unworkable. Then new plans were invented and measured, and discarded, but this time with insights and a fresh sense of what was a little bit possible and what might be achieved with the Fates' help.

One morning, a highly placed papio—a stranger until that moment—approached Divers with a battle plan in hand. That was the moment when she realized that for some papio and quite a few tree-walkers, Diamond was the greatest enemy imaginable. And that was probably the last moment when a phrase from her and one hard stare could have ended the plot.

But the proposed target was a single tree, and destroying Marduk seemed proportioned, even reasonable.

Divers gave her approval, and none of the Seven attempted to stop her.

Twenty days before the attack, during a final meeting of conspirators, one grinning lieutenant revealed that with so much fuel and manpower on hand, a far wider attack had been mandated. "In case the little boy wanders or escapes every trap," was the excuse offered.

Divers couldn't disagree with the logic.

Tritian couldn't agree. He said nothing, but even his silence felt disapproving. Yet Divers was secure enough to invite her brother's opinion: one last chance to offer up whatever words that he wished.

Tritian responded with the obvious logic. "If this happens, and if everything afterward happens as you hope, then the humans and the world only lose everything that they might have gotten from that one boy."

No offspring, in other words. Which assumed of course that Diamond could father children . . . but waiting to find out meant waiting too long. If Diamond vanished, both human species would remain frail and mortal, which was exactly what Divers intended.

The Eight knew this: They had lived forever inside the old corona, implying they were in some fashion immortal. Immortal beings could afford patience. The forest and every soft mind around them would soon forget the carnage. The Eight would remember, and the other two siblings too, assuming they continued wandering the world for thousands and millions of days. And of course Diamond wouldn't actually be dead. That was a point worth making, worth repeating. The boy would survive fire and stomach acids. And a better day was coming, a perfect day when the world that Divers had created could dredge up an old corona, embracing that human child all over again.

That's where she put her thoughts. Every day until the trees fell, Divers reminded herself that the suffering would pass. Revenge was just a different kind of storm. Regrets mattered, but lumped together, the voices inside her—the Seven's voices and her own—were the world's smallest noise.

The attack was delivered on schedule, and the only important failure in that fine bold overgrown scheme was that against long odds, Diamond survived for another two days.

But that was best, in the end. The boy was a critical chore best done by Divers and Divers alone.

She ran through the night to meet *Bountiful*, but it fell short of her and she had to sprint to the crash site, finding Merit first. The slayer was sitting up and talking. And Divers killed him swiftly, without pain, and then she wiped the one hand clean on her trousers, thinking only about Diamond.

Because some moments have to be perfect, she misheard a nearby thudding, looking at the echo, not the cannon.

The boy was as obvious and tiny as she had imagined. He was perched high on the eroded crest of sourlip, big eyes bright from an endless flow of tears. Shame struck, but the sensation was brief and weak. Disapproving words danced about her. But there was no need to defend her actions, not to herself or any suffering witnesses. The adoptive father would have been a stumbling stone. There was no doubt in that matter. As every papio understood, dangerous stones should be kicked off the path, and nothing too wrong had been done. Yet Divers found herself wasting a few breaths arguing with the whispers coming from each of the Seven.

"Merit was disruptive," she said with her mind.

She warned, "He would have fought us now, and he would have led the assault to recover his son tomorrow and the day after."

Then aloud, she said, "Time makes sense of every mess."

And she paused at that point, waiting for Tritian's response, or anyone's. But the only voice came from a weak sister and her steadiest ally.

"You're talking," said the girl. "But you're not talking to us."

Divers laughed.

"None of us spoke," the sister insisted.

She laughed out loud, mocking the liars.

Meanwhile the boy hadn't moved, which was hard to believe. Diamond was staring at the Eight. Fresh smoke was standing tall behind him. He should have run into the smoke while he had the chance. Divers had foolishly given him enough time to flee, or better than that, hide. If that little body wormed its way deep inside a crevice, it could keep out of her reach for a little while. But no, he was standing on the same knoll, too stunned or sad to think, much less act on the simplest instinct.

At last, Divers began climbing to the ridge's crest. The reef beneath her was as narrow and keen as an old medical scalpel, and she couldn't run fast. The boy watched her coming, and then he yelled, one hand high over his head and waving, as if that motion helped fling his word into the high bright morning air.

"Here," he shouted. And again, "Here."

Divers glanced over her shoulder. Two fletches were closing on the boy, but they were still too distant to matter.

She sprinted on feet and hands.

Then the hard chugging rattle of rotors took away every other sound, and three whiffbirds came from behind, sweeping low over her, two of the craft pivoting before settling on the ridge in front of Divers, stubbornly barring her way.

The unit banners told her everything. These were birds from a distant base, and none of these soldiers could be trusted.

Divers stopped for an instant, pretending obedience.

To the Seven, she said, "Suggestions."

No one responded.

Then she broke into a hard sprint, bounding down the slope to evade the big machines. Armed warriors jumped free, shouting commands at each other and at her. She was past the first whiffbird when the second machine launched again. A loudspeaker punched through the roar, the woman pilot shouting to her, saying, "Back away and let us take the prize. The prize. The prize."

Divers paused, listening for the other Seven, listening carefully, but she heard nothing. Not disapproval, not agreement. Not rage or fear or even an empty gray sound inviting her to do what she wished.

What she wished.

The world's largest hands grabbed and yanked, a lump of coral wrenched free of the weathered reef. Her aim felt wrong, and as soon as the projectile left the hand, she began hunting for more ammunition. But the pilot never imagined being attacked by something as stark as one tossed stone. She couldn't guess Divers' power and flew straight until the canopy shattered and the airship dove, striking nose-first, rotors shattering and scattering before the wreckage came to rest on the broken, worn-out ground.

Divers picked up one of the rotor blades—a long piece of corona bone, white in the body and whiter along the sharpest edge—and ran on. The third whiffbird had settled just under the knoll, on a tiny patch of half-flat ground. Diamond was surrounded by papio soldiers. He didn't run from them either. Then a big loudspeaker blared, a tree-walker yelling from the nearest fletch, the worst possible rendering of papio saying, "Ours, ours, ours."

Divers arrived at the base of the knoll.

Two soldiers lifted their rifles, and she chopped them with the blade.

An officer fired into her body, and she knocked him down with her sword's blunt face, yanking the gun away before lifting his body—a proud papio warrior held kicking in one hand.

The Seven said nothing.

The officer rose and spun once in the air before landing in the whiffbird's whirring rotors, and the reef was splattered with pieces and mist.

Panicked, the remaining soldiers scattered.

But Diamond remained where he had always been, rocking side to side and then not rocking, setting his feet apart and his hands at his side.

"What are you doing?" Divers called out.

"Standing like soldier," said the weeping boy.

"You should have run," she said.

"You should run," he said.

"Your people aren't close enough to help," Divers said.

The boy wiped his eyes with his fingers, the right eye and then the left, and that hand dropped to his side again.

Divers started to climb the steep slope.

And then at last, finally, one of the Seven spoke. Quietly, firmly, that loyal little sister asked, "Are we certain that Diamond is alone?"

• • •

Feet stood their ground, and it became their ground. No other place was worth so much courage and strength, passion and the unalloyed need to make the world understand its value. This one space was precious, and he said so with his entire body, including the hand clinging to the polished brass tube.

Father's officers had temporarily become Prima's officers. One officer was watching *Bountiful*'s long fall and its fiery crash. King studied the human working the controls, moving dials that engaged tiny motors that moved a telescope lashed to the *Ruler*'s skin, changing directions and focus and the magnification. Several large telescopes were feeding light into the *Ruler*'s bridge. Each had its officer watching a distant critical part of the world. Then once King understood the mechanisms, he made the officer move aside. King didn't lift the man, and he certainly didn't strike the uniform or the face. But the human discovered that he had lost his space, and several soldiers saw the incident and came forwards, discussing how to force King aside.

But wisdom won, and that tiny army retreated without a fight.

Peering into the telescope, King watched Diamond run away from one piece of wreckage, heading straight for the fire above.

The *Ruler*'s bridge was filled with bodies and voices. Every human was scared, sounding more foolish than usual. King listened to voices that mattered, keeping tabs on the battle's progress. If war was a circle drawn on the floor, then the world was standing on the ring's edge, toes touching the paint. Important generals were making plans for full-scale battles. Prima as well as Father shouted orders, trying to keep the fighting at a lesser, less combustive stage. Once and then again, King lifted his face to glance out the big windows. Half of the world's weapons had been jammed into the same sliver of air. Guns fired but never steadily, and most remained silent. Flares and signal lights and individual men waving bright flags added to the chaos. Both species were screaming for something called *Order*, for respect of the rightful leaders, for hesitation instead of haste, and all the while everyone was aiming for neat resolutions that were never possible to begin with.

Prima was a little more in charge than anyone else.

Again and again, she ordered her fleet to move together and claim the wreckage, rescuing survivors and recovering bodies. But the papio were closer to the *Bountiful*, more abundant and very short-tempered. The telescope operator beside King named units and counted bodies, telling an assistant where to place each enemy soldier on a big map of the reef. She was scared enough to make mistakes, and nobody heard much of what she said. Then Prima asked about Diamond, and the operator confessed that she couldn't see the boy, that he had vanished inside the heavy smoke.

King gave a huge wet roar, telling the entire bridge, "I see him fine."

"You can't," his colleague said.

"I see where the smoke curls around him," he replied, laughing in his best human fashion.

Every one of King's ears listened to the bridge, and he had memorized where everyone stood. Father was protecting ground a little bit ahead of Prima. But that didn't fool anyone. Everyone was talking and every voice was scared, but when the tiny woman spoke, the entire bridge grew a little bit quieter, and if she talked about strength or perseverance, the mood calmed for the next few moments.

A young lieutenant acted like Prima's shadow.

Sondaw was handling papers. King heard the papers moving, and then Prima asked for a summary, and her shadow read that the base at High Coral Merry was signaling only one message. Nobody wanted war, the papio said, but there was a rescue mission of grave importance underway and to please let their brave people do their important work.

Some generals scoffed, but Prima demanded opinions.

A colonel named Meeker came forward, pointing out that nobody was positioned for a fight. Formations were scattered, and other formations were crammed far too close together. If true war broke out, both fleets would have allowed themselves to begin in awful circumstances.

"Like a mist of fuel in the air," he said.

"One spark," Prima said, understanding the image. Then in a louder voice, she told her fleet, "We aren't the spark today, people."

King began to like this brave, fierce female human.

Then the officer beside him said, "There he is. I see the target again."

Diamond was running back the way that he came before, emerging from the smoke and swirling ashes.

Breezes bent the smoke, causing it to gracefully follow after the boy.

Every day before this day, imagining war, King dressed armies in majestic colors and marched them forwards with great purpose. In his mind, the papio and humans were two combatants standing beside contested ground, and they would trade blows and insults and bleed each other before inflicting even worse wounds, and one species would win and the other would retreat, and there was order to what he envisioned, and the imagined drama sometimes left him joyful.

But now, experiencing the thinnest example of real war, he found nothing honorable or orderly. This was mayhem. This was waste on a fabulous scale. Real war was more like a storm than any fair contest between warriors. Storms rose to sweep through the world, and they had no souls, and they were idiots—mindless, changeless impulses to be endured, or they would crush everything in their path. War was very different from one brave soul standing on his important floor, guarding the lens and his telescope for no reason except that this was the most interesting place to stand.

"What am I seeing?" the operator asked.

"A female papio," said a third operator. "But no, she's huge . . . isn't she . . . ?"

King's telescope was the last to see the apparition running over the barren, uptilted coral. But he noticed Merit before the others, and he had enough time to bring the focus to the old slayer as he fell and then recovered. A crisp shout of directions pulled the other telescopes to the scene, and every little telescope and pair of binoculars were raised, people claiming to see nothing or everything.

Father and their leader moved to the pilot's window.

"What is that?" asked Prima.

The giant papio had stopped beside the old slayer.

"List," she said. "What is that thing?"

The officer beside King said, "Oh. She's trying to help Merit."

Then the slayer was dead, and after the shared hollering, shock fell into anger and the bridge turned quiet enough that only one voice was audible.

Prima said, "You know. I think you do know. Is that the papio's child?"

Father said, "Yes."

"Tell me about it," said Prima.

Everyone wanted to hear the answer. King wanted to hear. For all of his insights and honest chatter, List had never mentioned this creature, at least not in earshot of his son.

"It's physically huge," Father said.

"Gigantic," Prima said.

"Female in appearance."

"What else?"

"The creature's inhabited by different minds, different personalities."

"What does that mean?" Prima asked

"She's stranger than ours," said Father. "Your child, and mine."

King kept the one eye fixed on the papio, watching it climb farther up the ridge. Diamond was standing on higher ground, and the whiffbirds descended, and the giant easily dropped one of war machines.

King stepped back from the lens.

What was apparent needed to be words, and he spoke them. To his father, he asked, "Could the attack from two days ago . . . could that belong to this creature?"

"I don't know."

"Well, Father, what do you *guess*?"

List didn't like the subject, the tone. Something caused him to straighten his back, and King knew that more secrets were being hidden from him.

Five leaps and then King lifted his father overhead, pressing him near the ceiling. Just short of screaming, he asked the squirming man, "What else do you know?"

"Nothing," Father insisted. "We have an agent, he'll report again soon."

Then the indignity was too much. With a stiff voice, the Archon of Archons said, "You will put me down."

King dropped him and then caught him just before he struck the floor.

More leaps and he was standing back at the telescope, watching his tiny brother do nothing while that bizarre sibling climbed closer.

Diamond was facing his father's killer.

And that was the moment when Prima pulled her shadow across the bridge, finding an empty piece of floor where she could talk and the lieutenant could listen. Everyone else was watching the scene below play out. King watched, and he breathed in great gulps, trying to make sense of what glass and his eyes showed him.

But all that while, he listened with every ear.

Prima said, "If we discover that this is . . . "

"Yes, madam," Sondaw said.

"The criminal."

"Yes."

"We need options," she said.

"Of course, madam."

"I need someone outside the normal lines of command."

The lieutenant breathed, saying nothing.

"You. I need you. But only if you're ready to carry out my orders."

"Madam, of course," said Sondaw.

And after a moment's reflection, with the slowest, most careful voice in the room, the young man asked, "What do you want my hands to do?"

• • •

The smoke and black ash stood tall, ignoring the wind and the wash of propellers. Twisting currents made the smoke swirl, and from deep inside came a rumbling, low and purposeful and almost too soft to notice. The boy stood on the dead coral. Divers charged up the rugged raw slope, and the soldiers tried to block her route. The papio didn't want Diamond injured. *Bountiful*'s gutted belly was scattered across the landscape below, flames dying, survivors moving slowly. Save for a few fingers of stubborn reef, there was nothing beyond the wreckage but air. The morning was staggeringly brilliant. Graceful airships flew under the shaggy green and happy wilderness, and most of the forest was nothing but healthy. Slice away the violence and pain, the stark emotions and dangerous trajectories, and what remained was a lovely picture that a mind could swallow and then cherish for the rest of its days.

Divers threw a massive lump of coral, and one whiffbird dropped and died.

The smoke swirled within itself, and it shrank, growing denser, the rumbling turning into a familiar voice.

"I'm here," said Quest.

Diamond glanced over his shoulder.

There was no smoke behind him. Particles of coral dust and ash were suspended on a framework of narrow airborne fibers. Quest had eaten bodies and consumed a fat portion of the ship's stores, and while the fire raged, she discovered that heated corona skins had an appealing flavor, bits of them incorporated into her huge new body. She was vast, she had never larger, and she was still trying to gauge what she could make from these far flung ingredients, and how quickly she could work, and which shape would do the most good.

Divers chopped up two papio with a makeshift sword.

"I'll help you," Quest said.

Diamond shifted his weight, saying nothing.

Divers threw a third soldier into the rotor, and she sprinted toward their brother, one hand grabbing at the rising coral while the other brandished that bloodied piece of sharpened bone.

"What are you doing?" their enemy asked.

"Standing like soldier," said Diamond.

"You should have run," she said.

"You should run," Diamond said.

"Your people aren't close enough to help," Divers said.

The boy wiped his eyes and dropped his hand again. Divers paused, coming no closer while her eyes lost their focus. Then as their sister reached up with her empty hand, climbing again, Quest yanked every last thread to her center. She gave herself the shape and effortless grace of a jazzing—a black predator with black eyes and a forest of long milky teeth. Except she was far larger than the living jazzings, and louder, and for as long as she screamed, there was no louder voice in the Creation.

Half a day of careful labor and she could produce a beautiful body, larger than Divers and far more powerful.

But she had only moments to work, nothing but rough ingredients to weave into some kind of order.

Divers climbed close enough to swing the broken rotor.

She aimed for Diamond's narrow neck.

Quest shoved the boy down and absorbed the blow, the sharp edge burrowing into a damp matrix of muck and extra water.

She felt nothing but the nagging pressure.

Divers retrieved her sword with a hard yank, and Quest leaped at her, nothing on those feet but the illusion of claws. She used her mass, and she used surprise, the impact driving their sister off her feet and the rotor from her hand as they tumbled across the jagged ground.

Red blood mixed with sooty water. Divers was extraordinarily strong—far beyond what a mortal jazzing could match. But she struck nothing of importance, and she bit what didn't matter, and then both of them lay sprawled together in a broad bowl where clay lay beneath trapped rainwater. Divers squirmed until she was on top, one hand holding down what looked like a face while the other hand struck and struck and struck all of the body, searching for any weak point.

A cannon on the nearest fletch fired, the shell impacting beside them.

But before the debris stopped falling, whiffbirds and wings began pummeling that fletch, corona scales scattering like shiny leaves while one of its engines dragged smoke in its wake..

Short of breath, Divers quit striking her enemy.

An idea offered itself, and from a human-style mouth deep inside, Quest shouted to her brother, "Run now. Fast as you can."

But Diamond had already vanished.

Divers invested a moment laughing at this unexpected puzzle.

"You're the ghost," she said.

"My name is," Quest said.

Divers dipped her head, genuinely intrigued. "Yes?"

And Quest turned back into smoke again. She was huge and dense, and then an instant later she was everywhere and vaporous. The world went black, and Divers was swallowed up by the amorphous twisting flesh. Shock became panic. Divers breathed in reflex, ingesting fibers and charred twists of corona skin, and then her lungs rebelled, a string of brutal coughs striking her like body blows.

And once again, Quest shrank.

Her plan, the inspiration, was to shrivel and compress, smothering her enemy in a dense black blanket. Without breath, Divers would collapse, and by then there would be more soldiers crawling about, probably from both species, and Quest could slip away in the midst of that chaos.

She was proud of her plan, even after it failed.

Compressing and smothering was work, and it took too much time. Divers swung into the pressure and kicked hard and reached out, using memory in place of eyes . . . and getting hold of the rotor, she pivoted and lashed out once more, hard and then harder.

The smoky body began to tear and collapse.

The giant papio body stepped out, filthy red with her own blood, and she swung at a likely point in the blackness, doing nothing. But then she pulled the rotor free, slicing at another angle, and Quest lost track of her half-born body.

Like black sap, she flowed into the bowl with the rainwater.

Divers stood on the shoreline of this living pond, and where she saw movement, she swung hard, each blow making Quest miserable and weaker and more scared.

Nothing in the world was bigger than her fear.

And that was when what was essential inside her climbed free from what was dying, and while Divers hacked and chopped at the black goo, the tiniest shred of her soul raced away on invisible feet.

• • •

One scared soldier had dropped his big rifle before fleeing.

Diamond was standing in the little gully when he lifted the weapon with both arms and a knee. He couldn't outrun Divers, and that's why he needed to fight. But the rifle was heavy, and it was covered with buttons with important, secret jobs. As an experiment, the boy tugged on the trigger, and nothing happened. So he pushed buttons and tried again, startled when a single round emerged with a sharp crack, and a bullet longer than his longest finger dug its way deep inside the old dead coral.

Soon Divers came hunting for the source of the gunfire.

With a deep breath and some luck, Diamond lifted the gun's barrel and fired eight quick shots, three rounds piercing his sister's chest.

She watched him.

The gun was too heavy, and it fell back to where it was happiest, left behind and useless.

Divers lifted her sword, and she stepped closer.

She was wounded, but the flesh was already healing.

"They're coming," said Diamond, and he pointed upward.

"Not fast enough," Divers said.

One cannon blast had started a full-scale battle. The fletch was limping away while more fletches arrived. Two whiffbirds collided with each other, and a swift wing was struck by someone's gunfire, screaming its way past the reef's edge, twisting down toward the demon floor and whatever lay beyond.

"Where's Quest?" Diamond asked.

"Is that the ghost's name?"

The boy nodded.

"I killed her," said Divers.

"You killed everyone on Marduk too," said Diamond.

"Hardly," Divers said. "I said a few words, wishing for your death, and the rest of it happened on its inevitable own."

She raised the sword higher, aiming with care.

"What are you going to do?" Diamond asked.

"Remove that brain from those little shoulders."

He stepped back, in reflex.

She stepped closer, laughing at the gesture, or maybe something else. "And then," she said. "Do you know what I'll do, brother? I'll throw that head of yours. Believe me, from this ground, I can toss you into a place where nobody will ever find you again."

Diamond was ready to drop.

And Divers swung the sword once, aiming high on purpose. There was no time to react, and the blade was past and back over her head before Diamond could think about moving.

He was doomed.

In that doomed head, he made wild little plans for his revenge.

Divers edged closer.

"Stop," the boy begged.

"When I'm finished," she said.

Then came a noise at once familiar and strange. The woosh began somewhere close, followed instantly by a solid thunk, wet meat absorbing some terrific momentum.

Divers and Diamond were equally startled.

For no apparent reason, the giant had fallen on her side.

Diamond saw the wound filling with urgent blood and the torn tissues fighting to reassemble themselves, and that long papio face was filled with doubt and a growing horror. Divers was still holding the makeshift sword. She used one end of the blade to dig into her body, widening the hole before it healed and closed.

Diamond backed away, but not far.

Divers began to weep, and she dropped the sword, ripping at the wound with both hands, making a gap wide enough to insert four fingers and then the thumb, and that was the moment when the metronome stopped counting. That was when the harpoon's explosive charge turned to gas and a white flash of light that left Diamond on his back.

He blinked.

Sore everywhere, he sat up.

Above him, the airships were firing salvos of three white flares at a time—the universal appeal for a truce.

From someplace close, Master Nissin called out Diamond's name.

And then a figure came out from the rain of coral grit and airborne blood.

A huge and fearless and infinitely capable soul strolled into sight. The launcher pulled from *Bountiful* was cradled in his arms, and the hair was burnt but the blistered face was grinning, and with a rough and very pleased voice, Karlan said, "Shit."

Staring at the shredded body, he said, "Now that's what I call a monster."

THIRTEEN

The Creation kept unleashing new tricks and ugly twists to make the next moments impossible. Alarms were sounding. Officers shouted conflicting orders, and civilians shouted for no reason but rank terror. A passing wing threw a burst of cannon fire at the *Ruler of Storms*, and against orders, three of the *Ruler*'s batteries returned fire. But those were little matters. On the reef, Diamond was being attacked by the Eight when the smoke floating behind him suddenly congealed into a second marvel. Every face with rank was pressed against the pilot's window. Prima propped her elbows on the glass, binoculars pressed against her exhausted eyes. The window glass was armored. The armored walls and floor would shatter before the window. But she felt utterly exposed, and her hands shook, and what she saw in the binoculars made her shake even more.

Ten times at least, she had demanded a general truce.

Every truce lasted for a breath or two, then fell away into mayhem.

And now a fresh papio squadron had appeared. A dozen Hawkspurs came from a distant base—narrow gray slips of metal and fire pushing at maximum velocity—and every onboard alarm found fresh urgency. The *Ruler* was the destination, the sole target. Slashing past the rest of the fleet, the wings ignored gunfire and every livid insult, reaching that perfect point in space where their munitions were released. But there were no cannons, no rockets. The enemy carried nothing but the brilliant white flares that tumbled away in threes—someone in the papio high-command just as desperate for peace as Prima was.

For the eleventh time, she demanded a fleet-wide truce.

And in that mayhem, an aide came forward with a file brought from the *Panoply Night*. The official document had been plucked from a tall pile of forms and scribbles and officious stamps. Ignoring the papers, Prima looked at the aide. This wasn't Sondaw, but Sondaw made it into her thoughts, and she wondered about his progress.

She didn't have to ask. A moment later, emerging from the turmoil, one of List's generals strode up to the little woman, explaining how furious he was about the latest miscarriage of authority.

"Your lieutenant is taking over our battleworks," he said.

"Yes," she said. "I know."

"A lieutenant and other soldiers . . . all yours . . . claim they have full authority to act as they want with our best weapons . . . "

"Not as they want," she said. "They'll follow my orders, no one else's."

The officer stood tall inside his glossy fine uniform.

And Prima said, "Listen."

Now at least four of the *Ruler*'s batteries were shooting at the enemy, the floor shivering with each sturdy blast.

"Are those gunners following your orders?" she asked.

The general couldn't look more imposing.

"I know what's inside the battleworks," she said. "The biggest, harshest weapons in existence, I know. But honestly, do you want to leave that power and so much misery in the hands of eager recruits?"

The general started to answer.

"There's no doubt," she interrupted. "Your flock of warriors needs a lot more training and a lot less fur on their legs, if you know what I mean."

"I resent that," he said.

"As you should," she said, once more gazing through the binoculars. The reef was closer and less visible. Real smoke mixed with vapors that might be something else, and there were countless long trails of white smoke too. And in the midst of it all was Diamond—a child standing between two very tall men, one of them cradling what looked like a harpoon gun.

She let the binoculars drop, landing hard on the floor.

"I trust my lieutenant," she told the general.

The general blinked and said nothing.

"Show me where I can speak to him, with a secure line. Then you can continue doing what matters."

"Which is what, madam?"

"Building this truce," she said. "And then maintaining the peace until everybody gives up this idiot dance."

List appeared. Or maybe he was never far from Prima. Either way, his voice was formal and loud.

"The Corona's Archon has the authority," he grudgingly told the general. "Give my colleague whatever she believes she needs."

A critical bank of controls stood in the middle of the bridge. A call-line to the front battleworks was opened, and Prima was handed the microphone and a headset so new that it was still wrapped in white paper.

"Sondaw," she said.

"Yes, madam."

The lieutenant's voice was clearer than any other in the room. And because the best lies wore smiles, she smiled.

"You know your duty," she said.

"Yes, madam."

"And that is?"

"Acquire the target, and hold the aim," she had told him earlier.

But wary of other ears, he lied now, quietly saying, "We'll keep the reef-hammers sheathed and safe."

"Very good," she said.

A young soldier was sitting at the adjacent controls. Her duty was to control the rear battleworks, but she was also eavesdropping on the conversation. Prima pretended not to notice. Smiling warmly, sister to sister, she said, "So that I know. Which button can I never push?"

The woman glanced at her general and then List. Then with all the scorn she could muster, she said, "The big red knob. But it doesn't matter if nothing's armed."

Playing the fool, Prima asked, "Is the knob a signal?"

"No, no. It's a straight wire to the weapons. Except in emergencies, firing mechanisms remain here, with our fleet commander in charge."

Prima began to examine the complicated panel with its one exceptionally red knob. Then she remembered that something else needed her immediate attention. What was it? She had honestly forgotten. King was still standing at the telescope. The armored boy was avoiding both Archons. She looked at List, and seeing confusion, he called out for the latest intelligence. Spectacular news was easy to find. The fighting had ebbed significantly. Truce flares were being launched by both fleets and from the reef too. Even the stubborn onboard batteries had stopped firing, and the fletches were finally in position to rescue *Bountiful*'s survivors.

"And where is the Eight?" she asked.

List asked King, but he didn't react. List's son said nothing and stood motionless as a statue, and then the officer beside him reported that nothing had come out of the narrow gully where she last saw Merit's killer. But several whiffbirds had landed nearby, and that miserable ground was teeming with papio.

She repeated that news to the microphone, to Sondaw.

"What about the Ghost?" List asked.

Everyone had one opinion, and the opinions were either that the creature was dead or it had fled.

Prima listened to the speculations, and turning, she noticed a civilian man standing nearby, not especially eager to be noticed. She set down the headset and walked to him without hurrying, smiling out of habit, and with a careful soft voice, she asked one of his ears, "What is it?"

The most important paper was on top.

But as he began to hand over the evidence, she said, "No. Just tell me."

Nobody seemed to be watching them. Everybody had important work or at least urgent worries, and every voice seemed busy, and she didn't want to test her eyes or nerves by trying to parse the handwriting of some blood-spattered torturer.

"We do have one prisoner on the *Night*," said the aide. "He might know something of value."

"Who and what?"

"It's a forester," the aide said. "And also a smuggler with long ties to the papio. Ten days before the attack, he met with a papio officer in an abandoned wilderness camp. He says they shared drinks, and the papio let himself get drunk. That's when our smuggler heard something about a creature called the Eight. The Eight had goals and a brilliant plan. The Eight was going to rid the Creation of that hated boy, and a lot of other bad souls would die too."

"The Eight," she repeated.

"Or a woman named Divers. Our prisoner's story keeps changing."

"Why wasn't I told this before?"

"Because our people assumed that the prisoner was drunker than the papio, and nobody trusted the testimony."

"The Eight did all of this," she said. "The Eight and Divers are the enemy."

"According to one alcoholic witness, maybe."

Except List had told her about the Eight, and she knew what was true. Nodding, Prima straightened her shirt and her smile before returning to the control panel. Then she stared at the red knob, imagining Sondaw and the other soldiers sitting inside the battleworks, acquiring targets as best as they could with machines that they had never handled before.

Prima had asked too much of the man.

To prove her humanity, she let herself feel a moment of sorrow.

Then came the hatred, fixated and relentless and pure. The trees were falling around her again. Thousands were dying, and the guilty remained free. Prima looked at the knob and made her fingers resist. No. The boy had to be rescued, and the other survivors had to be safe onboard, and then maybe another little while should pass just to earn some distance, a chance for perspective. But the Eight were inside that smoke and she couldn't stop believing that this was a remarkable moment:

Nothing would ever make the last days worthwhile.

But if she wished, one good woman could wring a measure of justice out of this madness . . .

• • •

The children sat with him. Some obligation was being fulfilled, or maybe they didn't have anything else to do. Diamond was neither happy nor sad about the company. He rarely looked at them, even when they asked harmless questions or offered a hopeful phrase or two. Sometimes he reacted to what they said. Occasionally his words were appropriate. But when he did look at their faces, it was as if for the first time. Names had to be summoned, by force. He had to remind himself that she was Elata and the boy was Seldom, and there was a long shared history between the three of them where nothing much had happened. In reflection, nothing about those lives seemed unpleasant or special. Then the nightmare descended. It descended, and what was leftover was a ragged jumble. Diamond felt sick inside, in places that didn't have names. Again and again, he looked at those faces while feeling deeply, eternally forgetful, and the confusion always ended with revelations that left him wishing that he could become lost all over again. Because whenever Diamond saw his two friends, he again remembered how both of them had just become orphans, and he was an orphan too.

The monkey sat on the coral dust, alone, eyes closed and the bruised body rocking back and forth. Master Nissim was injured, the pain inside his bones twisting his weathered face. Healing had never seemed so unfair. Diamond wished he could leave his skin cut, his ribs and fingers shattered. But he was whole and intact when everyone else was broken, and he caught himself wondering why his blood or the touch of his hands couldn't heal everyone. Wouldn't that be wonderful? It seemed wonderful until another memory was unleashed: Father claiming that the trick had been tried and didn't work . . . and again, without fail, the boy found himself looking about the reef, wondering where his father had gone . . .

He hadn't forgotten that one death, no.

But so many horrors lived inside him, and he didn't want to think about any of them.

Diamond scanned the terrain, and Karlan noticed. The huge boy had made it his job to stand guard over the survivors. Stepping close, Karlan dropped the gun's barrel and offered a broad smile that was just a little short of mocking, and with a man's rough voice, he said, "You don't have to thank me again. Once was enough."

"I didn't thank you," Diamond said.

"For saving your life. No, I guess you didn't." Karlan laughed and pointed the harpoon's tip at the fletches. "Anyway, they're lowering cages. At most, you'll be out of here in three recitations."

A Bloodwood fletch was hovering overhead, cages dangling from its belly. Wings were screaming in the distance but not nearby. Only a few whiffbirds were close, and most of them were resting on the higher slopes, surrounding the gully where Karlan saved Diamond. Meanwhile papio soldiers were walking the coral, talking with hands as much as words, and sometimes picking up pieces of Divers' wet flesh.

"Thank you," said Diamond.

"For which part?"

"Killing her," he said.

"Oh, your sister's not dead," he said, laughing in a slow awful way. "I just made her angrier, if that's possible."

Elata and Seldom always tried to find brave, hopeful words. Not Karlan. Karlan ground the truth until it had a keen edge, and Diamond had never appreciated the boy more than now.

Horns sounded, and human soldiers began dropping out of the fletch, riding the lines down to where they felt safe enough. Then they let go and fell, landing with guns in hand and packs bouncing and a few curses to lift their focus and practiced courage.

An officer looked at everyone before asking Nissim, "Any other survivors?"

"Honestly, I don't know," said the Master.

The officer gave his squad orders to search the wreckage below and then the burnt remains higher up.

Fighting various aches, Nissim stood and waved the officer closer. "There's one body that has to be recovered."

Diamond looked away, but he couldn't stop listening.

"Merit," whispered his teacher. Then louder, he said, "I won't leave until you find him. Understood?"

"Clearly," the officer said. "And I want you to understand something, sir. We have a truce with the papio and it lasts as long as it lasts. If they block us, we back away. Once we get the boy, everything else is negotiable."

The cages began to arrive, rattling on impact.

Two soldiers came at Diamond from the opposite sides, lifting him and carrying him without ceremony.

Diamond said, "Bring the others."

"First you," one man said.

He could have struggled, shouted or begged. But Diamond went limp, feeling as if he was floating over the hard ground. Then he heard a grunt and a familiar voice saying, "No no."

Good landed on his head, clinging tight to the dense filthy hair.

The first cage had room for several people, and most of them were soldiers. The prize stood in the middle, legs and torsos pressing in on all sides. An electric winch yanked the cable, and the reef fell beneath them, and almost too late, Diamond thought to look out between the uniforms, catching a brief glimpse of whiffbirds and papio soldiers carrying pink meat back into a gully covered with tent fabric.

Divers was hidden, and Diamond was glad for that.

Then he was inside the fletch, and two more fletches swept close, ready to loan covering fire, if necessary. Voices called out on loudspeakers, every mouth mangling the enemy's language. The air shivered with commands to stay back and honor the truce and honor the long peace, the status quo and the good lives of unborn children; and rolling inside Diamond was the idea that somebody would have to put every game piece back on the shelves where they belonged.

The other cages were chasing after him.

Diamond wanted to wait. He needed to speak to Master Nissim, though the best words kept slipping out of his grip. And he wanted to be near Karlan too, which was so unexpected. Elata needed to go home, wherever that was, and so did Seldom, and somebody should offer them a few encouraging words. But the soldiers were suddenly carrying him, almost running. They swept him into the hanger, and with no warning or explanation, Diamond was dropped into a little airship. Good climbed into his lap, feeling fit enough to snap at a careless finger. The new ship was tiny like the one that Fret and Father had ridden, but it was much quicker, engines roaring at the beginning and then screaming as he soared up and out into the sunshine.

Good cursed, and the pilot behind them echoed each word.

The *Ruler of the Storm* began large and swiftly became huge, covering half of Creation before they dove inside its enormous, heavily armored hanger.

More soldiers were waiting for the prize, but this time the boy evaded them, breaking into an easy sprint, diving under a pair of arms and reaching the hallway in the lead. Yet suddenly the strength in his legs was gone. His lungs refused to breathe, and his heart was a lazy muscle, and feeling as if he was weeping, he lifted one hand and then the other, wiping at the dry cheeks and dry unfeeling eyes.

Good caught him, barking some general complaints.

The quickest soldier fell in beside him, saying, "The boss wants to see you on the bridge."

"List," said Diamond.

"Not today," the young man said, smiling nervously. "Tomorrow, sure. But today, we've got your girlfriend ordering us around."

For no good reason, he remembered that little girl from school.

Prue was in charge of the world.

But of course his Archon was at the front of the pack. List was behind her, smiling as if his life depended on it, and various generals and aides took the trouble to look the boy over. The brown school uniform was in shreds, his feet bare and distorted by freshly grown callus, but the rest of his flesh and everything beneath the flesh was perfect. Not a scar to be found. Prima got down on one knee, which made her shorter than Diamond, and with concern and pain, she said, "I am so very sorry about your mother and your father. Those good people will always be missed."

Words hit him and flowed away, and he just nodded.

"The Eight," she said.

Diamond blinked. "Who?"

"I know this is hard, and too soon," Prima said. "But that creature down there. The one that murdered your father. Did she have a name?"

"Divers."

"Divers, yes." She glanced at List before looking at the boy again, and very carefully, she asked, "Do you think Divers is responsible?"

The question made no sense.

"She was trying to kill you too, wasn't she?"

"Yes, madam."

"And did she say . . . do you have any sense . . . did Divers have any role in the attack that dropped the trees?"

Diamond wanted to vanish and couldn't. Quest could disappear easily, and that was a fine reason to be jealous of her. "Others did the attack. She told me. But the ideas were hers, and she was in charge. Yes, madam."

"Well," said Prima. "Thank you. I needed to know."

Then she was on her feet, and gone.

List lingered.

"Where's King?" asked Diamond.

The Archon of Archons didn't answer immediately. He had to study the boy, his mouth working itself into a tight rough pucker. And then a new smile arrived, plus the words, "I'll take you to him."

King was using a fancy telescope. Nobody else stood near him. Nobody wanted to be close to him. King had never been taller or more powerful, dressed in shorts and those gorgeous bright scales, spikes jutting from his elbows and that spectacular head. Hearing Diamond approach, he took a step backward. "You can have a good look," he said. Then he gave his brother one long stare before saying, "I saw you and the smoke fighting all of them."

"All of them?"

"The Eight," he said. "It goes by the name Divers, but eight of them are trapped inside that one big body."

That made everything worse. Diamond listened to an explanation that his brother had harvested from various sources, various mouths. He learned how many brains were merged inside one body. The creatures were united, and once he understood that and accepted it, there was no purpose in listening to anything else.

Good dropped to the floor, quickly falling asleep under the telescope's mechanisms, where nobody could step too close.

Diamond wished that he could do the same.

Approaching the telescope, he discovered that the eyepiece was glad to get pulled down, and he looked ahead with that new eye, powerful but very narrow. Human soldiers were carrying bodies wrapped in bright white sacks. The landing party was heading back toward the cages, ready to abandon the reef. Then Diamond twisted his gaze to where the tent had been erected, except the tent was gone and the papio were standing in close ranks. Most of them wore uniforms, but one was larger than the others. One of the papio was wrapped in tent fabric and almost too weak to stand, knots of the complicated pink hair rooted in the rebuilt scalp.

"I see her," Diamond said.

"Let me," his brother said, easing him aside. Then after a moment, he asked, "Was the smoke our other sister?"

"Yes."

"Does she carry a name carry?"

"Quest."

"Well, that's a funny sort of name," said King.

Prima was standing beside the most important window, talking to generals with words and slicing hands.

King didn't look anywhere but through the telescope, yet he seemed aware of everything. With a calm slow voice, the one mouth said, "You know, she has a plan. She plans to kill Divers."

"Who does?"

"Your Archon. As soon as our people are off the reef and safe, she's going to launch the big rockets. Reef-hammers, we call them." Then because he was proud about what he knew, he told his little brother a string of details about hammers and firing mechanisms, each detail earned by being quiet and sly.

This news was important. Diamond felt the impact even if he couldn't piece together all of the meanings.

Then King stepped back. "Look again," he said. "Because I don't think the papio will let us see her any day soon."

Diamond stood very still, looking at nothing.

A smell was hanging on his brother, some pungent quality that meant something, and King moved differently than before. He wasn't trying to be human anymore. Gazing at the half-human face, King told Diamond, "You look tired."

"I am tired."

"And something else. I see something else."

"In my face?"

"And through your body too."

Diamond nodded and said nothing, and he glanced at the middle of the bridge, watching the tall control panels and their red buttons. But when he walked, he walked straight to Prima. A general was talking loudly about ship positions and the timetable to reach home again, and the woman was listening, satisfied if not happy. The Archon looked engaged and nervous, but she didn't jump when a boy's hot hand suddenly grabbed her by the elbow.

"Hello, Diamond," she said.

"Are you going to kill the Eight?" he asked.

There. She jumped, if only slightly. Then she glanced at the general beside her, letting her bottom lip curl against her teeth. Very carefully, she asked Diamond, "What did you say?"

"Are you going to use the rockets?" he asked.

Every general made some noise, and the one full of timetables asked, "What's our boy talking about?"

"Something overheard by his brother," Prima guessed.

Just then, List arrived.

"Will you try to kill her?" Diamond persisted.

"What is this?" List asked.

The generals started to explain the confusion with a confusion of words and gestures.

Prima ignored all of them. She bent just enough to bring their eyes close, and very carefully, almost patiently, she said, "I thought I should. I even hoped to do so. But no, no, it's too careless, too incalculable. Millions of people depend on me, and that's why as soon as we get clear of the reef, I will order Lieutenant Sondaw to disarm the weapons, and then I'll relinquish my command."

Diamond nodded slowly.

"Not soon enough," said one general.

And then List said, "Be gracious, gentlemen. These last days have been awful, but today will be better than most."

Good was still napping on the floor, and King was listening to every conversation while he watched their sister learn to walk on new legs. Diamond started to walk in their direction. He wasn't thinking about anything hard or certain. The adults behind him were happy to feud, and nobody thought about him again. Even when he broke into a casual trot, nobody noticed.

A woman was sitting near the critical panel, but she was talking into her headset, talking to an important voice.

Three more soldiers were between Diamond and the red knob.

Then there were only two soldiers left, and he was past King too.

Someone yelled, "Hey."

The boy moved a little slower.

"You," someone shouted.

And Diamond got up on his bare toes, running harder than he had ever run in his life.

FOURTEEN

Divers found herself awake.

Awake and upright.

Once again and forever, Divers was in charge of everything that mattered, and the rest of the world stood in mute amazement, watching her rapid recovery.

Then the flashes came, each flash brilliant enough to make the coral change its hue, and the light seemed odd and a little lovely. That's what she was thinking. Then one soldier told everybody to get down. It wasn't order or an alarm, it was just a request. But the body's position wouldn't help anybody. The reef was beneath them, ancient and stubborn, secure as any surface in Creation, and then something faster than any wing, faster and quite a bit larger, dug into the coral, burrowing into the slope beneath them, and at some preset depth the finest explosives anywhere turned into noise and wrenching motions that tore the coral and every other body to shreds.

With that first blast, Divers' flesh mimicked stone, holding her parts together.

Then she was falling back to the reef again. She was wondering where she would heal next. But a second rocket impacted and erupted, and still airborne, she was sliced by the flying debris, desperate hands clinging to pieces of her own flesh as she tumbled, as she fell, followed by a third blast that took away her eyes before flinging her remains out over the lip of the reef.

The Eight fell blind, together and never so close.

Out of the panic, Tritian spoke to the others. With a steady quick voice, he said, "We're going somewhere warm."

He said, "None of you can live there like I can live there."

He said, "Decide. I am the First and you are the Seven, or the coronas eat us all over again."

The vote was instantaneous and unanimous.

And the long fall continued while the body hurriedly wove itself into the beginnings of something new.

And in a sad fashion, Divers began to laugh.

"Is this what you wanted?" she asked her brother. "When you were walking me in the dark, in my dreams, Tritian . . . were you trying to step us off the edge of the world . . . ?"

• • •

Both species had played games and polished their best weapons, preparing for a moment rather like today, and here was a long day with plenty of opportunities to employ all of those lessons. Assumptions were tested as well as their own character. None of the details had been imagined beforehand; who would have dreamed up impossible children waging some ancient, deeply personal war? Yet the results were remarkably close to what had been planned. The tree-walker fleet deployed itself in battle formation, overlapping guns delivering withering fire. Every wing that attacked would be lost, so the papio shifted their aim, finding success in every other part of the world. The sickly Hanner tree was dropped with the first wave. By the time the *Ruler of the Storm* returned to the Corona District, the Hole had more than doubled in size, and the surrounding forest was riven with smoky stubborn fires. There was no thought of pausing, much less defending the ruins. Delays were another enemy. The combined fleet continued to push straight ahead, spitting off fletches and bigger ships to protect worthier allies. In every sense of the word, war had begun, and a general selected by List two days ago had become the dictator to every human clinging to the branches.

The boy watched the battles until the sameness and fatigue claimed his will. And then without announcing his attentions, he abandoned his piece of the bridge, walking quickly to the *Ruler*'s main dock.

Every face stared at him.

And reading every face, he saw hatred and fear and the keen paranoid thoughts of creatures that would never look on him with any shred of real trust.

The dock had always been a vast space, a gigantic room busy with small airships and the Archon's private fletch. But those lesser craft had been moved elsewhere, or they were burnt and lost. What had replaced them was a single vessel—the *Panoply Night*. The dock's largest wall had been peeled back to bring that great clumsy, heavily armored balloon onboard, and dozens of cables kept the *Panoply* secure, comfortable. Armed guards stood where they looked menacing, and other guards watched from high perches. Until they reached home, the *Ruler of the Storm* was only the second most important ship in the world.

"Stop," one guard said.

King continued walking. "Call and ask my father," he said. "He'll explain why I'm going up there."

"Your father doesn't have buoyancy anymore," said the next guard.

"Then please shoot me," said King. "Punch my hearts, and let's find out what happens next."

Guns were lowered, and he walked on. But every available call-line was opened, generals hearing news that would ensure a nice fresh panic.

The gangway led up to the public hallways, and King soon arrived at the steel door leading to the prison.

One hard blow with his palm, and the door shook in its frame.

From the other side, a scared man shouted, "I'll open. Let me unlock."

"I'll save you the bother," said King. "Stand back."

One moment of focused, harmless violence made him a little happier.

Every guard vanished after that. Three prisoners were sitting in the first cell. No charges had been named, but until the full conspiracies were dissected, they would be kept here for their own safety. Nissim was standing in the room's center—a sorry man suddenly older than his days. The two children were huddled against the back wall, staring at King without quite focusing on him, each holding the other's hands. Those creatures used to look frail and small. Not anymore. After today, after watching what the Eight and Quest could achieve against one another, King felt the sudden need to huddle with them, awaiting the next awful storm.

The next cell was empty, while the cell after that held the other boy, Karlan.

Like Nissim, he was standing. But he was far from defeated, and despite blisters and burns and probably no sleep, he looked happy enough. At least the smile was more convincing than some, and the humor came with a sharp, unaffected tone.

"Are we winning the war?" he asked.

With both mouths, King laughed, and he pressed on.

Prima and her lieutenant were locked together in the same cell. King's father and the generals weren't sure what blame to strap to each of them. The woman had ordered the reef-hammers armed, and her loyal lieutenant did nothing to stop the disaster. Neither had been interrogated, but Sondaw suffered some cracked bones between his last post and this bleak little space. Then they were thrown together so that careful people could listen to every word, waiting for them to convict each other.

The pair acted as if they hadn't shared one word all day.

But looking at the intruder, Prima sighed deeply.

"Do you know what I would do?" she asked. "If I could step back fourteen hundred days . . . what would I do without any regrets?"

"Throw us back to the coronas."

She nodded, dipping her head.

"And knowing what I know," said King, "do you think I'd crawl out of that stomach? Out into this miserable shit of a world?"

Her lieutenant rose, making ready to defend his lady.

But King pushed on to the end, to the solid door that he didn't break down once before and didn't need to touch this time. The door was unlocked and ajar. The prisoner and his monkey had been told to remain where they were, and both seemed happy to comply, sitting together in the farthest corner. Diamond was wearing a mechanic's jumper, sleeves cut short to suit his arms. The air smelled of toilet wastes. Monkey shit and human shit smelled mostly the same to King. He entered the cell where an old woman once beat up an old man. Boy and monkey stared at the dried blood on the floor. King approached, stopping a long stride short of them, and then he said, "They're afraid that I told you what to do. Starting the war was my idea."

The monkey looked up, one lip lifting to brandish the incisors.

"They don't want to think you could have done this by yourself. You're too polite, too kind. Too dull and plain and normal. I must have coaxed you somehow, and the guilt is half-mine."

"It's not yours," said the boy.

King laughed, asking, "Aren't you going to share with your brother?"

Diamond sighed and closed his eyes. "You're still walking free."

"Do they have a room that can hold me?"

"You're my brother," Diamond said.

King said nothing.

"And you tried to kill me once."

"I won't again."

"No?"

King needed to see the eyes, wanting this chance to measure the soul. That's why he said, "I killed ten men to come down here and tell you something, brother."

The pale eyes lifted.

King tried two smiles. "You're the scariest one among us. But you always suspected that, didn't you?"

• • •

She ate enough not to need food anymore, and she practiced shapes that she had never mastered, measuring her successes in the reflective surfaces sharing the storeroom with her. One shape was critical, and she didn't like the results. But this was the best disguise for the environment, and that's why she put it on and made it as close to perfect as she could before leaving the storeroom behind.

The long, awful day was finally drawing to an end.

Fear had always governed Quest's life, but this was no simple fear, urging her to flee to reliable safe havens. She knew that she couldn't continue living in the wilderness, not with a war screeching past every few moments, and she couldn't feel safe in any outlying District. But riding the *Ruler* back to its home berth wasn't the strategy of a desperate coward. This was one brother's home, and from the scuttlebutt and offhand statements of little officers, she knew that the other brother would soon live among the bloodwoods, biding his days until he was old enough to sire a new race of humans.

She needed to be close to Diamond and to King.

A thousand terrors had pushed her inside a white sack filled with dead parts, brought to the *Ruler* and a storeroom where field rations and bottled water made her halfway strong again. And now she was inside an endless hallway that cut down the middle of the world's largest machine, walking past soldiers, past civilians and mechanics and people whose lives were undecipherable to her. She wore a plain face for good reason. Men didn't look too carefully at her features or her bland fleshy body. Her uniform and the boots were stolen from a closet, and they helped hide most of her new flesh. But every step brought terror, every pause doubt. She smelled wrong, and her bones were wrong, and she didn't have any kind of life story to share with strangers.

Why did she even risk stepping out into plain view?

But then she happened across a crew lounge and its tall windows. As if she saw these scenes every day, she slowly crossed the open floor. The *Ruler* was approaching the first of the great bloodwoods, grand and powerful, dwarfing this assemblage of gas and corona parts, metal and more metal. The window was shaped to afford a fair view forwards, and for the first time in her life, Quest could see the center of the world up close, and her new heart slowed in response, fighting to keep her calm.

Another soldier, a female with a similar rounded build, joined her at the window and said, "Hello."

Voices could be difficult, but human voices weren't the hardest noises to mimic.

"Hello," Quest said.

Then she turned her head, looking back beneath the forest. In the late day sunlight, very little was understood. A couple orange flickers might mark wildfires, or maybe they showed fighting on the ever-shifting front. Questions needed to be asked, but soldiers weren't supposed to exchange information too freely. How could she phrase her curiosity and not end up in a wild chase?

Then the strange woman said, "And now I have seen everything."

She was looking down.

Quest followed the gaze with eyes that only looked human. The last light in the world rose up into her head and her mind, and she didn't understand what she was seeing. What was there was obvious enough, yes. But what were they doing?

With her new mouth, Quest asked, "What do they want?"

"A spectacular question," said her new friend.

Above the demon floor, floating or flying back and forth, were thousands of coronas. There were small coronas and giants and even another one of the dark ancient creatures like the one that had given birth to her.

"They're doing nothing but watching us," the woman said. "That's as simple and true as any explanation I can think of."

Countless necks were twisting, heads lifting, eyes fixed on the forest above.

"They know our hunters aren't flying," the woman said. "They're safe, and a war is underway."

"You're right," said Quest. "To the coronas, this must be a very beautiful evening."

• • •

The room belonged to no one. That point was made by several people, first and last by the Archon. The palace had many unoccupied rooms, but the voices claimed that this was one of the finest rooms, claimed or unclaimed, and there was an implication in those statements—a reason for celebration and importance, or at least some careful pride.

Diamond felt none of that.

After so much, Diamond sensed no emotion as he was shown the room. But the space was enormous. Every wall was distant, and even though the day had been finished for a long while now, the ceiling was filled with lights that hummed and glowed, working as hard as possible to make every bare surface shine.

Good walked to the middle of the room, looking hard for one thing.

"Where's the toilet?" Diamond asked.

List wasn't sure. He had to open three tall doors before he found the proper little room. But the bath was little only compared to this huge bright unclaimed empire of light and walls and curtain-covered windows.

Diamond expected to be left alone at any time.

But the Archon of Archons wasn't leaving. In fact, he was staring hard at the boy, with energy and the strangest joy that the man had ever displayed. On arriving at the palace, several aides had taken List aside. Diamond assumed that there was another meeting about the war or the Eight or an equally massive topic. But since then that odd encounter, the man had been nursing a smile that didn't seem to fit his face.

Diamond looked at the distant bed and the furnishings and the bookshelves that were covered with volumes but still looked only half-filled.

The Archon stepped closer.

From the bathroom came the sound of water running, in the toilet and then in the sink, and again in the toilet.

"I have news," the Archon said.

Diamond wanted him to leave.

"I want to show you something, Diamond."

The monkey emerged from the bathroom soaking wet. In one hand was a bar of perfumed soap, and with great precision, Good heaved the soap at the nearest light, glass shattering, glittering shards raining down.

Not even that violence bothered the smiling man.

Diamond followed List, turning off the lights on the wall switch as he left, telling the monkey, "Make a nest."

Good looked at him.

"Boy," he said.

Diamond stopped. "What?"

"I forget the sack," Good said. "I forget you putting me in the sack."

Diamond nodded.

"I forgive you," the monkey claimed.

Diamond made himself walk. He was heavy and cold and too tired to ever sleep again. The hallway was wider than most rooms, and nobody else was in sight. As they walked, the Archon said something about leaving behind orders, instructions. "On the faint hope of good news," he said.

The boy barely listened.

"A lot of things can't be controlled," said the man. "An Archon during war doesn't have the same powers as in peace, no. But I promise you: I will protect the people that you want me to protect, as much as I can protect them, and I will keep you safe. And in return, I want and deserve your cooperation too. This will be a partnership, an alliance. Do you know what I mean?"

Diamond wanted to be alone in a tiny room.

But List drifted nearer, and then he almost giggled.

"Refugees," he said.

What?

"It was chaos during that first attack," the Archon said. "Nobody was ready. A lot of civilian ships were pressed into rescue work. And then in the madness, people were carried to unexpected places. Some of these refugees were injured. Maybe they weren't able to identify themselves quickly enough. But everybody received medical care, and someone happened to recognize an important face under the bandages."

Diamond glanced at his ally, in profile.

"I left here with the fleet, and I left orders behind," said the Archon. "Without my knowledge, a certain woman was brought here by a special flight, on my personal authorization, to receive the finest care available anywhere. Anywhere."

They were walking, and then Diamond had stopped.

List found himself standing alone. His smile grew and he turned, and he winked, which was a decidedly unnatural gesture for the man. Then he came back to say, "She's resting comfortably inside my small, excellent clinic. I'm afraid that she's sleeping now, what with the sedatives helping her deal with the pains . . . "

The boy bolted down the hallway.

List couldn't match that speed, but he was happy to shout a last few directions.

Despite the warning, Haddi was awake and alert enough to recognize her son, turning her body on the mattress and reaching for him with the hand that wasn't buried inside a cast.

She said his name.

He stopped short of the bed.

She said, "You don't know how good it is, seeing you alive."

Diamond kneeled down. She couldn't reach him, and he couldn't touch her. Then from the floor he spoke with a steady flat voice, not crying, never crying, trying his best to explain just how wicked one boy could be.

BOOK THREE

THE GREAT DAY

PROLOGUE

She calls to her scions.

The children.

Her faded radiance and the divine, diminished music are still capable of saying quite a lot, including, "Let me see nothing but you."

This has always been a dramatic soul, certainly more public and passionate than the other Firsts. But the young ones do love her, or at least they love the idea that any meat and mind can be older than the world. Of course they obey, setting their lives aside the next little while. She waits inside the jungle, inside a bubble of still air. That is where they gather, pressing against one another. Firsts and their eldest children hang nearest the sun, while all others form the bulk of the magnificent sphere. The center belongs to her alone: a creature more female than male, softened by time and scarred by time and smelling of death. Heads are feeble, tooth-poor and half-blind. Flesh is drained, blood gray and bone frail. But she is the First among Firsts, the core from which all have risen. Her soul has always been strong and will remain strong forever, her wise voices filling this small good world with courage and rare wisdom.

The entire species waits for those voices.

She says nothing.

Youngsters and the stubborn begin to whisper among themselves. But those who know better use an irresistible scent to bring silence.

Yet of course silence is never silent, and what seems empty is full of true wisdom. The wise mind contemplates, hunting for the eternal in the wind and the echoes and finally inside the mind itself.

Now, at long last, the old one speaks, whispers and faint flashes of pale, exhausted light washing across her people.

" 'The mouth feasts and the flesh grows,' " she begins.

" 'Each of us is made from common meat,' " they chant, " 'and each of us wears the same body.' "

" 'Our bodies are small,' " she says.

" 'Our essences are great,' " they respond.

" 'No head,' " she begins.

And pauses.

Others complete that good true thought.

" 'No head reaches as far as the tiniest soul,' " they say. " 'When the youngster bursts from the egg, the inevitable, eternal spirit spills out from the body and across the Creation.' "

The egg is a sphere. Life is born from a sphere, and life is greater than the flesh. Any other possibility is wrong, is foolish madness and wrong. And every worthy soul encompasses this spherical world, echon and memory influencing the living long after the fragile body dies.

Holding the shape of an egg, the coronas remain steady.

And the First falls back into silence, chewing on great thoughts. Unless she is confused, which is an acceptable possibility. She is old and exceptionally weak. Firsts often struggle to pluck their next words from everything that might be said. The youngsters feel ready to ignore bewilderment and any embarrassing nonsense. But no, the old one is merely gathering her energies, and now she breaks the silence with vigor and clear, brilliant purpose, the mouth and every head shouting while flashes of rich high-purple light wash over the coronas.

"You must keep your work before you," she says.

All but newborns and the Firsts work. Noble, moral labor helps the mind survive this impoverished realm, and that has not changed since that day when the Firsts became the Firsts.

Sloth and madness are the coronas' only true enemies.

"Work as if ten billion days lie ahead," she commands. "But my flesh is leaving this world."

Including her, only five Firsts remain.

"Live as if a trillion days wait, but I am departing."

The other Firsts and their old, old children absorb this great news, making no noise or meaningful light. Most of the other coronas assume they understand. They assume that the gray flesh is doomed. The youngest are secretly intrigued: a First's demise makes for a very memorable day.

The high-purple light fades. Bladders empty, and the sick old creature becomes smaller and denser and darker. And now she is dead, the youngsters assume. Of course, of course. But as she falls closer, they realize that no, she still breathes. The message heard wasn't the message offered. Because leaving this world has two meanings, and what is she doing now? Descending. The Egg-of-all-eggs falls slowly and then quickly, and startled young coronas scatter beneath her.

A second world exists. It is a lesser, deeply feeble place. None of the First ever make the crossing. Why would they? Yet she continues to shrivel and plunge, escaping from the midday jungle, gaining momentum until nothing in the Creation will stop her. That black body punches through the shimmering demon floor. Old necks stretch out. Thin air and cold embrace her. Surviving eyes gaze at the wasteland. Other coronas gather above the floor, watching as she becomes gigantic, every bladder filled with hot nothingness while great gasps of whispery air explode from her mouth. Even for the fittest coronas, flight is endless work in that other world. Prey is scarce, foul-tasting, and sometimes dangerous. Should the children follow? Should they battle for the chance to give encouragement and help?

Four Firsts remain, and with high-purple words, they call out, "Leave our sister alone."

An ordinary day has become remarkably strange.

The First talk among themselves with touches and small scents, hiding their thoughts from everyone, including their oldest, most trustworthy children.

Secrecy is rare among the coronas, and unsettling.

But more urgent is the old female flying in that savage realm. Monsters rule that other world. Some monsters are tiny, clinging to the pale cold forests and scampering along the ring-shaped reef. Others are enormous—roaring machines built from corona flesh and corona bones, each buoyed up with gas bags and pushed forwards by little, oxygen-starved fires. The little tree monsters ride the huge gas machines. Which monster is in charge, the tiny or the vast, is a matter of some debate. But machine and flesh work together, killing coronas so their bodies can be sliced into little pieces that they will stitch together and fuse together to make new machines—a state of affairs that has existed forever, nearly.

That second world is thoroughly, appallingly mad.

There is no doubt in that pronouncement.

Yet the cold has value. Cross into that thin, nearly useless air. Let frigid winds flow past blood and furious hearts. Even a giant body like the First's cools rapidly. Muscles slow and thoughts slow, and the wandering corona passes into near-hibernation, time stretching out and out until each moment feels endless.

There is peace to be found inside that horrible second world. Clarity can arrive before the monsters, and most of the coronas survive the journey, the strong and worthy almost always spared.

A good chill strengthens the good soul, it is said.

Fly beyond the shimmering barrier, and the true world goes on living without you. The furious hot haste of jungle and words pass unnoticed. More than not, the pilgrim returns home energized, refreshed, more capable and self-assured. Some claim that the emptiness is a spiritual sanctuary—a place to be tested by solitude and monsters. But the old ones, particularly the Firsts, maintain that every place is a sanctuary. The monster realm mirrors some lost Creation, nothing more. On rare occasions, the Firsts describe days when both worlds were young and the coronas flew higher than anyone flies now. Back then, curious heads led the bodies up into that slow-growing forest, and they peered into the darkest reaches, and they ate creatures of every sort, just to know the taste of alien bones.

In those times, no monster dared battle against the coronas, much less abuse their glorious bodies. That second world was theirs too, and the little red-blooded beasts could do nothing but cower in the high branches or scramble into the sharp crannies of a younger, much smaller reef.

The Creation used to be a better, richer place.

The Firsts claim so, and perhaps they believe what they say. But the Firsts are subject to many beliefs, and they refuse to speak about times and realms from before the Creation.

The youngsters talk about every subject, and they watch the ancient female fly and glide through air that she hasn't tasted for a very long while.

Her body emits a weak golden light that normally means, "Help."

Against orders, several foolish bodies drag their souls through the barrier.

She tells them to leave her.

"You're asking for help," they point out. "We are helping."

"You don't understand," she warns. "The 'help' is not for me."

Baffled but compliant, they carry away their embarrassment.

Various monsters approach, mechanical and meat, but these enemies are still distant when the exhausted First returns to the true world.

"Not now," she says. "The proper moment still comes."

"Proper for what?" the youngest ask.

"Be quiet, and feed me."

The First among Firsts is bizarre and possibly insane, but they feed her the best meats, the richest treats, and several mature coronas guide her to a quiet eddy where the wind won't reach her, where she can float and sleep. Old flesh needs long rest, and meanwhile the coronas finish their work, cultivating the day's jungle. Only then can they can return to their homes, relishing the purpose and beauty that flows through each of them.

The sun is hidden behind jungle.

Night reigns, and as always, a portion of the corona pretend to be tiny furious fires churning in the holy void, and after a healthy time, night draws the next day into existence

The coronas do their work again. The jungle grows and every mouth is fed, and each day ends with them filling their homes with confidence, tending to private needs and private pleasures before passing into states that are not quite sleep.

Day and night, everyone talks about the ancient creature and what she wanted in the other world.

Bold voices find bold answers.

"She has decided to punish the monsters," they say. "One final battle for the flesh."

No other explanation seems likely for that kind of soul.

Twenty-nine is a blessed number. One third is a lovely partial number. Twenty-nine and a third days pass, and she is half-strong again. And again, she pierces the shimmering barrier, emerging at the Creation's center, working furiously to fly in a great slow circle. The monsters notice but they are too slow. Exhausted, she falls back through the barrier, and she eats again and rests, saying nothing about her mind or this crazed adventure. And the other Firsts never offer opinions about what their sister wishes. They want her left alone, and they talk quite a lot to one another, but always with private voices, wearing concern on their ancient bodies while they tell their scions to mind the jungles, to care for their own souls.

There is a third voyage and then a fourth. The old female leaves at night and each is uneventful. But she has established a ritual that even stupid creatures can understand. The final journey is buoyed up by sunlight. She emerges to be met by a great flight of monsters. The coronas drifting below count the approaching machines and the little beasts riding inside the machines. Never has the enemy been so numerous, so close. Young voices and harsh voices renew the arguments about what the First of Firsts wants, and more to the point, what she deserves. Plainly, everyone should follow her. The monsters are sick with urgency, racing to catch her and butcher her, and this is a rare rich chance for the good world to rise in force, destroying every machine and a small, critical portion of the tree beasts.

But that is not the coronas' way, of course.

The elders firmly remind everyone that they are tenaciously peaceful. Their power and speed are not attached to any rage. But talk doesn't stop the more belligerent souls. Calming scents are more effective, but even then not enough. The most violent coronas gather near the barrier, waiting just out of sight, each spotting the machine that he or she will kill first, and in their minds, in secret, they see themselves bathed in the searing white light that the coronas like to aim at their heroes.

A thousand young coronas make a momentous decision:

If the old female fights, they will fight too.

That is the honorable way.

But when the monsters arrive, not even one of her heads snaps against them. With bladders swollen and empty, she remains in one place, inviting them to pierce her with spears and explosives. Then the monsters grab her limp form with bags of gas—bags made from the bladders of her own scions. Every corona watches the murder. Then the monsters drag the dead gray flesh to the emptiest piece of reef. An ugly night arrives, and a few coronas sneak into the other world, watching knives hack the body to pieces and then toss the pieces aside. The First's glorious parts, too old to be given an age, are also too old to be used for even the ugliest purpose.

The waste is astonishing. What more proof is needed that the other world is ruled by insanity?

That wicked night is crossed at last, and other days and nights follow in turn. Another First is judged to be the eldest now. He is more male than female, and he might well be the same remarkable age. But his voice has never seemed as wise as the one who is lost, and where she was dramatic, he holds a duller kind of soul.

"She is not gone," he reminds them. "Can you hear her echoes? Do you see her bright voice roaming in your brains?"

But the old female is gone, and without that living breathing body in this world, something has changed.

The Creation feels diminished, feels a little wrong.

Young coronas grieve.

And the First only makes the suffering worse. "What she did did not need to do be done," he says.

Everyone aches. Everyone is unhappy with this tale's finish. The Egg-of-all-eggs died among the worst kind of strangers, and where is the value in that?

"It was a worthless waste," he says.

Every waste is worthless, is it not?

But then he offers something unexpected, unexplained. "I don't know why anyone should care so much about one old obligation."

"What obligation?" a few ask.

The old fellow acts confused by the question. Perhaps he didn't mean to speak. His thoughts leaked free of his skin, oblivious to his wishes.

"What old obligation?" everyone asks.

He pauses. He reflects. Then with all of his strength, he says, "Once and for good left-behind reasons, she made a promise to another. All of this nonsense grew wild from that one foolish promise."

"What promise? Which other?" the coronas want to know. And not just the young ones, and not just the loud brilliant ones. Even the elders beg for details, knowing nothing about this pact.

"Details are not important," the First claims with bright, defiant flashes of high-purple. "To act on a pledge after so long . . . under these circumstances . . . well, her judgment was rotted through."

One of his daughters is just a hundred days younger than the world. To him and everyone, she says, "I don't recall any obligations."

He says nothing.

"This promise was hatched in the other world," she guesses, every head gazing at the demon floor.

"Not in that world or in ours," he says. "I was with her when it happened. The other Firsts were elsewhere. I alone saw the agreement made. It was during the earlier Creation, and ask me nothing else."

But a singular opportunity is been exposed. In one voice, thousands say, "Tell us about the world before this world."

"It is not important," says the old corona.

His voices are solid, but his colors are less than confident.

"That world is gone," he says. "What value could it possibly have?"

No one in the world is working now. Bodies hold still and no one speaks, the jungle growing wilder by the moment while every eye and mind is focused on that ancient man.

"Our obligations are aimed at this day," he says. "This day reigns, and I will do everything possible to see your work fulfilled."

Days are like flesh. Each one is dressed in the same kind of flesh, and likewise, every night looks like every other.

But when have the coronas not done their important, eternal work?

Suddenly the old one flashes with rage. "We should have attacked those brutes," he says. "When the beasts came for my friend, we should have killed them. And we would have dragged her home again, and she would die among us, and that story would be finished."

He sounds crazy and looks crazy, talking this way.

"Those little monsters are getting strong," the First warns. Talking to himself as much as to the others, he says, "I won't surrender. Not to those little beasts, those foul murderers."

The world is silent, but for him.

"And I won't honor promises made to the dead, certainly not for reasons that I can't pretend to remember anymore anymore anymore."

"You made a pledge too?" one child asks.

Then another wants to know, "Who is dead?"

"Everyone is dead," says the crazed old corona. "Haven't you been damn well paying attention?"

• • •

Days are like flesh, worn for their time before dying, and the soul of the day, what matters most, is what lingers.

The Egg-of-all-eggs is dead and the days continue much as those following behind. The coronas measure each one of the days, and the Count of All Days grows larger by very little. What changes is allowed to pass, almost unnoticed. What matters is remembered as echo and idea. Pilgrims continue to leave for the other world and return again, claiming enlightenment. Nothing changes in either realm. But there are stories, scattered and occasional and perhaps dubious stories, where an odd creature gets noticed. Something that isn't known by sight or by scent is spied in the other realm. Then one young pilgrim returns with the tale about finding a tiny beast tumbling through the emptiest air. The pilgrim looks closely at the creature, noticing that it is young and small but in many ways different than its brothers. Tasting the boy with his smallest head is only reasonable. But then one of the tree monsters—a familiar hunter—falls through the air to fearlessly snatch the boy and claim him. The monster covers both of them with an intense drenching of fear, and the two creatures soon vanish inside a giant gas-bloated machine, and that day is made remarkable.

While telling the story, the pilgrim wonders if that odd new beast was falling on purpose. Maybe he was trying to reach this world. And if so, why did the hunter risk so much to stop him?

Explanations are invented.

Inventions are decorated in smart light and shared with the world. But no explanation looks true, and what is known is just enough to breed curiosity and arrogance.

For another four hundred days, nothing changes.

And then quite suddenly, for reasons that no corona can decipher, war comes to that mad, lesser world.

The battles are furious as well as beautiful. Burning forest and shattered pieces of the reef punch through the demon barrier, enriching the good world. War is an old story, something known and normally unremarkable. There have been many wars among the monsters, some as large as this and almost as fierce. Those in the trees and those on the reef are like siblings: they hate each other because they are too similar. Yet unlike the coronas, they have no good work that needs accomplishing. They do not have a jungle to cultivate or long days to cross. That is why they periodically fight until both sides run short of fire or hatred or willing bodies, and then the monsters weave a false peace that will last another dozen generations, or at least until the monsters again forget how horrible life becomes during war.

Six hundred days pass, and then the exhaustion arrives. Fights become less common, and big flying machines are scarce and fearful, and the coronas who have studied many wars can say with authority that neither side occupies any chance of victory.

Yet there is no peace.

The other world's madness has never been worse. Both species fight on, and what matters to the good world, to the corona world, is that the monsters have to make new machines. And to build machines, they need fresh scales and skins, bladders and blood from the only source in the Creation.

Both species actively chase the pilgrims, and they battle one another before and during and long after each of these hunts.

And there are many, many pilgrims for the killing: six hundred days of war have spilled minerals into the coronas' realm. Ash and reef rocks help fuel blooms of food, and nests are molded from fat and love, and every bright egg sprouts a child, and every new child grows to until they are slithering close to one another, fighting for the available space inside a jungle that cannot grow any larger.

Becoming a pilgrim, if only for a sliver of a day, helps calm the crowded soul.

Pilgrims leave by the hundreds, and some die.

Unlike earlier days, even the strong and swift can be slaughtered.

One day the Father-of-all-fathers holds council with the other Firsts and elders and certain important youngsters. Much is discussed. Nothing is decided. Every voice wants the normal ways to return, but the normal peaceful Creation seems impossibly remote. How can they ever fly so far?

Bold talkers wish for a new war.

Maybe this mayhem is a treasure, they argue. They have been given a rare opportunity. What if the coronas were to rise up and batter their weakened foes? If every one of their species plunged through the barrier—a great wave of focused, purposeful flesh—perhaps they could kill every last monster. Then the Creation would be freed of this scourge, and the Count of Days and the beauty of the nights would be assured for all time.

This is what teases, this promise of a peace that never ends.

The council speaks about these matters, other matters, and they talk long about nothing at all.

Nothing is decided.

The coronas will never change.

The Father-of-all-fathers delivers the final verdict. He gathers the coronas into a dense sphere while he floats in the center. Their multitude is a world onto itself, and it has never been so huge and worried. His worries have made him appear older than ever. But he takes his obligations seriously, reminding the coronas that they never kill for the sake of killing, and the other world cannot touch them or hurt them in any significant way, and he refuses to hear or see any words about making this ugly fight their own.

"Our obligation is clear," he says.

But despite the sounds that he makes, and the light and the stubborn scents—others can't fail to notice that the old one is offering the expected words, and in ways, he is distinctly unconvinced by his own words.

"Our flight path is set," he says. "Our world moves where it needs to move."

This is odd, unexpected phrasing, likening the world to an object passing through air. Why would the world move? The Creation is rigid, invincible and immobile. Just the image of motion strikes a few as being senile.

"We must do our work," he says.

Nobody doubts that the work is holy, and the Creation as well as both of its worlds depend on their unflagging devotion to the jungle and the food the jungle gives, and to the night that cools the world and lets the world rest before another day.

"Nothing can ever change," he promises.

Yet the very next day—in the midst of the most ordinary bright morning—one event leads to a place that no one envisions.

• • •

The coronas' world is rich with animals that float and that fly, and a thousand kinds of golden foliage gather as airborne jungles. Heat and endless moisture produce visible growth, moment-by-moment growth. The wooden forests in the other realm are sluggish, thin and impoverished. These jungles are far more productive. This is why so many giant coronas can live inside such a tiny place. Life is an explosion, magnificent and relentless, and on those rare days when the First mention the former Creation, they describe a paradise much like this one, only a thousand times larger, more wondrous and more magnificent than this.

Even when the world is crowded with coronas, like it is now, there are places where few go. The Creation is a sphere, and every sphere reaches its widest place. The demon floor rests against the world. Shadows rule. Wild creatures and weeds are the only inhabitants. A few children—odd, impulsive children as a general rule—like to investigate that useless terrain. They crawl into the tangles and crevices, and they hunt for the odd creatures that live nowhere else. The demon floor is close, slightly weaker than elsewhere, and that is an object of fascination too. But mostly, the odd children are there to make bright light in the darkness, be free of coronas and expectations, enjoying the company of souls just as peculiar as them.

The council of important souls was held yesterday.

Today, a trio of young coronas rise toward the sun with an unexpected claim. They found a creature unlike any other. What they describe is suitable for a dream, not for life. A few adults bother to listen. Then they dismiss the nonsense, offering candidates from among the known species. "No, no," the children say. "None of those animals fit what we saw." And not only did they see the beast, they spoke to it, and it spoke to them, after a fashion. Then they promised their new friend to tell no one about him, after which they hurried here with this fine new story.

The adults are too old and far too wise to accept any portion of this lie. But there are some curious details, and even the dullest adult can still enjoy a child's fantasy. That's why the stories spread. A corona day is exceptionally long, and everyone hears every story, and this is how the last of the Firsts eventually learn about this impossible business.

Three of them dismiss the whole matter without qualm.

But the Father-of-all-fathers turns silent, and against his usual nature, he turns contemplative.

The sun is shrouded and night arrives, and he leaves, presumably heading for his home. But he passes the cavity where he has slept for millions of days. In secret, the ancient one slips down to where darkness always rules, spending much of the long night throwing light into the crannies and calling out with words that he hasn't used in an eternity.

Just before dawn, what he seeks allows itself to be found.

The creature is exactly as promised—too strange to be real and barely comfortable inside its body. Noises rise from its peculiar mouth, and the Father-of-all-Fathers replies in various ways. Then the strange creature rises out of its hiding place, drawing images on sheets of gossamer weed, and the corona draws pictures on his flesh, each trading notions and truths until one of them is without hope.

The broken one starts home again.

He is devastated by the physical tolls, and those miseries are nothing next to the emotions roiling his soul. But his soul is a great thing, built large and everlasting in the world. How can such a soul change in one night?

The new day is well underway. Only the babies sleep, and he pauses in a pocket of still air, inside the half-born jungle, listening for his own essence living in the world. But all he finds, echoing in the air and in his mind, is that long-ago man.

A human, he is.

Human in shape, human in voice.

"These days will end," says the man. "But I will grant you a few more days, if you promise me one impossible, wondrous task, sacrificing everything for the slenderest chance to save All . . . "

ONE

He wore his age well, with gray lurking in the beard and a deep dark gaze that had witnessed more than most. The body still held its easy grace and most of that trusted strength, but the man inside was learning the benefits of filling a comfortable pillow, worldly eyes staring at a bare wall or the polished face of the floor. He had become a thinker. He often thought about his wives and their many children. Each wife had had a lovely name that he couldn't forget, and the older children had claimed proud names that he never bothered to remember. He had loved his family as well as any man could. He still cherished almost every portion of his former life. But that was long ago, in a very different place, and whenever he thought about his ladies and his babies, there always came that sorry moment when he remembered again that each of them was dead.

His type of women didn't live in this part of the forest. He had looked for them after arriving but always came home lonely. Some of the others talked about finding a girlfriend for the lonely man, but she would have to be brought from distant trees—in a bad humor, most likely. An angry and frightened bride would probably try to murder him before love had its chance, and that's why he said nothing positive about the idea, and maybe that's why the matchmaking had never happened.

There was quite a lot of talk in this place. Every subject was discussed in his presence, and he always listened to those pieces that concerned him. Words were very important, and he always worked to understand what he was hearing. Yes, he was a very smart man. But even familiar words were confusing when they were strung together, which was why he concentrated on simpler, surer qualities: he studied postures and hands and the colors of the voices and who was angry and who was most scared. That was how a smart man learned the others were thinking.

This new home was enormous, and that was just the portion of the palace where he was allowed to walk unattended.

The very important boy ruled one big room while the old-man teacher lived behind the next door. The very important man lived at the end of the long hallway, and entering his quarters only brought trouble. The giant with two mouths lived somewhere else inside the palace, and the orphans occupied two nearby rooms. There was a big rich-smelling kitchen and a small dining room to be shared by everybody, plus toilet rooms and playrooms, and there was one long room filled with fancy glass boxes and warm machines and huge cages where dumb animals lived and every kind of book—what he thought of as word-cakes—perched on the shelves. There was also space where three students could sit in their desks while the teacher stood before them, talking for half of the day at a time, saying very little that made sense.

The very important boy was owned. The man with the gray beard and dead wives was one of the owners. There was no disputing that fact. Ownership brought certain duties and obligations, including sharing a bed with the boy. The habit of sleeping together survived after they arrived in this place, but nothing was the same as before. The gray-beard was better than the boy about forgetting the past, but he couldn't forget that wicked time when the boy shoved him inside a dark sack, which was horrible. And more important, the boy was growing older. He had never smelled human, but as the days passed, he was acquiring the odor of a genuine man.

Grown men didn't sleep together. That rule was too old to measure.

Every creature had its rank, some distinct measure of worth and respectability, and that man-boy was becoming a potential rival. Snarls and curses were perfectly fine means to coax an enemy off the bed. A pair of fingers got eaten, but they didn't mean anything to the man-boy. It was the teacher who put a long arm over his favorite student's shoulder, explaining with words what teeth and violence had not made clear.

"You can't sleep with Good anymore," the teacher said.

The boy was sad before that news, and he was sad afterwards. Nothing had changed.

"You're going to have to find another bed," the teacher said to the other man in the room.

Stealing more fingers would cause useless trouble. The gray-beard surrendered the ugly bed to the stupid, ungrateful man-boy. But where would he sleep now?

One of the orphans used to be a boy, but he had grown up tall and thin as a stick, and his beard was finally coming in, giving him his own harsh, threatening stink. The other orphan was more woman than girl, and her scent was very pleasant, yes. But she didn't appreciate his odor or his honest manners, and that's why he was banished to a playroom, given a bed of cushions in the corner between bare walls—a space where a thoughtful man could lose his gaze in the middle of a long sad night.

The world was sad, and the world was very angry.

Every bad thing was blamed on the war. The war was everywhere and it seemed old and sure to last forever. Every visitor talked about battles and the big fires happening in far-off places. That kind of talk only made the sadness worse. Didn't they understand? The fire and fights happened in other places. This new home was strong, and there were soldiers here to keep it strong. The palace was at the heart of the world, and while there used to be gunfire and explosions, that was hundreds of days ago. Even miserable people agreed that the fighting was not as awful as it used to be, and the gray-beard understood that what became small often vanished, and that was what gave him hope.

Many nights were spent inside the playroom, but he didn't sleep well.

To claim that he grieved for his dead family was to miss the truth. Every wife had to die, and being his child meant that life would surely find its end.

Death was no mystery to a smart man like him.

His grief—the deep ache in his bones—was the irreparable loss of his fine, well-deserved life. Each day used to hold the promise of new women and the familiar blackwood tree and the sounds of being outside and the feel of wind and the endless easy joy that came with pissing into the morning sun. But this new life was lived indoors, more than not. And what was outside was not a happy realm for his kind.

The two-mouthed giant was a frequent visitor. He was called the man-boy's brother, except he looked and smelled like nothing else in the world. People plainly did not understand what the word "brother" meant, which showed how stupid they were. But a creature like him might make a good companion for the man. One day the giant came to the boy's room. He wanted to talk about the sister that nobody else ever saw. It was just the two of them and the tiny man with the fine old beard and the deep wise eyes, and that seemed like a good time to climb onto one of those slick armored shoulders, biting the first fingers that reached up to brush him aside.

The man's meaning was misinterpreted.

Thrown into the hallway, he decided to never try to claim any giant for himself. They weren't worth the bother.

A second door stood across from the boy's room. The door was closed, as usual, but it wasn't locked that day.

He eased the door open and peered inside.

The boy's mother was sitting on the edge of her bed. She had always been old, but she was badly hurt before coming here and she seemed much older now. Her wounds had healed, but what remained was tired and quiet. She often slept longer than anyone else, including her sad son, but she was awake just then, dressed and sitting on her bed, looking at the floor in the same staring fashion that he used during the longest nights.

Something in her posture and her eyes touched the little man.

He approached slowly.

The woman had never approved of him. Never once had she shown him more than grudging tolerance. But when she saw his face, she said, "Hello."

She didn't smile, but her expression wasn't as sorrowful.

"Haddi," he said.

That was her name.

"Good," she said.

That wasn't his name. The boy heard him say that word several times, and he misunderstood its meaning. "Good" meant *good*, nothing more, and his true name could only be spoken by the tongue of orange-headed men.

Once again, he said, "Haddi."

She thought of making the man leave. He could tell from her mouth and how the eyes got cold for a moment.

Without words, he jumped up on the bed, avoiding her reach while starting to pull gently at the softest blanket. Maybe if he were quiet and careful, she wouldn't notice his presence.

The old woman decided to say nothing about the interruption.

She stood slowly and did nothing, deciding what to do. Then she walked to a big box filled with little boxes. On top of the big box was a picture of her dead husband. The clearest, brightest pictures of Merit were lost with their home, but the very important man who lived down the hallways had found this picture. He had brought it to Haddi as a gift, and despite its age and the yellowing paper, she had squeezed the picture under glass surrounded by a frame.

The orange-headed man understood pictures, and better than some of his kind, he respected the magic people saw in such things.

"Sad face," he said.

Haddi didn't react. She didn't seem to hear him. But she picked up the frame, pulling the dust off with a fingertip, and then turning to him, she quietly asked, "Are you tired?"

It was still morning, and he was making a nest in her bed. Yes, he was tired, and saying so wouldn't lighten his burdens.

Haddi opened her mouth, golden teeth glowing. Something less than a smile broke out, and she asked him, "Do you ever think about our old tree?"

There were more important matters to think about than one lost tree. But the little man didn't have the energy or focus to explain even a portion of his busy mind. Instead he made one small and very mournful sound, hunkering down against the blanket, wishing for the chance to nap.

"All right," she said.

What did she mean?

"You can sleep here," she said. Then she gave both of them a good lie, saying, "Sleep here, but we're never going to be friends."

• • •

The past was jammed with lost belongings.

Diamond's father was trapped inside unreachable days. The boy's old room and simple bed and Mister Mister and all of the loyal lifeless soldiers were trapped there too. He used to be surrounded by trusted faces, and other people had been polite to him and often friendly, and the days were generally pleasant, and life pretended to be as stable and strong as a giant blackwood.

Any other child would be within his rights to cry about all that was gone.

But what Diamond missed as much as anything was an idea—the wrong silly stupid idea—that he was ill.

There were moments when he remembered being the weak child, a fragile little shadow of a boy who was sure to die any time, and he clung to that memory, wishing it could be true again.

But death wanted nothing to do with Diamond.

Even worse, an unbreakable brain lived inside his human-shaped skull, and that brain was powerful by any measure.

Waking in the middle of the night, normal people forgot sometimes where they were and who they were with.

Diamond always knew where he was and that he was alone.

Tonight he was lying at the edge of a giant bed. He was awake for a long while before opening his eyes, and then he looked across the room. Little splashes of light huddled near the door. Otherwise the vast space was filled with inky darkness. Good was sleeping soundly in Mother's room. When Diamond sat up, nobody noticed.

He sat up and rubbed at what his dream had done to him, and he stared at the dream, which was as ordinary and empty as any that he had ever experienced. He was standing inside the Archon's quarters with the faraway ceilings and the magnificent furnishings. List, the Archon, was standing beside King, the two of them discussing the war's progress. Nobody else was present. Every phrase had been yanked from overheard conversations. Battles that would win the war were about to happen. Except of course those battles had come and gone and nothing had changed. Every military ship named in these plans had been destroyed long ago. List and his son were firing giant bombs that didn't exist anymore. They were going to scorch papio cities that were already left as ashes. Key trees and installations had to be defended, except all of them had fallen into the sun hundreds of days ago. And most remarkably, father and son spoke as if they were generals, as if they had any genuine role in the endless waging of war.

Everybody in that dream was trapped in the past, and nobody knew it.

Diamond quit rubbing himself. A fancy metronome stood on the table beside the bed. Touch the button and it glowed inside. Even if this was a short night, the night was young. Why was he awake? Putting his bare feet against the fur-covered floor, Diamond shut his eyes again, listening intently. Eventually one sharp blast found him, followed by a bigger explosion that came rolling in from the same direction, passing through the room before hurrying across the darkened world.

The war wanted to be noticed.

The war was an angry baby that screamed loudest when it was ignored.

Diamond dressed in yesterday's clothes. His room's main door opened with a touch, and he stepped into the hallway. A sentry was at the end of the hallway, guarding List's door. There was just enough light that the sentry could watch a boy cross to the toilet. No rules were being broken. Nothing needed to be said. Other guards were nearby, but the rooms and passageways were designed to keep most of their protectors out of sight. What passed for home was a self-contained space buried inside the Archon's ancient palace. Only three routes led inside and out again, and each of those doors was kept locked. Home was a hard-shelled seed tucked in the middle of a giant fruit. The palace was the fruit wrapped inside a fortune in corona scales, but this interior house sported its own layers of scales and skin as well as cunningly hidden sacks filled with water—a stopgap means to frustrate the fire bombs that still hadn't managed to come this far.

List's quarters were in the center. Diamond's people lived on this side of List's quarters, and King lived on the other side, near the Archon's offices. Windows were forbidden, which was for the sake of security and very reasonable. But it was an absence that never stopped reminding Diamond of his first room, closed off and secret, and that made it easier to remember how small and fragile his body had felt in those times.

Diamond used the toilet and flushed the bowl, and he let the sentry watch him return to his room, which was his plan.

The door floated on greased hinges, and by turning the knob, he made the hard sounds that a sentry expected to hear when the bolt was resting in the jamb.

The nightlights were luminescent yogurts. He stared at them and waited for the sentry to begin his routine rounds.

Another distant rumble arrived, following the same pathway.

Diamond was no little boy anymore. He wasn't grown either, but the enduring body was showing interest in maturing. What had always looked small was gaining meat and strength. He would never be half as powerful as King, but when they trained together—and they trained every day, without fail—it was apparent that Diamond was going to wield more power than most fit men.

The curly thick hair was very long just three days ago, but then it was sheared off and sent to a factory making armaments for the war. Like everything else about Diamond, his hair only looked human. But it was as strong as the best kinds of silk, and if woven together in the right way, a mass of his hair could become the armor that an important soldier wore over his heart.

The world was that desperate. One boy's hair could win the war.

The sentry wasn't moving.

Diamond waited.

Humans, true humans, grew sick when they were sad. Beasts called grief and depression engulfed the soul with blackness, and the blackness could kill even the strongest among them. Mother was depressed for a long time after Father died. Diamond had worried about her. Everybody was concerned about her state-of-mind. But then Good couldn't sleep with him anymore, and somehow the monkey ended up inside her room. After that, she wasn't so sick with misery. Not that Good made her happy, because he didn't. But his face looked at Mother when she spoke, relating thoughts that she kept from others, and the monkey was older and better trained now, which helped the two of them live together. Mother was so comfortable with her friend that she had begun planning how she would have to change her life to care for an orange-headed monkey as he moved into old age with its endless, unremarkable problems.

Sadness and blackness and every shape of worry had found Diamond, and each clung to the deepest reaches of his mind.

Yet his mind was unbreakable, stubbornly free of numbness, or worse, the hopeless serenity that came to some people when they suffered an absolute collapse.

Diamond could not stop remembering who began this war. In his head, a button was waiting to be pushed or be left alone, and the boy pushed it willfully, without hesitation. There was no forgetting the moment or the very good reasons that shoved him into that moment. He could summon every doubt and every smart regret suffered over the last five hundred and ninety-one days. But doubt and regret didn't wipe away one event. The *Ruler of the Storm* launched its worst weapons, and the war eventually killed the airship and half of its crew, and most of the survivors had perished in a string of less historic, relentlessly tragic battles.

Diamond had memorized the crews' names, and because those tallies were published on occasion, he studied the pages for those names. That was an important, awful chore. And despite the misery, Diamond was prepared every day to read another long line of dead names.

The palace was ruled by security. No part of the world was genuinely safe, but these rooms were secure enough that hundreds of known faces could work close to the unbreakable boy, and every day brought strangers through the guarded doors. There were events to be attended—symbolic meals and symbolic meetings and audiences with dignitaries eager to see both of the corona's children. Standing beside Diamond, some visitors made it their duty to assure the odd boy that nobody blamed his finger for the war. That was a lie, of course. But sentries and servants, ambassadors, and various generals felt it was important to remind him that the Eight did horrible things to the world. It was the Eight who killed his poor father, and revenge was something that everybody understood. There was also blame for the papio and certain awful people among the human ranks, and there were plenty of hatred that was already ancient and would survive this business just fine. "As inevitable as the days," they said about war—a phrase too old to have any author. And then the optimists would claim that if Diamond hadn't punched that button—if his courage had failed him—then the next war would have certainly found them on even less decent terms.

Strangers could afford to share a single comforting position. But those who saw Diamond every day had offered a variety of opinions, conflicted and often contradictory. The Archon's aides and the generals had told him that he was blameless but wars should never be launched without planning and every advantage. Office workers assured him that vengeance was right, even noble, but a hundred days later, the same voices claimed that nothing right had been accomplished and nothing good could be found anywhere. Everyone liked to talk about evil people dying, yes, but they couldn't stop from praising the heroes and the innocent who died every day. Nissim and Elata and Seldom were trusted voices: each had held Diamond by a warm hand, claiming that their lives would have looked much the same without war. Or maybe they were talking to themselves, wrestling with doubt. With or without the war, this odd family would have come to the District of Districts. They were destined to stand behind heavy walls and locks and paranoia. That was the future and always had been, at least since Marduk fell, but it was hard to argue that the rest of the world would been the same tonight if one salvo of reef-hammers had remained asleep inside their tubes.

One simple story had been recited many times, and the Archon told it best. The narrow, shrill-voiced man thought it was a good story, a comforting explanation. He smiled as believably as he could manage, promising Diamond that this fierce, seemingly endless contest was inevitable. It had to happen. Because Diamond existed, this was nothing less than destiny. Nodding, List explained that whatever Diamond was, he had always been the irresistible prize: a human who wasn't quite human, a blessing that was going to remake one species and the Creation.

Perhaps. But nothing was known for certain, Diamond said.

List scoffed at that complaint and maybe at the weak will that made it. The great prize was the great prize because of belief. Reality was everyone's secondary concern. But of course Diamond would be a man soon, and everything might be answered soon. He would have a family of enduring, unbreakable children, or there wouldn't be any children and he would be just one great blessing, like King.

The Archon of Archons claimed that both of those destinies should make the boy smile now and again.

Diamond still smiled, but never for those suffocating reasons.

Habit and being polite were the only reasons to smile anymore.

Everybody held various opinions, except for Mother. She didn't pretend ten opinions, or even just two. There was one hard truth and nothing else: she was a widow who lost more than her husband. Everything but her only son was gone, and the son that she couldn't stop loving had proved himself to be as ugly as was every angry boy and boyish man who ever picked up a club.

Haddi didn't pretend to understand what was inevitable about the world. Where the war might have emerged, if it began on its own or with help, were questions not worth the trouble. What she did know—what her heart and mind and soul understood too well—was that inside Diamond, underneath everything special, waited a beast just like the beast inside the rest of them.

Standing in the darkness, touching that unfastened door, Diamond saw his mother. Several conversations replayed themselves inside the same intense moment. She was weeping while talking to her son. She was talking to him while her face was like coral, a pale coral, rigid and cold. And she was warm-voiced and calm, looking at the ceiling as she spoke. And finally, she was quietly talking to Good, pretending not to notice the beast standing a few steps away.

In each case, the same message was delivered.

"He would have been so disappointed," she said.

To her son, she said, "Your father."

To the monkey, she said, "Merit."

Then she said, "That good man despised violence against humans. It didn't matter if they were us or if they were the papio. He never wanted to raise a hand, much less incinerate hundreds of them. And he certainly wouldn't approve of you trying to murder one of your own siblings."

"The Eight were evil," Diamond said, trying to combat her logic.

"You knew that," she said skeptically.

"I did," he claimed.

"And that fact hasn't changed?"

There were papio soldiers who had protected the Eight, and now they were squatting inside tree-walker prisons and interrogation cells. They didn't describe a simple evil giant. Nothing about the creature was simple, including the mastermind—Divers.

"But Divers killed my father," Diamond said.

That was the day when Mother was addressing Good, not him.

"I saw Divers kill him," Diamond shouted, his voice livid, each word blended into the next.

Mother's face turned hard and cold. She stared at the monkey and then turned to her son. The pretty mouth was pinched, and the dark red-rimmed eyes refused to blink. Then very quietly, almost too softly to be heard, she said, "I know what you saw. But what your father would ask. If he were sitting next to me, if he could look at you . . . "

The boy's anger abandoned him.

He didn't intend to ask, "What would Father ask?"

But his mouth muttered that question just the same.

Mother's voice didn't answer. She changed the gait and color of her words, sounding very much like Merit when she said, "Diamond. Tell me. How many fathers did you kill that day?"

Wrenching endless sadness took his heart. Pain that would cripple anyone else became a weight, Diamond's massive and faithful burden. But the murderous boy kept living. He managed to sleep nights and eat every day, growing in little bursts like every other boy, and the hair changed on his body, and when he wasn't conscious about his grief and guilt, he became very much aware of new feelings—feelings as old as any species living inside the Creation.

The memories faltered, and the present returned.

In the middle of this night, Diamond took one long breath, holding the air deep inside his chest while all of its oxygen was married to his salty blood.

Then the sentry walked past the door, beginning his rounds, and the boy waited for half a recitation before slipping into the hallway, still not breathing, nothing useful left inside his lungs, his legs working with a magic that he couldn't hope to understand.

• • •

Important humans knew how to curry favor, and that was why the Archon used to receive gifts, enormous numbers of fine rare wondrous gifts.

That was before the war.

In those days, Father was the world's most important man, and it was fashionable among the half-powerful to give him portraits and sculptures of his extraordinary son. And that was why King's rooms were crowded with big canvas sheets slathered in paint, and tall blocks of carved wood and carved coral, and best of all, figurines built wholly from corona parts. Each work represented him, and they were usually competent and sometimes inspired. Few humans actually visited King inside his own quarters, but the typical reaction was to assume that the giant, heavily-armored beast was self-absorbed. Why else populate your home with thirty-seven portrayals of yourself?

Except none of these objects were King, and that's what he liked.

With paint and knives, King had altered each one of the gifts. An unsuspected artistic talent helped him adjust the lay of the armor and the color of spikes and the precise dimensions of legs and arms and the two mouths. Why this should matter was a mystery, particularly to him, but the creature never questioned his instincts. He considered these figures to be his family. Maybe they were ancestors; maybe they hadn't been born yet. Names and life stories mattered less than their presence, particularly the sense that he belonged to some abundant species populated with names and important stories.

King was taller than any human, tree-walker or reef-walker, and he weighed half again more than the largest papio. But three hundred days ago, this body that he barely understood had stopped growing. He knew that before anyone else. The butcher scale in the doctors' offices soon proved it. Eating more earned him nothing but more frequent trips to the toilet. His full-sized body was also showing other signs of maturity, and he had to assume that each stage was inevitable, natural, and healthy. Yet how could he be certain? A species of one had no guidelines, no history. He was alone in the worst ways, and alone in the best too, and maybe that's why it was easy to take pleasure from standing inside a magnificent room where King-like figures were set in rows—a pattern that felt right and proper and lovely.

"Did you hear the explosions?" asked his guest.

"They woke me," said the breathing mouth.

"How many?"

King raised both hands, implying twelve.

His brother nodded, leaving the door slightly ajar.

"Did he wake?" King asked.

"Not when I jumped over his bed," Diamond said.

It was an old joke. The Archon was a light sleeper, but both of them had experience slipping through the man's home without being noticed—unless List was aware and had decided not to challenge either of them.

"Where was the fight?" asked Diamond.

King pointed at the memory of each blast.

"My old home," the human said sadly.

Only little battles were fought in the Corona District. The blackwoods were dead, and the papio had all but abandoned that portion of their reef, which made this night a bit unusual.

"Maybe someone's starting a large offensive," said King.

Diamond nodded.

King had finished growing, but the human was only beginning. Everything that had been frail and small about Diamond was being swallowed by strong human muscle and a skeleton that was brawnier than anyone might have guessed. If the boy grew like his truly human cousins, he might end up tall. He could even find power, in some fashion. But he was also a species of one, which meant that nobody knew the answers. He could just as well grow until enormous, or he could transform into some unsuspected entity, like a thunderfly springing out of its chrysalis.

"Let's watch the war," King suggested.

Diamond was holding the fancy brass knob. He started to open the door but then closed it again.

"I'll get us to a spotter station," King said.

"No," the boy said. "I don't want to see the war now."

King waited, knowing what was coming.

"Put it out," Diamond said.

They had used the sign five nights ago, and this was too soon.

"Or I'll put it out," he said.

Saying nothing, King walked to the wall nearest the outside world, gently lifting a statue of himself made from silvery corals frosted with paint. This was the statue that resembled him best, which was why he called it Grandfather. It took a fair amount of power to lift his ancestor, exposing a small hole that had been surreptitiously cut through the wall and between the sacks of protective water, leaving a tube where a simple bell and tether lived.

With his breathing mouth, King blew into the tube.

The bell dropped and the rope straightened, and the bell rang out. Not even King's exceptional ears could hear the tiny clangor, not from indoors. Which was why they had settled on this signal.

The statue was set back in place.

Diamond was waiting in the empty hallway, patient but not patient.

A bolted steel door led to the rest of the palace. But they took a different route, climbing stairs to an observation tower built from corona parts and the strongest glass ever pulled from a furnace.

In other times, the District of Districts would have worn spectacular lights. Even in the belly of the night, a million people would have been awake, burning candles and electric fires, and the little public blimps would have been climbing and falling, taking insomniacs and drunks to whatever door seemed like a good idea. But this was wartime. Fuel wasn't scarce, but the generals demanded rationing to build character. Besides, just the glimmer of a few hundred lights would help the enemy wings navigate between the giant bloodwoods, and nobody wanted to make any attacks easier for the papio.

One window panel was unlocked. Diamond popped the latch and pushed the glass inward—a curved triangle rimmed with a rubbery white gasket made from corona fat.

They waited.

In the distance, in the direction of Diamond's former home, were several more blasts, each with enough punch and heart to be heard by human ears.

Diamond crossed his arms, saying nothing.

They might wait until dawn, of course. Or this could be a wasted night, although that would be unusual.

Because he wanted to talk, King said, "Dreams."

"None were interesting," said Diamond.

Sometimes the boy endured glimpses of an earlier life, or at least that's what he claimed. He told what he could remember and what he might remember, and sometimes he made allusions about a disembodied voice that came while he was awake, dispensing nuts of wisdom and nuts with no meat at all.

"What about your dreams?" the boy teased.

King had never suffered from those hallucinations. Sleep was oblivion for most of his soul, black and intense and relatively brief, while a lucid sliver of his mind remained on duty, constantly watching for enemies and potential allies.

The brothers stood together but not together. They looked like strangers who happened to share a destination.

Night held its pace, and talk fell away to bored silence, and King considered sleeping on his feet.

Finally the boy said, "She won't come."

"It's too soon," King agreed.

Five nights ago, while they stood exactly here, a pair of night-flying leatherwings had descended on the tower. One of the leatherwings circled nearby while his mate landed on the sill and reshaped her face, conjuring a human mouth and young woman's voice.

"Good evening, brothers," she had said.

Quest's skills never stopped improving. Any body shape was possible, rendered with the proper feel and scent and countless details. The male leatherwing had been fooled by her disguise. King had heard the high-high-pitched cries demanding caution, professing love, and endlessly promising to remain loyal whatever happened. And as always, he felt admiration for this marvelous creature. But it wasn't love, no. He wouldn't allow love to blossom ever, no. But there were secret thoughts where his sister grew brave enough to slip inside the palace with King. Diamond was anywhere else, and once inside King's quarters, she would summon a body like his, only female.

How she would look, he had no clue.

And the biggest part of his secret, what made his hearts race, was failing to imagine that wondrous moment.

Five nights ago, the brothers shared gossip about the war while their cautious sister described what she had seen. Tree-walkers had attacked the City of Round Roads, but they did it only because the city was already devastated. The papio didn't defend wastelands. Heavily armored airships pulverized the broken buildings, and all but one returned to base intact.

The secret consensus and the public consensus were very similar: the war was going badly for both species. The papio were always short of fuel and bombs, while the tree-walkers could make all the alcohol and explosives they wanted from what remained of their forest. But the tree-walkers had lost far too many airships, and there was nervous, consistent talk that the stockpiles of corona parts were just about spent.

"I don't see them preparing for any abduction raid," Quest volunteered.

The boy always asked about the imaginary raids. Five nights ago, he accepted the news the same as always: silently, nodding once and then once more before steering the conversation back to Quest.

Their sister wore endless shapes, but she never stopped carrying her fears. Even when it was just the three of them, escape routes on all sides, she remained guarded, anxious. She might talk about where she went at night, but her daylight haunts were her own business. She had dropped clues that she was human-shaped now and again, but whenever King brought up the possibility, Quest offered various reasons why that disguise was too demanding and far too dangerous.

"Humans don't notice leatherwings and epiphytes," she said. "All humans care about are their own faces and the sounds those faces leak."

King remembered every word spoken at the last meeting.

Diamond was probably doing the same.

The giant looked at his brother's face, reading the seriousness. "What do you want to ask her tonight?"

"Nothing," the boy lied.

Bright green eyes stared, King waiting.

Finally, Diamond admitted, "I wanted to talk about the Eight."

Just mentioning the name caused the plates on King's shoulders to life.

"Where is Divers?" the boy added.

They looked at one another for a long while. Then the human approached the open window, and King stood behind him, watching the naked hands touching the white gasket and the sill where their sister would perch, if she showed. But she wasn't coming tonight. They should give up the hope and sneak back to their quarters before their absence was noticed by someone who cared enough to sound an alarm.

In the distance—a different direction this time—King heard the screaming of a single papio rocket flying flat and swiftly into a flurry of cannon fire, accomplishing nothing, the rocket continuing on its important path.

Diamond probably only heard a murmur of the battle. But he tilted his head, listening intently.

And then the rocket struck its target or maybe a lucky cannon shell, and the explosion spread outwards, the blaze outraced by a roar that made the great bloodwood tree shiver slightly.

Diamond breathed hard, and he pushed his head into the open air.

King watched the back of the creature's close-shaved head, the tiny neck exposed. Was this a test? Was the boy testing if his brother could be trusted? Regret was a beast that preyed on other creatures, not King. He never once doubted his reasons for trying to cut off Diamond's head and throw the pieces back to the coronas. One moment demanded one action, but moments changed. Conditions slipped away, leaving new conditions. This boy might remake his species, or he would fail, but King would more than likely remain the largest and smartest brother. Eventually the war would end, and the Archon would die in his sleep, more likely than not, and his son would inherit whatever remained of this Creation. At that moment, inside a single breath, there was no other future worth cherishing.

They listened to the night.

Finally Diamond pulled his head back inside the tower, ready to close the window and give up on their sister.

But then he paused.

Diamond stood as motionless and King was close behind him, watching him, not thinking about anything at all.

Diamond was like a statue.

And King heard the voice.

Very quietly, the voice said, "This is the Great Day."

King couldn't tell which of his ears had heard the voice, if any. He didn't recognize the language, yet the words and meanings were perfectly understandable. Needing a worthy explanation, he decided that Diamond had pulled some trick on him, and maybe he should break Diamond's spine in a few places, as a warning.

But then that little neck turned, and nothing in that human face hinted at a joke.

"You heard it," said his tiny brother.

King said nothing.

"What did it tell you?"

King didn't want to say.

"What day is this?" Diamond asked.

Then he answered his own question, saying, "This is the Great Day."

King stared into the blackness.

"But you did hear it, right?"

"I heard something," King allowed.

Diamond smiled brightly.

"But if this looks like a great day," King said, "then your mystery voice damn well can't tell the time."

TWO

Human faces were difficult to mimic and human manners were impossible to duplicate. But early on and a million times since, Quest had witnessed how these myriad faces carried their own habits, unlikely quirks and singular tricks of the tongue. Being peculiar was normal. Being unique was ordinary. Humans had endless troubles trying to be human. Besides, the District of Districts had a reputation for its odd people, and war only made it more so: refugees fleeing the outlying Districts, particularly the wealthy and their grateful staffs; government officials sprouting from the shadows; officers too crafty to be sent into danger and young males learning to be soldiers in the high camps; plus the endless merchants taking "a little dust from every coin," making themselves even wealthier. Most of the world's tree-walkers were clinging to these the giant trees. There were even rumors about closing the borders to the outlying Districts, before the sheer mass of meat and money ripped the bloodwoods out by their roots.

In the midst of chaos, where almost every face belonged to a stranger, one fearful little soul could vanish easily, again and again.

Today and for almost six hundred days, Quest had wandered the forest by night, changing bodies and guises until dawn began to stir under the demon door. Forty-eight mornings ago, she found a chuckerhole and its owner, a ratty and selfish chucker monkey. The owner was waiting beside his escape hole, but he was also eager to defend his fortune of carefully hoarded trash. Chucker monkeys adored the color blue. That proud fellow assumed that Quest was here to steal his treasure, which was why he was easy to kill, and she ate him through the night, using the light of a fake glowdob to search the lost pieces of paper for anything useful.

Spotter uniforms were a deep wonderful blue, and the monkey had abducted several of those treasures.

The cleanest uniform carried the picture identification of a plain-faced woman. Quest donned the shirt and trousers, stolen boots and then a suitable body. With the plain face shining in the bright sunshine, she walked about in the human world. For ten days, nobody questioned her presence or her purpose. On the eleventh day, as she wandered the airy bottom of the forest, a genuine spotter called to her by her apparent rank.

Quest considered leaping into the open air, feigning suicide.

Suicides happened every day.

But the man kept talking, revealing his boundless ignorance as well as another possible stroke of luck.

"My shift's done," he claimed. "Please say you're here to replace me."

She carried a name and a woman's voice. Using both, she asked why he would grab that conclusion.

"You look lost," he said with considerable hope. "And I don't think anyone could find our station on the first try."

Hundreds of spotter stations occupied the low tips of the bloodwoods. These were not popular jobs. Crawling inside a big, overloaded room filled with telescopes and binoculars required a rare individual, someone who could stand the boredom and solitude, and this man was definitely not one of the best.

"I'll show you where you work," he said. "And I'll replace you come night."

She managed a believable smile, and later, when the grateful man in blue returned, Quest had a plausible life story to follow the smile. But the man never asked about where his partner came from or where she lived now, and he certainly didn't care about her sisters' names or why she voted for the Archon in the recent election.

Their relationship was instantly set, and perfect.

Quest roamed by night, changing form and directions while studying the sleeping world. She eavesdropped on small generals and linchpin clerks, massaging every word for meanings. She measured jet sounds and propeller sounds and the deep throb of the farthest battles. Every airship had a name that she knew, and every airship ran without lights in the darkness, trying not to be seen. But she noticed, and she often knew where the next battles would be fought, and because of her brother's questions, she watched the reef with neurotic care, hunting signs that the papio were about to launch some great final assault on the District of Districts.

There were respectable reasons for concern. Prisoners and two-faced spies talked about hidden fleets of wings, some bearing designs that had never been deployed. And the papio had captured fletches and blimps during the war, any ten of which might come here by night, pretending to be friendly. Every home was scared, but the mood was worse inside the Archon's palace. The treacherous and insatiable enemies were always coming tonight. Tomorrow. Soon. What was hiding inside those reef bunkers and surviving cities was beyond measure, which was why the citizenry and the high generals had no choice but think about little else.

That final night was the same as the previous thirty. Quest wandered and watched. Five airships and a squadron of wings destroyed one another among the dead blackwoods. Later she heard an important sound, but only once and she was far from the palace. By the time she arrived, the signal bell had been pulled back into its hiding hole, and she flew away, still wearing the leatherwing form.

Later, she plastered her body across a low limb, pretending to be an epiphyte, night-blooming flowers hiding an army of eyes.

Everything was memorable, but only because everything was always memorable.

Then the night felt done, and she was a different species of leatherwing gliding back to the chuckerhole, and after putting on the day's body and the blue uniform, she rode a descending rope, travelling down to where the rope bent and started up again. And that was the moment when the demon floor parted, raining burst upwards with a fabulous roar and the first ruddy wave of sunlight.

A woman in such circumstances was free to run.

She ran.

The rain was still rising when she arrived. But oddly, the male spotter wasn't waiting at the door. He was usually impatient to leave, preferring to escape before he was soaked, and his absence had to be a warning. Quest felt the strong urge to turn and flee, shucking off this over-trusted disguise afterwards. But the rain was just beginning, and it felt stronger than any storm from the last hundred mornings, and even her terrors had limits: nobody would be laying in ambush for her, not in this weather and with no place to hide.

The male spotter was indoors, but he wasn't waiting.

Unlike every other morning, he was doing real work. The station's largest telescope was fitted with special machinery, allowing spotters to see through the darkness half as well as any night-flying creature. The man's right eye was fixed to the final lens. His left hand was holding the call-line receiver. A voice at the other end of the line was talking, and then the spotter said, "Shut up. Shut up."

The distant voice shut up.

"You don't understand," the man said. "I see what I see. And it's there."

The telescope was supposed to be pointed at the reef and the papio. But instead the great brass gears had directed it straight down, aiming through a hole in the floor that had never made sense to Quest.

"When the rain stops, look," the spotter screamed.

Quest stood in the doorway, letting the water spray everything.

The voice on the line said, "But I won't sound the alarm."

"Then don't," said the spotter.

Quest made a sound inside her throat.

Then a man who couldn't even identify an alien standing in his midst looked up, noticing her and smiling at her as he reported with great joy, "It's another one of the big ones, the famous ones."

"Which ones?" she asked.

"The coronas," he said. "It's another big black ancient. You know. The sort that brought us the Children."

• • •

Coming into any room, Diamond always looked at Elata first.

Elata sat beside the long table. Her back was straight, a book opened where the plate belonged. Eggs and fresh crescents were cooking in the kitchen, making the air warmer, brighter. Chocolate eyes didn't look up. A finger and thumb were eager to turn the page. Diamond's eyes wanted to look at nothing else. He always embarrassed himself at moments like this. The girl was a younger, prettier version of her dead mother. The long black hair needed brushing, and she was wearing bedclothes and an old wine-colored robe, and nothing about her body was revealed . . . yet the boy spent a full breath doing nothing but absorbing her.

"It seems nobody can sleep," Mother called from the kitchen.

Thick windowless walls barely blunted the sound of water exploding upwards across the bloodwoods. The strongest wood in the world was twisting, and the entire palace groaned in response.

"Motion is a blessing," Father used to say. "Bending is stronger than being rigid and stubborn. And that's triply true with people too."

Other people were sharing the breakfast table.

Master Nissim sat beside Elata. Reading glasses rested lightly on the tip of his spectacular nose, bone frames holding bright new lenses. A tightly folded copy of the morning news was perched before him. Seldom was occupying the opposite chair, reading the opposite page. "Hi, Diamond," he said without looking up.

"Hi."

"Finished?" Nissim asked.

"No, sir," said Seldom, squinting at the tightly packed words.

The Master sat taller in a chair than anyone else. He had recently started to grow a beard, the whiskers emerging white and coarse. Removing his glasses, he told the newcomer, "You look well rested."

Diamond was walking towards the farthest chair.

Turning the page, Elata finally glanced at Diamond. "That's sarcasm," she said.

"Only if it's humorous," Nissim said.

Seldom rubbed his eyes. "Some battle woke me."

"Not me," Elata said.

Diamond began to sit, but then his mother called out. The words, "Come in here," were wrapped in a tone that could only mean him.

His bottom lifted off the chair.

Nissim was pouring bangle tea into his milk. Once more, he asked, "Are you finished?"

The tall boy leaned forwards, grinning. "Done."

"Do the folding, please."

Shaped like a giant funnel blossom, the news stood with its broad end down, flat outside faces defined by complicated folds hiding many more pages. Spidery fingers opened the blossom, hunting for fresh words.

"What did you read?" asked the Master.

"We shot down five of theirs in the Mists," said Seldom, "and only one of ours got damaged."

"What does that mean?"

"We lost two, and they lost three."

That battle was fought the day before yesterday.

"Anything else?" Nissim asked.

"I bet the fight wasn't far inside the District of the Mists," the skeptic said. "Probably near the border with our District."

"Our District." Seldom was the only one among them who claimed the District of District as his own.

Diamond stopped in the kitchen doorway. The room was bright and tall, with enough counter space for three servants to help prepare every possible meal. But the one lady who helped feed them was gone. Once Mother felt well enough, she made certain that their cook had a pleasant new job waiting, and then she fired her.

"You'll never eat as well as you did," she told her extended family. "But who deserves feasts, these days?"

Mother was finishing a wide skillet of eggs. Without looking up, she said, "Take the crescents out, put them in their bowl."

The oven door creaked as it fell open. The curled loafs of bread were resting on a sheet of black iron, their tips just beginning to burn. The mittens were hiding. Diamond used his hands, setting the iron on the polished coral counter.

Mother disapproved. He knew she would stare, and he imagined their conversation as he emptied the sheet two crescents at a time, the tips of each finger burnt worse than the oily bread. But Mother was ignoring him. Instead of the conversation that he expected, she said to her companion, "I told you two sweet nuts. How many was that?"

"One and one and one," said Good.

"Which is three," she warned.

The monkey looked at his best old friend, trying to share a grin. Then dipping his head, he moaned, "Sorry."

And he laughed.

"Take the crescents out," Mother repeated.

Blisters were already turning back into ordinary flesh. As Diamond matured, the healing came faster.

Mother shoveled the golden eggs into a matching bowl. "These too."

Diamond took the crescents, then the eggs. Mother had the nuts. Sweet nuts were the one indulgence—from one of the last happy blackwoods surviving inside their old District.

"Anything else?" she asked the table.

Reading wasn't allowed with food. Master Nissim set the news aside, and Elata closed her book and sat on it. Every chair was filled. There was room at the long table for others, but Mother didn't like how it looked. Empty chairs were just another item on that very long list of sights that made her sad.

Good sat on a box balanced on his chair. If he put one foot on the table, he would be sent to his room.

His room was Mother's room.

The carafe of oil was passed first, a little poured into the center of their plates, and after the food was claimed, the oil was passed a second time. Every bowl ended with Diamond. His plate was a serving platter, and his appetite was as big as any two others. Twenty days ago, he had visited the Grand University for the single purpose of sitting alone inside a special room—a sealed room built specifically for him—and he ate what he wanted and breathed naturally. Unseen people measured the oxygen used and the carbon dioxide coming out of him. The amounts were in balance, and what energy wasn't making new tissue went into heating his blood and stockpiling energy inside each of his busy cells. Numbers proved what everyone knew: his metabolism was like an hairyheart elf's, only on a giant scale. Scientists and doctors couldn't find anything that was genuinely, unabashedly magical, at least in that one narrow test. But all the same, the word "magic" was used quite a lot.

"Somebody needs to talk," Mother told the table.

She was sitting where she always sat, beside her son.

Master Nissim was the best hope. He smiled in a thoughtful way while looking at her, carefully measuring her state of mind. She didn't seem especially depressed or sensitive this morning, which was why he risked saying, "I'm taking my class on a little journey today."

That was the first word any of them had heard about this.

"The four of us are going to visit the Grand University. Again, yes. But we're exploring a different specialty. The world's leading expert on spheres and their mathematics has kindly agreed to make my students feel stupid."

Seldom laughed nervously.

Elata looked at Diamond. This was the first moment of the morning when she kept her eyes on him, and he felt her gaze, glad for it and not glad for it.

"Well," Mother said with a flat tone. "That sounds very entertaining."

Sarcasm, thought Diamond.

"Join us," Nissim said.

Diamond thought that was funny, at least a little bit.

She looked at him, letting a smile slip free. "You think I'll be bored."

"I will be," he said.

"Not me," Seldom had to say.

Elata's broad shoulder gave a shrug. "There's a lot more than math at the University."

"No," Mother said. "I want to hear about spheres."

She sounded earnest.

Diamond didn't know what to believe. He tried to laugh but ended up sounding dismissive when he asked, "Why?"

"Spheres are the perfect shape," she said. "Every child knows it, even before he learns so in school."

Nissim had opinions on the subject that he didn't dare mention.

Mother grabbed her boy by the hand, squeezing and staring at his face. "He told me," she began, and then she had to gather herself.

"Who told you?" Seldom asked.

Father, she meant.

"Merit," she said. But she didn't cry or look especially sad. The name was a pleasure to share and she might be able say it ten times without bending too much, shattering in the end.

Reading strength in her face, everybody relaxed.

"When he was flying," she said. "When he was beneath the District of Districts, and the sunlight was strong and the air clear, he would climb on top of his ship and look at all of the world at once. The hemisphere above covered with its the forest, and the reef wrapped the faintest gold mist, and he could almost see past the coral and wood, seeing the edge of Creation falling smoothly down into the demon floor, and that was one of the loveliest sights anywhere."

Then with a bittersweet edge, she said again, "One of the loveliest."

Nobody spoke.

Only time spoke.

Then out from the silence, she said, "Yes, I'd love to go with you."

Good understood. He was going to be abandoned at home, and that was the moment when he reached out with his bare feet, nabbing several of the sweet nuts off their plate.

Then he galloped off, the usual reprimands chasing after him.

There was pleasant talk after that. For several recitations, every subject was small and vital.

Outside, the rain was finally slackening.

Silence was trying to grasp the world.

Then from some distant place came the diluted roar of a siren. There was just one siren, the warning beginning in the direction of the Bluewind District, but quickly more and closer sirens joined in. And in another few moments there was nothing to hear but the wailing of hundreds of sirens and the first ominous firings of cannons—every gun aiming at nothing, doing nothing but mapping the winds.

• • •

Slayers had always hunted the margins.

The best hunting was beneath the Corona District, which was a respectable reason for the papio to burn blackwoods and burn hunter-ships and kill every human clinging to any burnt out tree trunk, in hopes of dispatching just one more slayer.

Survivors retreated into the District of Districts, finding sanctuaries where new hunters could be trained, building shops and hangers where military weapons could be lashed to their last ships. But the early days of the war didn't have much serious noise about chasing the coronas again. Fighting monsters was already difficult work, but it was familiar and halfway predictable. Slayers were not soldiers. Bullets and flame made the smallest hunt into a suicidal dash, and one little carcass wouldn't be worth any risk. Besides, the Archon and his wise ancestors had stockpiled corona parts, stuffing warehouses full of bladders and scales and skins and iron—a cache that would surely outlast the anger that had already eaten away at lives and wealth.

But then again, maybe there weren't as many warehouses as rumored. And there definitely was a shortage of visionaries—people who had imagined full-scale war being waged for six hundred days. Both sides were suffering from shortfalls, and both species were making brash plans. The papio had built ugly gas airships that hid inside bunkers by day, slipping out at night to hunt the margins of the reef. And meanwhile, the tree-walking generals had pulled some of their precious military fletches from service, adapting them to chase the coronas and fight the papio at the same time.

The young man was happy to learn how to hunt like a slayer.

But he already knew how to fight.

"Wake up," he told his roommate, shaking the bunk before giving the lazy boy one little twist of a fist.

Like a pill bug, the boy pulled himself into a ball, trying to protect his belly.

"So what, there's sirens," he complained.

Slayers didn't fire cannons with the ordinary troops.

"It's not the damn sirens," Karlan said. Then he dragged the boy off the high bed, watching him fall to the floor.

The boy was named Ticker, and he didn't like to fight.

"What's this about?" Ticker asked.

"Something's been spotted, and we've got to go."

They didn't hunt unless a worthy corona was flying directly beneath the District of Districts. Otherwise it was a sure loss of equipment and probably lives, and no spoils would come home in the end.

Pulling on trousers, Ticker asked, "How big?"

"Barely big enough," Karlan lied.

The boy did love to hunt though, which was the only reason he didn't find himself thrown him back with the common soldiers.

"Faster," Karlan said.

Clean shirts were too much of a challenge. Ticker threw on yesterday's shirt and then started lacing into the armor.

Then a voice pushed through the wail of sirens. One of the original slayers was down in the hanger, shouting, "The prize won't linger."

"Is it?" Ticker asked.

"They think so," Karlan said.

"Damn, you could have told me," the boy said, bursting through the door with his battle gear only halfway secured.

At his own pace, Karlan dressed. The armor was special-made for him, oversized and half again thicker than anyone else's. A fortune in corona scales had been fused together, and the helmet was a marvel of tiny interlocking scales harvested from the tiniest coronas. Karlan wasn't shy about using favors to get the best for himself. The hero who killed the Eight the first time deserved a lot more than accolades. Nobody else put an end to the rampage that murdered Merit, and he certainly didn't start any wars in the process. Merit's adopted son generated a lot of opinions among slayers, but in these ranks, Karlan was always offered free drinks and his pick of duties, and the women slayers had granted him a lot more than wine and the ship's prime gun.

The ship was a fletch called *Tomorrow's Girl*.

Once a warship, it had been reconfigured to hold double duties. The front high-hand turret had been dragged clear up to the nose, affording its gunner a grand view of everything. The harpoon gun was a marvel when it came to killing—a combination of the explosives to stun the prey and wires leading back to a bank of capacitors that would cook any corona to death. But that gun wasn't brought out until there was some beast to shoot. For the rest of the flight, Karlan was the master of a cannon that threw out fountains of hard rounds mixed with bursts of explosive rounds. Three shattered wings had been credited to his marksmanship, and he was confident that others had flown away injured, probably dropping through the demon floor before they got home.

Dressed for his day, Karlan was the final crewmember to stride into the hanger.

The captain considered words but didn't risk them. Whatever he thought about his big spoiled hero, he had learned not to complain too openly about these flashes of independence.

Besides, the *Girl* wasn't ready to fly. The big engines were running hard, but half of the crew was helping overfill the special ballast tanks, including Ticker. Too many hands were as bad as too few, and that's why the rest of the crew stood beside the open door. Karlan joined those admiring the new day. The morning light was even more staggering than normal, the rain having washed the air clear while the coronas' realm was less yellow than usual, slightly more transparent.

"See it?" one man asked.

Another man said, "Yes," and then, "No."

The prettiest woman smiled at the newcomer, offering him the smoked glass so he could stare down at the sun.

"Wait," said the first man. "Here it comes again."

What was coming?

Karlan wasn't often startled. But then the shadow swept over them. It wasn't total, and it certainly wasn't like the stories told from before. Night didn't come when the giant eclipsed the sun. But the sun's raw brilliance faltered for a blink, and inside the grayness were odd hints of motion and design, swirling according the titanic motions of what was possibly the largest entity in the Creation.

Karlan never had time to look through the darkened glass.

"Launch," the captain called out on the loudspeaker.

They broke into running gaits, taking their stations faster than they ever managed during the drills.

Karlan's oversized seat had extra belts and a piece of fur from a royal jazzing that everyone insisted would bring luck. But even when he was buckled in place, the *Girl* remained in its berth. Intercom noise was about new orders. Ticker waved at him from inside one of the back turrets, and the two men opened a gunner's line.

"We're with the second wave," the boy said.

More than that was obvious. Karlan could still hear the sirens over the roaring engines, and a lot of planning and more rambling conversations pushed into his thoughts.

"We won't get our shots," Ticker said.

"We will," Karlan said. "Don't worry."

But other fletches were already plunging out of the station's hangers, one and then another diving past their open door. If they left with their first chance, they already would have made it a long ways to the target.

"That other giant," Ticker said. "She was slow and didn't fight. Killing her was nothing. So yeah, the first wave is going to have this one dead and trussed up before we even get close."

"Trust me," Karlan said. "We're lucky people, and get your head ready."

And just like that, the *Girl* rose off the hanger's floor, the engines erasing every other sound in the world. That big fletch was ridiculously heavy, and most of its ballast wasn't even pulling yet. With Karlan at the nose, leading the way, the ship pushed into the scrubbed and blazing air. A thin trickle of rainwater hit the backside of the turret, splattering and then pooling against the flat scale-covered hull. Then the swollen ballast bags were dragged out behind them—six bags made from woven growler hides. Each bag was secured by short strong ropes, and each was filled with the cheapest, most disposable product in the world. Water leaked at the seams, but that wasn't important. The bags didn't have to hold together for more than a few recitations. The target was far below, probably flying weakly over the demon floor, and this was what slaying was today: drop hard and fast, making the kill without wasting a breath, and then fight to secure the carcass and bring it home again before the papio decided to attack.

Except today was different.

Karlan knew it.

The ballast bags were dragged across the hanger's floor, and then they fell, dragging the *Girl* downward at a staggering, wondrous pace.

Everybody screamed, at least inside themselves.

Karlan yelled heartily for a full recitation, loving the sense of motion and how the ship trembled at its core, and that was before he spotted the round black blotch of a corona that already looked huge from up high with a long way to go.

War loved secrets, and here was one of the big secrets that everybody talked about when they thought nobody was listening: what if someday, with warning or without, another giant corona surfaced?

One of those old beasts surrendered four dangerous children to the world. Another litter of cherubs could be hiding inside the next giant, which made everybody hungry and scared, and in ways that were definitely not normal, it made them smart. That first giant was just one of an ancient generation of coronas. Her peers were old and dying, and each one of them would emerge at the end. If one lady had a belly full of indigestible monsters, then all of them could be bearing gifts. Or curses. Whichever they were.

There was a point to all of this shrewd clarity: whoever won the next prize might win every war to come. That's why Karlan heard rumors and smart guesses about special plans for days exactly like this. It was even said that the generals who oversaw the war—the silk uniforms that controlled the world—were gathering around tables, playing elaborate kid games. They were testing what they should do when an ancient monster surfaced, and they guessed what their enemies might attempt in response, and they were trying to figure out the very best way to use whatever the carcass surrendered.

The fine long plunge continued.

The first wave was already approaching the target. Binoculars showed Karlan the blackish corona leaking its weak golden light, begging for someone's help, and then a single fletch dove into the scene, its ballast discarded and the big engines trying to coax it close enough for one clean killing shot. But those maneuvers were abandoned moments later. Suddenly the fletch tried to climb, banking hard to let its high-hands aim at other targets, and then came a bright flash as twin rockets struck it and detonated, the impact and blasts throwing the machine downwards, spinning as it fell.

The airship struck the demon floor, skimming for an instant before punching through and turning to flame.

Ticker cursed, complaining, "The papio never come this fast."

Why would they? They never had a worthwhile target.

"Do you see that, Karlan? There's got to be twenty wings below us."

More than twenty, and that didn't count aircraft still coming from other bases scattered along the reef. Karlan made one slow circle with his turret and cannon, getting a sense of the mayhem that had only just begun.

The papio were smart.

He had no doubts about that.

Smart meant coming here with at least two ways to win. The weak victory would be killing the corona, sending it back under the demon floor. Let it die with its own kind while keeping any treasures from being captured by the enemy. That wouldn't be the worst end. But the strong victory—the reason for parades and medals and maybe a few statues in the bargain—involved claiming the carcass for themselves and then against long odds, somehow dragging it home again.

At first glance, that was as impossible as any task could be.

But Karlan had already invested time wrestling with the problem. And seeing what was happening—the numbers of wings coming and their fantastic speed—he had a clear sense of what had to happen next.

To Ticker, he said, "Stow your cannon. Deploy the harpoon, now."

"But we're going to be under fire," the boy complained.

Arguing would waste time. Karlan stowed his cannon instead and pulled up the pneumatic gun, locking it into position.

Ticker noticed, and proving his stupidity, he called the bridge to warn the captain what the lead high-hand was doing.

Karlan's com-line started buzzing.

The *Girl* had dropped as far as the pilot dared take them, and with a single wrenching motion, the extra ballast was released. Massive sacks continued falling, bursting against the demon floor, and the water dribbled through, instantly turning to steam. But the ship continued to descend, slower now but willing to spend the last of its altitude. More water and soaked timbers came out of the belly as the machine and the men onboard tried to remember the magic of floating in one place.

The com-line fell silent.

They were following an arc, approaching the corona from above. The giant body was gray and yellow and perfectly round, inflated until it looked ready to burst. The mouth couldn't be seen, but no doubt the corona was pushing bursts of hot air out of its mouth, fighting for any lift. All that effort, but the demon floor lay just below, and the animal was plainly struggling not to fall back into its world.

The *Girl*'s first officer appeared beneath Karlan's turret. A young high-hand needed to suffer a good yelling, it seemed. "Kill the enemy first," the officer said. "Then we'll kill the corona."

"But look," said Karlan. "The monster's ready to fall back under."

"Ensign," the officer shouted. "Follow orders."

Harpoons were stowed on racks behind his seat. It was a clumsy, messy system put in place because the turret had two jobs. Gauging speed, Karlan guessed they were going to catch the corona in another half-recitation. Ticker had his turret opened up. He was firing at the papio, and it looked as if he was trying to kill all of them, filling the air with holes.

That voice below kept nagging.

Looking between his feet, Karlan said, "The cannon's jammed, sir. Come here, please. I need help."

The officer started climbing into the turret.

Karlan struck him with a fist, not particularly hard, and then the man was sitting in the hallway below, nursing a broken nose.

The *Girl* moved from falling into a climb, accelerating all the while. Somebody wanted to get them into position to defend their claim, which was stupid. Karlan spun his chair, digging into the harpoon stash. One harpoon was different from all others. It lacked explosives and the killing electrical line. Nothing rode that shaft but springs and barbed hooks that were folded tight, waiting to bite hold of the meat, and only that harpoon was coupled to a thick steel cable that fed straight from the fletch's bow.

Karlan loaded that harpoon and popped the compressor button.

A thousand deep breaths were squeezed into a tiny steel chamber, and the breech began to hiss.

Only then did he yank open the turret's canopy.

The corona was beside him—a vast looming dome-shaped piece of life. Dangling from the underside was a forest of long necks and heads, but every neck was limp, heads looking weak and sloppy. Only a few of those heads bothered glancing at the *Girl*. Scales were missing from the body, and bulges and discolored splotches showed where cancers had taken root. Plainly, the beast was on its final days. Karlan couldn't guess its mind. He shouldn't bother trying. But he suspected madness, maybe senility, watching the corona conjure the last dregs of its energies, trying hard not to fall back through the floor, perhaps lost forever.

Fletch engines throttled up, and the bow began to lift.

The high-hand aimed and the harpoon burst free. Steel screamed as the cable flew off the drum inside the ship's nose. Then the metal shaft pierced the old scales, weak and frail as paper, and the springs fired and the long hooks deployed inside a mass of ancient scar tissue.

The drum felt the slack line and automatically pulled in the tension.

In an instant, the *Girl* had been fused to its quarry, and feeling the weight, its nose dipped, unable to climb any farther.

The bloodied officer was standing again, pulling at one of Karlan's boots while screaming about this gross insubordination.

As if picking up a half-cup of tea, Karlan grabbed the man by his neck, lifting him into the turret while his dry steady voice said, "I'm giving you a present."

The officer struggled.

Karlan gave him a rough shake.

"You want the cannon?" he asked. "Deploy it yourself."

The officer managed to ask, "Why?"

"Because I'm insubordinate, and you relieved me from my duties."

Taking a sidearm and binoculars, Karlan went straight to the bridge.

The pilot and captain were sharing the controls. The captain looked miserable and a little lost, but seeing the high-hand gave him purpose.

"You aren't on station," he said.

"It's the corona," Karlan said.

"What's that?"

"The corona wants to stay up here with us. We need to put balloons inside it, give it all our help. Every ship needs to lash on and use their balloons."

The captain saw no reason to believe this noise. He seemed barely able to understand even the words, shaking his head as he asked, "How do you know what the creature wants?"

With a stern, certain voice, Karlan lied. "Merit was my neighbor. He taught me everything about coronas."

That name always had purchase among slayers. The captain wasn't sure how to debate the point.

Then the pilot interrupted, announcing, "They aren't firing on us, sir."

"What?"

"The papio are standing back," the pilot said, trying to be happy about the news.

Karlan joined the pilot, pushing binoculars against his eyes. Maybe the first wings were holding back, but a second wave was coming fast as bullets, and he didn't recognize their design.

Oh, he had to smile.

"Surrender your weapon, son," said the captain.

"I've seen this before," Karlan said. "The papio are going to board us. They want our ships."

"Impossible," the captain said.

These new wings were blunt but powerful, faster than any other wing that was capable of hovering, but that's what they intended to do, pushing close as the jets began to tilt, killing their terrific forward momentum.

"Oh, sir," the pilot said.

"Your weapon," said the captain, showing a trembling hand.

Karlan ran. Three strides and he was off the bridge, out of sight. The captain had so much free time that he could come across the intercom, telling his crew that the young ensign was insubordinate and possibly a traitor and to take all necessary measures to bring him under control.

The cargo hold was in the ship's belly. If Karlan had to jump onboard a moving fletch, that's where he'd make it happen. But a couple slayer/soldiers were waiting in the hallway just outside, automatic weapons aimed at the criminal.

Karlan stopped and dropped his pistol, and then his empty hands lifted a little higher than his waist.

He smiled until the faces relaxed. Nobody was about to be shot.

The roar of jets ended the peace, followed by one hard blast.

The *Girl* lifted and two slayers fell. Then Karlan was between them, grabbing up one of their guns and both of them, handing over his pistol to the unarmed man.

"What's happening?" that man asked.

"I don't know," Karlan said. "Let's look."

The doorway into the hold was jammed by the blast. Karlan stepped back and kicked it once, and it was open. Sunlight rose from what should be darkness. He stayed back and fired just one round, and a bullet came back at him, striking the metal doorframe before turning into coral dust.

Coral instead of metal; the papio didn't want punctured bladders by accident.

Karlan cursed and fired but stayed back, hiding his body.

The man with the pistol was much braver. Jumping into the opening, he screamed, "We're boarded," and fired once before sitting on the floor with his throat shattered and blood pumping down the front of his cheap, badly fitted armor.

Karlan put his free hand on the other slayer.

"Wait," he said.

Just as he guessed, a flash grenade came rattling out from below. He jumped on it and flung it back below, and one of those fine rugged papio curses could be heard just before the thump of the blast.

Smoke came next, thick and black.

Again, Karlan told his companion, "Wait."

Papio soldiers were shouting at each other. Karlan couldn't understand any words, but five distinct voices seemed to be arguing tactics.

The slayer beside him was shaking with nerves.

Not Karlan.

As a boy, he heard those stories about great warriors who were happy only when they were in battle. But what he had learned already as a fighter was that battles brought nothing that was happy. Gunfire scared him to the core, and he was no different than the others. But what attracted him—what found Karlan in these moments and what lingered afterwards—was the sense that most of existence was nothing. Life was an empty place full of nothing, like one of those heavy jars in the labs where they pumped out the air and the heat, leaving nothing but the void. Only in these little moments of terror did something true and real rush into the emptiness.

This moment wasn't joyful and it wasn't unpleasant. Now and for the next long while, Karlan would experience the absolute clarity that comes when life begins and nothing else has room. A mind could engage so fully that it would race past the ordinary, and that's why he left the trembling slayer behind. Crawling into the smoke, Karlan grabbed the shot slayer by the back of his armor. The man was still bleeding, still dying. He was easy to hold up high, and Karlan stood and fired into the clearing smoke just once, just to draw attention, and two soldiers shot the doomed slayer and Karlan kept holding him, pieces of coral finishing the job.

The papio had to steal this ship fast.

They advanced bravely, and Karlan used the dead man as a shield, putting down four of the enemy before his clip was empty.

The fifth soldier got into the hallway.

And then it was nothing but hands and feet and teeth, and yeah, maybe that part of the battle got to be fun.

THREE

The two of them had never touched.

"Hold my hand," she said, standing close to him but not close.

The spotter was already excited by everything happening below. Looking at the woman, he was startled and a little thrilled to discover that she was prettier than he recalled. She wasn't watching the battle through her little telescope. Looking at him, her hand was outstretched with those long fingers rippling, and that fine young face was showing some him some kind of smile.

He took the offered hand.

Something cut into his palm.

He said, "Ouch," even as he tried to hold on to her. But the pain was too intense, and he took back his hand, shaking it slowly, stoically.

"I'm sorry," she said.

The spotter meant to say that it was nothing, forget it. But his words started to pile up on his thickening tongue.

"Sit down," the pretty woman suggested.

Sitting was the last thing that he wanted to do. Blinking hard, he looked through his telescope's eyepiece. Except the giant corona had turned into one very dark blur, and the fletches and papio wings were nearly invisible against the yellow shine of the demon floor and the world beneath.

He rubbed his eyes, using the hand that didn't hurt.

Then he stopped rubbing, and without feeling any sensation, he quietly dropped to the floor.

The woman stepped over him. She was still quite pretty, except her face was wrong in the middle, dark human eyes replaced with bulging domes that resembled brightly polished crystal. And that was the moment when, for many fine reasons, the man lost consciousness.

Mayhem ants stung bark rats and other prey with this toxin. Creating the molecule was simple. Using it successfully was more problematic. The man could stop breathing, which would leave her with the unwelcome decision of employing the antidote or not. Or the man could die of cardiac failure, which would present her with another dilemma—whether or not to eat his empty body.

But thankfully the man's breathing remained steady.

Quest claimed his telescope—the big better telescope. Her new eyes were more powerful than anything a proud hawk would sport. Through the glass, she saw three fletches burning, bladders and torn hulls splattering against the demon floor. One more fletch was hovering above the great corona, a hair of steel tight between them. The corona was the greatest in Creation, its interior gorged with hot air and vacuum, and the circular body shook every time hot air roared out of its mouth, shoving it a little higher. Every strength was being spent to maintain its slight altitude above the glistening floor, and it spoke only as it breathed again, falling slowly—speaking as waves of yellow light that swirl across the bloated gray body, the effect pitiful and magnificent.

The papio had surrounded the corona, throwing cannon fire at the free-flying airships and flares at each other, and then they weren't firing anymore, circling their quarry at a wide, watchful distance.

Quest considered stepping outside, remaking herself with the sleek shape of a champion hawk and then leaping.

But one bold thought woke old fears, nailing her current feet to the floor.

And then as if proving her wisdom, new aircraft arrived at the battle site. They were swift despite being burly, odd bones riding some very powerful jets. Quest had studied every papio weapon, and these resembled nothing else—entities created just now, for this special day.

One of the new aircraft rushed the corona, jets pivoting as it slowed abruptly, parking beneath that lone fletch that had lashed itself to the creature.

The corona blew air and hovered, and the other fletches converged, making a larger circle around their round quarry. And the swift papio wings circled in the distance while the new ships hovered in a single watchful mass. All of the fuel in the world wouldn't keep the papio aloft for long, she thought. And then the corona let out a bright flash of yellow light, and one side of the body dipped far enough to slice into the demon floor. The floor broke, splitting like the face of water in a bowl, and the creature dropped farther, necks pulling back as if to avoid this fate, and then the great body flapped its edges and blew air and swelled even more, lifting up once again, defeating its weight and its drag for another few moments.

Flares were dropped from the other fletches.

A new plan was found.

Half of hunter ships attacked the corona, piercing it with harpoons tied to lines that dragged dozens of flattened bladders into the bright furious air. Pressurized hydrogen turned the bladders into taut white balloons. The miserable corona continued to flap and blow, but now a hand was lifting it from above. Altitude was bought, and the corona quit struggling for a moment or two, and it was easy to imagine thankfulness in those next flashes of blue light, and then more flashes far beyond purple.

Then the papio attacked again, en masse.

For Quest, time wasn't defined by how long it took one human mouth to finish one recitation. Time was the accumulation of incidents and activities, and if nothing happened, no time passed. Or like now, everything below her happened at once, and time had never been swifter. Those blunt new aircraft singled out fletches to attack from below, presumably to steal them from their crews. Other fletches were attacked by warrior pilots onboard the roaring hawkspur wings. She could hear the battle, the gunfire and explosions and the occasional blaring horn pushing through the morning air. She heard the concussive blasts of breath coming from the dying giant. What had been scattered fleets turned into a single confused maelstrom. Even her spectacular eyes and swift reflexes fought to keep track of every ship. Nothing was certain. But it seemed as if the papio had the initiative, tearing apart two and then another three fletches with no losses of their own. And every one of the new aircraft was positioned beneath a target—sometimes two underneath the same target. All the fuel in the world wouldn't keep them aloft for much longer, but this was a one-way mission. Papio soldiers must have drilled and drilled in secret, probably for hundreds of days, learning how to steal the fletches and save themselves while giving their species the spectacular gift.

The tree-walkers were losing.

Quest started making brave little plans to find her way to the reef, to watch any new siblings being born, although there wasn't much chance that she would actually dare it.

Then an eye that never blinked saw everything change.

The corona was doing nothing. It wasn't blowing, and the soft old body had shriveled, each of its bladders deflating slightly. And then every neck was moving, swifter than Quest imagined possible. They stretched and reached above the body, those old jaws grabbing what they could and holding as tight as they could with the few teeth left to them. They bit down on the papio machines, nothing else, and the necks tugged until the aircraft spilled one way or another, losing their trim.

Quest counted the ships plunging through the floor.

Every ship died.

One plan was ruined, and now the hawkspurs on the periphery swept in to attack the corona, trying to puncture the balloons keeping it aloft. But more fletches drove harpoons and balloons into the body, and the high-hands were ready with crossing fire and easy, bold targets already short of ammunition. The corona was suddenly limp and most certainly dead, but the papio were defeated as well. One species survived, and what had triggered the slaughter was adorned with a hundred swollen balloons that worked as one, forcing the carcass upwards, fast and then faster.

Quest stepped back from the telescope.

One last time, she looked at the man on the floor. Except for the achingly slow rise and fall of his chest, he didn't move. He was alive but with nothing to spare.

She knelt down, prying open one blind eye.

A taste of the antidote passed into the quiet, half-dead blood.

Then she stepped outside, looking up at the forest, each of the enormous bloodwoods wrapped with homes and stubby, bristle-leafed limbs, each one tapering down to a point like the point where she stood, as close to the sun as possible. Thousands of people were hiding. Thousands more were watching the marvels below. And meanwhile the dead corona was covered with balloons and rising faster by the instant, which was what Quest was watching when another brave plan came to mind—a plan that refused to be ignored.

• • •

Major engagements, regardless how distant, meant the immediate rooms were locked down. Public call-lines were disabled. Air vents were sealed. Toilets stopped working after the first flush. Without windows, the outside world was an invisible realm quivering with potential. One could imagine anything happening. But Diamond's thoughts always turned the long-feared kidnapping: a squadron of top-line fletches defending the palace, well-rested soldiers marshalling inside the palace hallways and ballrooms, and the papio arriving on columns of flame and thunder.

Most lockdowns were brief and dull, ending without explanation.

The resident sentries were as uninformed as anyone else trapped inside, though they worked hard conveying that guardly sense of stoic, unimaginative resolve.

But there were long attacks that brought endless sirens and little else. The adrenalin kick was soon swallowed by life, and because no room was considered safer than any other, life inside their home continued as best as it could. Elata dressed after breakfast.

The trip to the Grand University was out of the question, so Nissim suggested that school start early.

Mother informed the sentries that everybody would be in the classroom. She sat in back. Good made a bed between her and Diamond. The Master stood up front, and with an expression more calm than concerned, he contemplated the wailings. "This does seem longer than usual," he admitted.

"Maybe it's a drill," Seldom suggested.

Drills sounded the same as attacks, but they had more endurance.

Scratching his chin and the bristly whiteness, Nissim said, "I don't think a drill . . . "

And then every siren was turned off, the world filled with an abrupt, ear-rattling silence.

Everyone was ready for the soldiers' call-line to blare, announcing the lockdown's end. But what they heard was the grumbling chatter between a pair of men at the end of the adjacent hallway.

Mother excused herself and left.

Master Nissim grabbed a history book, naming a likely page.

Seldom dutifully opened his copy. Diamond had already read the book to the end, and putting his hands over the cover, he closed his eyes, flipping through the pages in his mind.

Mother and the guards were whispering. The guards' call-line was working, but nobody wanted to share any news with them.

A pad of paper and two pencils were on Elata's desk. Her textbooks were stowed, and nothing mattered but drawing what was inside her head.

The Master said her name.

"I heard you," she said, drawing faster.

Nissim wanted to be careful with Elata. Watching the girl, he felt a teacher's frustrations mixed with growing concerns. Nobody here should be happy. Tragedy had weight and power, and each face showed its effects hundreds of days later. For a long while, Elata was the bellwether, first to anger and quick to cry and quicker still to tell the Master that history was a ridiculous subject.

"It's all the same story, again and again," she would complain. "Why waste our little time with crap that never changes?"

"Because what can be predicted can be understood," he had argued. "And in little ways, the inevitable can be beaten."

They had some fine debates on the subject, yes.

But ten days ago, there was a change. The girl turned pleasant overnight. She still didn't want to read history, but she was polite, even sweet about her defiance. A smile kept surfacing, and what most alarmed Nissim was that he believed in her smile. But the girl had always been an accomplished liar. So long as Elata's true thoughts were a mystery, he intended to watch her carefully.

"Seldom," said the Master. "Would you please read the bottom passage?"

The boy's long back needed to be straightened, and Seldom always grew serious when reading. Even reciting a joke, words came out slow and heavy.

" 'The first person to define the natural motions of weight was not Akkan Cheen, as is commonly thought. At least three other scientists from three distinct earlier ages have been credited for making these discoveries independently. It seems as though each era of social order and relative wealth leads to the same epiphanies, and perhaps that is the mark of real disorder—when we forget what should be self-evident, and for the willing mind, what should be most beautiful.' "

Seldom finished with a grin.

Nissim once took Diamond aside, saying, "You deserve to be told. The best student that I have—the finest that I've ever known—is Seldom. It isn't you, and that probably won't ever change."

Diamond had the perfect memory, but Seldom adored knowledge.

Diamond could easily outthink his friend, yet he never outworked him or wrung half as much pleasure from an elegant thought found inside his own head.

To all three students, the Master said, "I adore that passage."

Diamond nodded, waiting.

"And why do I like it?"

Diamond was listening and reading in his head, and he was looking at Elata too. He saw her serious focused and very pretty face and how the long pencil swirled over the paper, creating the shaggy magnificence of a blackwood tree.

The girl habitually drew pictures of her lost home.

"Diamond," said the Master.

Diamond blinked and looked ahead, ready for an answer to pop into his mind.

Then Nissim said, "No. Not your first response."

The boy blinked, a little startled.

"Give me your eighth reaction. Will you try to do that for me?"

He wasn't sure that was possible, but he started to resurrect what had just happened inside his head, counting the ideas.

Then the sentries' call-line cackled.

A sour voice said, "Yeah?"

Something felt peculiar. Mother was standing in the hallway, leaning toward their protectors. Everyone listened as the sentry said nothing. They heard his boots sliding on the bloodwood floor, and the man taking a deep nervous breath. It was easy to imagine neck veins bulging, and maybe his hand shook a little. Then the same voice said one more word.

"Understood."

But the sentry didn't quite understand. He got as far as Mother before he stopped and delivered the news.

"That was the Archon," he said, amazed by the important voice. "They found another one and they're bringing it to big abattoir on Jakken's Tree."

"Another what?" Nissim asked.

"You know," the man said, trying to sound sharp and informed. "It's one of those special coronas."

What did that mean?

"A detachment's coming to take you," he continued. "All of you. The Archon and King are already leaving . . . but he wants all of you brought after him."

"What special corona?" Diamond asked.

But the answer had already popped into his head, and it was probably in everyone else's head too.

Another silence got started.

And then as they were sharing numbed, astonished looks, Elata suddenly stood up, throwing her pencil down, a loud grim half-happy voice saying, "Well, good. Now we can finally be outside."

• • •

Elata had known her intentions for the last few days.

As soon as she had the chance, whenever that was, she was going to climb over a convenient railing or open a likely window and then jump to her death.

The image found her one morning, clear and sharp and perfect. Her plan had one immediate benefit: for the first time in ages, Elata felt something that resembled happiness. She wasn't joyful or ready to laugh, but the massive ache dragging at her soul was gone. A decision was made. Like the old phrase said: "One branch left to walk." All that remained was finding the means while not losing her focus. She didn't want others watching her when she did it, because that would be mean. But she also couldn't afford to be picky with time and place. The others would try to stop her. Give them any warning, and they'd throw words at her, kindness and lies wrapped together, and they would use their own bodies too. But none of their warm-hearted efforts would work. Elata was certainly the dumbest person inside this house, and that might include Good. But better than anyone else, she didn't bother trying to find the best answers to every smart, unanswerable question, and when given an answer to what mattered, she would never waste time with doubt or thinking twice.

Life wasn't big enough for doubts, and after the first day of being alive, everything started filling up fast.

Elata knew that better than anyone.

Her bedroom was a mess of stuffed drawers and overflowing boxes and dirty clothes thrown over the clean, and standing in the middle of that unmapped chaos, she yelled at people who probably weren't even thinking about her, telling them that she would be there in another two breaths.

Where did she hide her purse?

There. The leather-and-brass satchel was tucked at the bottom of a wooden box filled with secondhand dolls. It made her a little sick, reaching past those brightly painted big-eyed faces. She never liked playing with dolls. They were nothing but fancy sticks. Real babies and grown people never looked this way. But some old woman decided that she was another orphan needing toys, and the gift came with a soft pat on the shoulders. Elata had threatened to throw all of them away. But that was when they first arrived here and everybody was trying to be nice. Haddi took Elata aside to talk. With her most reasonable voice, the despairing widow told the gloomy orphan girl, "You should keep them, in case you have a daughter someday."

Elata was living with strange, sick people, and talk about a daughter was just another example of how screwed up everyone was.

People they knew and people they didn't know were always looking at Diamond and then at her.

She knew what they were thinking.

And she knew even better what she was thinking, which seemed like a blessing lately. This was the day to leave the world, she knew. Unless a different day would be better. Either way, Elata had a fancy purse filled with folded up drawings—the big drawings of blackwoods that others had seen, and also the secret drawings of her mother and her long dead father, plus her friends, including half a dozen careful drawings showing Diamond at various ages.

Seldom called plaintively to Elata.

She ran back to the main doorway, except nobody was there except one young soldier, and his only duty was to wave her towards the half-secret emergency exit in the back of the house.

Haddi was the first person she saw. The old woman was telling the monkey to stay behind, and Good stuck out his chest, glad for the order. New soldiers had appeared, unfamiliar faces and muscles and office clothes bulging where the guns tried to hide, and only one of those men had a voice. He told Elata that she was wasting time. She smiled, making apologetic sounds. The hidden door led into a tunnel that existed only in reality and inside a few heads. No map or official diagram included this passageway cut through the bloodwood's trunk. She had used it twice before, and it emptied onto a private landing owned by a fictional citizen, and there were three routes off the landing, into the mayhem of this overpopulated District.

This group would take one of those routes.

It didn't matter which.

And that's where she would take her break for freedom. The decision would be made with instinct, with her feet. She let herself imagine nothing but the running. If she grabbed a lead, then the only person fast enough to catch her was Diamond. But on the list of what was important, Diamond was a thousand slots higher than whoever happened to be second place, and these soldiers would almost certainly wrestle him down before he could confuse the situation.

Bodies were waiting inside the tunnel. The space was narrow and infinitely long, the only lights carried by hand, and the black air was always stale in the middle reaches. Rough, hurried tools had punched through the bloodwood, the rounded walls bristling with splinters that could shred fingers or entire hands.

She got into the line.

Everybody walked down the tunnel's middle.

Nissim was ahead of Elata, his tall body hiding everyone else, and Seldom was directly behind her, long feet catching her heel once and then again.

"Sorry," Seldom said.

From the front, the boss soldier said, "Quiet."

Nobody could hear talking from inside the tree. But soldiers always wanted people to be quiet, if for no other reason than to keep their own heads clear.

The stale air got worse. Even good quiet soldiers coughed.

Diamond never coughed. That was one of those odd details in a boy who was built on oddities. Spending all of her days and nights with Diamond had made her understand just how strangely different he was.

Diamond was walking ahead of Nissim, she sensed.

Some kind of "good-bye" wanted to be said. But that would ruin everything. The perfect plan was to run away, buying distance and surrounding herself with strangers. And when nobody was paying attention to one girl, she would make the jump and be gone. The world could spend thousands of days hunting for her. Nobody could ever be sure what had happened, which was perfect. They would remember her with her purse. Maybe she had been carrying money. Maybe Elata was living somewhere close, or maybe she found some way home to the Corona District. The purse and the layers of mystery would help her friends imagine her living as an adult, wearing an assumed name and ten lives worth of happiness.

That's what she liked best about her plan. Everybody would be spared, believing whatever they wanted.

Coming out of the tunnel, Elata blinked and wiped at her tears. Everyone was walking on a landing that pretended to be attached to a normal rich home. The palace was on the far side of the bloodwood. Middle-of-the-Middle was this tree's name, which she never liked. What she liked for a name was Marduk, and just that name triggered an image of herself, grown up and prosperous. The war was finished, and in her daydream she was the person honored with the chance to plant a new blackwood at the top of the world, naming it whatever she wanted.

Marduk was the name floating in her wet, weak head.

"This way," the talking soldier told them.

They weren't taking any of the normal routes off the landing. This was better than she could hope. They were aiming for the landing's tip. A small, heavily armored fletch was moored there, waiting. Elata was ready. She felt her legs relax, preparing to sprint, and her eyes turned to the right long enough to make certain that the closest gate wasn't closely guarded. Ten good strides and she would be gone. She knew it. But then she made the blunder of looking ahead again, searching for the closely cut scalp of a boy who had almost stopped looking like a boy.

She didn't see Diamond anywhere.

Surprise made her gait slow, and then a very warm hand took her from behind, grabbing her by the elbow.

"Are you all right?" Diamond asked.

She hadn't been paying attention. Diamond was behind her all this time, probably watching her.

As much as anything, she hated living with his stares.

But now they were talking quietly. She assured him that she was fine fine fine, nervous but not too badly so.

Together, the two of them walked up the gangway into the fletch.

People noticed the two of them, and there were smiles.

Why did all this bother her so much?

FOUR

Mature bloodwoods were extraordinary in their length, reaching deeper into the Creation than any other tree, and even the youngest, most sun-starved among them were still giants. Each bloodwood was a spike of vibrant living wood. The wood was lightweight and indifferent to fire, and the brownish-red bark might be ten strides deep, while the branches resembled short burly trees growing horizontally, covered with dense tangles of blackish-green spines and needles that served as leaves. But no mere half-trees grew in the District's middle. Only the greatest of the grand were allowed, each hanging alone with its army of stubby branches. Every morning's light rose full and strong into the forest, feeding the overhead jungles and farms, and mouths and more mouths. This was abundance. Here the Creation had been mastered. Each mindless tree was endless and enormous, too old to count reliably, and even at a distance, too vast for eyes to hold.

From inside a quick fletch, the Middle-of-the-Middle seemed like a Creation in its own right, and Diamond almost believed that he could feel that mass of wood and brown bark and sap and people pulling at him.

And it was pulling.

The Master had explained: scientists manipulating wires and steel balls had proved that objects tugged at every other object, and these great pillars were cloaked with a power that revealed itself in the dance of every tiny sphere.

"Of course your bodies can feel none of this magic," Nissim said. "These impulses are everywhere, but they're minuscule. The demon floor is what we experience. The floor has its own relentless pull, and that's what wrestles with us every moment, and every object obeys it, and there are reams of strong, hard-to-see evidence that it is the same for the coronas too."

"They look up at the sun, not up at us," Seldom had said, gladly guessing at the Master's next words.

And grinning over her busy pencil, Elata had whispered to Diamond, "Which you knew all along, didn't you?"

But the sun was under his feet, and he didn't let himself think otherwise.

The ranking soldier had told Diamond to stand away from the window, letting him watch without being seen, and the boy thought about quite a lot while staring out at a rectangle of bark and landings and the critical government buildings that looked like toy houses pinned to the Creators' wall.

And then the fletch turned without warning, sprinting toward the adjacent tree.

This was not a long journey, but it seemed as if the roaring propellers weren't covering space nearly quickly enough. Diamond stood between Elata and Seldom. None of them spoke. Nissim was making friends with soldiers and of the crew. Somehow the Master was able to say a few words that meant nothing, and watching faces until clues were given, it was easy for him to pick the one person onboard this airship who might answer his questions.

"They told us all about the corona," Nissim said.

That wasn't quite true, and it wasn't a question. But there were slippery ways to steal what others knew.

Nissim smiled at his victim, saying, "It's the same kind of giant that gave us the children, that boy there."

The crewman glanced at Diamond.

"We heard the sirens," Nissim said. "Of course we couldn't see anything, buttoned up indoors like we were."

"Oh, there was a battle," the crewman volunteered.

He was younger than the various soldiers, probably in the fleet not more than a couple hundred days.

"Did you take part?" Nissim asked.

"Oh, no, sir," he confessed. "The slayers did the hunting, the fighting. They're the ones to be applauded."

Seldom started forward, ready with a question.

Nissim warned him away with a glance. Then he nodded, and with a low voice, he said, "*Tomorrow's Girl.*"

The crewman blinked, plainly impressed. "Oh, you heard what the *Girl* did?"

"Yes," Nissim lied.

"A bunch of heroes on that good ship," he said happily.

Soldiers knew better than expose the names of ships or their activities. But this wasn't their ship or their problem, so they retreated to distant parts of the cabin, watching for enemies they could fight.

"Karlan," said Seldom.

The crewman glanced at the boy, a trace of suspicion in his otherwise earnest, self-possessed face. "Who's Karlan?"

"That boy's brother," said Nissim. "Our last news was that he was stationed on *Tomorrow's Girl.*"

"I wouldn't know either way, sir. But I heard half their crew is dead." It was important to sound brave, which in his mind was the same as being caustic.

"But the survivors are what helped win the corona, and they're getting first honors cutting up that big ugly carcass."

A second bloodwood was slowly, slowly approaching. It was as big and ancient as the Middle-of-the-Middle, and a sweeping portion of its trunk was recently cleared of homes and businesses. That was an Archon project, huge amounts of capital and labor focused on a single structure that was nearly as big as the palace. Its exterior was armored with scales and adorned with cannons, while the vast interior was built around the world's largest room, lit with mirrors by day, and in the night, powerful lamps.

During peaceful days, coronas were butchered on the reef, the papio receiving two-fifths of the carcass. A few rough little abattoirs were scattered across the other Districts, but they were raided by the papio, and more and more targeted by bandits. Now the precious carcasses were brought to a worthy fortress, and List refused to be shy when it was time to take credit for this work.

Diamond approached the front window, fingers to the glass.

No soldier bothered to stop him.

A wide landing was perched at the bottom of the abattoir, eleven fletches moored in the air above. Some were damaged, and at least one engine was smoking. But none were Karlan's ship. Probably the *Girl* towed the corona inside, but every door and window was closed. The only traces of activity were a few deflated balloons dangling on the scaffolding outside and one broad vent spouting a thick stream of fumes—the exhaust from hard-running motors.

Seldom joined him at the window.

"Hi," they said in the same moment, with matching voices.

Something wanted to be asked. But the question remained hiding while Seldom stood tall, pushing out his long chest.

Diamond glanced over his shoulder.

Mother was sitting alone, carefully studying the floor.

Elata was standing beside the farthest window, hands wrestling with a leather purse as she stared back at the Middle-of-the-Middle. Nothing in front of them mattered.

Seldom groaned softly.

Diamond looked at his friend's face in profile. Seldom was thrilled and terrified, and when he felt the eyes, he grimaced.

Diamond asked, "What?"

"Inside the corona," Seldom began. Then he swallowed hard and looked into the sun, adding, "What if there's a stomach full of children like you? What do you think you'll do?"

Diamond inhaled. Suddenly and very clearly, he saw himself walking between cribs, and he was teaching odd creatures to speak and run, and in another instant he dared imagine a second King and another Quest. Then he blew out the long breath, imagining a human girl who became a woman so real that she had a name. In his mind, their lives were woven together, days without number, and these bloodwoods grew old, people mining out the wood before their cores fell, and holding hands, the two immortals watched new ranks of bloodwoods descending into the endless, wondrous days.

All that happened inside one gasp and sigh.

Then Seldom asked again, "What will happen?"

Just one answer deserved to be said.

Quietly but with all of his confidence, Diamond told his best friend, "My head doesn't know, or it isn't telling me."

• • •

Tomorrow's Girl was safe inside the abattoir and Karlan was alive.

Seldom wanted quite a lot more than that to be true, but he would happily settle for those two blessings. Losing this last shred of his family would be too awful, too unfair. His brother had to survive today and for ten thousand more days. But of course Karlan was a slayer and a warrior, and wishing for his survival, Seldom began to think in black directions, finding a keen awful hope that maybe the warrior had been wounded in some crippling but survivable way. His back was broken, maybe, but only his legs were dead, and now he was damaged and harmless and sure to live to be a very old man riding on a wheeled chair, and a selfish brother wouldn't have to go to sleep every night wondering when someone else he loved and counted on would suddenly die.

Diamond was the safest friend.

His birth proved his invincibility, and every splinter and grievous wound since verified his endless strength.

Not that he was an easy friend. Diamond had a distant, dreamy way, always a little odd and sometimes deeply peculiar. And there had been changes since Marduk fell. Everybody else changed, but this was Diamond. Gashes could be filled in and vanish without scars, but that singular face couldn't hide the sadness roiling inside. Loss after loss led him to one angry, vengeful act, and six hundred days later, Seldom was still arguing with the idea that the hand hanging at the end of the weirdly shortened arm had started a thousand awful battles.

Tragedy made Diamond seem more ordinary. And weirdest of all, being like other people made him only more difficult to be with. His silences weren't just the earned right of a deity dropped into their midst. He was a person and should be dealt with like any person, and Seldom never felt smart when it came to understanding people.

Too many others were standing close, or Seldom might have offered words of understanding or maybe asked good sharp questions. But they as unalone as any two boys could be, and now this trip was done, their ship falling towards a bright plain of bloodwood boards and gun emplacements, and soldiers and slayers, big slayer fletches riding on the high moorings. Smaller fletches and little airships were tied to the abattoir's landing. One ship had just settled—a blunt, underpowered balloon wearing an insignia of ten links of chain joined in an endless ring.

"That's a prison ship," Seldom said quietly.

Joining them, the Master said, "That's what it is, yes."

"But why is it here?"

Diamond took a breath, and it sounded like an important breath. But he said nothing.

"Maybe," Master Nissim began. "Maybe the Archon has invited someone special to share this great day."

Diamond straightened, as if a knife went up his spine.

Three passengers were embarking from the prison ship. None wore chains, but the little woman in the middle was easy to recognize.

"Prima," said Seldom.

Haddi rose and joined them. She looked at the prisoner and then her son, and she sighed deeply, saying nothing.

The Master watched mother and son in profile.

Elata was still standing at the back of the cabin. Her arms were crossed. She didn't care to join the rest of them. When Seldom looked at her, she turned away, staring back across at their tree. He assumed she wanted to be at the palace instead of here, but that was a funny way to be. This was an adventure, and Elata always, always liked adventures.

Their fletch slowed, and every hatch opened with a synchronized bang. Capable monkeys leapt to the landing with ropes in their mouths. Then the engines quit, and the monkeys and landing crew competed to see which species could warm the air the most with vivid, vicious cursing.

Once they were moored, the soldiers gathered them up before the leader said, "Between us, and keep moving."

The gangway was steep and brief, and the landing was washed in the sunshine reflected off the scale-encrusted building overhead. Everybody walked fast, the officer bearing toward a pair of closed steel doors. Engine smoke and ashes mixed with a rich stink that was like nothing but what it was: the blood of dead coronas.

The landing ended with small steel doors. The giant doors were high above. Prima was walking ahead of them, and then one guard dropped a hand on her head, much as a parent would do to a small child. The hand told her to stop, and she stopped. The second guard gave the doors a worthwhile kick. Inspired by the monkeys, he offered a few curses, and the steel pulled opened on hinges that were new and well-greased.

The criminal was led inside.

Haddi was close to her son, and she touched an arm. "Look at me," she said.

Diamond looked to the other side.

"See me," she said, and she reached up, grabbing his misshapen chin and pulling his eyes towards her.

The two of them weren't walking anymore.

Quietly, fiercely, the old woman said, "You know what I want."

"What?" Diamond muttered.

Seldom was past them, yet he couldn't help but look back.

"I told you," she said.

"I know," he said.

"Don't wait," she said.

Diamond grasped his mother's wrist, squeezing until she flinched and he flinched in turn. They were like one face shared by a distorting mirror, both feeling agonies far worse than any hurting bones.

Elata was beside Seldom.

Wanting to be helpful, he said, "We'll be home again soon."

A rough sound came out of her; she didn't act thankful.

"What?" he asked.

"Never mind," she said.

Everybody was a difficult friend. That was the only conclusion that Seldom could count on, or so it seemed.

New soldiers and one civilian emerged from that same door. The Archon of Archons was the only person in normal clothes, which made him look extraordinary. He was walking half a step behind the top general. General Meeker liked dull green silk uniforms and no special hat. As long as the humans were battling the papio, the Archon's office was subordinate to Meeker. Seldom didn't like politics, maybe because he was so bad at them, but he lived in a palace full of little else, and he had heard and heard and heard again that the two men were like married people. And everybody knew which partner was supposed to be in charge

"Not now, not under these conditions," said Meeker.

This was a marriage with a lot of public fighting.

List said a word or two that Seldom couldn't make out.

"Without my authority," the general said. Then he nearly bolted from the pack, fixing his eyes on Diamond.

"Get inside," he told the boy.

The rest of them didn't exist.

The Supreme Commander acted as if he was the only trustworthy guard. He put himself beside Diamond, and List stood waiting. The Archon's hair and eyebrows had turned gray since the war began, and wrinkles were thriving close to the bright smart eyes. But there was always a boy inside the man, not just in the high voice or his small body, but something in the way that most senseless, silly crap would suddenly make him happy.

List said, "I'm very glad you're here, Diamond."

Diamond muttered nothing sensible.

And then List was smiling, almost laughing when he said, "You should be here. You deserve this. Absolutely, this is where you have to be."

Meeker was taller than the Archon but even thinner, and the general's voice was ordinary, almost dull. But he knew how to be heard, telling everyone in the world, "The papio won't let this stand. They want what we have, and before today's done, they're going to try and take everything from us."

All of the soldiers seemed taller suddenly, every shoulder squared.

List kept grinning, acting as if this was his party. He welcomed Haddi by name, and he made a show of shaking the Master's hand before calling to Elata and finally Seldom. Without warning, without preparation, he was a charming man, right down to the way that he told an adolescent boy, "Your brother is the hero, you know."

"Karlan's alive?"

"Absolutely."

"Is he shot, or anything?"

"Not that I could see," the Archon reported. "And I'll tell you this too: without your brother, we might have lost everything."

Meeker disapproved of something, maybe everything.

"Indoors," he said. "There's room for heroes indoors."

They passed through the steel doorway, discovering stairs and sunlight. The sunlight's color changed, brightened and blued by an army of mirrors and lenses and the polished tubes that sent the easy light into what was the largest man-made space in Creation. The room was so large that five different fletches could float overhead, and dozens of balloons gathered into a bright white mass, waiting for their hydrogen to be piped safely away. Seldom blinked, holding a hand over his eyes, once again thinking how odd it was, this much sunlight pouring from above.

The stairs finished, and a noisy crowd stood beyond in little clusters and sloppy lines. Prima, the criminal, was gazing across the butcher floor. The largest animal in the Creation was sprawled out before her, dead and black and stinking in horrible ways. The body had been pulled out long, much like the corona that Seldom had seen on the reef. The heads and necks were the closest part of it. The body easily crossed that enormous space, great straps and little straps ready to secure its necks. But while younger, healthier carcasses were dangerous long after death, this creature would never move again. Each one of the heads was limp, jaws pulled wide, exposing shattered teeth and no teeth, eyes already turned to a pale slippery gel.

And that was when Seldom saw what was always willing to be seen. This vast floor and room and the entire oversized facility were designed to serve many jobs, but particularly this one. A corona twice as massive as any other could be brought here, and here it could be defended: those ancient guts full of treasures infinitely more valuable than any iron or flesh.

Seldom watched for a second giant.

King wasn't who he wanted, but that's who he saw first. Strolling on top of the corpse, wearing trousers but no shirt, no shoes, spines and the razored edges of his armor throwing sunlight around the Archon's son.

Softly, Seldom called out his brother's name.

And like magic, he spotted Karlan on the butchering floor, standing fearlessly beside the dead necks and dead heads. The young slayer was dressed in white clothes so clean they had to be new, one hand holding a power saw that was sleeping against his hip. Karlan wanted to get busy. That's what his body said. He was watching the various dignitaries and criminals and boys who just happened to be someone's friend, waiting for anyone's order to commence cutting.

Seldom waved at Karlan.

Noticing him, the warrior offered one crisp nod.

Then quietly but not softly, Haddi said, "Now Diamond. Now."

Diamond approached Prima, and she immediately turned to him.

With a grim gray voice, he said, "Madam."

She said, "What?"

"I'm very sorry," he said. "For everything, madam, I'm sorry."

The one-time Archon studied the boy. Or maybe she wasn't seeing anything. People did that sometimes when they were thinking. Then her eyes closed and pulled in a breath so big that her body seemed to grow. Alone among these people, the woman didn't look any older. Prison was easier than waging war, Seldom thought. But her voice had turned thick and a little slow, and the words came out sharp.

"What exactly makes you sorry?" she asked.

Diamond opened his mouth and said nothing.

"Then why say the word?" Prima asked.

Diamond glanced at his mother, but Haddi had no advice, just a hard coaxing stare.

Seldom's friend had never looked so foolish. In anguish, he managed to say, "I wish I hadn't . . . "

"All right, we agree," Prima said. And she turned her gaze, putting her focus on that vast beast. She was standing at the edge of the butcher floor—an engineering wonder made of bone planks with slits between to drain every fluid into sluices that would let nothing escape. She seemed to be staring at Karlan, and with what sounded like the beginnings of a laugh, she said, "And now, sorry as all of us are, we're glad to try this game all over again."

• • •

"All over again," she said.

Diamond heard nothing but those words. The rest of Creation had fallen silent, and nobody seemed to notice or they didn't care, and with that peculiar thought he put a hand to his eyes, waiting for the slippery kiss of fresh tears.

A second voice broke the stillness.

Someone shouted, "Sirens."

King was sprinting down the corona's back, bare feet slapping at the soft spent flesh.

"Sirens," King called out again.

Suddenly Diamond was again listening to machinery and generators working, and too many voices, and in the midst of the turmoil, a call-line began rattling inside a steel box painted an important red.

A soldier opened the box and handed the receiver to General Meeker.

King jumped off the corona, hitting the floor in front of Diamond. Sharp little teeth rode that mouth into a smile. "And I hear jets," the other mouth said. "Still a long ways off. But if I hear them, that means all of the wings in the world are coming."

Meeker was listening to the voice riding the wires. Nothing he heard was surprising him.

Stepping close, King said, "This is why."

"Why what?" Diamond asked.

"The voice was right," said his brother. "First the corona, and now this. What a great day."

"The papio—?"

"Are coming here to die." And King's other mouth made a hard wet sound that was laid over the next words. "The war is going to be won today," he said.

Meeker handed the receiver and its voice to a second general.

An aide was delivering reports to the Archon, but he didn't care to listen. List was first to shout at the slayers, at Karlan. "Rip into that belly now. No more delays."

Karlan already knew where he needed to cut. He broke into a sprint, tugging at the saw's handle, the engine sputtering and coughing before breaking into a piercing whine. He was past the dead necks when he shoved the long blade and furious chain into the torso, between two of the giant's long umbrella-style ribs; and a sudden long gash was torn open, fats and cancers and wasted muscle pouring out behind him.

King was beside Diamond. "Do you know what I was doing, walking on top?"

"I don't know."

"Listening for anything alive inside that corpse."

Diamond felt lighter. "Did you hear anything?" he asked.

"Blood pooling, guts rotting," said King. "Dead coronas are noisier than living humans, I think."

Karlan turned and came back again, shoving the saw deeper into the wound. Other slayers were scaling the black body, preparing to cut from above, tearing loose a mass of tissue and scars and swollen cancers.

King claimed a long pole topped with a bright steel saw,

"Let's help," he said to Diamond, or maybe to the saw.

Diamond followed. But the slayers noticed as they approached, and it was Karlan who stepped away from his work to face the intruder.

"We're the damned midwives here," he said. "Not you."

Karlan was small next to King.

"Out of my path," said King.

Karlan cursed.

Diamond's brother stomped at the floor twice, defending his ground.

And then Karlan smiled, suddenly and brightly. "I can't kill you, but I can take off those pretty legs before you get your shot at me."

King spat with his eating mouth. But the other mouth said, "No, I just wanted to bring you this tool."

The pole and blade struck the floor between them.

Saws quieted, and the other slayers shouted warnings. Then everybody ran away as a mass of hot rotting flesh slid free suddenly, save for two laughing men who rode the carnage all the way to the floor.

Diamond wondered if someone had blessed the corona.

Father would have by now.

The local sirens began to blow. Above them, one fletch and then its neighbors started their engines, getting ready to embark. But a lesser general started yelling at someone, telling them to signal those ships. "Nobody is leaving," she said, waving a hand in a circle above her head. "Gas protocols are in force."

In the course of the war, every weapon but one had been used. Just the word "Gas" made everyone move faster or stand stiller, and every soul contemplated a new set of horrors.

Karlan was wading through the gore, cutting still deeper while the other crews brought up timbers and fans.

Mother came close, needing to talk. Diamond assumed that another lecture about decency or shame was about to commence. But no, she tugged on his arm once, just to grab a bigger share of his attentions, and then she quietly told him, "You should be one of the first. Go closer. Go."

Diamond should be in the front, yes. But it took a startling amount of bravery just to cover the next twenty steps. He stopped beside King. Saying nothing, they watched the slayers set up fans to shove cool air inside, and then they were propping up the long wound, using timbers and sheets of wood to keep the limp body from crushing them. Then just enough had been done, and the men and women vanished inside, no more than one recitation passing before they began dragging out fresh masses of muscle and flower-bright organs that neither boy recognized.

This day had been imagined. A plan was in place, much-practiced and eager.

A dozen soldiers formed one tidy line.

"They search anyone who leaves the corpse," King said. "They don't want anyone slipping away with a brother in his pocket."

Diamond tried to laugh at the image.

King had a bigger laugh, and then he fell silent, suddenly standing taller, the plates on his shoulders beginning to lift.

"What's wrong?" Diamond asked.

King said nothing.

"You hear something—"

"Meeker," his brother said. "He's talking. Wait."

Karlan emerged from the hole. His white suit was black and shiny with the blood, and he was holding a rope and various hooks, a greasy tongue-shaped mass obediently following after him.

"Spotters in the little Districts," King said. "They're calling in. They see skulls riding long bombs and rockets. Papio nerve-killers. One whiff, and we're the only ones left alive here. And I'm not sure we'll be upright afterwards."

Diamond looked back at Elata, at Seldom. He wanted to catch his mother's gaze, but she was watching the butcher floor, arms crossed as her mouth offered silent words. She was holding an earnest conversation with her dead husband.

Beneath the floor, huge pumps began working.

The air inside the room instantly thickened, vents pumping in extra air to keep any toxic gases outside. The blowing air made the overhead fletches yank against their moorings, and the balloons spun like a flock of fat birds.

Slayers dragged more timbers inside the wound.

List came forward, standing among the soldiers. With his weak loud voice, he told everyone, "Hurry."

All of the world's sirens were roaring, but the attacks wouldn't happen immediately. Even the swiftest wings needed twenty or thirty recitations to cross half of the world.

But the Archon saw no reason for patience. Pushing the officer in charge, he said, "Get your people in there. Let the slayers do their work, but you build a roof. You drag and carry. I want the next children free before the papio arrive."

"What about security?" the man asked.

"Security we have. Time is scarce."

The order couldn't be obeyed without a general's compliant nod. But having received that, the soldiers marched forwards, glad to be busy.

Again Karlan emerged from the carcass. His clothes were dripping with iron-infused blood, and he was angry enough to glare at every invader. But a few withering curses was enough of a defense, and then he smiled, telling those miserable fools what to bring out next and what not to touch or trust.

List approached the boys, glancing at Diamond. Something like hope was building in the eyes, and the man even tried to smile. Then he looked at King, saying, "A lot of orders are at work here. But I'm giving you one important command."

The son couldn't have stood taller, waiting for the next words.

"Don't hurt them," List said. "You won't harm these next children at all. Is that understood?"

King stomped the floor ten times.

His eating mouth made injured noises, but the other mouth remained mute.

The soldiers had vanished. Karlan had vanished. But suddenly the soldiers were emerging. Bent low, the first few of them were sprinting, one stumbling and his companions jumped over his rolling body.

"We found something," several men cried out.

Generals and soldiers, government people and the resident staff pushed forward. Muttering sounds ended with questioning sounds. Meeker was at the front of the crowd, and with a tentative grin, he said to List, "There's news."

"Yes?" asked the Archon.

"The papio don't have as many wings as we feared. So we may, may be able to win everything today."

King told Diamond, "I was right."

Diamond stared into the black hole, saying nothing.

"Just like your mysterious voice predicted," said King.

Diamond started to shake his head. He intended to say, "No," before cautioning that the voice, whatever it was, stubbornly refused to speak in easy, obvious terms.

But there wasn't any time to explain. Karlan emerged from the corona, one rounded object cradled in his arms. Everybody saw him. Every conversation ended. There was a long fine moment when the prize looked like a baby, and the man covered in stomach wastes and rot looked like the proudest father in Creation. Standing at the edge of the wound, boots sinking into the soft old flesh, Karlan used the reflected sunlight to study what he was holding. He almost smiled, but the smile didn't have any purchase. So he decided to shake his head, and with no ceremony and no warning, he tossed the object onto the butcher floor.

The prize was round and stayed round, and it sang on impact, resembling a bell ringing in the distance. It hit the bone slats and rang each time that it bounced, and then it began to hum while it rolled forwards, dedicated to one straight line.

People caught in front of the wonder stared, and then when it came close, everybody turned, trying to leap out of the way.

"That's all there is," Karlan shouted. "Caught in some kind of cyst high in the stomach, all alone."

A single child would still be important.

Two of the coronas' older children came forwards, intercepting the ball, and List stayed at his son's side.

King stopped the humming and the roll with one bare foot.

A sphere was part of the object, but there was more than that. One of the sphere's faces was adorned with cylinders—fourteen cylinders—and that made it look less pretty and perfect than it would have looked otherwise.

"Do you know this thing?" King began.

Diamond said, "Maybe," and bent low.

"I know this thing," King said.

What Diamond recognized was the shape that made no sense other than looking distinctly familiar. Did he once have a toy that resembled this object? None came to mind, and the more he tried to remember toys, the less likely that felt.

But the object was definitely an object.

Not a child, no.

King played his toes across the top of the sphere.

Stomach juices clung to the round surface. Kneeling, Diamond put a hand against the grayness and pulled away the acids and a scrap of corona flesh. The sphere was wider than his forearm was long, but shorter than his full arm. It had weight but not as much as he might have guessed. Then a memory found him and took hold, a voice from some deep past—a human voice, female and familiar—and he heard her telling someone, "The one in the middle. That's the trigger."

"I know this thing," King repeated.

"Yes," Diamond said.

"I don't know the language, but I'm remembering a voice."

"A human voice," Diamond said.

"No," said King. "It was like my voice. It was beautiful."

List stood close to them, and Meeker had joined him. To nobody in particular, Archon asked, "Is it some kind of machine?"

"A weapon," the general suggested.

Instinct kept Diamond silent, and maybe it was the same for King.

"Any ideas, son?"

King didn't answer his father's questions. Saying nothing, he bent his legs until his knees were planted against the floor.

Diamond couldn't remember his brother ever holding this pose.

"The middle one," King whispered.

Diamond gave the ball a half-spin. Fourteen cylinders were pointed at their faces, offering no advice. But for the first time in the boy's life, his stomach felt sick, as if razors were bouncing in his middle, and the pain and accompanying dread grew worse when Diamond obeyed some imprecise, presumably ancient instruction, his right index finger slipping inside that middle cylinder.

The cylinder was smooth as a gun barrel, and it ended with a hard flat surface that did nothing.

He touched bottom and nothing happened, not to the ball or to them, and that felt like a wonderful stroke of luck. Like a monkey who leaps from one branch without knowing if another branch is below: Diamond had taken a gigantic chance, and he had survived.

List and Meeker were talking to Karlan and the other slayers, demanding that everyone climb back inside, to hunt through the stomach again.

With his smallest finger, King reached into the center cylinder.

Again, nothing happened.

But the ball remained a miracle. The gray surface was as perfect and smooth as any substance made by any human. All of time had been spent inside a beast's erosive belly, yet the sphere's mirror-like shine was spellbinding.

Diamond and King stared at their own reflections.

With a flat hand, King wiped away more acids, and he laughed at the distorted image of himself.

Then a third face joined their reflections. She was a plain-faced woman wearing a colonel's uniform, and what made her remarkable was the smile that was very much like their smiles. Whatever this mystery was, it thrilled her beyond all measure.

King turned to look at the officer.

"May I?" she said.

Against every instinct and all of her endless fears, Quest had sneaked into this facility. She came forwards with the chaos, and now she was kneeling between them, not caring who might notice. Her hand and just her hand had ceased to be human. It resembled the complicated limb of an insect, and her longest finger started to enter the cylinder, not quite touching bottom when she stopped herself.

"No," she said.

People began noticing the colonel kneeling with the boys. Bystanders were talking, and Seldom was poking Elata with an elbow, saying, "Look, look."

"No," Quest said once again, and she pulled her hand away, the finger hovering in the air.

One authentic general shouted.

"The sister's here!" she cried out.

And then it was King whose hand jumped ahead, grabbing what wasn't a wrist and shoving two smaller fingers into that center cylinder.

One last time, she said, "No."

Then she touched bottom, probably for no longer than a quick heartbeat, and an army of mirrors had nothing to reflect, and the huge building was plunged into darkness.

Startled, the world stopped talking.

And then a smart voice—Seldom's voice—shouted out, "It's out, it's gone. The sun is gone."

FIVE

This was a harder birth than the last birth.

Maybe in some remote past, one of them suffered more terribly. And the most miserable infancy could always be longer and perhaps, perhaps more painful. But all of that was conjecture, not memory. Memory gave them a stick with lines, a measuring rod to set beside their present burdens. The only other birth that they could remember involved the papio feeding them easy meals and simple conversations and some days filled with kindness, or at least the absence of outright malevolence. But nobody in this place pretended to be their parent. What they brought from their former life, knowledge about machines and science, human languages and human politics, offered less than nothing in this new existence. Existence was filled with endless, wrenching demands. The only goal was survival. Between every day's beginning and end, there were moments and sometimes long intervals when survival seemed unlikely, and the despair only worsened when night descended.

Even something as simple as one small escape was impossible.

For days and days and days, they were pinned inside a cavity—a slick-walled chamber empty of everything but the eight of them.

At first, they were barely joined. Flesh that was happy in cold realms and a thin atmosphere had been shredded, and then it was seared. The present climate was a furnace in darkness and even worse when the sun washed over the world. The toxic atmosphere was thicker than water, and it never quit pressing against the cooked meat and eight hapless brains. To lay at the bottom of this hole, unable to heal and unable to die, was a fate that made the bravest, most secure among them think the impossible:

This was deserved.

Just punishments were being delivered to the wicked.

Even the worst among them—Divers—was ready to accept that nothing would ever change. More brutal days were coming, and what remained of the body would keep baking and mummifying, leaving them to suffer endlessly inside a carcass discarded by some vengeful, unimaginative Fate.

Tritian was best suited for this furnace. But without food, without energy, his abilities went to waste.

Eyes were made, and nothing good was seen.

Various ears were woven, and there was nothing to hear but slow massive winds and little animals squeaking and the shredded remains of great voices—corona voices, everyone agreed.

"Something edible, something sweet, will come close," they told each other. "And we'll catch it and eat it and grow again."

Nothing came.

The hole was rounded like a ball, a partially squashed ball, broadest at the bottom and small at the mouth. Certain rare corals on the papio reef had the same blue-black color and the same slick-yet-rough texture. Those were the hardest, most precious corals, prized as jewelry and bullets. Maybe this was their native habitat. Maybe only a few stunted pioneers of these corals managed to push past the demon floor, struggling to grow in the sweet cold rarified air.

The Eight couldn't forget falling. Explosions and their momentum carried them into the corona world, and then the floor was below them again. The floor claimed them and brought them tumbling down again. Would they fall back into their world, like a toy tied to a rubber string? No, the Eight were suddenly flung sideways, hard as a cannon flings its shell. At least that was the sensation, what each of them sensed. They were above the demons and their magic, surrounded by blistering wet air, and a wind took them, or maybe it was the backwash or hard gasp of a corona, and then their senses failed, and time passed, and they settled here or they were set here, and they would likely remain inside this nameless hole for the next million horrific days.

Mortality was a blessing granted to others, not to them.

The Eight made simple eyes that didn't boil.

The days and darknesses between were counted.

The flesh that hadn't been lost or burnt was refashioned, attempting to become useful. But the best that could be managed was a single stubborn vessel with persistent eyes and ears, a rough grasp of taste and smell, and one weak mouth leading into a shared stomach.

Tritian was in charge of the wreckage.

More days were counted, and nights, and the frail strokes of each little heart.

But movement was impossible. Hunting was impossible. And no stupid animal wandered into their grave, offering its flesh as energy. Each day brought more weakness and less possibility. If not for the accidental charity of a passing corona, nothing would have changed until the Eight were as hard as the coral on which they laid.

Only the very young coronas had patience for holes and crevices and caves. And as holes were measured, the Eight had picked the bleakest, least interesting cavity in Creation. But a baby corona traveling to an interesting place was delayed by some social catastrophe common to young creatures everywhere. He/she paused where no corona ever paused. The creature needed a moment to nourish an insult and massage a bruised ego. Eleven heads saw nothing but embarrassment, while the twelfth head noticed a flat bit of colorless trash that wasn't expected and might have some interesting quality to fill the next half-moment.

That tiny creature approached.

Yet nothing about it seemed small. A magnificent, light-infused beast hovered overhead, and aching with hunger, the Eight imagined killing the creature, or at least ripping away the most curious head. But the visitor had a keen respect for danger, and the first twitch of the trash made it retreat again, and pause. The mysterious object was alive. Hard contemplation led to a quick journey through the roaring winds, and it caught one the gilled beasts rather like what the papio called "fish."

A simple mouth accepted the food, chewing in a very sloppy desperate and entertaining fashion.

Two hundred and six other fish followed that treasure, each delivered on a different morning, and then that dull hole inside the coral was filled with new flesh.

The corona wasn't so much a baby anymore. Presumably he/she had opinions about the discovery, and maybe that's why no one else was told. That might have been a second blessing. Or maybe not. But what mattered was that the fish were eaten in the greediest ways, and the secret creature changed shaped daily, and the corona enjoyed the ritual as well as the slow clumsy transformation of its helpless pet.

Only Tritian's flesh could endure the heat and pressure, but each of the Eight contributed little talents and sometimes an unsuspected brilliance. A shared metabolism had to be configured. Odd proteins and dense hot fats had to shredded with new chemistries. Those early fish offered little nutrition, but the last dozen seemed delicious, and they were rich with energy, and the latest stomach wasn't just happy for the work, it begged for more.

Arms and legs had to be contrived.

One quality about this remarkable place was how extraordinarily heavy the Eight had become.

Weight wasn't a constant, according to the papio Masters. They showed the Eight old compelling evidence that the demon floor pulled harder on the coronas. Maybe the Masters didn't know much about much, but they had been right about this fact. And once another sweet fish was delivered, the Eight began to climb, new limbs pulling the new body to the sharp edge of the hole. Then Tritian ordered everyone to stop and rest, waiting for the next morning's meal.

The next fish was carried by the baby's smallest head. Discovering its pet in an unexpected place, it rose and hovered. Coronas spoke more with light than sound or scent. The orange flashes were admissions of being startled. And then came a bright purple light edging into higher realms, and two heads that had never brought fish reached down, neatly wrenching free every limb on its pet's body.

The Eight were thrown back into the hole, and the fish was dropped on top of them.

Again, the vengeful Fate was in control.

Another forty-seven days and nights were spent making ready for the forty-eighth morning. Then when the baby arrived—a much bigger entity by then—it found nothing in hole but water and rough coral.

Its pet had fled.

Sorrow swirled inside anger, and not just one head reached inside the hole. Five heads decided to make quick work, examining the pit for clues about where the odd creature might have fled. Except the Eight hadn't escaped. What the baby hadn't seen was blue-black like the walls, and it grabbed the heads, the necks severed near the creature's body. What survived that wicked attack swam away. What might have been shame kept the corona from admitting what he/she had found and what he/she had done since. Meanwhile the lost pet was well-fed and now mobile, and the Eight moved between different holes and deep cool caves, hunting its way back to rough health.

The old world was the destination.

To make that journey, Tritian remade the body that had worked well before. At first glance, they looked like a papio made huge. But this papio didn't require lungs or big hearts. The hyperdense air gladly pushed its oxygen inside the orange blood and meat. Its mouth was only for eating. There was no one to carry on a conversation with, and no need for a voice. And the eyes only looked like eyes that worked well in the other world, but they could absorb energies far from the visible, pedestrian light.

This new realm was suffused with wonderful, endless colors.

Day was day, complete with the blazing roar of a great fire fixed to the center of everything overhead. Their brother, the little Diamond boy, had made noise about the sun belonging overhead. That tidbit was remembered from one of the many intelligence files brought by friendly hands. Thinking about old allies brought one mood, while thinking about the Diamond boy caused shifting, conflicted moods.

With Tritian in charge, the Eight would return to that other world.

"To make amends," he said to All.

And Divers remained silent.

By day, the edge of the world was a dome-shaped ceiling that ended only where the sun shoved its way into the Creation. The bottom of this world was vertical and coral-encrusted and difficult to navigate. The Eight considered climbing out on a long spur and falling, letting momentum punch them through the demon floor. But then the floor would pull at them again, and they would fall again and come back through again, and where was the point in that?

Thought narrowed the hopes. The only possibility seemed to be crossing where there were hard surfaces on both sides of the floor. Fortunately the papio reef and corona reef were strongest here. It was possible to climb down safely. Four hundred and nine days after its latest birth, a strong Eight reach their goal, standing on a coral spur and looking at a roughly equal spur on the other side. And as shadow fell across both worlds, with shared excitement, they knelt and reached down, touching the shimmering home of demons with one hand, then both.

The sensation was like touching very hot ice.

With one foot and then both, they stepped down onto the barrier.

In the world above, they would have melted through instantly. But the demons proved very strong, very stubborn. They didn't break with a single fist or a hundred hard kicks. Night came with the Eight still pounding away at the shimmer. They used coral lumps and boulders and their shattered fists, and they used a great deal of rage, and they even tried a sharpened piece of steel that must have fallen through from the other side—steel turning to rust and flakes at a fantastic pace.

This was not the same demon floor as above.

In the darkness, the dense air was a little cooler, a little less selfish about its moisture. A mist fell at the bottom of this world, and then hard fat raindrops that danced on the floor and settled, becoming a lake that was deeper than the Eight were tall.

The lake was no denser than the air, and it proved just as rich in oxygen.

Finally, admitting the hopelessness, the Eight took that fine new body across the floor, hoping without reason that it would weaken farther from ground and the world's edges. But if anything, the barrier grew stronger. Night was full. The last shred of hope was that the next day would bring rain to the human world, and maybe a tough young body could ride that storm a little ways, and maybe the swirling winds would prove lucky, flinging them against the papio reef.

They walked inside hot pressurized water.

The invincible shimmer was beneath them, and beyond the floor, they saw the soft ruddy glow of fire. The human forests were burning. Tritian wondered if a war was being fought, or maybe some other ordinary disaster had struck the tree-walkers. And he wondered if he was made of the same stuff as the demon floor. The Eight and the other Three could have been woven from that magical stuff, which could explain quite a lot, at least with the first glance. But no answer could be tested, and believing in magic left the mind heavier than ever, more questions and puzzles and feelings of deep stupidity riding on the next moments.

Night in the corona realm was very different from the human world.

Tritian cast those big eyes upwards, staring through the water, watching the sun's disk swallowed by the fully grown jungle.

Every night, the coronas hovered against the ink, sprinkling the Creation with pricks of light that spun around the center like a great silent wheel.

Sometimes that wheel seemed familiar.

Reassuring, even.

They surely had a purpose for what they did, what they did without fail. But the Eight didn't bother even dreaming up possible reasons.

Tritian was thinking how the big coronas could pierce the floor at will. Plainly it was a matter of simple size and strength. He was wondering if the Eight could learn the coronas' language and their desires, some sort of arrangement could be achieved. Then he laughed and told the others why he was amused. He imagined this body riding a corona up to the reef, to the trees. They were nearly dead once but born again, and they were stronger than ever, and the coronas were their new allies.

In that fashion, in an instant, misery and punishment seemed to have been transformed, nothing before them but promise and endless potential.

"But first, a taste of the cold thin air," Tritian promised the others.

Except the jungle exploded into fire, and the blast and steam broke through the floor without him. One moment, the water was all around, and then tiny pores opened up in the floor for no reason, it seemed, than to let out the flood and the wild energies that kept the trees alive, and the reef, and the human animals with their ancient grudges and small marvelous talents.

Suddenly it was day again, and the Eight were standing on top of the demon floor, shamefully exposed.

In a wild dash, they hurried back to the cover of the rocks.

And the coronas went about their hot important lives.

That was when the Eight finally, grudgingly began to study those languages of light and sound and scent.

Any code can be broken, particularly if gifted minds have nothing else to do.

Very quickly, the Eight realized that the aliens weren't empty monstrous mysteries, but instead they were endlessly strange and perhaps even more interesting than anything they had dared to imagine.

They learned about the old ones and the Firsts, and the Eight learned the Count of Days leading to these days.

The age of the Creation was revealed.

After that, a working voice was finally built.

Corona words emerged from the new throat.

A few curious babies came chasing the words, and the bravest stayed to talk, the coronas covering their bodies with swirling pictures, while the Eight drew simple, unlovely images on weeds and mossy corals.

At least one of those babies mentioned to others what she/he had witnessed. At least a few adults listened to her. Then one night, late in the night, one of the Firsts honored the Eights by seeking them out. A creature older than this Creation hung overhead, obscuring that wheel of tiny, holy lights. Tritian intended to ask about the lights and their patterns, wanting to understand the significance of this deep old habit. But there wasn't time that night. Instead, they managed a rough conversation with the greatest oldest grandest mind that they had ever met, and the Eight did their best to describe their first birth and first death, ending the tale with their rebirth here.

Nearly six hundred days had passed since that last birth.

Tritian promised to tell the rest of their story, as soon as there was time.

Then the First left, saying nothing about his/her mood or intentions or any great old promises made to vanished creatures.

Morning arrived.

The sun found the Eight sitting inside a favorite crevice. In this place, the coral had grown like a tree thrusting sideways from the wall of the Creation. The demon floor lay spread out below like a great basin filled with magical water. The Eight could look straight up at the sunlight, but what mattered were the coronas. Unlike every other morning, the corona gathered in a sphere formation, each of them doing nothing but talking.

One topic was fascinating to all.

Nobody understood why, but long ago one of the Firsts had left this world. She/he went to visit the cold, and her body never returned, and now she lived only as memory and wisdom and the great songs woven inside all of their minds.

Tritian and his siblings were parsing out the heart of the subject.

"She was our mother," each whispered to the others, to themselves.

And then the sphere of light and song was announcing that another one of the Firsts had left. Giving no warning, it had gone to the other world, and the central opinion in the midst of that confusion was the simple inescapable sense that it must be his/her time to leave flesh and join its celebrated mate.

Nobody inside this realm looked or sounded scared.

Tritian wasn't scared.

He led the body out into the glare of the morning sun. The coronas' everyday work had stopped, which was peculiar. Nobody was tending to the jungle. The day was as fiercely bright as it was after the jungle stopped burning. Squinting hard, the Eight spotted the last of the First—four giants hanging apart from the others, whispering with their bright high-purple lights.

The missing First was the same giant with whom they had just spoken.

Or it wasn't.

Tritian and his siblings still knew nothing about the Creation. In what was possible, they said very little, at least from their perspective. If nothing else came from their time trapped in this nightmare, it was to appreciate just how miserably slight their knowledge was.

"We are eleven simple, stupid idiots," Tritian muttered, speaking to the Seven but imagining the Three listening too. He imagined them so well that he saw Diamond and King and Quest standing at the lip of the crevice, tiny faces peering inquisitively down at them, taking his declaration to heart.

Something about that moment felt magical, which was not an uncommon occurrence. Every day had its moments when meanings seemed to raise their heads from the chaos. But that happened to be the moment when day vanished without warning, and in the same instant, the Eight fell out of the crevice, tumbling wildly through the black air, spinning toward a sun that had ceased to be.

• • •

"It's out, it's gone. The sun is gone."

Seldom shouted those words, and people laughed. Everybody was surprised and scared, and there was a lot of laughing, giggling and cackling with wild, mad voices making everyone feel even worse. Then an older voice, male and very deep, repeated Seldom's last few words. Diamond didn't recognize the man, but there was a defiant tone to the way he spoke, a booming dismissal meant for everyone to hear, and then the man delivered a string of withering curses, belittling and denying even the idea that anyone could sprout such a stupid thought. And the room that was on the brink of panic suddenly fell back to skepticism and sanity.

Meeker's shrill voice emerged, trying to gather control. He offered words that seemed to mean that the overhead windows had slammed shut, making ready for the papio attack. But darkness came in an instant. Diamond understood enough to know that windows couldn't close so quickly. Yet he joined in with the giggling, which made him feel better. And maybe that new mood would have lasted, but then some practical hand thought to test the principle, striking an important switch, and the great room becoming quieter as everyone listened to the throbbing of an engine and the hard rattle of chains that were lifting plates of interlocking steel

One of the giant access doors rose. Everyone could hear it lifting, and everyone felt the inside air flowing outdoors. But when light-adapted eyes stared at the door, nothing was visible, nothing waiting but a rich and perfect darkness that had claimed the entire world.

Five or six measured breaths had passed.

Time felt dense, leaden.

The initial shock and near-panic from before was nothing. It was a mild emotion compared to the mayhem that followed, chaotic and incoherent and shrill. Every mind was taken, every heart. One portion of the crowd surged for what should be the open door, but at least as many tried to flee back into the facility's hallways and safe rooms. No one could see past the wet depths of his own wide eyes. A small torch might be brought out of a pocket and lit, but that triggered ten hands grabbing for the treasure, and accidental collisions led to blind intentional battles, bodies dropping to the floor and a single gunshot—an accident, maybe, or warning shot, or somebody trying to win enough room to stand still and think.

Diamond was struck from the side by an anonymous adult, and he shoved back with an elbow and then his entire body.

King called his name, the voice tall but not as loud as it could be, and distinctly, richly frightened.

"Here," Diamond called out.

A vast hand dropped on his head, little scales cutting into his scalp.

Then Diamond called out, "Quest."

A dry angular hand brushed across his chest and his face, pinching shut the lips before he could say her name again.

Her invisible face came close. An odor like old flowers and mold rode in with quiet sharp words. "I didn't," she said. "I did not."

Of course she hadn't, no.

From overhead, King said, "I want to see." He was nearly begging, saying, "Sister . . . can you make a light . . . ?"

But she already had, it seemed. He asked the question, and a second hand opened, revealing a pale red globe. The globe resembled the fruit of the fungi that lived at the gloomy top of the world. The nearest few people noticed, surging like moths. King let go of Diamond and pushed back the first wave, and the second, and then he picked both up by their waists, asking, "Where is that damned thing?"

The gray ball wasn't where it was just moments ago. To Diamond, nothing was more reasonable than the gray ball riding inside the corona for one purpose, and having finally done the job, it had vanished. Or it became the world's darkness. Unless the ball sprouted legs and ran away . . . which was just as easy to accept . . .

"Brighter," King pleaded.

Quest's face was sprouting globes like sores and broad nocturnal eyes, and from the mouth that was still human, she said, "Put me on your shoulders."

Easily, yes. King dropped her behind his head, legs kicking his chest, and he turned once quickly, holding Diamond under his left arm.

"I hear it," he said.

Something that wasn't metal was being dragged and rolled along the clean floor of polished bone.

King followed the sound.

"Behind those soldiers," Quest said.

Half a dozen young men had surrounded the mysterious orb. The surging crowd must have kicked it to them. Maybe they didn't realize where it was, but they were standing in a rough ring, accidentally protecting what they couldn't understand. Then they saw an apparition wading through the crowd—massive below and glowing above—and one of the soldiers managed to lift his rifle and fire two shots before his rifle was flying across the room and one of his hands was shattered.

The soldiers backed up and fell over, and King grabbed the prize with his right hand. But the ball was a little too large, and it was slick as glass, and falling free, it again gave off that faint ringing sound as it bounced.

Diamond was dropped.

King scooped up the prize with both hands and spun it. Then with desperate conviction, he held it up before his face, saying, "Put your finger back in. Go on, now."

Quest did exactly that.

For a full breath, nothing changed. And then the room was bright again.

Scared faces blinked and bodies started to pick themselves off the floor, and for a fine stupid moment Diamond could believe that the problem was both simple and solved. The sun had returned, and not only was it back, but if anything, its light was more brilliant than ever.

He laughed.

But King knew better. He cursed and said, "No, it's just the lights."

The nearest big doorway was fully opened. The outside world was still black and mysterious, while the indoors was illuminated by a series of electric lights that hummed and sometimes flickered as their filaments grew white-hot.

One soldier turned to another, asking, "What do we do?"

King thought this was a fine question. Turning to his brother, he said, "Listen for the voice. The voice."

"Whose voice?" asked Quest.

Neither boy answered.

Quest was still riding King's shoulders. Her eyes kept shifting forms, shifting talents. She was watching every face, and in the uproar, nobody noticed her stares.

"Seldom," said Diamond.

King looked just at him. "What?"

Diamond wanted to find his friend, and a good smart reason helped him. "Seldom's wonderful with puzzles. This is a puzzle."'

That notion wore an appealing logic.

The three of them shouted, "Seldom."

Someone closer to the door called out, "Here."

King cradled the orb in one arm and pushed, his other arm sweeping bodies aside.

Diamond followed in his wake.

Meeker was standing with generals, with List. He was giving orders to one officer, but that important thought was interrupted as King and the others moved past. The general waved and said, "Follow," and obeying his own advice, he started out after them.

Mother and Nissim were together, arms locked and feet apart. The Master's size and strength had kept them very close to where they began, and Mother saw Diamond among the heads, her free arm lifting, a word or two shouted but not heard.

"Seldom," King roared.

A long arm lifted up ahead, and it dropped.

The crowd was flowing towards the open door. Sirens were screeching, as urgent as ever. But noise didn't matter so much anymore. Would the papio continue their attack? In a world where night could arrive without warning, would their pilots and soldiers hold to the mission?

King pushed slow people aside, and Diamond followed, and then King stepped over a row of bodies knocked off their feet.

Some of those people weren't moving.

Diamond started to leap before he saw her. Falling to his knees, he pressed his face next to Elata's face, blood from her nose bright under the lights.

She sobbed and grabbed at him.

Diamond stood, trying to lift her.

A mechanic's red uniform was holding a fat man, and the man came running up from behind and didn't like being stopped and didn't mind at all giving the faceless boy one hard shove, shouting, "Out of my way."

Diamond turned fast, and he swung.

A fist never enjoys hitting any skull. Even Diamond's clenched fist ached after it struck the fat and the cheekbone and that big eye that had only just begun to see the miscalculation. The mechanic's head popped back, and he staggered. But fear and rage had a useful target, and grabbing the boy by the collar, he hit that face three times before realizing what face he was fighting. Then he let go of the boy and cursed various deserving targets, and Diamond, feeling nothing so much as frustration, struck the man twice again, cracking a tooth and leaving both lips split.

"Stop that, stop," the mechanic said.

Diamond swung once more, slicing the air between them.

"I'm sorry," the bloodied man said.

Diamond turned away. Elata was on her knees, a little purse pressed to her belly. He grabbed her around the chest and lifted, and then the mechanic seemed to hug both of them, blubbering about how wrong he felt, bringing them to their feet.

Holding Elata's hand, Diamond climbed over a pair of bodies.

Where was King?

The giant had evaporated, and Quest too. Diamond grabbed that thought and believed it. The gray globe had taken them away. Nothing imagination could build was impossible anymore, and maybe his siblings were yanked out of this Creation, and he should have been with them, and that's when guilt struck. Even when he saw the crowd parting ahead of him and the broad armored back sprawled across the floor, he continued to grieve having been left behind.

But King was at the edge of the butcher floor, head down, hunkered in a low squat with one of his long elbow spines rising high as he moved his hand.

Orders were shouted across loudspeakers. Every giant door was rising, electric lights flooding out into the irrational black, and each of the indoor fletches began their engines as that great shouting voice ordered every fletch to embark and set up a perimeter. Only then would the doors would shut and seal again.

"Five recitations," the voice promised, "and we return to gas protocols."

It was Meeker's voice.

"The papio are still coming," the general claimed.

A small voice shouted, "Diamond."

Seldom.

King twisted his neck until he was looking down the length of his own back. Seldom was standing on the far side of King, waving excitedly. Then he kneeled, vanishing again. The other doors began to lift. The crowd stopped surging, people aiming for the other openings. More people fell but picked themselves up, and what began as a panicky rout became a simple migration to the nearest openings, everybody wanting to stand at the edge, gazing at what couldn't be real.

Elata pushed into the moving bodies, strong shoulders wedging through.

And now Diamond followed her.

All but one fletch was free of its moorings. They had to push lower before skimming under the rising doors. The fletches and little ships that had been moored outside had embarked. Maybe they were the aircraft visible in the distance, spotlights twisting one way and another while signal lights and flares gave orders, while beyond, out where the great trees hung, a few illegal flickers of light began to emerge.

"The enemy is still inbound," Meeker said across the speakers.

Even before this, the papio were desperate. Now what did they believe? That the tree-walkers must have found a great weapon—a prize that allowed them to suffocate the world of its sunlight. Of course their fighters would keep coming. How could they do anything else?

Elata reached King's feet and legs, and without hesitation, she shook free of Diamond's hand before climbing over the top of the giant.

Diamond went around.

Until the last step, he had no idea what he would find. Imagination was useless. He gave up using his imagination. He discovered Quest wearing a flat gruesome bug shape, the shell of a cockroach and twin eyes looking like domes of polished crystal, various fingers and hands busily pushing into the globe's holes and out again.

"All of them," Seldom said.

"I have," Quest said with a dry, startling human voice.

"Try different sequences," the puzzle solver said.

King added his littlest fingers, but one finger was caught inside one cylinder, as if in a sad-sack trap.

"I don't think so," Diamond said.

Seldom looked up at him, wearing a broad grin.

"It won't work," Diamond said.

Hearing his words, he felt absolutely sure.

King cursed about his finger and grabbed the globe with his other hand, yanking hard twice and then gathering himself before he jerked himself free of that embarrassment.

The globe rolled, stopping against the backs of random legs.

Seldom grabbed it.

The abattoir wasn't quiet and never would be. But people had found places to stand, and only one fletch—the wounded *Tomorrow's Girl*—was hanging overhead, engines sleeping. The rumble of generators and the urgent endless wailing of every siren in the human world ripped at the air, and there were conversations that after the mayhem sounded almost reasonable. Strangers talked about the darkness and why this darkness was different than night, and they discussed how would the papio respond, and with nervous caution, some claimed that nothing would come of this but a healthy scare and the total destruction of their enemies.

Elata was standing on her toes, looking outside.

Suddenly, with a loud laughing voice, Seldom said, "Hey."

Elata turned. "What?"

"Did any of you bother to look here?" the puzzle expert asked.

The other four children gathering around the gray ball, King remaining on his hands and shins.

"What?" Elata repeated.

Seldom took a moment, showing them his fine smile.

Everybody asked, "What is it?"

"Words," he said. "There's some tiny words here, on the smooth end of this whatever thing."

Words?

"I don't know the language," the boy continued. "But it's been my experience that usually, in some way or another, words really want to mean something."

SIX

Coming to the abattoir was exciting, and the dead corona was a wonder. Seldom was thrilled with his day, and then the world shattered. The papio were coming, the darkness was already here, and inside one impossible moment, everybody turned crazy.

Nothing about any of this should be fun.

Yet weird as can be, Seldom was still enjoying himself. Two bizarre creatures had shoved their way through the riot to find him. King had always been a looming entity, ugly and loud and too dangerous to touch. Diamond was practically ordinary next to his brother, but the giant was here, begging for any help he could find from the great Seldom. And then there was the mystery sister, Quest-of-no-particular-shape. After saying his name three times, loud and then loud again before one final near-whisper, Quest confessed that this madness was her fault entirely.

Seldom offered his first, most reasonable thought.

He said, "Sticking your pinky in a hole doesn't kill the sun."

Quest refused to believe simple words. She looked like a girl and like a beetle, and then she was more like a beetle than anything, jointed legs trembling as she stood before the mystery that Karlan carried from the corona's belly.

King was behind her, towering until he kneeled.

Both creatures talked about urges that sounded like dreams, and what might be instincts, and the keen shared feeling that they were playing out some ancient, mostly forgotten plan.

The aliens were rattled; Seldom was their best hope.

"Try your finger again," he suggested.

But she had already.

"Try different fingers, different combinations."

A simple suggestion, but these two marvels hadn't produced that strategy on their own. He watching them huddle, trying their best while the darkness, this uninvited night, kept its chokehold on everything. Yet this was maybe the finest moment in Seldom's little life. Strangers were staring at the two apparitions and their hysterical efforts. That one creature had to be the Ghost, they said. And nobody had ever seen List's son bowing down. And in the midst of that scene was a skinny human boy offering advice and little encouragements. The human was in charge, and Seldom didn't giggle but could feel the delicious urge slipping up and down his spine.

Then Elata found him.

Seeing her bloodied nose, Seldom instantly felt ashamed for having danced with joy.

He kept making suggestions, and then Diamond emerged from the crowd. Ordering his friend to try his fingertips seemed reasonable, but Diamond said none of this would work. He sounded as if he was sure. Then the ball got loose and rolled, and Seldom captured it first. The gray material felt like nothing else. Maybe this was what a diamond looked like when it was big, but it certainly didn't resemble the tiny glitters inside museum cases. This was hard and lifeless and he rolled it under both of his hands until he noticed what looked like a blemish at the bottom, opposite the cylinders. The overhead lights were at full strength, bright and blue-white. Kneeling down low, Seldom wiped away a last layer of slime, fingers tingling from the acid, and he announced finding a few lines of delicate, peculiar words.

Unless of course they were scratches, he thought in the next moment. But how could a substance that survived some long fierce burial inside a corona show nothing but those tiny marks arranged in what looked like six perfect rows?

King claimed the object, bright green eyes staring at the scratches.

"Can you read them?" his sister asked.

He said, "No," and spun it, letting the bulging glass eyes absorb the text.

"I can't either," Quest said.

The abattoir doors were open but not for much longer. The sirens were as relentless as always. The enemy was still pushing through the darkness. The papio trained for night raids, and maybe they preferred attacking when nobody could see clearly. Could they have pushed the sun into oblivion?

That wild thought had no time to grow.

A woman's voice fell from everywhere, urgent but not fast. "One recitation," she warned, "and then the doors will drop and seal."

Seldom looked over the heads of people lined up at the opening, and another sharp thought took hold of his brain.

Diamond was peering at the neat scratchy words.

He was as baffled as anyone else.

"Master Nissim," said Seldom.

The corona's children looked at him, that first bright sense of understanding emerging.

"He knows old languages," Seldom reminded his friend.

Diamond said, "Yes," and stood up.

King jumped to his feet, looking back across the great room.

Looking sorry and lost, Elata stood by the others, one hand holding the purse while she fought the running blood with her other sleeve.

Seldom was wicked for not feeling more sympathetic toward her. But as he approached her, trying to pick good words, Elata seemed to forget her present miseries. Something behind him was worth a good hard stare, and the bloodied arm lifted, two fingers pointing through the open door.

"What is that?" she asked.

At the same moment, with a roaring voice, King said, "I see him."

"Nissim?" asked Diamond.

"We'll take this to your teacher," Quest said.

The three creatures headed back where they had come from. Seldom wanted to follow. This was his puzzle, and he wanted answers, and he managed a long first step before looking his shoulder, following the line made by Elata's arm and fingers.

Night was ending. A faint but true, undeniable light was growing brighter by the moment, and other people were talking about the glow while pointing in various directions, but always outwards, away from this tree and this giant building.

Suddenly ten voices said, "The sun is coming back."

Even as the joy grabbed everybody, including Seldom, he suffered doubts. If this was sunlight, then it was peculiar just how weak the light it seemed, and odder still, there seemed to be colors inside the light, as if the sun was trying to awaken but not yet certain which face to put on.

There was a long drop from the big doors to the landing. The wall beneath was covered with sloping nets. Not everyone wanted to jump down, but dozens did. They leaped and others fell, and Seldom intended nothing but to get closer to the edge, finding a somewhat better perch to watch what still didn't make sense.

Bodies surged and he hurried, Elata settling in beside him. Even with her swollen, sore-looking nose, she was pretty. Seldom's life couldn't be awful when he was walking beside this girl.

They reached the edge.

The brave people had gone below, while the cautious and cowardly remained above, enjoying a lesser view.

Seldom was happy with the cowards.

But not Elata. Suddenly she was the girl that he remembered from

Marduk—the bright fear-nothing girl who would try any whim twice, just to see what would happen.

"Come on," she said, tugging at his arm.

Seldom shook his head. But the shifting light was definitely stronger. Not like daylight yet, no. But how many people had ever seen the sun killed and then rekindled again? Maybe this was just the way it was, the way nature was put together. Who could know? And because science mattered so much to him, and because a short pretty and very strong girl wanted this to happen, Seldom let his arm get yanked, sending him tumbling down the nets.

They bounced, and he felt the giggle sliding along his backbone again.

And then they were running across the long landing, chasing people and catching up with some of them, not taking the lead but still among the early few to reach the tall railing. They shoved their heads through gaps. A gun turret was directly under their feet, motors swinging it one way and then another, its vents opened to let the gunner breathe. And that was why they could hear the gunner shouting across a call-line, unless of course he was yelling at himself.

"I see them," he yelled.

See who? The papio? But it was too soon. Wings were fast, but the machines were flying from the ends of the Creation.

"I can't count them," the gunner complained.

Seldom was looking down. Elata was looking down. There was nothing to see but a great cloud of shifting lovely and deeply colored light. For one spectacular moment, Seldom could believe that he didn't know what he was seeing. He was free to convince himself that he was fortunate, that only the rarest of people got to see the birth of a new sun, and that this was going to be a better, much lovelier sun. Colors like he had never imagined were rising up into his spellbound face.

Elata cursed, and then she muttered, "Oh no. It's the coronas."

Seldom blinked, surprise taking his voice away.

"I don't know how many," the gunner screamed into his headset. "But it looks like every last one of the monsters."

• • •

No place was quieter, more remote or half so peaceful, as the vacated guts of a freshly killed corona.

Karlan didn't want to be anywhere else.

Maybe the earlier battle left him jangled. Maybe silence and the relative solitude was a tonic. But a lot of questions never interested Karlan, and that included why he was searching the same terrain all over again, and what he was feeling, and why it felt good to start walking from the gash in the monster's side, following this twisting space all the way down near the shrunken but still enormous anus.

Everybody understood that the corona flesh was different than other flesh, but that didn't do the stuff justice. There was strangeness woven into the muscles, into the organs. The entire body was stacked in odd ways, but that was just one factor. The pure feel of things was peculiar. Even in death, the stomach lining had a quality that Karlan didn't try to explain. Even when it was chilled, there was heat inside the flesh—a burning that could be felt in every way except with thermometers and touch. The corona's strength persisted long past its life. Time itself seemed thick and lazy inside the dead blood. The flesh had to be cut apart and its metals rendered before the weird sense of the alien dissolved, and there were moments when this unyielding stubborn and unreflective man wondered if any of these qualities ever really vanished: he was full of corona iron and calcium and copper. Everybody was. Maybe the alien magic was woven inside his world, and that's why it felt so special and good to kill one of these beasts. It was the only way to rejuvenate what really mattered.

He walked to the anus, and then slower than ever, he walked back again.

Nothing else had been found. Just that one odd ball was trapped inside ten layers of membranes, and nothing else.

But that didn't mean there was no point in hunting.

Every corona stomach had its odd twists, one-of-a-kind deadends. There were always folds where a human hand could push inside, feeling death that wasn't dead and the lingering heat as well as that second heat that refused to be measured. Maybe something tiny was buried inside one of these folds. Who knew? Stopped in no particular place, Karlan invested a long moment investigating several deep grooves that gave him nothing. He wanted nothing, and he certainly expected nothing. But his fingers were ready to find a tiny version of that gray ball. He knew what he would do. Before anyone could search his pockets, he would swallow the prize whole. It didn't matter what the object looked like. The risks were nothing he could measure, so why worry about them? Down the prize would go, and maybe it would take up residence inside his guts like it did before. Or maybe the little ball, or whatever, would endow Karlan with some grave, grand power that would transform him in staggering ways.

That was a thought worth imagining.

Only later, a long time later, did Karlan bother to wonder why the others were taking so long to relieve him, or at least check on his whereabouts. The outside world didn't exist. Corona flesh had an amazing capacity to deaden sound. Sirens and amplified voices and fletch engines were nothing. Raging gun battles would probably be heard as muddy little thumps in some gray distance. Still alone, puzzled but not worried, Karlan started walking back to the world, and only near the gouged hole did he begin to hear what sounded like a chorus singing in a distant tree.

Grown men and women were shouting.

Karlan emerged just as the newest panic took hold, the depleted crowd running back into the abattoir's interior.

He understood only that he must have missed quite a lot. The main doors were closing, which meant that they had been opened in his absence. Only one fletch was left indoors, which happened to be the battered *Girl.* What little could be seen outside was more puzzling than what was inside. There was far too much darkness, except for a curtain of light that couldn't decide on the right colors. Maybe Karlan had never been scared in his life, at least in any normal sense. But he was very much aware of being out of balance, and the effect was to make him numb and stupid for a few moments. One foot lifted and dropped again. More than anything, he wished he had found some ancient treasure, because nobody was going to bother searching him now.

The big general and little List were standing pretty much where Karlan last saw them. Each was holding one receiver while talking on a second receiver, and surrounding them was the usual collection of officers and aides who were working hard not to make their pants soggy.

Wanting the truth, Karlan headed for them.

But then he came across the old teacher and the old mother. They would work even better.

Karlan asked for an update.

Haddi couldn't talk. She didn't try to speak, standing with her arms crossed and hands wrapping into fists, the blood just about drained from her face.

Nissim told the story.

And Karlan interrupted him twice, laughing at what sounded just too strange. The sun was gone? And the coronas were coming too? The slayer laughed until he was sure that the retired butcher had finished spinning this story, and then he looked around again, waiting for his brain to catch up with everything that he was seeing.

Then the armored god showed up with the gray ball in both hands. And riding on top of King was a giant bug, except she was no bug. Karlan understood that easily enough, and looking up at that peculiar face, he said, "I've seen you look prettier than this. How have you been, girl?"

Quest dropped and flattened, and she changed color, half-vanishing into the butcher floor.

King turned the ball in his hands, and shoving the smooth end at Nissim's face, he asked, "Can you read this?"

"Read what?" the old man asked.

But then Nissim said, "Wait." The four-fingered hand was shaking, pulling a pair of reading glasses out of shirt pocket. Both hands were shaking. Not for the first time, Karlan decided the old guy was just about cooked, nothing left in his nerves anymore. But the glasses got to the nose, and the nose got close to whatever marks were on that peculiar ball. Karlan wondered if he should have looked the ball over more carefully, using his torch and young eyes. But he couldn't see anything from here, standing one step away, and what-maybes were about the biggest waste of time in life.

"Can you read it?" said the bug on the floor.

Nissim gave a half-hearted nod, and then he shook his head, meaning no.

"But you've translated old writing before," King said. "Diamond told me. Out on the reef, where nobody goes, you deciphered a message—"

Interrupting, Haddi screamed, "Where's my son?"

Diamond wasn't anywhere in view. But List was approaching, and the general wanted to join their little party. Except he first had to tell a handful of soldiers to find more soldiers, as many as possible. He was looking at Quest as he gave orders. Quest had never been easier to see, and Meeker wasn't the kind to allow this sweet opportunity to drip away.

The big steel doors had pulled closed and sealed.

Once again, bellows were filling the room with extra air, and the cadaver balloons spun in the air overhead while the *Girl* creaked against its moorings.

List arrived with his people. Like always, he looked clever and sneaky, ten ready sentences riding his tongue, each one eager to be said.

Between two aides was Prima, out of her manacles and looking pretty much disgusted with everything.

Karlan had always liked that tough little gal.

Haddi kept talking about her son. Could anyone see Diamond?

Nissim said, "Quiet."

The old woman didn't want to be quiet. She turned until she saw Meeker, and she hurried toward him, asking, "Did you put him somewhere? Is he safe?"

Meeker was getting his soldiers ready to surround Quest.

"Put who where?" the general asked the petrified mother.

Nissim had one eye pressed against the mad scratches, and there stood King, rigid as a statue, holding the lost ball motionless, as if it were set in a vice.

Quest got up on her long back bug legs, glass eyes peering at the mystery.

Meeker was making his own quick search for Diamond, as if his vision could be better than a mom's.

And then all of those eyes in the room stopped seeing anything. The big guns outside began punishing someone, but the cannons were a small mess of noises compared to what else came. Somewhere past the big steel doors wasn't one sound but a host of new sounds, none loud yet but heavy in nature, like big weights bashing against drumheads, and those roaring wails weren't just moving fast but they were rising past where Karlan was standing, soaring towards the highest reaches of the trees.

Every slayer in the room lifted his head or her head.

Coronas were outside, flying wild in a realm where they hadn't been since the beginning of civilization.

• • •

Diamond had stopped running. He had followed Elata and Seldom when they jumped over the edge but lost sight of them before anybody reached the landing's edge. The electric lights had abandoned him, every door down and sealed. A hundred faces were pointed away from him. Anonymous backs and hairy heads were silhouetted by a wash of pale light that tried to be red and tried to be purple and then blue. Crossing his arms, Diamond rocked slowly from side to side while struggling to find two small people. A military fletch was circling nearby, yellow spotlights aiming at targets moving swiftly below. Each beam dimmed as the open air brightened. Dozens of fletches and other military craft roamed in the distance. People standing at the railing were shouting. Some pointed below while others turned suddenly, fleeing toward the abattoir. A few voices shouted, "Coronas." Most people made incoherent noise, monkey noises, high-pitched and horrified and all the more bracing because of it.

Needing some idea to pin against the mayhem, Diamond decided that a flock of coronas was following the giant body up here. They were grieving. The coronas wanted revenge. Maybe they wanted to recover the globe or even the children that had been taken from them. Whatever was happening,

Diamond believed in purpose—clear and narrow and understandable—and that's why he could stand in one place, not calm but not panicked either, the arms coming uncrossed but nothing else changing as the first of the running, wailing humans raced past him.

A cannon set beneath the landing fired one round, and that seemed to set off every other gun. Emplacements on the distant trees began lashing out with tracers and flares, fireballs and concussive blasts. And then the big fletch finally decided on a worthy target, every spotlight pulling together, creating a single beam that illuminated something that was directly beneath.

The ship's guns fired while its engines throttled up.

Air was being explosively ejected from a giant's puckered mouth.

Diamond expected to see a corona and didn't. Instead he saw an unexpected shape following the joined beam of light. The shape had to be made of light because it was too quick to be real, appearing in an instant and chasing the spotlights toward the machine that was struggling in vain to get out of the way. Diamond didn't see trailing necks or heads, and the normally rounded body was distorted, made long by its velocity and the thin cold air rushing past it and the rapid sharp bursts of air that he still hadn't heard. He saw nothing clearly save for a brilliant flash of light that was purple laid over colors far beyond purple, and what was obvious was that these two objects would have to collide.

Now he heard the air thundering out of the corona's mouth.

The fletch's belly guns fired furiously, and at the last moment, someone thought to kill the spotlights, which accomplished nothing.

The corona was half-grown, riding on a column of jetted hot air, and papio wings couldn't fly that fast. The impact took no time. The fletch was intact, full of people and hydrogen and machinery and ammunition, and then it was bored through and torn to shreds, all of those pieces hanging fixed in the air while the corona continued to rise, giving no signs of slowing.

More coronas appeared. All of them were young, all rocketing past the landing, and Diamond put his hands on his stubbly head and yanked at his ears while his mouth twisted in anguish, leaking a moan, numbing breathless fear rendering him impossible heavy.

The fletch was shattered and now falling, but the sound of that titanic impact finally arrived—bladders bursting, the skeleton shattering—and buried inside that uproar was a voice and a name, and it took another moment for him to recognize the name.

"Diamond," said the voice.

Seldom was standing directly in front of him.

Elata was holding Seldom's arm, dragging him along. She hadn't noticed Diamond. She intended to pull her friend back to the building, and to help keep Seldom moving, she shouted, "Go," and, "Go," again with a furious hoarse voice.

The three of them ran.

And the coronas raced past, turning the landing bright and purple with red waves and twisting flashes of blue and gold. Giants by the hundreds were rising, and the air shook with their jets, and the entire landing jumped while the cannons fired as fast as they could, except it was easy to miss hearing any of them.

Elata was holding Diamond's hand now, not Seldom's, and nobody could remember how that happened.

Every doorway into the abattoir was closed. Desperate people were shoved against the small doorway where they entered earlier. The first row of bodies kicked the steel and begged in high shrieking voices, and then the next ranks pushed against them, leaving no room to kick and no breath to use in their pleading. Seldom tried to claim Elata's other hand, except she was still carrying her purse. She looked at him and then Diamond, surprised to find him joined to her. She wanted to be pleased. The beginnings of a smile shone in the corona light, and then something was above them, close and coming fast, and she flinched reflexively and the other two knelt with her, and a corona fell onto the landing, first with its heads and ropy limp necks and then its exhausted, doomed body.

Bloodwood boards sagged and shattered, but the massive framework beneath managed to weather the impact. The landing tilted before finding a stable angle that might last ten breaths or maybe forever. The corona's body radiated heat like an open smelter. A thick yellow light poured out over everyone. The corona's necks lay scattered, limp. The two heads closest to the abattoir and people did nothing for a long moment. Then the triple eyes opened and one head lifted and the other rose and fell weakly before pulling in the neck's slack, giving it the leverage to rise to its neighbor's height. The corona's light washed over every surface. The triple eyes took on a rich golden color. The triple jaws opened, each as long as a man was tall, and the teeth turned gold as both heads slowly examined the humans that were doing nothing but standing, not one arm moving and nobody daring to breathe.

One head closed its jaws.

The weaker head left its mouth open, bright sharp tongues emerging to taste the thin cold and nearly useless air.

A big turret was perched on top of the abattoir. Its gunners could see the corona below, but the cannons had safeties to assure that nobody would stupidly pummel the landing during some otherwise reasonable battle. Those safeties had to be unlocked. The work took cursing and muscle and memories that had never quite become routine, and then the frantic men who finally accomplished that job had no time or patience left to contemplate the fragile peace below.

The corona had done nothing but collapse.

Then the cannons began boom-booming, precious rounds of junk metal and explosives battering the helpless body.

A squealing roar came from deep inside the creature, emerging from the mouth and then every head, and the body twisted while turning a vivid blackish purple, and half of the remaining necks reached upwards, trying to kill what was killing it.

Then a second turret found its freedom and fired.

Another corona—smaller and stronger, already high overhead—turned and dove down to help its brother. Coming like a spear, its scaled carapace smashed armored glass and the men, and it got its body became trapped inside the ruined turret, badly wounded and furious and deeply unsatisfied by whatever revenge that it wanted to accomplish.

Necks and heads dangled down across the abattoir's front.

The first corona said quite a lot with its light, its mournful noise, and with potent scents that normally kept coronas calm and thoughtful.

It begged the world's coronas to do nothing more.

But there was no normal, no decency.

The trapped corona let twenty heads drop as far as they could on rubbery necks, jaws opened and then slamming shut again. Diamond hadn't moved since the three of them hunkered down for no good reason. Elata was in the middle. A big man in a government suit was standing on the other side of Diamond, and a sharp bright sound brought the barest sense of motion, and then the corona head was gone and the man was almost gone. Just his legs remained, the left leg managing to stand on its own an instant longer than its mate.

Inside the next moments, with scorching efficiency, that densely packed crowd of bodies was shredded, pieces of bodies scattered, and the few dozen survivors were lying on their stomachs, holding a little still or very still, begging the Fates for just one more recitation of life.

The second corona stopped the slaughter abruptly, retrieving its necks and its focus in order to try and pry itself free.

The first corona turned yellow again, but not as bright anymore. The two inquisitive heads pushed forwards, followed by many more. Corona heads were what saw the world and touched the world and sometimes made noises, and they were what guided prey and pieces of prey into the real mouth. Carefully, slowly, those heads passed over corpses and soaked red clothes. People's breakfasts and wet brown feces had been freed from various rectums. The triple eyes had turned red and brown, and the jaws were held shut, and the corona seemed to be counting the living, nudging each one, watching startled people react or not react. Curiosity might be at play. Diamond thought as much, when he thought anything. And then the strongest first head saw Elata and came close before the jaws spread and three tongues emerged, ready to taste her face.

She made a soft miserable sound but refused to move. Glaring at the creature, she closed her mouth tight and took a useless breath through her bloodied nose and held her face steady, just for an instant, summoning the will to tip her head into the mouth, inviting whatever came next.

Diamond reached out, grabbing the raspy tip of the nearest tongue.

The tongue jerked back and the head did much the same, putting distance between them. But a fresh thought or old notion took charge, and ten different heads came forward, wanting to examine the odd organism huddling with the dead and condemned humans.

Again, the corona's body changed color. What looked deep purple to a human eye was just the lazy end of the high-purple spectrum—a powerful scalding light that could carry a lot of meaning, or a single message repeated millions of times.

Fascination was a human word. But the heads and their necks pushed against one another, fighting to gain a closer viewpoint of a singular entity huddling in the gore. Corona flesh made the air hot and suddenly quiet. The roar of siblings and guns and every other nightmare was dulled when those many eyes came close to Diamond, and then seemingly as an afterthought, studying the tiny monkeys on either side of him.

"What?" Diamond said.

Then he climbed up on his knees and stared at the first head, asking again, "What?"

Bunched together, those heads provided easy targets. Soldiers fired from the gun ports beside the doorway, big slugs chewing away at the jaws and eyes. But even as the pedestrian doorway was opened, even as electric lights washed over the scene, the surviving few heads stared at Diamond and the other two children.

Once more, the first head pushed forward and opened.

Having no shot, the soldiers held their fire while watching three tongues embracing the alien face. Bristles even harder than corona teeth left Diamond's cheeks and chin bloodied, but not too deeply, and he was mostly healed after the corona slumped into death and the soldiers returned him to his mother.

SEVEN

Quest was ready.

Telling herself so didn't make it true. And confidence was always the worst trap that a soul could set for herself. But Quest spent effort and anticipation wondering what could happen and what she would do in response, and despite being more visible than she had ever allowed herself to be, she wasn't sick with worry. She was safer inside this one reinforced structure than anywhere else. One wretched event after another had arrived, and the human animals had no time or will to spare on one ghostly being. Besides, Quest was responsible for some chunk of this madness, and maybe all of it. An urge had claimed her and her siblings, but it was her finger that touched the bottom of a simple tube, which happened to be the moment when the sun vanished. Did she cause this torment, or was this coincidence? How could anyone know? But the point was that everyone believed she was culpable, including Quest, and the most hopeful thought in this wild unimagined set of nightmares was that the finger that ended the world might well bring it back again.

The giant room was filled with scared people doing nothing. The dead corona was strewn across the floor, its heat and its stench thickening the pressurized air. The Archon was standing close, and Meeker too. Sometimes the men spoke on call-lines, sometimes to one another. But mostly they did nothing except watch Quest help with the work. They wouldn't dare touch her. Not in these circumstances, not with their lives and every bigger thing at stake. That was the shell of her confidence.

"No," she said, looking at the big piece of paper. "That line bends here."

"You're certain?"

She said, "Yes."

The old teacher was preparing a large accurate copy of the message. Quest's eyes were best, and she copied what she saw with a sharpened pencil while he made notes between and beside the lines. Not one mark on the globe duplicated an existing letter, but there were passing resemblances that gave the game hope. And sometimes Nissim would go back and look hard at one word or two, muttering when he breathed, repeating a string of possible translations that gave their audience reason to bend at the hips, waiting for enlightenment. But so far, his best attempts only brought more questions.

Quest had never written with any implement. Now she was finishing the final line from a text that was as old as the Creation, or older.

Such an odd thought, and welcome. Her new hand slowed, trying to render the final symbols perfectly.

"And that's it," said Nissim.

It was. Yes.

King set the globe on the floor.

Meeker came forward, for the first time. He had unremarkable exterior, nothing to separate him from a million other soldiers, but he carried himself as if no one was half so important. Even List gave the man a careful gap in space and in noise.

"How close is the translation?" asked the general.

He only spoke to the human.

"This is an ancient language," Nissim said. "Ancestral, probably. Hopefully. But I don't have any of the books that I need."

"People have been sent to the library," Meeker said.

There was an excellent library below them. Quest had sneaked inside on several occasions, always at night, reading random volumes in the dark.

"If they survive the mission, you'll have everything from your shopping list," Meeker promised.

Nissim looked at the writing and then looked up. His eyes avoided every face. "All right," he said to nobody.

No one else spoke.

Then the old woman cried out, and Diamond ran up alone. A dozen soldiers were chasing him, losing the chase, and another dozen were accompanying the boy's human friends. Until that moment, Quest hadn't realized how worried she was. Then the unsuspected weight was gone, and she felt even more confident than before.

"But that is the full message, yes?" Meeker asked.

The Archon came forward, alone. He meant to examine the paper, but Meeker stopped him with the touch of a finger.

"Give our scholar some room," said the voice in charge.

The Archon put on a smile. "Of course."

Master Nissim stared at the carefully transcribed words. His own pencil was busy in his hand, spinning between fingers. But his face was calm and thoughtful, red-rimmed eyes dancing back and forth without any trace of order. Quest watched for order. The man wasn't reading what he could understand, and he didn't seem to be lingering over any piece of the text either. For a thousand days, Nissim had been growing older. Each time Quest saw that face, it wore more wrinkles and white hairs and broken, unhealing veins. But not this time. Under these awful circumstances, the man's exterior appeared peculiarly youthful, the blood behind the old skin helping smooth features by hundreds of days.

Quest didn't like human faces, but she liked his face.

She couldn't read human thoughts, much as she tried. But she had a clear sense of his mind when Meeker asked, "How close are you?"

"Not close," the old teacher said. "Not yet."

Nissim was lying.

"Well, we don't need to remind you about the urgency of this." Then with a general's sense for drama, Meeker tipped his head, giving everyone good reason to listen to the carnage outside.

Haddi was hugging her son.

King and Karlan approached the boy from opposite directions. The alien stomped twice at the floor, greeting his brother, while the giant human clamped his hand on top of the bare head, saying, "Stop being an idiot."

The irony was rich. Two souls that tried to kill Diamond were now rejoicing at his rescue.

Irony wanted Quest to laugh.

She didn't laugh.

Seldom arrived, and his brother slugged him in the chest, saying, "Stop being brave."

Haddi gave Elata a suffocating hug.

The girl bit her bottom lip, saying nothing as she stared at the floor.

Nissim's pencil had stopped moving. The youth in his face had suddenly drained away. He looked weary and then angry. The mysterious words needed one more long stare, and then he looked at the gray globe that was waiting patiently to the side, no longer needed and indifferent to the lack of attention. The object needed a long stare, and Quest tried to pull the insights out of the man's mind. And then, as if sensing the interest, Nissim turned towards her face, taking a moment to clear his thoughts. He meant to whisper something. Something very important needed to be shared. Great events and little ones had led to this moment, and Quest felt ready and lucky, even though she sensed that she wouldn't relish what she would hear . . . and that's when Meeker took one long step forward, pulling a compact pistol from under his bright green general's shirt.

The first round exploded on impact, throwing her across the floor.

She was lying alone on the butcher floor as the next nine bombs left her battered, unable to resist as the soldiers that came running at her from every direction, like cockroaches.

• • •

Slayer tools were slicing apart his sister's body, power saws and the finest knives in the world helping separate the unessential away from what seemed to be her mind. Impressive planning was on show. The soldiers worked quickly, some of them smiling to hide their fears. They wouldn't touch her body without rubber gloves or the heel of a boot. The bravest pair volunteered to drop the soulless meat into glass buckets filled with acid. Even the blood was worrisome. A woman soldier walked about the slaughter, cooking the dark blue spills with a handheld torch.

King barely watched his sister being eviscerated.

These circumstances needed a good polish, and that's why Meeker went to Diamond before anyone else. Not even pretending to smile, he said, "I didn't want this. I hate this. But the creature has been running free too long, and we know about a hundred incidents where she's done harm, by choice or chance."

Diamond was listening to the human, but his face was empty.

"I know the creature tried to help you before," the general said. "And I don't want you to believe that I would want it hurt in any lasting way. 'Her,' I mean. I don't want 'her' to be in pain, much less crippled. But she had to be contained. Do you understand me?"

Diamond seemed to nod, although the motion was very slight.

"Quarters have been built," Meeker continued. "There is a home waiting for a reduced, much safer version of her. No witness has seen the creature absorbing or manipulating glass, and so there's a glass room near the palace—"

"Glass," Diamond said.

"Everyone needs to be safe, including her."

"Quest," said the boy.

"Yes. Quest. Of course I know her name."

The conversation was just one set of noises that King absorbed and mostly ignored. He also heard the wailing of coronas and the dull concussive booms of guns, and there were several conversations and dozens of important faces nearby, not one of them mattering. What drew his hard focus was one man standing alone, standing motionless, one foot in front of the other as if he was planning to take a walk but still wasn't quite certain where he wanted to be.

King stared at his father, and he listened to the little man's breathing and the quick sorry racing of his heart. War had eviscerated the Archon's office. But instead of being dumped into buckets, the old powers were now worn by men in bright uniforms—warriors who had never killed another man with their own hands. The creature who once ruled the world had been sidelined by endless war. Civilian tasks were few, and List had no clear authority or even the right to speak. He was just another piece of the audience. He was almost pitiful, although what mattered to his son wasn't pity and it wasn't sorrow, much less any desire for greater, deeper understandings. All the miseries in the world, and what transfixed and saddened King was the cavernous gap between himself and that defeated creature.

The teacher was another important, disregarded face. Carrying the paper and its unknown words, Nissim approached the Archon.

"What?" Father asked, anticipating some demand.

The Master used a rough whisper, the intact hand hiding his mouth and the fur around his mouth. "I need to go below, sir. There's no time."

Something about the request amused Father, at least enough to draw out a wary smile. "I just spoke to a caretaker at the Antiquities Library. Those volumes are on their way now."

"No." Nissim had distracted eyes. "You don't understand."

Even weakened—particularly because of his lack of power—List retained a clear sense of people, what their sounds and various silences meant.

"You found something inside that text," Father said plainly, and not quietly.

The Master was careful to look only at the Archon's eyes. "The spotter's station," he said.

"At the bottom of this tree?"

"Yes."

The smile turned suspicious. "You want to use its telescopes."

"Yes."

"And a nearby window and binoculars won't do."

"They won't," the man said.

"You want to see if the sun is really gone."

"I know it's lost. What I need to see is what remains below us, and if I can, judge what's between us and there."

Their conversation was fascinating, but Meeker wanted words with Quest's other brother. Showing only the thinnest caution, the general said, "You were eavesdropping on me. I know you heard every word that I said to Diamond."

King said, "Yes."

"But I want you to appreciate something, young man. A lesson that your father undoubtedly knows: patience always has to surrender to wisdom. And that includes my patience with you."

The unexpected had arrived, and King's attentions had to split. He lifted one foot and dropped it again. "What do you mean?"

"The Quest creature has been visiting you at the palace," Meeker said. "I know this. For a long while, I've known how you and your brother dangle the bell and then slip away to meet with your sister."

"And you did nothing."

"Nothing to either of you, or to her. I thought it was best to bide my time, waiting until the hard decision had to be made."

King was rigid as a coral statue.

"And this had to be the time," said the world's ruler. "I took action, I take responsibility, and my only apology is that I couldn't give you either one of you children fair warning."

King had too many mouths to follow, too many shifting conversations. He was the largest beast in the room—the largest living beast—yet for the first time in his life, he felt like a whisper about to be swallowed by the echoes.

"Crush me or let me walk away," said Meeker.

King stared down at him.

"But be quick, please. There's a platoon of aides waiting to share their disastrous reports."

"Walk away," said King.

"Thank you," said his enemy, that tiny skeleton and the papery skin strolling past him, revealing little trace of fear.

The soldiers kept working. Quest's mind was a slick gray body, which was exactly like King's mind. That and a shattered skull and a sloppy length of what wasn't a spine were being laid inside a long and heavy glass trough—a reservoir used by slayers to catch the acidic milks from certain corona glands. Despite the intense damage, those bits of tissue began to move, flinching and crawling until one soldier was alarmed enough to smack the skull with a big iron mallet, and then ten big men carried a second trough over and nested on top of the first, leaving a gap barely thicker than a human hand. Once their safety was assured, the soldiers gathered around the prisoner, everybody looking through the thick glass, a few making the kinds of jokes that caused grown men to giggle.

Father was still explaining the world to Nissim.

"You don't understand," he said for the third or fourth time. "We assumed . . . we had to hope . . . that the coronas had been trying to reclaim their father or grandfather, whatever this is. But no, they're everywhere in the District of District. Thousands have come. And I've gotten reports that they're attacking the reef, and blessing of blessings, they're slaughtering the papio fleet too. But about the spotter's post, it went silent early on. The call-lines might be broken, but most likely, the facility has been destroyed. The monsters are murdering and wreaking havoc. And so even if I could give you permission, I wouldn't."

King walked away from the two humans.

Diamond saw him. What wasn't a smile revealed his icy white teeth, but King strode past, conspicuously ignoring him, and Diamond whispered to him, the same two words repeated again and again.

"Great day, great day, great day."

King walked on.

Standing apart from everyone else, still wearing the filthy coveralls, Karlan looked ready for any order or for no orders. He wasn't relaxed, but watching King step up to him, his nervousness showed only in the slow shifting of his feet and a lack of color in his voice. "What do you want?" he asked.

"Your ship," said King.

The man looked up at Tomorrow's Girl. "Yeah, and what do you want it for?"

"We need to escape."

Karlan tilted his head, inviting his companion to listen to the roaring coronas and the gunfire. Except there were few guns left with ammunition and crews. And in the same breath, one of the colonels was warning Meeker that the fully grown coronas had arrived—bigger than these babies that had already killed uncountable thousands.

"You want my ship," Karlan said.

"Yes."

"Tethered and too damaged to fly, and all of these big doors locked tight. You want to use that wreck to escape."

"Yes."

"Huh," said Karlan. "I never imagined you were stupid."

A wicked sound slipped out of his bottom mouth. Then King said, "You haven't begun to imagine my plan."

That earned a quiet nod, and silence.

"I've injured humans but never killed any," King continued.

"What's that?"

One giant to the other, he said, "I understand the mechanics. I don't need any help. But what I need from you is your expert opinion. When my enemies die, do I look at their faces or not?"

• • •

The final cannons stopped firing, out of shells or destroyed, and for an instant it felt as though the world would turn quiet again. But that illusion ended with a thundering that was heard and felt. A giant corona had jetted into the most distant door—meat and momentum driving into the steel plates, bending most of them and shattering a few before the bloodied carcass fell away, leaving gaps where the next three corona could shove their heads into the brightly lit interior.

Soldiers had to be given orders and encouragement and an officer to lead them.

Diamond walked toward the glass coffin, but one remaining soldier waved his hammer. "No, no. Go stand with the others."

The others were miserable, each in his or her own way. Seldom was sitting on a spare stool and Elata was standing behind him, each with arms wrapped around their own chest and both of them crying. Haddi needed to hug her son. Diamond let her cling, smelling her sweat and her breath. But the biggest smell came from the corona. The Archon decided to ignore Master Nissim, turning to a nearby aide just to ask some distracting question. Nodding wearily, the Master glanced at the copied text before trying to roll it up. But the cylinder was sloppy, so he opened it again and rerolled it two more times before he felt satisfied.

"This is awful," Mother said.

Diamond nodded, but that didn't feel like enough, so he said, "It is awful."

No words matched the mood.

King and Karlan were standing close together, talking quietly when the hammer-man approached them. Using rank and his confidence, the hammer-man told the human to get to work.

A curse was ready in Karlan's mouth. But what he did was hold his mouth closed while nodding, and then he look up at the ceiling once before walking away, apparently obeying that command.

And that's when Diamond understood.

There was no plan inside his mind, nothing so clean and neat as that, and if forced to explain, he couldn't have defined his own wants. But what he felt was the sudden warm lift that always came before the conscious idea—more instinct than language, simpler and truer. He saw what was important while everything else turned to vapor, drifting away. His mother asked him one question, and he answered it immediately and honestly but couldn't remember in another moment what she said or he said, and he couldn't even guess why she had to tip his head over so that she could kiss his eyes. But she gave him those two kisses, and then her hands released him, and as Diamond stepped away, he realized that Master Nissim had found someone else to talk to.

There was a second prisoner here, but she had been forgotten. Nobody would stop Prima if she tried to flee now. But where would she go? Looking up at the teacher, she found enough focus to listen to his careful pleads, but then as Diamond arrived, she reached up, waving her hand like a student might.

Nissim paused.

"Why waste your time with me?" asked Prima. "My vote counts for less than nothing."

Nissim wasn't cowed or embarrassed or even hesitant. He instantly explained, "I'm practicing my arguments. That's all. I want to be ready before I approach the generals with what I know and what I'm afraid of."

Prima considered laughing. But Diamond's arrival shifted her mood, and she fell into a keen scorching glare.

Diamond said, "Sir."

"Yes?"

"We don't need a telescope."

Nissim closed his eyes and opened them, and only then did he look at the boy. "Why don't we?" he asked.

But Diamond didn't answer. Instead, he turned to Prima. "You need to come with me, madam."

"Do I?" she asked skeptically.

"Both of you should please follow me, please," he said.

Karlan had returned. Diamond expected him to be carrying guns, but he wasn't. Corona skin had been pulled from the scrap pile—a long narrow skin salvaged from an old towing balloon, saved to make patches. He handed the skin to King, and King immediately began wrapping it around his chest, three circuits made before he bunched up the rest of the strap and walked toward the glass coffin.

Every soldier worried. Hammers didn't seem like enough weaponry, and the hammer-man put his hammer down and motioned for help. Suddenly ten men were warily staring at the Archon's son, every gun in hand, ready to lift.

King glanced through the glass as he walked past, aiming for Diamond and the others.

List stepped out to meet his son.

King touched his father on the shoulder with a finger, just that, and he walked past the man while calling to Diamond.

Again, that sense of deep knowing took hold.

King was breathing hard and that was all that he was doing. "This is what we are going to do," he said.

But Diamond said it to his brother first. There was no conscious thought until the words were spoken, and King opened both mouths while the dark green eyes grew even bigger, listening the basics of what he intended to do.

Then he was finished, and after a great breath, King said, "Unless there is a better way."

The brothers tried silence, wishing for inspirations that never came.

Karlan was speaking quietly to his brother and to Elata too. In the distance, soldiers began to fire at the invaders, killing the corona heads. Conversation became harder work, and looking about the room, a pair of officers noticed King standing with the civilians and how the other soldiers encircled the coffin, guns at the ready. But they didn't approach by themselves. The chain of command made certain that Meeker was alerted to the new danger, and he felt confident enough to approach, ready to disarm this situation with another few careful words.

The rest of the group was standing close to each other, watching King. Watching Diamond.

"We're going to retreat," Meeker began. "Unessential personnel are being pulled back into the tree. There's a bunker in that heartwood. It's older than everybody but you two, I'll wager. This attack can't last much longer. The coronas are too high, too cold. We'll outlast them."

As if to prove him wrong, another full-grown corona drove its body into the damaged door, a long steel shard cutting two soldiers in half.

The gunfire quickened.

Soldiers guarding the coffin wondered if someone should reinforce the defenders.

But Meeker told them, "No, come here," and then he began to wave at the nearest group of high officers.

King's left palm drop on top of the general's head.

Inside the abattoir, everyone stopped talking, and most of the guns quit firing.

"No," said King. "That won't happen."

List started to speak.

King's other hand covered his father's mouth and entire face. Then as soldiers pushed close from all sides, he told everyone, "There's a better shelter for these people. And anybody who stands in my way is going to die."

List put both of his hands on the smothering hand.

"You're welcome to remain with us, Father," King said. "Or if you wish, follow some other branch to its end."

Big rifles were set against strong shoulders, sights finding their marks on that armored face.

Meeker's voice broke when he said, "No."

"What?"

"You won't do this," Meeker said.

"What am I going to do?" King began.

Then a lone sniper took the easy shot. Rare metals burrowed into King's forehead and skidded upwards, leaving a clean gouge carpeted with white bone. Suddenly every officer was shouting, telling everyone to hold their fire, and King reacted instantly, angrily, lifting the general by his head and turning him, fixing that narrow body against the broad armored chest. But pulling that long strip of bladder skin around his captive proved difficult, particularly when a desperate man was squirming and every rifle in the room was pointing at his head.

Diamond jumped forwards to help.

In moments, Meeker was swaddled like a baby, two chests pressed together, and King adjusted the man's height and made a final hard knot before bending the head forward, allowing his eating mouth to engulf the entire scalp.

Razored teeth began to chew, just enough to let the man sense the kind of pain that would follow.

Meeker went limp.

"Now," said King with his breathing mouth. "Slow, but not slow."

Diamond followed the group, making certain that everybody was included. Elata and Seldom were holding hands. Karlan pivoted as he walked, counting the guns aimed at him. Mother said something to her son, and she said the same words into her cupped hands. Prima thought about running away and didn't, and List shuffled his feet until he half-tripped on a saw that had been forgotten on the floor.

"Father, be careful," King said.

Soldiers had the coffin surrounded. The hammer-man was shooting King with his imagination, practicing the motion and his aim while dreaming that he would be the hero to bring this monster to its knees at last. Right up until the end, that man was making himself ready, and then a young fellow beside him lifted his pistol, fast but not nearly fast enough, and a creature full of oxygen and nerves took two hard strides before swatting both of those soldiers in their faces, breaking every little bone.

Three snipers fired into King's back.

And he knocked every soldier off his feet and kicked their guns back at his companions.

Karlan picked up the biggest two rifles, and again, he spun in a slow circle, taking a census of his new enemies.

The glass coffin's top trough was jammed hard into the bottom trough. King's first yank did nothing, and the second yank lifted both of them off the floor. But then the top one let its grip slip, and he spun and flung it across the floor.

"Get her," he called out.

But Diamond already had his sister in his hands. She was no bigger than that first time when he knowingly saw her—a bug-like creature clinging to the window of that tiny awful cabin—and she seemed weak in every way. But the jointed legs clung to his forearm, while bright crystalline eyes captured his face, and he stared down at her, and the faint beginnings of a voice said nothing that made sense, but the sounds seemed hopeful nonetheless.

Prima hesitated, looking lost when she glanced at the boy who had ruined her world. But she needed him enough to ask, "Where's shelter? Where can we go?"

With his free hand, Diamond gave her a push.

The ancient corona was waiting. One hole led inside, and even though the scales and muscles were weak in life and very dead now, the body's bulk would supply protection against almost every attack. King turned to walk backwards, letting the room see the man strapped to his chest, that fragile head surrounded by teeth. And between more big breaths, he said, "Diamond. First."

Diamond climbed into the gouge, running a few steps before stopping. Nothing about the gut felt familiar. He didn't know this room. But to his sister, he said, "Home again," and heard a weak laugh.

His mother was next, and she took a moment looking about, probably wondering what Merit would have made of this remarkable place.

The others were coming, Karlan at the back.

King remained outside.

From a deep pocket came a long torch, and Karlan turned it on and handed it to List. Then to Nissim, he said, "Help me drop the ceiling."

Two timbers were kicked out, and soft old meat shut out the outside world.

Within the gloom, two lights shone.

Quest was glowing weakly.

Diamond kneeled on the gooey floor, and speaking in a whisper, carefully but quickly, he said, "I asked you once early on. 'How big can you grow?'

"Well, show me how big, sister.

"Show everyone."

EIGHT

A dead neck provided the way.

Despite living among tree-walkers, King had never walked along any branch, but running up the corona's neck had to be similar. Legs reached, feet planted. Sprinting was work, but balance was the greater trick. The first few steps taught him how the mind could grow peculiarly fond of any branch or neck, learning its curves and textures, anticipating what would happen next. Then the object to which he had pinned his hopes decided to vanish under its brothers, which was a small treachery, and King had to leap twice, finding a better neck that carried both of them to the top of the giant carcass.

Meeker's face was pressed against King's neck, and whenever his head twisted, teeth sliced into his scalp.

King tasted human iron and human salt. Running across the flesh, he told his prisoner, "Shout. Offer some final orders."

"You want them . . . to hold their fire," the general guessed.

"Not that, no," said King. "Reasonable. Tell them to be reasonable. The world's dying, and this is everybody's last chance to be sensible."

Meeker cursed.

King ran and then the corona's body fell away under them, and he half-jumped and half-slid back to the floor. By then, the other generals had to be realizing where he was going, if not why. But there was no time to react. The gangway to the *Girl* remained intact and unguarded. The only soldier in view was a recruit only a few days out of training, ordered to reinforce the soldiers who were being killed by living coronas. The boy was trotting towards the battlefield. Thinking like a soldier, he sensed that a slow, steady pace might save his life.

Then he saw King and the general dangling from the alien's mouth, and dumbfounded, the boy stopped, doing nothing but staring at the day's latest astonishment.

King sprinted past.

In the edge of an eye, Meeker saw the familiar green uniform. "Do what you have to," he screamed. "Shoot shoot shoot."

Nobody fired.

The gangway had a steep pitch, almost like a ladder. King needed both hands to climb. Speed counted, but he didn't hold any one pace. Snipers would have to work for their clean shots, and that's why he was better than halfway to the fletch before a signal was given, a dozen bullets launched at the same moment and battering his skull on three sides.

The humans wanted one sharp stunning blow.

The idea was respectable. But King's hands were locked on the heavy rope railing, and one foot never lost purchase. He dangled but didn't fall and a moment of empty blackness passed, and then he was conscious again, climbing again, and only when he was standing inside the fletch did he taste what was inside his eating mouth, understanding what happened when his head jerked.

King spat out the slivers of bone and the juicy remnants of brain. Then he unwrapped the skin around his chest, dropping the corpse to the distant floor.

Next he broke the heavy ropes, dropping the gangway.

One guard and three capable monkeys had been left on duty. The monkeys needed no excuse to jump away, limbs extended to slow their descent. But the human guard had the duty of firing at the invader while donning a drop-suit, and then he flung himself free of the abandoned ship.

Karlan's instructions led to the belly turret.

King was far too large to squeeze inside that bubble of glass, but he could lay on the floor above and grab the cannon's tiny handles, one thumb on the trigger.

A hundred soldiers were running below him, shouting and taking positions and then abandoning those positions for better ones.

Most of the civilians were retreating into the hallways.

The towing balloons that helped carry the corona up from its home were gathered nearby, rubbing each other and the highest portions of the ceiling. They should have been drained immediately, but people had been too busy and too excited to remember routines. And because all of the vents in the abattoir had been closed, making ready for the papio attack, every breath of leaked hydrogen was now puddling in easy view.

Three bursts of cannon fire shredded the bladders, unleashing fierce blue flames.

For the next recitations, the only duty below was survival. Fire triggered alarms, and pressurized carbon dioxide exploded from tanks waiting above the ceiling. People scattering, fighting for gas masks or simple distance. The heavy gas caused some people to pass out and drop. Scaffolding burned and rope rigging burned, flames draped across the giant corona, and the shredded bladders fell like dead leaves. But then the fires were suddenly finished, and the generals ordered their soldiers to approach the great black corona, carrying cutting tools as well as weapons, plainly ready to slice a fresh hole into its side.

King fired one explosive round and then ten more, and some of the soldiers ran.

Others lay still.

The coronas at the ruined door were wounded and weak, but no human was left to fight them. They squirmed and crawled inside, and they screamed mournfully while their dying flesh flashed gold and purple

Once again, desperate troops made a run for the dead giant. Snipers supplied covering fire, shooting at the turret, ignoring King while trying to kill the cannon. But the weapon was a tough proven design. Shells ricocheted, hitting King in the face and hands and across his shoulders. One eye was blinded briefly, but he became a quick expert with the cannon. That attack faltered, and he held tight to the handles, and because a relentless mind needs to be busy, he began to count the dead soldiers.

He stopped at fifty, well short of the answer.

And King was thinking this: generals were idiots at quite a lot, but not war. If they couldn't get inside the corona, they would try next to drop boarding parties from the overhead vents. To meet the attackers, he ran into the battered machine shop, claiming a long cylinder of steel to use as a battering club. But his enemies didn't even try to win back the *Girl*. Returning to the turret, he saw tubes in the doorways below, and out from the tubes, riding on columns of roaring smoke, were at least a dozen rockets.

The tree-walkers were so desperate that they were going to bring the fletch down on top of their own heads.

Tomorrow's Girl absorbed the first impacts and explosions, and the bladders seemed to be holding their gas. But then a peculiar smell hit the nostrils at the back of his breathing mouth—an odor that every human nose thought was sickening. But King had always found it to be a lovely smell, maybe the finest in the world, and the next blast would ignite this mess of a ship.

King imagined how it would feel to be burnt to the bone.

That's why he ran again. His trusted fear carried him down the hallway and out of the gangway hatch, using his mass and raw power to leap free.

Feet first, King plunged toward the distant floor.

The living coronas were still crawling indoors. He watched their necks wrap around machinery and each other, yanking with the last of their life. Then the other corona began to move—the gigantic black corona already in a place far beyond life

One of those dead heads rose up on the end of a dead neck
Impossibly blue eyes were gazing up at her brother.

• • •

They were falling and maybe the fall would never stop. There was no way to deny that possibility. And for a moment that stark, simple future not only felt possible, but inevitable and perhaps for the best.

The air had turned thin and cold to a corona's sensibilities.

The demon floor had vanished. The Eight were plunging towards what should be the sun, where the sun belonged inside the proper Creation, except up was down and nothing was below but chill perfect blackness that was working hard to drown a few weak smears of scattered, desperate light.

When the sun vanished, most of the coronas had fled upwards, either by panic or plan.

The Eight might wish for their own bladders and wings.

But there was no time for wishes.

The lost old world was above them—the hard-purple of corona voices mixed with fire colors and heat colors too. The human forest was full of violence and great voices and brilliant voices, every kind of light smeared together, rendered as a faint whisper that almost, almost had passed out of existence.

Wishing was a waste of time, but not memory. One of the small voices suddenly mentioned a certain day and one brief incident wrapped around an inchoate nut. None even the small voice understood why that mattered now, but it did matter. Eight souls were suddenly talking about a Procession of the Harvest, sharing perspectives about a ceremony said to be ancient and important, except nothing about the Procession had seemed critical. The papio were regimented creatures who appreciated order and orders and acts of devotion. This was just another ancient ceremony. Even on that poor, barely inhabited portion of the reef, the local papio were compelled to mark the passage of another one hundred and thirty days, carrying the symbolic harvest into the nearest village, and the Eight were allowed to watch.

That was before Diamond and King, when their body was still helpless, ruled by every soul and by no one.

One of the caretaker children was given the weighty task of describing what was happening below and would happen in the next few breaths. A line of papio was passing beneath the ravine where the corona's child could watch from deep shadows. At first, the only lesson seemed to be that the papio weren't what they claimed to be. The boasts about discipline, about being orderly and obedient, looked like lies. From the moment it appeared, the holy Procession was deeply, urgently sloppy. Children broke from the ranks to chase and play. Adults were little better, carrying their symbolic harvests in the wrong hands and with the wrong form. The old people chastised everyone for their failures, but they seemed to do that in glad, half-hearted ways that only made the chaos worse. At one point, a pair of small boys ran wild up the slope, past the markers that were intended to warn people away from the ravine. That incident made the caretaker nervous, but the boys—young enough to be blameless in everything they did—stopped short of the Eight and began to play a new game, standing on tall points of reef to see how far each of them could pee.

Into that mayhem came a young woman and the inchoate nut.

In the standards of papio, she was prettier than some but not most. There was a little too much beard and too much breast and scars that had been carved by accident, not by any artful hand. Yet she moved easily, carrying her nut in both hands, speaking to it and laughing while she spoke. The nut had a name. Her voice was quiet, too quiet, and thirteen hundred days later, each of the Eight remembered a different name. But they were certain that the nut was a stand-in for some young man, real or imaginary, and she danced with him as she moved up the slope, past the same warning markers, oblivious to two boys who were throwing their urine into a world grateful for every goodness.

Inchoate nuts took forever to ripen, and even in the best times and in the best ground, they were rare and exceedingly precious.

What the woman carried wasn't yet ripe, which meant that it wasn't edible. But as the caretaker explained with a quiet, know-everything-about-everything voice, it was her food to do with as she wished.

She was pretending that it was a lover's face.

Like any smitten young woman, she kissed the face to prove her devotion. "I will not bite you; you may trust your lips to mine," was what kisses mean. The rude boys saw her approach, and they tried to make her wet and angry. But discovering that they were out of ammunition, they threw out a few good insults, just enough to make their fierceness known, and then they scampered off, leaving the woman and her lover alone at the mouth of that shadowy, mysterious and forbidden ravine.

The Eight shared eyes but not every impression. What they had heard and what they imagined were rarely the same, which made the story worth repeating now.

The small voice inside them said, "This is what I thought would happen."

Then she confessed her guess, and the others told theirs in turn. Most of them had imagined something crude, and none proved right. In the end, the young woman kissed her dear nut once again, happy to the end, and then she set it on the ravine wall, exactly as high as her boyfriend's head would rise, and smiling, she made happy tears before pulling a pistol from a pocket, aiming at the imaginary boy before turning the gun on her rubbery heart.

Hundreds of days had passed since the half-pretty woman killed herself. The reasons for suicide were learned long ago: a boy had wronged her, and she left the world where he lived. What seemed important then had become just another small experience in a life full of more drama and suffering that any one failed love could ever cause. But only now, only as they tumbled into oblivion, did the Eight finally understand why the Procession was done this way and no other.

The papio deeply, truly believed in traditions and strictures and the value of old voices telling the species what to do.

Creatures with those qualities didn't need to practice what their instincts knew, what their blood and hearts understood from the moment of birth. The Procession of the Harvest was a wondrous chance to be less of a papio, not more. It was an unpracticed dance of bodies and inspirations, with beauty in this half-wild chain that was dragged past an entity that had thought itself brilliant.

The Eight had been foolish about the Procession and quite a lot more too.

That was never more obvious.

The Eight were falling, and the next little while was spent searching for some little moment, some past incident or lack of incident, where a different turn or words or maybe one unspoken phrase might have saved the world.

Because the world was dead.

Gazing upward, they saw the purple light of the coronas fading away, and the human fires were spreading through the dying forest, and a few columns of electric light were pointing down at them, searching for answers that did not exist.

No light lasts forever.

That was this day's meaning.

And maybe, hopefully, each of them hoped that no misery can outlast the end of All.

• • •

There was one light burning inside the corona. Master Nissim held the torch high until that arm grew tired, and then he changed hands and swung the beam in a circle, counting faces once again.

He wanted everyone to stay together.

Elata didn't want to be here.

She stood at the edge of the group, grieving the fact that she had made the walk with everyone else. She shouldn't have done it. Why did she? She could have walked in any other direction, and who would have stopped her? Nobody. Maybe Seldom would have tried to coax her back, but that's all. She knew the boy, knew that he'd call to her and ache when she ignored him, and grieve after she left him. But Seldom wouldn't have chased after her. Everybody but Elata would have stepped inside the dead animal, and the boy would have been too cowardly and too sensible to do anything else. And now she should be outside, enduring whatever awful thing that King was doing and the coronas were doing, and the soldiers, and the miserable sunless world.

A quiet voice said, "Tell me."

She didn't recognize List immediately. In this space, surrounded by alien meat, nothing sounded like it should.

"Tell me what it means," the Archon said, his voice smoother and more pleasant than usual, and by a long measure.

"The inscription," the Master said.

Yet his voice was more like it ever was, if that was possible.

"You made a translation," List said. "I know you did, and I don't see why you won't share it."

Nissim said nothing.

Noise passed through the stomach walls. The rumble might have been an explosion diluted by the creature's body, or maybe it was the body changing shape. Quest had vanished long ago. At least it seemed like long ago. Diamond had set his sister down, and she quickly ate her way into the floor and out of sight, taking her glowing light with her. And since then, very little had happened.

People and Diamond stood together.

Without fans blowing, the air was growing hotter, and each breath tasted staler than the one before.

With that strange voice, List said, "Master. Please. I want to know."

Nissim moved the torch again, changing arms and counting those scared sorry faces. Except for Karlan's face, which was hidden. Their bully-protector was holding one rifle, staring back at the collapsed hole, probably wishing that an army would give him another excuse to fight.

Haddi put her hand in the torch's beam, finger shadows dancing across the stomach walls. With a sharp impatient voice, she said, "Tell my son at least. He deserves to know, doesn't he?"

The gray ball was resting in the middle of them. It would be nice if the object glowed for them. That was a small trick to dream about from the object that had destroyed the world.

The torch tilted, its beam finding the inscription.

"Art has a tone," the Master began. "Even in translations, art and poetry have a distinct feel—one layer over another five layers. You often see that in the old works, the classics that people save and protect long after governments vanish and every tree and its grandchildren have died.

"But this is not one of those times. This is not art."

He paused, and the stomach around them shivered. For an instant it seemed as if they were moving with the corona, but then the meat wasn't shivering meat, nothing around them but a deathly calm.

What if Quest couldn't digest the corona?

The idea came into Elata's head, and she couldn't fling it out again. That's how true it felt.

"Okay," said Seldom. "But what does this mean?"

"These are instructions," said the Master.

The beam wasn't bright enough to reveal the etched words. When Elata looked, all she saw was the smooth timeless gray face of the ball.

"They are brief and very simple instructions about how to begin a purging or cleansing," he continued.

"Cleansing what?" Elata asked.

Except why did she talk? She didn't care one way or another.

"The cell," the teacher said. "Cleansing the cell."

"Like cells under a microscope?" Seldom asked.

People weren't real, Elata was thinking. Habits were what counted, and people were just convenient closets to fill up with important, everlasting habits.

And just like that, in this unimagined place, they were suddenly in class again.

"Not that kind of cell," Nissim said. "I can't be sure, but the text seems to refer to the kind of cell where prisoners are kept."

List made a soft, doubting sound.

Then Prima began to laugh—a long strange cackle leaving everyone else uncomfortable.

Nothing around them moved, and the heat was growing worse by the moment.

Nissim moved the torch to the other hand, and he looked at Elata's face longer than anyone else's. Then he pointed the beam at the ball, saying, "If I understand what I can read, then the sun's disappearance was just the initial step. Then the cell's floor opens, and every wisp of moisture and every breath of air is sucked out of the bottom, leaving the cell chamber ready for new prisoners."

"Prisoners," List said.

"Yes," Nissim said.

Karlan snorted, amused or angry. Who knew?

Haddi leaned away from the globe, brushing against Elata.

Elata couldn't remember where Diamond was. She turned her head one way and then the other, discovering him standing back as far he could be without being alone.

She looked at his face in the gray reflected light, and nothing about his manner seemed at all surprised.

Cold ideas got busy inside Elata's head.

"No wonder you didn't want to tell us," said Prima, not laughing anymore. Now she was miserable, saying, "All of our noise about the Creation being special, except this is just a cage with bars, and everybody is a prisoner."

"Children of prisoners," Haddi said.

Now the old lady was laughing, nothing happy in the sound.

Elata watched Diamond, and he looked at her until he grew uncomfortable, then turned to glance into the back of the corona's cavernous gut.

The corona was dead around them. No sound leaked in from the world outside, and maybe there wasn't a world outside anymore.

"But there's more," the Master said.

Everyone turned to him. Even Karlan.

"That's why I was desperate to look below with a good telescope. Somewhere past the sun is a mechanism, some kind of lock. The purge can be stopped. Like I said, this cell can be readied for new prisoners."

List sounded like his old self, shrill and tense when he asked, "And how do we manage that magic?"

"Use this key to engage the sun again," said Nissim.

"But how?"

The Master wasn't sure. He said so with his bouncing eyes, his silence, with the hard chewing that his bottom lip had to endure. And then finally with his voice, he admitted, "I don't have any idea how."

Elata looked back at Diamond.

This time the boy didn't look away from her.

"I don't understand," Seldom complained. "Do these instructions tell us how to use the key or not?"

"I can't decipher that last line," the old man admitted. "Not well enough, not even to guess."

Then the torch changed hands again, early this time. But both arms were very tired, and the beam dropped low and stayed down.

Elata approached Diamond. She could barely see the face. Grabbing his shoulders, she dragged him away from the others. Five long steps, and it felt as if they were far from prying ears. And then when she was certain that nobody else could hear, she said, "You know what the words mean. Or at least you think you know."

He nodded. But then he said, "No."

"You and your siblings knew to put fingers inside those holes," she said. "So I think you know a lot, even if you're too stupid to realize it."

The nearly invisible face lifted, staring at her.

And then an old thought came back to Elata—an idea the girl dreamed up maybe two days after she met Diamond. She had never mentioned it. It was such an obvious idea, simple and direct and obvious. In a world full of people who were smarter than she'd ever be, she couldn't believe that no one else had thought it. So the inspiration had to be stupid and wrong, and that's why she never brought it up.

Until now.

"Diamond," she said. "You have the power to do whatever you want. You could shape the world as it needs to be, or at least better than this shitty damned mess of ours. You had the power when I met you, and you didn't even know it, did you?"

"Know what?" he asked.

"You could have told us," she whispered. "You could have told us that you remember your life before, and you remember the Creators, maybe, and we would have believed a thousand smart instructions from the Creators. After that first day with me, you could have claimed anything. The Creators sent you here to share their blessings, and maybe you could have gotten some good things done."

He said, "No."

"No?"

"Because I don't remember any of that," he said.

Diamond's face was acquiring sharp lines. Leaking from the stomach walls and from the floor was a faint glow, and maybe it was Elata's imagination, but she felt cooler than just a moment ago. The air was fresher, wasn't it?

"I don't have anything to tell," he insisted.

She said, "You're not listening to me."

"I'm supposed to invent a story?" he asked.

Then she lifted her face into his face, and for the first time in her life, Elata kissed Diamond's odd mouth.

And having won his undiluted attention, she told him, "Every story is a lie. But if you could have done that one thing, given us a lie worth believing, then the world wouldn't be any worse than this, at least. If you just would have."

NINE

No flesh was stranger than corona flesh. Quest had lived inside one forever, but she plainly hadn't been able to consume what was in easy reach. Later, young and free in the wilderness, she would steal scales that refused to be chewed and bones that fought every stomach she could conjure. Even a thin shred of black meat proved too novel for metabolisms that thrived on every other kind of food. But where a monkey might dream about conquering undiscovered trees, Quest fantasized about acids and heat and wondrous enzymes that had never been born, and later, living in the District of Districts, she sneaked inside one of the factories that turned meat into guns, stealing a wide sampling of parts that slowly taught her how to consume the life that was like none other.

She imagined needing these skills, but never like this.

Not this scale

Wounded and tiny, scared beyond every fear experienced before, she was barely able to form any thought as Diamond carried her inside the carcass. She certainly didn't dream that he would let her go with the promise that she would grow as large as possible. She should have explained how unlikely that was, but then she astonished herself, blindly carving a path into the dead meat, wasting energy and time before the stomach's lining became a tumor wrapped around a stale mass of congealed blood.

Corona blood was the easiest meal.

One feast led to another five, each larger than the last, and faster, and more efficient. Energy collected was energy to be focused. Quest wove a wormy shape and stretched long before building branches. Every end hunted for delicious cancers and willing organs. The first neck found was infiltrated. Dead flesh was pushed aside by rubber and simple new tissues and neurons fat enough to carry images from big, unborn eyes. In less than a recitation, Quest fabricated new eyes inside the sockets of the old, and ears sprouted along the rubber skin, and with its fifth try, that reborn neck rose off the bone butcher floor, absorbing vibrations that sounded like explosions, and then a blurring image that turned clear and still made no sense.

King was falling, which was quite unexpected and a little funny too.

Why was her brother up in the air?

Then the fletch above him turned to flame and shattered.

King struck the floor and started to run. A length of pipe was clenched in his hand. Three strides were made, and then the fourth began before guns and soldiers began battering him from all sides.

King spun, and the pipe flew free, and he dropped and hands struck the floor, and he rose and again sprinted as the wreckage fell behind him and the fire stood tall and more guns drove metal into his armor, his muscle.

King was fighting to reach the dead corona.

To shelter against her.

She reached out with the neck, wanting to surround him, and then a cannon began firing quick concussive blasts. Her brother leapt sideways before a shell hit the floor and skipped and detonated, and he shrank down low and ran faster than seemed possible, fabulous long strides keeping him ahead of the next three blasts. But the reborn neck had too far to reach, and the last round dug low into King's back and emerged again in front—a timed round meant to punch through the armor on papio wings—and the explosion left two of her eyes blind and King thrown back onto the floor, exposed and limp, both hands thrown across a hole that filled with bright purple blood.

Three more of the corona's necks had turned to rubber sleeves and new muscle.

Fresh easy food lay everywhere, and she feasted in ways no corona could: the heads bolted down dead soldiers and several mortally wounded soldiers, and one dead general, and all of that monkey meat was suffused inside a vast new body that was barely begun.

Soldiers came out of hiding places, shooting King at will.

Then they were too close to his body to shoot.

Quest's first neck stretched toward those soldiers, and the triple-jaws opened wide, and the new mouth said its first clumsy first word, "No."

A familiar soldier stood before her, his face bloodied and a hammer in his favorite hand. He was happily swinging the hammer against the spikes on King's head.

Again, Quest said, "No."

The soldiers took note, and with new enthusiasm, they left King alone to kill the talking corona.

One last time, she told them, "No."

They fired at the carcass and the neck and that opinionated mouth, and hiding soldiers fired down on both of the corona's children.

That was the moment when hard decisions became simple.

A tiny portion of Quest's new flesh needed a good shake, one kind of molecule turning into another.

From the bullet-riddled mouths came a thin vapor—wet and swift and almost as loud as the gunfire and cannons—and every mortal creature that breathed had to pull a taste of that stew into their lungs, their blood. The genius of mayhem ants had been tweaked, made stronger and far quicker. Paralysis was the first symptom, and in some cases, the prey would stop breathing forever.

But at this moment, looking across the battlefield and two thousand days of relentless fear, Quest could find no reason for any of these hateful beasts to ever wake again.

• • •

Blackwood leaves were large as rugs and nearly as durable. But eventually they wore out, and the tree would scavenge their nutrients and precious salts, leaching the green color out of them, revealing a vivid orange shade that stood out in the canopy—a rare color that Diamond always found pleasing.

The corona's stomach walls had begun to glow with that same telltale orange, soft and warm and steady, and everyone was painted that deathly shade.

Diamond had no idea what he wanted.

Then he saw the strongest face, and he knew a little more. Just a little. Saying nothing, he stared at that face until the eyes gave him a suspicious glance, and then Diamond stepped past his mother and Master Nissim, saying, "You did a wonderful thing, trying to kill me. I'm sorry I never thanked you."

Suspicion gave way to surprise and a brief, half-sweet grin.

"Then you're welcome," Karlan said.

Mother said, "No."

For a moment, no one spoke.

"No," she repeated, anger stretching the simplest word.

Diamond watched Karlan. "You showed everyone my nature, including me. Nobody else did that."

"He was trying to murder you," Mother said, emphatic and furious. "Whatever happened afterwards, it wasn't what he intended."

Diamond smiled, and he said, "I don't know."

No one spoke.

The stale hot air had been replaced. Everyone was comfortable, everyone breathing easily.

Diamond turned to look at every face before returning to his tormentor. "I remember everything. My room is still inside my head, and every day that I lived there alone lives here. Every time my parents came to feed me, I remember. Every time the door was locked. I was their secret, and they talked to their secret, and they tried their best to keep the world secret from me. They had reasons, their sensible decent reasons, and I accepted their judgment until you came through that door and cut me open and proved what I was. Maybe you had some other goal in mind. That doesn't matter. I once tried to give my face a fine brave scar, to look more like my father. I took a secret knife from its forgotten drawer and cut and cut and cut, seeing my skull and peeling back my flesh. But what I wanted wasn't important. What was leftover was the same lesson that you'd already given me."

Diamond paused, unsure what to say next.

His mother made a low sound, anger mixed with anguish, and then he knew.

Turning to Haddi, he said, "I dream about my parents. My real parents, and I've never told you, no. But sometimes they come to me while I'm sleeping, and they talk to me or they don't say anything. They're just there."

"You never told me," she said, dismayed.

Diamond agreed with a nod, nothing more.

"In one dream," he began. Then he paused, pretending to think even though he found the next words waiting. "In my favorite dream," he said, "I would crawl inside the chamber where there were little drawers and my knife, except there was a secret doorway that I hadn't ever noticed before. Everyone has secret doors in their dreams, and maybe that's why I thought nothing was remarkable. But that door was gray. And not just any gray, but it was this color and it had exactly this feel." He kneeled suddenly, both hands against the ball. "It looks orange now, I know. But in sunlight, this was the same magical gray as that gray door, and one night my father was waiting behind it."

Diamond let silence have its moment.

"He was a strong man," he said. "His body was like mine, the long legs and short arms and the same kind of nose and mouth, and he spoke to me. He said that this was the best place me for now, that I was safe here. He warned that everything was stranger than I realized. And not only did I have to come find him and find my mother, but I had to bring all of them with me."

Again, silence.

" 'All of them,' " Seldom repeated. "You mean your brother and sister too?"

Diamond said nothing.

"And the Eight," Prima guessed, bristling at that possibility.

But Diamond didn't want to talk about lessons buried inside dreams or one nameless gray orb. And he didn't want to talk anymore about his old room or locked drawers and how the Creation had to be one secret room inside something quite a bit larger. He had a goal, a destination, and he was as eager as anyone to discover what it might be.

Once again, the boy looked at Karlan.

Karlan shifted his grip on the rifle, as if making his hands comfortable. With rare caution, he asked, "So what's the monster's big plan now?"

"I'm going to turn the sun back on," Diamond said.

No one made sound.

And he turned in a circle again, slowly. Every face was important. Mother was worn out and doubtful. The Master was wishing that he could believe, but he couldn't. The two Archons were standing beside each other, each watching the orange stomach floor. Seldom did believe, which made him the only one, while Elata was offering a thin smile, not quite nodding but plainly glad that Diamond had taken her advice and was trying to weave a fictional tale, no matter how gloriously silly and pathetic it seemed to be.

Karlan waited for the gaze.

Again, both hands needed to shift against the weapon.

"I want you to throw me into the air again," Diamond told him.

That won a big laugh, and Karlan asked, "Is that so?"

"Yes," Diamond said with enthusiasm. "And I'll hold tight to this ball and plunge to the bottom of the world, and I'll make the world live again. Or I won't. But that's what I'm going to try."

Each person took a small step backwards.

But then the orange light became white, the walls of the dead stomach vanishing in the glare, and from some new mouth, a close and strong mouth, Quest said, "No, that's crazy talk. I have to be the one to take you down there."

Which was the moment when Diamond realized to whom he had been talking all along.

• • •

Doctors had drawn maps of his body, but when King was still a living secret, isolated inside the palace, he insisted on naming each of his organs and bones and even the spikes and individual plates of armor. The project demanded a language of its own, each word built from sounds that felt comfortable inside his *ffaffar* and his *woooloo*, and once finished, he rarely thought in those terms. But for a long while, maybe always, that one day was the best day of his life.

Now those remarkable organs were healing.

He was sitting in the open, alone. Generators were thrumming in the distance, but critical wires had been severed or circuits were disabled and the entire abattoir had given up the fight against night. Sitting in darkness, King realized that he was more durable than this building, but perhaps not the tree. That was the first bright thought sparking in his mind: the giant bloodwood was ancient by any fashion, and as tough as he was, and he was just a frail sack full of smaller sacks that didn't know their true names.

The darkness was imperfect. Quest blushed when the necks ate and when the main body shuddered, shimmers of color hinting that energy was being ripped free from one great meal. Also glowing were the coronas that had crawled through the shredded doorway, still living, still making weak threads of light, their bodies plainly struggling to survive just the next moments.

When he felt strong enough to stand, King remained sitting, touching his new chest and belly, measuring how much bulk had been lost before he climbed up onto his feet and was disappointed.

Then his sister made one astonishing sound, wet and massive, prolonged yet impatient—amorphous flesh rising high, ready for invisible hands to give it some final, perfect shape.

The new, somewhat shorter King stood easily enough.

The butcher floor was bloodied but otherwise empty. Every dead soldier had been ingested, and there was no reason to feel uncomfortable about the dead becoming meals. But other soldiers had gasped while the necks swallowed them whole, and King considered what to say to his sister later, if there was any such thing as later.

He took one short step and two long steps toward his sister, and then he paused.

The necks were being absorbed, and a long groan rose from that tall body. A titanic new shape was forming from the rank and raw.

Did Quest name her organs as she worked?

That was a question worth asking, if he ever had the chance.

King turned and strode toward the obliterated doorway. Twisted steel plates squealed with the wind. Corona blood flowed like water and stank of metal and felt slick underfoot. The abattoir's enormous landing had been wrenched free, unless it had collapsed under too much wreckage. Dark empty air was everywhere. The neighboring bloodwoods seemed remote, illuminated by clinging, half-dead coronas and countless little fires that would never do more than consume buildings and walkways. Bloodwoods didn't like to burn. But looking out into the black air, gazing hard at the Middle-of-the-Middle, what impressed the boy was the feeble, smoky nature of each fire.

For the first time, an organ that wasn't any human lung pulled in a long breath, and King realized that the air was markedly thinner than usual, and it was too chilly, oxygen present but not nearly enough.

The atmosphere was draining from the world.

Sounds were draining away, thin and too slow. He listened. A thousand humans were begging in the dark, beseeching the Creators to make a new day, and ten thousand more voices were passionately cursing the Fates. Other humans said nothing, but he heard the noise they made as they fell, clothes flapping and dropsuits flapping. Despair or madness or maybe just stupid mistakes caused people to tumble free from this tree. Those ten carefully named ears heard individual bodies knifing through the thin air, and King wished he was deaf, and in the next breath, he wished that he could hear every sound inside this big room of a world.

A piece of steel cable offered itself as a handhold, and planting one foot, King dangled into the open air. No demon floor glimmered below. The corona realm was missing, and beyond was an emptiness that didn't require any sun. But the dark air was perfectly empty. Past the sharp tips of the trees were ships—tree-walker airships and papio wings that had survived the coronas. It took time and some thought to realize what had happened: desperate hands had overloaded these machines with extra ballast, or the papio had pushed their aircraft into endless dives. There wasn't enough air up here, but maybe there was below. Maybe that's what this cluttered fleet was chasing. Unless this wasn't a survival strategy. Maybe it was as simple as before they died, these people wanted to see what lurked below.

King imagined a dirty steel floor and some important hatch foolishly left open, letting the air leak away.

He couldn't stop remembering how his hand pushed Quest's hand into the ball.

King had never shared the maps of his body. He never mentioned them to Father or Diamond, and certainly not to anyone else.

Each of his hands had its own name.

The hand around the cable wanted to let go, allowing his body to plummet to the world's floor.

The rest of King overruled that hand, and he came back inside.

His reborn lung had no trouble finding adequate oxygen, at least for the present moment. His feet sounded different, walking across the slick black floor. The nearest corona let loose a long exhausted sound, complications woven into the misery, and he was thankful that he didn't know what sad words were being said.

The giant creature was inflated with emptiness, scales pulled apart and the body rising like a building before him. The dying flesh was hot but not hot enough, and it was velvety black save for the peculiar imperfections—spots too miniscule to be bright, yet brilliant enough to shine against the blackness.

With the razored tip of a finger, King touched the brightest light.

An old thought came near enough to be felt, and then it was gone just as suddenly, and maybe it never existed.

But the urge to fall remained relentless. He felt it in his limbs, his reflexes. Ignoring that insanity took work. To distract himself, King drew an arcing line from the first light to a bright neighbor and then to others still. This was a puzzle that couldn't be a puzzle. These points of light felt random. Yet with stubborn cleverness, the alien boy managed to write his name once with the tree-walker language, and then he began drawing the long, self-invented word that meant "King." Slicing deep into the wounded flesh, every gesture was precise and a little desperate. But the perfect little specks were fading, and the blackness surrounding them was losing its vibrant sheen, and before King would finish that simple task, the corona was dead, deep bladders collapsing and the body slumping, crushing both of his names.

TEN

White light filled the stomach.

Diamond asked what was happening outside.

"The world is dying," Quest said, her voice small, sorry.

"Can you see where we need to be?" he asked.

"I pushed a few eyes through the abattoir's floor. I'm looking now. But the shape of everything below us seems different, and I can't see enough to know."

Nobody spoke.

"I'm hurrying," his sister said.

She was furiously rebuilding herself.

"But all of you need to leave," she said. "I'm becoming clumsy. If you stay here, I'll likely digest you."

Karlan blew air through his teeth, almost laughing when he asked, "So are we going to get shot when we show our heads?"

"You won't be shot," Quest said firmly. "I promise you."

Nobody asked why.

Then she said, "Diamond. Take the key with you and explain the situation to King. As soon as I'm ready, bring him and the key back with you."

The world was insane, but that sounded reasonable.

Why?

She said, "Now, please. Get out of me."

The slayer-made gash in her side lifted, white light spilling across the white bone floor. The warm damp interior air led the way. Karlan waved for Diamond, wanting him to emerge first. "In case your sister happens to be wrong," he said, thumping his scalp with imaginary bullets.

With both hands, Diamond lifted up the ball.

But then Mother hurried past him, one arm waving as she told the darkness, "We surrender, we surrender."

Nobody fired.

There was no one to raise a weapon, much less beg for mercy.

King was alive but noticeably smaller. He was standing near the open door, standing beside one of the attacking coronas. The corona was motionless and dark, and it had to be fascinating, judging by how his brother stared at the carcass.

Diamond let the ball fall and roll, but the alien ignored the noise.

"Can you breathe?" Nissim asked Mother.

"If I work at it," she said, wheezing as she walked.

Quest closed the opening. Save for a faint ruddy glow leaking from her entire body, the gigantic room was dark and cold.

"Butcher's weather," joked the Master.

Seldom followed Diamond. But then he noticed Elata standing apart from everyone, and he turned and went back to her. For someone's sake, he said, "This will get better."

"Better than what?" she asked.

King was a statue. His breathing and his hearts might have stopped, still as he was.

Diamond approached him, talking quickly. "The gray ball is some kind of machine, maybe a key. And Quest is taking us below to rekindle the sun."

King didn't respond.

"What are you doing?" asked Diamond.

The statue didn't react.

Then another voice said, "You know me."

List.

"I'm not a gracious man," said the human, hurrying to stand beside the statue, one hand stroking the sharp plates high on one arm. "And I won't pretend graciousness now. I know the world is built on numbers, and the counting and the weighing are what I do better than most people. Which is the heart of the reason why a clerk would invest so much and risk so much in a child unlike all others."

Two fingers bled, and he sucked on them for a moment.

Then the man said, "You saved me. Today, you took a huge risk and saved all of us. But that's not what is important. What matters—why I should feel grateful—is that you knew what to do. You couldn't know the sun would leave. But then that happened and everything was collapsing, and the three of you had the clearer, cleaner sense of these events. And if I can make myself hope, I'll hope that despite being an ignorant and ungracious calculating monster, I nonetheless helped put you where each of you can help us."

A breath emerged from King's high mouth.

Words followed.

"In no way is this about you," King said.

"Not about me personally," List agreed.

"And it isn't about any of you monkeys." King was facing the corpse, and then he turned, gracefully and with no sound. He ignored his father. The eyes were fixed on his brother.

Diamond took a reflexive step backwards.

"We are supposed to do this thing, whatever this thing is," said King. "But we can't remember what the duty is. We forgot because too much time passed. Because the corona kept us locked inside her belly longer than she should have, than was intended, and even our great minds couldn't keep every memory clear and fixed."

Diamond looked at the satin black corona flesh.

"Too many days have passed," said King. "I've looked in my mind, poked and looked, and I don't remember enough even to know what we're late for.

"But I can't believe it has anything to do with these damned monkeys."

• • •

Karlan didn't feel like moving. Watching the monster remaking herself, guessing what she would become, seemed like a suitable game.

Then somehow the one-time Archon ended up standing nearby. She wasn't doing anything, but she was breathing quickly nonetheless, like someone halfway up an unwelcomed set of stairs. He didn't know the woman from a can of paint. If they ever talked, he had forgotten the conversation. Yet something about her being a prisoner—one of the great enemies of the modern world—made her fascinating.

Karlan approached, and when he had her gaze, he said, "I'm going to leave with them."

She blinked, saying nothing, probably building her own response.

"This world is dead," he said. "But from what I hear, our little friends might be heading someplace else."

Now she laughed.

Good.

"You should come too," Karlan said.

The next laugh died. Prima used both hands, wiping at the short hair that prisons liked to mandate for criminals and guards alike. Then with a quiet smiling voice, she asked, "Why should I? Because there's no reason for me to stay?"

"If you think there isn't," Karlan said, laughing.

Then he turned, both of them watching Quest.

Like any woman, she kept changing appearances. She became a narrow and very tall cone, and then the cone collapsed into a rounded mass, flesh swirling around some stubborn core. But where were the legs? Why wasn't the girl making legs or living ropes, anything that could drag her to ruined doors?

Karlan thought that part through, finally seeing what was simple.

There really wasn't enough air to breathe, was there?

• • •

Staring out into the killing night, Diamond waited for Quest to finish her preparations. Distant fires were struggling to survive. A dead corona fell past, limp and dark and almost soundless. Then a civilian blimp followed, two heavy timbers strapped to its underside, helping drag it toward thicker air. For an instant, Diamond saw inside the brightly lit cabin, saw packed bodies and desperate faces and hands holding guns.

Haddi approached him, stopping short of the door and the endless fall. She was breathing in long, weak gasps, but once she began to talk, nothing about her seemed weak.

"You need to know," she said. "I am proud of you."

Diamond watched the blimp turn small with distance.

"I was foolish, holding you to such a high standard," she said. "Whatever you are, you are a child, and I shouldn't have expected so much."

"But you should have," he managed.

"Look at me, Diamond."

She wasn't alone. Master Nissim stood behind her, his big frame surrounding her body, both lit by the weak glow of burning wood and Quest's ongoing metamorphosis. The gray ball was on the floor where he left it. And nearby stood Elata and Seldom, one of them clinging to the other one's free hand.

"You're my mother," Diamond said. "Nobody else is."

Haddi straightened a back that was rarely straight anymore, and her breath came even faster than before.

"Thank you," she said.

Everyone was suffering. Speed mattered, and Diamond wanted to leave now, which was why he tried to walk past them.

But the Master put a hand to his shoulder, saying, "I have something to give you."

Diamond paused. "A lesson," he guessed.

"But not as a teacher," Nissim said.

The entire facility began to shake. Quest was violently twisting, the body burrowing through the abattoir's floor.

"A butcher's perspective can help you," Nissim said.

"All right," Diamond said, sick of waiting.

The butcher said, "Wherever you happen to go, show up on time and sober, and do all of your work with an artful amount of complaining. And when you're working with other butchers, remember: everybody has knives and cleavers."

Diamond stared up at that worn old face.

"When there's trouble," said Nissim, "and there always is trouble among butchers, your advantage comes in realms that don't involve the steel."

Diamond closed his eyes, thinking.

With no warning, Quest plunged through the bone floor.

Was his sister leaving without him? And without the key too?

But no, she was inside the rooms below, grabbing hold of the building's foundation, and her body hadn't finished making ready for whatever she was planning.

King was holding the gray ball in his hands.

King ran, and then Diamond ran. Nobody else could even try.

The two Archons had found each other in the gloom, converging beside a booth where call-lines ended. One circuit was working, and like dear friends, they put their ears to the same earpiece, listening to some quick voice.

Diamond stopped running.

Until his mother caught him, he wasn't sure why he was standing still.

Her hands had never felt colder, every little bone struggling to be felt. She squeezed him and panted for a long moment before saying, "Good-bye." Then she said, "Good-bye," again, with a softer, sadder voice.

"I do remember your face," he said. "When I was looking up from the toolbox, I saw you watching me."

With that. Diamond had to turn and run again.

He didn't dare do anything else.

• • •

Only at the end, by accident, did Seldom suspect what Elata wanted.

The moment they emerged from the giant sister, the girl began to chase after Diamond, and a familiar, reassuring jealousy fell across Seldom. He always felt inadequate next to any corona's child, but particularly his best, almost-human friend. He had no choice but assume that she wanted nothing but to be near Diamond. Which would have doomed her, maybe. And maybe all of them. But then Seldom began to think how Elata stood apart from everybody all day, saying nothing unless forced to talk, and he remembered how she had acted every day for what seemed like a long while. She was far from happy. Almost nothing in her life was pleasurable, and the world since Marduk fell was horrible, and maybe Seldom wasn't as sensitive about people and emotions as he should be, but had one talent not shared by the perfect-brained Children: he was a genius when it came to misremembering the past.

That's what Seldom did then. He thought he remembered Elata turning to him once, confessing that if life became too unbearable, she would simply jump.

Later, replaying the abattoir and his faltering memories, Seldom would realize that the girl had never said anything of the kind. He couldn't figure out where that non-memory came from, unless instinct or intuition were talking. But the recollection felt genuine then, and that's why he forced himself to run, catching her and grabbing her hand.

"What are you doing?" she asked.

"Nothing," he lied.

"Then stop," she said.

Too graceless to invent an explanation, Seldom simply told her, "No. I want to keep you close."

Elata considered fighting and didn't.

They were standing together, not talking, when Quest sank through the floor. Then Diamond finished talking to his mother and to Master Nissim. He trotted past his friends, seeing them without seeing them. Diamond had a way of noticing everything, but he didn't even make eye contact with his only real friends. Elata watched him pass them, and then she started to follow Diamond.

Seldom allowed himself to be dragged along behind her.

The Archon of Archons had dropped a call-line receiver, and he hurried to catch his son, presumably to share more of his political genius.

Karlan appeared, placing himself in Diamond's path. Loudly, very happily, he announced, "I'm going with you."

Seldom stopped running, and Elata shook free.

Quest was almost invisible, her body squirming under the floor, destroying rooms and machinery as she made herself ready.

Diamond told Karlan, "No."

Seldom watched his brother and the rifle that he was carrying. He knew his brother. Karlan was considering shooting Diamond and maybe King too, giving him the freedom to do whatever he wanted. Seldom shivered, watching the rifle barrel drawing little circles in the air.

Again, Diamond said, "No."

King came past both of them, saying, "He is coming. With a gun. We need soldiers."

Diamond asked, "Why?"

From under the floor, a giant mouth roared at them.

Quest said, "Hurry."

Everybody was walking towards her.

Diamond asked King, "Why do we need guns?"

"The spotter station below us survived. They just got their com-line fixed, and they're reporting. After the sun vanished, after the coronas were done rising, the papio started launching their slayer ships. Maybe they're trying to save their people, looking for better air. Whatever the reason, we aren't going to be alone down there."

Diamond gave no reaction.

"So I am going," Karlan said, showing a smile to his little brother.

Elata was past all of them. Before anyone could stop her, she jumped into the fresh hole in the floor, vanishing inside whatever Quest had become.

Karlan laughed while picking up ammunition belts.

King and the key plunged into the hole.

Diamond ran a little ways and then stopped, turning in one circle and half of another before asking, "Where's Elata?"

Seldom caught up and said, "She already got onboard."

Diamond didn't want to believe him. "Why?"

"She doesn't like here," Seldom said reasonably.

From below, Quest roared, "Now," and as if to prove the urgency, beams of bloodwood and bone pegs began to shatter.

"Out of my way," Karlan shouted, and he vanished.

Diamond ran and jumped after him.

And then Seldom sprinted to the hole's edge, finding what looked like an ordinary wooden trap door flung open, and the only surprise was how little surprise he felt, watching himself fearlessly leap after the others.

ELEVEN

They fell past the lost sun, mesmerized eyes absorbing the endless night. Seven of them noticed nothing else, but with the same vision, the eighth teased out a thin sliver of pale golden light.

Tritian fixed the eyes on a narrow patch of ink, and the light was a little brighter.

Whatever it was, they were closing the gap.

Two moments of debate ended with a plan. The glow was below them but not beneath. Aligning the head while extending arms and legs, the Eight allowed themselves to fall like the world's weakest bird, fast but not straight, and time made the corona become real—one of the last and the oldest, too weak to flee the gaping wound in the world, far too stubborn to give up and die.

The Eight planned for a graceful collision.

The disk-shaped body sang in painful colors, in sharp yellows, and the bladders expanded for lift and then collapsed, and it sounded as if the last of the world's air was exploding out of the giant's mouth.

The Eight believed in inevitable successes. Their aim was perfect and true until they missed the giant corona. But the ancient creature noticed motion and ended up catching them instead, its longest, strongest neck stretching as far as possible, the last of its teeth removing a hand and foot before bringing the Eight close.

The corona might be the last living First.

Why it would grab this miserable creature was a mystery, and what it thought about its quarry remained unknown. But the leviathan kept the Eight close, and they fell together. The Eight clung to the neck that had damaged them and saved them, and they grew a new hand and a worthwhile foot. The giant mouth was close, wide when it caught the air and roaring when the air jetted free. In the presence of vast memory and every answer, there was no chance to piece together even the barest conversation. The world remained built from puzzle, from ignorance. Yet the Eight had never felt closer to any organism than this desperate doomed wondrous soul.

In Creation, no fall is eternal.

In the end, in terror or exaltation or maybe by sheer chance, the First emitted a single pulse of scorching purple light, showing its passenger what was rising fast from below.

The chamber ended with a barren floor, and all nine died.

And time flowed and eight of them were less dead.

More time was crossed while the shared body wasn't just repaired but reinvented, the old papio-form given lungs for this air and a mouth gifted at cursing.

The body crawled out from beneath the corona's smashed remains. The Creation loomed overhead. Walls defined a finite, knowable space. The space couldn't be seen but was felt, invisible every way but in the mind. Tritian made the new body stand, and they enjoyed the first shared breath. The floor beneath was slick and gray and a little cool against just-born flesh, and it seemed far too flat. A perfect sphere had been promised, but the wise Masters were again proved wrong. They were standing at the bottom of a pipe, and a steady wind was blowing across the floor, one direction in mind. In the distance, in the darkness, great masses were slamming against the floor. Not just the coronas were falling. With the forest overhead, dead trees were falling, and downed aircraft, and it was inevitable that one object or a thousand more would crash down on top of the Eight. They would die again and crawl out into the open again, nothing ahead but work, hellish laborious work that would not end until the starved forest was safely dead underfoot.

The Eight practiced running, covering a short distance before a new sound made them pause.

A papio wing was diving from high overhead.

Divers fell silent inside them.

Tritian told the others to give him the only voice.

The jet engine throttled down, and the nose sprouted a column of light that pivoted, finding the gray floor rising, and then the machine landed in the distance, skidding sharply and then crashing into piece of debris.

Unused munitions detonated.

The violence washed across the landscape, and overhead, dozens and maybe hundreds of aircraft took sight of the goal.

They came in waves, exhausted wings followed by overloaded airships full of tree-walkers, and there were individuals riding beneath parachutes and inside drop-suits. Most of the refugees landed badly, dying instantly or after some plaintive wails. But others touched down successfully, and only time stood between now and that moment when some survivor, standing amidst the carnage, noticed the Eight

Those lucky eyes belonged to a papio crew riding inside what looked like a slayer-hunting aircraft. Motors and gas bladders held several dozen soldiers aloft, and they fixed their spotlights on a big papio body, a woman's magnified voice shouting at them and echoing across the gray plain, asking if they were the great missing Eight.

Tritian demanded calm from his siblings.

Each of the Eight helped raise one hand high, friend to friend.

And then Tritian told a useful lie. Shouting over the roar of engines, he said, "We are the Seven. Divers is dead."

Human memory forgot quite a lot after one day, and six hundred days could wipe away much of the past. But these creatures knew how to nourish old emotions, keeping them raw enough to last for generations.

Divers or not, one of the papio gunners opened fire, gutting the creatures that had helped ignite this endless war.

And once again, the Eight became dead.

• • •

Inside the Creation, in this one tiny realm, perhaps nothing had ever moved so swiftly.

Quest fell like a dart.

Massive and narrow, wearing a skin that slipped through any air, she plunged faster than the papio wings, and soon faster than every rocket. Distances that should have felt enormous were crossed in moments, crossed and found empty and barely noticed as a consequence. She spawned eyes that didn't interrupt the precious airflow. She spat out brilliant flares to throw light across the walls of the world. And what she saw was shown to her passengers: the intricate, lovely reefs that had infested the corona world; the formerly high-realm where the sun ruled and where a great hole now waited; and beneath that hole, an expansive but not spectacularly wide cylinder leading down for another enormous journey, swiftly crossed.

"But do you see Them?" asked Diamond.

"If I do, I will tell you," Quest said.

"See who?" asked Seldom.

Nobody answered.

Then Seldom looked at Elata, and she mouthed, "The Eight."

The rounded chamber was intended for two bodies, plus the unfathomable gray ball. Crowded together, everybody touched everybody. The humans occupied one side, King and Diamond the other. The gray ball lay on King's hands. Karlan's rifle looked at home in his arms. The ceiling and floor were flat, but beyond each was a bubble that bore a strong resemblance to Quest's crystalline eyes. They could see what she saw, except for the details that their speed that washed away, and the total exhaustion that stole their focus, and the limited numbers of eyes in their few heads. The reef wasn't built from coral, it was woven from countless holes, and Diamond worried that the Eight were hiding inside any one of those holes, or they were lost in some other way.

Suddenly the reef was above, left behind.

The man in the dream had told him to bring everyone.

But if Diamond couldn't . . . ?

What might have been the moorings of the sun passed on all sides—a washed-out gray scaffolding, without weakness and without beauty, looking cobbled together by gigantic but ordinary workman hands.

The cylinder beneath was the same slick gray as the ball.

A steel pipe would have more character than this.

Nobody spoke.

Elata set her purse on top of her own foot, and she reached for the gray ball, for the tubes that had held the trap.

King said, "No."

She nearly tried anyway.

Diamond said, "No."

She picked up her purse, and after turning it once in her hands, she threw it aside, in that way people use when they will never pick an object up again.

Then with a quick flat voice, Quest said, "I see Them."

"The Eight?" asked Seldom.

"And everyone else in the world, too."

A long study of rockets and momentum had inspired this body. This was the opportunity to learn if the lessons and Quest's plans were any good. She told her passengers, particularly the human three, to lie flat on their backs and do nothing until they were safe or they were dead. There was no room to spare. One swollen stomach beneath them was full of freshly built perchlorates and metabolic rubber and aluminum, and she set that mess on fire. And nozzle made of corona scales dilated, the largest rocket in existence trying it best to remake the missing sun.

Karlan and the human children briefly lost consciousness.

Every refugee beneath them looked up and then looked down, and every bone, living and dead, shook with the roaring.

In the end, Quest managed to hover above a plain covered with battered aircraft and refugees and a thousand ugly fires. There was enough oxygen for easy breathing, but the world was still draining through some undiscovered vent. Quest hovered and then lifted, edging closer to her target, and as the last of the fuel was burnt, she pulled herself free from the huge body. Wearing nothing but a new carapace and strong little body, she lay across her brothers as the ship ended its descent.

The three of them held hands, just for a moment.

The humans were sick to their stomachs, bruised. Even Karlan let his pain show. But after the fleshy rocket was down, the six of them cut their way free and came out together. Tree-walker blimps and forester blimps and one papio airship were covered with lights, and they were parked around one body that had been repeatedly shot and chopped and then drenched with alcohol that still stank in the air long after the fire went out.

The Eight saw their siblings.

Mournful words came from a broken mouth.

"When it all can't be worse, it is."

There was no war here. The papio and tree-walkers had been united in one clear task, delivering endless pain to an entity that couldn't die. And suddenly three more guilty monsters had stumbled into their midst—a parade of bodies and potential delivered by the best Fates.

One of the foresters was a big man carrying a little papio in his blood. He instantly ran forwards to take away Karlan's rifle.

In reflex, the warrior aimed at the attacker.

Faster than any human, King grabbed the barrel and wrenched it from the hands, and then he tossed the rifle so far that only his ears could hear it hit and slide away.

But that gesture won only moments without violence. Revenge was left to float, waiting for the next opportunity.

Every sort of human followed after them.

The Eight were burnt and bleeding, several colors brightening skin that refused to look human.

"All of them," said someone. "Make all of them . . . feel . . . "

Several papio repeated the verdict, and the world stood together.

Karlan cursed, and Seldom whimpered.

Elata did both. This day began with her wanting to die. Death or something far worse was about to claim all of them, and she hated the idea and despised herself for ever walking so close to darkness. She was standing between King and Diamond. The alien wasn't as huge as before, but he was still taller than any monkey, standing with his feet apart, holding the dangerous ball with one hand. King was probably deciding which of these little necks to break first. And Diamond was even worse, staring ahead and breathing fast out of nervous energy, probably thinking about what to say or what to do that would defuse the situation. But that too-smart brain was generating a thousand more ideas than the one good answer that she had already offered him.

"Put me on top of you," she told King.

Her voice wasn't loud, but of course he heard her. And like his brother, he didn't immediately understand what was obvious and right.

The brave strong and endlessly impulsive girl grabbed those spines and dragged herself on top of the giant. King didn't try to stop her. His hands were filled with the precious ball, and he assumed that she would feel safer above. Elata put her feet on the alien shoulders, her balance barely surviving the next moment. But she righted herself and grabbed the spines on his head, and she glanced back at Quest and the battered Eight, and then she stared ahead at what seemed like all of the faces left in the world.

"Do you know what these creatures are?" the girl cried out. "Do you understand their nature?"

Curiosity and fatigue kept every gun from firing.

"I know what they are," she lied. "They are not leftovers from the Creation, and I promise you, promise you that they are not monsters. No. What they are and have always been is simple simple simple, and you are idiots not to see it, and maybe they are right. What they said. What they said when we were coming here to put the world back together again. They talked about letting all of you ungrateful, unthinking excuses for monkey shit die. Letting you die in the way you were made, which was in the dark and stupid as can be."

Papio who understood now whispered rough translations to the others.

Then silence took hold, but not for long.

A voice in the back called out. A tree-walker tongue said, "All right then, what are they?"

One hand gesturing, she announced to the world, "These are the Creators themselves."

Her words rushed across the gray plain.

Whispers chased after her voice.

She needed to be believed. Elata needed to believe herself. And that's when she spoke again, crafting the finest lie of her life, shaping a universe and the greatness of gods while inventing all of the sterling reasons why even the lowliest life, particularly the lowliest life, should give their Creators some measure of help, or at least stop trying to murder what simply could not die.

• • •

In the orange-headed tongue, his name was The-Man-Who-Stood-Tall. But a long while had passed since he stood that way.

The old woman and man/boy left him, taking the others away too. Alone inside the big rooms, he could nap where he wished and eat whatever he found for himself, and this seemed like the best kind of day. Even when the sun died, he was happy. There were no windows to scare him. The electric lights remained strong, and he was accustomed to the sirens and banging of cannons. But then the panicked monsters flew high, attacking the palace, and the power failed, and two soldiers ran through the darkened hallways, arguing about foolish human matters. One man or the other had done something wrong. Who would wear the shame remained undecided, but an important door was left open, and The-Man-Who-Stood-Tall was brave enough to walk where he wasn't allowed, finding a window and jumping up on the sill long enough to see the unexpected night and a thousand giants trying to kill him and nobody else.

The little man with the gray beard hid where he felt safest.

He was in the man/boy's bed, inside a fortress made of pillows and blankets. Eyes closed tight, he saw nothing except for what he imagined, which was terrible enough. Cannons fired and wood burned and fuel was spilled nearby and then set ablaze. Great pieces of the palace were torn away. He felt the bed jump and the floor tilt. He fully expected to die. Then a human came into the room to sit on the edge of the bed. The hiding man didn't recognize the newcomer's scent. He was a stranger who talked to himself and to the Creators. Suddenly a nearby portion of the palace fell away, and the stranger fell silent for a moment, and then he sobbed, and then he shot himself with one bullet. But it took a very long time for him to bleed to death.

After that, the world fell silent.

Soon the hiding man felt a chill, and despite his fine big lungs, he felt as if he couldn't breathe fast enough.

Death was everywhere.

Even under the blankets, the world appeared doomed.

Then after a very long wait, after no sleep and no food and one ugly moment where he peed in the corner of his fortress, a light came on somewhere. The light passed through the heavy blankets, and the man heard a voice calling. He knew that voice, and he crawled out slowly, cautiously, ready for quite a lot but not for a bird with a blue head and green body—an usher bird that had wandered far from home.

The bird flew away.

Avoiding the corpse, the orange-headed man gave chase.

Haddi's room had been stolen. The far side of the hallway was gone. But he stood on the last of the floor, gazing down at a brilliant sun that seemed wrong and felt lovely, and he smelled moisture in the wind, and after more time passed, he smelled at least one human that he knew and loved.

• • •

Elata demanded a ride to the world's edge, and the papio from the slayer ship volunteered, out of respect as well as simple terror.

Diamond told the lady captain to let the wind pick her direction.

Every hallway in the ship was wide, every room huge. The papio never stopped watching their bizarre guests. The Creators and their tree-walking attendants were led inside the cargo hold where they could watch the gray floor sliding beneath them. Time passed, and the Eight healed completely. More time was crossed, and the airship stopped where the giant cylinder ended. A towering gray wall stood before them. But the wall never reached the floor. There was a gap at the bottom, and the spotlights couldn't find any end to the gap. Perhaps it went all the way around the world's bottom. The gap looked large enough to let the ship to pass, but the captain refused to try. So the passengers embarked, and Elata thanked the papio for the kindness, and Seldom thought to ask the captain to wait for them. "We might be back soon," he said hopefully.

Seven bodies walked with the wind. King carried the gray ball. Their only lights were handheld torches, and nothing changed. Even the humans sensed that time was running out. The Eight offered various opinions about Diamond's guidance and the trustworthiness of old memories and dreams. But what worried the boy was when the Eight stopped talking, and his friends didn't say a word to defend him.

That's when Diamond ran as fast as he could, alone and happy enough. And that was why he came first to the room at the end of every possible route.

The room was small and very dark until he stepped inside, and then it was smaller and quite plain, round and brightly lit and made of the same mysterious gray material. There were no furnishings. A simple fire pit waited in the middle of the round room, empty of ashes or logs or old coals. Diamond was standing beside the far wall when the others arrived. He was hunting for a door that didn't exist. King asked some question that Diamond didn't quite hear. Then one of the Eight said that this felt like the right place, although she wasn't certain why.

Then Karlan said, "Hey, have a look."

The fire pit was smooth before. But now there was a hemispherical depression in its middle, and at the bottom were fourteen holes.

"Say something," King said, nudging his brother.

"Like what?" Diamond asked.

"This is a great moment, a historic moment," King said. "Give us some important words."

But the boy couldn't think of anything to say, except, "I was waiting for something stranger."

King handed him the key.

Diamond climbed into the ring, setting it inside the locking mechanism. And time passed without passing, and everybody was left naked, and everybody was weak, lying on a different floor.

Far above was a smooth gray ceiling.

The ceiling fell away on all sides, vanishing behind ground that also fell away in the distance. They seemed to have been dropped on top of an enormous hill, and the land was black and glassy, dotted with great pools of water and the occasional pool of molten red rock, and strange creatures flew and screamed, and trees stood strong beneath the sky that had no sun yet couldn't be brighter.

Walking towards them, wary but curious, were too many children to count.

Each child wore clothes made from leather and hair and bone, and each carried some little machine that made light and made noise. Those noises were words, Diamond sensed. The machines were talking to each other, and the new world was full of sound. But not the children. The children were silent and a little cautious and very curious, marching barefoot across the sharp volcanic rock, every foot being cut and every cut healing in an instant.

ABOUT THE AUTHOR

Robert has had eleven novels published, starting with *The Leeshore* in 1987 and most recently with *The Well of Stars* in 2004. Since winning the first annual L. Ron Hubbard Writers of the Future contest in 1986 (under the pen name Robert Touzalin) and being a finalist for the John W. Campbell Award for best new writer in 1987, he has had over two hundred shorter works published in a variety of magazines and anthologies. Eleven of those stories were published in his critically-acclaimed first collection, *The Dragons of Springplace*, in 1999. Twelve more stories appear in his second collection, *The Cuckoo's Boys* [2005]. In addition to his success in the U.S., Reed has also been published in the U.K., Russia, Japan, Spain and in France, where a second (French-language) collection of nine of his shorter works, *Chrysalide*, was released in 2002. Bob has had stories appear in at least one of the annual "Year's Best" anthologies in every year since 1992. Bob has received nominations for both the Nebula Award (nominated and voted upon by genre authors) and the Hugo Award (nominated and voted upon by fans), as well as numerous other literary awards. He won his first Hugo Award for the 2006 novella "A Billion Eves."